By Larry McMurtry

Hollywood: A Third Memoir
Literary Life: A Second Memoir
Rhino Ranch
Books: A Memoir
When the Light Goes
Telegraph Days
Oh What a Slaughter
The Colonel and Little Missie
Loop Group
Folly and Glory
By Sorrow's River
The Wandering Hill
Sin Killer
Sacagawea's Nickname: Essays on
the American West
Paradise
Boone's Lick
Roads
Still Wild: Short Fiction of the
American West, 1950 to the Present
Walter Benjamin at the Dairy
Queen
Duane's Depressed
Crazy Horse

Comanche Moon
Dead Man's Walk
The Late Child
Streets of Laredo
The Evening Star
Buffalo Girls
Some Can Whistle
Anything for Billy
Film Flam: Essays on Hollywood
Texasville
Lonesome Dove
The Desert Rose
Cadillac Jack
Somebody's Darling
Terms of Endearment
All My Friends Are Going to Be
Strangers
Moving On
The Last Picture Show
In a Narrow Grave: Essays on
Texas
Leaving Cheyenne
Horseman, Pass By

By Larry McMurtry and Diana Ossana

Pretty Boy Floyd

Zeke and Ned

THE
BERRYBENDER
NARRATIVES

Larry McMurtry

Simon & Schuster

New York   London   Toronto   Sydney   New Delhi

Simon & Schuster
1230 Avenue of the Americas
New York, NY 10020

First Simon & Schuster hardcover edition November 2011

SIMON & SCHUSTER and colophon are registered trademarks
of Simon & Schuster, Inc.

For information about special discounts for bulk purchases,
please contact Simon & Schuster Special Sales at
1-866-506-1949 or business@simonandschuster.com.

The Simon & Schuster Speakers Bureau can bring authors
to your live event. For more information or to book an event,
contact the Simon & Schuster Speakers Bureau at
1-866-248-3049 or visit our website at www.simonspeakers.com.

Designed by Meredith Ray

Manufactured in the United States of America

1   3   5   7   9   10   8   6   4   2

Library of Congress Cataloging-in-Publication Data

McMurtry, Larry.
The Berrybender narratives / Larry McMurtry.
p.   cm.
1. Berrybender family (Fictitious characters)—Fiction. 2. Eccentrics and eccentricities—
Fiction. 3. British—West (U.S.)—Fiction. 4. Women immigrants—Fiction. I. Title.
PS3563.A319B47 2012
813'.54—dc23   2011033049
ISBN 978-1-4516-4772-3
ISBN 978-1-4516-4843-0 (ebook)

These titles were previously published individually.

The Berrybender Narratives *is dedicated to the secondhand booksellers of the Western world, who have done so much, over a fifty-year stretch, to help me to an education.*

Contents

THE
BERRYBENDER
NARRATIVES

Characters

Berrybenders

Lord Albany Berrybender
Lady Constance Berrybender
Tasmin
Bess (Buffum)
Bobbety
Mary
Brother Seven
Sister Ten (*later,* Kate)

Tintamarre, *Tasmin's staghound*
Prince Talleyrand, *parrot*

Staff

Gladwyn, *valet, gun bearer*
Fräulein Pfretzskaner, *tutor*
Master Jeremy Thaw, *tutor*
Mademoiselle Pellenc, femme de chambre
Cook
Eliza, *kitchen maid*
Millicent, *laundress*
Señor Yanez, *gunsmith*
Signor Claricia, *carriage maker*
Venetia Kennet, *cellist*
Old Gorska, *hunter*

Gorska Minor, *his son*
Piet Van Wely, *naturalist*
Holger Sten, *painter*
Tim, *stable boy*

Captain George Aitken
Charlie Hodges, *boatman*
Mery-Michaud, engagé
George Catlin, *American painter*
Toussaint Charbonneau, *interpreter-guide*
Coal, *Charbonneau's Hidatsa wife*

Jim Snow (The Raven Brave; Sin Killer)
Dan Drew, *prairie hunter*
Maelgwyn Evans, *trapper, Knife River*
Master Tobias Stiles, *deceased*
Father Geoffrin, *Jesuit*

Indians

Big White, *Mandan*
The Hairy Horn, *Oglala Sioux*
Blue Thunder, *Piegan Blackfoot*
Nemba, *Oto*
Pit-ta-sa, *Teton Sioux*
Blue Blanket, *Teton Sioux*
Neighing Horses, *Teton Sioux*
White Hawk, *Sans Arc*
Three Geese, *Sans Arc*
Grasshopper, *Sans Arc*
Cat Head, *Sans Arc*
Big Stealer, *Sans Arc*
Little Stealer, *Sans Arc*
Step Toe, *Mandan*
Rabbit Skin, *Mandan*
Draga, *Aleut-Russian*
The Bad Eye, *Gros Ventre*

French

Georges Guillaume, *trader*
Simon Le Page, *Hudson's Bay Company agent*
Malboeuf, *his assistant*

John Skraeling, *trader*
Malgres, *Mexican/Apache*

mud, though in fact it was no worse off than the steamer, grounded for the night on what the river men called a riffle, or sandbar. Mr. Catlin, though mildly ridiculous, had not been wrong to call the Missouri a plain of mud. The Berrybender family, with all its get and chattels, was, for the moment, stalled.

"What shall we do, Tasmin?" Bobbety asked, as usual referring all questions of procedure to his older sister.

"Let's examine the matter from the point of view of logic," Tasmin said. Her beloved mama and papa—Lord and Lady Berrybender, that is to say—were, of all the great race of human beings, the least likely to accept the severities of logic. Whim alone was their lodestar and their guide—whim it was that caused them to pack up and leave their great house in Northamptonshire; whim had brought them through America to their present resting place on a sandbar in the Missouri River—and only so that Lord Berrybender could shoot different animals from those he shot at home.

"This pirogue won't move, but our legs will," Tasmin pointed out.

She was going to suggest that they wade back to the ship and join the evening's carouse when little Mary walked out of the dusk holding an immense, vicious turtle above her head, a creature half at least her own weight, which she promptly flung amidst them, into the pirogue—no boat was ever emptied of its human occupants more quickly. Tintamarre, Tasmin's gallant hound, set up a violent braying and attempted a lunge or two at the turtle, of course to little avail. The Berrybenders were in the water, and the turtle was in the boat.

"It's entirely your fault, Bobbety," Buffum said. "Why *will* boys attempt to thrust frogs down little girls' dresses?"

Bobbety made no reply—he was sucking his bitten finger, so that no drop of his noble blood would drip into the Missouri to tempt the piranhas from their watery homes.

There seemed nothing for it but to swim back to the steamer, leaving the outraged turtle in possession of the pirogue. The water proved so shallow that no swimming was required, though Mary, perhaps amphibian by nature, dove and bobbed like a dolphin. Tintamarre floundered off after a mud hen, which eluded him.

The fact that the four of them, muddy as muskrats, arrived in the midst of dinner and rushed to their seats at the great groaning table aroused no comment at all; the group, as usual, was going at one another hammer and tongs: Lord Berrybender was profane with Gladwyn, who had dribbled the claret;

Master Jeremy Thaw, entirely overcome with drink, was slumped amid the salads, snoring loudly; Mr. George Catlin was attempting to make it up with Lady Constance by explaining the Hindu doctrine of reincarnation. The fat Fräulein Pfretzskaner and the skinny Mademoiselle Pellenc were shrieking at each other: the two despised everything that their respective nations stood for. The dank Dane, Holger Sten, annoyed to find that another painter had presented himself on board, was staring daggers at Mr. Catlin, while the two Mediterraneans, Señor Yanez and Signor Claricia, having drunk far too much of Lord Berrybender's excellent claret, were directing looks of frank concupiscence at Miss Venetia Kennet, who sat with her cello at the ready, waiting for the din to subside before favoring the group with a little Haydn. Piet Van Wely, aroused by Mademoiselle Pellenc's fiery rages, puffed rapidly at his foul pipe; and of course, there was Lady Berrybender's ancient, raggedy parrot, Prince Talleyrand, who was allowed the freedom of the table and was liable to pluck tidbits virtually off the tongues of inattentive diners.

Lady Berrybender's brow was furrowed, always a sign of intense and unaccustomed mental effort.

"I don't think I should wish to come back as an eel, if I must come back at all," she was saying, rather querulously. Late in the day Lady Constance was apt to grow careless with her dress; one of her great dugs was at the moment almost fully exposed, a fact not lost on the Mediterraneans, or even the normally monkish Holger Sten.

"Madam, the eel is only one of many possibilities reincarnation offers," Mr. Catlin said, rather stiffly.

"I will endeavor to come back as a mosquito and bite Mary and give her malaria and cause her to foam at the mouth," Bobbety announced, failing, as he often did, to correctly match his symptoms with his disease.

Tasmin had never lacked appetite. The goose was excellent—Cook had even been rather clever with some sweetbreads. Delicacy was the last thing wanted at the Berrybender table; Tasmin shoved, grabbed, elbowed, ate her fill, and then got up and left. A restlessness seized her—though she had nothing much against Venetia Kennet, she felt like avoiding Haydn for once and so went out on the upper deck, to take the rather humid air.

Below her on the underdeck was the rabble who would be expected to do most of the work on the Berrybenders' grand expedition: the smelly *engagés* in their greasy pants; Tim, the randy stable boy; Old Gorska and Gorska Minor, the former quite drunk; the shambling Monsieur Charbonneau, taller than the *engagés* but no less smelly; and a few scowling boatmen,

Tasmin was, as she had often asserted, the one competent Berrybender; even if she now disclaimed the family connection, she hoped to retain the competence. She had never made a fire, but she *had* read several of Mr. Cooper's novels, and supposed that, with application, she could soon master the essentials of flint and steel, the very objects contained in the young frontiersman's small deerskin pouch.

Remembering, as best she could, her Cooper, Tasmin assembled a sizable pyramid of grass and twigs, whacked away with the flint and steel, and was rewarded, after only a few minutes, with a respectable column of smoke. She was down on her knees, puffing at the pyramid, encouraged now and then by a tiny tongue of flame, when the young man came back with a dead doe over his shoulders, the arrow that had killed her still wagging from her side.

No sooner had he dropped the doe behind the log where he had been praying than he bent and with a flick or two reduced her grassy pyramid to one half its size, after which, immediately, a sturdy flame shot up.

"Too much grass," he explained. In only a few minutes he had the liver out of the deer, seared it over the blazing fire, and offered it to Tasmin on the point of his knife. A lifetime of eating amid the violent contention of the Berrybender table had long since rid her of any pretentions to ladylike etiquette when it came to food. Well used to fighting off her siblings with elbow and fist, Tasmin seized the dripping liver and ate it avidly; no meat had ever tasted better.

Her host and victualler watched in silence, then quickly butchered the little deer, which was already beginning to attract a green buzz of flies.

"Do you know that girl that sniffs out roots?" he asked, watching Tasmin closely.

"Yes, that's my sister Mary—she seems to have an unusually keen smeller," Tasmin said. "How did *you* know she could sniff out roots?"

"I seen her last night—she was talking to a snake," he said. "The snake led her to that turtle. A turtle that size could have bitten her arm off, but it didn't."

"No doubt she took it unawares," Tasmin said, a little puzzled by the drift the conversation had taken.

"A child that talks with serpents has a powerful sin in her," the young man said. His brown eyes had suddenly turned to flint. The look was so hard that Tasmin, of a sudden, got goose bumps. Who *was* this young fellow, who looked at her so?

"I still don't know your name, sir," she pointed out, meekly, hoping that such a normal inquiry would make him mild again.

The young man shrugged, as if to suggest that a name was of little importance.

"Depends on where I am," he said. "Round here I'm mostly just Jim—Jim Snow."

Intrigued, Tasmin ventured another question.

"But Mr. Snow, who are you when you're somewhere else?" she asked, coquettishly.

"The Assiniboines call me the Raven Brave," he said—"they're way north of here. Some of the boys just call me Sin Killer. I'm hard when it comes to sin."

Tasmin could see that, just from the change in his eyes when the subject of sin came up, a subject Tasmin had never given even a moment's thought to, though growing up in a family of flagrant sinners had given her plenty of opportunity to observe the phenomenon at first hand.

"You've got no kit," Jim Snow pointed out, more mildly. "I expect you could use some help, getting back to the boat."

"Why, yes . . . if it wouldn't be too much trouble," Tasmin said, but Jim Snow was already shifting some of the more edible portions of the butchered deer into the pirogue. His rifle, bow, and knife seemed to be his only possessions. In a moment he had settled Tasmin in the front of the pirogue and quickly moved the small craft toward the middle of the river: they were on their way to catch up with Tasmin's wandering kin.

4

As there was only one paddle, and Mr. Snow had it . . .

As there was only one paddle, and Mr. Snow had it, Tasmin could be of little assistance—she sat idly in the front of the pirogue, in a mood of indecision. Her oarsman soon demonstrated a keen eye, easily anticipating sandbars and hidden trees, obstacles he skirted with a few flicks of the paddle.

"I say, who was that gentleman you were wrestling with, Tassie, in the year of our Lord 1832?" Bess asked, in her most grating tone. Tasmin at once slapped her sharply—she had quickly acquired the American habit of addressing all problems as violently as possible.

"When I require a calendar I can quite well acquire one from the stationer's, Bess," she informed her stunned sister.

"But Tasmin . . . ," Bobbety began; he stopped at once when Tasmin doubled up her fist and shook it at him.

The wicked Mary smiled.

Tasmin raced as quickly as she could out onto the prairie. Mr. Snow had been gone but a minute, it seemed—perhaps she could catch him yet. Perhaps the temper aroused by her careless words would have cooled—if she could just find him, there might yet be hope.

Gone he was, though—as far as she could see there was nothing but the sighing grass. Tasmin could scarcely believe it—where had he gone? All around her was featureless plain and empty sky. So confused was Tasmin by this emptiness that, once she gave up and stopped, she would have been hard put even to find her way back to the river, had it not been for the loud braying of Tintamarre, who had found a muskrat hole and was attempting to bark its inhabitants to death.

"But who was it, Tassie . . . mayn't I even ask?" the tearful Buffum said, when Tasmin returned. Still in a dark temper, Tasmin did not reply.

"*I* know who it was—Sin Killer," the sinister Mary said.

Without another word being spoken, Tasmin rowed them back to the steamer *Rocky Mount*—all, that is, except Tintamarre, who was still barking into his muskrat hole.

8

In her red fury Tasmin had forgotten . . .

Bobbety and Buffum Tasmin quite refused to forgive—in her view it was entirely their fault that the Raven Brave had got away, leaving her to examine her own surprisingly turbulent feelings. Could she be falling in love with this scarcely articulate young American? Since she reached the age of twelve, men Tasmin had no interest in had been falling in love with *her*—could it be that matters were now reversed? Had she been making a fool of herself over a man who didn't want her?

Or *did* he want her? A day or two more and she might have had him, she told herself. Three days more and he would have been happy to take her to Santa Fe, or Samarkand, for that matter.

Yet now the Raven Brave was gone, tramping alone somewhere on the great pallid prairies.

Tasmin had yanked little Mary up by her scruff and flung her into the pirogue, curious as to how this malignant sprite could have known that the man who was shaking her was called the Sin Killer.

"Big White talks of him," Mary said. "All the Indians do."

In her red fury Tasmin had forgotten that they had three wild chiefs on board—all three had been to Washington to meet the president, and were being returned, under Monsieur Charbonneau's care, to their respective tribes. All three chiefs were old: they lounged around the lower deck all day, amid the greatest disorder, smoking long-stemmed pipes, spitting, snoring, painting themselves up most garishly, and occasionally rolling a kind of dice made from elk bones.

"And since when do you speak the languages of the Mandan, the Blackfoot, or the Sioux?" Tasmin asked. She knew that, in Master Jeremy Thaw's opinion, Mary was the family's best linguist, able to babble tiresomely in Greek, but Tasmin tended to disregard Master Thaw's opinion.

"Big White is teaching me Mandan, and the Hairy Horn helps me to comprehend the dialects of the Sioux," Mary said. "The only one who won't help me is Blue Thunder, who is a Blackfoot of the Piegan band."

"It is hardly ladylike to conspicuously display one's knowledge," Tasmin reminded her. "Do I flaunt my Portuguese?"

In fact she could scarcely utter a syllable in that peculiar tongue, though it was true that a skinny hidalgo, of a vaguely Iberian nature, had seen her once at a horse race and proposed marriage immediately.

"Are you going to fornicate with the Sin Killer?" Mary asked—she had ever been strikingly direct.

"Perhaps I shall—we'll see," Tasmin told her.

"If you plan to travel the prairies you had best take me," Mary said.

"You brash mite, why would I?" Tasmin asked.

"So you won't starve—I can sniff out tubers, tasty tubers," Mary said, as they pulled alongside the steamer *Rocky Mount.*

9

He lumbered away like some small dirty bear . . .

Tasmin's first thought, once getting on board, was to rush down to the underdeck and question Monsieur Charbonneau closely about her new acquaintance, Mr. Snow—but of course she had scarcely stepped on deck when a garrulous regiment rushed at her, each member eager to relate to her various iniquities that had occurred in her absence.

"Why, Tasmin, you look wild as a deer," Lady Berrybender said—she was already walking unsteadily from the effects of her morning tipple.

"I was just picnicking, Mama . . . exploring the prairie glades a bit," Tasmin said—she had no intention of mentioning the Raven Brave to her mother, though she *did* gossip a little with Mademoiselle Pellenc, who drew her a bath and combed the many tangles out of her wild hair.

Mademoiselle Pellenc was the only female on board whose cynicism matched Tasmin's own. For all that, the violently hot-blooded Frenchwoman flew like a shuttlecock from Señor Yanez to Signor Claricia and back again; the latter was rather too garlicky, the former a good deal too quick, but Mademoiselle was not slow to inform Tasmin that she had just acquired a fresh prospect.

Tasmin supposed for a moment that she might mean Lord B. himself, supposedly still fully occupied with the languid cellist, Venetia Kennet.

"*Non, non,* Herr Sten!" Mademoiselle said. "He presented himself to me in the laundry—he is a fellow of modest dimensions, I am afraid."

"I wouldn't expect too much in the way of passion from a Dane," Tasmin said. "What else is new that I should know?"

"The German slut, she gives herself to the big American—Big Charlie," Mademoiselle said.

Tasmin found herself completely unmoved by this news, or by various other tidbits of gossip that Mademoiselle offered. She no longer much cared what this rabble of displaced Europeans did with themselves. As soon as she was dressed in a clean shift she hurried down to the underdeck to locate Monsieur Charbonneau, the man who knew Jim Snow.

Toussaint Charbonneau was a tall, graying man of a decidedly shambling nature, kindly, but never really clean or wholly sober. His buckskin shirt was invariably stained, his leggings often torn. On this occasion Tasmin found him soon enough, sitting at a filthy table with his plump young Hidatsa wife, Coal. Old Gorska, equally untidy, had been sitting with them but he hastily moved away when Tasmin appeared; she had more than once given him notice that she would tolerate none of his low Polish insolence. He lumbered away like some small dirty bear the moment she appeared.

Tasmin liked Coal, a girl round of form and merry of eye; she was perhaps fifteen, and greedy for trinkets, an appetite girls seemed to share. Tasmin had won her for life by presenting her with a tortoiseshell comb, which she wore to splendid effect in her shiny black hair. To Tasmin it seemed a pity that such a lively creature had been taken to wife by this pettish old fellow, Charbonneau, no prize that Tasmin could see.

"Bonjour, monsieur," Tasmin said at once to the old tippler. "Could you please tell me what you know about the Sin Killer?"

Tasmin had spoken politely; she was hardly prepared for the pandemonium her words produced among the chiefs. The old Hairy Horn jumped up as if pricked, brandishing a gleaming hatchet. Big White rose too and took up his great war club, referred to as the "skull smasher" by Monsieur Charbonneau. The Piegan Blue Thunder looked wary—even a few of the *engagés* drew their knives, as if expecting immediate assault.

Old Charbonneau, the man to whom Tasmin had put her question, seemed, for the moment, quite paralyzed—the pinch of snuff he had been in the process of carrying to his nose rained like powder on his untidy tunic.

"Why, miss," he said, in astonished tones, "how would you be knowing Jimmy Snow?"

"I went rather adrift in my pirogue," Tasmin explained. "Mr. Snow found me and brought me back—if he hadn't come along I expect I'd still be adrift."

At that point Charbonneau, the Hairy Horn, Big White, and several *en-*

gagés all rushed to the rail—they all stood gazing at the somber but empty prairie.

"Which way did Jimmy go, miss?" Charbonneau asked.

"I am not a compass—I did not ascertain his direction," Tasmin said— she had thrown the red nations into turmoil without learning even one useful fact about the Raven Brave.

"Jimmy's sly—he might be lurking—that's what's upset the chiefs," Charbonneau stammered. "Jimmy can sneak up on a prairie chicken and catch it, which is a rare skill. It's best to be watchful with Jimmy around."

At that point they all heard a high whistling—a great flock of swans, hundreds and hundreds, were passing directly overhead, a fact which seemed to stimulate even sharper anxiety amid the chiefs and the *engagés*. They clearly did not like being beneath so many swans.

To Tasmin all this stir and hubbub was quite ridiculous. It was a fine day—the boat was moving steadily—what harm could come from a flock of birds? What astonished her was that her rescuer, Mr. Snow—who was only one man—inspired such fear that half the men on the boat felt they must rush to arms—yet still, she didn't know why.

It occurred to her then that there *was* one person who might be helpful, the cheerful and muscular Captain George Aitken, the master of the steamer *Rocky Mount*.

Less than a minute later, to George Aitken's mild surprise, Tasmin presented herself on the bridge.

10

"Our West is not much like your gentle England."

Mr. Catlin's easel and paints were set up on the bridge, but of that silly cackler there was no sign—Tasmin was alone with sturdy Captain Aitken, who was studying the river with a practiced eye.

"Oh, Mr. Catlin—no, miss," he said. "Mr. Catlin's gone ashore with your father on a hunt. I believe they are hoping to scare up a bear."

"How thrilling—we've so few in England now—just what the Gypsies have," Tasmin said. "May I ask if you're acquainted with Mr. Jim Snow? I mentioned him to Monsieur Charbonneau and I'm afraid caused quite a stir."

"Jimmy, why yes, I know him pretty well," Captain Aitken said. "I thought that was Jim you set ashore this morning—bit of a tussle you were having, it seemed."

Tasmin blushed—she had not supposed this honest captain had seen her violent shaking. Of course he had a spyglass—no doubt an indispensable tool on such a river.

And yet Captain Aitken quietly went on with his job. He did not appear to feel that a tussle on a riverbank between a lad and a lass was a thing much out of the ordinary.

"That was my fault—I fear I let slip a mild oath—it was more than Mr. Snow could tolerate," Tasmin admitted.

"That's Jimmy—he's preachy unless he's drunk," Captain Aitken said. "Best not to cuss in his company unless you have to, though he's a riproaring cusser himself when his blood is up. Smacked you on the cheek, I see—didn't he, miss?"

Tasmin did have a bit of a bruise on one cheek, though this bluff professional man had been the only one to mention it. Her mother might well have mistaken it for dirt, but Mademoiselle Pellenc, no stranger to slappings, must surely have seen it for what it was.

Tasmin found that she liked Captain Aitken the better for his candor—she gave him a smile and he returned it.

"When I mentioned Mr. Snow's name belowdecks it stirred up quite a fuss," she said. "Can you tell me why?"

"Jimmy's an Indian fighter," Captain Aitken said, speaking as casually as if he had just informed her that Mr. Snow was a butcher, a baker, or a candlestick maker. "Oh, Jim can trap and he can hunt as well—he and Pomp Charbonneau have trapped all the way up on the Green River, and not many can say that."

"I have heard of young Monsieur Charbonneau," Tasmin said. "Is he an Indian fighter too?"

Captain Aitken looked at her for rather a long while—something of the weariness that had been in Jim Snow's face when she challenged him to take her with him could be seen in Captain Aitken's face as well, though the captain's gaze held no trace of unfriendliness. He just looked tired—nothing seemed to tire men so quickly as even a few minutes' questioning by a persistent woman.

"You're new to our country, Miss Berrybender," Captain Aitken said. "Our West is not much like your gentle England. If a man's got killing in him, the West will draw it out."

"And is Monsieur Pomp Charbonneau an Indian fighter too?" Tasmin repeated.

"Oh, Pomp will kill in battle, if he has to," the captain said. "So will I— and I have. But most sensible men will walk around an Indian fight, if they can. I will, and Pomp will too."

"But not Mr. Snow, I take it," Tasmin said.

"No, not Jimmy," the captain said. "It's the Indians who will walk around Jimmy, if he'll allow it."

"What happens when he won't allow it?" Tasmin asked.

The poor man heaved a sigh.

"When he won't, then there's likely to be hell to pay," Captain Aitken said.

11

. . . Cook brought up a squab and a squash . . .

That Indians feared Jim Snow, the Sin Killer, did not surprise Tasmin— she had seen the cold fury in his eyes when he turned to face the four painted warriors by the hill of devils. She very much doubted that there were devils about that rocky bluff that could have bested the Sin Killer when it came to dealing out carnage. Perhaps he had only held back that day because he didn't want her to see him at his killing.

Once she left the bridge Tasmin spent the morning sitting under a little awning outside her bedroom, a victim of very uneven moods. She looked far out onto the plains to the west, the plains that she had trod but for a day. At lunch Cook brought up a squab and a squash, the latter article having been obtained from some mild river Indians a few days earlier. Tasmin ate only a bite or two. The appetite that had led her to rip at a deer's liver with her teeth had now quite deserted her. In a room nearby Buffum and Bobbety were attempting their Latin, under the droning instruction of Master Jeremy Thaw—she could just make out rhythms that seemed to suggest Horace. From time to time the boat would have to back off a riffle, or else the *engagés* might need to saw off a snag. Fräulein Pfretzskaner and Master Thaw had their customary spat—the Fräulein wanted him to finish up with Latin so she could begin with their mathematics. At the end of the spat Fräulein burst into tears; salty floods drenched her great bosom, an interruption which gave Buffum and Bobbety time to attempt to make peace with their sister.

"We are so sorry, Tassie, that we interrupted you with your gentleman," Buffum said. "We will never be so brash again."

"What will *that* matter—as you can see, my gentleman is gone," Tasmin said, in her iciest tones.

"I suppose he meant to carry you away to Samarkand," Bobbety said, in his most grating voice.

"Samarkand is in Persia, you ignorant nit," Tasmin told her brother. "The city west of here where I had hoped to be taken is Santa Fe—but now you two have ruined everything."

"Perhaps Papa would hire you a guide," Buffum said. "It is said that Monsieur Charbonneau's son is a fine guide. He was brought up in Germany by a prince, I believe."

"Yes, the brilliant Pomp," Tasmin said. How a son of Charbonneau's had got to Germany was rather intriguing but it did nothing to mollify her for the loss of Jim Snow. Though her siblings were virtually prostrate with guilt, Tasmin did not immediately unbend—such pious virtues as forgiveness did not appeal to her. Besides, there was the distinct possibility that the Raven Brave was gone for good, driven off by her cursing. He may have felt that such a hell-bound woman deserved no guide.

These unhappy thoughts produced in Tasmin an almost unendurable restlessness. It was a sultry day—after a time she napped, slipping into an impatient, swollen dream. She seemed to hear great wings beating, and then a hand was on her, near the dark entry. She waited, but just then the steamer bumped hard against a riffle and Tasmin woke. Her sister Mary sat by the rail, licking clean the last greasy bones of Tasmin's squab.

"Who offered you my bird, you greedy wretch?" Tasmin inquired.

"The Hairy Horn says that we shall see a million pigeons this afternoon," Mary replied—of all the family she took the least notice of Tasmin's moods. "Old Gorska can easily shoot you some."

Tasmin, hungry again, made no answer.

"I expect you'll soon be leaving this old boat, won't you, Tassie?" Mary asked. She was but a little thing, yet she made up in ferocity what she lacked in size. Bobbety was of the opinion that she might be rabid—but of course, Bobbety's opinions were rarely accurate.

In this case, Mary was right. Tasmin did mean to leave the boat, which was just a floating Europe. Even the smelly *engagés* were merely Frenchmen at one remove.

"The chiefs are hoping you will lure the Sin Killer on board," Mary said. "They hope to fall on him and kill him."

"Oh tush," Tasmin said. "The chiefs are old men. I doubt they would be a match for my Raven Brave."

"It is only the Indians to the north who call him the Raven Brave—Mr. Catlin told me that," Mary said. "And he told me why."

"Well, if Mr. Catlin said it, then it must be knowledge beyond challenge," Tasmin replied. "His learning is quite encyclopedic, in his own view at least."

"I like Mr. Catlin," Mary said. "Once we locate some buffalo he means to make me his assistant. We'll tramp off into the prairie and I'll carry his paints."

"If you're going to wake me up, stick to the point," Tasmin said. "Why do the Indians of the north call my friend Mr. Snow the Raven Brave?"

"Because there are no vultures in the north," Mary said, giving the bones of the pigeon one last lick. "In the north the raven is the bird of death."

"You needn't sound so melodramatic about it, Mary," Tasmin said. "Even in England crows are carrion birds. Nor is it a bad thing that Indians fear my friend. I myself would be a captive of the noisy Osage now, had Mr. Snow not saved me."

"Mr. Catlin says Papa is not to shoot the great swans," Mary said. "He says the Indians believe that swans are the carriers of souls."

"Tut, they only want to sell the feathers," Tasmin said. "Your new friend Mr. Catlin is a fine exaggerator. Take that plate to Cook and ask her to fix me a chop—a large chop."

"Cook was just thrashing Eliza," Mary informed her. "Eliza broke two plates this morning. If she is allowed to go on in this way we will soon be without a plate to our name."

"Trot along and do as you're told," Tasmin said, and then at once retracted her command, having just remembered something.

"Mr. Snow claims he saw you talking to a serpent," she said. "Is that true? Can you communicate with serpents?"

"It was merely a moccasin—I told it to go bite Bobbety, since he assaulted me with a frog," Mary said. "But the moccasin did nothing to Bobbety, otherwise he'd be dead."

"Mary, you are a violent brat," Tasmin said.

12

. . . far to the west, on a low hill, three antelope stood.

Long before the pigeons came, every member of the hunting party was in a crashing bad temper, none more so than Lord Berrybender, who was not accustomed to tramping around for hours without once firing his gun. He did not, at least, have to *carry* his gun—Gorska Minor shouldered the two fowling pieces, while Gladwyn took the rifles. Old Gorska had his own weapon, Belgian-made and of the finest workmanship; Mr. Catlin, who merely carried an ordinary musket, had several times complimented Gorska on his excellent Belgian gun. These compliments did not entirely please Lord Berrybender, who did not see why the help should have better equipment than his own, although it was true that the company would soon be dependent on the Polish hunter for meat, and possibly even for defense. Had he been allowed to blast away continually at buffalo and bear, or even antelope and elk, Lord Berrybender might have been less envious of Gorska's Belgian gun; but such, emphatically, had not been the case. The prairie grass that from a distance looked so silken was more nearly like a carpet of needles, and nothing appeared to be abroad to be stuck by the needles but themselves.

"I say, Gorska, can't you send that boy off to beat the bushes and scare up a stag or two?" Lord B. inquired impatiently.

"What bushes? No bushes," Gorska said. He had honed his hunting skills in the employ of a petty prince, ruler of a pocket duchy in the foot-hills of the Carpathians, in whose heavily forested glades it was easy to surprise the local game: boar, stag, even bear. But how was anyone to surprise game on this treeless prairie, where the wind was always blowing, for hunting purposes, from the wrong direction and where the animals—who, after all, were not blind—could see the hunters coming when they were still far out of range of even the best Belgian rifle?

"Well, if there are no bushes, then it's somebody's fault," Lord B. complained. "Poor planning, I say. Somebody should have come out here and planted a few bushes."

George Catlin, though he considered Lord Berrybender to be a rude, crusty old fussbudget, also knew that he was reputed to be one of the richest men in England; a hand-to-mouth painter such as himself, often dependent on extremely whimsical patronage, could not afford to be rude to the richest man in England, however great a fool he might be.

"Of course, of course—such an excess of visibility is a great inconvenience," he said. "It's a pity Mr. Jefferson was never in the West—I imagine he would have at once foreseen the necessity of bushes."

Just then Old Gorska held up a hand: far to the west, on a low hill, three antelope stood.

The efficient if moody Gladwyn, who was never more than a step behind Lord Berrybender, immediately held out a rifle.

"Antelope . . . about time they showed up," Lord Berrybender said.

"We're in luck, sir," George Catlin said. "Saddle of antelope is a most excellent American dish . . . first rate, excellent, tasty." When nervous, and he was usually nervous, George failed to see that his habit of using three words where one would have done was apt to irritate some people.

"They are a mile away," Old Gorska pointed out—he saw no hope of a successful approach to the jittery antelope.

"Quite inaccurate, they are but half a mile from us at most," Gladwyn said. He did not approve of the Pole.

"Mile," Gorska repeated, though he had no idea how far away the animals were.

The antelope appeared to be watching the English party—to George Catlin's eye they seemed poised for flight.

"My gun won't shoot a mile—or half a mile either," Lord Berrybender said. "The beasts must be brought closer."

"There's an old hunter's dodge that sometimes works with antelope,"

George said. "I believe the mountain men use it with frequent success . . . they're curious, you see, the pronghorns. I will advance a little
way toward them and then stop and stand on my head. If I waggle my legs
at them they may be disposed to come and investigate. Crouch down and
have your guns ready while I make the attempt."

"All right," Lord Berrybender said. "Perhaps I'll just say a prayer or two,
while I'm kneeling. I've been rather wicked with Venetia lately."

George Catlin advanced some fifty steps and then, laying aside his
floppy hat, quickly stood on his head. The antelope had not moved. Carefully, he began to waggle his legs and was just getting the hang of it when
the antelope, unattracted, turned and fled.

Sobered by the suspicion that he had not only lost three antelope but
several fat commissions as well, George Catlin brushed the grass off his
hat and rejoined the group.

"I fear they winded us," he said.

"Next time I'll bring my horse—at least I could chase the brutes," Lord
Berrybender said.

Gorska Minor proceeded to kick up a badger, an aggressive creature
who bared its teeth and snarled. While Gorska Minor poked at it with his
ramrod the sky darkened; the sounds of millions of beating wings was
heard. From the north the pigeons came, in a cloud that blocked the sun
and cast a shadow far across the prairie. The hunting party stood and
looked—some half an hour passed and still the cooing pigeons came.

"Where are they going, Catlin?" Lord B. inquired.

"Perhaps Indiana—someplace where there's grain," George said.

Lord Berrybender took his fowling piece and fired carelessly into the
air: twenty-two pigeons rained down. Gorska Minor was forced to scamper, in his efforts to gather them up.

"It won't do, Gorska—I think I might have hoped for something better
than squab," Lord Berrybender said, turning in disgust toward the river
and the boat.

13

. . . news of the Sin Killer's approach had stirred them up.

The *engagés* were bitter because the English lord was so stingy with his grog—the splenetic Mery-Michaud, who had never been closer to France than the Hudson's Bay Company's trading post at Three Rivers, had heard of a big revolution and wanted to cut the old lord's head off. He came to Toussaint Charbonneau ranting about grog and beheadings; it was a message the tired interpreter received more and more wearily, every evening. The chiefs were in a disorderly mood too—news of the Sin Killer's approach had stirred them up.

It seemed to Charbonneau that he had spent far too much of his life listening to the endless complaints of *engagés* and Indian chiefs. If it wasn't grog they lacked, it was women, or money, or vittles.

"Shush that blab, Mery, unless you want a fine flogging," Charbonneau said. "I ain't the boss of His Lordship's liquor—there's a whole keelboat of it, alongside. Go steal some if you're that dry."

Big Charlie Hodges smiled at that suggestion—if Charbonneau had ever been fully sober himself he would have realized that the *engagés* had been going regularly over the side, to nip bottles of Lord Berrybender's claret from the keelboat. Charlie Hodges was the only American among the crew—George Aitken had hired him because he needed at least one boatman who spoke English, to give him precise information about the riffles and the snags.

Charlie didn't care much for the *engagés,* but he had a certain sympathy for Sharbo, an old, tired man, not unkindly, who had the hard job of managing the three surly chiefs and the English family too.

"That liquor boat is already sitting higher in the water—I'm surprised nobody's noticed," Charlie said.

Tim, the stable boy, who looked after Lord Berrybender's two thoroughbreds and his fine pair of carriage horses, knew that the rascally Frenchmen were stealing the old lord's liquor, but he hated the old man, who had often cuffed him rudely, and didn't care.

"How long before it's all gone, Charlie?" Tim asked.

"A month, maybe," Charlie said. "I expect most of the *engagés* will be long gone by then—they'll want to be trapping up the Red River of the North."

Though he didn't say it, Charlie Hodges meant to be long gone by that time too. Tim could stay in his stables and play the beast with two backs with Miss Elizabeth Berrybender all he pleased—Charlie had heard them huffing and grunting several times. Tim, for his part, had been equally discreet when he saw Fräulein Pfretzskaner slipping Charlie Hodges a big sausage or a leg of goose. It was clearly Charlie that the Fräulein favored— he was the only man on board built to her own ample dimensions; the day rarely passed but that she found a way to offer her Charlie some tidbit from His Lordship's table. Most nights they managed to enjoy at least some fleshly probings in a private corner off the pantry.

Charlie Hodges, though he closely concealed his intentions from every- one, did not intend to remain much longer with the steamer *Rocky Mount*. Charlie was no river man—he had headed west to farm, having heard that the Ioway soil was rich and fertile. The forests were said to be light, the Indians not too fierce. Though fond of Captain Aitken, Charlie did not feel he could allow such an opportunity to be missed. Somewhere above the mouth of the Platte, a stream they would very soon pass, he meant to leave the boat and tramp off to the east. His hope was to find land close to the Mississippi, which would make for ease of shipping, and as surely as he would need a plow, he would also need a wife—and he wanted no skinny slip of a girl, either. What he wanted was a fine sturdy woman of height and heft, someone who would bear him six to a dozen children to help him work the land. For such a task the big Fräulein seemed ideal; she hissed like a kettle whenever he touched her, steamed like a stove when they could enjoy a full embrace. For the Berrybenders, her employers, the Fräulein expressed only loathing. She would leave with her Charlie in an instant—if it should be that they must escape with only the clothes on their backs, then the Fräulein was ready. She could cook, she could sew, she could wield an axe; no more lessons with the stupid English children, no more quarrels with the skinny, stuck-up French whore. Charlie's secret was safe with her—it was her secret too.

Meanwhile Charbonneau, tired and tipsy, was trying to convince the Hairy Horn that the Sin Killer would not attack the boat.

"Jimmy's got no call to fight us," he said. "He just found that English girl and brought her back, that's all."

"A warrior who has eaten the lightning doesn't behave like other men," the Hairy Horn said. He himself had no fear of the Sin Killer. Such a warrior would gain nothing by killing an old man like himself. His interest was mainly in the lightning. Among his own people the belief was that a warrior who had eaten the lightning and survived was impervious to ordinary weapons. In the Hairy Horn's long lifetime he had known only one other man—a Sioux named Burnt Eagle—who had been struck by lightning and lived to fight again. Burnt Eagle had finally been killed by a white bear, but not before he had stolen many horses and counted plenty of coups.

"Only the white bears can kill a man who has eaten the lightning," the Hairy Horn remarked, before retiring to his blanket for the night. What he really wanted was for Sharbo to offer him his woman; such a fine plump girl would be good, but Sharbo, though he had lived long among the Mandans, was like other whites in that regard. He did not share his woman, which was a pity. A girl so young and bouncy would be a good thing, for an old man.

When the old chief left, Gorska walked over to Charbonneau.

"When the buffalo?" he asked, in his limited English.

"I can't say," Charbonneau admitted. "It's been a wet year—lots of the little water holes are full. The buffalo don't need to come to the river yet."

Gorska shuffled off, not satisfied. Every day Lord B. asked about the buffalo. He seemed to think it was Gorska's fault that there were none for him to shoot.

Charbonneau walked over and said a few words to Big White, repeating what he had told the Hairy Horn about Jim Snow. Big White hardly listened—he was a vain old fellow who still believed that the strength of his own arm was all the security he needed against an enemy. He had even put it out that he had single-handedly killed a white bear with his great club, a claim that made even his own young warriors snicker: they knew that the bear was barely quarter grown, little more than a cub, and had been groggy from a winter's sleep when Big White clubbed it.

Charbonneau understood that Big White, the Mandan, was a braggart, and that the Hairy Horn was just a loquacious old man who babbled on to anyone who would listen to him. The only one of his native charges who worried him was the Piegan, Blue Thunder, a powerful man given to sudden, explosive rages. The first wisdom he had been offered about the tribes on the upper Missouri was that the Blackfeet were those who should be given the widest berth. Though there were many beaver in the streams

west of the Yellowstone, few white men had harvested many and escaped
with their own hair. Captain Clark had particularly warned the English
lord about the Blackfeet, but who knew what an English lord would do?

The tall Piegan had passed through Washington in silence—the president's flattery had not impressed him, though he did consider the white
man's axes very superior tools and had been quick to gather up a good
supply.

Though Toussaint Charbonneau had been up and down the Missouri
River more than twenty times he had never enjoyed the luxury of such
a fine boat as the steamer *Rocky Mount*. He and Coal had a snug bunk
under an overhang. Coal kept their baggage neat, busying herself to see
that he was as comfortable as possible; though her efforts were appreciated they did not keep Charbonneau from feeling old, tired, and overbur-
dened; he felt he might be making his last trip up the capricious river on
whose banks he had spent much of his life. It seemed to him that there
was a sadness about these long plains that seeped into men who traveled
them too long. That sadness had seeped into him. Too much was expected
of him—too much. In his memory Charbonneau had begun to loop back to
the time when he and his Bird Woman, Sacagawea, whom Captain Clark
called Janey, had made the great trek to the ocean, with their boy, Pomp,
just a baby on Sacagawea's back. Of all the women he had known, his Bird
had been the quickest of mind; even when she did not know the words that
were being spoken she could figure out what was intended, what was at
stake. None of his other women had had so lively a mind.

Coal knew that her husband was a man of many sorrows, sorrows too
old for her to grasp. Her main hope was that she would soon be with child.
She dreamed of a fat little boy—once her husband saw that he could still
be a maker of sons some of his sorrow might go away. To ensure that there
would be a child, and a male child, Coal did everything the old women told
her to do. She watched the moon, she took certain herbs. Sometimes when
Sharbo was drinking with the boatmen Coal would try to entice him away
before he became too tired. Sometimes when he came to their pallet ready
to sink into sleep Coal would manage to arouse him just enough that he
could be a man for a few moments, long enough to fill her with his seed.

Yet Coal sometimes felt that her husband's sadness must have come
into her, along with his seed. She was by nature a cheerful girl, and yet,
sometimes, lying by Sharbo and listening to him snore, she could not keep
sadness away—could not choke back her tears. Her husband was old, he

might get drunk and fall overboard; someone might kill him; he might simply die, as old men did. Then, whether she liked it or not, she might have to become the wife of some cruel warrior, like Blue Thunder. Every night Coal listened carefully to the call of the night birds; she was listening, particularly, for the trumpeting of the great tundra swans, birds that came every year to the Swamp of the Swans. The old women told her that if, mating, she heard the call of the tundra swans, it would be the best of omens. Then she would soon deliver a fat little boy; then maybe her husband would cheer up.

14

. . . George Catlin, his death at hand, took the only course open to him . . .

George Catlin felt bold enough one morning to ask Lady Tasmin at breakfast if she would care to sit for her portrait—he was at once rebuffed so rudely that he promptly went below and cajoled—with an offer of a new musket and some blue beads—the Piegan Blue Thunder to sit in her stead. After all, it was Indians, not English ladies, that he had come west to paint. Mr. Gainsborough had painted plenty of the latter.

Tasmin knew that the cranky painter was becoming rather too fond of her—even sharp rudeness didn't really discourage him. A week had passed since Jim Snow returned her to the boat—a week during which she had remained so snappish and surly that both family and servants did their best to stay out of her way.

"Blue Thunder will be my first attempt at a portrait of a Western Indian," George said—he did not allow himself to be discouraged by Tasmin's rudeness and had gone back upstairs to finish his coffee. "You can come and watch me work, should you care to, Lady Tasmin."

"Why would I want to watch George Catlin paint a picture of an Indian when I can see the Indian for myself?" Tasmin asked Mary, when George had gone off to assemble his equipment.

Nevertheless, since there was little to do on board except stare at the muddy water of the featureless prairies, Tasmin and Mary drifted down to the lower deck. The Piegan was painting his face in vivid reds and yellows, in preparation for the sitting. Big White and the Hairy Horn ignored these preparations—both were sulking because the painter had not chosen them instead of Blue Thunder.

"I think you and I should gather up our kit and immediately leave this boat, taking only Tintamarre as our protector," Mary said.

Tasmin ignored the comment. For a week she had thought of nothing but escape, and yet she had had just enough experience of prairie life to convince herself that escape, at the very least, might prove impractical.

"Eliza has now broken three more plates," Mary continued. "Mama and Papa will soon be eating off the bare boards—and besides, if we don't hurry, we'll never catch your Mr. Snow."

"In a logical universe I would not be pursuing Mr. Snow, Mr. Snow would be pursuing me," Tasmin observed, noting that the painted Piegan was a strikingly handsome man.

"Perhaps he's following us, even now," Mary said. "Perhaps he means to kidnap you and ravish you."

Tasmin could not suppress a laugh at the wildness of the little creature's imagination.

"You've been spending too much time with Vicky Kennet," Tasmin said. "It is she who secretly dreams of wild ravishments—I believe she is growing rather tired of our old papa."

On the lower deck, near the rail, Mr. George Catlin was waiting with clear impatience for Blue Thunder to finish adorning himself. The Piegan wore a beaded war shirt and had draped himself with a great necklace of bear claws.

"I do believe it will take him longer to paint himself than it will take me to paint *him*," George said.

"I wouldn't mind sitting, I suppose, should you tire of painting these aboriginals," Venetia Kennet, a new arrival, declared. She had unloosed her auburn hair, which fell well below her waist. Both Señor Yanez and Signor Claricia had offered to slave untiringly for her throughout their lives, and yet neither had yet been admitted to the sanctum of her boudoir.

"I'm surprised you aren't at your scales, Vicky," Tasmin said. "Such a demanding discipline, the cello."

Venetia Kennet ignored that thrust. The humid air induced in her a heavy languor. For Tasmin Berrybender she felt the blackest hatred, of the sort one beauty is likely to harbor for another. Vicky's principal hope was that Lord B. would soon get off on a hunt, sparing her, for a day, his heavy but inattentive embraces.

Just then Mademoiselle Pellenc came down from Lady Berrybender's cabin carrying Prince Talleyrand, the ill-tempered old parrot, to allow him his daily airing. Mademoiselle detested the flea-bitten old bird, but Lady B. insisted that Mademoiselle be the one to air him—after all, they both had French names.

No sooner had Prince Talleyrand been released from his cage than he hopped up on the rail near where George Catlin was rapidly sketching in Blue Thunder's wildly tinted profile. The parrot seemed to take more interest in the likeness than any of the other spectators—the scraggly old bird tipped his head curiously, from side to side.

"Good morning, Prince Talleyrand," George said, hoping that a great eagle might sweep down and relieve them all of the filthy bird. It was hard to get a profile right while enduring the scrutiny of a querulous old parrot.

"*Schweig, du blöder Trottel!*" Prince Talleyrand said, raspily but distinctly—even Mary Berrybender gaped with astonishment, while Fräulein Pfretzskaner, who sometimes amused herself by teaching the bird random insults, blushed a very bright red.

"What did he say?" George asked, in shock at having been rudely addressed by a parrot.

Holger Sten, the Danish painter, let out a roar of laughter—to his mind the parrot's remark was quite appropriate.

" 'Shut up, you silly fool,' that's what he said," Holger informed them.

"It's just a country phrase—customary," Fräulein Pfretzskaner mumbled, departing at once to seek her Charlie.

George Catlin, always a quick worker, thought he had Blue Thunder's profile just about right—it only needed a little lengthening of the chin. He was well aware of native impatience; for the moment speed was more important to him than finesse—he could always touch up the likenesses once he got back to Philadelphia. He meant to call his portfolio *Vanishing Races*, and he knew the native races *would* vanish—the very fact that he was traveling up the Missouri in a steamboat meant that, for these wild, warring peoples, the end was not far off.

Lord Berrybender, trailed by his man Gladwyn, came slowly downstairs, feeling rather heavy in his bowels, just as George Catlin finished his adjustment of Blue Thunder's chin. Lord B. tramped over to the easel and took a look.

"Why, hark the heralds, you've got the brute to a T," His Lordship remarked.

Pleased by this unexpected compliment, George Catlin picked up his little canvas and handed it to his sitter, Blue Thunder, hoping the Piegan would like it too. In this he was to be disappointed: instantly the Piegan's passive manner turned to one of horror and rage. He slapped at his painted cheeks, as if to assure himself that they were still part of his face; then he grabbed a hatchet and advanced on the horrified painter, uttering a high, chilling shriek—George Catlin, his death at hand, took the only course open to him, which was to vault over the rail into the river.

Lady Berrybender had been following her husband down to the lower deck, a glass of gin in one hand. Blue Thunder's wild shriek startled her so that she missed her step and plunged straight downstairs, knocking Mademoiselle Pellenc into Señor Yanez, who in turn fell against Gorska Minor, who had been cleaning a gun. People toppled like dominoes; Big White and the Hairy Horn dashed to Blue Thunder's side, and the three of them began to gobble like angry turkeys—at least that was how it sounded to Tasmin's ear. Blue Thunder seemed disposed to leap into the water and finish off the sputtering painter, and he might have, had not Monsieur Charbonneau rushed up and restrained him.

"I say, what a racket—what's upset them, Charbonneau?" His Lordship asked.

"Why, it's just that in the picture Blue Thunder only has half his face— that's the cause of the racket," Charbonneau explained. "Blue Thunder thinks Mr. Catlin has stolen the other half of him—once he *feels* himself good and knows that he's all there, I believe he'll quiet down."

Holger Sten turned to wink at Piet Van Wely, who shared his dislike of the cranky Catlin—but Piet Van Wely was staring hard at the fallen Lady Berrybender, whose eyes were open, whose mouth gaped, and whose neck was bent at a most startling angle.

"Oh, Constance is always fainting; eats too much," Lord Berrybender said, hardly glancing at his wife. "Gluttons frequently faint.

"Do get up, Constance," he insisted. "I'm about to leave for my hunt— mademoiselle, perhaps you might better fetch the smelling salts."

But Mademoiselle Pellenc, Señor Yanez, Signor Claricia, Gorska Minor, Tasmin, Mary, and even Bobbety and Buffum, alarmed by the Piegan's shrieks, all knew what Lord Berrybender had not yet realized, which was that his wife, Lady Constance Berrybender, a heavy eater, would never need smelling salts again. She lay on the lower deck of the steamer *Rocky Mount,* stone dead of a broken neck.

15

... *Mademoiselle Pellenc, whose duty it had been to tend the bird* ...

It was hours later—after the dripping George Catlin had come back on board, after peace had been restored with the chieftains, after Lady Berrybender had received one last kiss from each of her children, after her hair had been combed one last time by Mademoiselle Pellenc, after her shroud had been sewn tightly shut by the skilled seamstress Fräulein Pfretzskaner—that someone happened to remember Prince Talleyrand, Lady Berrybender's parrot. A search was made, but to no avail. Prince Talleyrand had evidently flown away.

"It seems you were right to begin with, George," Tasmin said to the painter, so stunned by what had happened that he had not even bothered to change out of his wet clothes.

"It *is* the river Styx we're traveling on," Tasmin continued. "Not only has it taken poor Mama in the general direction of Hades, but we've lost her parrot too."

George Catlin was silent, for once. His comment about the river Sticks had been only a rather poor jest.

"As for Prince Talleyrand, good riddance, I say," Bess piped. "Smelly old bird."

But Mademoiselle Pellenc, whose duty it had been to tend the bird, could not accept the loss of her once-despised feathery charge.

"Now I am the only French," she cried.

"Well, no, there are the *engagés*," Tasmin reminded her, but she gave the poor half-crazed woman a comforting hug anyway.

16

Now, in the bright morning, a grave was being dug . . .

Jim Snow watched the burial party from a sizable thicket of plum bushes. For a moment he feared the big red dog might catch his scent, but the dog merely looked his way for a moment before trotting off behind a large procession of children and servants, their goal a low bluff where several *engagés* were laboring to dig a grave.

The old parrot had alighted at Jim's campfire the night before. Now that the family whose pet the old bird had been were trooping up a hill, in plain sight, Jim rather expected the bird to rejoin them, but the parrot showed no interest in the grieving group. Instead it happily plucked the ripe, tart plums.

Though Jim Snow had walked briskly south most of a day he had been unable to get the bold, barefoot English girl in the muddy dress off his mind. In truth, his conscience was bothering him somewhat, where Tasmin was concerned. When she cursed he had shaken her so hard he feared she might have cracked a tooth; and yet he doubted that his shaking, or anything else, would long prevent her from leaving the boat and striking out for Santa Fe. Clearly she was a young woman of uncommon determination. Jim could not imagine why such a girl, or such a family, would be traveling up the Missouri River with winter coming on. There was nothing to be expected in the high Missouri country except wild tribes and bitter cold. Santa Fe, with its bustling trade, made a far likelier destination, and yet the big steamboat had already passed the usual embarkation points for Santa Fe. What the passengers meant to do in such wild country was a puzzle to Jim. Of course, the men could hunt, but it was hardly necessary to travel two thousand miles upriver to find good prairie hunting—the Osage were even then killing buffalo in abundance not a day from where the boat floated.

After a night of brooding—a night spent so close to the Swamp of the Swans that he didn't dare make a fire—Jim had retraced his steps to the Missouri. He caught up with the steamer on the afternoon of the fifth day, watching the prairies carefully for any sign that a party had headed west.

Since then he had quietly followed the steamer, expecting, any day, to see Tasmin and some of the company disembark and strike out. When the old bearded hunter, the great lord, and the others had tramped ashore to hunt, Jim hung well back, watching. It was obvious that none of the party had the slightest notion of how to conduct a prairie hunt. The old lord tramped around smoking a long pipe, whose smoke any animal and many men could smell from a great distance; besides that, the group had made no effort to keep quiet. The most they could have expected from such a noisy approach was to surprise a greedy black bear in a plum thicket. Bears were sometimes inattentive, but deer and antelope, hearing such loud voices, would be unlikely to linger until the hunters came in range.

Jim had hidden himself in an overgrown buffalo wallow while the hunting party passed—the old lord was upbraiding his servants at every step. They passed within forty yards of him, quite unaware that they were being watched; for Indians bent on war they would have been easy prey. A little later, while the party was returning to the boat, Jim killed a young antelope with an arrow. He considered taking a haunch out to the boat, but decided against it, and dried the meat. If he went to the boat it would only stir up the three chiefs, whom he could see plainly enough, standing in their blankets and paint. He felt it would not be long before the adventurous girl came ashore—maybe, despite the risks, he could devise a plan for taking her to Santa Fe. He was wading across a little creek when he heard, just faintly, the Piegan's high war cry and saw a man jump off the boat into the river. The Piegan was enraged, that was clear, but Jim could not make out what had stirred him up. From the boat there came a babble of voices but there were no more war cries; the hubbub soon died down. The steamer made no progress for the rest of that day. At dusk Jim waded into the river and gigged a fine catfish, using a gig made from a two-pronged willow branch. He was eating the catfish when the old parrot sailed in and made himself at home.

Now, in the bright morning, a grave was being dug and a line of mourners was filing up to it, led by the old lord, who was still smoking his long pipe. Someone was dead, but Jim could not determine who it might be. Tasmin strolled behind her father, followed by her brothers and sisters, several servants, Charbonneau, the chieftains, and George Aitken, the captain of the boat. Behind them came a tall girl carrying what appeared to be a giant fiddle.

Jim kept low—he knew that if one of the Indians saw him there would be a great uproar. He worried that the parrot, who fluttered boldly about the plum bushes, would give him away, but none of the mourners noticed. Soon there was hymn singing—then low, sad-sounding notes from the big fiddle. The burying didn't take long. The mourners, in scattered groups, were soon filing down the long slope to the boat. Charbonneau had been entrusted with the big fiddle. The young woman who played it was strolling arm in arm with the old lord.

"You best go back—they'll be leaving you," Jim said, giving the parrot a nudge.

"*Schweig, du blöder Trottel!*" Prince Talleyrand replied.

17

"Merely fornication—wouldn't interest you, Bob."

Let us declare war immediately, savage war!" Tasmin said, addressing herself to Bobbety, Buffum, and Mary. George Catlin came around the corner just at that moment and heard the shocking comment.

"War?" he asked. "War with whom?"

George had a jumpy look—having a war hatchet raised over his head had been an irregularity from which his nerves had not recovered.

"That comment was not meant for your ears, George," Tasmin said. "Do go along."

"Why must he twitter so?" Bess asked, when the painter had taken himself away.

"Oh, the artistic temperament, I suppose," Tasmin said. "Artists ain't rough, like us aristocrats."

She had summoned her closest siblings for a council of war. Lady Berrybender had been in her grave less than half a day, and yet Venetia Kennet had already moved herself and her cello into Lord B.'s stateroom, with the plain intent of becoming the next Lady Berrybender. Lord Berrybender, their father, was, as they all knew, no sentimentalist. His true feeling for his deceased wife, whose loins had yielded him fourteen children, had been summed up at breakfast, which Lord B. had tucked into with his usual appetite just before the funeral.

"Constance, your dear mother, had no head for cards," Lord B. remarked, as Cook served him his kidney. "An even weaker head if she happened to be drunk, which was often the case. I could always beat her at whist—don't recall dropping a single hand these past twenty years. Very comforting to have a wife one can invariably beat at whist—so relaxing."

Tasmin doubted that the import of that remark was lost on Venetia Kennet, who possessed an excellent head for cards.

"The point of this savage war is to prevent Vicky from marrying Papa," Tasmin told them. "Should that dreadful event come to pass I fear we should all be put to work in the scullery—Vicky has many insults to avenge."

"*Your* insults, Tasmin," Buffum said. "I am always most polite to Vicky myself."

"Oh, slap her, Bobbety," Tasmin said, and Bobbety *did* slap her, though not hard.

"Why can't we just kill her?" he said. "Any of the *engagés* would be glad to do it."

"No, let's sell her into slavery, perhaps to the violent Comanches," Mary suggested. "She would be sure to suffer gross indignities—ravishment among them."

"Do shut up about ravishment, you don't even know what it means," Tasmin said.

"I do—it's what Buffum suffers at the hands of Tim, down in the horse stalls," Mary said. "It makes her whimper and squeal."

"What *is* she talking about?" Bobbety asked. He spent his days cataloguing his growing collection of snails and spiders, a pursuit that left him little time for shipboard intrigue.

"Merely fornication—wouldn't interest you, Bob," Tasmin said. She was beginning to regret having called the council. Help from her siblings was apt to be sporadic at best. If they meant to compromise Venetia Kennet it would be best to do it soon, before the conniving cellist managed to get with child. And Mademoiselle Pellenc had assured her that the statuesque Vicky was quite expert at the seductive arts.

"I wish Mr. Snow would come and take me off this dull boat," Tasmin said. "The parched prairies would make a nice change."

"They ain't parched, it just rained yesterday," Buffum reported. "You are so bossy, Tasmin, and that's the very reason men don't like you."

"The fact that I don't fornicate with stable boys doesn't mean that men don't like me," Tasmin replied cooly.

Just then George Catlin came round the corner again, looking distressed.

"There's been rather an uproar," he said. "Mademoiselle flew at Fräulein and scratched her cheeks quite badly—then Fräulein snatched up a club belonging to one of the chieftains and smashed Master Thaw with it. Master Thaw lies unconscious, bleeding from both ears. Fräulein vows to leave the boat at once, and Mademoiselle declares that she will not travel another mile until Prince Talleyrand is found."

"If Master Thaw is injured, that means no progress with Horace," Bobbety said.

"I've a fine suggestion," Tasmin said. "The Missouri River has two banks—deposit Mademoiselle on one and Fräulein on the other. Then we'll never have to listen to their wild harpings again."

George Catlin gave a start. A tall man had appeared on the western bank. He thought it might be the frontiersman who had brought Tasmin back, but before he could comment the steamer struck a sandbar so violently that they were all thrown off balance. When George recovered his footing and looked at the western shore again, the tall man was no longer visible.

"I say, Tasmin, I thought I saw that fellow who brought you back," George said.

"What? Where?" Tasmin said, rushing to the rail.

"I saw him just as we hit the riffle," George said. "Can't seem to spot him now. He can't have gotten far."

Tasmin wasted no words and no time. In a flash she was in her stateroom, rummaging up a kit. She grabbed a laundry sack and stuffed a few articles of clothing in it. If she could just get ashore quickly, perhaps she could catch Jim Snow.

She went racing down to the boat's ladder, trailed closely by Mary and Tintamarre, only to discover to her vast irritation that two *engagés* had taken the pirogue some distance off, in order to probe the sandbar with long poles.

"Bring back my boat this minute!" Tasmin shouted, with such outrage in her voice that the *engagés* immediately obeyed. One man was so abashed that he jumped out of the boat and was soon mired in mud up to his thighs.

"I'm going along, you'll need me to find the tubers," Mary said. The second *engagé* was about to relinquish the pirogue when Captain Aitken, looking rather at his wit's end, came rushing down to stop them.

"You mustn't go now, miss—there's weather coming," the captain said.

"Look, Tassie—what a violent cloud," Mary said.

Tasmin saw that a great black cloud, with lightning dancing in it, and thunder rumbling, had stretched itself across the whole of the northern horizon. The sight vexed her extremely—why *would* such a storm come just when she had a chance to rejoin the Raven Brave?

For a moment she was of half a mind to go anyway—what could a storm do but get her wet? It was true that the wind, merely a breeze with the breath of summer yet in it, had increased in force and become as chill as November, but what was a bit of a blow compared to the loss of this miraculous opportunity?

Sensing the drift of her thoughts, Captain Aitken went so far as to grasp her arm.

"You mustn't try it, miss—there's apt to be terrible hail!" he said. "We've all got to batten down and stay inside."

Just then there was a thunderclap so loud it seemed it might split the earth. The rain was advancing rapidly across the river, a wall of gray water hiding the brown Missouri. The *engagé* who had foolishly jumped out of the boat was struggling desperately to get aboard. Captain Aitken rushed over and threw him a rope, shouting for the other men to pull. Even Old Gorska took a hand—the poor muddy fellow was reeled in just before the torrent struck. Tasmin, though bitter, realized she had to give way. She and Mary and the dog raced for the cover of the lower deck. After a brief violent deluge the wall of water passed them—tiny hailstones the size of peas began to pepper the steamer, striking the water like a million pebbles. Mademoiselle Pellenc was wild with fright, the Hairy Horn hid under the stairway, the *engagés* cried out to their God for mercy, and the size of the hailstones increased, first to the size of pigeons' eggs, then to the size of ducks' eggs; at the climax of the storm the hail was as large as turkey eggs.

"We shall be battered to bits! We have come to the end of days!" Mary whispered in mad glee—there was a light in her eyes that Tasmin couldn't regard as entirely sane.

The roar of the hail became so great that no speech would carry. Big White and the Piegan drew their blankets over their heads, and Charlie Hodges, snug under the stairs with the Hairy Horn, was heartily glad he had resisted the Fräulein's demand that they leave the boat summarily. On the open prairie, hail was what all animals feared—even elk and buffalo fled such storms.

Then the hail slowed, became intermittent: soon the hailstones were merely peas again, and the cloud, still black, now darkened the plain south of them—the plains were as white as if there had been a snowfall. On the lower deck some of the *engagés* crunched the smaller hailstones when they walked.

So intense had been the storm that when it passed no one moved at once. They sat as though numbed, at first scarcely able to credit that they were still alive and the boat not smashed. Tasmin, who had resolved to put out for shore the moment the storm passed, found that she had lost some of her resolve. The impulse that seized her so strongly had diminished as the storm battered its way past them. Her hastily assembled kit sat at her feet, but she made no move to rush to the pirogue.

"Ain't we going, Tasmin?" Mary asked.

"In a bit, perhaps," Tasmin said, feeling decidedly glum. Where would Jim Snow have got to, in such a storm? Were there not other men on the Western plains besides her Raven Brave? Trappers were always passing them, headed downriver with peltries piled high in their small boats. Probably it hadn't even been Mr. Snow that George Catlin saw. The thought, logical and sensible as it was, made Tasmin want to cry.

"I wonder what Papa is doing," Bobbety said, wandering up. "Do you suppose he misses the mater?"

18

Another half minute and the thing would have been achieved . . .

Lord Berrybender, in fact, had been indulging in a leisurely act of fornication with Venetia Kennet when the violent clatter of the storm struck their roof. In Lord Berrybender's case it was a particularly ill-timed clatter—surrounded by such a roar, he lost his stroke; the fires so regularly induced by Venetia's white languor were damped by the pounding of hail just at the moment when Lord B. himself should have been pounding.

Another half minute and the thing would have been achieved; and yet, though Vicky Kennet turned quite rosy, the thing had *not* been achieved; her sly attempt to lock him in with her legs did not deceive Lord Berrybender, an amorite of vast experience. Noise of such a level was, at such a moment, unwelcome. He seemed to recall that a cannonade—where had it been? Egypt, perhaps, or was it the Peninsula?—had once had the same effect. In that case there had been no remedy, Lady Berrybender, with the help of her laudanum, having dropped into a deep unconsciousness, leaving Lord B. alone with his disappointment.

In the present instance, though, there was still hope. His ingenious Vicky had invented a little variation which sometimes stimulated His Lordship to second or even third efforts.

"Venetia, that damn storm undid me," Lord Berrybender said. "Do be a good thing and get your bow. I believe success is still within my grasp if you'll just help us a bit with those ticklish horsehairs."

Oh rot! Venetia thought but she obediently slipped from the bed. Tired as she was of the old fool's sluggish embraces, she had no intention—with Lady Berrybender miraculously removed from her path—of allowing the richest man in England to escape her. She took up her cellist's bow and returned to the bed.

"Mustn't get it sticky now, Your Lordship," she said. "I fear my Haydn would suffer."

She drew the bow just lightly a few times across Lord Berrybender's floppy member. Reaction was not immediate, but Venetia—employing just the lightest of touches—persisted. Though other methods of resuscitation were available, she put her trust in her bow, deftly devoting a stroke or two to His Lordship's hairy balls.

"That's it, that's a good girl," Lord Berrybender said. "I believe I feel life returning."

"Now just lie still, this is merely the overture," Venetia said. "Soon we'll get along to the first movement."

"First movement be damned, we had *that* before the thunder," Lord B. said. "It's the crescendo or whatever you call it that's wanted now."

A few more strokes and the laggardly organ gained at least a rather knobby strength; when Venetia Kennet judged that it was as high as it was

likely to rise she carefully put down her bow—*not*, of course, the bow she
actually played Haydn with—and flung herself astride His Lordship before
he could go floppy again. If there was seed in the old brute she meant to
have it; and very soon, the thing was, after all, achieved.

"Damn useful that you're a fiddler, Vicky," His Lordship said, before
dropping off to sleep.

19

She would not trade her Pope . . . her Akenside or Shenstone . . .

Mademoiselle Pellenc could not be calmed. Buffum, who could usually mollify the high-strung *femme de chambre*, was helpless before her
abject despair. The loss of Lady Berrybender, coupled with the departure
of Prince Talleyrand, had quite undone the poor woman—the violent hailstorm seemed to have been the last straw. She raced around the boat in
hysterics, scaring the *engagés* and demanding to be put ashore to search
for the lost bird. Big White wanted to strike the noisy woman with his big
club, the very club that, in the hands of Fräulein, had deprived Master
Jeremy Thaw of his powers of speech. Charbonneau pleaded with the irritated Mandan, a warrior not easily restrained.

"She'll run down soon, I expect," Charbonneau said. "Women do, you
know . . . like clocks. They run down."

"She grieves for our dear mama," Bess said. "Such anguish is most af-
fecting. Since we're stuck on a sandbar anyway, couldn't we mount at least
a small expedition and go in search of Prince Talleyrand?"

Tasmin found, to her considerable vexation, that she herself could think
of little besides the Raven Brave. Never before in her life had a man occupied her thoughts for any length of time. Master Stiles, at best, seldom
lasted half an hour. Various balladeers, poetasters, Portuguese, Frenchmen, or the male nobility of England could rarely tempt her from her studies for more than an hour. She would not trade her Pope, her Erasmus

Darwin, her Akenside or Shenstone, her Scott or her Byron for all such male attentions. Yet now, in America, through the caprice of travel, she had stumbled onto a man she could not get off her mind.

But where was he? The American plain was vast, her own experience slight. The terrible hailstorm had reminded her of how vulnerable one was on the naked American plain.

"I suppose I could just ask Captain Aitken how long he thinks we might be stuck," she said. "If it will make Mademoiselle feel any better I suppose we could go tramp around a bit."

She found Captain Aitken sitting on the bridge, smoking a pipe so short it almost seemed an extension of his chin. The poor man looked exhausted, and no wonder, with such a bunch to supervise. Below them, in water as brown as burlap, a number of *engagés* were pulling with great ropes and pushing with long poles—but to no avail. The steamer *Rocky Mount* was firmly stuck.

Tasmin could not but like Captain Aitken. By dissuading her from her impulsive dash he had probably saved her life—but that was not why she liked him. What she liked was his evenhandedness, a rare quality in men of her acquaintance. He neither ranted nor fawned; the excitable, even hysterical behavior of the Europeans neither impressed him nor offended him, as far as Tasmin could tell.

George Catlin had set up his easel some ways down the deck—he wanted to capture the summer plains covered with white hailstones. Piet Van Wely stood behind him—he liked to study the painter's effects as he worked. If George Catlin minded the plum botanist's scrutiny, he didn't show it.

"I have to thank you, Captain—what a fearsome pounding we had," Tasmin said. "If I had pulled for shore I fear the consequences would have been dire."

Captain Aitken tipped his hat.

"You've no experience here, miss," he said. "Probably the weather's not so fickle, in England."

"It's certainly not so violent," Tasmin replied. "A storm such as that one would have broken half the windowpanes in London."

"Yes, and it damaged two of our paddles, as well," the captain said.

"Mr. Catlin spoke of seeing a man on shore just before we struck the sandbar," Tasmin said. "Did you perhaps see him too?"

"I saw him—that was old Dan Drew," the captain said. "He's a hunter—supplies passing boats with game when the season's fair. Dan will soon be round, I expect, once he sees we're stuck. Perhaps he'll bring us an ante-lope."

Tasmin's glumness returned. It had not been the Raven Brave after all, just some ancient hunter. Her wild impulse had only been folly, after all.

"Since we're stuck we were thinking of going ashore for a bit, to look for Mama's old parrot," Tasmin said. "Perhaps we'll meet this Mr. Drew."

"If you do he'll talk your ear off," the captain said. "Dan gets lonesome, walking the river. I wouldn't mind a word with him myself—he keeps up with the moods of the tribes . . . knows who's at war and who ain't. It's use-ful information."

"I wonder if he knows Mr. Snow?" Tasmin asked.

Captain Aitken gave her a thoughtful look. Tasmin felt awkward—per-haps too much eagerness had showed in her face or her voice.

"Dan buried Jim Snow's parents—they were massacred by the Kicka-poo," Captain said. "Jimmy was just a babe. They hid him in a cactus patch—was Dan found him and took him to the Osage, who adopted him. He was pretty full of stickers before he got out of that cactus, Dan said."

"My goodness . . . what horror," Tasmin said. She waited, but Captain Aitken volunteered no more information, so she went down to call for the pirogue.

Gorska Minor, who was occasionally disposed to be helpful, brought the pirogue round and helped Tasmin store her kit, which she decided to bring along just in case. Gorska Minor had a tendency to leer at the girls—he often stationed himself just below stairs, the better to peer up petticoats; it was he who spread the rumor that the massive Fräulein Pfretzskaner had quite dispensed with undergarments.

Tasmin, Bobbety, Buffum, Mary, Piet, and the hound all came trooping down to the pirogue, but there was no sign of the hysterical French maid.

"Where *is* she, drat her?" Tasmin asked.

"Locked in her room—I suspect she is taking poison," Mary said.

"Quite likely it's merely constipation," Bobbety declared. "I suffer from it myself."

"It's this American diet," Piet suggested. "What we all need is some good cabbage soup."

"I am hardly in the mood to delay this trip just to hear you two specu-late about Mademoiselle's bowels," Tasmin said, as she took up the paddle and commenced to row toward the distant shore. "If Mademoiselle wants to join us in the search she'll have to swim."

Almost at once there was a loud splash from behind them.

"She's swimming," Mary said.

20

Jim Snow had known the storm was coming . . .

Ever been in a cloud, Jimmy?" Dan Drew asked. The two of them sat out the big hailstorm in his dugout, cozily enough; but the hail had receded and it was possible to converse again. Dan Drew was not one to waste an opportunity, conversation being one of his favorite pursuits.

"I can't fly, Dan—how would I get in a cloud?" Jim asked. The dugout, which Dan Drew claimed had once been a snake den, was hidden beneath a low shelf of rocks on a little ridge. Quite a few hailstones had bounced into the dugout. Now and then Dan picked up one of the smaller hailstones and crunched it between his teeth.

"Well, the way to get in a cloud is to climb up one of the Rocky Mountains," Dan went on. "I've been in several clouds in my day—I've even been above them. I was right on top of a storm like this trying to get up one of them high peaks near the South Platte. I was up there looking for eagle eggs."

Jim Snow had known the storm was coming when he crossed a prairie dog town without seeing a single prairie dog. When the burrowing creatures went to ground it was time to seek shelter. Dan Drew's dugout was not far away, so Jim ran to it, accompanied by the old parrot, who resisted all efforts to make him return to the boat. With the storm no longer a danger Jim was impatient to be off, but no one escaped Dan Drew without hearing seven or eight of his stories—most of them stories Jim didn't believe.

"Why would you want eagle eggs?" he asked.

"Oh, they weren't for me, they were for the professor," Dan said. "Tom Say his name was—he was traveling with Major Long, collecting birds' eggs and such."

"Why take birds' eggs, with a hunter like you to kill game?" Jim inquired, to be polite.

"They didn't gather them to eat, they gathered them to study," Dan informed him. "The professor particularly wanted eagle eggs, but the best I could do was an eaglet. It worked out well enough, though—Major Long tamed the eaglet. The major would stick bacon in his hatband and that eaglet would fly around his head and even land on his shoulder, trying to get the bacon—it made a big impression on the Indians. None of them had a tame eaglet."

Jim was ready to crawl out of the dark little room—it was lit by a single candle, floating in a cup of tallow.

"That professor even collected bugs and mites," Dan said. "He caught a louse and put it under a microscope—he let me look but it was a thing I didn't like to see. Bad enough to have to live with lice—why study them?"

"The storm's over, Dan—I'm off," Jim said. "Will you be visiting that steamer anytime soon?"

"I might, if I can knock down a deer to sell them," Dan said. "There's a passel of grandees on that boat. I expect George Aitken has his hands full with 'em."

"This old bird belongs on the boat," Jim said. "I'd be obliged if you'd return it for me—I suspect it's somebody's pet."

The parrot pecked at some of the smaller hailstones, crunching them much as Dan did.

Dan Drew reached over to get the bird, but the parrot waddled out of reach.

"I don't know, Jimmy—I think that old rascal has adopted you," Dan said.

"Well, I can't be bothered to keep up with somebody's parrot," Jim said, irritated that the bird would behave so queerly.

"Old critters have minds of their own," Dan said. "I expect this one's going to go where he wants to go."

No sooner had the two of them crawled out of the dugout than Prince Talleyrand took wing, flew high, and was soon out of sight.

21

A bloody death fit for an opera seemed the only way to proceed.

Mademoiselle Pellenc locked herself in her room, meaning to cut her throat in privacy. Feeling that Lady Berrybender's death had deprived her of any reason to live, she meant to finish herself with some darning scissors. As Lady Berrybender's *femme de chambre* she had naturally stood first among the servants; but with her mistress gone the skinny young Frenchwoman knew that she could only expect the worst. Cook, who hated her for her finical demands, would give her only gristle and gruel. Señor Yanez and Signor Claricia had already grown bolder in their advances. Lord Berrybender, who had once dallied with her familiarly, was now besotted with the tall, untalented cellist, a woman who seemed quite unfamiliar with any music except Haydn's. And now the German slut had smashed the head of Master Thaw, the one nice man among the Europeans. Master Thaw had often paid Mademoiselle fine, elaborate compliments, but now, thanks to Fräulein, he had lost all power of speech.

A bloody death fit for an opera seemed the only way to proceed.

The darning scissors, however, quickly proved inadequate to the task Mademoiselle set them. They were quite dull; they wouldn't cut. Instead of a great operatic gush of blood, the scissors merely pinched, raising an ugly bruise, which she was forced to slap over with powder before rushing out to join the boating party, her suicide postponed.

Mademoiselle was no sooner out the door than she saw that the pirogue had departed without her, an injustice that quite wrung her heart. It was her compatriot, Prince Talleyrand, that they were searching for. Mademoiselle had often fed the old bird hazelnuts—she felt quite sure he would come to her call. But there the boat went. Lady Tasmin hadn't waited—Lady Tasmin never waited! Without a moment's hesitation Mademoiselle jumped over the rail, realizing only at the last second that she might have been wiser to descend to the lower deck before jumping. But the die was cast. She jumped, she was falling!

Toussaint Charbonneau, Old Gorska, and the diminutive Italian, Signor

Claricia, were all standing at the rail smoking when the skinny Frenchwoman came falling and fluttering right past them, to strike the sandy
water with a resounding splash. They were all astonished—none of them
had ever seen a *femme de chambre* fall out of the sky before.

"Now *that* was a splash, Gorska," Charbonneau said. "I was near to getting water in my eye."

Mademoiselle was not hurt by her wild leap, but neither was she pleased
to find herself the cynosure of so many masculine eyes. Big White, the Hairy
Horn, and even Charlie Hodges rushed to witness this curious spectacle.
Mademoiselle had jumped into no more than three feet of water; the channel was not deep enough for easy swimming. The laughter and ribald comments of the *engagés* she ignored, but just as she struggled into deeper water,
something brushed her leg; with her wet hair in her eyes Mademoiselle
could just distinguish three ominous gray shapes. Convinced that they were
crocodiles, she emitted a wild shriek and began to swim toward the pirogue
as fast as she could, while behind her, the three gray logs floated silently on.

22

Hearing the wild shrieks . . .

Hearing the wild shrieks, Tasmin stopped the pirogue until the crazed
Mademoiselle Pellenc swam, waded, and floundered her way to them. Getting her on board was not easy—as she crawled in, Tintamarre leapt out,
amid a general splashing that left no one entirely dry.

Though the smaller hailstones had by this time melted, some of the
larger ones remained. Soon, once the bank was reached, Bobbety and Buffum amused themselves by throwing hailstones at each other.

"What sport, we can pretend they're snowballs," Bobbety said, only seconds before Buffum hit him smack in the forehead with a well-directed
hailstone the size of a goose egg.

"You're a regular David without the slingshot, Bess," Tasmin said. "Go-
liath now lies vanquished."

"Come along, Piet, it is time we sought the delicious Jerusalem artichokes," Mary commanded. "Come along—we'll dig together."

"Is she not uncanny, the little one?" Piet said, before stumbling away.

"It is not every day that I have hailstones to fling," Bess said, looking down at the unconscious Bobbety. It was her habit never to admit wrongdoing directly.

"The crocodiles wanted to eat my legs off," Mademoiselle Pellenc insisted, as she got undressed. Wet clothes were intolerable to her, far more so than immodesty. The sun was now bright. She soon had her dress spread on the grass to dry and surveyed the empty skies clad only in her chemise, hoping to see a flash of green.

Tasmin fervently hoped that Jim Snow was not witnessing such dubious proceedings. They had been ashore no more than five minutes and yet, already, her brother was unconscious, a lump almost as big as the hailstone rising on his forehead. Mary and the botanist had disappeared, Tintamarre had managed to get a thorn in his foot, and the *femme de chambre* was almost naked.

"Mademoiselle, why is it that you have hardly any bosom?" Buffum asked.

"It is because I am so intelligent," Mademoiselle responded, icily. "The brain gains, the bosom loses."

Tasmin, occupied for the moment with her whimpering hound, did her best to ignore both women. In fact she had already decided to take the pirogue and leave them. Other boats could be sent ashore to pick them up when evening came. The balm of summer was still on the prairies. Tasmin had stuck some biscuits in her kit bag; she had in mind to sleep in the pirogue again. Perhaps the miracle would repeat itself; perhaps the Raven Brave would appear again in the splendor of the dawn. Other, less happy possibilities—bears, Indians, floods, snakes, chiggers—she refused to allow her mind to dwell on. The prairie at least offered the hope of surprise, pleasant or unpleasant, ecstatic or fatal, while their little floating Europe offered only sameness: quarrels, sulks, spite. In the freshness of the West old ways could be peeled off as easily as Mademoiselle had peeled off her wet dress.

"*Voilà! Voilà! L'oiseau!*" Mademoiselle Pellenc exclaimed, pointing to the far, far distance.

Tasmin looked: the bird in question was so far away as to be no more than a black speck in the sky.

Bess had meanwhile been making a mud poultice for Bobbety's great lump. Though the trip ashore had been her idea, finding Prince Talleyrand had not been her main motive. She had come ashore in hopes of locating a shaggy frontiersman who would shake her and slap her as Tasmin had been shaken. Hearing of Tasmin's shaking, all the women aboard the boat had become deeply envious; they all hoped to get ashore and find men who would shake them thus dramatically. Buffum was particularly anxious to find such a shaggy swain; Tim the stable boy's rough embraces had become rather too mechanical; a good shaking by a passionate frontiersman might yield tremors far more interesting than anything Tim could induce.

Clad only in her chemise and her shoes, Mademoiselle Pellenc had begun to hurry across the prairie, on toward the distant speck, crying, *"L'oiseau! Voilà!"* as she ran.

"It's a *oiseau* all right, but I doubt it's Mama's parrot," Tasmin said. "More likely just a crow. Go get her, Buffum—if we're not careful she'll get lost. These plains are quite featureless, I assure you."

"But our dear brother is stricken—what if his brains ooze out?" Bess complained.

"Oh, stop dithering, he's merely got a little bump on his forehead, and you put it there," Tasmin said. "Go after Mademoiselle and don't lose sight of her—we're in danger of becoming dispersed."

"Pythagoras," Bobbety muttered. He often spoke in his sleep, intoning the names of the great.

Bess left reluctantly. She didn't trust Tasmin, who would no doubt desert them and take off in search of her young man; but in fact Mademoiselle was racing on across the prairie and could not be callously neglected. The need to recapture the old bird lent strength to Mademoiselle's skinny legs. Bess began to run too—if the indispensable *femme de chambre* should be lost, who would comb their hair in the morning, or before balls?

The prairie, which had looked so level, wasn't, and the grass, which, to the eye, seemed so silky, was full of unexpected brambles which scratched her calves as she ran. In what seemed like seconds Bess began to feel that she was being swallowed up by the Western distance, as Jonah had been swallowed by the whale—though being inside a whale might be cozy, whereas being on the great prairie alone was *not* cozy. The sky above her seemed larger than England itself. She seemed to have suddenly been sucked into a great emptiness as by a gust of wind—and what would the outcome be? When she began to run she had looked back often to the river, but now she feared to look back. What if she only saw the same distance, the same grass?

The only element of hope was Mademoiselle Pellenc, who showed signs of having run herself out. Now she was merely trotting. Soon she stopped altogether. Bess saw, as she approached, that the same brambles that had scratched her calves had torn the poor Frenchwoman's chemise away. Her skinny legs were naked, her small bosom heaved, and her wet hair was much in need of a combing.

Bess had every intention of delivering a stinging reprimand, informing Mademoiselle in no uncertain terms that her mad pursuit of Prince Talley- rand was a capricious act for which serious amends must be made. Bess considered herself a polished deliverer of reprimands. Among the servants only Cook—who possessed powerful powers of retaliation—was spared. But on this occasion, alone with the sweaty Frenchwoman on the vast prairie, Bess realized that she lacked the breath required for a proper rep- rimand. Though sentences of censure formed distinctly in her mind, she could not get them past her lips. She was out of breath.

Mademoiselle, who had been more or less stumbling along, suddenly stopped stock-still.

"I think we should go back now, *oui*?" Mademoiselle said, in a small, subdued voice. "Yes, at once, let us return to *le bateau*. It is almost time for tea."

"Yes, let's return—it was foolish of you to venture so far," Bess said, and stopped. Running, she had seen nothing on the prairie; stopped, she sud- denly saw the men, risen as if from the earth. There were six of them, small and dark—their scrawny horses grazed nearby. A great shaggy carcass lay on the prairie; the dark men had been cutting it up, their arms bloody from the task. All had stopped their work, dripping knives in hand. They looked at the two stunned white women silently.

"Yes, mademoiselle, let's excuse ourselves to these gentlemen," Bess said, taking Mademoiselle's arm. But when they turned to leave, the prairie was empty. There was no sign of the Missouri River, of the steamer *Rocky Mount,* of Tasmin, Tintamarre, Bobbety. There was no sign of anything.

The six dark men watched.

"Mademoiselle, we must run for our lives," Bess said.

Mademoiselle Pellenc, French and fatalistic, shook her head.

"I am runs out," she said. "I have no more runs."

Bess had no runs herself, but it didn't matter. The two of them were in the belly of the prairie—before they could stumble ten steps, in a rush the dark men came.

23

Scamper off? Scamper off where?

The sight of the dead, butchered buffalo enraged Lord Berrybender so terribly that he threatened to thrash Old Gorska with his stick—and perhaps thrash Gorska Minor too. Informed by Captain Aitken that repairs must be made before the steamer could proceed, Lord Berrybender had at once insisted on setting out on a hunt; he even insisted that Monsieur Charbonneau, the expert plainsman, accompany the hunting party.

"You ain't from Poland, you'll find me buffalo, won't you, Sharbo?" His Lordship said.

Somewhat to his own surprise, Toussaint Charbonneau did just that, and almost immediately, too. The only trouble was that the buffalo, a nice young cow, was not only dead but thoroughly and competently butchered, too. Tongue, liver, sweetbreads, haunches, and saddle had been neatly removed by people who knew their job.

"They left the guts, that's unusual," Charbonneau observed.

"Why, I don't see that it's odd," Lord B. said. "I always leave the guts myself, when I kill a stag. Rather foul on the whole. Not much Cook could do with a great pile of guts."

"Indian children slice them in sections and eat them quick as candy," Charbonneau told him. "My boy, Pomp, was always mighty fond of gut. Captain Clark always saved a good section of gut, when he killed something, just for Pomp."

"What do you say to this, Gorska?" Lord B. said, pointing at the carcass. "I've been telling you all along there were buffalo here, and this proves it— only this one's already dead. I'd like you to scamper off now and find me a live one to shoot."

Old Gorska looked around at the prairies, endless and empty, and felt his heart sink. Scamper off? Scamper off where? No buffalo were in sight. Nonetheless, there was little he could do but obey. He shouldered his fine Belgian gun and was about to tramp away when Charbonneau stopped him.

"Might be best to wait, Your Lordship," Charbonneau said.

"Wait? I'll be damned if I'll wait!" Lord Berrybender said. "I've traveled from England to kill buffalo and by God I want to kill some. Finding them's Gorska's job—why shouldn't he do it?"

Charbonneau had never ranked himself high as a tracker, but with the prairies muddy from the recent rain, it would have taken a blind man to miss the horse tracks around the carcass. Several Indians had run the cow down and killed her, leaving only the guts. They might have run the cow several miles before making the kill. Undoubtedly the hunters had a camp—it might be a mile distant, or it might be forty. No doubt the hunters were aware of the steamer, which had been belching black smoke all afternoon. Once the boat left, the Indians might come back for the tasty innards, not to mention the useful sinews and such. What was left of the buffalo cow might not interest a white man, but that didn't mean it wouldn't interest an Indian.

"From the look of the tracks six or seven hunters made this kill," Charbonneau said. "They haven't been gone long. If Gorska was to go rattling off now he might be in for a scrap."

"What of it? The man has a weapon!" Lord Berrybender said, his fury rising. "I suppose my expensive hunter's capable of beating off a few savages—if not, then I've wasted money bringing him all the way from Poland."

"I will go!" Gorska said, fed up with the insolent old brute.

"It is my fate," he added somberly, once again shouldering his gun.

Once Gorska left it occurred to Lord Berrybender that Charbonneau might be right—it would be a nuisance to lose his hunter to some wandering band of savages.

"Gorska Minor, step lively . . . go with your father," he said. "Gladwyn, give the boy a fowling piece—I'm in no mood to shoot birds."

Gladwyn at once handed the shotgun to Gorska Minor, who looked surprised.

"Go, boy . . . find me some buffalo and do try to guide them back this way," Lord Berrybender said. "I won't be satisfied until I've brought one of the shaggy brutes down."

Gorska Minor was startled by his new assignment. Every few days he was required to clean all His Lordship's weapons, but he had never even been allowed to fire a pistol. The sight of the great dead beast with a huge pile of guts beside it had very nearly undone him. The thought that it was now his duty to tramp across the empty prairies, locate such a beast, and somehow urge it back within range of Lord Berrybender's gun was terrifying—but his father was moving at a steady pace across the grasslands and he had no choice but to follow.

The Poles had scarcely left when Charbonneau's eye fell on a piece of white cloth, stuck on a bramble not far from where the buffalo lay. It was only a scrap, but it reminded Charbonneau that Lady Tasmin and her party were somewhere onshore. The possibility of kidnap did not at first occur to him—plenty of Indians had cloth of one kind or another, from the traders, and in any case, it seemed unlikely that the girls from the boat would have advanced that far into the prairies. The scrap of cloth was no more than a reminder that the young ladies had to be safely rounded up when the hunt was over.

"I believe Lady Tasmin and some of her sisters and that jumpy Frenchwoman are around here somewhere," he remarked.

"Looking for that damn parrot, I suppose," Lord B. said, gesturing for Gladwyn to set up his hunting seat, a small leather folding seat with a sharp point that could be thrust into the ground; the nobility customarily used such seats at horse races but Lord B. found them perfectly suited to hunting, as well. When Gladwyn had the seat ready, Lord B. was more than glad to sit down—there had been that trouble with the fornication, requiring rather prolonged exertion. Having his nice sturdy seat was a handy thing. He felt, all in all, rather tired—from now on, with the hunting prospects improving, he meant to hunt first and fornicate later. A solid hunting seat, when a man was tired, was a mighty welcome thing. Lord B. sank onto his gratefully; a bit of rest wouldn't hurt.

"Gun, Gladwyn . . . gun!" he said. "I want to be ready if a great shaggy herd comes loping by." Gladwyn provided a gun; Lord B. yawned and took it. Even keeping his eyes open was proving rather difficult.

Charbonneau took his knife and went over to the buffalo and cut off a few sections of gut. As a part-time cook for the famous Lewis and Clark expedition he had once been rather famous for his *boudin blanc*, which needed fresh buffalo gut to be done properly.

While he was slicing, Charbonneau heard an unusual sound—a snore.

Lord Berrybender, his head tilted back, his mouth wide open, was fast asleep and snoring loudly.

"I guess a nap won't hurt him," Charbonneau remarked.

"Possibly not, sir," Gladwyn said, in a chilly tone. As His Lordship's man he felt it best to stand aloof from the help—particularly the American help.

"A nap never hurt anyone," Charbonneau said, turning his attention to the gut pile.

A moment later he was proven wrong. Lord Berrybender, dreaming of buffalo, allowed his rifle to droop. While he dreamed, a horsefly settled on his hand. Lord Berrybender twitched, the fly rose, Lord B. twitched again, and the gun discharged. Lord B. fell off his seat and writhed on the ground—he had discharged the heavy ball directly into his right foot.

"I guess naps ain't as safe as all that," Charbonneau amended.

"Clearly not," Gladwyn said.

Charbonneau had scarcely had time to run to His Lordship and assess the damage—three toes, at least, seemed to be missing—when they heard the sound of running feet.

"It's Gorska, he's carrying something," Gladwyn said, in a weak voice. The sight of His Lordship's noble blood—at the moment gushing out of the wounded foot—caused him to feel rather faint.

"Must have kilt an antelope, or maybe a doe," Charbonneau said. He was in the process of making a tourniquet, using his own belt.

"Or even a buffalo calf," he added—Gorska had something across his shoulders, but Charbonneau, busy with his tourniquet, could not tell what.

A moment later Gladwyn fainted dead away.

Old Gorska, drenched with sweat, very red in the face, stumbled through the high grass and dropped his burden, which proved to be his son, Gorska Minor, a short, bloody arrow through his throat. Charbonneau saw at once that the boy was dead.

"Well, now that's a great pity, Gorska," he said, carefully twisting the tourniquet. Lord Berrybender had lost most of a foot—it wouldn't do to misapply the tourniquet and have him lose a leg. Charbonneau considered himself a fair doctor, having been trained by the great Captain Lewis himself.

"And now His Lordship's shot off his foot, too," Charbonneau said. "I guess we're having us a day."

24

Tintamarre barked from a distance; Bobbety occasionally uttered a Greek name.

Tasmin's escape succeeded, with only the mildest effort. Buffum and Mademoiselle were gone in one direction, Mary and Piet in another. Tintamarre barked from a distance; Bobbety occasionally uttered a Greek name. The lump on his forehead was of a size to be of interest to science, Tasmin felt sure, but no scientist was there to appreciate it. She waded out to the pirogue, shoved it into the stream, and was soon drifting pleasantly away, a circumstance which brought her deep relief. Above her, swans were calling, and geese as well. A great yellow fish, of ugly demeanor, surfaced briefly beside her boat—a harmless big fish with whiskers. With the sky bright above her and the air balmy, Tasmin felt that few things could be better than floating in a boat. The beauty of the day was extraordinary. She wondered how far New Orleans was—there were said to be some very distinguished Creoles in New Orleans.

It was a little gusty. The pirogue rocked this way and that; occasionally a small wave splashed her, but Tasmin didn't care. She thought of taking a swim, but felt too lazy. Being away from her family, with their interminable screechings and whinings, was rather sedative. The warmth of the sun and the gentle rocking of the pirogue lulled her into what seemed the briefest of naps. For a few moments at most she closed her eyes, and when she opened them, the miracle she had dreamt of happened. Jim Snow, in water to his waist, had hold of her boat and was pulling it to shore.

"Why, hello!" Tasmin said. "My chevalier has come to save me, just as I had hoped."

Jim Snow was not amused. His look was iron. Tasmin was at once reminded that he was not an easy man.

"You need to stop this wandering off, you little fool!" he said.

The cutting way he said it caused Tasmin's temper to flare.

"Don't speak to me that way, Mr. Snow," she said. "I'm a free woman and I'll go where I please. Why *are* you taking me ashore—I *was* ashore."

Jim Snow flashed her a look, but was too intent on the business at hand to respond.

"Get out of the boat and don't be talking," he whispered. "You've got one of them carrying voices."

Tasmin, still rather miffed, grudgingly stepped out of the pirogue. To her astonishment Jim Snow at once hacked a sizable hole in it and sent it spinning back out into the current, where it slowly sank.

She was about to protest this ruthless scuttling of her vessel, but for once held her tongue. Jim Snow seemed to know exactly what he was doing, and he was in a hurry to do it too. The decisiveness of his actions convinced her it was no time to bicker. Instead of pulling her ashore he hurried her, still in the shallows, upriver for a hundred yards or more, where the bleached trunk of a tree was lodged against a muddy point. His rifle, pouch, and bow and arrows were there, nicely concealed. He listened for a moment, put his finger to his lips, and then, bending low, led Tasmin across the prairie, pausing when a clump of weeds offered a little cover, to listen and look.

From upriver Tasmin noted some stir about the steamboat, which was still stuck. Various canoes, keelboats, pirogues clustered around the main vessel, but Tasmin could gain no conception of what was wrong. Though the country still seemed empty and peaceful, both the Raven Brave and the people on the boat seemed to be acting in response to unseen threats.

Their silent but purposeful travel continued for another half hour. Though somewhat exasperated, Tasmin kept quiet. They had drawn almost level with the steamboat when Tasmin saw an unexpected flash of green amid the gray prairies—it was Prince Talleyrand, sitting on a rock. The old bird seemed to be waiting for them. Before Tasmin could comment Jim Snow pushed her into a kind of hole, under the little ridge of rock where the parrot sat.

"But I don't want to go into a hole," Tasmin protested. "I've always been singularly afraid of holes."

"It's all right, Tassie . . . it's quite roomy once you've squeezed in," said her sister Mary, from somewhere in the bowels of the earth.

"Get in—they're close now," Jim whispered.

"Well, I do hate holes," Tasmin repeated, wondering who it could be that Jim referred to. The Raven Brave observed no niceties. Once Tasmin dropped to her knees he put his hands on her rump and shoved her into a dimly lit chamber, he himself crowding close behind—Prince Talleyrand soon waddled in too, avoiding Mary, who sat with a number of smelly wild onions in her lap.

"Where's Dan?" Jim Snow asked Mary. "And where's the little fat man?"

"Mr. Drew was of the opinion that he ought to have a look around," Mary said. "Piet suffers violently from claustrophobia, so he went too, though I don't think Mr. Drew much wanted him."

"All this I find quite puzzling," Tasmin said. "I was enjoying a peaceful boat ride and now I'm in a hole in the ground with my wicked sister. What's it all about?"

"You are *so* impatient, Tassie," Mary said. "It's the reason you are rarely well informed. Buffum and Mademoiselle have been kidnapped by the red savages, Gorska Minor has been killed quite dead, and Papa has shot most of his right foot off—all this while you were boating."

Tasmin's inclination was to disbelieve every word the little wretch said—Mary had long been noted for the extravagance of her reports. But then there was Jim Snow, who offered no contradiction, and who *had* exercised unusual caution in pulling her off the river and rushing her into this hole.

"The Pawnees and the Osage are at war," Jim said quietly, as if discussing a change in the weather. "Them and some Kickapoos. The Bad Eye has stirred them up."

"Who is the Bad Eye, may I ask?"

"An old prophet—he's made a war prophecy," Jim said.

Tasmin felt that somehow events which belonged only in the fantastical fictions of Mr. Cooper or Mr. Irving had somehow surged into her well-ordered English life. Instead of rejecting suitors in Berkeley Square or Northamptonshire, she sat in a hole in the dirt, somewhere in America, being asked to believe things which hardly seemed credible. Her sister and the *femme de chambre,* last seen chasing a bird, had somehow been kidnapped? A harmless Polish boy killed? Her own father abruptly and inexplicably minus a foot? And all this had happened in the brief, happy hour she had spent drifting in her boat on the brown muddy river?

"May I remind you that this is the child you claim talks to serpents," she said to Jim Snow. "I wouldn't believe a word she says."

"Oh hush, Tassie—I scarcely said two words to that snake," Mary protested.

Jim Snow's thoughts, as usual, were severely practical.

"That fat fellow should have stayed here," he said. "There are Indians on the prowl all along the river—that's why I sank your boat. If they'd seen it they'd be trying to hunt you down."

"If they find me I'd rather like to run," Tasmin said. "I can't run far in this hole."

"No, Tassie . . . we are in sanctuary," Mary said. "Mr. Drew says no savages will bother us here."

"Be that as it may, I still don't like holes," Tasmin repeated.

All the same, she was pleased that the Raven Brave had taken it on himself to rescue her. She had convinced herself that he was hundreds of miles away and indifferent to her fate—but it wasn't so. She felt a sudden urge to comb his long, tangled hair, though she knew that it was a license unlikely to be permitted.

Prince Talleyrand suddenly fluttered out of the cave.

"Be quiet," Jim Snow whispered. He was listening hard, a wariness in his look. Tasmin found him intensely appealing.

"Jimmy, you there?" a voice asked.

"We're here—is it safe to come out?"

"It's safe, the Pawnees have gone north," Dan Drew said. "We best be getting these young ladies back to their boat."

The prairie sun, once Tasmin squeezed out, was so intense after the dimness that for a few moments she had to shield her eyes with her hand. Only slowly did her focus accept the strong light. Jim Snow seemed to have forgotten her. He stood some distance away, talking to a tall, kindly-looking old man with gray hair down to his nape, whose buckskins were very well kept, in contrast to Jim's.

"That is Mr. Drew," Mary said. "He is extremely knowledgeable—he has already taught me how to whistle prairie dogs out of their holes."

"Very useful, I'm sure," Tasmin said. "I hope he won't mind escorting you back to the boat so that you will be out of harm's way."

"Where will you be, Tassie?" Mary asked.

"Oh, hereabouts, I suppose . . . I do hope for a moment or two with Mr. Snow," Tasmin said. "We have our trip to Santa Fe to plan, you know?"

"He seems a rather stern gentleman," Mary said. "Probably he'll get round to giving you another good shaking, very soon."

"Get back on that boat, you impertinent brat," Tasmin said.

"You don't seem very concerned about Buffum and Mademoiselle," Mary said. "Very likely they are enduring cruel ravishments, even now."

"It's only your opinion that they were taken, and your opinions are rarely reliable," Tasmin said. "If they *are* taken I will immediately ask Mr. Snow or Mr. Drew to arrange their release."

"I must get Piet—he was intending to hide in a plum thicket," Mary said. "It would be most vexing to lose our botanist at this early stage of the trip."

The old hunter, Dan Drew, in conversation with Jim, stopped and made Tasmin a very decent bow when she approached. For a man who lived in dangerous country, he seemed mild—lazy, even.

"How do, miss?" he said. "The little one and I will just go locate that Dutchman and then I'll get them back on board—I guess Jimmy will look after you, in the meantime."

"I hope he won't mind," Tasmin said. "I know that I'm rather a lot of trouble."

Jim Snow ignored her remark. He seemed rather embarrassed about something—Tasmin couldn't guess what, though in fact she felt rather embarrassed herself, a condition she rarely experienced. Usually she preferred to brazen her way through dubious situations, and yet now she felt constrained and rather uncertain. What would happen? It had been an afternoon of kidnap, injury, and violent death. All logic suggested that she ought to hurry back to the safety of the steamer *Rocky Mount* as rapidly as possible; and yet, if there was one thing she *did* know, it was that she didn't want to hurry back to the boat just yet. Though hardly tranquil in spirit, she felt she was exactly where she wanted to be: on a small ridge above the Missouri River, in a country filled with warring savages, and in the company of her unusual gentleman, Mr. Jim Snow.

25

. . . and here was this talky girl again.

When it came to Indians, Jim Snow trusted old Dan Drew's judgment—if he said they were safe for a time, then they were—but the mere fact of safety did little to relieve the turmoil in his spirit. What *was* he doing, standing there with this English girl, a troublesome sort he had supposed himself well rid of ten days earlier? Why *wasn't* he rid of her, when it was clear that the safest place for her was on the boat? The Osages, Kickapoos, and Pawnees were at war, with the Omahas and Otos likely to be drawn into the conflict. Even the river wasn't safe, but it was far safer than the prairies. Two women had been taken already—at least that was Charbonneau's opinion, and Dan Drew's as well. A boy had been killed, by which tribe no one knew.

Jim had known nothing of these tribal warrings until he had happened to spot a dozen Osage warriors, moving north and painted for battle. He hid, and once the war party passed, sought out Dan Drew, who knew the various Indian bands well; he often brought meat to them in times of famine. Because of his great generosity Dan Drew was safe, where other whites would soon have come under attack.

Now the immediate danger had passed, but not without cost to the English, who had casually drifted ashore right into the thick of things; and here was this talky girl again. Though Jim Snow liked Pomp Charbonneau and Kit Carson and some of the other trappers, and could even tolerate talkative old Dan Drew, the fact was he usually liked to keep some distance between himself and his fellows; and yet that rule did not apply to the English girl, who had somehow taken over his attention in a way no one else ever had. There she stood, meek—for the moment—as a doe, having contrived to show up alone in her boat again just at the most dangerous moment possible. He *should* send her back to the steamer, and yet he didn't want to. There was something about her he liked—why else had he come back for her?

Tasmin, who had been censured countless times for her impatience, now waited patiently for Mr. Snow to decide their fate. Defiant when he awakened her in the boat, she now felt calmly passive. Whatever course of action they were to pursue was for Jim to suggest.

"You still ain't got no kit, but at least you've got shoes, this time," he said, with an effort.

"I *had* kit—you sank it when you sank my pirogue," Tasmin said pertly. "It's probably rather soggy now but if we could find the boat we'd find my kit."

"I'll get it tonight," Jim said.

Without another word he turned and started walking away from the river. Tasmin felt confused—was she to be abandoned again? Had he rescued her only to leave? Disappointment was so sharp that tears started in her eyes, but then Jim Snow stopped.

"Ain't you coming?" he asked.

Tasmin came—so little was her Raven Brave a man of words that he had not thought to ask her—and yet he must have followed the boat for days, waiting for an opportunity to see her, a realization she found deeply satisfying.

When she caught up, Jim set a steady clip straight out into the prairie. Though she wore shoes this time, Tasmin still found it a rather scratchy experience.

"Are you taking me to Santa Fe after all, Mr. Snow?" she asked.

"Nope—just want a look at that dead buffalo," he said.

"Oh, did Papa at least kill one—he's been so keen to," she said; and then she saw the butchered beast itself, stiff in death, dried blood everywhere, and a vast cloud of black and green flies buzzing over the carcass.

"He didn't kill this one," Jim said, lifting a snatch of white cloth off a weed. He had handed it to Tasmin.

"This might be from Mademoiselle's chemise," Tasmin said. "She was in a rather immodest state, I'm afraid. I sent my sister Bess to make sure she didn't get lost."

Then, to her surprise, Tasmin saw her father's fine leather hunting seat, poked into the ground some little distance away. The sight startled her far more than the little scrap of chemise, for if there was one thing her father was particular about it was his sporting equipment. A catastrophe so great as to cause him to forget his hunting seat must have been a very considerable catastrophe indeed.

"Why, they left Papa's seat, careless fools," she said. "We had better return it, when we go back, else someone will probably be flogged."

But *were* they going back? she immediately wondered. She could not in the least predict what Jim Snow's intentions might be. The discovery of the scrap of chemise and the hunting seat was enough to convince Tasmin that something pretty drastic had occurred on the prairies. Jim Snow had walked off to the north, scanning the terrain. After a time he returned.

Feeling a little weary, Tasmin sat for a moment on her father's seat. The emptiness of the country seemed brutal—indeed, overwhelming. Tasmin, who had seldom been at the mercy of anything more powerful than her own moods and passions, felt suddenly at the mercy of those great prairies and the wild men who inhabited them. The plains had power of a different order than any landscape she knew; they made her feel melancholy and small. Without warning, her spirits slid. Had she been alone she might have cried, in puzzlement and misery—but she wasn't alone. Jim Snow was nearby, looking rather carefully over the ground. He stooped and picked up a piece of black ribbon, which Tasmin at once recognized. Buffum had worn it as a choker, when in dramatic moods.

"That's my sister's ribbon—she's excessively fond of black," Tasmin said.

"Whoever took 'em went north," Jim said. "Probably those scoundrelly Kickapoos."

On the steamer *Rocky Mount* all the talk of kidnap by wild savages had served mainly as a source of stimulation—idle blather from the women of the group. Tasmin had given the matter no real credence. Of course, they were forging into a stark frontier, where such things as abductions by savages were bound to happen now and then; but gleeful talk of ravishment and speculation about native proclivities and equipment had only been a mildly titillating part of shipboard life. Even now, holding what was plainly her sister's ribbon, Tasmin could not quite accept the fact of kidnap. Bess might merely have dropped it—perhaps she and Mademoiselle had just taken fright and scampered back to the boat.

"But it's only Monsieur Charbonneau's *opinion* that they were taken," Tasmin said. "They might be on the boat—someone ought to look, at least, before leaping to dire conclusions."

In fact she didn't want her tiresome sister or the frantic maid to have been kidnapped—it might produce a disappointing interruption of her time with the Raven Brave.

"Nope, they're gone," Jim said. "Charbonneau was right."

"But how do you know—you said yourself that he was a fool," Tasmin argued.

"He *is* a fool, but not that big a fool," Jim said, surprised yet again by Tasmin's determination to argue every arguable point. Neither of his own wives, Sun Girl and Little Onion, both Utes, had exhibited anything like such a level of temperament. But then, the two Utes had been trained to obedience, whereas this good-looking English girl had evidently been encouraged to dispute even the most obvious facts.

"Look at the tracks, miss," he said. "There were six Indians here, with horses—they ran down the two women and they took them.

"You need to get better sense," he added mildly, a comment that stung

Tasmin to sudden fury. She jumped up, yanked her father's hunting seat out of the ground, and faced her rescuer.

"Do please stop accusing me of lack of sense!" Tasmin raged. "I won't hear it! If there is one point generally agreed on in our family it is that I am the one with sense.

"It's not that *I* lack sense, it's that this dreadful place lacks *everything*!" Tasmin continued, fiercely, bosom heaving. "There's not even a magistrate to summon, which is the usual procedure in instances of kidnap. If my sister's gone, then there's nothing at all to be done about it, that I can see."

Still in a high fury, she flung the leather seat as far as she could throw it.

"I came ashore hoping that I might find you and that we might have a nice time together," Tasmin said. "I assume you must want something of the sort, since you troubled to follow our boat. *Don't* you want a nice time with me, Mr. Snow? I want our nice time very much, and I'm disgusted with my blinking sister for getting abducted and spoiling everything."

Tasmin felt the anger drain out of her—dejection immediately took its place. She it was who had insisted on her own good sense, and yet what sense did it make to have so strongly declared herself to a man she scarcely knew? A man, moreover, who had no fondness even for conversation and who seemed to possess nothing except a rifle and a bow—not much to put against the Berrybenders' vast estates.

Jim Snow flushed—it was such a long speech to sort out—and yet he was not one to deny joy when he felt it; and he *did* feel it.

"If you mean you want to marry up, I'll do it—sure!" he said. "I thought you might want to marry up with me—that's why I followed the boat. But right now we need to go—this is warring time. More Indians could show up, and catch us like they caught your sister."

Tasmin was stunned. Did she, as he put it, want to marry up? Whatever could it be like, to marry, in such an absence of all context, this appealing but perplexing young man, when what she mainly wanted was to trim his hair and beard? Though the impulses that brought her such an unexpected proposal seemed wildly fanciful, Tasmin was pleased—deeply pleased—by Jim Snow's frank statement. Dejection and rage turned to joy—though joy not unmixed with confusion. Her Raven Brave *did* want to have a nice time with her—it was the most honest acceptance Tasmin had ever received, a big improvement over the sort of fopperies that had come her way in England.

But before the nice time could happen, the warring time had to be surmounted. She no longer felt the need to dispute it. It was time to trust the Raven Brave.

Jim picked up the hunting seat, took Tasmin by the hand, and led her quickly back toward the river, stooping low and stopping whenever there was a bit of cover, to scan the prairies around them for whatever enemies might be.

26

Alarums of the most violent kind were heard from the near shore . . .

Captain George Aitken, with the patient exercise of care and skill, had at last managed to ease the steamer *Rocky Mount* off the clinging sandbar when, it seemed, pandemonium suddenly rained upon him. Alarums of the most violent kind were heard from the near shore, shortly after which a canoe arrived, aslosh in bloody froth from Lord Berrybender's foot, which seemed half shot away. Charbonneau was doing his best to manage a tourniquet, but the old lord's outraged thrashings made it difficult. Venetia Kennet, leaning far over the rail to catch a glimpse of the nobleman she intended to marry, saw the bloody froth and the mangled foot and fainted dead away, toppling over the rail just beside the boat. It took three *engagés* to retrieve the heavy but momentarily lifeless cellist.

Hearing the hubbub and sensing that something was terribly wrong, Fräulein Pfretzskaner began to blubber, upsetting Cook, who seized her heaviest ladle and rushed out on deck, prepared to defend her honor and perhaps even her life. Cries and lamentations soon reached the ear of George Catlin, who was on the upper deck—he was near to finishing the landscape he had labored on since the hailstorm passed; rattled by the intolerable noise, he ripped the canvas up and flung the pieces overboard. The pieces drifted down toward a pirogue that seemed to be filled with blood, from which several *engagés* were attempting to lift the body of Gorska Minor; the boy, an arrow through his throat, was evidently quite dead. George regretted the hasty destruction of his landscape—it had not been *that* far off—but how could a painter be expected to make delicate adjustments amid such a racket?

Just then Captain Aitken came off the bridge, surveying the chaos below with his usual calm.

"I believe there's been an attack, Captain," Catlin said.

Captain Aitken continued his calm inspection.

"Well, the West ain't Baltimore, Mr. Catlin," he said. "These English *will* go ashore."

He went down to the lower deck and administered the violently annoyed lord a dose of laudanum sufficient to put an elephant to sleep; then he attempted to comfort Gorska, who was crying out to his God and weeping bitterly over the loss of his son.

"Who was it killed the lad?" the captain asked, once they had carried the old lord up to his stateroom, where he sprawled, mouth agape, across his bed in dope-induced sleep.

Toussaint Charbonneau had no sufficient answer.

"Gorska never saw an Indian—just looked around and saw the boy gasping for breath—that arrow cut his windpipe," he said. He had been attempting to instruct Gladwyn on the correct use of the tourniquet, but Gladwyn was so worn out from having to help carry his master over more than a mile of prairie that he was in no state to comprehend a lecture on medical technique.

"A Polish hunter wouldn't know one Indian from another anyway," Captain Aitken said. "Is someone bringing the young ladies, or are they dead too?"

"Well, Lady Tasmin and little Mary are fine—Jim Snow and Dan Drew have them," Charbonneau said. "I don't know about the other two—most likely they were taken."

"Taken?" George Catlin said. "Taken?" Suddenly the stories of kidnap took on a different weight.

Before Charbonneau could say more, Venetia Kennet, her clothes soaking, her long hair a wild wet tangle, stumbled into the stateroom, eyes wide with shock. Lord Berrybender's right foot, or what was left of it, was extended off the bed, dripping into a bucket—the sight filled her with sudden horror. Her husband-to-be, once the handsomest nobleman in England, was now a deformed old man.

"It's only toes, mainly," Captin Aitken said. "Many a man has lost a few toes, Miss Kennet. In a month His Lordship will be as good as new."

Black bile rose in Vicky's throat and she stumbled away.

"He's not bleeding much now—ease off the tourniquet," Captain Aitken said. "You best go talk to the chiefs, Charbonneau. I imagine they want calming."

"Yes, and so do the tribes," Charbonneau said. "Dan Drew thinks it's a general war—Osage, Pawnees, all the fine tribes."

When Charbonneau got downstairs he found every man on the lower deck armed to the teeth, which rather vexed him. Señor Yanez, evidently convinced that attack was imminent, had distributed muskets freely to the *engagés,* many of whom had only a rough idea of how to use them. The lower deck bristled with muskets and knives, a grave danger to the English party but hardly a threat to the Indians, who, in any case, were not in evidence.

Worse yet, in the confusion, they had lost a chief: Big White. Either from impatience with being stuck on so many sandbars, or from disgust with the noisy company, he had taken his great war club and gone. Neither the Piegan nor the Hairy Horn expressed the slightest interest in Big White's whereabouts or intentions. And yet Big White was the chieftain Captain Clark had strongly urged Charbonneau to protect. Charbonneau, calm in the face of the old lord's injury, the young ladies' kidnapping, and the young Pole's death, was rattled considerably by the disappearance of his famous charge.

"I was told not to lose him and now I've lost him," Charbonneau said. "If he gets kilt there'll be hell to pay with the Mandans. I better go locate him, if I can."

At this Captain Aitken balked.

"Sharbo, I can't spare you," he said. "I've got to have somebody handy who can parley with the red men, if they come. Big White's an able man—I expect he can look out for himself."

"Damnation, I had meant to have him sit," George Catlin said. "Full face, of course—no more profiles. I've learned my lesson."

In fact George was talking mainly to distract himself from a painful attack of nerves. Lady Tasmin had not reappeared, nor the brash little Mary, and as for Bess Berrybender and Mademoiselle Pellenc, the general view was that they were quite gone—"taken," in the stark expression of the frontier.

Toussaint Charbonneau and Captain George Aitken, each with his own worries, ignored the talkative painter—in Charbonneau's view the man was lucky to be alive anyway, considering the rash liberties he had taken when he attempted to paint the volatile Piegan.

Just then a second pirogue came slowly back from shore, this one carrying old Dan Drew, Mary Berrybender, a dazed, semiconscious Bobbety, and a rather scratched-up Piet Van Wely, his face much marked from the thorny thicket in which he had hidden during the time of anxiety, while the Indians were milling about.

"Oh good, there's Dan . . . just when we need him," Charbonneau said. "Dan knows the country as well as any Indian—perhaps he'll hunt Big White for me."

"If it comes to a choice, I rather hope he'll help us to get the young ladies back," Captain Aitken said. "Wouldn't want them to be ill-used, any more than we can help."

"Drat Big White anyway," Charbonneau said.

27

He thought he might just have a nip of grog—maybe two . . .

Bobbety Berrybender claimed that the blow from the hailstone had left him afflicted with triple vision.

"Trios, trios, I only see trios," he insisted. News that neither Tasmin nor Mademoiselle Pellenc were there to make him poultices alarmed him so much that Captain Aitken gave him a dose of laudanum not much weaker than that he had given the old lord himself, after which Bobbety was deposited on the upper deck with Master Jeremy Thaw, whose power of speech had still not returned. Piet Van Wely, iodine on his scratches, joined them, the little group being viewed with stern contempt by the unmarked and fully operative Holger Sten.

Charbonneau disarmed as many of the *engagés* as possible. Señor Yanez and Signor Claricia, both very drunk, inquired about the fate of the missing women; both still had passionate designs on Mademoiselle.

"But what of Lady Tasmin?" George Catlin inquired.

"Oh, I wouldn't worry about that pretty lass," Dan Drew said. "I expect she and Jimmy Snow are just courting."

"Courting? Surely not!" George said, much disturbed by the suggestion. Bold as Lady Tasmin might appear, it was scarcely credible that she would have started a romance with some raw product of the Western frontier.

"It's the other two that worry me," Captain Aitken admitted. "I suppose there's no hope of bargaining for their return?"

"Plenty of hope, if we can find 'em," Dan said. "I imagine they've taken them to the Bad Eye—he's the main trader in women in these parts. I expect when you get upriver you can strike a bargain—if that's where they are."

"We'll be three weeks to a month getting to the Bad Eye," Captain Aitken said. "And that's if we're lucky with the currents. Rather a long time for two tender ones to suffer."

Dan Drew didn't answer—a month's captivity was not long, as captivities went. It was white women who had been held a year or two that there was scarcely any good reason to bring back. They were usually broken by then, not equal to the scorn of their luckier sisters, once they were returned.

"The Sin Killer might get them back," Charbonneau said. "Jim throws a powerful fear into some of the tribes."

At this Mary Berrybender broke into her strange, high laugh.

"But the Sin Killer is Tasmin's new gentleman," she said. "She is unlikely to allow him time off just to rescue her sister—though I suppose Mademoiselle is another matter."

"Why'd that be, little miss?" Dan asked.

"Why, because Mademoiselle is so good with Tasmin's hair," Mary replied.

She then raced upstairs to have a look at Bobbety's lump.

"Who makes a warmer friend, an English girl or a fish?" Captain Aitken asked, once the strange child was gone.

Charbonneau didn't answer. The day's disturbances had left him weary. He thought he might just have a nip of grog—maybe two nips—and then retire to his cozy pallet. Perhaps Coal, his bright-eyed wife, would bring him his pipe and some vittles—she might even rub his aching feet.

28

For a moment she had hoped there might be a kiss . . .

When she saw that they were making for the river, Tasmin became fearful that Jim Snow—in the interest of her safety—might mean to return her to the boat after all. She didn't want to go back to the boat, and was much relieved when he merely hid her in Mr. Drew's cave while he went downriver and retrieved her sopping kit.

Tasmin spent the little wait feeling rather blank—she had often been accused of dissecting her suitors rather as if they were frogs. But now something momentous had happened—a man of whom she knew almost nothing had offered to marry her, a thing so surprising that all capacity for analysis seemed to have left her. She merely waited. In Jim Snow's presence past and future got squeezed out. The present—intense, exciting, huge—took all her attention.

"Come out," he called, when he returned. "You'll want to spread these clothes to dry."

Tasmin at once squeezed out of the cave. The sun was just setting—afterglow was golden in the Western sky. Over the river a bright moon had risen. Jim quietly helped her spread her wet clothes on the grass to dry. His wariness had left him; he seemed to feel confident that the warring tribes would not disturb them.

"We've got no vittles tonight," he said. "I might try to gig a fish."

"There's something else I'd like you to try," Tasmin said mildly.

Jim looked up, curious but not hostile.

"I'd like you to call me by my name, Tasmin—you've never said it," she told him. "It would please me if you would just say my name."

"Tasmin, okay—I'm Jim," he said. "Pleased to meet you."

To Tasmin's astonishment he took her hand, shook it firmly, and returned to his task of spreading out wet clothes—she had packed only the roughest and simplest. For a moment she had hoped there might be a kiss—but for that, it seemed, she would have to wait. She hardly knew what frontier custom allowed to the betrothed; perhaps she could not immediately expect any kissing. She found herself assailed by powerful doubts. Perhaps his offer to marry up with her had been only a momentary inclination on his part—perhaps he had only said it to calm her fury. It had *felt*, at the time, like a true offer, but was it? Did he still want to?

"Look here, Jim—did you mean it when you said you'd like to marry up with me?" Tasmin asked, feeling that she might burst into tears if the matter were not immediately confirmed.

"I meant it—I sure did," Jim said, as if surprised that there could be the slightest doubt about the matter.

"So we're truly to be married? I need to know it!" Tasmin said. Some jelly of doubt would not quite leave her; she wanted to be fully convinced that Jim Snow intended to make her his wife.

"That's right—we'll get hitched," Jim said, smiling at her for the first time—a shy, becoming smile.

"The only reason I followed that boat was you," he admitted. "I've a notion you'll make a fine wife."

"Well, I do hope so," Tasmin said. "As your fiancée, then, might I just ask one favor? Might I just trim your beard a little, so as to see your face better? I have some scissors with me—I'm just in a fever to do it."

Jim was a little startled by Tasmin's request. He had never given a thought to his beard—it was just there, like the hair on his head. So far it had required no attention; neither of his Indian wives had even mentioned it, and yet Tasmin, his new bride-to-be, was waiting expectantly. She would surely think it rude if he said no—perhaps, independent as she was, she would even refuse to be his.

"I guess you can cut it, if you want . . . if it will please you," he said.

"Oh, it will please me exceedingly," Tasmin said, immediately getting out her scissors, at the sight of which Jim Snow looked startled.

"You mean cut it now?" he asked.

"Why yes, at once—just sit on one of those rocks," Tasmin said. "I shan't take long."

"But it's nearly dark," he said. "Wouldn't the barbering go better in the morning?"

"Sorry, can't wait," Tasmin said. "There's plenty of light, really."

Jim obediently sat on one of the rocks near the entrance to Mr. Drew's cave and Tasmin was at last allowed to do what she had been longing to do since the day they met; she got her fingers in Jim Snow's tangled beard and began to comb it straight.

"Don't take too much off, now," he said, very surprised to find himself the object of such attentions.

"Hush now . . . how can I trim a beard with you chattering?" Tasmin said.

Jim made no further protests. Tasmin stood so close to him that he could smell her; she had a light fragrance, probably from the use of some fine soap. She wasn't greased like his other wives. She was quick with the scissors too—masses of his beard seemed to be falling away. It seemed to him that she hardly meant to leave him a beard at all.

"There . . . I'm rather content with the beard," Tasmin said. "You are so handsome, Jim, only one could scarcely see it for the tangles. Now you could pass for a prince in any court in Europe."

The compliment embarrassed Jim deeply—he doubted that anyone would ever mistake him for a prince. But he liked it when Tasmin stood so close.

"Now that the beard's right it's obvious that you have rather an excess of hair," she said. "Do be sweet and oblige me for just another minute—I mean to give your hair just the lightest trim."

Jim didn't protest. He had given himself over to a new power—a good-smelling power, Tasmin, his wife-to-be. Soon again the scissors snicked and his hair, like his beard, seemed to fall in masses. Tasmin snipped, she didn't speak. She had rarely felt happier than at that moment, while at the simple task of barbering the young man who was to be her mate.

"There, you're sheared, Jim," she said.

Her eyes seemed to have widened, as she stood close. To Jim they seemed as large as the moon.

"I just must kiss you—I must," she said, and she did kiss him, his fresh-cut locks tickling her cheeks.

"I should have brushed you off, you've hair everywhere," she said, lifting her face from his. But then, hair or no hair, she kissed him again.

"Jim, when can we marry?" she asked, her voice rather husky. "I fear I'm cruelly impatient. I don't want to wait too long to be made a wife."

"Old Dan can marry us, when he comes back," Jim said. "He was a justice of the peace, back in Missouri—he's married up two or three of the boys."

"I hope he hurries back, then—I am so impatient," Tasmin said.

29

. . . soft echoes of pleasure that left her rather dreamy . . .

Dan Drew married them just as darkness fell, using Jim's little Bible. Then he lent them his cave for their nuptial night, and appeared again shortly after dawn, with three rabbits and two fat grouse as wedding presents.

"Well, you're hitched now—first couple I've married in five years," Dan observed, once he had a rabbit and a grouse cooking on a spit of wood.

"I guess that means the country will soon be settled up," he added, with a smile.

Tasmin could still feel the effects of the hitching in her body, soft echoes of pleasure that left her rather dreamy but also keenly hungry. She could hardly keep from grabbing the grouse. Jim Snow was washing himself in the river. He claimed that most of his hair had gone down his shirt and was itching him ferociously. Tasmin watched him bathe with a proprietary eye. By the time he came back, his newly cut hair shining with droplets of water, Tasmin was already ripping into the first of the grouse. Though grateful, of course, to the tall frontiersman for marrying them and then supplying their wedding breakfast, Tasmin was rather hoping that the old fellow would soon run along. She wanted to be alone with her husband, to kiss him and kiss him, and more.

Of the steamer *Rocky Mount* there was no sign—it had disappeared into the early morning mists—the day promised to be cooler; the breeze held a hint of autumn.

"They'll pass the Platte today, if they don't stick," Dan said. "Big White's loose somewhere—jumped ship during the commotion. Charbonneau's mighty upset about it."

"That boat's stuck most of the time," Jim said. "Big White probably thinks he can make better time afoot."

Like Tasmin, Jim was hoping Dan Drew would soon go on about his business. Decisions would soon have to be made, but for the moment he felt too lazy to think about them. It would be nice just to sit with his wife for a while, watching the river flow. Eventually he and Tasmin would de-

cide which way to go: back to Council Grove, across to Santa Fe, or upriver
to the Mandan villages, where Tasmin's sister and the Frenchwoman were
most likely being taken.

Tasmin was impatient with any mention of the steamboat, or her family, or Monsieur Charbonneau and his problems. She had escaped that
world, that tiresome fuss; now that she had secured her prize, a fine young
husband, she meant to glut herself with him. The Berrybenders, with their
endless complaints, were fetters that she had at last shaken off.

"George Aitken's exercised about the two women—I told him I'd help
try to get 'em back," Dan said. "The old lord's roaring about lost dowries
and such."

Tasmin, sucking the greasy bones of the fat grouse, could not but be
amused at this report. It was not hard to imagine how loudly her papa would
roar if he knew that she herself, who would surely have commanded one of
the most lavish dowries in Europe—from a Bourbon or a Borghese, a Ho-
henzollern, a Romanov, from any number of Hapsburgs—had married, will-
ingly and boldly, a penniless American, who probably didn't even know what
a dowry was. The virtue that might have brought the highest price in Europe
had been given away for love. There was much that she meant to teach her
young husband, and much that he must teach her about prairie ways—but
the base, at least, was solid; the sweet ache in her body told her that.

Dan Drew knew that the young couple wished him gone. Oh, they liked
the breakfast he had brought them, but they wished him gone. They had
just discovered each other—they wanted no one else. It was only the way
of the world. The young lady was too absorbed in the love that was just
beginning to really grasp her sister's peril, or that of the Frenchwoman.

With a smile, Dan stood up and turned to go.

"Where will you be heading, Dan?" Jim asked.

"I may go parley with the Bad Eye—buy those girls back, if that's where
they are," Dan said.

"I may have to go kill that old liar, someday—he's bad about spreading
false prophecies," Jim Snow said casually, as he took the rabbit off the spit.

Such talk made Tasmin uneasy—she wished Mr. Drew would just go.
She liked her mild Jim best; surely their raptures would soon gentle the Sin
Killer. She didn't want her husband to be seized by violent passions. She
wanted to tame him with passions of another kind. Wrapped in her young
arms, flushed by her quick kisses, rocked in her eager loins, he might soon
lose his dangerous impulses.

Dan Drew gave them a nod and turned to leave.

"Good-bye to you, young folks," he said.

"Thanks for hitching us, Dan," Jim said, as the old plainsman turned and walked swiftly away.

Tasmin at once laid her cheek against her husband's soft wet beard.

"You smell so sweet when you're clean, Jimmy," she said.

Just then the old green parrot flew down and settled on the rock by Dan Drew's cave.

"Go away, filthy bird!" Tasmin demanded, but the parrot took no heed.

30

The stars above were secure in their courses . . .

At night, with the steamer *Rocky Mount* safely moored, George Aitken liked to sit on deck and study the stars. With his erratic crew he could do little; with his even more erratic passengers he could do nothing. His relaxation came at night, when he could get out his little book of tables and constellations and contemplate the heavens. As they moved north of the Platte the North Star, his favorite star, seemed to increase in brilliance nightly. Captain Aitken respected the river, but he loved the stars. As summer passed into autumn the nights grew chill, but Captain Aitken had a great thick coat; he wrapped himself up in it warmly, filled his short pipe, and let starlight be his balm.

No one else on the boat, it seemed, was susceptible to being soothed by the heavens. Since the capture of the two young ladies and the departure of Lady Tasmin, the painter George Catlin had become increasingly frantic. He often interrupted the captain's restful stargazing with futile pleas involving Lady Tasmin—he wanted a search mounted, an effort Captain Aitken knew to be quite futile. Lady Tasmin had left of her own accord—if she ever reappeared it would also be of her own accord.

"The ice, Mr. Catlin—the ice," Captain Aitken repeated. "We mustn't let the ice catch us. We must get to the Yellowstone, where there's a fort. If the ice catches us with no fort to winter in, the Indians will pick us like berries. They'll not only take the rest of the women, they'll take the guns and all the provisions. We'll be eating shoe leather, if we ain't lucky."

George Catlin scarcely listened. The loss of Bess Berrybender and Mademoiselle Pellenc was bad enough, but Tasmin's apparently willing departure shook him so badly that he considered going ashore himself to mount a search; he was only dissuaded by Toussaint Charbonneau, whose own efforts to locate the missing Big White had convinced him that the shores were too dangerous to risk. Charbonneau said the prairies were cut by many horse tracks, signifying warring bands, who would not be likely to deal gently with a white man so green as to suppose a huntsman could attract antelope by wiggling his legs.

"Best to stay aboard, Mr. Catlin," Charbonneau advised. "Probably we'll find the young ladies when we get to the Mandan villages—there's a pretty brisk trade in captives goes on there."

Old Gorska, since the death of his son, had given himself up to drink and weeping, weeping and drink. Over and over again he repeated to anyone who would listen that he had never seen an Indian—he had merely looked around and discovered that his son was dead.

Mary Berrybender was devoting a great deal of time to the Hairy Horn, receiving instruction in the Sioux language. With Lady Berrybender dead and Lord B. just able to hobble about with the aid of a crutch fashioned by the skillful Signor Claricia, chaos had descended on the English company. The boy Seven, he of the cleft palate, could not be located—one theory was that he had been playing near the great paddle wheel and had been swept over and drowned. Others thought that the Piegan, who disliked the boy, had quietly dispatched him and dropped him overboard. The loss—if it was a loss; Seven had always been adept at hiding—weighed on Captain Aitken particularly. His employers in Pittsburgh were not paying him to lose noble English passengers—this George Aitken well knew. They were not much past the Ioway bluffs and several were already dead, missing, or damaged—Master Thaw still showed no signs of recovering his power of speech.

And now Dan Drew, who showed up occasionally to sell them meat, insisted that Lady Tasmin and Jim Snow were married—Dan himself claimed to have officiated. If true, this represented a calamity for Lord Berrybender's dynastic hopes—so great a calamity that no one had yet worked up to telling the old lord, the brunt of whose towering ill temper, since his accident, had been borne by the increasingly haggard cellist, Venetia Kennet, now constantly subject to the old nobleman's many whims, some of them decidedly gross in nature. Lord Berrybender could scarcely walk, which meant that he couldn't hunt, which left the two of them nothing to do all day except to play whist and copulate. Though perfectly willing to lose at cards, as Lady Berrybender had obligingly done for years, Vicky Kennet found to her horror that, despite herself, she sometimes won, Lord Berrybender's attention sometimes wavering just as he had to play the critical card.

"What . . . you treacherous wench, I'm sure you cheated!" Lord B. would yell, when he noticed to his distress that Venetia had actually won a hand, after which he was apt to pinch her cruelly the next time he had her alone—and he always had her alone. Venetia, so recently determined to marry Lord B. at all cost, had come to doubt that even the vast acres, the carriages, the castles could really be worth such constant stains to her dignity.

It was just after a rather onerous afternoon of fornication that Venetia happened to hear the *engagés* shouting about something. Looking out the stateroom window, she saw a buffalo standing in the water not fifty yards away. At once she yelled for a gun—Gladwyn, hurrying in with a rifle, was rewarded with a glimpse of her white bosom before she could cover herself. Lord B., naked except for the bandage on his foot, took the gun, opened the window, and shot the buffalo, a bit of marksmanship that improved his mood immensely.

"By gad, that's the answer!" he said. That evening claret flowed—the next morning Lord Berrybender settled himself in a chair on the lower deck. In the course of the day he shot two elk and a beaver—Cook was rather put out at being asked to cook the beaver tail; Charbonneau, who had cooked many, was finally allowed to assist. Lord Berrybender even offered a slice to Old Gorska, in an effort to cheer the old hunter up.

"Now, Gorska, that boy of yours is gone," he said. "My Constance is gone, my Bess is gone, the Frenchwoman is gone, and it appears that even my son Seven may be gone. We all must live with our losses, we all have crosses to bear. I myself have to put up with a damnable woman who cheats at cards—you must buck up, man, the hunting's just starting."

Gorska declined the beaver tail—he had no intention of bucking up.

"But what of Lady Tasmin?" George Catlin put in. "Lady Tasmin is not presently among us, as I'm sure Your Lordship has noticed."

Lord B. gave an airy wave.

"Oh, Tasmin's just picnicking," he said. "No worries on that score. I'd like to see the savage who could handle Tasmin—there's no one in England who can handle her, else I'd have collected a fine dowry by now. She's a peach, Tasmin is, matrimonially speaking, and I'm not one to sit by and allow matrimonial fruit to grow overripe. Pluck it, I said, just as I plucked Lady Constance. I liked that fine bosom of hers."

That night Captain Aitken sat long on deck—the North Star and its millions of pale companions cast a fine light over the swelling prairies. He and his party would be among the river Indians soon—the Arikaras, then the Mandans, plus whatever tribes might have come to the river to trade—the Teton Sioux perhaps. Though the river Indians had long been accustomed to trading with the whites, the possibility of some sudden conflict was always there. Some of the young warriors, hot to prove themselves, were likely to be indifferent to trade; they might prefer to take scalps. Or one chief might seek to gain position over another by demonstrating his boldness with the whites. Indeed, the very size of their party might be taken as a threat. The Hudson's Bay Company wisely sent their traders south in twos and threes. Greedy for goods, the tribes saw no reason to fear two or three Frenchmen; but a whole boatful of Europeans might be seen as a threat, as it had been ten years earlier, when the Arikaras had soundly defeated General Ashley and his company of mountain men.

Fortunately the English lord, on Captain Clark's advice, had laid in an expensive stock of presents and trade goods—perhaps lavish bribery would work, as it had before.

Despite the solace of the stars, Captain Aitken found himself assailed by doubts. The stars above were secure in their courses, whereas, on the Missouri River, nothing was secure. Lord Berrybender had not yet grasped that he had come to a place where English rules did not apply. The rules of the wilderness were less forgiving than those of any Parliament or Congress. It might be that, of them all, Lady Tasmin was best off—no one was abler on the prairies than her chosen companion, Jim Snow.

The fading moon was just being reddened by the rising sun when Captain Aitken rose from his chair and went back to the bridge to refill his pipe. He was just tamping in a shag of tobacco when a shot rang out from the lower deck—Lord Berrybender, up early, had evidently found something to shoot at.

Charbonneau, hearing the same shot and fearing trouble, jumped up at once; but it was only the old lord, his hair wild, in a bed suit of red flannel, brandishing his rifle. On the bank lay a dead wolf.

"Got him! Would you just be a good fellow and go fetch him, Sharbo?" Lord Berrybender asked.

"If your cook won't broil a fine beaver tail I doubt she'll appreciate a wolf," Charbonneau said, a little puzzled by the request.

"Oh, I don't want to cook him, man—I mean to stuff him!" Lord Berrybender said. "My first wolf—gets the blood up, you know. I believe I'll go wake up my cheating Vicky and show her a thing or two."

31

The plains were covered with the great brown beasts . . .

Bess steeled herself—the fat, friendly puppy was licking Mademoiselle Pellenc's face. Mademoiselle could not seem to move; she let the puppy lick her.

"Mademoiselle, we *must*," Bess said, well aware that the half-breed woman, Draga, was watching them impatiently. Any delay and Draga would seize a stick from the fire and beat them with it—beat them with the smoldering stick until she could no longer lift her arm. Then Draga might direct one of her daughters to seize other sticks and continue the beating until Bess and Mademoiselle were scorched, scarred, and almost insensible.

"*Mademoiselle, s'il vous plaît!* Draga is watching," Bess insisted. Finally Mademoiselle seized the puppy and held it firmly. Bess at once hit it sharply in the forehead with the blunt end of the hatchet. The puppy barely squealed. Mademoiselle flinched, but at once took up the skinning knife and began to skin the warm, limp carcass of the little dog.

Draga stood by the campfire, watching. Bess glanced at her fearfully—Draga was just waiting for some sign of sloth, waiting for any excuse to beat them—even without an excuse she would beat them, sooner or later. Bess had become inured to the blows themselves, but not to the hot sticks, which left blisters all over her back.

"Maybe they will let us have a little of the *petit chien*," Mademoiselle said. In three weeks she had gone from being a woman of such refined appetite that she had thought nothing of returning a loin of pork to Cook if she thought it a moment overdone to a woman so racked with hunger that she would eat anything—bones, guts, any cast-off morsel. Always skinny, Mademoiselle had grown so thin that the warriors scarcely bothered to amuse themselves with her anymore—the chubbier Bess drew more of their attention now. Terrible at first, these assaults had come to seem minor when compared to the threat of Draga, who had left no doubt in either of their minds that she would beat them to death, stab them, or even burn them alive if they faltered and were slow to do their chores.

"Hurry, Mademoiselle—she's watching," Bess said.

Mademoiselle hurried—in her country childhood she had often watched peasant women cutting up hares or lambs; she soon disjointed the puppy and took the pieces to Draga, who dropped them one by one into the stew pot.

The weather had turned cold—there had even been sleet in the afternoon, which meant a hard night for Bess and Mademoiselle. They had to huddle together in whatever little nest they could make in the long grass. They had no blanket but had managed to capture a deer hide that the dogs had been worrying. Mainly they used it to wrap their feet, which were bloody, scratched, and cold. They had to be up early, to scour the plains for firewood. Both of them knew they would die when the real cold came, unless they were rescued or managed to escape. In the night, whispering, they talked only of escape but had not been able to develop a plan that offered much hope of success. Mademoiselle wanted to try and steal a horse, but Bess could not convince herself that such a plan would work. Neither of them had any idea where to go if they did escape; and if they fled and were recaptured their punishment would undoubtedly be terrible, perhaps fatal. Even if they somehow reached the river they would have no way of knowing whether the steamer was upstream or downstream. Nor were their captors the only Indians in the area—twice other raiding parties had stopped at their camp. Bess and Mademoiselle had been made available to the visitors but the raiders had been hasty and skittish. They didn't linger.

Twice buffalo were killed. The plains were covered with the great brown beasts but the raiders who had taken them were not mainly on the prairies to hunt. They traveled hard and made only hasty camps.

Since escape seemed at least as perilous as captivity the two women did not attempt it. They did whatever chores were set them, and endured the beatings and indignities as stoically as possible. Never friends, or even amiable when on the boat, adversity soon brought them close. They agreed that, had either of them been taken alone, they would have died, from hopelessness, filth, violation, hunger, chill, and Draga's implacable cruelty. Together, they had survived, and had forged an intense determination to keep surviving. Degraded they might be, but they were alive.

At night, huddled with their deerskin, they whispered and made various plans, most of which were abandoned in the morning. Their only real plan was to live, and if possible, to be revenged on Draga, the cruel old half-breed woman who blistered them with hot sticks and laughed with her two dusky daughters when one or another of the warriors took a lustful interest in them. Mademoiselle's tenacious haughtiness provoked Draga's most violent attacks.

"If only Tasmin would come with the Sin Killer," Bess said. "I'm sure he'd soon put these brutes to flight."

Mademoiselle didn't answer. She didn't think anyone would come—not until they reached the trading place, where she supposed they were being taken. Monsieur Charbonneau spoke of it often, the big trading place of the Mandans. He said Frenchmen often came there from the north, a fact which gave Mademoiselle hope. How far away it was she didn't know, but she hoped it was not many more days. She feared the coming cold; every morning the frost on the grass seemed heavier. Soon a big snow might come. And how would they survive a big snow?

"I want to be warm again, Bessie," she said. "That's all. Just to be warm."

32

Near the Little Sioux, not far ahead . . .

Dan Drew smelled smoke—not much smoke, but enough to alert the curiosity of a hunter with a sensitive nose. He was near the Little Sioux River—game had been scarce along the Missouri so he had moved farther out, away from the big river. So far he had encountered four raiding parties, none large, none threatening to him, and none with any white captives to trade.

Near the Little Sioux, not far ahead, was a fine grove of willows, which was where the smoke came from. Dan went tramping loudly toward the smoke. In his view it was better to announce oneself as noisily as possible when approaching a camp, even a very small camp. In warring times folks were apt to get jumpy.

He thought he might find some Omahas or Otos, smoking a deer or an antelope, but to his surprise, the solitary man by the campfire was Big White, Charbonneau's missing Mandan. Big White was cooking himself a fat duck for breakfast.

Dan reckoned he and Big White were about the same age; over the years they had encountered each other many times, usually in the Mandan villages, where Big White had long been a prominent chief, much spoiled and flattered by the subtle French traders who had been slipping down from Canada along the Red River of the North.

"I'm surprised you ain't home by now," Dan said. "I heard you was lost."

Big White didn't answer. The notion that he might be lost in his own country was an absurdity. He was annoyed that the old hunter had stumbled on his camp. What was he doing on the Little Sioux anyway? Big White was on a serious vision quest; the last person he wanted to see was Dan Drew, a good hunter but a man who talked much and said nothing important. Among the tribes he was known as White Tongue, because of his loquacity. It was true that he was generous, often sharing his meat with the Mandans and other tribes. For that reason Big White didn't wish to be rude to him, although he was already impatient for the man to go.

"I am fasting," he said. "I don't know why I killed this duck. You are welcome to it if you are hungry."

"Let it cook awhile," Dan said. "Sharbo's looking for you—he's upset that you left the boat."

"If you see him tell him to leave me alone," Big White said. "I have to make a fast. I am not going home right now."

Then he turned the duck. Actually he was hungry—he didn't believe in fasts. But it would be worth a duck to get Dan Drew to leave.

"They've lost a passel of people off that boat," Dan said. "Two dead at least, maybe three. And two white women taken—they may be dead too."

"No, Draga has them—she is with some Gros Ventres," Big White said, annoyed that he would have to interrupt his meditations to explain even the simplest things to Dan Drew.

"Uh-oh, Draga," Dan said. "That vile old hussy needs killing."

Dan knew Big White wanted him gone, but the fat duck smelled better with each turn of the spit.

"Why ain't you going home?" he inquired.

"I waited too long to return—Captain Clark couldn't find me a boat," Big White said. "All the boatmen said the Sioux would come and kill them if they carried me. Even old Lisa said it—even old Lisa was afraid of the Sioux. This boat took me but now it is too late."

"Why, it ain't too late," Dan said. "You still got your hair, and you could still bash heads with your war club."

He saw the great war club, propped near a log nearby.

"I have been gone too long," Big White said. "Probably my old wives are dead. No one in the village will want to see me. They have a new headman. None of the young warriors will remember my deeds. The young women won't want me. I am old. Everything that I did has been forgotten."

He looked at the old hunter, who had pulled off a leg of the duck and was munching it. In fact, Dan Drew was one person who had known him long. Dan Drew would remember his great feats. He wondered if he ought to trust the hunter with a potent piece of information. He wanted to tell it to somebody.

"A bird spoke to me this morning—a meadowlark," he said. "He spoke to me in my own language."

Dan Drew had a cold feeling suddenly. He wished he had not found Big White. When Indians spoke of talking birds who could speak in Sioux or Mandan, the message was never likely to be good. Birds only talked to those who would soon be dead.

"What business has a meadowlark got, blabbing to people?" Dan asked. "Meadowlarks should mind their own business."

Big White could tell the old hunter didn't really want to hear the meadowlark's prophecy, which had been bad. No one wanted to hear bad prophecies.

"He said I would soon be killed by a man from the south," Big White said—he wanted to tell someone what the bird had said.

"Birds can be wrong," Dan said. "Anybody can be wrong."

Big White didn't answer.

Dan Drew found that he had lost his appetite for duck. To be polite, he smoked a pipe with Big White and then got up and left.

33

Tasmin awoke shivering, covered with goose bumps . . .

Nemba, the Oto woman Jim had insisted on visiting, was noted among the river peoples for her skill at working hides; the doeskin shirt she made for Tasmin was indeed very soft and supple, but also baggy, much too loose at the waist in Tasmin's opinion.

"Does she expect me to get fat?" Tasmin asked, once she put on the shirt.

Nemba had no fear of the Sin Killer, though she did fear the ruthless Sioux. She told Jim quickly, in sign, why she had left the doeskin shirt so loose at the waist. There was no end to the ignorance of white women, in Nemba's view. This one the Sin Killer had taken to wife did not even seem to know that she was with child, though only that morning Nemba had seen her puking near the corn patch.

Jim Snow was startled by what Nemba told him. A child already! The moon was only in its second cycle since he and Tasmin had been behaving as man and wife. Because the tribes near the river were warring he had taken Tasmin far out into the prairies, where no one would threaten them, to spend the last weeks of warmth. There they had only the roaring of the buffalo bulls to disturb them—they could behave as man and wife as often as they wanted. But frost had soon begun to whiten the grass in the morning. Tasmin awoke shivering, covered with goose bumps, so they had come back to the Oto village, to arrange with Nemba for warm skin garments, kit to protect them in the deep cold.

Tasmin felt a flash of jealousy—she didn't like it that the Oto woman was talking to her husband in sign; indeed, she was rather vexed by the whole business of skin clothes. On the boat there were plenty of warm clothes: great capotes, oilskin jackets, waterproof boots, all acquired by

Lord Berrybender and his agents in Saint Louis. All they needed was to go upriver until they caught up with the boat; Charbonneau or Gorska or Gladwyn or someone could have brought them plenty of winter clothes.

But Jim Snow had brushed aside the option of provisioning themselves from the steamer; he brushed aside so many of Tasmin's suggestions that she had begun to wonder why she even made them. She loved her sweet-breathed husband and responded to him deeply when they were joined in love—her one serious frustration was that he had no use for words. He ignored her opinions and only occasionally responded to her queries. Tasmin had not forgotten her mild inquiry about theology and the slap that greeted it, but she was rapidly reaching the point where she had rather be slapped than ignored. And it seemed to her her objection to the baggy shirt was being ignored. Nemba was comely, though short and rather heavy—Jim seemed on familiar terms with her, which Tasmin found disquieting.

"What were those obscure gestures supposed to mean?" she asked, anger in her voice. Jim heard the anger—it was always a shock, how quickly women angered.

"She left the shirt loose on account of the baby," he said.

"Baby?" Tasmin asked. She looked again at Nemba, wondering if it could be true—and if it *was* true, how had the Oto woman known? Was *that* the reason for her nausea in the mornings—a recent nausea but consistent?

"A baby?" Tasmin said again, convinced suddenly that it *was* true. "But what will we do? We have no domicile—not even a cabin."

"I guess we won't need one, for a while," Jim said. "You'll be droppin' it in the warm months, at least."

"Drop it? Is that what I'm expected to do?" Tasmin asked.

All around them, when they were far out on the prairies, the cow buffaloes had been dropping their calves. Was she herself now locked into this old, inexorable cycle, expected merely to squat at some point and squeeze a human infant out of her body? She remembered the wild screams that had accompanied her mother's regular lyings-in. Teams of nursemaids brought water, toweling, sheets, steaming basins, while the two placid, hammy midwives sat in low chairs at the foot of the bed. Tasmin doubted that she would be able to avail herself of any such help, if indeed Nemba was right and a baby was coming. Would Jim help her? Would anyone?

In her time on the prairies with Jim Snow she had made some progress toward wilderness skills. She could clean a fish, remove the liver from a

buffalo, and the tongue as well. Jim had even made her a bow and fashioned her some arrows. In time she felt she might be a decent archer,
though, so far, her only victim had been a skunk, which she shot at as a
joke but pinned to the earth.

All that had been fun, but she doubted that she was yet equipped to
be her own midwife. The very thought of such a crisis made Tasmin a bit
wistful for the Berrybender resources—at the very least, before her time
came, she meant to pluck a servant or two off that boat. Probably Cook,
herself the mother of twelve, would be the most practical choice. Of course
it would enrage her papa—no English gentleman could happily tolerate
the loss of his cook.

That night they camped on the river, some distance above the village
where Nemba lived. Gray chill squeezed out the sunset; Tasmin was glad
of her warm new shirt, even if it was baggy. The weeks on the prairie had
been a time of deep content, but now she felt restless, tight, unsettled.
Other than to reveal it to her, Jim had said nothing about the baby. Did it
please him that a small human, conceived in their passion, was even now
forming itself inside her? He had made no response at all—he just went
about, securing the night's firewood, which he did every night, whether she
was pregnant or not. Memory of the quick way Nemba had talked to him
with her hands still annoyed her—it had put her in the mood to quarrel.
Better a quarrel than long hours sitting in silence by a little fire, waiting for
the stars to shine in their brilliance. Tasmin had never long allowed herself
to be squelched by any circumstances, and she didn't intend to allow such
a thing, even if her husband *had* been quick to slap.

"Was Nemba your woman?" she asked, abruptly.

Jim thought he must have misheard. "My what?" he asked.

"Your woman—wife, even," Tasmin said, making a blind strike.

"I've heard that many frontiersmen take Indian wives," she went on.
"It seems quite reasonable, since no other wives are likely to be available."
She tried, with no great success, to keep heat out of her voice.

"Oh no, not Nemba—she's just good with skins," Jim said. "I've got two
Ute wives, though, up near the Green River."

They sat close together by the campfire. One of Jim's hands rested lightly
on Tasmin's knee. Instantly the knee was jerked away. Her blind strike had
worked so well that Tasmin was completely stunned. She had thought she
might provoke Jim into admitting to a dalliance with Nemba—caught the
Sin Killer sinning, as it were. But Nemba at once vanished from the equa-

tion, only to be replaced with two wives, and a third who was dead. Tasmin was so shocked that she could not at once find her tongue. The man beside her, a self-confessed polygamist, had married her too, and got her with child, a child she was expected to "drop" somewhere, when the time came.

"Could you repeat what you just said, Jim?" Tasmin asked, not hotly. She was still stunned—her tone was subdued.

"I married two Ute women when I was up on the Green River, trapping with Kit Carson and Pomp Charbonneau," Jim said, pleasantly. "The women kept the camp, while we trapped."

"And did Mr. Charbonneau have wives too—they seem to have been so useful," Tasmin said.

"Not Pomp," Jim said. "Plenty of the Ute girls wanted him but Pomp's finicky. He wouldn't have them."

"How fortunate that you aren't so finicky, Jim," Tasmin said.

"Such an accommodating man you are. I fear I must be rather a disappointment to you, Jim. I have so few skills, compared to your other wives."

"You're learnin' quick, though," Jim said with a smile, giving her a pat on the knee.

At that Tasmin stood up and walked blindly into the night.

34

With her feelings so roiled, the fact of darkness was a comfort.

Tasmin spent a cold night huddled in the Oto corn patch. Several dogs snarled at her, and a few barked, but then they quieted down. She heard Jim calling for her, but she didn't answer. Her feelings were in riot—one moment she was hot with anger, the next chilled by the thought of her own folly. In Northamptonshire, English custom had somewhat kept her native recklessness in check; but she was in America and there was *no* American custom. What system of manners could possibly prevail in a place where there were only savages and buffalo? That she had rushed to accept Jim

Snow as a husband now seemed absurd; and yet, only weeks ago, accepting him had felt right and felt wonderful. And as she herself had said only moments before the fateful revelation, it was no blemish on Jim's character that he had taken native wives—on the frontier *that* was customary. How could he have known that he would someday meet Lady Tasmin Berrybender—or any English woman? He had not tried to hide the fact of his Indian wives, particularly—to him it was a matter of so little importance that he had not thought to mention it—until questioned. And the wives—two surviving—lived far away, in a place unimaginable to Tasmin, where the Utes lived.

With her feelings so roiled, the fact of darkness was a comfort. Tasmin needed time to think, to recover, if possible, her famous command of logic; but it was not easy to think logically with her emotions running first hot and then cold. They were hardly the small, quiet feelings that might be expected from some country squire's daughter. One minute her blood—whether Berrybender or de Bury—was up and she wanted to fight the man she had just come to love. The next minute the very forbidding facts of the actual situation cooled her anger and left a dull listlessness in its place.

The insult that had driven her away from the campfire—Jim's casual assurance that her progress at practical tasks meant that she might someday hope to equal the performance of his two native wives—had of course not been intended as an insult at all; it had clearly been meant as a compliment, and yet it was a compliment that starkly revealed to Tasmin that the great plains of America, where she had enjoyed several very happy weeks, were no wider than the distance that lay between herself and the young man she had joined herself to. Could the frontiersman from the New World ever really know and appreciate a woman of the Old World? And the child, when it came—which world would it belong to?

That query and others just as painful and perplexing raced through Tasmin's mind all night. She did not sleep a wink. Finally the sun came, and nausea with it. When Jim found her she was bent over amid the cornstalks, throwing up.

35

Then, out of nowhere, the storm came . . .

According to your friend Nemba the steamboat passed several days ago, which means that it's upriver," Tasmin said. "I am going to it—if you have other plans, please pursue them.

"I'm afraid you married a very obstinate woman," she added, a fact that Jim Snow, halting and confused, could hardly have been unaware of.

Jim was purely stumped. He supposed most women were changeable but none he had met so far were nearly as changeable as Tasmin. When she learned from Nemba that she was with child, she was naturally a little startled, but seemed content enough. Then, out of nowhere, the storm came, and was still storming. She had first wanted to be taken to Santa Fe, a possibility now that fall had come; only now she *didn't* want to go to Santa Fe with him, or anywhere else with him, it seemed.

"The boat will be nearly to the Mandans by now, I expect," he said, confused. Tasmin had stuffed her kit into the sack she had brought it in. She showed every indication of being about to leave.

Jim had killed a small deer the afternoon before. He had been about to smoke some of the meat when Tasmin declared that she was leaving.

"What about meat? I can smoke you some," he said, deeply puzzled.

"I don't care to wait, thank you very much," Tasmin said. "I have my bow and arrow—perhaps I'll manage to pierce something a little more edible than a skunk."

There was a crispness in her tone which startled Jim—he had never heard a woman speak with such crispness. Her words were like shards of ice. He didn't want Tasmin to go, but he could not think of anything he might say or do that would cause her to change her mind. A fit of some sort had come over her—he decided it was best just to let her go. Once the fit passed she would probably come back.

Tasmin drew some faint amusement from the fact that she had managed to quell the Sin Killer. The terror of the prairies just looked tired and confused, and all it had taken was a little English ice.

All Jim could think to offer was a little practical advice.

"Stay on this side of the river," he said. "If you do the Sioux might let you be."

"Now, now . . . no instructions," Tasmin said. Then she walked away. Only two days before she could hardly get enough of kissing him—but now there she went.

When Tasmin had proceeded along the river some fifty yards she turned and looked back, half expecting to see her husband following her. But he wasn't following her—he was methodically smoking the deer meat. Her intent had been to leave him so broken that he would be incapable of practical actions—but in that she had failed. He might be heartbroken, but it didn't keep him from curing his jerky. She had no interest in justice—she had meant to break him utterly; that he was capable of merely turning to some mundane task was itself an insult. For a moment she considered turning back, for the sole purpose of goading Jim some more; but she didn't turn back—her pride wouldn't allow it. If her husband repented, let him track her.

A brisk wind, carrying more than a mild suggestion of winter, was in her face. Tasmin, still angry, struck a brisk pace. Twice she passed small groups of Oto women, gathering nuts and acorns from beneath the scattered groves of trees. She thought she might gather a few nuts herself, once she got farther from Jim.

As she walked her anger subsided. For six weeks or more she had scarcely been out of Jim's presence for an hour. He had only left her when he hunted, and then not long. Slowly, an old happy lightness infused her spirit, a joy much like that she had felt when she awakened alone that first morning in the pirogue. She felt again the happiness of being solitary—dependent only on herself and answerable to no one. It seemed strange, at that moment, that she had forged a union so intense as to make her forget how much she liked solitude—cherished it, in fact.

In her haste to be off the steamer she had failed to grab a book—once out on the prairie with Jim it was that oversight that irked her most. The great spectacle of nature was all very well, and Jim Snow's embraces were also very well; but she missed her books, her Scott, her Byron, Mrs. Ferrier, Southey, even silly Marivaux, whom she picked up at the urging of Mademoiselle Pellenc. Any book would have provided some diversion during the sultry prairie afternoons. The first thing she meant to do, once she got back, was lock herself in her stateroom and glut herself with reading. Her body had been sated on the prairies, but her mind had been starved; now she was anxious to get upriver and feed it.

Just as Tasmin was ripping along, buoyed by the thought of what a fine thing it would be to have a good soak and then shut herself in for an orgy of reading, she saw, not far ahead, a small, black-clad figure sitting on a fallen tree. It was a man, though a small man. Tasmin took up her bow. In such a wilderness all men were to be approached with caution; and yet Tasmin considered that it would be rather too theatrical if she were to stride up like Diana and loose an arrow at him. When she drew nearer she saw that the man wore priest's robes, and was doing just what Tasmin had been anticipating. He was reading. When he looked up from his book and saw Tasmin he was very startled indeed and immediately stood up to greet her.

"Queen and huntress, chaste and fair," the small priest said. He had a narrow face, and a carbuncle on his chin.

"Bonjour, mademoiselle," he added, with a quick, frank smile.

"I hope we can speak English, Father, since you seem to know it so well," Tasmin said. "What is that book you're reading?"

"Oh this, my little duodecimo?" the priest said, with a self-deprecating look. "Why, it's only Marmontel, the *Contes Moraux*—it would be *Moral Tales* if one were to English it. I cannot seem to get enough of him, ma'am—no author is more acute when addressing the challenges we all face in our attempts to lead a moral life."

Tasmin smiled. "I like the way you put that, Father," she said. "Got any more books with you? I've been touring the prairies and I confess I'm rather book-starved."

"Only a tiny Testament and an even tinier catechism," he said. "I am Father Geoffrin and you, I assume, are one of the missing Berrybenders."

"Yes, I'm Tasmin—eldest of that nearly innumerable brood," she said.

"I saw your esteemed father only the day before yesterday," Father Geoffrin said. "The brood is not quite so innumerable as it was. Your papa, I fear, is rather vexed with you for being so long about your picnicking."

Father Geoffrin had the habit of squeezing his own fingers as he talked—his fingers were long and thin, and the nails well kept, a novelty on the frontier, in Tasmin's view.

"Oh well, Papa is more or less always vexed," Tasmin said. "Fourteen children and nineteen servants hardly make for a simple life—but what's the latest?"

"The Fräulein is the latest," Father Geoffrin said. "She disappeared on the morning of my visit—eloped with one of the boatmen. Monsieur Charbonneau considers it a very ill timed elopement, due to the violent state of the tribes."

"That means we've lost both tutors—unless Master Thaw has recovered," Tasmin said.

Father Geoffrin shook his head. "Master Thaw, I'm afraid, remains as silent as the grave, mademoiselle."

"I'm no longer mademoiselle—I'm madame now," Tasmin corrected. Even if she never saw Jim Snow again she meant to insist on her married status.

Father Geoffrin was plainly startled by this news. He looked Tasmin up and down frankly—more frankly than was to be expected of a man of the cloth.

"Madame?" he said, lifting his eyebrows.

"Madame," Tasmin said firmly. "Would you have any food?"

"Only a humble corn cake," the priest said. "I was yesterday among the Omahas, attempting to harvest souls, and they pressed it on me."

He extracted the corn cake from a small pouch and handed it to Tasmin—though it looked rather grubby in appearance, she munched it hungrily.

Father Geoffrin was still pondering the unexpected news that Tasmin was a married woman. He looked intensely thoughtful, as if he were working out an equation of the higher mathematics.

"Have you met my countryman Monsieur Simon Le Page?" he asked, wrinkling his narrow brow. "Of course, he isn't really *my* countryman—he's a Québecois."

"Never heard of the fellow—what does he do?" Tasmin asked, to be polite.

"He's a fur trader," Father Geoffrin said. "From time to time he manages to ransom white captives. He is said to be making some effort even now, in regard to your sister Elizabeth and Mademoiselle Pellenc."

"Look here, Father, I'm feeling rather anxious to get back," Tasmin said. "Won't you come with me? I would like to hear more about Fräulein's exciting elopement—and I'm sure there are other scandals as well."

"Oh yes, your brother Seven has disappeared," the priest said. "Dire forebodings there."

"Tell me . . . but let's walk while we talk," Tasmin said. "You don't seem to be very busy here, on the whole. After all, you were just sitting on a tree reading a book of tales, when I came along."

"Ah, but Lady Tasmin, they were *moral* tales . . . *moral*," Father Geoffrin insisted.

"There's nothing very moral about a tale, that I can see," Tasmin said. "Not if it's a good tale."

Father Geoffrin looked rather downcast. He slipped the little book into a pocket.

"A fine, subtle point, madame," he said. "I'm a Jesuit—we thrive on subtle points. I suppose that's why I hate the wilderness so. There's nothing subtle about a tomahawk."

"I'm going, Father, subtle or not," Tasmin said. "Are you coming?"

"Happy to stroll along with you, madame," Father Geoffrin said.

36

. . . a company of fiends sprang from the dense morning mist . . .

Fräulein Pfretzskaner awoke to horror—a company of fiends sprang from the dense morning mist and began to hack at her Charlie—she saw his blood on their hatchets as they struck again and again. The trek east had exhausted them both. All day they had pushed on through heavy grasses, weeds, briars, little swamps, mud; everything that grew clutched at them—even the grasses were waist high.

"Charlie, we will have to do much chopping before we can farm," Fräulein said, looking far to the east and seeing only the high waving grass.

"Then we'll chop, I guess," Charlie Hodges said. He himself was a little startled to find the prairies so resistant, the going so slow. By nightfall they had scarcely traveled ten miles toward the distant Mississippi. The hard going had made them both ravenous—in one meal they ate nearly all the cold pork and thick sausages Fräulein had smuggled off the boat. They camped near a little copse of trees—Charlie thought he heard wild turkeys gobbling, not far away.

"Might get us a gobbler, in the morning," Charlie said, before falling asleep with his head on Fräulein's ample shoulder. She herself was still munching corn bread and sausage; she always liked to eat a bit before falling asleep. Better dreams came to sleepers with full stomachs. She munched as their campfire dwindled, the coals glowing. Being off the boat, in this wilderness of grass and weeds, had not yet brought the quick happiness that Fräulein expected. Of course it was good to be free of the English—the English she was done with. But the sky seemed too wide. Munching corn bread helped put down the occasional pulse of apprehension that rose in her now and then, like nausea. Afoot, far from the boat, the wilderness she had been observing seemed more threatening—less easily turned into a prosperous farm. Still, they had traveled only one day. Happiness needed patience. Soon they would build a snug cabin, clear a neat field, produce some jolly, chubby *Kinder,* stout boys who would soon grow big enough to help Charlie in the rich fields they would plant. They would be so happy together, she and her Charlie, on their good American farm.

By the time Fräulein awoke and began to scream the hatchets had made an end to Charlie—he opened his eyes in surprise just as death came. Fräulein Pfretzskaner fought to reach him—she wanted at least to close his eyes, but the Indians were around her like a wolf pack.

Pit-ta-sa, their leader, was surprised at the size of the white woman— usually it was easy enough to capture a woman once her man had been killed, but this large woman was willing to fight. She smashed Blue Blanket's nose with a skillet and hit Neighing Horses such a blow with her fist that the wind left him; he had to sit down. Pit-ta-sa himself grabbed the dead man's rifle and hit the woman three times with the butt; but even that, though it staggered her, didn't make her fall.

Blue Blanket bled so freely from his nose that thick blood covered his chest and belly. After that day he would be called Bloody Belly. Pit-ta-sa hit the woman again with the gun butt—the blow would have killed a deer, perhaps even a horse, but the woman only sank to her knees. She still held the skillet.

"I don't want her, let's go now—she would eat too much," Neighing Horses said, when he had regained his power of speech. The woman lurched over, on her knees, and closed her dead husband's eyes—or one of them, anyway. The other eye had been knocked partway out by one of the hatchet blows.

Pit-ta-sa ignored Neighing Horses, who often got discouraged if a fight didn't immediately go his way. Pit-ta-sa thought the big woman was about through fighting; she had begun to realize that her man would never be alive again. Her time with him was over; her fury was already changing to sorrow.

"No, wait a minute," Pit-ta-sa said.

Neighing Horses hated having his opinions questioned, but Pit-ta-sa was always questioning them. He had never seen a woman as large as the one there on her knees, sobbing over her dead husband.

"Put her on your horse, if you want to keep her," Neighing Horses said. "She is too big for my horse. She might break his back."

"I don't need to put her on any horse," Pit-ta-sa reminded him. "It is not far to the Bad Eye's camp. We'll just tie her good and let her walk."

None of the young braves wanted to use the large woman—they all said they had had enough of women for a while. Pit-ta-sa found this amusing. What they didn't want was to have their noses broken by a skillet.

Then Fräulein sat down. Her Charlie was dead; all her dreams were broken for good. No amount of corn bread, or sausages, or anything else could hold back her hopelessness. Nothing was any longer any good. When the skinny Indian came toward her with leather thongs, Fräulein meekly held out her hands and let herself be tied.

37

Draga, a violent woman whose origins were obscure . . .

Monsieur Simon Le Page, though a young man of only twenty-four years, considered himself to be a master of trader's protocol; he believed himself to have the delicate sense of precedence necessary to deal successfully with native tribes. He would have appreciated the assistance of some intelligent man with whom he could discuss diplomatic niceties and analyze strategies, when tricky situations arose—in a large trading encampment such as the Mandans', with many chiefs vying for position, tricky situations were bound to arise.

Unfortunately Simon Le Page had no such bright assistant—he merely had the phlegmatic, incurious, pipe-smoking Malboeuf.

"Malboeuf, do you even know what protocol is?" Simon had asked, more than once.

"Monsieur, I just row the boat or skin the beavers," Malboeuf replied. "I don't care for fine words."

Young Monsieur Le Page had scarcely walked into the large encampment—followed by a horde of filthy children and packs of skinny, slavering dogs—when a delicate situation came to his attention.

Draga was beating two nearly naked white women with a hot stick just pulled from a campfire. The women, filthy and bruised, seemed too glazed to respond. They each gave a grunt when a blow fell, but only a grunt. To Simon's eye one looked English, one French. He considered himself a fair student of nationalities, as any trader must be if he were to succeed.

"Look at the old slut, we should shoot her, monsieur," Malboeuf said. "Beating those pretty girls."

Simon merely nodded to Draga, who paused in her chastisement for a moment to look at him hostilely.

"If I shot Draga the Bad Eye would have us torn apart sinew by sinew," Simon reminded him. "I'll see what can be done for the young ladies in good time. First we have seven chiefs to visit, presents to distribute, and furs to inspect.

"That's our reason for being here, Malboeuf," he repeated. "Furs. Charity will have to wait."

In fact it was the distribution of presents that worried Simon most. He would need to make a careful assessment of the ever-shifting orders of precedence among the chieftains. It would be no easy task.

More than sixty solidly built earth lodges were scattered along both banks of the Missouri River. This great village of the Mandans had been a busy trading center for many years; from it thousands of choice pelts had made their way north to the Hudson's Bay Company's great depot at Three Rivers, the place from which Le Page and Malboeuf had been dispatched.

Young Simon Le Page stood high in the estimation of his superiors at the Hudson's Bay Company—otherwise he would not have been entrusted with the Mandan territory, an area where there was sure to be competition from many experienced traders.

Though Simon's future looked bright—he hoped to someday direct all the company's trading operations in the West—he knew that everything depended on precise and careful judgment. The Indian leaders were all jealous men; if one thought another had received better presents, then resentment might smolder or violence flare. Any slip—a musket with a broken trigger, blue beads given to a chief who preferred red beads, an insufficient offering of tobacco—could mean that, instead of a bright future, Simon might have no future. The order of precedence had to be estimated correctly—failure in this task might get one hacked, shot, scalped, killed. Simon was not fearful, but neither was he reckless. One must be supremely alert, and not allow oneself to be swayed by momentary sentiment, as Malboeuf had been when he saw Draga beating the two women.

Draga, a violent woman whose origins were obscure, could do what she wanted with captives—whip them, torture them, even burn them alive—because of her impregnable position with the Bad Eye, the old, blind, murderous prophet who stood first among the leaders whom Simon had to woo. The Bad Eye was convinced that Draga could talk with the dead and hear what they were plotting—for the dead were always plotting, in the Bad Eye's opinion. A woman such as Draga, who could inform him of the plans of the dead, was a woman who must be protected, which is why Simon Le Page walked past the two white women, as they were being beaten, without giving them more than the briefest glance.

"I don't like this Bad Eye," Malboeuf said, as they approached the old man's lodge, the whole surface of which had been piled with buffalo skulls, long since bleached white by wind and sun. There were said to be more than a thousand skulls piled on the humped, earthen lodge. Whenever a chieftain or leader wanted a good prophecy he brought the Bad Eye a buffalo skull. The old man—gross, surly, indolent, suspicious—would feel the skull carefully and then deliver his prophecy. Draga claimed to know what the dead intended. The Bad Eye, for his part, was said to know what the buffalo thought. Together they were capable of producing powerful fears.

"Do you think they fornicate? Draga and the Bad Eye?" Malboeuf asked.

"What a thought, Malboeuf," Simon said.

Did the prophet copulate with the witch? It was a distracting thought—so distracting that Simon at once put it out of his mind. He had his tasks to think of. He intended, personally, to inspect every peltry before allowing it to be sent north. This was the kind of thoroughness his superiors expected of him. If the trading went well, if the Bad Eye liked his presents, then it might be possible to do something for the two bruised white women, who were even then grunting under Draga's blows.

38

. . . that same long mane of shining auburn hair . . .

The steamer was almost in sight of the Mandan encampments—another day would have put them there—when the scuffle occurred with the Teton Sioux, six of whom Captain Aitken had taken aboard as a courtesy three days earlier. He had done so on Charbonneau's advice—a very large party of Sioux, some two hundred, Charbonneau thought, were milling around on the western bank, showing every sign of hostility.

"It's take the six or fight the two hundred, I expect," he said.

"The filthy wretches, what right do they have to interfere with us?" Lord Berrybender said, much vexed because the marauding Sioux had driven all the game off the river, where he had become accustomed to taking his sport. Almost every day, from his position on the lower deck, he had managed to bag a buffalo, an elk, or a deer. With Gorska now a drink-sodden wreck it was mostly helpful to have the game within rifle shot—and yet this admirable system had been disrupted by these wild men of the prairies.

George Aitken had been dubious about the wisdom of taking the six Tetons aboard—but the Sioux had spotted the Piegan and the Hairy Horn, one of their own chiefs, and were jealous. When the six came aboard no one was less happy to see them than the Hairy Horn himself, who refused them even tobacco. He was almost as annoyed at their arrival as Berrybender himself. In his view one Sioux on board the steamer *Rocky Mount* was plenty—and the Sioux should be himself.

"Six Sioux can get into a lot of mischief, Charbonneau," Captain Aitken said. But he knew the interpreter was probably right—better six minor miscreants than two hundred warriors bent on war.

George Catlin was the only one thoroughly glad to have the new Indians on board, for the simple reason that he was running out of Indians to paint. He and Holger Sten had set up rival ateliers on the upper deck, vying with each other to sketch such trappers or vagrant watermen as came on board. George and Holger had become rather chummy of late; soon they were trading brushes, critiquing each other's efforts, comparing techniques. George Catlin still mainly stuck to portraits, while Holger Sten executed many rather pallid landscapes. In the absence of Tasmin—an absence that had begun to vex Lord Berrybender exceedingly—both painters had been slyly attempting to get Venetia Kennet to let them paint her with her glorious long hair down.

"Why she's a very Rapunzel," Catlin exclaimed one morning—the two of them had caught a tantalizing glimpse of Venetia shaking out her auburn mane.

It was that same long mane of shining auburn hair, stretching down to Venetia's derriere, that produced the brief but unfortunate scuffle with the visiting Sioux. Venetia, feeling rather languid thanks to Lord Berrybender's excessive attentions, was standing outside their stateroom, brushing out her hair—a process that took a good hour—when a Sioux named Half Man walked up, saw the astonishing mane, and casually began to inspect it with fingers greasy from a scrap of pork Cook had flung at him.

Venetia, who was hard put to keep her lustrous hair clean in the primitive circumstances that prevailed on the boat, was so outraged by this indignity that she smacked the man hard with her silver-backed hairbrush.

"Leave off, you filthy savage!" she yelled, with such force that Lord Berrybender at once rushed to her aid, grabbing Half Man by the arm. Half Man was called Half Man because one of his testicles remained hidden in his body; spells, herbs, and incantations had failed to coax it down. Fortunately the novelty of a man with only one testicle greatly appealed to the Sioux women—Half Man had four wives and had been seduced many times by curious girls. He thought his novelty might appeal to the tall white woman with the long hair—he had been about to show himself when she whacked him on the hand, an insult not to be tolerated. Half Man at once drew his knife—he meant to kill the woman, scalp her, jump overboard, and wade ashore with his great trophy scalp; but the old white man lurched out of the cabin and was so rude as to grab Half Man's arm. Half Man's knife was sharp—he whetted it carefully every night, since skinning buffalo or other game could easily dull a knife. Half Man shook free, but the old man lunged for him, intent on getting him in a stranglehold. Half Man whacked hard at the hand, and his stroke was good. Three of Lord Berrybender's fingers dropped to the deck, among them his trigger finger, a sight which caused Venetia Kennet to scream at the top of her lungs—and her lungs were very healthy. Piet Van Wely, just coming up the stairs, saw an Indian with a bloody knife—Piet at once reversed direction. The deafening screams unnerved Half Man—instead of scalping the tall woman he quickly followed the small fat man to the lower deck, where he sought out his fellow Sioux. The six tribesmen, knowing that the old lord was a powerful chief, decided it might be time to go ashore. Charbonneau, without knowing the extent of the disaster—Miss Kennet was still scream- ing—at once saw that a boat was provided.

"I didn't hurt that old man much," Half Man explained to Charbonneau. "It was only three fingers. That woman is too loud."

"Well, she's a musician," Charbonneau explained.

Half Man was not mollified. "Who wants racket like that?" he asked.

Venetia Kennet's screams continued for several minutes. Tim, the stable boy, was forced to stuff straw in his ears, as a means of shutting them out.

Captain Aitken, meanwhile, had once again assumed the duties of a medical officer; he bound up Lord Berrybender's hand, in this task assisted by Cook, who had carved a great many joints in her day and was quick with opinions on matters of a surgical nature.

Venetia Kennet screamed from shock—then, once she stopped scream- ing, sobbed for quite some time, not from shock but because she was faced with a deeply unappetizing situation. The loss of half a foot had greatly increased Lord Berrybender's impatience; what tolerance could she expect now that he had lost more than half the fingers on his right hand?

The old lord himself wandered distracted around the upper deck, won- dering whether the stump of what remained of his finger would be long enough to reach a trigger.

"*Can* I shoot—that's the question, Captain—can I *shoot*?" Lord Berry- bender said. He had already disturbed Captain Aitken's neat bandage by trying to wiggle his trigger finger—or the stump that remained of it.

"You must just be patient, sir," Captain Aitken said. "Must not get the bleeding started up again."

"Patience be damned!" Lord B. cried. "Patient is the one thing I'll *not* be! Had my way more or less instantly my whole life—don't intend to stop now! Vicky, stop that bawling and get me Señor Yanez. He is said to be a fine gunsmith—perhaps he can devise me a trigger that I can reach with my little stump."

Later, after an extended conversation with Señor Yanez about modifica- tions for the triggers of Lord Berrybender's many guns, the small Spaniard hustled off and got busy. The old lord, having, by then, drunk a consider- able quantity of brandy, sank into a lachrymose state. As he wept, little Mary Berrybender plunked a mandolin lent her by her friend Piet.

"It's Tasmin's fault, don't you agree, Mary?" Lord B. said. "Filthy girl, always selfish, picnicking and gamboling about while her own father goes to rack and ruin."

"I expect she's been marrying her gentleman, that's what I expect," Mary said—"so Tasmin shall have no title, no throne, but there's a great fat dowry you won't have to pay . . . I suppose our wild girl's flown away, just like old Prince Talleyrand."

Lord Berrybender belched and gave a start. No notion had been farther from his head than that a daughter of his would betray his noble interests in that way. There had once, he knew, been murmurings about Master Stiles, but that was, on the whole, given country tradition, rather the expected sort of thing.

But an American? It was not to be tolerated.

"Pretty Tasmin, such a desirable girl," Mary said. "I doubt a Bourbon or a Hapsburg would give much for her now."

"Egad, how sharper . . . ," Lord B. said, before drink overcame him and he slumped down, dead drunk.

Having stirred the hornets' nest, Mary slipped down to the lower deck and had a very satisfactory hour of instruction in the Sioux tongue from the old Hairy Horn, who had just decided that he wished to spend the rest of his life aboard the steamer *Rocky Mount*.

39

His skull lodge stood well above the river . . .

Most boats are quiet—why is this new boat roaring like that?" the Bad Eye asked. He could hear the steamboat plainly, belching like a great beast. His skull lodge stood well above the river—and yet the boat sounded like it was just outside his lodge.

"It's a new kind of boat," Draga said. "New and big."

"It must be big or it couldn't roar like that," the Bad Eye said. His lodge had a long mud platform on it, covered with buffalo robes. The robes were old, filled with fleas and lice, but the Bad Eye was not bothered by such trifles. He had grown so fat that he no longer cared for walking; his legs would still carry his weight, but they wouldn't carry it far. Though Draga still brought him women, he now had little interest in copulation. The Bad Eye had known the great boat was on its way to the encampments—he had had many reports. But he had not expected to hear a boat roar like a beast.

"How many men does it take to row it?" he asked.

"No one rows it—it is a steamboat," Draga said. "It eats wood. If there is no wood it eats coal."

The Bad Eye didn't like the sound of that at all. A boat that ate wood could not be a normal boat.

"It sounds like a god," he said.

Draga was contemptuous of the old fat fool, a man who had spent an idle life making up prophecies that his people were superstitious enough to believe. Blind from birth, he had never seen the world. He learned what he knew by feeling—how a puppy was shaped, or a fish, or a woman—or by listening. He took in food through his mouth and knowledge through his ears. His hearing was very acute, so acute that he could hear a mouse scratch in its burrow or identify a fly or wasp or bee by the sound of its buzzing. Because he had never heard the sound of a steamboat, he thought the boat might be a god, or else a great water beast of some kind.

Draga came from the West, her father a Russian trapper, her mother an Aleut. As a young woman, coming south with the Russian fur traders, she had seen great seagoing ships in San Francisco Bay. She had come to the Russian River in a skin boat with her parents and some other Aleuts—but a great swell capsized the boat and only Draga made it to shore. For a time an old Spaniard kept her, but he choked on a grape and died. Draga, thinking herself Russian, tried to reach the Russian fort, but she first fell in with some Modocs and then with some Nez Perce and gradually drifted east. Two white trappers bargained for her and kept her for a year, until one of them was killed by the Blackfeet. The other trapper hid his furs and fled, taking Draga with him; in time she came to the Mandans and the skull lodge of the Bad Eye. An old crazy woman of the Modocs, who had convinced herself she could talk with the dead, had taught Draga a few spells and recipes. The old one knew of a cave where there were many bats; she taught Draga how to pick the hanging bats like fruit, kill them, dry them, mix them in potions. The old half-crazed Modoc woman thought that the bat cave was connected with the world of the dead. Draga was not convinced, but she had learned early that she could either surrender herself to the appetites of men or else become a sorceress; the choice was not hard. She had a few dried bats with her, which she used to good effect in the Mandan village. She saw that the Bad Eye was as crazy as the old Modoc woman had been—only the Bad Eye was cruel as well as crazy. She herself saw him strangle two men and a woman—it was the Bad Eye's way of dispatching those who disregarded his rambling prophecies. Draga soon gained more power over the fat prophet than anyone had ever had. From listening to his ramblings she learned the names of many Mandans who had fallen in battle; it didn't matter to Draga whether these dead men had been great warriors or merely fools and braggarts: she gathered names as the other women picked berries, and used them to convince the Bad Eye that she was in communication with the spirits of the departed. In time he came to trust no one but Draga—in fact the Bad Eye was more than a little afraid of the strange sorceress from the Western waters.

Draga knew that the steamboat was just a boat. It posed no threat to the Bad Eye; the Mandans would never have let anyone harm their prophet. But the unfamiliar sounds it produced upset the old man. Draga thought it might soothe him to hear a rare but not wholly unfamiliar sound: the screams of a burning captive.

"I want to burn one of the white women—we have three now," Draga said. "Pit-ta-sa brought in a new one last night, a big one. Why not let me burn one? The cold is coming. The people would enjoy a good burning, before it gets too cold."

The Bad Eye had no intention of going along with that suggestion. The custom was to trade for captives, and these women had all come off the great belching boat. No doubt the whites would give many blankets, many rifles, to get them back. It irked him that Draga would even mention burning one of the whites. Let her go catch an Omaha or an Oto if she wanted to burn somebody. White captives were too valuable to waste. Besides, he himself had never liked the smell produced by burning people. A burned human left a bad smell in the village for days—a thing he had never understood. A roasting goose or haunch of antelope smelled good when it was cooking, but a cooked human left a sickening, sweet odor that was not pleasant—once it got into his nostrils it lingered for days.

"No burning—the Frenchman will buy these captives," the Bad Eye said. "We can sell them for a good price."

Draga knew the old man would reject her suggestion. He was greedy now for the things the whites gave him—guns he couldn't see to shoot, axes he couldn't see to cut with, beads whose color he could not define. She had mentioned the burning merely to remind him that there was another way to deal with captives: the old way, the way of the torture stake. Warriors used it to build their power. The wild tribes—those who grew no corn but lived by the buffalo—still used it: Sioux, Cheyenne, Comanche. Despite the power she wielded, despite her hold over the Bad Eye, Draga thought she might leave these corn-growers, these bargainers, someday. What the whites brought didn't interest her. She thought she might go west again, to a place where she could do what she wanted with a white girl, if she caught one.

"No burning, did you hear me?" the Bad Eye repeated. "Beat the women if you want but don't ruin them. I don't want any trouble with the whites on that big boat."

The Bad Eye waited, but there was no answer from Draga. Draga's breathing was husky—he could hear her if she was still there—but now he heard nothing; the sorceress had left. The fact that she left so silently made him a little uneasy. A woman who moved that quietly was a woman to beware of, particularly if she spoke with the dead.

40

"All those tears over a little tupping."

Oh fiddle, a pox on Samuel Richardson," Tasmin said. "I confess I could not get through *Clarissa*. All those tears over a little tupping. A great bore, I say."

The first of the low, brown earth lodges of the Mandans were visible not far upriver, and a trace of smoke in the air indicated that the steamer *Rocky Mount* was just around the next bend. The two of them, Tasmin and Father Geoffrin, had taken only two days to catch up with the steamer— days during which they had talked incessantly about literature, only paus- ing now and then to consider a collateral issue—that is, morals.

"Lady Tasmin, it is not the tears or the tupping, it is the sensibility of Clarissa one admires," Father Geoffrin protested. "A young lady of fine intelligence torn apart by virtue."

"Would you say I have a fine intelligence, Father?" Tasmin asked, with a smile.

"Oh, indeed," Father Geoffrin said. "As fine as Pompadour—*tendre et sincère,* as Voltaire said."

"Oh now, hardly *that* fine—you mustn't flatter me," Tasmin said. Indeed, the little priest had been a very fountain of compliments, so far. All her accoutrements, mental and physical, he judged to be of the finest. Tasmin's modest denials grew more and more routine. If this diminutive Jesuit wanted to be in love with her, so be it—but she still had no intention of indulging his taste for Samuel Richardson.

"I suppose I'm rather too hardy for all that moping and scribbling," Tasmin said. "If the lustful Mr. Lovelace wanted *me* so badly I'd find a bed and have him. Nothing wrong with a bit of pleasure, that I can see."

In fact the absence of just that sort of pleasure was making her a bit fretful. Her brief weeks of marriage had accustomed her to regular and fervent attentions in the arms of Jim Snow. From time to time she turned and looked back downriver, half expecting to see her husband trailing after them. In the heat of her jealousy at hearing of Jim's native wives, she had lashed out too cruelly. Life among the fourteen young Berrybenders had not encouraged in her any disposition to share. She did not regret marching off—it had been necessary to make her point. Pleasant as it was to talk about books with the little priest, Tasmin found that her attention kept returning to her husband and his other wives. Jim Snow had made their home on the Green River seem quite remote. Perhaps these distant wives no longer really existed. Perhaps they had taken husbands. Perhaps they had run away, been drowned, been eaten by bears.

"I expect you know your geography, don't you, Geoff?" Tasmin asked—they had quickly agreed to proceed on a first-name basis.

"I fear in this case that I am very vague as to longitude and all that," Father Geoffrin said. "The Green River is very distant—that I can assure you."

"I am equally vague when it comes to the Jesuit doctrines," Tasmin said. "What do you Jesuits think about polygamy?"

"Our doctrines are very complex," Father Geoffrin admitted. "Hopelessly complex, I fear. I myself have not mastered even the hundredth part of them."

They had just come level with the first of the Mandan earth lodges. Several filthy children were staring at them. An old crone was hobbling about, attempting to kill a skinny dog. The sight of these ragged scraps of humanity seemed to overwhelm Father Geoffrin. To Tasmin's astonishment, he suddenly burst into tears. One of the small, filthy children immediately threw a stone at him.

"Go away, you little wretches!" Tasmin yelled.

The children stood their ground. The old crone, more nimble than she had at first appeared, succeeded in braining the skinny dog. Father Geoffrin's sobs slowly diminished. He wiped his eyes on a corner of his robe.

"A mistake . . . ridiculous . . . a mistake," he said to Tasmin. "Do I look like a priest to you? Of course I don't. I'm a man of the boulevards and the coffeehouses. By inclination and habit I am very clean—but in the wilderness it is rarely possible to remain clean. Then there are my skepticisms. I harbor the gravest doubts about the Deity. I have studied the works of the greatest thinkers and philosophes and yet I doubt."

"Geoff, this is ridiculous," Tasmin told him. "I merely wanted to know about one river."

Father Geoffrin ignored her.

"And then there are these people, these savages," he went on. "A little boy just then threw a rock at me. Am I to attempt to save his soul? I, who have no notion of what a soul is, or whether these savages *have* souls? It's all very well for Father de Las Casas to argue that they do, but then he probably knew better Indians . . . Aztecs, you know."

"Shut up, Geoff . . . this babble is intolerable," Tasmin said. "If you don't wish to be a priest, then you must simply leave the order."

Much as she liked the little Frenchman, her immediate urge was to give him a good smack. The steamer *Rocky Mount* was in sight, not a mile away. She herself had an inclination to cleanliness. Rather than stand around watching a dog being butchered, she wanted a good bath. She did not care to indulge Father Geoffrin in an ill-timed crisis of conscience.

The little father, however, was not to be easily checked.

"When I agreed to come among the Mandans I thought I might just manage a glorious martyrdom, but that won't do either," he went on. "Even the mildest toothache causes me to reach for my laudanum—I have some here in my pouch. If I were to suffer martyrdom my behavior would be anything but glorious. I would rather renounce many gods than suffer a twinge of pain."

All around them, in the strung-out village, heads were turning. Many Indians, their mood difficult to judge, were staring at the white woman and the priest. More and more warriors emerged from the lodges, men of uncertain disposition. The boat, which had seemed so close, now seemed far. A gauntlet of a sort would have to be run—or walked, at least—and her companion was hardly in a state to put a crowd of savages to flight.

"Hello, miss—you're back," a familiar voice said, from just behind her. She turned and saw Monsieur Charbonneau. Though he was as greasy and unkempt as ever, Tasmin was very glad to see him. He said a few words to the old crone and led them safely through the crowd.

41

Draga, spitting out teeth . . .

N o, no, Fräulein . . . submit!" Bess cried, but too late. Draga, for once, had misjudged the demeanor of her victim. All night Bess and Mademoiselle had tried to soothe Fräulein for the loss of her Charlie, but they made little progress. The Fräulein's grief was bottomless. When Draga took a stick and began to beat the new captive, Fräulein's grief boiled into anger. Draga at once discovered that she was beating a woman with the strength of an ox. Fräulein Pfretzskaner, eyes blazing with hatred, yanked the stick away from Draga and smacked her with it—right in the mouth, dislodging two of Draga's none-too-numerous teeth. Through a gurgle of blood Draga managed a strangled yell and several warriors came running, hatchets drawn. Fräulein Pfretzskaner whirled on them like a very Boadicea, knocking two men senseless with her stick. Draga, spitting out teeth, yelled at the men to catch her—she wanted a long revenge—and the men tried but failed. The Fräulein's arms were slippery with blood; they couldn't hold her. Pit-ta-sa thought for a moment that the huge woman might defeat them all, but then, as she turned, he saw his chance and killed her with a hard hatchet blow to the back of her skull. The other warriors, their blood up, continued to hack and slash.

Buffum hid her eyes through it all, but Mademoiselle Pellenc stared.

"The end came—they chopped her dead," Mademoiselle said to Buffum, when the yelling stopped.

"It was only one beating," Buffum said, her eyes still hidden. "She should have waited. The steamer's almost here—she might have waited. Think of the beatings we've stood."

"She wanted to be with her Charlies," Mademoiselle said. "Now she is with her Charlies. It may be for the best."

That same day, as they were selecting a dog for the stew pot, the young trader Simon Le Page came and got them.

"Mademoiselles, your liberty has been secured," he said, with a smile. "If you'll allow me I'll escort you back to the boat."

Draga, her mouth swollen, her eyes terrible, did not dare to interfere.

42

Venetia cast a look of great helplessness . . .

T he grand reunion—or what should have been a grand reunion—on the steamer *Rocky Mount* was turning sour. Never had the various temperaments of the Berrybender ménage more glaringly failed to mesh, and this despite the fact that Cook, overjoyed to have the missing women back— Tasmin particularly—had outdone herself, preparing a suckling pig and a great haunch of buffalo. There were quantities of fresh smelly bread, and even some mint jelly. But only Tasmin, Mary, and Simon Le Page addressed these edibles with respectable levels of appetite. Bess and Mademoiselle, who had seen nothing of such rich food during the weeks of their captivity, barely managed a nibble. Mademoiselle, though Simon Le Page was paying her sensitive attentions, could not forget the bloody hatchets as they descended on the expiring Fräulein; the smells of the rich food were so overpowering that Bess had to excuse herself several times in order to rush to the rail and be sick.

Bobbety and Father Geoffrin, discovering that they shared a passionate interest in the new science of geology, talked of nothing but sediments and fossils.

"You *would* bring this Papist back to us, Tasmin," Mary said—"I fear you were never solidly lodged in the Anglican faith."

"Shut up, Mary, you're a rude brat," Tasmin said, carving herself another hot slice of the piglet.

Simon Le Page was at once dazzled by Lady Tasmin, but knew, sadly, that such a noble beauty was far beyond the aspirations of a humble young trader. Mademoiselle Pellenc, despite her ordeal, struck him as very pretty—there, he thought, there might be hope for an ambitious Québecois.

George Catlin's heart had leapt up when he saw Lady Tasmin come aboard with no young frontiersman in tow; he had rushed down and gushed out effusive welcomes, only to be greeted so coolly that he had spent the afternoon in a sulk.

Venetia Kennet, who had hardly drawn a bow across the strings of her cello since Lord Berrybender shot his foot, had been required to dust off her Haydn and play a bit for the reunited company, which she did embarrassingly badly, with many a piercing shriek from the cello as she mangled her chords. Venetia had rather hoped that Tasmin would come back humbled—skinny, bruised, and starved, like Bess and Mademoiselle. But Tasmin wasn't humbled—and even more annoying, she looked to be in vibrant health.

"Father, do have Vicky leave off the Haydn just this once," Tasmin said. "She's all atremble with happiness at our safe return, I expect—she can hardly be expected to control her fingers at a time of such abounding joy."

"She's just lazy, Vicky . . . ought to practice more," Lord Berrybender replied.

Tasmin saw Venetia Kennet flush at that remark—everyone on board knew what Vicky Kennet was required to do.

"You should try a few weeks ashore, as I just have, Vicky," Tasmin said. "The cool prairie air is such a balm to one's complexion—brings the color right to one's cheeks."

"Oh well, Tasmin, I have not got the milkmaid spirit quite to the degree that you have," Vicky said. "I should need a very trustworthy escort—in fact I've already had a horror of stepping in a bog. One could be so quickly swallowed up."

Venetia cast a look of great helplessness at handsome young Monsieur

Le Page when she said it—a rather daring look, considering that Lord B. was alert to the merest suggestion of a rival. Simon Le Page thought it best to ignore the look; he continued his attentions to Mademoiselle Pellenc.

Lord Berrybender considered Monsieur Le Page—rescuer of his daughter and his *femme de chambre*—as something of a popinjay—but then, all French had a measure of the popinjay in them. Lord Berrybender had been assured by a local antiquary that, at some distant genealogical point, the Berrybenders themselves had been French, a suggestion he didn't welcome.

"Don't care to look behind me—no interest in the Conqueror or any of that 1066 rot," he said; he did, however, take pride in the fact that Berrybender seed had flowed only into the most dynastically appropriate wombs—bastards, of course, did not count in that reckoning. And yet there sat his daughter Tasmin—if she *was* his daughter; he was, of course, aware of certain rumors concerning Lord de Bury—so willful as to dare breach this long trickle of noble seed to noble womb. Lord B. had a bad feeling about Tasmin, and had had it from the minute she stepped on board, as casual after an absence of several weeks as if she had merely strolled down to the village to buy a ribbon or a sweet.

Lord Berrybender rarely suppressed an inquiry for more than a few seconds—and damn the company!—and yet he found himself unaccustomedly cautious in the matter of Tasmin's prairie marriage, a great calamity if true. Still, what evidence for it was there? Only Mary's comments—and Mary was known to be inventive, with a sort of genius for planting seeds of disquiet. Such seeds were even then sprouting like spikes in Lord Berrybender's vitals—he felt he might even be getting indigestion, though he had eaten very little of Cook's great feast.

Now, restless, drunk, troubled by a growing distemper, Lord B. reminded himself that he, not Tasmin, was lord of the manor. He looked directly at his daughter, hoping to catch her out, to learn the truth—but Tasmin, to his annoyance, merely stared straight back at him, bold as brass, with even a touch of defiance in her light smile. Spears of disquiet stirred even more sharply in Lord Berrybender's bowels. In his annoyance he remembered how casual his late wife, Constance, had been when it came to discipline, never smacking Tasmin as she should have been smacked. And now Constance was dead, Tasmin was grown, the days grew short, the winds blew cold, it was too late. Tasmin was not some social-climbing wench like Vicky Kennet, who would allow him any number of liberties in hopes of marrying him. Tasmin had no need to climb; unless she married some prince, she could go no higher. But the horrid thought occurred to Lord B. that Tasmin, in her defiance, might have climbed in the wrong direction: down, into the embrace of some American.

"Were you wanting to ask me something, Papa?" Tasmin asked. "It's rare we see you so deep in thought when the table is spread with such an array of excellent vittles."

"Ah, Tasmin . . . ," Lord B. said, appalled to discover that he was rather quailing before his daughter—he who had fought seventeen duels without a tremor.

"I expect Papa is fretting because you have not chosen to bring your gentleman home for inspection," Mary said. "Of course, he *isn't* a gentleman in our good English sense, though perhaps presentable in his own way."

Tasmin gave her sister's ear a cruel pinch.

"I would like to take you to a high place and drop you headfirst on a rock," she said. "Perhaps the Rocky Mountains will provide an opportunity—we'll see."

"What's this, Tasmin? A fellow of some sort? Not a bounder, I hope—shouldn't want my fine girl compromised," Lord Berrybender managed to mumble, well aware that Tasmin sometimes flew into prodigious rages when her behavior was questioned.

"Oh, no . . . I'm not at all compromised, just rather blissfully married," Tasmin said. "My husband, Mr. Jim Snow, is occupied at the moment with his many duties but I expect him in a few days. I do hope you'll approve of him, Father."

Her comment silenced the table. George Catlin started as if pricked with a pin—he felt all hope slipping away.

"And if I don't approve?" Lord Berrybender growled—the audacity of the girl was not to be borne.

"But Papa, why shouldn't you approve?" Tasmin asked, not about to be cowed by a drunken parent. "You can't have been planning to sacrifice me to our enfeebled nobility, once we get home, I hope—you know I can't tolerate these pale, sickly English nobles."

Venetia Kennet's heart gave a leap. Tasmin had ruined herself; that was clear. Venetia felt suddenly filled with new resolve; she *would* triumph, become Lady Berrybender after all. Lord B. *would* marry her yet!

Lord Berrybender could not immediately decide what answer to make to the insolent girl across the table. Sometimes, when he carelessly mixed brandy with wine, the combination made his head rather whirl. At the moment, despite a strong inclination to thunder and rage at Tasmin, not only his head but the whole table seemed to whirl. He gripped his chair firmly, but the whirling continued.

"Tasmin has been very bad, hasn't she?" Mary said. "Do rise up, Papa! Do produce one of your purple rages. Smite her hip and thigh! Reduce her to silence and shame!"

Father Geoffrin could not suppress a giggle.

"The *petite mademoiselle* is very quick to turn a phrase—she would be much applauded in France," he said.

Mary received this compliment coldly—she had no intention of accepting any familiarities from the silly Jesuit that Tasmin had dragged home with her.

Lord Berrybender stood up—stood up only to sway. The table was whirling, more or less like a carousel. Yet he knew that he must say *something* chastening to his upstart daughter. Rarely in a long life had his authority been so directly challenged.

"Can't allow it—not acceptable," he managed to mumble. "Have to throw the bounder out."

"Your opinion is quite irrelevant," Tasmin informed him. "The thing is done. I'm married."

"Then I'll *unmarry* you, you insolent wench," Lord B. managed to thunder. "You can't just fob off the nobility of Europe like that. I'll seek an annulment—consider yourself confined to your room.

"Here's a priest . . . he must know how to arrange annulments," he added.

Father Geoffrin merely chuckled.

"Oh, not I, Your Lordship," he said. "I should think you'd have to apply to the Holy Father directly, in a matter of that significance.

"The Holy See is unfortunately rather distant from the Missouri River," he added, unnecessarily, Mary thought.

"Wouldn't work anyway—not only am I married, I'm with child," Tasmin said. "Pregnant, to put it bluntly."

"What? You harlot, I'm ruined!" said Lord Berrybender. "Where is the fellow? I'll kill him!"

"You're not ruined at all, you're just drunk," Tasmin informed him.

Seconds later Lord B. began to sway, then to sway more, and finally to heave. The remains of his modest dinner, and a great deal of wine besides, came up in Simon Le Page's lap, to the horror of Mademoiselle Pellenc, who at once took command of the young trader and led him away, meaning to clean him up.

Tasmin found that she missed the clean, cool air of the prairies: no centuries of Europe, no squalid family scenes, no yelling. She took herself out on deck, followed by Mary and the hound, Tintamarre. It was snowing lightly, the breeze quite chill.

"I wish you would let off goading Papa," Tasmin said. "He knows well enough he can't tell me who to marry."

"Are you missing your husband, Tassie? Tell me," Mary said. She had become the meek Mary again.

"Yes, quite sharply," Tasmin admitted. "He can be a silly boy at times. I left him in a moment of pique."

"No doubt you were jealous of his other wives," Mary commented. "Monsieur Charbonneau mentioned them to me."

"I was, but it's hard to remain properly jealous of two brown women who may be a thousand miles away," Tasmin said.

"They can't be as pretty as you, anyway," Mary said. "Rather squat girls, I imagine."

Tasmin looked into the darkness. Snow was melting on her flushed cheeks, on her hair, on Tintamarre's red coat.

"This snow will make Captain Aitken very anxious," Mary said. "He fears we will get stuck in the ice and be unable to make our fort, in which case many of us will perish."

"None of that's happened yet," Tasmin said.

If she were with Jim, she reflected, they would be sitting close together, listening to the way the campfire spat as the heavy snowflakes fell into it.

"I do hope my Jimmy is warm," she said. "If I were with him I might at least keep him warm."

Mary went belowdecks, to seek the Hairy Horn. She never tired of conversing with the sly old chieftain.

Tasmin, with Tintamarre beside her, stood by the rail a long time, watching the snowflakes disappear into the dark waters. In her breast was a sharp regret. How silly she had been to leave her Jim.

43

Captain Aitken had no patience . . .

The day Old Gorska killed himself—messily, by cutting his own throat with a razor in his filthy closet on the lower deck—was a day so rife with alarums and distempers that no one had time to mourn the drink-sodden old hunter except Cook, who had lost two sons herself and knew the grief it brought. The silent arrow that killed Gorska Minor fatally pierced his father too.

What drew the company's attention away from the suicide was the untimely discovery of the parlous state of the stores—a discovery made on the very morning of the day when the seven chiefs of the Mandans and a few from neighboring tribes would be lining up to receive what they were sure would be splendid presents from the rich whites on the Thunder Boat, the name given the steamer by the Bad Eye, who was still much distracted by the belchings of the boilers. The great bulk of trade goods they had laid in in Saint Louis had not been examined since the voyage began. Toussaint Charbonneau was horrified when he saw the state of the goods. Rats had been into the blankets—half of them were riddled with holes. An undetected leak had left the crates of muskets covered with water, leaving the great majority of the guns too rusty to use. There were plenty of beads, of course, but the native women had been receiving regular deposits of beads from many sources—unless the beads were spectacular, the natives were apt to yawn and carp—and the Berrybender beads were the cheapest variety, thanks to Lord Albany's fine sense of economy; in his view a bead was a bead and a savage a savage. Instead of buying better beads he had bought himself a fine new rifle, made by a Pennsylvania gunsmith—even Gorska had conceded that it was a fine gun, though not, of course, as good as his own Belgian gun.

The Belgian gun was the first thing Lord Berrybender mentioned, when informed of Gorska's suicide.

"Bad news, of course, alas and alack—set in his ways, Gorska was," he said. "Preferred the Carpathian bear to the American bison—odd fellow. Doesn't do to be set in one's ways—life doesn't always go smooth . . . adjustments frequently necessary . . . I lost my Constance, after all, and the boy Seven too. Meanwhile, since Gorska will no longer need it, I'll just have that fine Belgian gun. Of course, it's selfish of me to mention it immediately . . . but then, why wait? Besides, I *am* selfish . . . ask Vicky."

Venetia Kennet set her teeth—she was not going to be tempted into a rash remark. She had already put up with much and was prepared to put up with more: she meant in time to be Lady Berrybender, and that was that.

Captain Aitken had no patience, either with the old lord or his aloof consort; but he held his temper. The company faced a serious threat—he determined to keep a cool head.

"Sir, there's trouble besides Gorska," the captain said. "The stores are mainly ruined and today is present day. The chiefs are expecting rather a lot—and we haven't got a lot."

"Why haven't we? I laid out quite a sum for presents, I recall," Lord B. said.

"Rats and leaks," Charbonneau said. "The blankets are chewed and the muskets rusted up. The chiefs are likely to be riled. All we've got that they like are axes and hatchets."

"What about grog—I suppose I could spare a few bottles of claret," Lord B. offered.

"No sir . . . if we give them grog they'll use the axes and hatchets on us," Charbonneau said. He was so appalled at the situation they were in that he had considered taking his two charges, the Hairy Horn and the Piegan, and leaving the boat. The Mandans knew him—they didn't expect *him* to provide presents. It was known that he was a poor man who worked for Captain Clark. Leaving might be the safest thing. Nothing enraged powerful chiefs as quickly as inferior presents.

"This is somebody's fault, I'm sure," Lord Berrybender said. "Gladwyn, what about it?"

"Why, sir, Señor Yanez is the gunsmith—the muskets were his responsibility," Gladwyn said, smiling a thin smile. "But I fear Señor Yanez rather scorns the muskets—he says they aren't really guns, just clubs that shoot."

"Damn it all, get the whips—I'll have the skin off everyone's backs," Lord B. said, but Captain Aitken shook his head.

"We've no time for floggings," he said. "We may all have the hair off our heads if we are not resourceful."

"There's that Frenchman, Le Page . . . I rather ruined his trousers," Lord B. said. "Perhaps he has baubles to spare."

"No sir, he's a Hudson's Bay man," the captain said. "They keep a strict inventory. Besides, he's already ransomed the women. I'm sure he's already distributed his presents. I hear he got six thousand fine peltries for them. That young man will go far."

"Can't we just go far ourselves?" Lord Berrybender inquired. "Charge past them and run for it—full steam ahead and all that!"

Again, Captain Aitken shook his head. "I have to think of the boat, sir—can't put her at risk," he said. "There's a thousand Indians in these villages. They're the river keepers. They expect their toll."

"I'm damned if I have an answer, then," Lord B. said, looking out his window. It was snowing still—the low ridges beyond the river had turned white. The sky whirled out snow and more snow.

"I've a thought, sir . . . clothes," Captain Aitken said. "The Indians do like finery. You and Lady Constance brought aboard substantial wardrobes, couldn't help noticing that. Fine garments, I have no doubt. Perhaps some of the jewelry is cheap enough that it could be spared."

Lord Berrybender was aghast and Venetia Kennet not pleased. She had already made a hasty selection of Lady Berrybender's jewelry—was the rest of it merely to be flung to painted savages?

"Give them my clothes, and Constance's gems?" Lord B. said, deeply shocked. So far as he could remember he had never parted with a single possession in his life, and here the captain was suggesting that he give his clothes to savages?

"They want me to give them my *clothes*, Gladwyn . . . speak up, man, you're my valet," His Lordship said.

"Though of course a grave loss, it may be the most sensible suggestion," Gladwyn said, with as much restraint as he could muster. Year after year he had taken care of Lord Berrybender's wardrobe. Though he didn't show it, his spirit soared at the thought of garish red Indians wearing those same wretched clothes.

Tasmin, once informed of the dilemma, stared down her father and managed the divestiture herself, assisted by Father Geoffrin, a man of unexpectedly strong opinions when it came to clothes.

"Terrible, terrible, awful garment," he said, casting aside one of Lady Constance's embroidered ball dresses. "Send it away!"

"*Atroce! Atroce!*" he shrieked, when Tasmin opened a drawer devoted entirely to Lady Constance's pantaloons—they were all in vivid colors.

"*Atroce*, maybe, but they might be our salvation," Tasmin pointed out.

"Perhaps the Mandans can be persuaded that Mama's ugly pantaloons are garments of prodigious rarity and value."

Lord Berrybender, in a dark fury, wept, drank, and swore as the process of selection proceeded. Parting with the most insignificant garment went entirely against his grain.

"Take plenty of Tasmin's dresses . . . no, take *all* of them!" he raged. "Extravagant wench—always buying dresses. Now that she's married a yokel she'll have no need for respectable clothes."

"Do hush, Papa, you'll disturb Father Geoffrin's concentration," Tasmin said. "Don't you see that these clothes are all that's going to save us from the savages?"

"Humbug, don't believe it . . . Give it all away if you want . . . ruin me entirely," Lord B. said, clutching his one consolation, Gorska's excellent Belgian gun. He had already fired it off at a Mandan dog, killing the cur where it stood.

"Of course, one of the great attractions of Paris is the sewing shops," Father Geoffrin said. "I admit I could never stay out of them—it's the patterns that ravish one, you know. I'd much rather spend an afternoon in the sewing shops than worrying with my rosary or attempting to redeem prostitutes."

"What about this, Father Geoff?" Tasmin asked, holding up a vivid yellow blouse.

"Awful. How I do despise yellow," Father Geoffrin said, flinging the bright blouse on the take-away pile.

44

. . . and yet there had been an élévation, impossible to conceal . . .

Mademoiselle Pellenc in no way intended the thing to happen, but the fact was, Lord Berrybender's voluminous vomiting quite drenched Monsieur Le Page's best trousers. It was Mademoiselle's view that the trousers were beyond cleaning: they must be thrown away and others secured. Mr. Catlin gallantly offered to lend Monsieur a pair, and in fact handed them over, his cabin being only two doors from Mademoiselle's.

"Should fit well enough," George said; he saw that the young French-man was deeply shocked by what had occurred. Though he must have seen some sights in his life as a trader, he had certainly not expected his noble host to vomit in his lap. His embarrassment was intense.

It was Mademoiselle's impatience that provoked the incident. She couldn't wait to get the reeking garment off the young Monsieur. Shy about finding himself in a lady's cabin, he was even more shy about undoing his buttons—in fact he proved so clumsy that Mademoiselle knelt down and assisted him. He wore his trousers tight—it was the fashion in Quebec. Mademoiselle had to peel them down his fine muscular legs. In an instant, once his legs were free, Mademoiselle rushed out and flung the smelly garment into the river; *les poissons* could nibble them if they liked.

It was when she returned to her room that the thing happened. Young Monsieur Le Page, blushing deeply, was struggling into the trousers Mr. Catlin had lent him; and yet there had been an *élévation*, impossible to conceal. The trousers quite refused to contain the young Monsieur's imposing staff. Moreover, he was gazing at Mademoiselle with a look of shocked tenderness, as he did his best to conceal this awkward sign of budding affection. In an instant Mademoiselle decided: she would marry Monsieur Le Page! Though the foul attentions of her captors had made her feel she would be unlikely ever to want a man again, she had not supposed her rescuer would be someone so sweet, so young, so blushing, so *agréable*, and yet at once so firmly made as this young Québecois who now stood in her bedroom, struggling to stretch his trousers over his prick.

"No, no, monsieur . . . let me," Mademoiselle said. He was but a boy—she herself was thirty-five, tied to a bunch of worthless English, beset by the garlicky Italian and the lustful Spaniard. Monsieur Simon Le Page was her hope. She hastily shut the door, went back to the trembling boy, and took him in hand—the conclusion, almost immediate, was quite copious—but for her skillful handling Monsieur would have messed another pair of pants.

"Monsieur, it is decided—I am yours," Mademoiselle said. "Where you go, I go too."

Simon Le Page was not quite sure *what* had been decided; but his heart swelled in his breast. Thoughts of the company he hoped to rise in were for the moment put aside. He would deny Mademoiselle nothing, they would have a snug log house in Three Rivers, children would come.

The next day—with ten of the *engagés*, who would be dropped off to trap the northern streams; with six thousand pelts, every one of which had survived Monsieur Le Page's exacting inspection; and Mademoiselle Pellenc, by this time busily bossing all the French, including the surly Malboeuf—the French party left the Mandan villages, themselves much brightened by many pairs of Lady Berrybender's colorful pantaloons—red, pink, blue, green, and lavender. The pantaloons had been a great hit with the Mandans, Rees, Hidatsas, Gros Ventres, and a sprinkling of wild Sioux. The Bad Eye had been given Lord Berrybender's great plaid cape, the one he usually wore when hunting stags in Scotland; and the lesser chiefs had been mollified with very proper umbrellas, a score of which Lord Berrybender had laid in before leaving Portsmouth.

Several of the party waved at them as they left.

Only Lord Berrybender sulked.

"Never cared for losing servants—can't have too many servants," he said, as he sat with his claret and his fine Belgian gun.

45

"She does look disagreeable," Bobbety observed.

The steamer *Rocky Mount* steamed north, beyond the Mandan encampments, on a bright, cold day when the plains shone white with frost. Tasmin, Bobbety, George Catlin, and Holger Sten stood and watched— Lady Constance Berrybender's bright pantaloons were on flagrant display among the Mandan women. The Indians lined up to stare at the Thunder Boat—even the Bad Eye had dragged his great bulk, some of which was covered now by Lord Berrybender's great plaid cape, to the door of the skull lodge to listen as the great water beast belched. Draga stood beside him. She scorned the English clothes; what she wanted was English scalps.

"She does look disagreeable," Bobbety observed.

"Not disagreeable, evil," Tasmin said. "I fear she's ruined our sister Bess. I can hardly get her to say a word."

"Yes, it's annoying," Bobbety said. "She does not even care to hear my theories about the Mesozoic Age."

"Don't care to hear them myself," Tasmin warned. "You're lucky I brought you Father Geoff, who is interested in everything."

"Count on a Jesuit for a nimble mind," George said.

"He's only a faux Jesuit," Tasmin said. "Not much of a credit to his stern order. He seems to be one of those gentlemen who take a great interest in clothes."

On the deck below, Tim, the stable boy, was being flogged—the lashes firmly laid on, at Lord Berrybender's insistence, by Captain Aitken, who approached the task with some reluctance but a strong hand. George Aitken didn't believe the young lout was much at fault in the matter of the blankets and the muskets—the thoroughbreds, after all, were his responsibility—but he laid the cat on hard, anyway. The boy was certainly not worth much, and the captain had the remaining *engagés* to consider; they'd be into all sorts of mischief if they thought they could get off with a light whipping. Young Tim was hardly stoic; he was soon blubbering and wailing, but he was young and the stripes would soon heal.

Bess Berrybender, staring at the white, chill plains, heard the blubberings, but they aroused little sympathy for her former lover, Tim. She herself had hardly been stoic when Draga beat her. She had wailed and shrieked, and Mademoiselle had done the same, but no one in the Mandan camp came to their aid.

The liberties Bess had allowed Tim, in the time before her capture, seemed very distant memories. Though she was safe, warm, and comfortable again, she was gripped by a great passivity. Once much given to declamation, she now said nothing. When Bobbety tried to interest her in fossil fish she made no response. When Cook inquired about Fräulein Pfretzskaner, Bess only sobbed a little—she remembered the bloody hatchets.

The sly Mary had caught a baby raccoon and made it a pet. She came along with the little creature while Tim was blubbering, but Bess was not responsive to its furry antics.

"It is sad that you don't like my raccoon," Mary said. "I have named him Agamemnon."

"I enjoy nothing," Bess said. "I shall soon go in a convent and become a handmaiden of the Lord."

"If that is your aim you should have left with Mademoiselle," Mary said. "I have no doubt that there are convents in Quebec, since the French seem to require a great many nuns."

"I shall attempt to find an order enjoined to silence, so I shall never have to listen to noisy brats like you," Buffum answered.

Mary at once flung the small raccoon over the side—after a second, a splash was heard.

"If you don't even like my little pet, Agamemnon, why keep him?" Mary asked.

Bess didn't answer.

"You are rather a loss, good-bye," Mary said. She ran downstairs and persuaded one of the *engagés* to rescue her little coon, which was swimming desperately.

"Do you think my sister's eagerness to take the veil is genuine?" Tasmin asked Father Geoffrin. "Or might we expect her to become her old contentious self, someday?"

Father Geoff had been reading Crébillon—he had found the volume in Mademoiselle's stateroom, which was now his.

"Fornication seems constantly to be on this odd fellow's mind," he said, closing the book. "I have no opinion about your sister's faith, but if she does take the veil I recommend the Carmelites—they have such elegant vestments."

"There are times, Geoff, when you are less rewarding than even Mary's coon," Tasmin said. She was quite put out with the little priest—it occurred to her that if she had not encountered him and begun to babble about books, she would have cooled off, changed her mind, and gone back to her husband, Jim Snow, whom she had begun to miss quite severely.

As evening drew on—chill and dank—Bess bestirred herself and asked Cook for a little salve; she felt it would be only Christian if she applied some to Tim's bloody back.

"At least you weren't blistered by hot sticks," she told the apathetic stable boy. Tim, taking this as encouragement, grabbed Bess's hand and forced it against his groin—that being his usual, indeed his only, method of dalliance.

Bess drew back a fist and gave him a solid punch—so solid that he looked shocked.

"I came to this dank hole merely to treat your wounds, as a Christian would, Master Tim," she said. "I will tolerate no more coarseness—I intend soon to become a bride of Christ."

"What? Be a nun? But we had such times afucking," Tim said.

"Those pleasures will be no more, not in the year of our Lord 1832," Bess said, as she left him.

46

. . . even in their pleasure she was noisy . . .

Jim Snow did not miss Tasmin much, in the first days after her departure. The truth was, her constant talk wore him out. She was forever talking, asking, interfering, insisting, opposing, suggesting. Some nights she talked on and on, when all Jim wanted to do was go to sleep. He had never known such a woman—even in their pleasure she was noisy, unlike his Indian wives. He had cracked his bow and needed to make a new one, which would be easier to do if he could give it his whole attention and not have to continually be answering questions. He didn't suppose Tasmin would be gone long, or encounter much danger. The night she had spent in the Oto cornfield had done her no harm.

Tasmin was scarcely out of sight before the old green parrot showed up. In the daytime the bird would vanish, but every morning, when dawn came, the old bird would return for an hour, nodding by what coals still glowed in the campfire, like an old man by a hearth.

When two nights passed and Tasmin had not returned, Jim grew doubtful. Perhaps he had underestimated the danger—perhaps the Sioux had come upon her. He walked a few miles up the river, following her tracks, and soon discovered that she *had* fallen in with someone, someone with very small feet who had been wearing sandals. It could hardly have been Charbonneau, whose footprints were a laughingstock among the trappers because of their great size.

"A buffalo could follow Sharbo," Dan Drew claimed. "I can barely track a moose, but I can track *him*."

There were no signs of conflict, which suggested to Jim that Tasmin had merely fallen in with someone from the boat, which by now was surely at the Mandan encampments. Probably she was back with her family, safe for a time. The steamer, he knew, could not afford to linger long at the Mandans, if George Aitken hoped to get it upriver to the Yellowstone before the thick ice formed.

Though Jim's new bow was finished, he had no sinews with which to wrap it or string it. For sinews he needed a buffalo—even an old one would do. He decided he had better go west, kill a buffalo, finish his bow, and then swing wide around the Mandans and catch up with Tasmin and the steamer somewhere near the Knife River. Then he could ask Charbonneau or one of the hunters to tell his wife that he had come for her.

That night he dreamed of her—in the dream he could even smell her sweet breath—and then woke, cold and disappointed, to see the old parrot, nodding by the coals.

In the afternoon it began to snow—a wind came up from the north and blew so hard that not much of the snow settled; instead, it whirled in clouds. One moment Jim could see far across the prairies, the next moment he could see only white. It was only by luck that he noticed the buffalo, twenty or thirty of them, their coats already carrying a thick blanket of snow. Moving with the flurries, Jim came within thirty yards of them and killed a bull and a calf; the bull he took for the sinews, the calf to eat. He found a little wood near a small frozen creek, enough to warm him through the blowy night. Not long before dawn the wind settled, the sky cleared, and the cold deepened. That morning there was no parrot by the fire. Jim drew the sinews, dried them, and finished wrapping his bow—he felt quite out of sorts with his wife, who could have been of help had she not gone storming off, for no reason. He intended to speak to her sternly about such impulsive behavior, the next time he was with her. A wife had the duty of obedience. Bow making could not be rushed. It required steadiness, a good eye, and a clear mind. Jim took his time with the wrapping.

He was moving northeast, toward the distant river, when he heard Indians singing—not many of them, five or six at most. A minute later their dogs caught his scent and began to bark. The song, faintly heard across the cold prairies, was no war song. It was a death song, a song meant to send a just-released on to the Sky House, to the company of other spirits. An old person, an elder of the little band, tired, his spirit fluttery, must have passed on. Growing up as a captive of the Osage, Jim had heard many such songs of passing. The song he was hearing now—repetitive, keening, sad— was, he felt sure, a song for a chief. And yet if a great chief of the Mandans had died the whole tribe would normally be there, wailing out this death song—not just these few singers. The dogs still barked—the singers knew he was near. Rather than turn west into the snowfields, Jim moved toward the sound.

The six old men who had been singing were just lifting a body onto a burial scaffold—a heavy body, too. They were struggling with it, but finally got it lodged securely on the poles of the scaffold. Three old women stood watching. Jim raised his hand in a sign of peace. The singers, out of breath from their lifting, paused for a moment and then resumed their singing. Jim recognized one of them, an old warrior named Step Toe—the old man often traded for tobacco with Dan Drew. The men with Step Toe were also old. Before many winters all of this little group would be on just such a scaffold themselves. Jim could make no sense of it. Why was this little group so far from their villages, burying an important chief?

To Jim's astonishment, the old Berrybender parrot came flapping over his head, out of a clear cold sky, and landed on the corpse. No sooner had the bird landed than he said the same four words that he had said to Jim, at the earlier burial service, which had been for Tasmin's mother.

The Mandan mourners were shocked—they stopped singing at once and fell back from the scaffold.

For a brief moment, Jim felt his own hair rise. Was the bird some kind of harbinger, trained to speak over the dead? He expected that one of the Mandans would immediately kill it, but they didn't. Instead, they drew farther back, watching the parrot nervously. The parrot repeated the same mysterious words: *"Schweig, du blöder Trottel!"*

The Mandans retreated a few more steps, watching this strange talking bird warily. The parrot made no further comment—it bent and picked at a button on the corpse's coat, and when it did, Jim suddenly realized that the dead man was Big White, Charbonneau's escaped Mandan. Big White *was* a great chief, worthy of much ceremony—but why was he dead, far from his village, attended only by six old warriors and three old crones?

47

. . . a talking bird was walking back and forth . . .

Jim at once laid all his weapons on the snow-flecked, stubbly grass, in an attempt to reassure the Mandan mourners, who were terrified. Who could blame them? Their great chief Big White, absent for years, was now dead—and many miles from the village he was thought to be returning to. The Sin Killer had just appeared, out of a snowstorm, and a talking bird was walking back and forth on the corpse of Big White. It added up to a combination of events that might have shaken stouter hearts than this frail old bunch could muster. None of them looked capable of defending themselves from a foe of much ferocity.

Jim approached the Mandans slowly, indicating again, in sign, to Step Toe, that he meant them no harm. He stopped and waited, allowing the Mandans a minute to settle their nerves. Finally Step Toe came over—he was short and very thin.

"No tabac?" he asked. "We need tabac."

"No tabac," Jim said.

The old man looked disappointed.

"We have been to the springs," he said. "We like to go to the springs before the cold gets too bad. I am not old myself but these others are old. The warm springs are good for their bones."

Jim knew the springs Step Toe was talking about—there were several bubbling, foul-smelling sulfur springs in the barren country five days' travel to the west. Many Indians used the springs, and some trappers liked them, but Jim himself found the smell so strong that he avoided them.

"We found Big White—he was already dead," Step Toe said. "He killed a Ponca—broke open his head with that big club of his. The Ponca is over there.

"There is not much game near the springs," he added. "We have been living on roots."

Jim saw that in fact the little band was starving. He at once gave them what was left of his buffalo meat and the old women immediately set to cooking it. Two of the old women and one of the old men were almost blind—they were the smoke starers, people whose vision had been weakened by too many years spent in small, smoky lodges. The parrot still paraded on the corpse of Big White—it occurred to Jim that the chief might have played with the old bird while both were on the boat.

The dead Ponca's head had indeed been broken open—there was ice on the clotted brain matter. Jim made a thorough search but did not find the old chief's famous war club.

Except for the fact of two corpses, there was little sign of struggle. Jim noticed the tracks of four horses—that was all.

"Was Big White shot?" Jim asked, after studying the horse tracks to no purpose. The Mandans were gulping down the half-raw buffalo meat. They all looked exhausted, and one old woman, blood on her chin, was already snoring loudly.

Step Toe held up a finger, jabbing with it three or four times.

"Somebody stuck him with a little knife," Step Toe said. "The wound was no wider than my finger—it went between his ribs and bit him bad."

"You didn't see the horsemen?"

"We saw no one," Step Toe said. "When we found Big White his spirit had gone, but he was still warm. At first we feared that someone might come and try to kill us too, but they didn't. I guess we were too worthless to bother with. Big White was a heavy man—it was all we could do to get him on that scaffold."

"Have you heard of a man called Malgres—a dark man from the south?" Jim asked.

Step Toe shook his head, but another of the old men, old Rabbit Skin, who had been half nodding, came awake at the mention of Malgres.

"I saw him once with some Poncas," Rabbit Skin said. "Some Poncas and the Twisted Hair."

"That's right—he works for the Twisted Hair," Jim said.

"A Frenchman was there when I saw them," the old man said. Being full had made him feel sleepy. He could barely remember the dark man, Malgres—he had been butchering a horse at the time, he seemed to recall.

"Malgres has a little thin knife," Jim indicated. "They say he's quick as a snake, when he strikes."

"I wonder if Big White really killed a grizzly bear with that club?" Step Toe said. "He was a great man, but he was always bragging. I knew him years ago, when I was younger."

48

Among excitable people, calm was the first requirement . . .

John Skraeling, known among the tribes as the Twisted Hair, from his habit of twisting his long gray mane into a knot so it wouldn't blow in his face on windy days, or spoil his aim if he was hunting, was annoyed when Draga told him that the steamboat had left the Mandan encampments three days earlier. All the river tribes were talking about the great Thunder Boat, with the rich English family on it. Skraeling had meant to be in the Mandan villages two weeks earlier—he, Guillaume, Malgres, and the two Poncas, one of whom was now dead—but the trouble between the Osage and the Pawnees had slowed them down. In any case, traveling with Guillaume—Willy, to the English—was never fast. Guillaume refused to be rushed; he was seldom willing to leave camp before noon. Malgres wanted to kill him because of his sluggish habits, but Skraeling forbade it.

"Don't you be cutting on Guillaume," he said. "We need someone who can talk to the Sioux. I can't, and you can't either."

"I don't want to talk to these filthy Indians," Malgres said—he himself was said to be part Apache. Malgres was small, quick, hotheaded, and deadly. Skraeling tried to avoid long conversations with him; he had been looking for a safe way to be done with Malgres, but hadn't found one yet.

Georges Guillaume, the man Malgres wanted to kill, had been in the north country forty years, as hunter, trapper, trader, guide, slaver, spy. He spoke more native dialects than any man in the north, far more than Toussaint Charbonneau, Captain Clark's interpreter. Skraeling knew that Malgres's Santa Fe bravado would not help them much if they ran into forty or fifty Teton Sioux on a day when the Sioux were in a warring mood—as they usually were.

"The Bad Eye made me give two white women back," Draga said. "We had three but one attacked me and the warriors killed her. There are many women on that boat. It has only been gone three days. Some of the women would bring a good price."

"I'm more interested in that keelboat full of wine the men are talking about," Skraeling said. "That much wine would keep a fellow warm all winter. It's gonna get bad cold pretty soon."

John Skraeling hated the cold. Son of a Norwegian sailor and a Creole mother, he had been born to the humid warmth of Galveston. He himself had been a captive, taken by the Comanches when young; Comanche was the only native language he spoke. When he grew up the tribe let him go— very soon, with more and more settlers crowding into the Comancheria, Skraeling became a ransom specialist, buying back young captives for the frontier families or small settlements from which they had been snatched. He was paid for his work, but not much; it soon occurred to him that he could make a good deal more money if he snatched the children *and* rescued them. Generally the return would be made quickly—else the children might die, from the mere shock of captivity itself. Keep them three weeks and their families might consider them hopelessly tainted by contact with the Comanches; this was particularly true if the children were female. Comanche women became wives very young.

John Skraeling soon tired of the uncertainties that went with the trade in captives. He struck the old Spanish trail to Santa Fe and became a trader in everything *but* captives: pelts, silver, weapons, blankets, even spices. Six times he crossed from Saint Louis to Nuevo Mexico. He had been in Kansas when he heard about the great steamboat with the rich English family and its keelboat full of fine wine. With Malgres, Guillaume, and the Poncas, he had decided to follow it, mainly out of curiosity. A steamer on the shallow Missouri might encounter a lot of setbacks—there might be much to scavenge, if things went wrong.

But they had arrived late, and now the boat was north of them, with the bitter cold at hand.

"We could catch it," Draga said. "Take me with you if you go. I'll see that you're warm."

Georges Guillaume sat comfortably by the fire, carefully scraping the rich yellow marrow out of a buffalo leg bone. He lifted an eyebrow at Draga's remark. Long ago, before she had begun to smell old, Draga had been his woman. What was the old slut suggesting? That she would build Skraeling's fires—or find him young women; or was she offering to be his woman herself? John Skraeling showed little interest in women anyway— why would he want a harsh, toothless old witch?

"Thank you," Skraeling said politely. "I'll let you know what I decide."

He had no intention of taking Draga with him, but he didn't want to offend her, either. Draga had the ear of the Bad Eye, a fact no trader could afford to ignore. In any case, as he had tried to explain to Malgres, courtesy and good manners did not go unnoticed in the Mandan encampments—modesty got one more than bluster or rage. Among excitable people, calm was the first requirement—the unfortunate encounter with Big White showed that clearly enough. Big White had actually been on the English boat—Skraeling had merely been waiting for Guillaume to catch up so Guillaume could ask the old man about the treasures on the steamer. But then one of the Poncas had foolishly insulted the old Mandan, an act of aggressive folly that immediately cost him his life. Then Malgres, whom Big White hardly noticed, struck with his knife before Skraeling could stop him, and the one man who could have given them valuable information about the treasure boat slumped down in the snow and died.

"Draga wants you to catch her some more white girls so she can beat them," Guillaume said to Skraeling. "She hates these white girls that the young men want."

Draga ignored him—she might lack the beauty of her youth, but she was not too old to please men. Almost every day, if she went to the shore to gather firewood, some young warrior would follow and seek to couple with her. Some she allowed, some she rejected. She knew, of course, that Skraeling didn't want her for himself. He was not a young man—in fact, he looked sick. Draga meant to watch him, observe where he squatted, see if there was blood in his excrement. Skraeling's cheeks were sunk in, and there was a rasp in his breath. Skraeling no longer wanted women, but he did still want money.

When he left the lodge to go visit the Bad Eye, Guillaume cracked another buffalo bone—he could not get enough of the rich marrow. Outside, the wind was howling—Guillaume was happy to be in a warm lodge, even if the old witch, Draga, was staring at him with hatred in her eyes.

"The Bad Eye made a terrible prophecy," Draga informed him.

"I don't want to hear it—I don't like bad news," Guillaume said. "I need a new wife, Draga—nobody skinny. Can't you find me a young woman with some flesh on her bones?"

"Why should I find you wives?" Draga asked. Then she left the lodge—she wanted to hear what Skraeling said to the Bad Eye.

Guillaume threw a big piece of driftwood on the fire. His lodge was a good solid lodge of well-packed earth, warm even on the coldest days, though perhaps a little smoky. If Skraeling decided to chase the English boat, then let him do it with Malgres and the Ponca. Guillaume meant to stay in his warm lodge and eat buffalo marrow until the warm weather came. When Draga came back she found him sound asleep and snoring.

49

The sky to the north was bluish, like a gun barrel . . .

Tasmin woke to the snorting and snuffling of buffalo—many thousands of them crowded both banks of the river and covered the plains to the west as far as the eye could see. Those nearest the river had icicles hanging from their chins, and more icicles dangling from their shaggy sides, where melting snow had frozen hard. It was so cold that Tasmin's breath soon frosted up her windowpane.

To her annoyance Bobbety and Mary came bursting in, admitting air so frigid that to breathe it was like drawing fire into her lungs.

"My thermometer is quite smashed—the mercury kept sinking until the glass broke," Bobbety said. "That means it is very cold indeed."

"I believe I could have deduced that without a lecture from you, Bobbety," Tasmin said.

"The Piegan is rather annoyed because he can't paint himself today—his paints are frozen, and so are Holger Sten's, but Mr. Catlin had the forethought to trust his to Cook, who kept them in a warm place," Mary informed them.

"Even so he is not painting these numerous buffalo—his fingers are too cold," Bobbety said.

For some days now Tasmin had been feeling the kind of restless frustration that she had felt on the day of the big hailstorm. Once again, just as she had resolved to go ashore and search for her husband, an unignorable impediment had been thrown up. Then it had been hail, now it was this terrible cold. The sky to the north was bluish, like a gun barrel; it offered no suggestion of warmth. Tasmin felt herself to be a hardy, healthy woman, but she was not so foolish as to suppose she could survive such cold. Besides, she was with child, her abdomen just showing its first slight curve. The Oto woman had been right to make her shirt loose. Vexed as she was at having to deal once again with the inanities of her family, frustrated as she was at not being with Jim, she knew there was nothing much she could do about it. Only that morning Captain Aitken, himself much disturbed by the sudden, brutal end to the fallish weather, had put it to Tasmin bluntly.

"You'd not last a night on shore," he said. "The Indians can stand it. Oh, sometimes they lose a toe or two. But they don't die. You'd die, Miss Tasmin."

"Captain, you must stop thinking of me as a Miss," Tasmin reminded him. "Cook can't seem to remember that fact, either. The one who remembers is Papa, and that's because he's lost a great fat dowry."

"Sorry," the captain said. He had a great deal more on his mind than forms of address. They were still more than one hundred miles, as the river flowed, from the snug trading post on the Yellowstone that was their destination, and yet the river *wouldn't* flow, if the cold didn't moderate. The edges of the river were crinkled with thick ice—it had happened in only one night.

Charbonneau came up to the bridge as the captain was talking with Tasmin.

"The Mandans said it was going to get bad cold," he said.

"I'm going to start running all night," George Aitken said. "I'll send some *engagés* in front of us, in a pirogue—they can feel out the snags and sandbars."

"But really, gentlemen, we can get out and walk, if we have to, can't we?" Tasmin asked.

"We can, but I don't know how many of us would make it—depends on the blizzards," Charbonneau said.

"We stayed a day too long at the Mandans'," the captain said. "Fixing that paddle was the devil of a bother. Little delays tell against you, when the season's failing."

"I'm sure my Jim is out there somewhere," Tasmin said, a little anxiously. "I hope he's not met with an accident. *He's* not likely to freeze, is he?"

Captain Aitken almost slipped and called Tasmin "miss" again—she looked so young and blooming. It was rather a mystery what sort of marriage she was intending to have with Jimmy Snow—a skilled young guide, certainly, but hardly the man to provide this smart young Englishwoman with a comfortable home life.

"Oh, Jimmy can handle weather," the captain said. "I'd be happy to see him myself, to tell you the truth. If the weather stays this cold we may ice in—Jimmy could be a big help if we have to tramp it."

Later, in her cabin, Tasmin locked herself in and withdrew into memory, as she had many times. She did her best to recall everything that had happened in her time with Jim. No book now interested her—she could think of nothing but her husband. She wanted intensely for him to come to her and remain her husband, and yet she could not decide, from a review of his behavior, whether such an appearance was at all likely. He had mentioned casually, in the midst of her pique, that he only expected to see his Ute wives every two or three years—what if he were intending to be similarly lax in regard to conjugal life with her? The thought of waiting years, months, even weeks to see him was intolerable! Didn't he miss her? It was a matter she had no way of judging.

In her life as a much-courted English beauty, Tasmin had rarely been prone to self-criticism. Guilt was an unknown emotion. She had taken Master Stiles away from her mother without a moment's qualm.

Now, in her chilly stateroom, surrounded by the vast plains—bare except for the milling buffalo—Tasmin, long accustomed to blaming others for everything that went even slightly wrong, now turned her considerable skill at blaming herself. Why had she allowed the revelation of these distant Indian wives to upset her so? Why had she been so foolish as to leave a man who had been, on the whole, rather considerate of her, and who pleased her deeply? The obvious explanation was that she herself was an excessively spoiled piece of work. Her feelings of abandonment and loneliness were her own fault—Jim, after all, hadn't left her.

In her turmoil of spirit Tasmin struck out ruthlessly when any member of her family made the slightest demand. The pale, passive Buffum—already nunlike—she avoided. Bobbety she ignored, Mary she smacked; and she had nothing to do with her father, who in any case remained closeted with Vicky Kennet most of the time, nursing his stumps. George Catlin she froze out; the other specialists she rarely saw. The one person she took into her confidence, regarding her pregnancy, was Cook—no gossip, and gynecologically experienced as well—and Coal, Charbonneau's wife, made rounder and much jollier by the fact that she too was with child. The tundra swans had blessed her, Coal believed.

Coal and Tasmin had no language in common: what they had was a common state, the old, old state that came only to women. On sunny days Tasmin often went down and sat with Coal, comforted by her cheerfulness and impressed by her industry. Coal had insisted that her husband bring her rabbit skins—she had already made a warm pouch for her child, and assured Tasmin—in sign—that she would make her one too. Old Charbonneau was rather put out at being required to scour the plains for rabbits, but he did his duty and Coal worked the skins until they were supple and soft. Sometimes Tasmin helped a little, accepting Coal's instructions. Then she conceived the notion of making Jim a cap. Monsieur Charbonneau was required to secure two beaver skins from some Indians. Tasmin racked her brain over the question of head size. When her Jim did come she wanted his cap to be right, neither too small or too large. The final product looked rather Russian to her, but Tasmin was proud of it anyway and slept with it under her pillow at night. Somehow just having a fine cap waiting made her feel a little more hopeful that someday soon her Jimmy, her Raven Brave, would come back to his wife.

50

Insults, slights, teasings, rudeness she had borne in studied silence . . .

Venetia Kennet, five years now in service to the Berrybenders, had not once lowered herself to ask a favor of Lady Tasmin. Insults, slights, teasings, rudeness she had borne in studied silence, a haughty dignity her only refuge. Now and then she might lash out at Bess, slap Mary, curse one or another of the Ten; of course, she had always felt quite free to abuse the tutors, the *femme de chambre,* the kitchen help, the valet, and lesser riffraff on the boat. But Tasmin she let be—it was most unfair, of course, that Tasmin had been born noble and herself of common stock; but there it was, and Venetia felt that the best response she could make to this unanswerable injustice was to ask Tasmin for nothing—not even the loan of a book. This policy she had held to rigidly for the whole five years. On rare occasions, when Tasmin unbent and *offered* to loan her a book, Venetia Kennet had nobly, serenely, icily refused, and would have refused to the very portals of eternity had the family only remained in England, where life proceeded according to long-established rules.

But now the deep deep cold, so intense that when Venetia went on deck even for a few minutes, the very roots of her teeth ached, was forcing her to break this rule of rules in the interest of keeping alive her hopes of someday being Lady Berrybender—which could only occur if Albany Berrybender himself stayed alive, and Lord B. was even then insisting, over Captain Aitken's strong protests, that he *would* go hunting immediately, taking Gladwyn, his man, and Tim, the stable boy, who, between them, would be expected to carry the guns.

"What, come thousands of miles to hunt buffalo and then not hunt them when they veritably blanket the plains?" Lord B. asked. "Of course I'll hunt them, despite this spot of weather."

When pressed to go with the hunting party, Toussaint Charbonneau flatly refused.

"I've lost one Indian and I expect he's dead—I'm sticking with the other two," Charbonneau said. "It's a bit frosty for hunting, anyway."

Lord Berrybender was hardly pleased by Charbonneau's refusal. He liked to suppose that everybody on the boat worked for him and him only. That a man would refuse to hunt with him because Captain Clark had enjoined him to look after two mangy savages hardly showed the proper spirit, in Lord B.'s view. Charbonneau might have a French name, but he exhibited a very American sense of independence, a national trait that Albany Berrybender had no use for at all, since it led commoners to ignore the wishes of their betters, as Charbonneau had just done.

It was Captain Aitken—worried for His Lordship's safety—who asked Venetia Kennet to see if Tasmin would attempt to talk sense to her father.

"He doesn't know what he's letting himself in for, Miss Kennet," Captain Aitken said. "He thinks because the sun's come out for a few minutes he won't freeze—but he *will* freeze, and so will his men."

Tasmin had been brushing the fine cap she had made for Jim Snow, enjoying the soft feel of the furs; she was not pleased to hear a pounding on her cabin door—very probably it was only Father Geoff, wanting to complain about the tedium of Walter Scott, whose *Kenilworth* he found lacking in both concision and wit. She opened the door with some reluctance and was astonished to see an obviously distressed Venetia Kennet standing there. Never in the years of their troubled acquaintance had Vicky Kennet pounded on her door.

"Goodness, Vicky! What is it?"

"It's His Lordship," Vicky said. "He proposes to go off hunting, despite this fearful cold. Captain Aitken thought he might listen to you—that you might try to dissuade him."

"Captain Aitken has an exaggerated view of my influence over Papa, I fear," Tasmin said. "I've never talked him out of doing anything he wanted to do, and no one else has either."

"I know—he is *so* willful," Vicky said, fearing that the case was hopeless.

"In my opinion a man as soaked with brandy as Father is very unlikely to freeze—but that doesn't mean the help won't," Tasmin said. "We can ill afford to lose many more servants—at least they can shoot guns if we find ourselves under attack."

She shrugged on one of the great gray capotes and followed Vicky Kennet to the lower deck, where a pirogue with two freezing *engagés* in it waited to ferry the hunting party to shore. Except for Lord Berrybender himself, the hunting party was in low spirits. Gladwyn and the lad Tim also had been issued the great gray coats, but both were shivering violently despite them. They looked like men about to ascend the scaffold. Yet Mary Berrybender, wearing only a thin sweater, stood by the almost naked Hairy Horn and neither seemed at all bothered by the extreme chill.

Tasmin wasted no time on niceties.

"Papa, do stop this folly," she said. "It's so cold it broke the bottom out of Bobbety's thermometer—it's obviously quite insane for you to go ashore."

"No business of yours, that I can see," Lord Berrybender said brusquely. "Anyway, the sun's out—things will soon be melting, I expect."

"No sir, no!" Captain Aitken pleaded. "The sun will be gone by the time you reach shore."

Lord Berrybender ignored him and turned toward the ladder, but Tasmin quickly blocked his access.

"Here's the count," she said. "You've already lost your wife, one child, a boatman, two Poles, our good Fräulein, and a smattering of toes and fingers. Now you stand ready to deprive us of Gladwyn and Tim, neither of whom is likely to survive such profound chill."

Lord Berrybender flushed red at her words—the impertinence! To the horror of the company he grabbed Tasmin by the hair and gave her a violent shaking; then he shoved her so hard that she spun across the deck and fell in the startled Piegan's lap. The man just saved her from a nasty fall.

"I *will* hunt, and I will hunt *now!*" Lord Berrybender shouted. "I don't think I've quite sunk to the point where I must carry my own weapons, either."

Without another word he descended into the pirogue and settled himself. He too wore one of the great gray coats. Gladwyn and Tim, offered no options, climbed slowly into the boat, being careful with the guns.

"Cold as it is you'll have to do the butchering quick," Charbonneau advised. "Otherwise the meat will freeze."

"I don't propose to butcher them—I just propose to kill them," Lord B. said. "Might take a tongue or two, if I'm in the mood."

With that he waved impatiently, and the pirogue made for the icy shore. The buffalo had moved off the river, but thousands were still in sight, a mile or two west.

"Best not to lose sight of the river, sir!" Captain Aitken shouted, cupping his hands. His voice echoed off the low bluffs to the west.

"Well, Vicky, so much for my influence," Tasmin said. "All I got was my hair pulled."

Father Geoff popped out of the galley, licking one of Cook's great spoons. Lately he had been spending a good deal of time with Cook, feeling that the shipboard cooking might profit from a little French expertise.

"What's the fuss?" he asked.

"No fuss, particularly—what's on that spoon?" Tasmin asked.

"Pudding," Father Geoffrin said.

As they watched, the sun disappeared. A dark blue bank of cloud, moving over them from the north, swallowed it so completely that no ray shone through. On the shore they could just see the three gray forms slipping and sliding on the ice. Soon the three men were dots against the shallow snow.

"I fear that's the end of Papa," Mary said. "I can't think why he is so unwise."

Captain Aitken, heartsick, said nothing. He stood at the rail, watching the deep cold cloud. Soon he heard the first distant pops from Old Gorska's Belgian gun.

51

He heard a kind of snuffle . . .

Great sport! Great sport!" Lord Berrybender yelled, in high exuberance. "Never had such fine sport in my life. Keep loading, man. How many would you say are down, so far?"

"Tim would be the one to ask, Your Lordship," Gladwyn said, feeling that his hands might simply snap off, like twigs. He could not load properly with gloves on, and yet when he took his gloves off, his hands got so cold they would barely grasp a gun. Young Tim had already peeled half the skin off one hand by foolishly grasping one of the freezing gun barrels with an ungloved hand. Now, of course, the gun barrels were warm from Lord Berrybender's rapid fire, but that was no consolation to Tim, whose peeled palm burned like fire.

"Forty, I'd say, Your Lordship," Tim yelled. All around, within a radius of less than one hundred yards, great brown beasts lay sprawled, some dead, some still belching bright crimson blood into the snow.

"Good lad—do take a few tongues," Lord B. instructed. "Cook will be impatient if we neglect such a fine opportunity to bring back tongues."

As soon as Gladwyn handed him a rifle he turned and fired, this time killing a buffalo cow that was no more than thirty feet from where he stood. Instead of fleeing, as most animals did when under assault, the buffalo seemed quite indifferent to the shooting. Of course, the wind had risen, snow was beginning to blow a bit. Still, the odd thing was, the buffalo *did* seem to be massing together, milling around in a formless herd. One cow passed between himself and Gladwyn—another nearly stepped on Tim, who had not yet mastered the knack of neatly severing a buffalo's tongue from its bleeding mouth.

"I say, Your Lordship, they do seem to be crowding rather close," Gladwyn said, becoming alarmed. Buffalo were everywhere.

"The wind's keening so—I suppose they can scarcely hear the shots," Lord Berrybender said, as a great shaggy beast ambled past him, its coat snow-streaked, not ten feet away.

"I do rather wish they'd spread out," Lord Berrybender said. "It's rather more sporting if I have to do at least a bit of aiming."

He took a gun from Gladwyn—the man was shivering damnably—and shot the great shaggy bull, only to experience a startling change: the immediate disappearance of everything. Snow suddenly whirled around him so blindingly that when he held out the empty rifle to Gladwyn, not merely Gladwyn but the rifle and even his own arm disappeared into a swirl of white. He heard a kind of snuffle, then a buffalo just brushed him as it went past. Lord Berrybender felt it but could not see it. For a moment he thought he just glimpsed Gladwyn, but then the man vanished again. Lord Berrybender stood stock-still, his arm still extended, the empty rifle growing heavy in his hand. He expected, of course, that Gladwyn would take it and reload it, and yet he didn't. Lord Berrybender withdrew the gun and tried to pull up the big floppy hood of his capote, only to have the hood fill with snow before he could even pull it over his head. He pulled it over his head anyway—the snow melted and then froze again as it dribbled down his cheeks, forming an icicle just below his chin—it was the first time his chin had sprouted an icicle in his life.

Then he felt a hard bump and was sent sprawling—a buffalo had stumbled into him in the blinding whirl of snow. Lord Berrybender just managed to keep his grip on the rifle. When he tried to struggle up he found that someone else had a grip on the rifle too—the briefly lost Gladwyn it was! The two men were less than three feet apart, and yet could not see each other.

"Am I to reload, Your Lordship?" Gladwyn yelled, and then realized at once that the task was hopeless. He could scarcely see the Belgian gun, and could no longer manage the powder and shot. Fortunately he had clung grimly to a second rifle, which was loaded. This he handed to Lord Berrybender.

"Wrong gun! Wrong gun! Where's my Belgian?" Lord B. wanted to know. He had become extremely fond of Old Gorska's excellent gun.

Gladwyn was shaking so hard that he couldn't answer; in fact he had no idea what he'd done with the Belgian gun—though a moment later he realized it was squeezed between his shaking legs.

"Have to use this one, sir," he screamed, and Lord B. *did* use the second rifle, firing point-blank into the side of a great beast that had just loomed out of the snow, only feet away. The buffalo fell just in front of them, its shaggy coat steaming. Gladwyn could not resist—he thrust his freezing hands into the wounded animal's shaggy fur. Lord Berrybender, his own hands far from warm, did the same.

"Getting a bit thick, in fact," he said. "I believe I've killed forty-two buffalo, if Tim's count was right—perhaps the prudent thing would be to make for the boat."

Gladwyn's teeth were chattering so violently that he feared they might shatter. In the privacy of his modest quarters Gladwyn sometimes wrote verse; he thought he might just have a rhyme—"chatter, shatter"—if he could just hold it in mind until he could write it down.

"Where exactly is the boat, sir?" he asked.

Lord Berrybender, his hands warming as he pressed them against the buffalo, looked about and saw only white—uniform, monotonous white.

"I'm afraid I haven't the faintest notion," he admitted. "Never much of a head for directions . . . got lost in my own deer park more than once. I expect Tim will know—just the kind of thing a stable boy *would* know."

"But where is Tim, Your Lordship?" Gladwyn asked.

"Gad, can't be far," Lord B. said. "He was just taking a tongue."

Suddenly a moment of absolute panic seized him. Where was Tim? More important, where was the Missouri River, the pirogue, the *engagés*, the steamer *Rocky Mount*, the languid but pliable Venetia Kennet?

"Tim, Tim, Tim!" Lord B. yelled, at the top of his voice. "Time to retreat, lad—come lead us home."

The howling, keening wind snatched his words and whirled them away so swiftly that even if Tim had been on the other side of the fallen buffalo he might not have heard them.

Tim, for his part, had lost not only the tongue he had just cut out of the buffalo, but the knife he had used to remove the tongue. Both dropped from his freezing fingers and were instantly lost. He was too cold even to yell—when he opened his mouth, cold filled it. By inadvertence he made the same discovery Gladwyn had made: the buffalo he knelt by was still breathing and still warm; also it was large enough to form a kind of barrier. Tim squeezed as close to it as he could get, even warming his icy cheeks in the thick fur. Though a moment before he felt certain that his would be a frigid doom, the fact that the animal he was pressed against still pulsed with the heat of life gave Tim a little hope. The buffalo would be his shelter and his stove. He thought of his three jolly brothers, all safely back in England, cheerfully shoveling out the Berrybender stables and making crude assaults on the milkmaids' virtue now and then. What a happy lot was theirs! Just faintly, once or twice, he thought he heard His Lordship calling, but Tim didn't answer; he knew he mustn't be tempted to leave his shaggy stove.

"The lazy rascal, where is he, now that he's needed?" Lord Berrybender complained. A great many buffalo were trampling and snuffling around them, on the whole rather welcome since they somewhat broke the chilling wind.

"Lost as us, I expect, Your Lordship," Gladwyn said, his teeth still chattering-shattering. "Lost as us."

"I wouldn't object to a spot of fire, if any wood could be found," Lord B. said. "Expect they'll send a party to get us, soon. Stout Captain Aitken knows his job—he won't desert us."

"Perhaps not, but how will he find us, sir—I mean with the atmosphere being so thick?" Gladwyn asked.

Lord Berrybender considered the comment, unhappily. The atmosphere was damnably thick—the sun that he had been counting on to melt things was absolutely gone; darkness was not far off. A shore party might stumble around for hours before lighting on them, crouched as they were behind a fallen buffalo.

"Kick around a bit, Gladwyn . . . there must be wood around here some-where," His Lordship said. "Kick around, won't you? Be cheery to have a spot of fire."

52

She remembered the terrible wind that had keened and roared . . .

Despite the bitter cold, as the great inconstant wall of storm advanced toward them from the north, one by one the company aboard the steamer *Rocky Mount* left the warmth of cabin, galley, and bridge, to stand by the rail on the lower deck, watching the terrible storm come.

"Wotan is angry," Mary said. "He means to bury the whole world in snow."

"Don't know about that, but it's a fine blizzard, I guess," Charbonneau said. "The Bad Eye predicted it."

"Bosh, I don't hold with these red prophets," George Catlin said. "Why not predict a blizzard, since it's winter?"

"They say he can hear a snowflake form," Mary said. "They say he can hear the swan's breath."

"And now our own Papa has very likely gone to his death in this year of our Lord 1832," Buffum said.

"The spirit of the hunt was on him," Señor Yanez remarked, startling everybody. Señor Yanez rarely spoke.

"Yes, and the old brute's taken two innocents with him," Tasmin said.

She remembered the terrible wind that had keened and roared, underneath the hail. Now the wind was keening again, and the snow wall had snuffed out the sun's light—there was only a ghostly glint on the snow.

Father Geoffrin shivered violently.

"So desolate, these plains—such melancholy," he said. "I often weep, and I don't know why. Snow is so much more a thing to be welcomed when it falls on cobblestones . . . or ancient walls . . . or lamplighters . . . or the shawls of prostitutes."

"Any chance we could find them, Charbonneau?" Captain Aitken asked. The light was almost gone, the snow wall advancing fast, and the black watery lead that would take them up the Missouri was narrowing by the hour. Still, he could not steam away and leave a noble patron. The loss of Lord Berrybender would mean the end of his career. His employers would not forgive such a calamity—none of them had been west of Cincinnati; they had rather rosy ideas about life on the wild Missouri.

"No chance, George," Charbonneau said. "The snow'll soon be blowing so thick you can't see the length of your arm. His Lordship *would* go."

"That he would—he nearly yanked my hair out when I tried to reason with him," Tasmin said.

Cook came out for a moment, took Father Geoffrin by the sleeve, and led him back inside. She had begun to rely heavily on his advice in the matter of sauces and spices.

"It could not get this cold in Holland," Piet Van Wely announced. "The people would not stand for it—there would be protests and someone would lose his position."

"In Denmark also there are no such snows," Holger Sten declared. "Only where the Lapps live are there these snows—knowledge of the Lapps I do not claim."

Remembering, suddenly, Fräulein Pfretzskaner's terrible end, which could so easily have been her own, Buffum began to sob.

Venetia Kennet began to cry also. The thin, fading light filled her with the deepest melancholy, the darkest sorrow. His Lordship, her great hope, was gone, doubtless to be frozen—and now she found herself pregnant with his bastard. Cook had confirmed her status only that day. The pregnancy that had once been her hope was now her despair. The seed at last had sprouted, but the noble seeder was gone.

As Buffum sniffled and Venetia Kennet sobbed, a new sound reached them over the roar of snow—a high chant of some kind. They all turned and there was the Hairy Horn, calling out a high, eerie chant. He had thrown off his blanket—he faced the storm almost naked.

"The Hairy Horn wishes to end his life's journey soon," Mary said. "The melody he offers up now is his death song."

"Wouldn't pay too much attention to *that* claim," Charbonneau said. "He's said as much before and yet he's still eating a good portion of vittles, every day."

Venetia Kennet, too distressed to stand on ceremony, flung herself into Tasmin's arms and gasped out her secret.

"I am going to have a baby—you are not the only one, Tasmin," she said.

Tasmin gave the weeping cellist a consolatory pat or two. At least the woman was not without vigor, a desirable quality in the New World they were voyaging into.

"I wasn't the only one anyway, Vicky—there's our merry Coal," Tasmin said. "If you ask her she'll make your baby a snug fur pouch. Why, we can establish quite a nursery up on the Yellowstone—at least we can if we survive this desperate weather."

53

Getting the bear out proved a challenge . . .

Maelgwyn Evans liked to claim that he got through the bitter winters along the Knife River through the precaution of having taken six hundred pounds of wives: three Winnebagos and a Chippewa. Maelgwyn himself was skinny, but his lodge north of the river was well caulked, and the warm poundage of his four wives was proof against even the coldest night.

Of course, this stratagem only worked if he was *in* his lodge when the bitter weather struck. He and Jim Snow had gone three or four miles north, meaning to take a fat buffalo cow, before the blizzard hit. They easily killed a cow, took the liver and sweetmeats and a bit of flank, and were hurrying back to shelter when they saw the three men from the steamer come crunching ashore and start shooting into the buffalo herd, evidently oblivious to the fact that a high plains blizzard was swiftly advancing toward them.

"The one doing the shootin' is my wife's pa," Jim said. "The old one."

"She says he's stubborn," he added, watching the scene across the snowy plain.

"A man from the north, I expect," Maelgwyn said. "No one stubborner than a northman. Not practical minded, like us Welsh."

Jim eyed the hunting party, eyed the approaching storm, eyed the boat. He was calculating as to whether he had time to race over and try to get the hunting party to safety. He had had a chilly tramp north; once he knew that he was upriver from the steamer he rested for a day, allowing Maelgwyn's wives to feed him thick stews and rub him well with bear grease taken from a fat grizzly that Maelgwyn had killed in its den earlier in the fall. Getting the bear out proved a challenge, even for a Welshman with four stout wives.

"It was a wide bear in a narrow den," Maelgwyn said. Always eager to talk, he described the adventure at some length, while Jim dozed and got his rub. His Ute wives had the same habit; he could expect a good rub when he showed up. Tasmin had never rubbed him in that fashion, but of course he had yet to supply her with the fat of a hibernating bear. He wondered, as he dozed, if it was not more practical—as Maelgwyn claimed— just to have Indian wives, women well able to cure skins, pick berries, gather firewood, tan pelts.

"One of the benefits of life out here on the baldies is that not many English come this way," Maelgwyn said. "But now there's a steamer full of 'em. I don't know that I like it."

Maelgwyn was respected by all the beaver men, north and south, because of the high quality of his pelts. Other trappers sometimes brought in more pelts, but Maelgwyn's were always prime—he secured the silkiest beaver, the fox pelt with the most shine, weasel tails, and pelts taken from wolves with their long winter hair. He traded no pelts with flaws—even John Skraeling, who didn't like the north, stopped at Maelgwyn's from time to time, taking his excellent furs back to Santa Fe.

"It's the wives," Maelgwyn claimed, modestly. "I've trained every one of them. I've my own little fur factory, here on the Knife."

Jim concluded that there was no way he could get to the foolish hunters before the storm engulfed them. Nobody, white or Indian, could do much in a whiteout. The only thing to do when a blizzard came was find a warm place and wait. He and Maelgwyn had to make haste themselves. The whirling snow was waist high when they got back to Maelgwyn's lodge.

"I expect those English will freeze," Jim said.

"It's likely, unless the buffalo save them," Maelgwyn said. "Buffalo crowd up in a storm. If the English can stay in the midst of them it'll knock some of the wind off. I was saved that way myself once, up on the Prairie du Chien—got in among two or three thousand buffalo. I had to keep moving, but I survived.

"If it clears by dawn, then the bad cold will hit," he added. "They have quite a few buffalo down. I expect we could find them by starlight, if the blow lets up."

"I don't know that old man, but he's my wife's pa," Jim said. "When the wind dies we might better try."

54

"Not a cork broken, not one"

The buffalo Tim crouched behind was cooling—it had died. Snow blew over the dead beast and over Tim. By chance his hand fell on the knife he had dropped earlier. Though he felt little hope, he grasped the knife with both hands and began to try to scratch out a little cave, beneath the carcass. He couldn't feel his feet, but still had some feeling in his hands. His ears stung like fire. He pressed his face against the dead buffalo and sucked in his breath as he worked. Slowly the trench deepened. He could just squeeze a little way beneath the hairy, inert body. He raked and raked, but then somehow lost the knife again. He tightened his coat around him and crowded in under the buffalo as best he could, shivering so violently that he thought his bones might snap. At moments he wondered if he had already died. He seemed to hear Lord Berrybender talking, going on about some great Spanish battle he had fought long ago. Tim heard him, then didn't hear him, then heard him again. Until the two men came in the starlit night and tried to get him to his feet, Tim had not been aware that the wind had died. He was at first not sure whether he was alive or in heaven, though surely his hands would not hurt so if it were the latter.

"Come on, you've got to walk," Jim told him. "It's not far to the river—we can't carry both of you."

"It hurts too much, I believe I am frozen," Tim said, very surprised to see Lord Berrybender staggering around, only a little distance away.

"Mustn't forget that Belgian gun," Lord Berrybender was saying. "Expensive, that fine Belgian—belonged to my hunter. Rather sentimental, my hunter. Lost his boy and killed himself."

"We can come back for the gun, sir," Maelgwyn said politely. "We have to get you shipboard and see to your feet, and the boy's."

Lord Berrybender just then noticed Tim, stumbling along supported by another stranger, a prairie fellow of some kind.

"Why, Tim . . . stout lad, stout lad," he said, feeling for a moment like weeping. The small fellow was hurrying him away, allowing him no time to gather his possessions.

"Might just grab that Belgian gun, Tim," Lord B. said. "Can't manage it myself, with my stump."

"Can't hold it, Your Lordship, hands won't work," Tim admitted.

"Nonsense, blow on your fingers, that'll do the trick," Lord Berrybender instructed. "Not disposed to lose that gun."

"You won't—I'll get it later," Jim said, annoyed at the selfish old fool.

"A savage could pick it up—thoroughly wasted on a savage," Lord B. began; but then he noticed that the two rescuers were looking at him in a not entirely friendly way. He could always send Charbonneau ashore to gather up the weaponry—or even Señor Yanez.

"But where's Gladwyn, sir?" Tim asked. "He usually carries the guns."

"Stout lad, you're right, of course," Lord B. said. "Gladwyn's job, quite clearly. But where is the fellow?"

"Gladwyn?" Maelgwyn asked. "That's a Welsh name, a bit like my own. Was the fellow Welsh?"

"Possibly Welsh—or was he a Cornishman? Fear I'm too cold to think clearly," Lord B. said. "Haven't got a spot of brandy on you, I don't suppose? Might clear my head."

Neither Jim nor Maelgwyn were encouraging on the matter of brandy.

"But mustn't we look for him, sir? Gladwyn, I mean," Tim blurted. It seemed to him a dreadful crime that the two of them were being saved while Gladwyn was being left.

There ahead of them, not half a mile away, sparkled the lights of the steamer *Rocky Mount*. It was by far the most welcome sight Tim had seen in his life. And yet no effort was being made to assist Gladwyn back to the warm haven of the boat.

"Gad, what became of the man?" Lord Berrybender wondered. "He *was* there, of course. We both rather clung to the buffalo—it was warm for a bit, before it died."

He looked behind him for a moment, as if a glimpse of the prairie where he and Tim had almost frozen might refresh his memory; then it came back to him!

"Why yes, I remember now," he said. "It was rather discouragingly cold. Then Gladwyn stood up and said he had someplace to go. Someplace to go. And off he marched."

"Where could he have had to go?" Maelgwyn asked. "There was no place to go."

"Yes, that's rather a puzzle," Lord Berrybender replied. "A good man in his way, Gladwyn. Never broke a cork, in all the years I had him. But up he stood. Said he had someplace to go and that he might be some time. So off he went. Unusual man. Never quite knew what made Gladwyn tick. Greatly skilled with the claret, though—greatly skilled. Not a cork broken, not one."

55

"Sons of Madoc, habeas corpus, kitchen maids in love with valets . . ."

Tintamarre's barking brought Tasmin out of a sound sleep, though it was scarcely dawn. The window in her stateroom was quite frosted over. Tintamarre had taken to sleeping in a corner by the galley, with the Charbonneaus. Now he was barking furiously.

When Tasmin opened her door she was greeted by air so cold that she was reluctant to go out, but when she did skip to the rail, just for a moment, to investigate the commotion, she saw, with an immediate deep flush, her husband, Jim Snow, attempting to boost her wobbly father high enough that the *engagés* could grasp him and pull him aboard. Not only was her father alive, but so was Tim, being assisted up the ladder by a small man in buckskins.

All sense of cold vanished: Tasmin knew her husband had come for her, just as she had hoped he would, and by some miracle, he had even saved her father. Without even waiting to put on her slippers, which she could never find when she was in a hurry, Tasmin raced downstairs. Jim Snow had only just stepped on board, among the Charbonneaus, Cook, Captain Aitken, and the *engagés*, when Tasmin flung herself into his arms. To his extreme embarrassment she kissed him hard on the mouth—Jim quickly pushed her away and reached down to lift the shivering Tim into the boat. He gave Tasmin only a furious glance, a look that confused her. After such a long absence, was she not to be ardent? For a moment she felt on the verge of tears, so disappointed was she, but the small man in buckskins who had come aboard with Jim spoke to her in a kindly fashion.

"You'd be the wife, I expect," he said. "I'm Maelgwyn Evans."

"I'm the wife—not much wanted, I guess," Tasmin said.

"Ah, it's just his shyness," Maelgwyn said. "Bashful Jim is what we always called him."

Tasmin passed rapidly from hurt to indignation. Jim had turned away; he was helping her father hobble on to his stateroom.

"You are always too forward, Tassie," the wakeful Mary said. "Your Mr. Snow was in no mood for such a brazen display."

"Shut up, I was just glad to see him," Tasmin said.

Before she could even follow her husband a great cry went up from the kitchen. Eliza, Cook's buxom assistant, the one who was always breaking plates, came sobbing out of the galley and attempted to fling herself over the rail into the icy Missouri. Only quick action on the part of Maelgwyn Evans kept Eliza from fulfilling this desperate design. Maelgwyn caught a foot, just as Eliza was going over the rail—George Catlin, disheveled and confused, stumbled over and helped the small fellow pull the sobbing scullery maid back on board. The Hairy Horn, who, during the night, had concluded that his death song had been premature, was smoking his pipe as if nothing untoward was happening at all.

"What can it mean? Is the girl insane?" George Catlin asked.

"Not at all," Mary said. "Eliza was merely in love with Gladwyn, who is now lost and presumed frozen."

"But perhaps he *isn't* frozen," the rattled painter said. "It is very wrong to jump to conclusions where life and death are concerned. *Habeas corpus,* you know."

"If you don't shut up I'll certainly punch you," Tasmin told him. "I'm in no mood for pomposity just now."

"I'll go look for Mr. Gladwyn—he might be a countryman of mine," Maelgwyn said. "There's not too many of us Welsh, in this wild region."

"Many! I'm surprised there are any," George said.

"Oh yes, we were once quite a group—came over to seek the sons of Madoc, you know. There's a lost tribe here somewhere, but we can't seem to find it. We're rather dispersed now—I rarely see a Welshman. I'd be glad for a talk with this Gladwyn, if he ain't frozen to death. Always curious about my countrymen."

"Sons of Madoc, *habeas corpus,* kitchen maids in love with valets, old chieftains singing their death songs and then not dying . . . I'll soon be insane myself if I have to listen to much more of this talk," Tasmin informed them. She stared hard at the Hairy Horn, who had just accepted a large saucer of porridge from Cook, who went on cooking no matter what the frenzy.

"Don't frown so at the Hairy Horn, Tasmin," Mary pleaded.

"But *wasn't* it a death song he was howling last night?"

"It seems he was merely practicing," Mary replied. "His death is now postponed until the summer."

Just as she spoke there was a fluttering of feathers and a green bird landed on the railing. *"Schweig, du blöder Trottel!"* Prince Talleyrand remarked.

"If only Mademoiselle were here to welcome him," Mary said.

56

At this Tim began to blubber loudly.

Damnable method! . . . damnable!" Lord Berrybender insisted loudly, between howls of pain. Jim Snow and Toussaint Charbonneau had cut his clothes off and were vigorously rubbing snow on his frostbitten limbs, while Captain Aitken and Maelgwyn Evans did the same for Tim, who yelled even more loudly than Lord B.

"Yes sir, but it's the *only* method that gives frozen flesh a chance," Captain Aitken reminded him, as he went firmly on with his rubbing. Careful attention had to be paid to even the smallest patch of frostbite: cheeks, ears, hands, feet, groin, toes all had to be checked.

"You *would* go ashore despite the chill, sir," Captain Aitken reminded His Lordship, whose groin area presented a particularly ticklish problem due to an evident leakage of urine, which had of course frozen hard on the noble lord's legs.

"Of course I went ashore, why not? Killed forty buffalo, too—only proper sport I've had on this wretched expedition," Lord B. insisted. *"Somebody* ought to be fetching those expensive guns instead of harassing me with this damned snow."

Then he howled more loudly as Charbonneau began to address his yellowish legs.

Tasmin, Bobbety, Buffum, Mary, and Venetia Kennet all watched the proceedings impassively, from a corner of the stateroom.

"I had not expected to look on my own father's nakedness, not in this year of our Lord 1832," Buffum intoned, in her new nun's voice.

"Leave, then—who asked you to stay?" Tasmin said.

"Father *is* rather a horror," Bobbety said. "Very foolish of him to piss himself. If I am ever faced with an extreme of cold I will endeavor to empty my bladder immediately."

"Good for you," Tasmin said, painfully aware that her husband had scarcely glanced her way; he concentrated on rubbing snow on her father's cheeks and hands. Though she maintained an icy demeanor, inwardly Tasmin seethed. It was all very well to attempt to save her father's few remaining appendages, and the stable boy's too; but Jim *could* have spared her a look, even a smile—only he hadn't.

Venetia Kennet stared straight ahead—she meant to maintain her station as Lord Berrybender's loyal wife-to-be, but she didn't feel she had to follow the hospital work too closely. Her stomach, in fact, did not feel entirely settled; like Tasmin she was experiencing some queasiness in the mornings. She declined to look directly at Lord Berrybender's body, but it did occur to her to wonder whether he would be in possession of any toes and fingers at all, by the time she managed to coax him to the altar, an ambition she had by no means abandoned, despite the steady diminishment of appendages. Captain Aitken did not appear to be overly optimistic, when it came to fingers and toes.

"I expect the boy will lose two fingers, perhaps three, and about as many toes," he said. "There is also some doubt about his right ear."

At this Tim began to blubber loudly.

"Oh, don't let them saw on me, Bess—I can't endure it."

"Now, Tim, Captain Aitken must do as he thinks best," Buffum said, in cool tones.

"I fear His Lordship will lose two toes on his good foot—the leg itself is worrisome, for that matter," Charbonneau said.

"No, the leg is lost—the quicker we take it off, the better," Jim said flatly. This opinion shocked Vicky Kennet and so outraged Lord Berrybender that he immediately struggled off the bed.

"Nonsense, you shan't have my leg—be damned if I'll surrender my leg!" he said. "Who are you anyway, you young fool?"

"He's your son-in-law, Father—my husband, Jim Snow," Tasmin said.

"What? Son-in-law—and he wants to take off my leg, which is a perfectly good leg . . . perhaps rather numbed at the moment but a very adequate leg . . . carried me faithfully on many hunts," Lord B. protested. "The damn young butcher, why would he want to take my leg?"

"Because it's frozen," Charbonneau said, as matter-of-fact about the matter as Jim had been. "Apt to go putrid on you when it thaws. Last thing you'd want is a black leg—that'll kill you pretty quick."

"Get out, all of you! Take that blubbering stable boy and go!" Lord Berrybender demanded. "My Vicky can manage a touch of frostbite well enough . . . fortunately not squeamish, my Vicky. Nothing wrong with me that a fast bout with Vicky won't fix."

"Sir, vigorous rubbing is your best chance," Captain Aitken pointed out. "It won't save your toes but it just might save your leg."

"Vicky can rub me, then," Lord Berrybender insisted. "None better than my Vicky when it comes to rubbing."

"I do so dislike the word 'putrid,' " Vicky Kennet said in a somewhat strangled voice; suddenly her vision began to wobble. Lord Berrybender was ordering everybody out. There he sat, almost naked, his leg possibly putrid. The thought of a putrid appendage caused Vicky's queasiness to increase. She seemed to see the people in the room through an ever narrowing circle. Narrower and narrower the circle got until finally she could only see Lady Berrybender's old parrot, perched on the headboard of the bed where Lord Berrybender had received his rubbing. The circle shrunk to a pinpoint and then there was blackness, deep restful blackness.

"Quick, Jim, catch her . . . Vicky's fainting," Tasmin said.

Jim Snow spun and caught the collapsing cellist in his arms—in a moment he had deposited her on the bed from which the old lord had just risen. Lord Berrybender was far from pleased by this event. He didn't like seeing his Vicky in the arms of a young peasant, even if she *was* fainting. This same young peasant had somehow married his daughter, cream of the Berrybenders—and, were that not enough, the young upstart advised cutting off his leg. All in all it was too much—how inconvenient of Vicky to choose such a moment to faint.

"Mary, quick, run to Cook—the smelling salts!" Lord Berrybender commanded. "Why must this damn woman faint, just when I need her to be rubbing my leg?"

He stumbled back to the bed and began to slap Venetia Kennet's face—light slaps, to be sure.

"Wake up, Vicky . . . that's enough now . . . important job to do . . . no fudging, my girl," Lord B. said. "Get out, the rest of you."

One by one the company obeyed: Tim, still blubbering, Buffum, Bobbety, Captain Aitken, Maelgwyn, Charbonneau.

"Stop that, Father—Vicky's worn-out from worry," Tasmin said—her father was still fitfully swatting the unconscious girl. "Be generous for once. Allow her a little nap."

"None of your business what I allow her," Lord B. responded. "It's all your fault anyway, you disobedient wench."

Jim Snow whirled, grabbed Lord Berrybender by the shoulders, and shoved him so hard that he reeled across the room, smacked hard against the wall, and sat down. Tasmin saw the flinty look in her husband's eyes.

"You old devil, I ought to cut your stinkin' heart out," Jim said.

Lord Berrybender had not, in many years, received quite such a shock.

"What did the fellow say, Tassie?" Lord B. asked.

"He said he ought to cut your stinking heart out, and I expect he will unless you promptly correct your behavior."

"Cut my heart out—cut my leg off—and you married this butcher?" Lord Berrybender said, in rather subdued tones.

On the bed, Venetia Kennet was just beginning to stir.

"I married him, I'm very glad to say," Tasmin replied. "First man I've met who knows how to treat a selfish old brute such as yourself."

As they passed out the door she shyly took her husband's hand. This time Jim did not shove her away.

57

. . . dresses, hairbrushes, combs, mirrors . . .

I'll say this, Jimmy—being married to you ain't like anything else," Tasmin said, once she had her husband in her bedroom. "Perhaps that's why I crave you so—I was always the one for novelty.

"I admit that I am somewhat untidy," she added. "But then I've always had a maid to pick up after me, and now I don't."

Tasmin's plan had been to coax Jim immediately into conjugal activity, but in fact the bed where such activity could be best pursued was at the moment a distressing litter: dresses, hairbrushes, combs, mirrors, several novels, slippers, an intimate garment or two, a spyglass, this and that. Jim seemed thunderstruck at the mere sight of so many things—her room, Tasmin realized, was the very opposite of his own spare existence.

Once inside the bedroom, with the door shut, Jim had permitted a kiss, but just as Tasmin was settling into it, hoping even sharper intimacies might follow, Jim pulled away and stationed himself at the window, as if to spy out the approach of enemies. Tasmin was quite vexed.

"Oh, Jimmy . . . why mightn't I kiss you? I've waited so long!" she protested. "We're quite secure here—no one would dare disturb us."

"You don't know what you're talking about," Jim said. "You never do. What's that funny smell?"

"Oh, it's just Mama's scent—I took it under protection so Mademoiselle wouldn't be tempted to steal it," Tasmin admitted. She had taken to daubing a little on, now and then, to block the various stenches from the river.

"Makes my nose prickle," Jim said. "Can't you wash it off?"

"Good lord," Tasmin said, a bit exasperated. "You said yourself that Indian women anoint themselves with various greases. Why is my mother's scent so much more objectionable? You smell rather greasy yourself, but *I* don't care."

She rushed over and began to try to straighten her bed, or at least reduce the disorder on its surface; then, in her annoyance, she simply swept everything she could reach onto the floor—combs, books, brushes—a happy result of which was the rediscovery of a ruby brooch, once her mother's, that she had also chosen to protect from Mademoiselle Pellenc. She had looked for it for days, and there it was, beneath a small volume of Miss Edgeworth's edifying stories.

Jim Snow watched with frank curiosity, as if he were observing the activities of some new animal whose den he had just discovered. Tasmin felt herself growing distraught—she had never made a bed and found the process more complicated than she would have supposed. In fact she felt like crying because of the general resistance everything—sheets, objects, her husband—seemed to make to her efforts.

"I don't understand it, Jim—why can't you ever like *anything* I do?" she stammered—and then burst into tears. She had waited for this man through many lonely nights—all she craved was his sympathy, a touch, a look. That she couldn't just *have* it seemed too cruel.

Jim Snow was taken aback. He had been mild with Tasmin—why on earth was she crying? The fact was he didn't like being in small, close rooms. Except for his brief stay with Maelgwyn and an hour in Dan Drew's cave, he had not been indoors in several months. It meant adjusting his breathing and his looking: his habit was to study the distant horizons, where the first signs of danger were likely to appear, but the only way to do that, in Tasmin's room, was to stay by the window, which is where he stationed himself. Being on a boat crowded up with people, one of them a dangerous Piegan, made him feel tense, wary. He felt he ought to stay on the alert—and yet there was nothing in his caution that should have made Tasmin cry. He pulled a curtain across the glass and sat down by her on the bed, wiping her tears away with his finger.

"Sometimes it feels so easy, being with you, Jimmy," Tasmin said. "But other times it feels so hard. I forget what to say. I don't want you to slap me again . . . it's very confusing."

"Now, I just slapped you the once, and that was for talking wrong," Jim said. "You've been flapping your mouth ever since we met, but you haven't talked wrong except that once."

"What did I say? I don't know what talking wrong means," Tasmin said, feeling that the whole thing was hopeless. "Couldn't you just explain your-self, rather than slap me?"

"Ever seen ferrets rut?" he asked. The question took Tasmin by sur-prise.

"Why no, I haven't, Jim—where would I see ferrets rut, and why would I want to?" she asked.

"You've got that musk smell on you," Jim said. He carefully sniffed the soft flesh of her neck—Tasmin was so surprised that she shivered.

"It's just Mama's scent," she said, hoping it was not going to be a reason for fresh reproaches.

Jim continued to sniff her neck.

"I expect you've been missing our ruts," he said, after a moment.

"I have . . . of course I have," she said, startled that he had put it so baldly. "I *have* been missing our ruts."

She turned to face him, then. The tension that had gripped him when he first came into her room—a kind of caged animal tension—had left him, but another, different kind of animality was in his look.

"Is that why women cry? Because they're missing their ruts?" he asked.

"It's one reason, I suppose," Tasmin said.

"Then hush up crying," Jim said. "We can have us a good long rut, right now."

"Oh, Jimmy, let's do," Tasmin said, blushing deeply at the thought that at last she would get what she craved.

58

"The white people will die like the grasshoppers die in the summer . . ."

White Hawk, the best hunter in the Sans Arc band, was pursuing six wolves when he came upon the small bloody white man. It was very cold— the wolf pelts, if he could take them, would be at their best, deep and soft. Wolves were hard to shoot, it was true, but White Hawk preferred hunting them to trapping beaver—with wolves, for one thing, it was not necessary to get one's feet wet, an important consideration when the cold was so bitter.

White Hawk had come across the wolf tracks only a little after dawn. He was hunting with Three Geese and a boy named Grasshopper. They saw the wolves some distance ahead—they were eating something. The three Sans Arc hunters had provided themselves with wolf skins for just such an eventuality. By pulling the wolf skins over them they might be able to crawl in rifle range, particularly since the wolves were making a meal and not paying too close attention.

On this occasion Three Geese refused to crawl—he was often finicky on a hunt, likely to pout if things weren't done his way.

"Suit yourself, stay with the horses, then," White Hawk said. He was rather fed up with Three Geese—nonetheless he and the boy, Grasshopper, hidden beneath their wolf skins, crawled close enough to the wolves to see that they were eating a just-born buffalo calf. Four of the wolves were skinny, but two of them were nice fat wolves, with excellent pelts. White Hawk had a good musket, supplied by his French friend Monsieur Sacq, but Grasshopper's gun was old and unreliable. The boy had tried to borrow Three Geese's musket, but the touchy warrior wouldn't lend it.

"I had better keep it, some bad people might be coming along," Three

Geese said, an excuse that merely exposed what a stingy fellow he was, since no people at all were likely to be coming along, with the cold so bitter along the Knife River.

When they had crawled close enough, White Hawk killed his wolf neatly, but Grasshopper's gun misfired, causing him to say bitter words about Three Geese—he would have liked to have a nice wolf pelt to trade at the Mandan villages in the spring. It was while the boy was spilling out bitter words that the small bloody white man appeared, startling them both. Grasshopper wanted to shoot him at once, but White Hawk waved him off. He was interested in how the small man had got so bloody, a mystery that was soon solved. A dead buffalo cow lay not far away—probably the cow had died giving birth to the calf. The cow buffalo had not been dead very long. It looked as if the small white man had stumbled on the dying cow and had tried to warm himself by trying to squeeze into the place the calf had just come out of, which of course was a sensible thing to do if you had no fire on such a cold night. Finding the split-open cow, a large cow that had kept pumping warm blood, was probably what had saved the little white man.

The small bloody man did not seem hostile—he was very bloody and also very cold. White Hawk had no particular interest in him—he had his wolf to skin—and would have been happy enough just to let the man wander off and freeze; but then Three Geese came racing up and jumped to the wrong conclusion, which was that the buffalo cow had given birth to the small white man, along with the dead calf. It was typical of Three Geese's poor thinking that he could imagine such a thing. Three Geese often leapt to ridiculous conclusions, which he clung to stubbornly, sometimes for years.

Grasshopper, a boy of only fourteen years, became so confused that he didn't know what to believe. This did not surprise White Hawk—Three Geese could be very convincing when he jumped to a wrong conclusion.

"We must take him to the camp," Three Geese insisted. "I think the Bad Eye made a prophecy about this. I think he said that someday a buffalo would give birth to a white man."

"No, that was not the prophecy at all," White Hawk told him—he was working carefully with his skinning knife, so as not to mar his fine wolf pelt. The last thing he wanted was to argue with Three Geese about some old prophecy of the Bad Eye that Three Geese had got all scrambled in his memory.

"What *was* the prophecy, then, if you know so much?" Three Geese asked. Seeing the fine wolf pelt White Hawk had taken made him angry with himself—he should have crawled up and got a nice wolf pelt himself.

Grasshopper built a little fire, thinking they might as well cook a little of the dead buffalo. No sooner did the fire flame than the small white man came and huddled over it, shivering violently.

"What the Bad Eye said was that someday a white buffalo would be born," White Hawk explained, patiently. "When the white buffalo is born it will be a sign for all the tribes to band together and kill all the white people. The white buffalo will bring us all the power we need. The white people will die like the grasshoppers die in the summer, when we set the prairie on fire."

Three Geese refused to accept White Hawk's version of the prophecy, even though he dimly remembered that someone had talked about a white buffalo—it had been idle talk, very likely. He himself had seen millions of buffalo and none of them had been white. Of course, the tribes were always talking about killing all the white people; there were many councils on that subject, but the chiefs could never get together and decide on a time to do it, or a way to do it, either. Personally Three Geese thought there were just too many white people—an old witch of the Brulé band told him once that there was a great hole in the earth where white people swarmed by the millions, like hornets. The old witch woman of the Brulés said that no matter how many white people were killed, more would just come swarming out of the hole. But the old woman had been more or less crazy—most prophets, including the Bad Eye, were more or less crazy in Three Geese's view. Nonetheless he was not prepared to yield to the bossy White Hawk in the matter of this particular white man.

"He wouldn't be that bloody unless he came out of the buffalo," he declared.

Three Geese was so firm on that point that the boy, Grasshopper, began to have doubts himself. Perhaps the white man did come out of the buffalo. Grasshopper didn't know it for sure, but he was anxious not to get on the bad side of Three Geese by disagreeing with his opinion too openly. Three Geese was known to be vengeful—he held grudges against many of the Sans Arc people and other Sioux as well. Grasshopper didn't want Three Geese to get a grudge against him, so he tried to be respectful of his belief about the white man.

"We need to find somebody who can talk to this buffalo man," Three

Geese insisted. "Guillaume or Draga or somebody. We had better take him with us until we know what his story is."

"Oh, all right—leave me alone," White Hawk said.

Three Geese went over to the fire and tried to talk to the little white man in sign, but the white man had not the slightest ability to converse in sign—in Three Geese's opinion this fact alone proved his point. If the white man was at all normal he would know how to talk in sign.

"He must have come straight out of that buffalo," Three Geese insisted. "He cannot even talk in sign."

"All right . . . all right . . . ," White Hawk said. Why argue with a fool? He was not feeling particularly well, and even if he had been feeling better, would have had quite enough of arguing with Three Geese. He finished taking his fine pelt and ate a bite or two of buffalo liver that Grasshopper cooked for him, though his appetite was not strong.

By the time White Hawk and the others, with their small white captive, got back to the Sans Arc lodges, White Hawk had begun to feel hot and weak. He nearly fell when he got off his horse—his wives had to help him to his lodge. That night his fever soared and he began to have strange dreams—he dreamed of a white buffalo, and then of a white man who had buffalo horns coming out of his head. The medicine men came and gave him strong emetics, hoping to force the terrible fever out of him; but the medicine men failed. Gripped by a great illness, White Hawk died before dawn.

Privately Three Geese thought White Hawk died because he had scorned the prophecy about the buffalo man. Grasshopper became very worried; after all, he too had been doubtful of the prophecy. What if the big fever took him too? To give himself the best possible chance he told everybody that he agreed with Three Geese: the white man, still shivering, still bloody, had undoubtedly been born of a buffalo cow.

The women of the tribe cleaned the white man up, gave him some clothes of skins, and fixed him a small lodge, so he wouldn't be cold. They also gave him two twin captive girls, fat ones, just to make sure he stayed warm.

Soon people from other bands—Brulé, Miniconjou, Oglala—trickled into the Sans Arc camp, to hear the story and examine the miraculous being. News of the miracle soon reached Draga, who was very annoyed. She had no aversion to miracles, but if a miracle was needed she wanted to produce it herself, not have it happen in some remote camp of the Sans Arc.

"It's your fault," she informed the Bad Eye bitterly. "You talked about a white buffalo so much that it confused everyone. Now the Sans Arc think they have a Buffalo Man."

The Bad Eye immediately pulled the great cape the Englishman had given him over his head.

"I am going in a trance now," he said. "I'll listen to the spirits—they might know about this."

He didn't really know what to think about the strange news that the Sans Arc had themselves some kind of Buffalo Man, but he did know that when Draga used that deadly tone with him it was just as well to hurry up and get in a trance.

59

Three horsemen on unshod horses had recently passed...

Despite the deep cold, Maelgwyn Evans and Toussaint Charbonneau went ashore and dutifully gathered up Lord Berrybender's expensive guns. Then they made a bit of a search for Gladwyn—a search made with not much expectation that they would find the lost valet alive.

"I guess we ought to try and scratch him out some kind of grave, if we find him," Maelgwyn said. "It's a hard way to go, froze in a blizzard like that."

"The wolves may not have left enough to bury," Charbonneau said.

They had gone not more than half a mile from the circle of dead buffalo dropped by Lord Berrybender when they came upon a puzzling scene. Three horsemen on unshod horses had recently passed. There was a dead wolf, newly skinned; a dead buffalo cow, not skinned, but partially butchered; a dead buffalo calf, mostly eaten by wolves; and one of Gladwyn's shoes, covered with frozen blood. The shoe was close by the dead buffalo cow. A few live coals still glowed in the campfire.

"I guess he ain't dead, your Welshman," Charbonneau said. "He's just half barefooted."

"And besides that he's taken," Maelgwyn said.

"That beats being dead," Charbonneau replied.

"Maybe . . . it depends on who took him, and what kind of mood they're in," Maelgwyn said. "Some Indians can be pretty mean—he might escape the ice and get the fire."

"That's the chances a fellow takes—this Knife River country ain't for me," Charbonneau said. "It'll cheer up Eliza, though . . . she'll be glad to know that the fellow might be alive."

"Oh, you mean that girl who tried to jump overboard—the one I caught by the foot?" Maelgwyn asked.

"That's the gal, our clumsy Eliza—she's bad about bustin' the crockery," Charbonneau said. "And here we didn't even know she fancied the fellow till overboard she went."

60

"Who says our pleasures are languid?"

Once coaxed to bed, Jim Snow was not stingy with his attentions—Tasmin felt that her wait had been well worth it. They were at their conjugal occupations most of the morning, the satisfactions of which were intense; and yet all their sweet meltings and mergings did not quite reconcile Jim Snow to the closeness of the stateroom, or make him much less wary where possible enemies were concerned. His rifle was propped by the head of the bed, a circumstance that made Tasmin nervous. She was in the mood to let herself go and didn't want to have to be worrying about a rifle.

"What if it falls and goes off, like Papa's did?" she asked. "What if I buck around too wildly and knock it over?"

"Buck all you want—it won't shoot," Jim assured her. It was far too close in the stateroom—their bed was now a swamp of sweat. Jim wanted to open the window, or even the door, but people were always passing along the walkways—with the window open anyone would be sure to hear the sighings and squealings that went with a good long rut. As soon as they satisfied themselves for the day Jim meant to take Tasmin and get off the boat, back into the open air, where he could breathe better; but they were not soon finished.

In one interlude Tasmin made Jim sit up in bed so she could trim his beard again. It was one of her favorite activities as a wife, trimming Jimmy's beard and snipping a vagrant lock or two of his hair.

"Where will we be when I drop our child, as you put it, Jimmy?" she asked.

Jim Snow shrugged. "We'll just be where we are—somewhere on the Yellowstone, probably, unless you're still in the mood to go to Santa Fe—and this ain't the best place to start from, or the best time of year to start."

"I just mean that I hope you'll be with me and not off on one of your rambles," she said. Though she still felt tremors of pleasure in her body, and was for the moment a happy wife, the thought of the child worried her. She did not want to be without him when it came.

"Don't be walking off like that, you hear?" he said, looking her directly in the eye. "I thought you'd soon come back or I would have chased you down."

As for where they would be when the baby came, what could he say? The baby was six months away, and they could all be in bad trouble within six hours, if the Sioux showed up in an ugly mood. Where they were when the baby came was not too important, as long as they were somewhere where game was plentiful.

"Get your warmest clothes and let's go," he said. "I feel like I'm choking, from being in this close air."

"All right, Jimmy," Tasmin said. "But all this rutting's made me a little weak in the legs—I'm not sure I can tramp very far today."

She began to rake around in her tiny closet for anything that looked warm. Jim watched her pull out garment after garment, amazed at the supply of clothes his wife had. He felt sure he could get through his whole life with fewer clothes than she had just piled on the bed.

Tasmin stuffed a valise, then put on the loose shirt of skins the Oto woman had sewed for her—she was gathering up hairbrushes and combs and a book or two when there was a knock on the door. Jim immediately took his gun, but Tasmin peeked out the window and saw that it was only her sister Mary.

"It's only our brat," she said—"might as well let her in."

Mary, once in the room, stopped and sniffed.

"I smell lubricious secretions," she said; the look in her eye, as usual, was not entirely sane.

"What of it?—there are very likely to be such odors when husbands and wives have been about their natural work," Tasmin said.

Jim Snow had never seen anyone quite like this little English girl who used strange long words; he recalled that when he first saw her she seemed to be talking to a serpent—a white-mouthed moccasin, in fact.

"We have all been waiting patiently for you and Mr. Snow to finish fornicating—a number of crises need attention," Mary said. "Are you through yet?"

"For the moment," Tasmin said. "Jim wishes to leave the boat—he finds the air rather close. What's this about crises?"

"Well, there's Father's amputation," Mary said. "He still opposes it but medical opinion is that the limb will soon rot. And then there's the ice—we're stuck fast now. Captain Aitken was very much hoping Mr. Snow would visit him on the bridge before he departs. You can come too, Tasmin."

"Of course I can come," Tasmin said. "I hope I don't need you to invite me."

"Fortunately Monsieur Charbonneau and Mr. Evans have found all Papa's guns," Mary said. "Papa was much reassured."

"What about that third man—did they find him?" Jim inquired.

"No, Gladwyn they did not find—merely one shoe, rather bloodstained."

"How odd," Tasmin said. "The rest of Gladwyn must be somewhere."

"Abducted by red savages of the Sans Arc band, that is the theory," Mary said. "Unfortunately the Piegan, Blue Thunder, left this morning, while you two were about your languid pleasures."

Tasmin gave her a thump on the head.

"Watch your tongue," she said. "Who says our pleasures are languid?"

"That's two out of three of Charbonneau's Indians gone," Jim observed.

"Yes, Monsieur Charbonneau is very upset—the Piegan disappeared while they were looking for the guns—Monsieur feels the failure keenly," Mary said.

61

"It's win all, lose all, in this game, Sharbo..."

Captain George Aitken, not entirely sober, had to face the fact of defeat. Upriver there was no longer an open flow: the ice had come. Already several buffalo were sniffing around where, only the day before, there had been rushing water. With the Yellowstone still more than one hundred miles away, the captain had to admit that the race had been lost, and the boat might be too, unless he was lucky. He knew that no excuse available to him—sandbars, mud banks, broken paddles, ice that formed earlier than had been expected—would move his employers to tolerance. Sandbars and ice were merely words to them; they had never stood where he stood, looking at the unforgiving line of cloud and a few cautious buffalo, already testing their icy bridge over the Missouri. All his employers would consider was the fact that the steamer *Rocky Mount* had not got where it was supposed to deliver its expensive human cargo. The failure would be reckoned his fault—indeed, he reckoned it so himself, although, tracing his way back day by day, he could not fault any of his hour-to-hour decisions.

"It's win all, lose all, in this game, Sharbo," he said. "Win all, lose all. And we ain't winning."

Toussaint Charbonneau, upon discovering that the third of his charges— Blue Thunder, of the Piegan Blackfoot—had left the boat and vanished, immediately took to his cups. He felt himself beaten. Only the Hairy Horn, the one Indian he would have been glad to lose, remained on—indeed, could not be persuaded to leave—the boat. Captain William Clark was not going to like it.

Only two weeks before, steaming past two villages of the Omahas, Charbonneau had awakened in the dawn, stirred, as he always was on that stretch of the river, by the memory of his Bird, Sacagawea. There, on the shore, were the remains of the fur king Manuel Lisa's old fort, now fallen badly out of repair. It was in that same fort, twenty years before, that Sacagawea had been seized by a putrid fever; she had died just at dusk and had been buried that same night, outside the fort, as a precaution against the spread of the fever. Charbonneau could never float past her grave, as he had several times, without heaving a sigh and shedding a tear. He had been far from alone in mourning his Bird Woman. All the rough trappers vied to carry her to her grave; all acknowledged that she had been the finest woman in the fort. Even Manuel Lisa, who had seen more death on the Missouri River than any other man, came out of his quarters and stood in silence by Sacagawea's grave.

Every time he passed the spot where she lay it seemed to Charbonneau that Janey—as Captain Clark had called her—stretched out a hand to him, as if asking him to join her in easeful sleep—yet, somehow, his stubborn body kept living, despite many ills and discontents.

Now here he was, stuck in the ice north of the Knife River, more than a week's hard march from adequate shelter, with a bunch of English he didn't much like, having lost two of the three Indians that had been specifically entrusted to his care by Captain Clark. They were important Indians, honored guests of the nation, and losing them was no small thing—if the Piegan happened to get killed, as Big White had, it would surely affect relations with the Blackfeet, and relations with the Blackfeet were never easy. It seemed to Charbonneau that he could have managed better if only his Bird had lived. Coal was a fine healthy girl, but only a child, really. It was not to be expected that she could manage things as well as Sacagawea, who, after all, had carried their boy, little Pomp, all the way from the Mandan villages to the Western ocean and back, on their great trek with the captains, while managing to keep himself in good order and half the company besides.

When Tasmin and Jim, led by Mary and trailed by George Catlin, went up to the bridge they found that neither Captain Aitken nor Toussaint Charbonneau were in particularly good repair.

"We're stuck, Jimmy—stuck," Captain Aitken said. "I was too slow about the river, and now we're stuck."

He looked at Jim Snow and Lady Tasmin, blooming and blushing as if they had just awakened from a fine wedding night—the sight made George Aitken feel old.

"Why is that so bad, Captain?" Tasmin asked. "You have a snug boat, and there seem to be plenty of buffalo around, in case we run low on vittles. We brought lots of ice skates—our brats can go ice-skating now and then."

George Aitken scarcely knew how to reply. Lady Tasmin was in a state of high health and happiness—she had no inkling of the perils that awaited them in the frigid months ahead. Jim Snow, her young mate, seemed to offer altogether the best hope. If Jim would agree to guide a land party over to the Yellowstone they might get through the winter without much loss. There was a wagon and a buggy in the hold, and four horses. If they could only get a little break in the weather, a few days of warming, the situation might yet be saved.

Captain Aitken was about to ask Jimmy Snow to help them when pandemonium suddenly broke loose on the lower deck. There was a gunshot—then another gunshot. Then came a chorus of high screams, merging with low French curses and exclamations of despair from the *engagés*. Those on the bridge rushed to the rail and were astonished to see several *engagés*, evidently wild with terror, piling into one of the pirogues, which of course was immovably stuck in the ice.

"Quick, Sharbo, go see!" Captain Aitken ordered. "Is the Hairy Horn running amok?"

"Not the Hairy Horn—it's our papa, I expect," Mary said, darting fleetly down the stairs.

Charbonneau tried to follow, but got his feet tangled up and fell flat on his face.

"Get up, Sharbo, this won't do," the captain said, though he was none too steady himself.

"Very likely it *is* only Papa—he's always more or less amok," Tasmin said. "I think that's Vicky Kennet screaming—there's no telling what outrage the selfish old brute has committed."

"He must be shooting at the Frenchies . . . they all look pretty scared," Jim said.

"Perhaps Father Geoff could speak to him—priests are supposed to soothe unruly souls," George Catlin suggested.

"You're an optimist, George," Tasmin said. "Our fine priest is probably hiding under a bed—either that or he's in Mademoiselle's room, reading indecent literature.

"I expect you think we're all crazy, we English, don't you, Jim?" she asked, looking shyly at her husband. "These alarums are merely the stuff of day-to-day life, when the Berrybenders are assembled."

"We ought to be getting ashore," Jim said politely.

Tasmin was right—he *did* think the English were more or less crazy. His own main desire was simply to get away with Tasmin, to the emptiness and peace of the country, where it was easier to breathe and even easier to think.

"Ha, the great theft is revealed," Mary said, popping back up the stairs. "It's the claret. Papa sent Vicky to fetch him a bottle from the keelboat, whereupon it was discovered that there *is* no more claret. The *engagés* drank it all, every bottle."

"All? A thousand bottles?" Tasmin asked.

"All," Mary repeated.

"But why is Vicky screaming so, she's not an *engagé?*" Tasmin asked.

"No, but she's being blamed," Mary said. "Papa's chasing her with a horsewhip."

"I wouldn't mind if we left now, myself," Tasmin said. Jimmy had taken her hand, which she liked very much. Once again she felt like a wife, wanted. She did not intend to make the mistake of leaving her husband again.

"But Jim, we've the amputation to do, when His Lordship quiets down— and then we'll be needing a guide, to get this bunch to the fort," Captain Aitken pleaded.

Jim looked at Tasmin—it was mainly her family involved. George Aitken was in a bad spot—it would be hard to deny him a little help.

"Drat! Not for a minute of my life has Papa managed to do the convenient thing," Tasmin said. "What should we do, Jimmy?"

She gave his hand a squeeze, and to her delight he squeezed back.

"He's your pa, and he'll die if we don't get that leg off," Jim said. "I guess we better sharpen the saw."

62

Draga had brought some poison with her . . .

When the dark woman, Draga, came to the Sans Arc camp to attempt to discredit him and have him put to death, Gladwyn confounded her by speaking in Gaelic. In the whole time that he had been captive not a word of English had passed his lips; if the people thought he was just an ordinary Englishman, they would probably kill him.

In fact he knew little enough Gaelic—just a few songs and scraps of legend and rhyme, but to the Sans Arc it sounded like the babble of a Buffalo Man; it was enough to save him.

There were, unfortunately, a number of skeptics in the Sans Arc camp, older people mostly, who didn't believe for a minute that this skinny stranger had been born of a buffalo. But the Gaelic at least made them uncertain— no one had ever heard such strange speech. Three Geese, Gladwyn's main sponsor, considered the fact that the stranger spoke an unearthly language proof enough of his extraordinary origin.

"You see?" Three Geese said. "He is not speaking white man's language. That's buffalo he's speaking."

Old Cat Head, the most flagrant of the skeptics, was not convinced.

"I have never heard a buffalo speak like that," he pointed out. "I have never heard a buffalo say anything."

Cat Head didn't want to yield any ground to Three Geese, who had been much too full of himself since he brought the small white man to the village; but even he *was* rather startled by the strange language the white man babbled. At first Cat Head would have been happy just to hit the white man in the head with a good hatchet, but the strange babble caused him to waver. Even if the white man hadn't come out of the womb of a buffalo, he was still a peculiar man. Cat Head thought he might be some kind of holy fool—there was no point in acting rashly. Killing a holy fool could bring all sorts of calamities down on the people.

Draga did not welcome the presence of this Buffalo Man in the Sans Arc village. She knew he had come from the white men's big boat—the Thunder Boat, the Bad Eye called it—and she told the people as much, but to her annoyance, she was greeted with insults and sneers. The Sans Arc had always been independent and aloof. They scorned corn growers such as the Mandans; they were people of the buffalo and did not consider themselves subject to Draga's wishes, or the Bad Eye's either. Draga had brought some poison with her but the Sans Arc were not about to let her poison their holy fool. They never let her near the little man, lest she stab him or try to interfere with his food.

Draga had not expected to have much luck with the Sans Arc—like all the Sioux bands, they were difficult; but she had made the trip to the camp anyway, in order to bring the Bad Eye a report. Now that he was too fat to move around much he had begun to worry about messiahs and other prophets. It made him anxious to think that there was a Buffalo Man of some sort living with the standoffish Sans Arc. Any little threat caused him to build a new sweat lodge or go into a big trance. In two minutes Draga could easily have beaten the little white man to death with a stone, or even a big stick—but the Sans Arc maintained a good guard, so good that she was forced to go back to the skull lodge and report complete failure.

"A Sans Arc named Three Geese started all this," she said. "And that's not all."

"What else?" the Bad Eye asked. He hated bad news.

"They have given the white man two wives," she said.

"Is that all?" the Bad Eye asked. "Why should I care how many wives they give him?"

"These wives are twins," Draga continued. "They are called Big Stealer and Little Stealer, although they are the same size."

"Why are you bringing me all this terrible news?" the Bad Eye exclaimed. That the Buffalo Man should be married to twins was the worst possible news. Twins always had formidable powers—twins married to a Buffalo Man could lead to any number of calamities: wars, pestilence, flood. The old women were already talking about the likelihood of a great flood in the spring; there was too much snow upriver, they had heard. A terrible flood might even threaten the skull lodge—the Bad Eye might have to move himself to higher ground, which would be a lot of trouble.

"Maybe this Buffalo Man will just get sick and die, twins or no twins," he said.

"We won't be rid of him that easily," Draga said darkly.

Gladwyn was not quite sure what kind of special person he was supposed to be, but it was clear that the people who had taken him were determined to treat him well. They made him a warm tent and fed him tender buffalo liver and their fattest puppies. His bloody clothes were taken away and a suit of soft, warm skins was fashioned for him. He was not required to do any work at all. The most they required of him was that he come and sit outside his tent, by the campfire, when visitors came to see him. The boy Grasshopper was given a lance and made to stand guard so that no one could threaten him or get too close. He was always guarded; Three Geese saw to that. It was no secret that the Brulés and the Miniconjous were jealous of the fact that the Sans Arc had a Buffalo Man. There was danger that some envious warrior might just walk up and stab him out of pique. Grasshopper was told to lance anyone who made a suspicious move.

All Gladwyn had meant to do, when he stumbled away from Lord Berrybender in the terrible blizzard, was die somewhere out of range of the old man's hated voice. Lord Berrybender continued to give him orders even as they were freezing, orders about guns, orders about firewood. Gladwyn, His Lordship's man for many years, decided to die as his own man. He was about to curl up and let the blowing snow cover him forever when he had the great luck to stumble on to the buffalo cow just as she was laboring to get her calf out. Something had gone wrong in the birthing; the calf wouldn't quite come free, and when it finally did, with Gladwyn pulling and tugging at the warm calf, the cow's lifeblood came too, only slowly—so slowly that Gladwyn was able to use her warmth to keep alive. She was still alive when the six wolves came and began to eat her calf, though she died and was growing cold when the Indians came.

At first, when he was not sure what his captors meant to do with him, Gladwyn gave some thought to escape—but his half-formed plans were soon abandoned. He would probably just get lost and freeze after all, and even if he were very lucky and managed to get back to the boat, what would it gain him? He would once again be merely Lord Berrybender's man. When the theft of the claret was discovered, very likely *he* would be the one blamed.

Once in a while he did miss Eliza, Cook's fumble-fingered assistant, who readily offered her ample body to his embraces; but once the Sans Arc presented him with twin wives even Eliza soon faded from memory. It was true that the twins, Big Stealer and Little Stealer, bickered constantly, and sometimes grew so hot that they came to blows—but that was only to be expected of sisters. Him they never neglected. When he wasn't on show for envious visitors he lounged in his tent, naked amid warm robes. His efficient wives rubbed him with oils, attended quickly to his lusts, and even fed him with their fingers—tender morsels from the stew pot.

Gladwyn had no way of knowing how long his comfortable celebrity would last, but he didn't trouble himself by looking ahead. His lodge was warm, his wives competent, the prairies thick with buffalo. The tribe gave him a pipe and ample tobacco; his wives kept his pipe filled; Gladwyn smoked and rested. Blizzards blew, snow fell, geese probed in the Mandan corn, wolves howled, the hunting birds—eagle, hawk, owl—hung in the white sky or came dropping down on sage hen, quail, hare, or the incautious rat; the great bears slept in their dens, buffalo pawed the snow and grazed, while the Sans Arc hunters made many kills; slowly, in this way, the winter passed.

VOLUME TWO

THE WANDERING HILL

Contents

Characters

Mountain Men

Hugh Glass
Tom Fitzpatrick (The Broken Hand)
Jim Bridger
Kit Carson
Eulalie Bonneville
Joe Walker
Milt Sublette
Bill Sublette
Zeke Williams

From *Sin Killer*

Lord Berrybender
Tasmin
Bess (Buffum)
Bobbety
Mary
Sister Ten (*later,* Kate)

Gladwyn, *valet, gun bearer*
Cook
Eliza, *kitchen maid*
Millicent, *laundress*
Venetia Kennet, *cellist*
Señor Yanez, *gunsmith*
Signor Claricia, *carriage maker*
Piet Van Wely, *naturalist*
Tim, *stable boy*

Father Geoffrin, *Jesuit*
Jim Snow (The Raven Brave; Sin Killer)
Toussaint Charbonneau, *interpreter-guide*
Coal, *his wife*
George Catlin
John Skraeling
Malgres

New

Pierre Boisdeffre, *trader*
Pomp Charbonneau
William Drummond Stewart
Prince Maximilian zu Wied-Neuwied
Karl Bodmer, *his painter*
William Ashley, *trader*
Herr Hanfstaengl, *Pomp's old tutor*
David Dreidoppel, *Prince Maximilian's hunter*

Indians

The Hairy Horn, *Oglala Sioux*
Little Onion, *Jim's Ute wife*
Otter Woman, *Minataree*
Weedy Boy, *Minataree*
Squirrel, *Minataree*
Blue Thunder, *Piegan Blackfoot*
Climbs Up, *Minataree*
Skunk, *Assiniboine*
Bad Head, *Assiniboine*
Red Crow, *Assiniboine*
Old Moose, *Piegan Blackfoot*
Antelope, *Piegan Blackfoot*
Two Ribs Broken, *Piegan Blackfoot*
The Partezon, *Sioux*
Limping Wolf, *Piegan Blackfoot*
Quiet Calf, *Piegan Blackfoot*
Red Weasel, *Piegan Blackfoot*
Bull, *Piegan Blackfoot*

Red Rabbit, *Piegan Blackfoot*
Wing, *Piegan Blackfoot*
Three Geese, *Sans Arc*
Grasshopper, *Sans Arc*
Cat Head, *Sans Arc*
Big Stealer, *Sans Arc*
Little Stealer, *Sans Arc*
Greasy Lake, *shaman*
Walkura, *Ute*
No Teeth, *Ute*
Na-Ta-Ha, *Ute*
High Shoulders, *Ute*
Skinny Foot, *Ute*

1

. . . tall, gaunt, furious, snow in his hair and beard, and murder in his eyes . . .

The old mountain man—tall, gaunt, furious, snow in his hair and beard, and murder in his eyes—burst into the big room of Pierre Boisdeffre's trading post just as the English party was sitting down to table—the table being only a long trestle of rough planks near the big fireplace, where a great haunch of elk dripped on its spit. Cook had just begun to slice off generous cuts when out of the winter night the wild man stormed. Tom Fitzpatrick, called the Broken Hand, had just been filling a pipe. Before he could fully turn, the tall intruder dealt him a blow that sent him spinning into a barrel of traps—man and barrel fell over with a loud clatter.

"Good Lord, it's old Hugh Glass," Pomp Charbonneau said, turning, Tasmin thought, rather white, a surprising thing to see. Pomp Charbonneau, educated in Germany, as correct with knife and fork as any European, was a man not easily discommoded.

"Hugh Glass he may be, but why has he struck down the Broken Hand?" Mary Berrybender piped, in excited surprise.

Before Pomp could answer, the furious stranger rushed past Tom Fitzpatrick and leapt at young Jim Bridger, who, with his partner, Kit Carson, had been nodding on a pile of blankets—both youngsters, tired from a day of trapping, came unwillingly awake.

"Why, Hugh!" Jim Bridger said—he leapt up just in time to keep the invader from grabbing him by his throat. Pomp Charbonneau half rose from his chair, but then settled back. Several of the mountain men—bald Eulalie Bonneville, Bill Sublette and his brother, Milt, Joe Walker, all of them as shaggy in their tattered buckskins as bears—stumbled hastily out of the way of the combatants. Kit Carson, who managed with difficulty to get his eyes open, soon opened them wider when he saw that his friend Jim Bridger was locked in mortal combat with Hugh Glass.

Kit immediately jumped into the fray, as did Tom Fitzpatrick, once he got free of the traps. Soon several mountain men were clinging to old Hugh's back; they smashed into a shelf, pots fell, crockery broke, and the old parrot Prince Talleyrand, a great favorite with the mountain men, flew up into the rafters to escape the commotion. Pierre Boisdeffre, the proprietor and landlord, rushed out of a storeroom and began to declaim indignantly in French; he surveyed the spreading carnage with dismay. For a moment it seemed to the startled spectators that the old man, in his terrible anger, might defeat them all. Five mountain men clung to his back; soon all of them crashed to the floor and rolled around in confusion, scratching, biting, kicking, as Monsieur Boisdeffre continued his futile protests.

"Hugh Glass is supposed to be dead, killed by a grizzly bear," Pomp explained. Several mountain men now contented themselves with sitting on the old fellow, waiting for his fury to subside.

"If that disputatious gentleman's dead, then he's pretty active for a ghost," Tasmin remarked, indicating to Cook that it was time to serve the cabbage—cabbage was the only thing in the way of a vegetable that the Berrybenders had been able to bring with them on their hard trek overland from the steamer *Rocky Mount,* though a happy consequence of unloading the cabbages was the discovery of their missing sister, Ten, aged four years; little Ten had evidently been living happily amid the cabbages for some weeks, missed by no one.

Some vittles, of course, had to be left with stout Captain Aitken, who had stayed behind to defend his icebound vessel during the chill months ahead. Marooned with him were seven *engagés,* the old Hairy Horn, Toussaint Charbonneau and his young wife, Coal, Master Jeremy Thaw—too damaged from his clubbing at the hands of the late Fräulein Pfretzskaner to survive a hard trek in deep chill—and the Danish painter Holger Sten, who argued that if he came ashore his paints would surely freeze, a consideration that had not deterred the American painter George Catlin from disembarking with the English party. Throughout the lengthy packing and departing the Hairy Horn, half naked, had annoyed them all by repeatedly singing his death song, though everyone had long since stopped expecting the old chieftain to die.

"Tell us, Pomp—why is Mr. Glass so very angry with Jim Bridger and the Broken Hand?" the ever-curious Mary piped.

Pomp was about to attempt an answer, but Tasmin, out of patience with her inquisitive sister, picked up her fork and warned him off.

"We're eating, Mary—no interrogations," Tasmin said. "It's hardly to be considered surprising when mountain men fight—I can think of one I wouldn't mind fighting with myself, if only he'd show himself."

She meant her husband, Jim Snow, known to some as the Sin Killer, who refused absolutely to take his meals at the trading post, or to sleep under its roof, either; a life spent almost entirely outdoors on the raw Western frontier had unfitted Jim Snow for life of an indoor, or civilized, sort. Walls and roofs made him feel so close that he got headaches; he quite refused, despite Tasmin's pregnancy, to contemplate an indoor life, a fact that Tasmin found decidely vexing. Jim cooked his meals at their modest camp overlooking the Yellowstone River, more than a mile away from Pierre Boisdeffre's well-chinked log trading post. Though Tasmin would have preferred to dine with her husband, she was not about to forgo Cook's excellent victuals when she could get them; nonetheless, the fact that her husband refused even to consider coming up the snowy slope to dine with her put Tasmin in a testy mood—a fact of which everyone in the post was by then well aware.

At the far end of the great table the other members of the party—George Catlin, Lord Berrybender, Bobbety, Buffum, Father Geoffrin, Señor Yanez, Signor Claricia, Venetia Kennet, and their nominal host, the tall Scotsman William Drummond Stewart, watched the ongoing struggle of mountain men against mountain man with varying degrees of interest. Lord Berrybender, sitting just across the table from Drum Stewart—as the tall sportsman preferred to be called—took only a momentary interest in the fight, though he did take care to keep his one leg and his good hand under the table, in case knives were drawn. Lord B. had lately become wary of knives—fortunately the struggle seemed to be moderating with no one having recourse to edged weapons as yet. The several trappers now sitting on Hugh Glass were talking to him soothingly, as if to reassure him of their friendship. Even Pierre Boisdeffre had managed to rise above the loss of his crockery—he too spoke to the fallen warrior in mild tones.

"Glad there's no slicing tonight," Lord B. remarked pleasantly. "Every time there's slicing I seem to lose an appendage—how many is it now, Vicky?"

"One leg, seven toes, three fingers," Venetia Kennet reported, without enthusiasm. Venetia had not adjusted well to her young pregnancy; the trip across the frozen wastes had been, for her, a horror. Her cheeks were hollow, her eyes dark-rimmed, her smile now only the mockery of a smile.

And yet Lord Berrybender casually assumed that she would be pleased to keep up with his ever diminishing number of fingers and toes.

"Hear that, Stewart?" His Lordship asked. "I find myself rather whittled down, although fortunately there's been no threat to the principal—perhaps I should say the indispensable—appendage."

"Which would that be, Papa?" Tasmin inquired. In her testy mood she saw no reason to spare her tablemates whatever grossness her father chose to come forth with.

"Why, the organ of generation—you know what I mean, Tasmin," Lord Berrybender insisted. "My favorite appendage by a long shot, I can tell you that."

"I hardly see why you should be so proud of a mere prick," Tasmin told him coolly. "All it's got you is a collection of violent brats and bitches. I'm sure you know how our sainted mother used to refer to it, within the confines of the nursery, of course."

"Er . . . no . . . why would my dear Constance call it anything?" Lord B. inquired, growing rather red in the face. Tasmin's shocking impertinence often took him by surprise.

"'Papa's big nasty,' that's what she called it!" Mary yelled, before her sister Buffum could drive her off with a few sharp slaps.

"Thank you, Mary—you're precise for once," Tasmin said.

"I don't thank her," Buffum said. "How painful to hear obscenity out of the mouth of a child, here on the Yellowstone in the year of our Lord 1833," she intoned.

"My daughter Tasmin has a tongue like an asp," Lord B. observed, under his breath, to Drum Stewart. "Don't argue with her, Stewart—just slap her if she annoys."

Drum Stewart made no reply—he was happy, at such time, to take refuge in Scots taciturnity. Though he was soon to be the seventh baronet of Murthly, the vast family seat in Perthshire, Drum walked with the trappers, slept with the trappers, waded in icy streams with the trappers, ate what the trappers ate, and starved when the trappers starved. He did nothing to set himself apart from the hardy group of mountain men—Bridger, Carson, Fitzpatrick, Bonneville, Walker, and the Sublettes—with whom he had traveled north. Most of them were now sitting on Hugh Glass, trying to persuade him to let bygones be bygones where Jim Bridger and the Broken Hand were concerned. His own understanding was that Hugh Glass—oldest and, by some accounts, wildest of the mountain trappers—had been killed by an enraged mother grizzly some years before, while trapping with Major Henry's men; clearly this was a misjudgment, since the man was alive and kicking—literally kicking, whenever he could get a leg free. Neither Bridger nor Fitzpatrick was any longer engaged in the struggle—both stood by a table, looking somewhat stunned, as would only be natural in the light of the violent return of a man they had supposed to be dead.

"You know, Stewart, it's a goddamned nuisance, having to drink whiskey with my meals," Lord Berrybender complained. "I miss my leg, of course, but the plain fact is that I miss my claret more. Never thought I'd be reduced to a life without claret—when we fought together on the Peninsula I distinctly remember that you were a man who drank claret—no small amount of claret, either. You wouldn't have a few bottles hidden away, now, would you? For your private use? Come on, man, confess. . . ."

"Oh, do shut up about that claret, Papa," Tasmin said sharply. "It's gone, and good riddance. You've drunk more than enough claret for one lifetime, in any case—overconsumption explains why you're such a gouty old brute."

"Didn't ask you, asked Drum Stewart," Lord Berrybender insisted. "A man who's fond of claret doesn't change. I expect you've got a few bottles secreted away here somewhere . . . now haven't you, Drum?"

"I *walked* here, Albany," Drum said bluntly. "We had a few ponies, but we needed them to bring out the pelts. Can't clatter around with a lot of bottles, in country like this."

Drum Stewart did warm to the way Lady Tasmin's color rose when she heaped abuse on old Albany Berrybender; and he was hardly the only man in the post who liked to hear her heap it. When Lady Tasmin spoke in her spirited and witty way, all the mountain men fell silent and became shy. The purity of her diction, the flash of her wit, the bite of her scorn all fell so naturally from her lips that no one would have dared interrupt, particularly since her fulminations were often accompanied by a heaving of her young bosom. Young Carson, young Bridger, and the Sublette brothers were so smitten that they scarcely dared breathe, when Lady Tasmin spoke.

Despite his admiration for Lady Tasmin's looks, and those of Vicky Kennet's as well, Drum Stewart could not but be vexed that the English party was there. When he came to the Yellowstone valley with the Sublettes and the other trappers, he had supposed himself to be in a wilderness so remote that it would be years before the English rich arrived—getting clear of the English rich was one reason he plunged so eagerly into the Western wild. But then, before he had been at the post even ten days, who should arrive but Albany Berrybender himself, a man whose high title alone had kept him from being cashiered in Portugal for grand disregard of even the most elemental military discipline. No sooner had he settled in at the trading post than here the Berrybenders came, with Lady Tasmin herself driving a wagonful of servants and attendants. Old Albany—his left leg having been recently removed—bounced up in a buggy driven by an Italian of some sort. To Drum Stewart's dismay a Little England was immediately established at Pierre Boisdeffre's trading post, where, to the astonishment of the mountain men, a callow American named Catlin set up his easel and began to paint the various Indians who wandered in to trade; lordly Piegans, squat Minatarees, wild Assiniboines from the northland, all virtually jostling for positions in line in order to allow the American to render their likenesses.

It seemed to Drum that everything he had traveled six thousand miles to escape had caught up with him before he could even draw his breath in the high West. Far though he had traveled, he had only beaten the English by little more than a week—already the one-footed old lord had taken to racing across the prairies in his buggy, with the Italian applying the whip to two fine mares. Albany, of course—in the normal way of English sportsmen— shot at everything that moved. Already the buffalo and elk had learned to avoid the vicinity of the post; the pot hunters had to forage farther afield every day, in order to find game.

That Lady Tasmin had already managed to locate and marry a frontiersman judged to be wild and untamable even by the loose standards that prevailed among mountain trappers did not greatly surprise the worldly Scot. English ladies could always be counted on to seek out wild meat; there was little left in the East that could qualify, when it came to wildness. He had to admit that he *did* still admire the white throats and long legs of the Englishwomen, two of whom, graceful as swans, sat at that very table: the voluble Lady Tasmin and the somber cellist, Venetia Kennet. In Drum Stewart's view there was no escaping a certain moral equation: with beauty came difficulty, and with great beauty came great difficulty. Thus he looked aside from Lady Tasmin and let his gaze linger now and then on the admirably long-legged cellist—she was said to be with child but hardly showed it yet. Lady Tasmin *would* keep talking, whereas the silent cellist spoke only when required to. Drum Stewart was, after all, a Scot of the Scots, taciturn by nature. Ten minutes of Albany Berrybender's selfish ramblings made him want to cut the old brute's throat.

"Are you fond of cabbage, Miss Kennet?" Drum asked politely.

Not the least of the woman's attractions was a soft, full lower lip—on the long trek north from Kansas, Drum had largely held aloof from native women, put off by their short stature and the grease with which they liked to anoint themselves. To a man not naturally celibate, Vicky Kennet's full lower lip suggested the possibility of quickening passions and tangled bedclothes.

"She better like it, it's the only vegetable we're likely to have through this long winter," Tasmin said—she was quite aware of how frequently the tall Scot's gaze sought out Vicky.

"It'll do, sir, when there's naught else," Vicky said, allowing, just for a moment, her full lips to curve in a smile.

"Well, if there's no claret we'll have to make do with brandy, I suppose, Drum," Lord Berrybender said.

2

. . . a wife, wanted—simply a wife, wanted.

Pomp Charbonneau had formed the pleasant habit of walking Tasmin back to her camp at night, a courtesy Tasmin found both reassuring and yet obscurely irritating.

"Pomp, you needn't—Pomp, it's quite unnecessary—Pomp, don't bother," she protested, though never with much force. Not once did she strictly forbid this polished, friendly, very polite young man to take this trouble on her behalf. Tasmin liked Pomp very much, and yet why was it Pomp, rather than her husband, Jim Snow, who felt she needed protection on the easy walk from the trading post to the modest camp by the Yellowstone? Why—besides that—were she and Jim, in the coldest months of a northern winter, living in a tent on a riverbank? Because Jim found indoor lodgings "close"?

"You've now bewitched our good Pomp, Tasmin," Buffum said, once the elk and cabbage had been consumed. Pomp himself had hurried over to join the conclave of mountain men around Jim Bridger, Tom Fitzpatrick, and Hugh Glass—evidently some long-held grudge on the part of the latter was being adjudicated by a kind of trappers' jury.

"Shut up, Buffum, I've done nothing of the kind," Tasmin retorted. "Why would it matter to you if I have? Last I heard you were entering a nunnery, as I recall."

The fact was that, with the passage of time, Bess Berrybender had begun to feel considerably less nunlike; she would happily have allowed Pomp to pay *her* a good deal more attention, and Tasmin a good deal less.

"That's right, Tasmin—not fair to hog Pomp," Bobbety said. "When spring comes he has promised to take Father Geoff and me to some excellent fossil beds."

Bobbety and Father Geoffrin had become an inseparable pair, constantly babbling on about geology, vestments, or licentious French literature, over which they were prone to giggle and smirk.

Tasmin found the two of them increasingly hard to tolerate, though the rest of the company was not much more to her liking—always excepting Cook, who followed the progress of Tasmin's pregnancy with the attentiveness of the seasoned midwife that she was.

Tasmin had spoken sharply to George Catlin so many times that the disappointed painter seldom uttered a word while in her presence—why give the woman a target?

Mary Berrybender, her young breasts just budding, was not so easily squelched.

"I fear you may commit adultery with Pomp, if you aren't careful, Tassie," Mary said. "Indeed, I fear it very much."

"Hush, you minx!" Tasmin said. "I have no improper feelings for Pomp."

Mary turned aside and began to kiss and stroke the gloomy botanist, Piet Van Wely, her special friend. Numbed by the cold and depressed by the short winter days, the Dutchman had fallen into a deep melancholy. Now and then Mary could coax a sentence or two out of the sad fellow, but no one else could persuade him to speak a word.

Seeing that Pomp Charbonneau was deep in conversation with Eulalie Bonneville and Tom Fitzpatrick, Tasmin left the table and strode briskly out of the trading post into the cold Montana night—she had scarcely passed beyond the gates of the stockade when the ever-watchful Pomp appeared at her elbow, which irritated her. She liked the young man very much; but she didn't like him coddling her. Coddling was her husband's job, though one he entirely refused to do.

"What was all that stir?" she asked.

"Hugh had a grudge against Jimmy Bridger and Tom Fitzpatrick," Pomp informed her. "It was Jim and Tom who left him for dead, after the bear clawed him. His whole chest was ripped open—the boys thought he *was* dead, and the Sioux were close, so they took his gun and left, hoping to save their hair."

"Aha, but he lived to chase them down," Tasmin replied—Hugh Glass's survival did not seem all that surprising. Even in her own short time in the West she had observed the sort of things human beings could survive, provided they had sufficient vigor. Her own father had roared like a bull while his leg was being sawed off, and yet, scarcely a week later, he was hobbling around on his crutch with considerable agility, shooting unwary buffalo from the boat and assailing Vicky Kennet, who was plenty wary but had no place to run. Vigor did seem to be the necessary factor. Tim, the stable boy, only lost two fingers and a toe to the bitter frost, and yet came near to dying, and even now looked like a haunt of some kind, a man not sure whether he belonged to life or death.

"Yes, Hugh chased them down," Pomp said. "It's lucky there was a bunch of the boys handy to jump on him—otherwise there might have been blood spilled. Jim and Tom convinced him they did their best—it's not always easy to say when a man's alive, not when the Sioux are in the neighborhood."

They walked on. The winter stars were tiny pinpoints in the dark sky. Their feet crunched the crust of a light snow. Pomp Charbonneau's manners were so easy, so nearly infallible, so European, that Tasmin found herself rather resenting them; it seemed to her that those manners masked a certain neutrality, a preference for standing apart, a trait she could not but disdain. Pomp had been educated in a castle near Stuttgart; perhaps the castle was the trouble, Tasmin reflected—when had she *not* disdained men raised in castles? Drum Stewart had also been raised in a castle; he too was eligible for her rich scorn. She had not liked the cool way the Scot had skipped past her in order to focus his charms on Vicky Kennet. Glances were not neutral acts, where grown men and women were concerned.

"Pomp, have you never lusted!" Tasmin burst out suddenly. She could not tolerate neutrality and was determined to smash Pomp's, if she could.

"Not strongly, I suppose," Pomp said, with a quick smile. The question did not seem to surprise him, a fact irritating in itself.

"Oh, hell—why not?" Tasmin asked. "Inconvenient as men's lusts frequently are, there's not much else a woman can trust about them."

Tasmin picked up the pace of their walk, stung by Pomp's refusal to be ruffled by her pique.

"I don't mean I want you lusting for *me,*" she said. "But I'd like you better if you lusted for *someone*—perhaps a wild Ute, of the sort my Jimmy once found so appealing."

"I did once care for an Italian girl, but she died on the Brenner Pass," Pomp said, a little sadly.

"Not good enough—you're young and handsome—there are native beauties aplenty," she told him. "Besides, it's no good loving a dead woman—indeed, it's quite unfair to those of us who remain alive. We might need you."

"You're just annoyed that it's me that's walking you home," Pomp said. "I expect you'd rather it was Jim."

"You've hit it!" Tasmin exclaimed. "Only I'm more than annoyed—I'm furious. Why isn't it Jimmy? After all, you *are* a very good-looking man. Unlikely as it seems, a sudden lust might overwhelm you—overwhelm *us* for that matter. I'm flesh and blood, after all: nothing I respect more than sudden lusts. Yet this possibility never occurs to Jim—does the fool believe he's the only one subject to sudden lusts?"

"Jimmy and I have roamed together—I expect he just trusts me," Pomp said—whereupon Tasmin felt her fury burn even hotter.

"You, certainly—he can quite clearly trust *you,*" she said. "But it's *me* he's married to, and I'm rather a more volatile animal! I won't be taken for granted, not by Jimmy Snow or anyone else. He can't just entertain me with a little conjugal sweat and assume I'll be docile forever. Others are quite capable of working up similar sweats—wouldn't a good husband know that?"

Pomp gave a polite chuckle.

"Jim, he's different," he said. "I expect he'll walk you home himself, once it warms up a little."

"Why would the weather matter—cold doesn't affect him," Tasmin said.

"No, but the grizzly bears will be coming out—Jimmy's careful about bears—so am I," Pomp told her.

Tasmin was in no mood to receive such vague assurances. That her husband would prefer that she not be eaten by a grizzly bear hardly checked her fury; Jim had always been alert in protecting her from Indian abduction and other local dangers—she granted him that normalcy, at least. But the notion that she might need to be protected from her own strong feelings was a notion her husband simply didn't grasp. She was his wife— it was settled—and they would live where he chose. At the moment that meant a drafty tent by a frozen river. If Pomp chose to walk her home, that was fine—so there she was, being walked home, every night by a neutral, amiable chaperone, in this wintry wilderness.

It made Tasmin furious, and yet, when they reached the camp and Jim turned his mild eyes up to her, and moved so as to make a place for her on the robe beside him, Tasmin failed, as she usually failed, to sustain her hot feelings, and quickly forgot all the things she had meant to thrash out with Jim once Pomp was gone.

"Hugh Glass came by," Jim said. "That bear didn't kill him after all—he's mighty hot about the boys that left him, though."

"Oh, we noticed that," Tasmin said.

"He busted Tom in the jaw and tried to strangle Jimmy Bridger," Pomp said. "It took about all of us to get him calm."

Pomp chatted only a few more minutes, and then slipped off into the night. Tasmin sat on the robe her husband offered, her anger melting away like snow in a teapot. It was easy enough to be mad at her husband when she was away from him and could examine his actions coolly—and yet she could rarely manage to sustain her hot angers once she was with him. Instead of bursting out in fury, she leaned her head against his shoulder and all too meekly subsided, worn out from the turbulence of feeling she had just experienced.

At the trading post it was easy enough to feel like a woman rather undervalued, or misunderstood, or not taken seriously. She might complain to Cook about the drafty tent or various other aspects of their domestic arrangements, and yet once Pomp was gone and she and Jim crept into the tent and turned to one another, beneath their warm robes, Tasmin forgot her complaints. In the tent, amid the furs, with her husband, she felt like a wife, wanted—simply a wife, wanted. In the nighttime, at least, that was enough.

3

Otter Woman was old now, cranky and almost blind . . .

In the still night, once he had delivered Tasmin to her husband, Pomp could already hear sounds of the coming carouse at the trading post—naturally the trappers would want to welcome old Hugh Glass back to the land of the living. Pomp, not much of a carouser, did not immediately return, though he liked Hugh, a man who had seen much and was not loath to share his information. Hugh Glass had fought with William Ashley and Jedediah Smith in their great defeat at the Arikara villages a decade earlier—it had been that defeat that drove the trappers off the Missouri River and forced them to seek out beaver streams deep in the Rockies. It was at one such stream that the enraged mother grizzly left Hugh so torn and broken that Jim Bridger and Tom Fitzpatrick left him for dead.

Even now, at the fort, Hugh was trying to convince the skeptical trappers that he had crawled and hobbled some two hundred miles before being rescued by friendly Cheyenne. Already, before Pomp left with Tasmin, he had seen Joe Walker and Eulalie Bonneville rolling their eyes and shaking their heads at old Hugh's claim of a two-hundred-mile crawl. Some of the boys were so glad to see the old man that they pretended to believe him, while privately regarding the story as just another tall tale. No doubt the story of Hugh Glass, the bear, and the two-hundred-mile crawl would be told around Western campfires for years to come: the bear, the desertion, the crawl, and the search for revenge seemed to Pomp to have the makings of a play, or an opera even—he had seen plenty of the latter in Germany.

Though glad, of course, that Hugh Glass was alive, Pomp felt no inclination to join in the party. Tasmin, in her annoyance, had stated an awkward truth about him: he was not often lustful, and he had rarely been able to join in the spirit of any group celebration. The English girl stated clearly what he himself had never quite articulated: he stood apart, not hostile or critical of the lusts or greeds of others; his gaze contained no stiff judgments, as her husband the Sin Killer's fierce look was apt to do. Pomp would have liked to love a woman, feel a brother to a man, and yet he never had—or at least, he hadn't since the death of Sacagawea, his mother; and that had occurred when he was only a boy.

Down the Missouri, a few miles from the post, a small band of Minatarees were camped; one of them was his old aunt, Otter Woman, his mother's sister, who had also, for a time, been married to Pomp's father. Pomp thought he might just visit the Minataree camp and talk with his aunt a little. The cold was sharp, but Pomp didn't mind it. Otter Woman was old now, cranky and almost blind, but she had been at Manuel Lisa's fort the day the sudden fever had carried Pomp's mother away. Pomp was in Saint Louis, living with Captain Clark at that time; his father, Toussaint, had been there as well. When the trapper John Luttig came in with the news of Sacagawea's death, Pomp's father wept, and then Captain Clark wept too. The two men drank much whiskey that night; more than once they wept, a thing that surprised Pomp—he knew that Captain Clark was a very great man, and yet he wept for the death of an Indian woman. Seeing the two men, both drunk, so bereaved, caused a kind of breaking in Pomp—after that he saw his mother only in dreams; she became a woman of the shadows, a phantom he could never see clearly; though he could remember the warmth he had felt when she carried him close to her body in his first years.

Later, looking back, it seemed to Pomp that it was on that night in Saint Louis, when he had realized his mother would hold him close no more, that he had begun to live at a distance from other men, the distance that Tasmin Berrybender noticed and complained about. In Germany his kindly old tutor, Herr Hanfstaengl, had cared for Pomp deeply; and though he liked Herr Hanfstaengl and the jolly cooks in the castle of the prince of Württemberg, who, with William Clark's consent, had taken Pomp to educate, he could not really close the distance between them. The cooks all wanted to hug him, but Pomp would rarely let them.

Now, a grown man, he was back on the river of his birth, the great Missouri. Much had changed since his mother and father had brought him to Saint Louis so that Captain Clark could see to his education. The whites were in the West now, exploring every stream and trail. In his office in Saint Louis, Captain Clark, old but still alert, kept a great map of the West tacked to his wall; this map he amended constantly, as reports came in from trappers, priests, military men, merchants, informing him about a river or a pass that had escaped his attention. The old captain, tied down by his duties as commissioner of Indian Affairs, talked longingly of going out again, making one last, great trek, perhaps this time to California; it made Pomp sad to hear the great captain talk so—for it was only an old man's dreaming.

It was in Captain Clark's office that Pomp had met Drummond Stewart—Pomp had just been helping Captain Clark amend his great map again, putting in one or two of the tributaries of the Green River, where he had gone trapping with Jim Snow and Kit Carson only the year before. At once the tall Scot had asked Pomp to guide him on a hunting trip, a great expedition meant to last three years. The Scotsman didn't just want to kill the great beasts of the West, the bears and the bison; he wanted to capture specimens of all the Western animals—elk and antelope, cougars and wolves, mountain sheep, hares, and porcupines, even—and take them back to Perthshire, where he planned to establish a great game park on his broad northern estates. Of course, they would hunt for the table as they traveled but Drum Stewart was a man who had no interest in slaughter for the sake of slaughter—his enthusiasm for the West was so keen that Pomp happily agreed to go with him as a guide. Drum Stewart's questing spirit had so far never faltered, though here they were, more than two thousand miles from Saint Louis, at Pierre Boisdeffre's new trading post where the two waters joined, the brown Missouri and the green Yellowstone.

Only ten days before, as Pomp was just starting off on a hunt, who should surprise him but Jim Snow, trudging along the Missouri at the head of a shivering party of English, trailing behind him in a wagon and a buggy.

Jim Snow took to groups even less readily than Pomp, which is why the sight of him at the head of such a party was such a surprise. Word had reached them from some wandering Hidatsa that a big boat was stuck in the ice somewhere downriver; two or three of the trappers had been vaguely planning to investigate this wonder—but here the whole party came, with Jimmy Snow well in advance of the others. Kit Carson and Jim Bridger had been playing a game of kick ball with some Assiniboines when the Sin Killer suddenly appeared, carrying only his rifle and bow.

The sight of Pomp, his old friend, seemed to cheer Jim Snow up.

"Are you hired?" Jimmy asked at once. "If you ain't I want to turn this bunch over to you—all except my wife."

"So, Jimmy—got a fresh wife? What tribe would she belong to?" Eulalie Bonneville asked—he assumed, of course, that Jim would have taken a native woman—he himself had several native wives.

"The English tribe—that'll be her driving the wagon," Jim admitted.

The statement quite flabbergasted all the trappers. To see such a beauty as Tasmin on the Yellowstone was miracle enough; but then to hear that Jimmy Snow, a man who never bothered much with women, was married to her at once set the fort abuzz.

There were more than a dozen people in the wagon this English beauty drove; in the buggy was a tall woman, a short Italian, and the old lord himself, his left leg now a heavily bandaged stump.

"Jimmy, I *am* hired," Pomp admitted. "I've been engaged by a Scot—we mean to be out here three years, catching critters for his zoo."

Jim Snow felt a little disappointed—Pomp had lived in Europe and would no doubt be the best man to deal with a lot of Europeans.

"Well, there's Kit—I might try him," he said. "Kit's polite, at least."

Before the wagon even reached the stockade Jim Snow had shaken hands with the boys, said a few words to Kit Carson, privately, and left, headed, evidently, for the nearby Yellowstone.

"Dern, Jimmy left before he even got here," Eulalie said.

"That's our Jimmy—he don't linger," Milt Sublette remarked.

"Jim's married—I expect he just intends to make a separate camp," Pomp said. "He's shy—not like you, Bonney."

"He could have told us the news, at least," Jim Bridger said, rather annoyed. He always liked to get the news.

"At least he brought us a circus, though—let's watch it," Tom Fitzpatrick observed. "I wonder who that old one-legged fellow could be."

Then, as they all watched, the sprightly English girl stopped the wagon, jumped down, and sprinted off after her husband, Jim Snow, by then nearly to the frozen Yellowstone.

"Why, look at her go—she's a regular antelope," Billy Sublette allowed.

"She don't mean to let Jimmy skip out, does she?" Joe Walker observed.

Kit Carson was astonished—he had never seen a woman run as fast as the English girl.

"Why's she chasing after Jimmy so hard?" Kit wondered. "I expect he'll come back and get her, if she'd just wait."

"You'll learn this soon enough, so I'll tell you for your own good, Kit," Tom Fitzpatrick said. "There are some girls who won't be made to wait."

4

In fact, the mouse was sleepy too . . .

When Pomp walked up to the campfire, three young Minataree braves were playing a game with a mouse. They had three leather cups and were shuffling them rapidly, singing a kind of mouse song to distract the boy who was trying to guess which cup the mouse was under. It was an old game. The boy who was supposed to guess which cup the mouse was under proved to be a very bad guesser. He was wrong three times in a run—the quick boy who shuffled the cups laughed at such ineptitude.

"You try," he said to Pomp. "This one will never beat me."

"I'm sleepy, or I could beat you," the first boy said. His name was Climbs Up.

Pomp sat down and immediately won three games, merely by keeping his eye on the place the mouse had been. In fact, the mouse was sleepy too—or bored. The mouse ignored the cups and stayed in the same place. The cup shuffler, whose name was Weedy Boy, soon grew irritated at the lethargic mouse whose idleness had cost him victory. He picked the mouse up by the tail and flung it off into the snow.

"You put a spell on our mouse, so you could win three times," Weedy Boy said to Pomp.

Pomp just smiled. He liked the three gangly Minataree boys and sometimes took them hunting when they were camped nearby. Some of the Minataree braves considered Pomp a Shoshone—his mother's tribe—and were rude to him accordingly, but the three boys accepted him and badgered him to let them shoot his gun, a fine rifle Drum Stewart bought him while they were in Saint Louis. The Minataree band owned only a few guns, and they were just old muskets, in bad repair.

"There are too many Assiniboines around here," Weedy Boy commented. "They have been stealing our horses."

"We want to go to war with them, but we don't have very good guns," Climbs Up complained.

There were several bands of Assiniboines north of the post, most of them far better equipped than the Minatarees—a war was unlikely to turn out well for this little band. Pomp was careful not to say as much to the three boys, who would have regarded his apprehension as an insult.

"The old woman will be up pretty soon," Weedy Boy said, referring to Pomp's aunt. "She never sleeps very long."

Two of the boys retired to a lodge, but Weedy merely took a blanket and curled up by the fire.

Pomp seldom slept much, either. Some nights he merely rested, neither fully awake nor sound asleep. The pure silence of the winter night, broken only by the sighing of the wind over the snowfields, was a restful thing in itself. In summer the nights were never silent: insects buzzed, night birds called, and the buffalo bulls, in their rut, set up a roaring that could be heard for many miles.

Weedy Boy had been right about Otter Woman. Long before dawn she crept out of her lodge and shuffled up to the fire. It irritated her that Sacagawea's boy had shown up again, smelling of white man's soap, an unpleasant thing to smell so early in the morning. He looked like his mother, her sister, and that annoyed Otter Woman too. Though she and Sacagawea had been married to the same man, they had never been close. Sacagawea was not a bad person, but she was cunning and could always get her way with men, a skill Otter Woman did not possess. Though Sacagawea had had only one husband, this smelly boy's father, and Otter Woman had had several, it still annoyed her that Sacagawea had always been able to get her way.

"If you are going to come around here and burn up our firewood you should at least bring me a new blanket," Otter Woman said. "There were too many mice last summer—some of them nibbled holes in my blanket."

"I'll buy you one, Aunty," Pomp said. "If you want to come to the trading post you can take any blanket you want."

"Too far," Otter Woman said. In the cold weather her knees didn't seem to want to bend. Let this boy of her sister's choose a nice blanket and bring it to her. As long as it was warm and had blue in it, it would do very well. She had a fine buffalo robe, which she had tanned and worked herself, but it was too heavy to sleep under, except on the coldest nights. A nice blue blanket would be a comfort on days when the wind blew sleet or fine snow through the camp.

Pomp knew his aunt didn't particularly like seeing him—his father claimed she had never liked seeing much of anyone; she was often rude to guests and, besides that, was slipshod about her chores. Now her face was as wrinkled as a dried apple and she rarely had two words to say, unless they were words of complaint. Also, she was greedy—the last words she spoke to Pomp, as he got up to leave, were to hurry up and bring her the new blanket he had promised. Minataree braves were in and out of the post—any one of them would have been glad to bring her the blanket if Pomp asked them to, but that wouldn't do, either. Otter Woman didn't trust the Minatarees, even though she lived with them. She felt her nephew should hurry up and make the delivery, although she still resented the fact that his mother had been so clever about getting her way with men.

"Bring it today, and don't lose it, either," she warned.

"Why would I lose a blanket?" Pomp asked, a little taken aback by his aunt's stridency.

"Your father was a big gambler, he was always losing everything," Otter Woman said. "It's going to be cold tonight and I'm tired of this old blanket the mice have nibbled."

Pomp was almost back to the stockade when the very thing Weedy Boy predicted happened right before his eyes. From just inside the stockade, war cries suddenly rent the morning silence. A musket went off, and there was the snarling of dogs, the neighing of a frightened horse, another gunshot, and loud sounds of battle. Pomp raced in, expecting to see a party of besieged mountain men under attack, but in fact not a mountain man was to be seen—only the painter George Catlin, cowering under his easel, his paints spilled everywhere, as six or seven Minataree braves chopped and stabbed at as many Assiniboines. One man, an Assiniboine, had already fallen; a stout Minataree was just taking his scalp. One horse, a bay, had taken an arrow in the neck, its split vein spewing blood over the nearest combatants, as if they stood under a fountain. As Pomp watched, an Assiniboine boy no older than twelve picked up the fallen warrior's musket and shot a Minataree right in the stomach, blowing the man backward. The man screamed so loudly that combat froze, allowing Pomp to rush in and drag George Catlin out of the fray.

The man whose portrait he had been working on, a vividly painted Piegan, stood calmly over by the posts of the stockade, evidently not much interested in the sudden conflict between Assiniboine and Minataree.

"Thank God you came, Pomp, I thought I was lost," George Catlin said in a shaky voice. "Hadn't we better get inside, before they start up again?"

"I don't know what it was about, but I think it's over—for now, anyway," Pomp said. Indeed, the two bands had stepped back from each other, though they still brandished hatchets and knives. The wounded horse continued to bleed, and the skinny dogs to snarl. Two men lay dead, but the urge to fight seemed to have left the warriors as rapidly as it had come. Both groups retreated warily. An Assiniboine went to the wounded horse, jerked the arrow out, and stuffed a rag into the wound. The dead warriors were picked up; no more threats were made. A retreat took place, by silent and mutual consent.

The Piegan who was waiting to have his portrait painted suddenly voiced a raucous curse.

"Better get your paints, Mr. Catlin," Pomp said. "It's safe now, but that customer of yours doesn't look like a patient man."

"None of them are patient—they all rush me," George Catlin said, before picking up his scattered paints and motioning the Piegan to stand in front of his easel again.

5

"Boys, do you see an angel over there?"

Hugh Glass got so drunk that he began to have visions of heaven—he looked up and saw an angel making sweet music over by the English table. She was tall and fair, this angel, with long auburn hair hanging down her back; the sweet music came from a big instrument, rather like a swollen fiddle. Hugh Glass watched, entranced; it was warm in heaven, and there was plenty of grog, as there should be.

Drum Stewart had persuaded Vicky Kennet to bring out her cello and favor them with a little Haydn, a development which vexed Lord Berrybender considerably. He was impatient for bed, and perhaps a spot of copulation just beforehand; but he held his tongue for once, mainly because he was still convinced that the Scotsman had a few bottles of claret tucked away somewhere; he didn't want to offend the man until the question was firmly settled.

"Boys, do you see an angel over there?" Hugh asked the company, some of whom were nearly as drunk as himself.

"What would an angel be doing up here on the Yellowstone, in the dead of winter?" Eulalie Bonneville wondered.

"Why, playing the harp, I guess—ain't that a sort of harp she's got?" Hugh inquired.

"That's no angel, that's an Englishwoman," Tom Fitzpatrick informed him. "I expect she's the old lord's whore."

Hugh looked at the Englishwoman again, his head lolling slightly to one side. Now it seemed to him that he saw two female angels—one slid out of the other and then slid back in again, as his vision wavered.

"No, it's an angel—maybe two," Hugh declared. "The reason you can't see 'em is because none of you have been dead. I'm the only man here that's been dead."

This claim made Jim Bridger indignant.

"Dern, Hugh—you come bustin' in here and tried to strangle me because you claimed me and Tom left you for dead when you was alive all the while."

"Jim's right, Hugh—which was it?" Tom Fitzpatrick said, with a smile—he was well aware that Hugh Glass was far too drunk to make good sense. He was so drunk he was even seeing double. He himself, while on a carouse near the Tongue River, had once shot at a careless elk and missed entirely because he had shot at the double and not the real animal.

"You were right, boys! Here I've been hot after you for months when at the time you left me I *was* dead," Hugh declared, more humbly. "I was floating up to heaven, only an angel with feathers like a prairie chicken came and lowered me back to earth."

Jim Bridger and Kit Carson—the only trappers who weren't drunk—looked at each other in amazement. Why would Hugh make up such a wild lie? After all his hot accusations about being deserted, now he was trying to claim he had been dead after all.

"No, you're off, Hugh—angels don't have wings like prairie chickens," Joe Walker said. "Prairie chickens can hardly fly at all—angels have wings like them big white swans."

"Who's seen one, you or me, Joe?" Hugh said, his temper flaring.

"I agree with Joe," Bill Sublette said. "There's plenty of books with pictures of angels in them, and they all have them big white wings, like swans."

"Yes, and the damn fools that drew the pictures had probably never been killed by a grizzly bear, like I was," Hugh protested.

"You're a mouthy old fool, Hugh," Jim Bridger said—he was getting hotter at the thought of the injustice of the old man's claim.

"Don't bait me now, Jimmy," Hugh said threateningly. "It ain't easy to remember being dead. I'd forgotten it until I seen that angel over at the English table, playing that big fiddle."

"If you were dead why didn't you stay dead, like most people do?" Milt Sublette said, a little spooked. If old Hugh *had* been dead, then maybe they were all talking to a ghost.

"Heaven didn't want me, I guess—nor the other place either—so that prairie chicken angel just lowered me back down, and that's when I started my crawl," Hugh said. He sensed a rather uneasy skepticism among his listeners, one of whom, little Mary Berrybender, had just joined the crowd.

"Oh, Mr. Glass, that's transubstantiation you're referring to," Mary said. "Few among us have been granted such an interesting experience."

Mary's long word stopped the conversation dead.

"Young miss, could you say that again?" Eulalie requested. "I reckon that's the longest word any of us has ever heard spoke."

"Transubstantiation," Mary repeated. "The soul departs the body, but decides to return. Only the very holy experience it."

"That leaves Hugh out, then," the Broken Hand said. "I doubt he's got a holy bone in his dern old body."

"Point of order, Mary—point of order!" Bobbety cried out. "Many Hindus experience transubstantiation on a regular basis."

Both Sublettes looked pale, took their guns, and prepared to leave.

"If you're a ghost, then, Hugh, I believe I'd rather sleep outside," Bill Sublette declared.

"Now, Bill, there's no need to worry—I've settled back into myself now," Hugh assured him—though in a slurred voice. He saw that everyone was looking at him strangely. The room seemed to be rocking slightly. The English angel had put away her big fiddle and was leaving the company, with the old one-legged lord stumping along behind her on his crutches. Hugh was hoping to see the auburn-haired angel fly up toward the ceiling, where the parrot was—instead, after a moment, his head hit the table.

"Hugh didn't see no angel—the liquor got him," Tom concluded. "In my own opinion, a man that's dead stays dead."

"Exceptions do exist, Mr. Fitzpatrick," Mary said politely. "There's Lazarus, for one—gospel of John, chapter eleven, verse seventeen."

All the trappers had been staring at Hugh Glass—now they turned and began staring at Mary, whose face wore an unearthly but—in Kit Carson's opinion—very unholy expression.

"Things are sure changing around this trading post," Kit Carson said, in bemusement, when Mary had gone back to the English table.

None of the trappers disagreed.

6

. . . a hand went immediately and accurately under her gown . . .

Damn it, a most unsatisfactory copulation," Lord Berrybender complained. "Came off before I even got inside. We mustn't let this get to be a habit, Vicky."

Venetia Kennet kept silent. What was there to say? Lord Berrybender's effusions, though copious, were mostly now premature, one inconvenience of which was that the sheets were permanently sticky, a fact the laundress, Millicent, could hardly fail to notice.

"Do try your bow, just a bit," Lord B. requested. "Accustomed to far lengthier pleasures, as you know. Don't relish these goddamn foreshortenings."

Vicky tried her bow—tried and tried; she could have managed a concerto in less time. In this instance, though, flaccidity prevailed. Much tickling of His Lordship's balls only produced a slight lumpiness—nothing that was likely to result in penetration.

"Effect of that whiskey, I'm sure," Lord B. said. "Never spunked in such a hurry when I was well primed with good red claret. I'll just sleep a bit now, I suppose—expect we can go at it well enough first thing in the morning."

Finding no water in the basin—it would never have stood empty had Mademoiselle Pellenc still been in charge of the rooms—Vicky pulled on a flannel robe and stepped into the corridor, meaning to refill the basin from little Mary's room, which was just next door. But she had scarcely put her foot out the door when lips found hers, lips with a stiff red beard below them—and a hand went immediately and accurately under her gown, while another squeezed a breast.

"Chilly here, Miss Kennet—my room's not far," Drum Steward whispered, his hand still squeezing and probing.

"I imagine old Albany takes a bit of pumping these days, as drunk as he gets," the Scot suggested.

"Oh yes, pump pump, that's all I do, sir," Vicky Kennet agreed.

7

Jim's slap came quick as a snake's strike . . .

God damn this weather—now I'm stuck!" Tasmin said, without thinking. Jim's slap came quick as a snake's strike, before she could even close her lips; one of them split slightly, a dribble of blood ran down her chin, but Tasmin was too stunned even to dab at it. She had just been leaving for the post when the wind rose to a howl and snow began to swirl around their tent, blotting out the river and, indeed, the world. The trading post, only a mile away, might have been a hundred—in such a whiteout she could never find her way to it. This was vexing; Cook had been going to make her a kind of porridge bath, thought to be beneficial to women in her condition. Angry at having to miss her porridge bath, she had let slip a casual curse and been slapped for it.

And yet, only the moment before, they had been happy; they had been singing, in fact. Jim had a fine tenor voice. Tasmin was teaching him "Barbara Allen" and one or two other old ballads. Song one minute and then the slap, harder even than the first one she had received, for transgressing his powerful but, to Tasmin, mysterious religious beliefs.

Tasmin sat stock-still, her eyes wide, staring. Through the flap of the tent she could see only white—the snow enclosed them like a cocoon. The night before, when they were amid their robes, being a wife, wanted, seemed a fine thing; but in the howling blizzard, being a wife slapped was a very different article. Jim Snow watched her with the flinty eyes of the Sin Killer—Tasmin had the sense that if she misspoke he would at once strike her again. With many men—even some stronger than herself—her fighting nature might have caused her to fling herself into battle—but not with Jim Snow, the stranger with whom she was mated. If she deliberately provoked him she could not guess where it would end. She sat, staring, leaking a tear or two of embarrassment and shock, struggling to regain her composure.

"You ain't to cuss—you've been told," Jim said, gently wiping the blood off Tasmin's lip with a finger.

Tasmin, still struggling with her emotions, didn't speak. She didn't yet dare. Her bosom heaved; she held back tears—were it not for the blizzard she would have immediately run out of the tent, but now she feared to. If she ran into the whiteness, would her husband find her? Would anyone?

After a bit she calmed and reached into her bag for a tiny mirror. Her lower lip was puffy, but the bleeding had stopped.

"You ain't to cuss—you was told," Jim said again.

"I'm a mere human being, Jim," Tasmin said unsteadily. "Like most humans, when I'm frustrated I sometimes slip and utter words I shouldn't say. Your friends the trappers curse constantly and rather colorfully. I myself was brought up in a family that cursed a great deal—it's only natural that, now and then, a bad word escapes me."

"There's vanity in you too," Jim said, ignoring her comment about the trappers.

He reached for the mirror, meaning to smash it and end her preening, but Tasmin jerked the small glass away.

"This is my mirror—I'm prepared to be beaten rather than surrender it," Tasmin said. "Of course there's vanity in me—and in you, too. You're rather vain about the way your beard is trimmed."

"I wasn't until I met you," Jim replied.

"I see—so your vanity is my fault too," Tasmin said. "You seem to think everything is my fault."

Jim Snow didn't answer. There was still hostility in his look, so much hostility that Tasmin felt rather despairing; and yet she was determined, now that the die was cast, to speak her mind.

"I'm human, I'm fallible, I admit it," she said, staring straight ahead. "I *will* slip in my language—now and then I may even commit worse sins. There is, I believe, a Christian virtue called forgiveness—I guess it isn't in the part of the Holy Book you possess—perhaps you tore the forgiveness pages out to make our campfires."

Jim said nothing. As usual, he felt at a terrible disadvantage. He could not possibly speak as well as his wife. He had slapped her hard and yet it had not knocked the vanity out of her, or curbed her rebellious spirit. The Book said a wife should be submissive, and yet Tasmin, *his* wife, was defiant.

"There's forgiveness, I guess, but there's punishment too," he said, without confidence.

"I see," Tasmin said. "You like the punishment parts best—I suppose that's why you're called the Sin Killer."

Jim's eyes were softening a little, and yet the prospect of a return to their easy union still seemed distant and bleak.

"I don't want to get slapped every time I'm vexed and speak out," she said. "Somehow you've become convinced that it's your duty to punish sinners—which can make it hard on a wife—though I do think mostly I make a decent wife."

Jim didn't answer. He wished Tasmin could just be silent, and not always be spilling words out of her mouth at such a rate. Lengthy talk just made it harder for him to hold the simple articles of faith in his mind, the faith that Preacher Cockerell had beaten into him at an early age. Preacher Cockerell never hesitated: he took the horsehide whip to his own wife and children as readily as he took it to Jim. Sin was to be driven out and violence was the way to drive it. Sin was also constant; violence had to be constant too. Preacher Cockerell whipped in the morning, whipped in the noontide, whipped at night; when members of his congregation sent their unruly young to him, he whipped them too. Jim grew up fearing the whip but not doubting the justice. Before the morning meal and the evening, Preacher Cockerell read from the Holy Book, terrible passages about punishment, sin, hell, Lot's wife, the whore of Babylon, wars and floods and banishment, all the punishments that man deserved because of his sinful nature. Preacher Cockerell even whipped himself, for he had fallen into adultery with the wife of Deacon Sylvester. For such a sin even the whippings had not been enough, so Jehovah sent the lightning bolt that fried Preacher Cockerell and turned him black; the same lightning bolt threw Maudey Cockerell and Jim Snow aside as if they were chaff from the grain. For three days Jim lay unmoving; he seemed to float in red water, though there was no water where he was. Even the Kaw was low that year. Maudey Cockerell lived, but her mind died, destroyed by the heavenly flash. From that time on Jim had felt it was his duty to punish sin, whenever he met it in the violent men of the West, red or white; the Indians feared him because of the ferocity of his attacks. He was particularly feared by the medicine men, because it was the heresy of their spells and potions that angered him most.

But he was not in battle with heathen savages now; he was with Tasmin, his wife, a woman who had just carelessly taken the Lord's name in vain. Her quarrelsome words had not really been checked, not even by the sharp blow he had struck her. His Ute wives, receiving such a blow, would have immediately ceased their disputes; they would have known to be quiet. But Tasmin was no Ute—she could outtalk him, make him feel a fool if he even tried to justify his behavior by reference to the Holy Book. Both slaps had shocked her; but not enough. He had no whip; he couldn't lash her as Preacher Cockerell had lashed his Maudey. Even then Tasmin was looking at him boldly, a little scared perhaps but not compliant, as a chastised wife should be. Jim made a fist, but then held back. He didn't strike her.

Tasmin saw the fist—she watched, rather numb, as battle raged within Jim Snow. His face had darkened. She could only wait, she couldn't run; if she ran into the blizzard the best she could hope for was to lose a toe or two. If there was to be a beating, better to stay and take it. All the same she felt herself trembling as she watched fury darken her husband's face. She didn't look at Jim; she looked at nothing, said nothing. She hoped that if she held a strict neutrality the crisis might pass—and it did. Jim Snow relaxed his fist—his face slowly cleared. He seemed as numb as she was; he started. When his knee accidently brushed hers he jerked back, as if burned.

When Tasmin thought it safe to speak she did so as gently as possible. An element of real danger had suddenly come into her union; she had become afraid of her husband, afraid that in him were angers she couldn't anticipate or soothe. These angers might have little enough to do with her; still, she was the wife who was there to meet them. She didn't like being fearful, and yet she was not sure that she understood Jim well enough to avoid setting him off.

"You've just made me scared of you, Jim—that's the most honest thing I can say," Tasmin began. "I accept that you don't like cursing, and that you disapprove of vanity."

"No, it's that I don't like you to *talk*!" Jim said—why would the woman keep on? "It's prideful, the way you talk. The Utes don't let their women babble like you do—a Ute man would likely cut your tongue out."

"I'm lucky I haven't married a Ute man, then," Tasmin said quietly. "I'm afraid speech is a habit I'm unlikely to be able to break. I was brought up in a talky family—I've been babbling, as you put it, from an early age. In England I was much admired for my wit, which I must say I enjoy employing. Silent is one thing I can't honestly promise to be."

His fist came quicker than his palm; it struck Tasmin squarely in the temple and knocked her partway out of the lodge. She did not entirely lose consciousness, but her vision blurred for a moment—she scraped her knee on the frozen snow as she struggled back into the tent. The world had become gray, like a thick soup; Tasmin's only thought was to crawl back under the robes and rest. The one thing that was clear was that her husband didn't like her to talk; his tolerance in that regard had abruptly ended, leaving her with a split lip and a lump forming on her temple. The injustice of it overwhelmed her: she had only been trying to understand Jim's feelings, so as to be a better wife! Tasmin began to sob—she could not stop the warm tears from flowing, although she knew Jim couldn't be expected to like her crying, either. She longed so for Jim to comfort her, to talk to her normally— just that morning, they had been singing together! But then, as her vision cleared, she saw that this hope of comfort was in vain. Except for herself, their tent was empty. Blizzard or no blizzard, Jim Snow was gone—his gun, his bow, and his quiver were gone too.

8

Who but a haunt would come visiting . . .

U h-oh, who is it, Kit?" Jim Bridger asked—in the dim blue light of the storm, the man all white with snow who suddenly pushed into their lodge seemed ghostlike, at least from what Jim knew of ghosts. Who but a haunt would come visiting in such a blizzard?

Kit Carson was startled too—since old Hugh Glass's return from the bounds of death all the trappers had become a little jumpy. Now a man all icicles and snow came pushing in out of a blizzard so severe that no normal man would attempt to travel in it; he and Jim Bridger had taken one look at the storm and decided to make do with jerky for another day.

"Oh, wait—it's Jimmy Snow—I recognize his gun," Kit said.

"Well, Jimmy—I'd say you picked a bad day to get restless," Jim Bridger allowed to the guest.

Jim Snow courteously tried to shake all the snow off himself without sending too much of it into the small campfire. Carson and Bridger, the youngest and the soberest of the trappers, prided themselves on their ability to live rough. The lodge was small and makeshift, and they seldom bothered to lay in extra firewood.

"I ain't restless," Jim Snow said. "I just thought I'd visit."

Jim Bridger received this news skeptically. Jim Snow, the Sin Killer, was by far the least sociable trapper in the Rockies. No one could ever predict where he might turn up, though it would usually be somewhere west and north of Saint Louis.

"You're smart about directions, Jimmy," Kit said. "I *might* could find your camp in a blow like this—but if I wasn't lucky I'd miss it."

"How is that pretty wife of yours? She *is* a treat for the eyes," Jim Bridger inquired. He distrusted his own grasp of manners, where married folk were concerned, but thought he might be permitted a polite inquiry.

"I just hit her a good stout lick, to stop her chatter," Jim Snow admitted.

Bridger and Carson received this information in silence. The world of marriage was a world they knew not. That husbands and wives sometimes came to blows was a circumstance they had heard rumored. Among the native tribes, of course, women were frequently beaten; whether excessive chatter was a principal cause of these beatings they were not sure. Their own experience, not extensive, had so far been solely with native women; no beating had as yet been necessary.

Privately, both Kit Carson and Jim Bridger admired Tasmin beyond all women—in both their daydreams and their night dreams she made frequent appearances. They considered her to be quite likely the fairest woman on earth. Now her husband, the Sin Killer, had walked out of a blizzard to inform them that he had just silenced his wife with a good stout lick. What could the man expect them to make of such startling information?

"Silence is a comely thing, in a woman," Jim Snow informed them. "Silence before the Lord. It's in the Book."

Neither Carson nor Bridger could read—what was in the Book came to them in scraps here and there, at second hand.

"My wife don't know when to shut up," Jim Snow continued—clearly

Tasmin's proclivity for talk was bothering Jimmy a good deal, but their roles in this matter left them feeling increasingly embarrassed. On a day of blizzard, when no man could see two feet in front of his face, Jim Snow had made his way to their lodge mainly in order to complain about his lovely wife.

"Tasmin talks all the time," he went on. "I had to crack her just to get a little peace.

"Knocked her out of the tent—didn't mean to," he added.

The two young trappers considered this information somberly. Neither man could imagine hitting Tasmin, much less knocking her all the way out of a tent. It was clear that Jim Snow was not entirely comfortable with what he had done—he had plunged into a blizzard in order to tell them about it, and now was looking at them expectantly, as if waiting for them to assure him that knocking a talky wife out of a tent was perfectly proper behavior in a husband, a judgment neither felt qualified to make.

"I expect she'll have a pretty fair lump on her noggin," Jim Snow went on—he seemed unable to get his mind off the fact that he had struck his wife.

"What is it she talks about, Jimmy?" Kit inquired cautiously. Excessive talk on Tasmin's part seemed to be the heart of the problem; Kit felt it might be appropriate to inquire about the subjects she dealt with in her chatter.

"Stuff—I can't remember much," Jim Snow confessed. In fact what Tasmin talked about was usually beyond his powers of description.

"Sometimes she cusses," he added. "That's what started it today."

"A woman shouldn't cuss," Jim Bridger agreed.

"Nope, it wouldn't be good etiquette," Kit Carson agreed. He had recently learned the word "etiquette" from Tasmin's sister Bess, who had objected to his habit of spitting out gristle or other unsatisfactory foods while at the common table.

Outside, the blizzard was moderating somewhat. The snow still swirled, but the wind blew less fiercely.

"The blow's about over," Jim said. "If you see my wife tell her I'll be gone for a while. I promised George Aitken I'd check on him and the boat once I got the folks safe at the post."

"You're headed back to the Knife River *now*?" Jim Bridger asked, surprised. Both he and Kit felt that they had received a heavy commission. Neither trusted themselves to utter a word in Lady Tasmin's presence.

"Yes—I told George I'd come check on him when I got a chance," Jim Snow said. "If the wrong bunch of Indians was to show up, it might go hard with George and the others."

"It might," Kit Carson agreed.

"Don't forget to tell my wife where I'm going," Jim Snow insisted. Then he slid out of the lodge and disappeared.

"You go tell his wife, Kit," Jim Bridger said at once.

"No sir, not me," Kit said. "You go—you're far smoother with the womenfolks. I might spit in the wrong direction or do some other bad etiquette. You go."

After wrangling for an hour, during which the debate grew heated, they decided to draw straws, which they did later that day, at the trading post. Joe Walker held the straws.

"Short straw tells her," Kit said—the words were hardly out of his mouth before he drew the short straw.

"That wasn't a fair draw," he protested. "Joe was jerky."

Jim Bridger, however, refused to redraw.

Though oppressed by fears about his own shortcomings in the area of etiquette, there was nothing Kit could do but plod down to the Yellowstone and give Lady Tasmin the bad news.

9

The wind had become inconsistent . . .

Tasmin sat in the chilly tent all day, well swaddled in robes, nursing her hurt. Though her lower lip was puffy and her head ached, the deeper hurts were inside. Her feelings swung back and forth, regularly as a pendulum. One minute she longed for her husband's return—the next minute she feared that very event, for he might very well hit her again. The wind had become inconsistent as the blizzard lost its force. Several times, in moments of quiet, Tasmin convinced herself she heard footsteps. Twice she crawled out of the tent, hoping to spot Jim.

In the afternoon the wind stopped blowing, the sky cleared, and the sun shone with unusual brilliance on the snowfields. Tasmin could have walked on to the fort and asked Cook for her porridge bath, but she didn't—a lethargy seemed to take her; she merely sat, now and then putting a few sticks on the fire. At least Jimmy had left her plenty of firewood. Ordinarily she would have been ravenously hungry by that hour, but she didn't feel hungry. She made little snowballs and applied them to her puffy lip and lumpy temple. When she did go to the fort she didn't want any of her relatives to notice evidence of violence.

Even when the sun began to sink, Tasmin continued to wait. She felt that to leave her tent just then might mean leaving her marriage, which, despite the day's trouble, was a thing not wholly to be despised. There was little accounting for men's tempers, it seemed. Her own father, unprovoked, often fell to slapping and whacking. Perhaps it was merely a flaw in the male temperament—perhaps Jim Snow had awakened to some obscure anxiety having to do with sin which, unwittingly, her profane chatter had exacerbated.

It might be that enduring such unjust attacks was merely a part of women's lot—her mother had sported many a black eye over the years, and yet, somehow, it had never occurred to Tasmin that a man would hit *her*. Now that one *had* she felt that her best bet was to achieve a better understanding of her man—perhaps if she could penetrate to the cave of her husband's angers she would learn what set him off.

It was nearly dusk when next Tasmin heard footsteps approaching the camp. They seemed rather timid footsteps—perhaps Cook had sent Eliza to see about her. But when Tasmin cautiously peeked out she saw Kit Carson standing nearby, evidently in deep perplexity of spirit. He wore a little rag cap, such as a shop boy might wear. Tasmin felt immediate relief. Kit was her favorite of the trappers; such a polite boy he was. Already Buffum, no longer nunlike, had conceived a passion for him.

"Why, hello, Kit," Tasmin said. "Were you looking for Jim?"

"No," Kit admitted. As usual Lady Tasmin's beauty caused a paralyzing shyness to seize him. He knew exactly what he was supposed to say—he had rehearsed it many times in his walk from the post, but he could not bring himself, bumbler that he was, to launch into speech.

Tasmin saw this—standing just by her tent, as the cold shadows of evening stretched over the snowfields, the young man seemed incapable of either speech or action.

It occurred to Tasmin that if she could just get him moving again he might make a useful escort. She no longer felt that leaving the tent meant leaving her marriage—that view was too dramatic. If she could persuade Kit to walk her to the post she might enjoy that porridge bath after all.

"It's a great convenience to me that you've been so thoughtful as to stop by," Tasmin said. "Jimmy's off somewhere and I was just heading for the post. I wonder if you would be so kind as to escort me—I'll just get my little bag."

"Went to the boat," Kit managed to say, as they started along the path.

"What's that?" she asked. "What about the boat?"

"Jim, he gone to the boat—said to tell you not to worry," Kit managed to bring out. "Said he had to go to the boat to see that George Aitken was all right."

Tasmin felt a flash of warmth—she had not been entirely forgotten, after all.

"Jim came by our camp and told us—he didn't want you to worry," Kit added, his tongue loosening, rather to his surprise.

"How nice of you to bring me this reassurance—he mentioned nothing of the sort to me," she admitted.

"Gone to the boat," Kit said again—he clung to this simple piece of information as a drowning man might cling to a spar.

"Marriage is not always a smooth path, Kit," Tasmin said—she now felt quite confident of her power over young Kit, and inasmuch as he had become putty in her hands, she felt a devilish need to twist him just a bit.

"Not always a smooth path at all," she repeated. "I confess that my husband and I had a tiny quarrel this morning—what you might call a spat."

"I know," Kit said—the comment popped out before he could think.

"Pardon me—how can you have known about our quarrel?" she asked.

"Jimmy told us," Kit said, startled by his own volubility—his tongue, like a skittish horse, now threatened to run away with him.

"Well, goodness me," Tasmin said, watching Kit with surprise. Her devilish mood had not passed—she wanted to discommode this polite young fellow in some minor way—perhaps snatch his ridiculous rag of a cap, or even ruffle his hair.

"You mean my husband came to see you, in a howling blizzard, just to tell you about our quarrel?" she asked.

"Yep," Kit said. "Jimmy Snow can find his way around better than most. Mainly he came because he didn't want you to get all worried."

Having delivered the longest speech he had ever made to a female, Kit felt rather proud of himself.

"He said he knocked you out of the tent," he added, having just remembered that detail.

"Yes, I have a fine lump on my head and scraped my knee besides," Tasmin said. "Since he seems to have been so forthcoming, did he happen to mention what the quarrel was about?"

"Didn't like your chatter," Kit said nervously. "Hit you to keep you quiet."

"And yet, you see, I'm not really quiet, am I, Kit?" Tasmin said, favoring him with a brilliant smile.

"I am not quiet and I doubt I ever shall be," she went on. "You've heard my father roaring and my sister Bess, who's taken rather a fancy to you, complaining. We Berrybenders just happen to be a noisy lot—forthright in our appetites too. It wouldn't surprise me at all if my sister Bess attempted to become familiar with you soon."

"Familiar?" Kit said dubiously; he had no idea what sort of behavior Tasmin was predicting.

Kit's solemnity was so comical that Tasmin felt an irresistible urge to tease him. Just as they entered the stockade, with several trappers watching, she suddenly linked her arm in Kit's and strode boldly toward the post. Kit was too stunned to protest. Eulalie Bonneville, who had been sharpening his skinning knife on a whirling grindstone, stopped his sharpening and just let the grindstone whirl. Tom Fitzpatrick was so surprised he dropped his pipe. Hugh Glass, who had been bent over, trimming a corn on his toe, forgot about his toe.

Kit didn't dare withdraw his arm; but his gaze became unseeing as he contemplated the disgrace that had overtaken him—walking arm in arm with Jim Snow's wife, with everybody watching.

Happy with the consternation she had wrought in the breast of this too solemn young man, Tasmin released his arm just as Kit, still unseeing, tripped over a wagon tongue—it was half hidden in the snow—and fell absolutely flat on his face.

No comedian could have achieved a cleaner pratfall. The sight was so funny that Tasmin could not hold in a hearty peal of laughter—various trappers whooped and chortled too. Bess Berrybender, chatting with Father Geoffrin about the exciting levels of depravity in the dark Gothic fictions of Ann Radcliffe, saw Kit fall and felt very vexed with her sister. Here again Tasmin was misbehaving, teasing a nice young man she had no business teasing, the result being this sudden ignominy. Bess immediately rushed to Kit's side—ignominy, after all, sometimes led to opportunity—retrieved his shop boy cap, and tried to help him staunch the flow of crimson that was pouring copiously from his smashed nose.

"Bend over, bend over—no need to bleed on yourself, Mr. Carson," Bess said. "We'll just apply a bit of this handy snow and have the bleeding stopped in no time."

"It's broke, I guess," Kit said, wiggling his nose and bending over as instructed—soon a considerable patch of snow was stained with his blood.

"My God, Kit," Joe Walker allowed, "I've kilt buffalo that didn't have that much blood in them."

"I'm so sorry, Kit," Tasmin put in. "I thought for sure you saw that wagon tongue."

"You are so wicked, Tasmin," Bess said hotly. "That's what our bad Tasmin does, in the main, Kit—she causes people to smash."

"What nonsense, anyone can trip on a wagon tongue," Tasmin replied coolly, before going in to see about her porridge bath.

10

"I'd call that a bad dream, all right."

Jim Snow tramped east, through the fading, thinning storm, very uneasy in his mind. He strode past herds of buffalo and elk but shot nothing, although it would soon be dark and he was hungry. He intended to walk on through the night until he felt calm again in spirit. He felt he had been right to slap Tasmin for her cursing—it was the other blow that troubled him. The Sin Killer had failed to heal sin in himself, in this case the sin of anger. Preacher Cockerell had strode through life angry, whipping, roaring, condemning—Preacher Cockerell believed his angers were righteous but Jim wasn't so sure, though he himself could always summon a just anger against the wild old native medicine men, with their snakes and bats and poisons.

But hitting Tasmin to stop her chatter was not the act of a holy man who was battling some great sin. There was no great sin in Tasmin—a mild shaking, to persuade her just to keep quiet, would have been enough. But he had made a fist and used it, and now could not get the memory of her shocked face out of his thoughts. It was, of course, true that Tasmin found it difficult to be meekly obedient—she was not at all like his Ute wives, who said little and obeyed him without question. The difference perplexed him. Some adjustment to a new mate was normal, but he and Tasmin had now been together for several months and she didn't seem to be changing. Worse yet, she was always trying to get *him* to change, to let her cut his hair a certain way, to be more sociable, unbend a little with her family. Nor was she a match for his Ute wives, Sun Girl and Little Onion, when it came to getting the chores done efficiently. Tasmin skinned game sloppily at best; she could barely get a fire going, and was no good at working hides. When it came to the daily practicalities of wifehood she failed every test; and her chatter and frequent defiance had to be put in the scales against her. In the nighttime, though, things were different. In the darkness, amid their robes, Tasmin pleased him far more than the two Ute girls, neither of whom were enthusiastic wives in the nighttime sense. Sometimes, in the deep night, Jim would come half awake to realize that Tasmin was beneath him, the two of them in the midst of an embrace whose beginnings were lost in sleep and whose long rapture carried them back into sleep again. Jim was not sure about such powerful and frequent lustings. Preacher Cockerell would have said that such strong lusts were sinful, even though sanctioned by the bonds of matrimony. It was all perplexing, and Jim did not enjoy perplexity. In the main he had lived alone because he liked things simple, but from the moment he had first seen Tasmin, naked in the Missouri's waters, nothing had been simple at all. His mind had become clouded, his actions confused; if only Tasmin would recognize her place and improve in her duties, the confusion in his breast might subside.

Lately, though, confusion had only been increasing. That morning it had reached an intolerable intensity; he had struck his wife and left, and yet, with him still were the very feelings that had caused him to strike out. Such tension was not what he wanted; there must be change, and yet where Tasmin was concerned he had no idea how it could be effected.

Just as the morning star appeared, Jim suddenly tired. He felt he must have walked nearly forty miles; he stopped, built a small fire near a frozen creek, curled up beside it, and slept. He had not slept long, though, when a throb in his ear brought him awake. Someone was coming, on horseback; the throb he had registered was the hoofbeats of a loping horse. It was puzzling. He was far from any camp. Why would the horse be loping?

Then the horse—it was Joe Walker's short-legged mare—became visible, with Pomp Charbonneau on its back. The mare's breath steamed white in the frozen air.

"You are a walker, Jimmy," Pomp said, sliding off the mare. "I knew I'd never catch you on foot, so I borrowed Joe's best mare."

Jim Snow would not have been prepared to welcome any of the other trappers—they were too garrulous and quarrelsome for his taste. But he was always glad to see Pomp; he was able and he knew when to keep quiet. Besides, Pomp had been reared in the old country, where there must be other women like Tasmin. Though not a womanizer himself, perhaps Pomp would have some advice on how to live with an old country wife.

"Why'd you want to catch me?" Jim asked. "I'm just on my way to the boat."

"That's why—Pa's on the boat," Pomp reminded him. "At least I hope he is."

"Oh, I expect he's there—he was guarding the Hairy Horn when we left," Jim assured him. "His wife was with him and we left them plenty of vittles. Why be worried?"

"Bad dreams," Pomp said. "Bad dreams for two nights. I dreamt of the Partezon."

"I'd call that a bad dream, all right," Jim said. The Partezon was the leader of the most aggressive band of the Brulé Sioux. His only pleasure was war, and his dislike of whites was well known. There had been talk of him on the boat, but the Hidatsa scouts all claimed that he was far out on the prairies, in the midst of many buffalo. Why would Pomp be dreaming of him, just now? It was deep winter—the tribes seldom raided then.

"I wouldn't expect him to show up now," Jim said—and yet he knew that dreams were not to be carelessly disregarded. Preacher Cockerell had dreamed of the lightning bolt, and not three weeks later it killed him.

"A raid may not be likely, but when I heard you were headed for the boat I thought I'd just come with you," Pomp said. "Sometimes people do what you don't expect them to."

"Particularly if they're Sioux Indians—that's right," Jim agreed.

11

"Shut up, you wretched little catamite!"

Tasmin's hope that the evidence of Jim Snow's violence toward her would go unnoticed at the dinner table was soon dashed—no one, it seemed, could talk of anything else, the exception being her father, who habitually took not the slightest notice of any wounds except his own. Indeed, when Mary, with her usual malice, pointed out that Tasmin had a puffy lip and a lump on her temple, Lord B. merely chuckled.

"Well and good," he said. "High time some fine fellow got the best of Tasmin. Might knock some of the willfulness out of her—a very sensible thing to do."

"No one got the best of me, Father—I merely slipped on some ice and fell into a ravine," Tasmin replied haughtily.

"Liar—black liar!" Buffum cried. "Your husband beat you—all the trappers are quite unanimous on that point."

"Dear Buffum, your grammar continues to erode," Bobbety said. "'Quite unanimous' is, of course, redundant. A judgment is either unanimous or it isn't."

"Hear, hear, good point," Father Geoffrin cried. He and Bobbety had drawn even closer—they frequently applauded each other's modest flashes of wit.

Tasmin regarded them coolly.

"Very likely both of you, and Bess too, will fall into a ravine someday," she replied. "Let us hope it is a deep one. In fact, I'll go further—let us hope the earth swallows you up, so those of us at table will no longer have to listen to your idiotic chirpings."

"Oh, don't say it, Lady Tasmin," Vicky Kennet pleaded. She had long had a morbid fear of earthquakes, and could not bear the thought of the earth swallowing people up.

Father Geoffrin had long since exhausted his early fascination with Lady Tasmin Berrybender. He now saw her as the very embodiment of English arrogance and lasciviousness.

"What would a fellow such as our Mr. Snow know to do with such a one as Lady Tasmin *except* beat her?" he asked in his whispery voice—though he directed his remarks to Bobbety, Tasmin overheard.

She studied the priest silently for a moment, hoping her malevolent stare would wither him, a hope that was disappointed. Aided by Bobbety's flattery, Father Geoff had convinced himself that his own rhetorical powers were equal to those of an Aquinas or an Augustine.

"Your Mr. Snow," he went on, "accomplished though he undoubtedly is in the ways of the wilderness, has never read a book, seen a picture—if we except George Catlin's poor daubings—listened to an opera, heard a fine symphony, worshiped in a great cathedral, or visited a dress shop. If I may be permitted a little mot, his fists are his paintbrushes—as we can all see, he has sketched a rather vivid bruise on Lady Tasmin's temple. To which I say, tut, tut . . . it's what she gets for marrying an unlettered American."

"Shut up, you wretched little catamite!" Tasmin yelled. "If you insult my husband again, I'll come around there and smother you in your own filthy vestments."

Father Geoff merely gave one of his whinnying laughs, but Lord Berrybender came abruptly awake at the mention of the word "catamite," the practices it suggested bringing to mind certain brutish experiences he had suffered while away at school.

"What? Catamite? Surely he's not *that*, Tasmin!" Lord Berrybender said—the brutish experiences had occurred long ago, but had by no means been forgotten.

"Of course he's *that*, Father," Tasmin insisted sternly. "Surely you must have noticed that this little French whelp has enticed our Bobbety into the ranks of sodomites."

"Not Bobbety . . . not possible!" Lord B. bleated. "Not my son and heir!"

"Now, Papa, pay her no mind," Bobbety said. "Father Geoffrin has merely been introducing me to subtleties of Jesuitical doctrine—things it can't hurt to know."

Bobbety smirked at Tasmin and then leaned over to whisper some piece of naughtiness into the smiling priest's ear, a bit of defiance, or dalliance, whose consequences were immediate and terrible.

Lord Berrybender, enraged that, under his very nose, his son might have been subjected to the same foul practices that he himself so much abhorred, grabbed up the long fork that Cook had been using to turn the goose and, leaning across the table, thrust it like an épée, his intention being to jab the fork right into Father Geoffrin's jugular vein. Instead, because of Bobbety's ill-timed whisper, the tines struck *him*—not the priest—full in the right eye. It was no gentle thrust, either—when Lord Berrybender withdrew the fork, Bobbety's eye came with it. Venetia Kennet screamed and fainted, as did Buffum. Father Geoffrin, fearing that Lord Berrybender might thrust again, slid out of his chair and fled. Piet Van Wely turned very pale and George Catlin looked 'round for Cook, who was always reliable in emergencies.

"Egad . . . 'scuse me . . . what's this now?" Lord B. asked, rather unclear in his mind as to what he had just done. Bobbety emitted a single piercing shriek; before it had ceased echoing, Drum Stewart had rushed over and covered his empty eye socket with a napkin.

Tasmin herself felt the room swirl for a moment, but she didn't faint.

"Be damned, what have I done?" Lord Berrybender cried. His son, one-eyed now, sat sobbing.

"You've made Bobbety a cyclops, Papa," Mary said coolly—"only his one eye is not quite in the middle of his head, as it should be in a proper cyclops."

"Loss of an eye is only an inconvenience—many men have borne it," Drum Stewart said, resolving, privately, to take his meals with the mountain men from then on, their tempers being somewhat more reliable than that of the Berrybenders. All the same, he liked the way Tasmin had threatened to smother the priest.

The mountain men, alerted by the shrieking, watched the proceedings from a respectful distance. No strangers to sudden mutilations themselves, they were nonetheless rather shaken by what Lord Berrybender had just done.

"Somebody needs to shoot that old fool," Tom Fitzpatrick observed.

"Good thought," Eulalie Bonneville agreed. "If he's left loose he's likely to do for us all before he's through."

"They're worse than the Blackfeet, them English," Joe Walker commented.

"*Blitzschnell! Blitzschnell!*" Prince Talleyrand croaked, startling the trappers.

"I've always been against forks," Jim Bridger remarked.

"Seeing a thing like that makes me wish I'd stayed dead," Hugh Glass observed. "The thought of getting an eye poked out gives me the shivers."

"I wonder if we could procure some smelling salts?" Drum Stewart asked. "Venetia Kennet's unconscious and so is Lady Bess."

Tasmin went to the kitchen and secured Cook, who came and surveyed Bobbety's injury as calmly as if she were making soup. Towels, soft rags, and warm water were soon supplied in abundance, though no smelling salts could be located.

"Mademoiselle took it," Tasmin said. "I believe she intended on doing a lot of fainting, up in Canada."

Bobbety was whimpering quietly. "I need Geoff, where's Geoff?" he kept asking.

"Hiding like the coward he is, I've no doubt," Tasmin said.

She soaked a rag in vinegar and managed to get Vicky Kennet awake, but vinegar had no effect on Buffum, or on Eliza, the plate breaker, who had managed to faint while no one was looking.

All through the crisis, as she dealt as best she could with the situation, Tasmin felt Drummond Stewart's hot eyes upon her, a fact which annoyed her considerably. The man had the look of a rank seducer—she was hardly in the mood for such attentions.

Cook made an excellent bandage for Bobbety's empty socket; soon he was led away, still calling plaintively for his Geoff.

To Tasmin's great annoyance her father, after pounding the table a few times, began to sob.

"Buggery, nether parts, buggery—there's a curse upon our blood, I'm afraid!" he cried. "Between Constance and Gladwyn I believe I miss Gladwyn the most—impossible to find a valet with his qualifications in these parts."

Tasmin had just noticed that Pomp Charbonneau was missing. Irritated only last evening by his determination to walk her home, she now found that she wanted him back. She didn't mean to allow the hot-eyed Scot to catch her alone, and Pomp could have been some help in that regard.

"Let me see that nose, Kit," she said, walking over to the mountain men.

"It's stopped bleeding—wiggles funny, though," Kit admitted.

"If I promise not to wiggle it, will you walk me home?" Tasmin asked.

"What an odd place your country is," Tasmin said, as they neared her camp. "I was struck, you broke your nose, and my brother lost an eye. Makes one feel lucky to be alive at all."

Kit Carson, silent and shy, merely tipped his cap when he left Tasmin at her tent.

12

. . . naked, mutilated, frozen, scalped . . .

They found the first two *engagés*—naked, mutilated, frozen, scalped, eyes gone, genitals gone, leg bones split—more than ten miles from the river.

"These two made a good run for it," Jim observed.

"Not good enough," Pomp said—he was worried about his father.

"Your pa's got along with the Sioux for thirty years," Jim reminded him. "They wouldn't be this hard on your pa."

"When someone like the Partezon gets in a killing mood, thirty years may not mean much," Pomp said.

Tasmin's staghound, Tintamarre, they found not far from the river, speared and frozen stiff.

"That dog was bad to run off," Jim said.

The steamer *Rocky Mount* was now just a few piles of charred planks, scattered over the river ice. Master Jeremy Thaw had had his skull split open with an axe. George Aitken and Holger Sten were both scalped, burned, and cut.

"I liked George Aitken," Jim remarked. "He ought not to have traveled so slow."

"Probably the old lord's fault," Pomp said. "He kept George waiting so he could hunt."

None of the other *engagés* could be found, nor was there any sign of Toussaint Charbonneau and his wife, Coal. The Hairy Horn was missing as well.

"I expect your pa left," Jim reasoned. "Maybe the Hairy Horn finally decided he wanted to go home."

"That's the hopeful view," Pomp said. Most of the plainsmen he knew considered his father an old fool who could barely find his way from one river to the next; and yet his father had survived when many a better-equipped man had fallen. Some lucky instinct seemed, at the last moment, to propel him out of harm's way. Perhaps it would be so this time, as well.

They wrapped the corpses of George Aitken, Holger Sten, and Jeremy

Thaw in a few scraps of blankets, hasty and imperfect shrouds, but all they had. Since the ground was frozen hard, burial presented a problem.

"George was a waterman," Jim said. "Maybe we can cut through the ice."

They carried the corpses far out on the ice, hacked holes with their hatchets, and shoved the bodies through. Neither felt quite right about it but there was no better option.

Jim Snow noticed another thing. The victims had been hacked and burned and stuck with arrows, but no one had been shot.

"That's the Partezon's way," Pomp reminded him. "I expect he may have a few guns but he don't use 'em much, and he won't let his people take nothing from the whites. His womenfolk still use bone needles. I think he may trade for a little corn with the Mandans, but otherwise he lives way off in the center of the plains. He tries to keep his people true to the old ways."

"Probably that's why he came all this way to burn a steamboat," Jim suggested. "Once steamers start coming up this river there won't be any Indians left to keep to the old ways—or any ways."

Jim had never met the Partezon—he had just heard tales. Though not a large man, he was said to be able to shoot an arrow clean through a running buffalo, which suggested a powerful arm. He himself had tried the trick a number of times but with no success—he could only get the arrow to go in to the haft. A chief powerful enough to keep his people from trading their independence for the cheap baubles of the whites was a man to be reckoned with. That he killed with a vengeance was evident from the bodies they had found. Plenty of Indians would kill their enemies in a painful manner, but the Partezon had brought his warriors several hundred miles for a purpose—to keep the steamboats out. He had come with at least a hundred warriors, too, judging from the tracks. Few chiefs could boast of full control over their warriors—the young ones, particularly, were apt to bolt and spoil a good ambush. But the Partezon had kept control. Just knowing he was there gave the plains a menacing feel.

"Let's follow the Partezon a ways, and see where he's headed," Pomp suggested; but then he recalled that Jim Snow had a wife to think about.

"I suppose you might be needing to get back to Tasmin," Pomp said. "I can track the Partezon for a day or two and then go look for my pa."

At the mere mention of Tasmin, Jim felt filled with confusion again. He wasn't yet clear in his mind or his feelings, when it came to Tasmin—he felt in no hurry to go back.

"I guess I'll stay with you," he said, a little awkwardly—but Pomp seemed not to mind the awkwardness. He was staring at a small, conical hill about half a mile away. The hill was mostly bare, but had a gnarled tree—cedar, probably—on top, a single tree with a dusting of snow.

Pomp looked troubled.

"That hill looks familiar," he said—"but it ought to be farther south. There's a hill just like that down by Manuel Lisa's old fort, where my mother is buried."

Jim looked at the tree—it seemed to him that he had seen a hill remarkably similar to this one—hadn't it been near the South Platte?

"Maybe it's the wandering hill—they say you usually find it where there's been killings," Pomp said.

Jim had heard of the wandering hill several times—it was a heathenish legend that many tribes seemed to believe. The hill was said to be inhabited with short, fierce devils with large heads, who killed travelers with deadly arrows made of grass blades, which they could shoot great distances.

"If that's the hill with the devils in it they'd have a hard time finding grass blades to shoot at us, with all this snow," Jim said.

Pomp was still staring at the strange, bare little hill.

"My mother believed in the wandering hill," he said. "She claimed to have seen it way off over the mountains somewhere—near the Snake River, I think."

"Well, I thought I saw it once myself—on the South Platte," Jim admitted. "What do you think?"

Pomp shook his head.

"I don't know," he said. "I just don't remember that particular hill being here the last time I came this way."

They had not gone a mile more before they found the other *engagés*. They had tried to make a stand in a thicket of tall reeds but had been burned out by the Indians and treated as the other *engagés* had been. Wolves had been at the corpses.

"I hate to leave men just laying dead on the ground," Jim said. "It feels unholy."

"I agree," Pomp said—he was still troubled in his thinking about that odd little hill.

They covered the dead *engagés* with driftwood and rocks. The wolves would eventually dig through to them, but it would take them a while.

That night, from a ridge, they saw the Partezon's campfires, red glows far ahead.

"Look at those fires," Pomp said. "That could be two hundred Sioux. The Partezon sure wasn't taking any chances."

"Nope—why would he?" Jim said.

13

Gladwyn felt a prickle of apprehension . . .

Gladwyn felt a prickle of apprehension when the old warrior on the white horse rode into the Sans Arc camp. Many warriors, from many bands, visited the Sans Arc to look at the Buffalo Man—women came, and small children were brought here for him to bless. When visitors stared at him Gladwyn spoke loudly in Gaelic to impress upon everyone that he was a god, a holy fool, born of a buffalo cow.

Always, when there were visitors, Three Geese, his discoverer, and Grasshopper, his protector, kept up a constant chatter, describing the miraculous birth which they both now claimed to have witnessed. With White Hawk dead of fever there was no one to contradict them, yet skeptics remained, old Cat Head in particular. Cat Head often proclaimed his disbelief, but he was not a popular man; the council of elders refused to listen to him.

But it was Cat Head who, losing patience with his gullible tribesmen, went off into the prairies and returned with the old warrior on the white horse, an old man who looked at Gladwyn with unflinching hatred. The old one had brought only a few young warriors with him, but Gladwyn felt frightened anyway. The wild newcomers looked as if they could easily wipe out the whole Sans Arc village, should they choose. Gladwyn didn't even bother with his Gaelic—these were not men to be impressed with a little babbling.

"You see, I told you," Cat Head said to the Partezon. "As you can see he is just an ordinary white man, and yet these fools believe he came out of a buffalo."

Three Geese was horrified at the situation he found himself in. Cat Head, without asking anyone, had gone off and persuaded the Partezon to come look at the Buffalo Man. Long ago Cat Head had ridden with the Partezon's band, but then he had hurt his back during a hunt and ever since had been leading an easy life in the Sans Arc village, with three wives to see to his needs. Cat Head was vain and sharp spoken—he was always causing trouble, but rarely this much trouble.

"What is this foolishness?" the Partezon asked Three Geese. "This is just a white man."

"He is a white man, but he came out of a buffalo cow. I saw it and so did Grasshopper," Three Geese said.

"If he came out of a buffalo cow once then he ought to be able to do it again," the Partezon declared. He spoke sharply to his young warriors, who immediately wheeled their horses and raced off into the prairie.

Gladwyn could not understand what was being said, but one thing was clear enough: the old man on the white horse didn't like him. In fact his dislike was so strong that the Sans Arc themselves began to dislike him as well. The whole tribe stopped whatever they were doing and waited idly to see what would happen. His own wives, Big Stealer and Little Stealer, always so eager to get him whatever he wanted, now backed away, waiting, with the other Sans Arc, for the old man's verdict.

The old chief did not bother to dismount and take a close look. He waited, his cold gaze unchanged.

Three Geese began to feel very uncomfortable. It seemed to him that people were turning against him—even Grasshopper had left his position behind the white man. Three Geese, who had found the white man and witnessed the miracle of his arrival, was losing status by the minute. The Partezon was the most respected of all living Sioux. No one challenged him. Thanks to the meddling Cat Head, the Partezon was now there, in the Sans Arc village. Three Geese felt like leaving—he thought he might go live with his brother in the Miniconjou band. Only, for now, it was too late. Whatever test the Partezon intended to make would have to be waited out.

Soon, from the prairies to the north, came the ti-yiing of the hunters. A great cloud of dry snow was being kicked up by the racing horses. The young warriors the Partezon had sent away were now coming back, running a large buffalo cow between them. Three warriors raced on each side of the big cow, driving her straight into the Sans Arc camp. People fell back in astonishment, but the Partezon's young warriors knew what they were doing. As the big cow, almost exhausted, lumbered into the camp, the lead hunter leaned over so close that he was almost touching the buffalo and loosed an arrow, then another.

The buffalo cow ran a few more yards, then stumbled and went to her knees. For a moment she knelt, her breath steaming, coughing blood onto the snow, and then she fell over. The Partezon made a gesture—the six young warriors jumped off their horses and rolled the cow onto her back, at which point the Partezon dismounted and walked over to the buffalo, now spread wide as the young warriors pulled back her legs.

"I need a sharp knife," the Partezon said. "Mine is dull from cutting up those Frenchmen we caught."

He looked at the Sans Arc women—his tone was mild. In a short while, to Gladwyn's horror, his own wife Big Stealer emerged from their lodge and gave the old man a sharp butcher knife, a blade he inspected critically.

"I can make a better knife than this, but right now we have to make a good womb for your Buffalo Man," he said.

Gladwyn felt terror seize him—he didn't know what the old man was saying, but he knew that his days as a holy fool for the Sans Arc were over. He wanted to leap to his feet and flee, but the whole band was close around him now—he would not get ten yards. All he could do was sit, numb with fear, waiting.

The Partezon, working hard with what he considered an inadequate knife, slit the buffalo cow up her whole length, from anus to nose. He made the cut as deep as he could, and then instructed his young men to lift out the guts, armful after steaming armful. The warriors were soon bloody to their shoulders. The Partezon had them string out the guts in long lines and coils—he waved, and the hungry Sans Arc children rushed on them. Those who had knives cut themselves sections—others gnawed at the slippery coils with their teeth.

While the children of the Sans Arc feasted on gut, the Partezon had the buffalo cow—which was still breathing—cleaned out as completely as possible, opening the rib cage wide, making a large red cavity. When the cow died the old warrior borrowed an axe and broke off most of her ribs—then he turned to the Sans Arc and pointed at Gladwyn.

"Sew him in the buffalo," he said. "If he is a Buffalo Man, like Three Geese believes, then he will soon slip out again. Then I will know that I have been wrong and that he is indeed a god."

It seemed to Gladwyn that a thousand eyes were on him—all he saw were the eyes, as he began to scream. All the eyes were hard now, like the old warrior's eyes. Though he screamed and screamed, the warriors stripped him naked, removed the nice skins his young wives had sewed for him, and then shoved and squeezed until they had pushed him into the red carcass of the ripped-open buffalo cow. The same blood that had once warmed him and kept him alive now filled his eyes, his mouth, his nostrils—he gasped in blood when he tried to breathe.

"He is too large—he won't fit in this buffalo," one of the Partezon's warriors complained.

"Then cut his feet off—if he is a god he can grow more feet when he comes out," the Partezon instructed, handing the warrior the axe. The chopping was soon done, but even when Gladwyn had been crammed into the cavity of the dead buffalo, sewing him in did not prove easy. He struggled far longer than anyone had expected him to. His own blood now flowed into the buffalo, whose warm blood had once saved him. Even when the women pulled the sinews tighter Gladwyn somehow managed to gasp in air. When the sewing was nearly finished he managed to thrust a hand out—but this was a last effort; with the loss of blood Gladwyn slowly weakened; his staring eyes did not close, but he slowly ceased to see.

"I want that hand—I have never had the hand of a Buffalo Man before," the Partezon said. "Perhaps it will help us in the hunt."

The hand was easily cut off, but the young warrior who removed it began to have uneasy feelings about the whole business.

"He hasn't been in there long—I think he might come out when we leave," the young warrior said. "His eyes are still open—I don't like it."

"If you think that, then you are as big a fool as Three Geese," the Partezon said. He cleaned the butcher knife in the snow before giving it back to Big Stealer. Then he mounted his white horse and left the camp.

Later that same day Three Geese and his wives also left the Sans Arc camp and went to live with his brother, among the Miniconjous. In the eyes of the Sans Arc his disgrace was complete. If he stayed with the Sans Arc old Cat Head would never let him forget that he had been foolish enough to suppose that a man had been born of a buffalo.

Three Geese and his wives were not the only Sans Arc to relocate. The dead buffalo lay right in the middle of the Sans Arc camp, with the dead man inside it. The stump of his arm still protruded and his eyes were still open, staring at nothing.

"This is a pretty bad thing to look at," Cat Head concluded. "I don't want to get up every morning and see that buffalo, with that arm sticking out of it and those eyes staring."

For once, Cat Head expressed a sentiment shared by the whole tribe. In two hours' time all the Sans Arc tepees had been folded, goods were packed on travois, and the tribe was on the move. As they left their camp it began to snow heavily. By the time Cat Head himself was ready to leave the old camp, the dead buffalo was only a mound in the snow. Leaving it behind made Cat Head feel so good that he decided to make Big Stealer and Little Stealer his wives. After all, they were competent girls, and they had no husband now.

14

. . . a Hidatsa boy had just come running up with news . . .

"The Partezon is my half brother, but he doesn't like me," the Hairy Horn informed them. They were in the trader John Skraeling's camp—a Hidatsa boy had just come running up with news that the steamer Rocky Mount had been attacked and burned. Toussaint Charbonneau shook his head sadly; it was just as he had feared, from the moment they heard that the Partezon was on the move. He and Coal and the Hairy Horn had left the boat just in time.

"Why don't he like you?" the trader, Skraeling, asked. He too had taken precautions when he heard of the Partezon's advance, camping near the Mandan villages in what he hoped was a neutral zone.

"He didn't like it that I went to see the president," the Hairy Horn replied. "He thinks he is better than the president. He doesn't bargain with the white men, or make treaties with them, or smoke the peace pipe."

"He sounds like he needs to be taken down a notch or two," Malgres said. "I expect he's just an old bluffer."

Both Skraeling and Charbonneau looked hard at Malgres, a killer, but a man of little judgment.

"If you think he's a bluffer, why don't you pay him a visit?" Skraeling suggested. "If you're hot to kill somebody, go kill the Partezon."

Malgres didn't answer. John Skraeling was yellowish and thin. No doubt he would die soon. Malgres and the Ponca had discussed killing Skraeling and taking his money and the two young Hidatsa girls he had acquired; but the Ponca advised caution. Even sick, Skraeling was still quick with gun and knife. Besides, all the tribes trusted him and brought him furs. Let him get a little sicker and a little richer: then they could kill him.

Toussaint was not at ease in Skraeling's camp, but he had to stop somewhere until the threat from the Partezon passed. In a day or two, when it was safe, he meant to take Coal and rejoin the English party on the Yellowstone; the only impediment to that plan was the Hairy Horn, who was still officially Charbonneau's charge. There were plenty of Sioux around; the old man could have easily made it back to his band, but now the old fool was resisting all efforts to send him home. Captain Clark, safe in his office in Saint Louis, had specifically instructed Charbonneau to take the old chief home—but it was not easy to make an Indian go home if the Indian didn't want to.

"My people chase around too much," the Hairy Horn said, when pressed on the matter. "I might just stay here, near the river, where there is no danger of thirst. There is some pretty dry country out where my people live."

"If you need a wife I'll sell you one," Skraeling suggested. "I've got one to spare."

This offer annoyed Malgres—if Skraeling was going to dispose of one of his girls, Malgres felt his own wishes should have been considered.

The Hairy Horn didn't want either of the skinny Hidatsa girls. The best woman around, in his view, was Sharbo's plump little wife. For some reason it didn't occur to Sharbo that he ought to share her, and this despite the fact that the Hairy Horn had made his interest plain enough. White men were often obtuse when it came to the common business of sharing women.

"I hope the Partezon wasn't too hard on George Aitken," Charbonneau said—he had a guilty conscience on that score. If he had just been a little more persuasive, George and the other two white men might have left the boat and come with him to safety. George's concern had been for the boat, but after all, his employers were rich men and could always build another boat.

"If the Partezon caught any white men he probably burned them," the

Hairy Horn said. "He doesn't like to parley with white men, but he doesn't mind burning them."

"Well, at least George is dead—past suffering," Skraeling remarked. It had begun to snow a little. They all stood around outside the lodge, idle but anxious. Whatever business they might pretend to be conducting, what they were really doing was watching for any sign of the marauding Sioux. No one wanted to be caught snoozing in a lodge if the Sioux riders came flying through the snow.

Suddenly they all saw the Ponca, running as if for his life from the direction of the river—his leggings were loose, evidently he had just been with a woman and had to pull his pants up in a hurry. They all thought of the Partezon, but surely the Sioux would be coming from the prairies, not from the river.

The Ponca, out of breath, babbled his news, and Charbonneau relaxed.

"It ain't the Partezon," he said. "It's Pomp. My boy's coming."

Tears started in the old man's eyes, at the thought of seeing Pomp, his dancing little Baptiste, as Captain Clark had called him when Pomp was an infant. The thought of Pomp reminded him of Sacagawea, and of the fine family life they had had, so long ago.

"Why, that's good news, Sharbo," Skraeling said. "I like Pomp. We'll kill a buffalo, if we can, and have a fine family reunion."

The Ponca grabbed Skraeling's arm—he was not through reporting, evidently.

"Oh, Jim's with him," Charbonneau said. "I guess that's why this fellow's upset."

"Jim Bridger—I thought he was over at the Yellowstone," Skraeling said. He knew that Jim Bridger and Pomp Charbonneau were good friends—it was merely surprising that the lanky young Bridger would be at the Mandans' instead of deep in the mountains where the rich beaver streams were.

To Skraeling's surprise the Hairy Horn, after chattering for a minute, suddenly launched into his death song, a tiresome chant that none of them wanted to hear.

"No, not Jim Bridger—it's Jimmy Snow that's with him," Charbonneau said.

"Well, well—this will be interesting," Skraeling said. "We don't get a visit from the Sin Killer every day."

15

Far in the distance, now and then, they saw a few brown specks . . .

The buffalo, so plentiful for the past weeks, had suddenly become scarce, Jim observed. Perhaps the fact of the Partezon and his two hundred warriors scared them off. On the trek over to the Knife River the two of them had seldom been out of sight of the great herds; but now, as he and Pomp moved cautiously downriver, toward the Mandan camps, they saw no buffalo—or at least none close. Far in the distance, now and then, they saw a few brown specks, many miles away. Other game was scarce also—scarce enough that when they saw a strange mound in the snow and discovered that it was a dead buffalo, their first thought was food. Cold as it had been, the meat would likely not be spoiled.

Pomp got out his knife and kicked at the carcass, to knock some of the snow off, when he got a bad surprise. The stump of a man's hand protruded several inches from the dead cow's belly.

"Jimmy, look here," he said.

Jim Snow looked—they poked tentatively at the frozen carcass a time or two. Though it was plain enough that the man inside the buffalo would have to be dead, they still moved cautiously. Both had seen numerous instances of decapitation and dismemberment; but neither of them had ever seen a man sewn into a buffalo before. It was impossible to say how long the man and the dead cow had been there, but thanks to the deep chill, they were now frozen together.

"Do you want to try and hack him out?" Pomp asked.

"What would be the point?" Jim said. "We've got no way to bury him. It must be that little fellow from the boat, the one who carried the guns for Tasmin's pa. He was lost in the storm and never found."

"Someone found him, I guess," Pomp said. "Didn't there used to be a good-sized Sans Arc camp around here somewhere?"

"I think so," Jim said. "I wonder where *they* went."

The two of them wandered around the area for a while, hoping some clue to the mystery might turn up. But they found nothing, and it began to snow. Soon the buffalo, with the small man sewn into it, was once more just a mound on the snowy plain.

When they left, drifting south with the snow on their backs, both felt that somehow things were drifting out of kilter. They had not managed to save Captain Aitken or anyone else from the boat, or even managed to bury them properly. The fate of Pomp's father and his young wife remained to be determined. The best place to start a search seemed to be the Mandan villages, and yet, as they went south, Jim Snow seemed so uneasy with the proceedings that Pomp stopped to consider what best to do.

"You don't have to come with me, Jimmy," he said. "Pa's probably at the Mandans'—I imagine he's safe, otherwise we'd have found him. You've got a wife and all. If you want to head back for the Yellowstone, suit yourself."

"No, we better stick together for a while yet," Jim said. "There could still be some of the wild men on the loose."

In fact he didn't believe his own answer—he just didn't want to go back to Tasmin yet. When he tried to think about what to do with Tasmin he felt tired—the complications of marriage took the spring out of his step, a thing that didn't happen when he thought of his Ute wives; but then he almost never thought of his Ute wives. They didn't fill his mind in the way that Tasmin did.

As things stood Jim was glad to have an errand to help Pomp with. It allowed him to put off, for a while, having to deal with the forceful English girl he had married, a woman who didn't understand that the duty of a wife was to be silent before the Lord. What if she never accepted that duty? What if she never obeyed? It was a problem Jim didn't want to think about too much, and yet he couldn't get it out of his mind as he plodded along behind Pomp.

To Pomp the fact that Jim Snow and Tasmin Berrybender had somehow proceeded into a marriage was one of those perplexing facts that no amount of reasoning could explain. That such incongruous matings happened, and happened often, was obvious, though. In Europe great princes were always confounding their subjects by marrying Gypsy dancers or Turkish slave girls—even, now and then, a French whore. If well-born princes couldn't manage to align their fancies with dynastic needs, there was no reason that a frontier boy such as Jim would be any more likely to choose a wife suitable to the circumstances of a mountain trapper or Santa Fe trail guide—professions that were sure to entail long absences from the domestic hearth. Of course, Jim had two Indian wives, but he seldom saw them and they were very likely much easier to deal with than Tasmin Berrybender.

It was a puzzle—on the whole Pomp felt glad that it wasn't *his* puzzle.

The snow, after a last intense flurry, suddenly stopped falling. The sky cleared, the sun cast down a thin winter light, and to the south, a dog barked.

"Hear that?" Jim said.

"Yep, a Mandan dog, I suppose," Pomp said.

Just then an Indian who had evidently been copulating with a woman jumped up from behind a snowbank, pulling at his leggings—the woman, short and almost square, scurried off like an outraged prairie chicken.

"Why, there's Pa," Pomp said. His father stood a head taller than many prairie travelers and was usually easy to spot in a crowd. He was standing with an old Indian and three or four other men near a Mandan earth lodge, but the bright sun on the new snow made it hard to see exactly the people they were approaching. A thin, high chant reached them, and the dog continued to bark.

"That's the Hairy Horn singing," Jim said. "At least your pa managed to keep up with one of the three chiefs."

"I believe I see John Skraeling," Pomp said, squinting against the glare.

"Be watchful of the little Spanish fellow who's with him," Jim cautioned. "He's the one who punctured Big White's liver."

"Skraeling don't usually run with killers," Pomp observed.

"He probably picked this one up by accident and ain't figured out how to get rid of him," Jim said.

16

"I shall never look noble now," Bobbety complained . . .

Since Jim Snow was gone, and Pomp Charbonneau too, Kit Carson quietly appointed himself Tasmin's guardian; he stuck to her like a burr on her walks from tent to trading post. Most days he waited with her while Cook dressed Bobbety's socket, a task Cook performed imperturbably, while Tasmin distracted her deeply depressed brother by reading him long passages from Pope or Prior.

Father Geoffrin soon made a cautious reappearance, in the main keeping well clear of Tasmin. Once he ventured to suggest that Bobbety might enjoy a snatch of Rousseau, but Tasmin greeted the comment with a look of such chill that the little priest retreated. He began to spend more time with George Catlin, who, despite the bitter cold, seldom passed a day without doing three or four Indian portraits. Some of the sitters had traveled long distances to be painted by the likeness maker.

"I shall never look noble now," Bobbety complained, though in fact the kitchen girl, Eliza, clumsy with plates but skilled with the needle, had made Bobbety a very practical eye patch out of the soft leather on one of Lady Berrybender's old purses.

"You never did look noble, Bobbety," Tasmin told him frankly. "At best you looked silly."

"Quite right," Buffum agreed. "If anything, Eliza's eye patch lends you a particle of dignity."

"Something sorely lacking up to now," Mary remarked. "Now you look like an evil pirate—one of a sodomitical bent."

"You are all cruel, too cruel," Bobbety complained, though without force. "I wish Father would come and lash you with his horsewhip."

"Not likely—he is off lashing his horses with it, in hopes of catching up to some wild beast he wants to shoot," Tasmin told him.

"Ha ha, perhaps he'll run off a cliff, in which case the title will be mine and I'll make you all pay for your cruelty," Bobbety said. "I'll immediately parcel you out to minor curates and vicars. All frivolities will immediately cease—from then on you will be expected to walk the modest path of piety."

Kit Carson could only stand in wonder when the English spoke to one another in such fashion. What it meant he had no idea, though he did think it likely that Lord Berrybender might someday run his buggy off a cliff. Even the mountain men, well accustomed to the dangers of the wild, looked sharp when in close company with Lord Berrybender. A man who could casually poke out his own son's eye was to be allowed a certain space.

Kit did not understand the business about vicars and curates, but he didn't think that Bobbety stood much of a chance against three such forceful sisters. It was odd how the English could keep on insulting one another hour after hour—insult feeding on insult, rising now and then to an occasional slap or pinch. Among the mountain men ten minutes of such slanderous talk would have led, at the very least, to fisticuffs, and knife fighting or gunplay would not have been out of the question; but with the English it seemed to go no further than words. One thing Kit saw clearly was that Tasmin could easily outtalk anyone in her family—even the old lord grew tongue-tied and red in the face when he tried to match words with Tasmin, the woman with whom Kit was now so deeply in love that he spent most of his nights and days thinking about her. He was not so disloyal as to wish Jim Snow dead, but he did allow himself to hope that Jim would be a while getting back. Perhaps a desire to trap the southern Rockies would come over him—some task that would occupy him for several months. Kit knew that this was unlikely—Tasmin, after all, was with child—but he couldn't help hoping. The mere fact that several of the mountain men had begun to exchange pleasantries with Lady Tasmin had begun to annoy him, a fact not lost on his friends and colleagues. Jim Bridger was huffy about it—not only did Kit no longer have time for *him,* but he had also begun to ignore the camp chores the two of them had been sharing.

"Kit wouldn't bring in a stick of firewood unless he stumped his toe on it," Jim observed to Eulalie Bonneville.

"Men in love need no firewood," Eulalie reminded him. "Their nuts keep them warm."

"Yes, but what keeps their *compañeros* warm?" Jim Bridger asked—though he himself had begun to think rather warmly of the pert Eliza, Cook's brown-eyed helper, who frequently allowed plates and platters to slip through her grasp. She had twice managed to spill gravy in Jim Bridger's lap, a sure sign of ripening affection, in Bonneville's view. Both times Eliza had made a great flutter and tried to daub Jim dry, attentions that embarrassed him and provoked caustic comment from the other mountain men.

"She's wanting pokes, I expect," Tom Fitzpatrick allowed, as the old parrot wandered up and down the long table, seeking scraps. "I suppose she thinks that if she spills enough gravy in Jimmy's lap he'll rise to the task."

"Anybody can spill gravy," Jim replied—he did not like the imputation of coarse motives to his Eliza, although it had to be admitted that his own thoughts often took a coarse turn when Eliza was about.

Tasmin knew, of course, that young Kit was deeply smitten—she had only to let her eyes meet his for a moment to bring a deep blush to his cheeks—even his ears turned a fiery red. When once she gave way to an

irresistible impulse, grabbed his silly cap, and flung it onto the snow, Kit
was so astonished that it seemed he might pass out.

Of course, in such a place, with the winter deep and the company limited, it was only to be expected that attractions would form and affections
flourish or even rage. Tasmin saw with amusement that Drum Stewart,
the overheated Scot, had unleashed a tigress in Venetia Kennet. Cook confided the colorful truth to Tasmin: Vicky had obtained some potent sleeping drafts from Monsieur Boisdeffre; these she stirred liberally into the
old lord's brandy each night, putting him deeply under and leaving Vicky
free to pursue strenuous nightlong tourneys of carnality with the highborn
hunter—so strenuous were these tourneys that Drum Stewart only now
and then had energy left for the hunt.

For the first week or so after Jim Snow's departure, Tasmin took an
amused and lofty attitude toward what she observed at the post. After all,
whatever her immediate differences with her husband, she was a satisfied
woman, one who did not have to seek casual heats. But as the weeks passed
she began to feel less amused, and also less serene—where *was* he, Jim
Snow? News had reached them through native runners of the destruction
of the steamer. Though too late, Jim had done his duty by Captain Aitken—
why didn't he come back and take up his duties to his wife?

For three weeks she went every night to the tent, escorted by the faithful
Kit. She knew that when Jim returned he would expect to find her there. It
was their home; he had chosen the campsite; so she waited through more
than twenty nights, never feeling quite safe, not sleeping very deeply, always half on guard against whatever threats might arise.

But Jim didn't come. Every night, walking out with Kit, Tasmin's spirits
sunk a little lower. Why didn't he come? How *could* he leave her in such uncertain circumstances? That old raunch Hugh Glass had begun to follow
her boldly with his eyes. Her noble blood did not impress old Hugh, nor
did the fact that she was the Sin Killer's wife. To a man who had survived
a bear, Jim Snow may have seemed like small beer. Tasmin did not want
to make too much of what, after all, were only looks—but she didn't want
to make too little of them, either. In one respect Hugh Glass was like her
father: he was all appetite.

"I don't quite like that Mr. Glass," she said to Kit. "He has the look of a
criminal, that man."

"Hugh's a rough cob," Kit agreed. "It's all three of us can do to whip
him, when he's drunk."

"What about my Jimmy?" she asked. "Do you think my Jim could whip him?"

"Not in a wrestle, no—Hugh's a biter and a gouger," Kit said. "Jim might kill him, though—with a knife maybe. Killing him might be the only way to stop him."

Tasmin thought of the wild old man, watching her. What if he came, caught her before she could even wake up?

"I've made you walk all this distance for nothing, Kit," she said one night. "I'm going back to the fort—after all, I need to be careful. I have a baby coming."

On their way back, their feet crunching in the snow, Kit imagined himself killing Hugh Glass in a savage fight over Tasmin. Once imagined, the vision wouldn't leave him—he dreamt it by night and dreamt it by day. Sometimes he shot Hugh, sometimes he stabbed him. In one vision Tasmin even gave him a warm hug, as he stood over the corpse of her attacker.

In the next weeks, as winter edged toward its end and the snows began to melt, Kit nourished his fantasy of rescue. Only in battle, he felt, could he show Lady Tasmin that he was worthy of her. With Tasmin living at the post and old Hugh often about, Kit felt that he did not dare relax his vigilance.

"Why's that Carson boy so itchy, when he's around me?" Hugh asked the Broken Hand. "He comes in puffed up like a rooster, ready to peck. Why would he think I'd need to fight a pup like him?"

"Oh, young men are like dogs—they go round snarling, half the time."

"*Blitzschnell! Blitzschnell!*" the old parrot said.

"It ain't you he's itchy about, Hugh," Tom Fitzpatrick replied. "It's Jimmy Snow's pretty wife he's itchy about. I expect Kit thinks you've got the randies for her."

"No, it's Kit's got the randies for her," Jim Bridger said. "He follows her around like a puppy. Won't hardly even speak to me, and I'm his partner."

"All the same, she is a fair beauty," Milt Sublette declared.

"Jimmy Snow got lucky," his brother said.

"Maybe he's lucky and maybe he ain't—maybe he's just got trouble," Hugh allowed. "If he's so lucky, why'd he run off?"

No one had an answer for that question.

"Jimmy Snow leads his own life," Joe Walker said. "Always has. Holy matrimony may not suit him particularly. It never suited me."

Across the room Tasmin was having an animated dispute with George

Catlin—the two of them could hardly discuss any subject without quarreling, it seemed, a fact the mountain men took note of.

"I hope I've got better sense than to take up with a quarrelsome woman—and that one's quarrelsome," Hugh Glass declared. "In the dark one woman's as good as another, I expect, provided the hole ain't plugged."

This sentiment required considerable thinking over. The mountain men gave it seasoned consideration, thinking back over their experiences with women, quarrelsome or docile. Most of these experiences had been so brief that a clear statement of principles was hard to arrive at.

"Hugh may be right," Bill Sublette allowed.

"Hasn't Jimmy Snow got some Ute wives somewhere?" Joe Walker asked.

"That's right—I believe they're down on the Green River," the Broken Hand said. "They're sisters, I believe."

"Probably went back to them," Hugh Glass concluded. "Probably got tired of listening to that English girl yap."

17

"That would be the missing valet."

Jim Snow and John Skraeling were startled by the warmth of the reunion between Pomp Charbonneau and his father, Toussaint. The old man hugged Pomp tightly, as he wept, his tears wetting Pomp's hair and dripping onto his shoulder. The old man was too choked up to speak, and Pomp, usually so shy and reserved, wasn't shy at all about his father's teary welcome. He held the old man close, patted him, whispered to him.

This long embrace of father and son, and the delight they took in being together again, was a wonder to Jim Snow, whose own parents had been killed when he was four. As a captive child, with the Osage, he had had to fight the camp dogs for scraps of food; when the Cockerells ransomed him from the Osage he had become an indentured boy, fed and worked but not loved. He saw in the Charbonneaus' sudden happiness something he had never known—perhaps the lack of it accounted for the fact that he had always felt a man apart. The trader Skraeling must have felt something of the same surprise—he turned away from the Charbonneaus and questioned Jim closely about conditions upriver, the movements of the Partezon in particular.

"He's gone back out onto the plains," Jim said. "We followed him and saw his fires. Coming down here we saw about the derndest thing I've ever seen—a man sewed into a buffalo. Frozen hard, over by where that Sans Arc camp used to be."

As he talked he noticed that the Spaniard, Malgres, was following him with his eyes.

"That would be the missing valet," Skraeling said. "I heard of him from Draga. The Sans Arc—or some of them—believed he was born of a buffalo. I guess the Partezon decided to test the story."

"I guess," Jim said. He wanted to leave, though he wasn't entirely sure where he wanted to go. The sight of Pomp, so happy to be with his father, made Jim restless. While he was trying to make a plan the old Hairy Horn walked over.

"The Partezon is my brother," he said. "How many warriors did he come with?"

"Plenty of warriors," Jim said. "Could have been two hundred."

"He's mean, my brother," the Hairy Horn said. "So is that Spaniard who's with the Twisted Hair."

"You're right about him," Jim said. "He's the man who killed Big White."

"He's a bad one but he won't kill me—it's you he wants to kill," the Hairy Horn said. "You're more important. I am just an old man who will soon die anyway."

Jim glanced at Malgres again—the old Hairy Horn was probably right. Many men killed in battle, but only a few for reputation. Perhaps Malgres was one of that sort—he himself wasn't worried about the Spaniard but he thought it might be well to warn Pomp about him—Pomp, after all, was a highly respected guide, someone who, in Malgres's eyes, might be a reputable target.

Jim said as much to Pomp but Pomp dismissed the threat.

"He won't bother us while we're at the Mandans'," Pomp said. "I want to stay with my father a few weeks—we may go down and visit my mother's grave. If you're expecting to see the boys anytime soon I wish you'd take Joe Walker back his mare. Pa and I and Coal, we'll walk along and take our time."

He didn't mention Tasmin—Pomp tried his best to be tactful, where Jimmy Snow's domestic arrangements were concerned. His tact was appreciated, too. Jim didn't know what he was going to do about Tasmin. Sometimes he felt that Pomp should have married her—after all, he had been raised in Europe and could talk about all sorts of things of which he himself knew nothing; but Pomp, for all his education, didn't seem to be the marrying kind.

"Joe Walker's particular about horseflesh," Toussaint Charbonneau commented, when Pomp handed over the mare. "If that's a Joe Walker horse she'll carry you a good long way."

"Guess I'll find out," Jim said.

"Tell Mr. Stewart I'll meet him on the Yellowstone somewhere, when it's warm enough to start gathering up his zoo," Pomp said. Father and son stood watching as Jim rode away.

He soon learned that old Charbonneau had been right to applaud Joe Walker's judgment where horses were concerned. The little mare had an easy gait which she seemed able to hold indefinitely. Jim had never been able to afford the luxury of a horse of his own, though he had occasionally been given a mule or a burro to ride, when he was with one of the Santa Fe expeditions. In trapping, workhorses were used mainly for packing out furs—the trappers themselves usually walked, which meant that twenty miles was about as far as they could expect to get in a day.

The mare's name was Janey—the day after he left the Charbonneaus, Jim calculated that she carried him a good fifty miles. Such a pace would bring him back to the Yellowstone in only a few days—but was he ready to go back to the Yellowstone? The weather was warm, the skies absolutely clear. Being alone in such a great space brought Jim a sense of calm that he knew he would soon lose once back in the small tent with his talkative wife. If only Tasmin could learn to behave like Sun Girl and Little Onion, his Ute wives, behaved.

That evening, while spitting a prairie chicken he had managed to knock over with a rock, a new thought struck Jim Snow. The little mare was hobbled some fifty feet away, grazing avidly on the brown prairie grass. Now and then she pawed away a patch of snow, to get at a few more stems. The thought that occurred to Jim was that, with the mare to carry him, the whole West was open to him. Why not cut south and west to the Green River and join his Ute wives? In fact, the best plan of all might be to take them with him down the Yellowstone to where Tasmin waited. Tasmin was no slow-witted girl—no doubt she would quickly learn by example how a good wife should behave. Also, of course, the child was coming—his Ute wives could be a help with the birthing if they could all get there in time.

It seemed such a perfect plan that Jim was at a loss to know why it hadn't occurred to him earlier. His Ute wives could train his English wife, not only in how to work skins or sew leggings, but in how to behave with modesty in relation to her husband as well.

Well before dawn Jim slid onto Janey and was off to the southwest, down through the Sioux country toward South Pass and the regions below the Great Salt Lake, where Sun Girl and Little Onion lived. The steady little mare carried him almost twenty miles before the morning freshness faded. The weather was warm, spring not far off. The Utes would soon be planting their little plots of corn. Jim felt a sudden, deep relief. Thanks to the energies of Joe Walker's little mare he had seen a way out of his dilemma. For the moment all he had to do was be watchful and let Janey cover the ground.

18

"At the moment he is devoting himself to lichen . . ."

P iet is very gloomy still," Mary Berrybender confided to her sister Tasmin. "He only smiles now if I fondle him under the lap robe, which frequently produces some spunk."

"That's a detail you might have spared us," Tasmin replied. "It's hardly wise to provide casual services of that sort."

"Of course it isn't—and why, may I ask, is he gloomy?" Buffum said. "There's plenty of botany around here, let him study it. That's why Papa brought him, after all."

"But he *is* studying it," Mary assured her. "At the moment he is devoting himself to lichen—fortunately there's an abundance of lichen quite near the fort. He won't go farther afield for fear of the great yellow bears."

The fact was that, despite the warming weather, all the Europeans wore gloomy looks. They all lingered at table as long as possible, a much-smudged and diminished company, in Tasmin's view. Señor Yanez, Signor Claricia, and Piet Van Wely were nowadays mostly silent and sad.

"I see no reason why I shouldn't do Piet these little favors, since nothing else makes him smile," Mary said, annoyed, as usual, by her sisters' unyielding attitudes.

"Come to that, it is not only males who are frustrated in this lonely place," Buffum remarked. Unable to arouse much interest in the younger mountain men—Kit Carson was in love with Tasmin, Jim Bridger with Eliza, and young Milt Sublette with Millicent, the laundress—Buffum had been forced to have recourse to Tim, the stable boy; a mostly unsatisfactory recourse, as it happened. Tim had not yet recovered from the forced removal of his frozen digits—he no longer cared to grab Buffum's hand and hold it against his groin. When she herself attempted to remind him of that useful technique, he burst into tears and thrust her away, a rejection that did not improve her temper.

"I can't think why they're all so gloomy," Tasmin said. "The post is snug and the winter's nearly over. Cook, of course, sees that we're well fed."

"Material comforts are not enough, Tasmin," Bobbety said. "I expect they all despair of seeing good old Europe again—I myself will only be seeing it with one eye next time, if I'm fortunate enough to see it at all."

"The fact is, none of them expect to see Europe again, ever," Mary said. "They think Papa will succeed in getting every one of them killed on these harsh prairies, somehow."

"Well, we all have our troubles, in this year of our Lord 1833," Buffum declared. "Even our fortunate Tasmin at last can be said to have troubles."

"Oh, and what might those be, Bess?" Tasmin asked. "I'm aware of no troubles—certainly none worth complaining about."

"Really? It matters so little to you that your husband has deserted you while you are heavy with child?" Bess asked. "I consider it most unlikely that we will ever see the handsome Sin Killer again."

"Of course we'll see him—he's only off trapping somewhere," Tasmin said lightly. "Americans can hardly be expected to live strictly by the calendar, as we Europeans are apt to do."

Her remarks were met with looks of skepticism from her siblings, none of whom appeared to believe a word she said.

"Besides, I am hardly one to tie a man to my apron strings," she went on. "Jimmy and I agreed at once to keep certain freedoms for ourselves.

It would be foolish to marry a mountain man and expect him never to roam."

Such statements—not the first Tasmin had made on the subject of Jim Snow's absence—were served up mainly for the sake of defiance; privately she was furious with Jim for leaving her in such an embarrassing situation. Of course, in the literal sense her statements were true enough: freedom to roam was what defined a mountain man—in fact, most of the other trappers were now leaving too. Only two, Kit Carson and Tom Fitzpatrick, remained at the post. Hugh Glass, Eulalie Bonneville, Jim Bridger, the Sublette brothers, and Joe Walker had all drifted off, up the Yellowstone or along the Milk River, or the Tongue—anywhere they could expect to find beaver. Jim Snow's absence was merely a normal part of the spring exodus, though that didn't keep it from rankling, and rankling deeply, with Tasmin herself. Inwardly she raged one moment, despaired the next. The fact that the two of them had quarreled on the morning Jim left to do his duty by Captain Aitken no longer seemed to have much bearing on the matter. She had known, in fact, that he meant to check on the steamer soon. But almost a month had passed without news of Jimmy, though news did frequently trickle into the trading post through various natives. Only the day before, one of the Minatarees who was related to old Otter Woman had brought news to Drum Stewart: Pomp Charbonneau and his father were waiting for him near the headwaters of the Yellowstone, ready to begin trapping animals for the Scotsman's zoo.

No news could have been more welcome to the red-bearded Scot—to Tasmin's amusement he was packed and gone from the post within three hours, leading two pack animals. His fervor for Vicky Kennet's embraces had long since abated—it weakened even as Vicky's determination to become, someday, Lady Stewart grew stronger. In a fairly short time, though large with child now herself, Vicky had worn Drummond Stewart out—he could hardly wait to escape to the peace of the prairies.

Of course, Tasmin also was great with child. She and Vicky strode about the trading post, heavy and majestic, like two goddesses of the corn, overawing the skittish mountain men by their vast fecundities. Lord Berrybender, offended by the sight, had even attempted to ban the two of them from the common table.

"Takes my appetite, looking at you two great cows," he complained. "I always sent Constance to Dorset until the brats were birthed."

"It's rather a long way to Dorset, Father," Tasmin said.

"Perhaps I'll have Boisdeffre set up a tent—confine you until you've given birth," Lord Berrybender said, ignoring Tasmin's point. "Most unappealing sight, pregnant women. They look like melons with heads."

"Yes, and sometimes the heads even presume to speak, as I myself frequently do," Tasmin said crossly. "Vicky and I intend to stay where we are—*you* move into the tent if you don't like looking at us."

"I'll do better than that, you insolent hussy," Lord B. told her, turning rather red in the face. "Drum Stewart left and so will I. I'll go on a hunt, while the weather's nice and cool. You'll soon have brats at the teat, a sight I don't want to see. Of course, I'll take Millicent with me, to see to the laundry."

Due to her swollen state Vicky Kennet, it seemed, had ceased to appeal to Lord B.; he had abruptly transferred his attentions to the black-haired Millicent, a sturdy, solid girl with no pretentions to wit.

"And of course I'll need Cook," Lord B. went on. "And Señor Yanez and Signor Claricia, in case something goes wrong with the buggy or the guns."

"Cook's not going," Tasmin informed him. "I'll keep Cook."

"What's that? Of course she's going—whose cook do you suppose she is, anyway?" Lord B. thundered, half rising in his chair.

Kit Carson, watching the scene from a distance, felt sure there would be violence; he edged closer—for a moment it seemed it might be her father that he would have to save Tasmin from. But before Lord B. could whack her—which he showed every intention of wanting to do—Tasmin grabbed the same fork that had half blinded her brother and thrust it to within an inch of Lord Berrybender's nose. When he tried to grab it Tasmin drew back, only to lunge again, this time marking Lord B. slightly on the cheek.

Lord Berrybender, in disbelief, sank back into his chair. He touched his cheek, then regarded his bloody finger with surprise.

"You will do well to let be, Father," Tasmin said, still holding the fork. "I am with child, Vicky is with child. We shall each be needing a competent midwife in the not too distant future, and Cook is our best hope. You shan't have her."

Lord Berrybender stared at Tasmin in shock. The tines of the fork seemed to be pointed straight at his eyes.

"Signor Claricia is an accomplished Italian," Tasmin said. "We have all profited from his lectures on garlic buds and olive oil. I'm sure he can cook your bears or your stags or whatever varmints you kill. Cook—I repeat for emphasis—will not be going."

"Insolent Tasmin, so disloyal to our pater," Mary cried, hurrying over to wipe Lord Berrybender's bloody cheek with a napkin.

"Do smite her, Father—smite her hip and thigh," she added.

"God damn you, miss," Lord B. said, looking at Tasmin. "Take my cook, will you? Next I suppose you'll be telling me I have to do my own laundry."

"I am hardly a miss, Father," Tasmin said. "You've heard the long and the short of it. Cook stays with us."

"And so will my good Piet," Mary said, giving the gloomy Dutchman a peck.

Lord Berrybender rose from the table, took his crutch, and stumped away. He said not another word. That his own daughter would threaten him with a turning fork was such an appalling thing that it put him off for the night. Of course, he meant to have Cook anyway—no child of his was going to tell him what to do with his own servants—it had merely seemed best to leave the field until all the cutlery had been gathered up. Napoleon, he recalled, had been reluctant to leave the field, when circumstances called for retreat.

When Millicent, in due course, presented herself for amorous service in Lord Berrybender's room, she found the old lord deep in thought. Millicent's way was to accept all duties placidly, whether that meant lying beneath Lord Berrybender while he groaned and grunted a bit, or else gathering up the soiled bedclothes. Duties were best done without fuss, but this evening, she had scarcely lifted her skirt when Lord B. waved her away.

"Go along with you, Milly—I've had enough of girls for one night," Lord Berrybender said. "We're off hunting tomorrow—you'll pack for me, won't you?"

"Yes, if you'd like me to, sir," Milly said.

"That's what I like, Milly . . . a good girl like you, no fuss, no airs," Lord B. said. "We'll have some fine tupping, we will, once we're well out of this fetid hole. Prairie breezes, that's what I need—I'll stir up a bit, I assure you, once I'm out where the wind blows free."

"I dare say you will, sir," Millicent agreed.

19

. . . a few vagrant flakes of snow . . .

Lady Tasmin and Miss Vicky, they'll be needing me once the little ones come," Cook said firmly. The hunting party was set to depart the trading post.

Lord Berrybender was stunned—a servant of his had just refused a direct order. A brisk north wind was blowing, carrying a few vagrant flakes of snow.

Tasmin, also firm, stood on one side of Cook; Venetia Kennet stood on the other. Pierre Boisdeffre, who had developed warm feelings for Cook, lurked in the background.

A wagon piled high with guns and blankets and other kit stood near. A great keg of brandy, acquired at great cost from Monsieur Boisdeffre, was lashed securely in the wagon. Señor Yanez and Signor Claricia, neither of them happy men, waited in the buggy. Both were convinced that their deaths awaited them somewhere on the plains to the south.

Tim, the stable boy, utterly miserable, sat on the wagon seat, grasping the reins as best he could with his damaged hands. Beside Tim, entirely sheathed in an all-enveloping fur coat, sat Bobbety, a Russian cap pulled down so far that his features were scarcely visible. He had been forced from his warm quarters by Lord Berrybender, who was determined that his son and heir should give up foppish ways and test his manhood in pursuit of buffalo and bear. Bobbety's protests and Father Geoffrin's horrified remonstrances were ignored.

"You'll come or I'll disinherit you—doubt you'd like being penniless," Lord Berrybender told his son.

"But, Father, I am accustomed to aiming with my right eye and now I don't have a right eye," Bobbety protested.

"No excuses now, we're off," Lord B. said. Millicent, like the good girl she was, had installed herself meekly in the wagon, next to the brandy keg. All was in readiness, until Cook, to Lord B.'s amazement, informed him that she wouldn't come.

"I'll just stay with Lady Tasmin," Cook said again. "And besides that, sir, Mr. Boisdeffre has been kind enough to offer me a position here at the post."

"A position?" Lord Berrybender said. "I don't give a fig for positions. "You're *my* cook, and so was your mother before you."

"I'm sure Millicent will do well enough, sir," Cook said. "Were it Eliza I might be worried, she's such a tendency to drop the plates."

"This is all your doing, Tasmin," Lord Berrybender shouted. "Cook has always done what *I* told her to—or what your sainted mother told her to. She is *our* cook—quite irrelevant what you want or what Boisdeffre offers. No more of this nonsense—it's time to be off. Cook, please get in this wagon now."

"Do remember, Milly, just to turn the kidneys a time or two—that's how His Lordship likes them," Cook said, and then, to Lord Berrybender's bafflement, she turned and walked back into the post.

"Here now, none of that!" Lord B. thundered. But Cook, a person of unusual firmness, merely kept walking.

"She can't do that! I forbid it! I won't have you stealing my cook," Lord Berrybender repeated to Tasmin, but his voice lost conviction once the sturdy little figure disappeared into the trading post.

"You will just have to get used to the inconveniences, Papa," Tasmin told him. "You've strayed into a democracy—a great mistake from your point of view, I'm sure. The citizens around here are rather determined to do as they please."

Lord B. didn't answer. He was remembering a great rich pudding, filled with plums and cherries that he had eaten once in his great house. Had it been a victory pudding? Trafalgar, perhaps—or Waterloo or something even earlier? His Lordship could not remember who had cooked this pudding—had it been Cook, or her mother, or, even, her grandmother? There had been some victory—or was it only a wedding . . . perhaps it had even been for his own marriage with . . . with . . . ? He could not, for the moment, recall the name of his fine wife. It was as if the brisk wind of the prairies were blowing away his memories, one by one. Constance it had been; he felt sure that *that* much was was right. About the victory . . . if it had been a victory . . . he was not now sure . . . only sure, in the end, that the pudding had been wonderful, filled with cherries and plums . . . sugary and juicy it had been . . . never had he had such a pudding . . . and now Cook had left, and Constance had died, and such puddings as that, with their plums and cherries, would not be for him to eat again.

"Look out! The old boy's crying . . . now what?" Tasmin said. She was wondering what more they would have to endure before her father finally went on his hunt.

Lord B. stood by the buggy, indifferent to Señor Yanez and Signor Claricia. Tears streamed down his face—memories light as thistles seemed to be blowing 'round his head, memories of damsels blithe and jolly whores long dead, or puddings perfectly baked and kidneys correctly turned, of fine, velvety rich claret, of the duke . . . Some duke! . . . Which duke? Had it really been Trafalgar when Cook . . . some cook. . . . baked that great pudding, or was it merely a wedding, perhaps even his own?

The gunsmith and the carriage maker were horrified—were they fated to journey into the country of the great bears at the whim of this old man who couldn't stop crying?

Tasmin was merely disgusted. It was hardly the first such maudlin display she had witnessed of late—once Lord B. found some slight excuse to feel sorry for himself, buckets of tears were sure to flow.

Meek Millicent saw at once that it was her duty to put His Lordship in order.

"Here, sir . . . come on now, just sit by Milly," she said encouragingly. "There's plenty of room here on the blanket."

Grateful for a kind voice, Lord Berrybender did as he was told. He crutched his way over to the wagon and sat on the blanket Milly offered.

"Stop crying now, don't wet your shirt, please, sir," the girl continued. "Might miss your target if you catch cold."

"Let's be going now, Tim . . . snap to!" Milly ordered. Like Cook, she believed in speaking with authority when it came to lax young men such as Timothy.

Tim was not quite so broken in spirit that he enjoyed taking orders from a laundress, even though it was clear that she was His Lordship's new favorite. The old wild head was even then resting itself comfortably on Millicent's substantial shoulder. Tim popped the reins on the horse's rumps.

"Alas, I go! Au revoir, Geoff!" Bobbety cried.

Señor Yanez and Signor Claricia looked at each other and shrugged. It seemed that, for better or worse, the hunt was on; neither of them doubted that it would be for worse.

"Now, there's a turn. Papa's got a new bawd," Tasmin said to her sisters, as the wagon bounced off into the prairies.

"That's right, our wicked laundress," Buffum agreed. "Now who do you suppose will fold our clothes?"

20

. . . quietness and calm were at last to be met with . . .

With the departure of the mountain men, and then of Drummond Stewart, and finally of Lord Berrybender and his attendants, quietness and calm were at last to be met with in the nearly empty rooms of Pierre Boisdeffre's trading post; the calm would have been complete but for the fact that the early spring winds blew fiercely over the northern lands, sighing and roaring through the nights so violently that Tasmin was sometimes kept awake. Deep sleep, indeed, was not easily obtained; if it was not the winds that awakened her it was apt to be the baby, turning and stirring in her womb.

Venetia Kennet, almost as far along as Tasmin, experienced similar disquiet. Often the two of them found themselves in the kitchen in the early morning, letting Cook make them tea as dawn reddened the windows. Sometimes trader Boisdeffre, who had taken a great fancy to Cook, would play melancholy tunes on his Jew's harp. Buffum might appear, pale in her gown, then Mary, then George Catlin; and last, invariably, would be Father Geoffrin, who would immediately announce that he hadn't slept a wink due to his anxieties about Bobbety.

Often Tasmin would suggest cards. Buffum would usually drift off with Boisdeffre; she was helping him organize his stores—so far rather scrambled—in return for which Monsieur Boisdeffre taught her songs of the *voyageurs* who paddled the northern streams in search of furs. Frequently, once the cards were brought out, Tasmin teamed with Vicky Kennet against the painter and the priest. Vicky, freed of the necessity of losing endlessly to Lord Berrybender, proved a skilled and savage competitor. As Tasmin herself was no mean hand at whist, the two women generally routed the men. With many of the Indians now gone away to hunt, George had little to paint except the landscape. Sometimes the card play went on all morning and well into the afternoon, entailing much lively banter. Even when Mary sided with the men, as a kind of coach, the women usually won. Occasionally George would let Mary play his hand; then he took out his sketch pad and did the scene in a few strokes.

"There, how's that?" he asked, handing the sketch around. "I shall call it *Three Ladies and a Jesuit at Whist.*"

"Don't call it anything until you fix my chin," Tasmin told him. "I'm sure my chin isn't *that* sharp."

"Nor is my bosom that *heavy*," Vicky Kennet protested.

George smiled, but held his ground. "I am sketching now not only the present but also the future," he told them. "I see you not only as you are but as you will be. That, after all, is the portraitist's gift—even his duty, I'd say."

"And you practically didn't put me in at all," Father Geoff complained. "You've made me so mere, you know . . . I'm only a wisp."

"Your spirit is particularly elusive, Father," George admitted. "Developments there will no doubt be in your life—they're not likely to make you markedly heavier, though."

Mary alone seemed happy with her likeness—so happy in fact that George Catlin gave her the little sketch, an act that annoyed all three of the other sitters, who would have liked to have it.

In the days round the card table, near the big fireplace, Tasmin found herself feeling more friendly toward her three companions, whom, previously, she had dealt with rather cavalierly. On the boat and in the trading post, crammed in with so many musky males, Tasmin had had little patience with Vicky, George, and Geoff; but with the musky males removed—the mountain men had been, of course, the muskiest—the talents and personalities of her companions could be better appreciated. Vicky Kennet, freed from amatory pressures long enough to get in some practice, was a more than decent cellist; and George Catlin, of course, though sometimes too hasty, was a more than decent painter. Father Geoffrin, though vain as the day was long, *did* have a subtle French mind, and *had* read many books. Though the little priest coveted Tasmin's attention all the time, and was filled with malice and spite when she denied him, he was not, on the whole, a bad companion.

On occasions when conversation bogged down, Tasmin and Vicky had their rapidly advancing pregnancies to fall back on, the uncertainties of which provided much grist for talk.

"The absence of wet nurses is rather shocking," Vicky observed one day. George Catlin's hasty pencil had not much exaggerated her bosom, which every day grew heavier still as it filled with milk.

Tasmin was experiencing the same phenomenon.

"There aren't any, if that's what you mean," she said. "I suppose we'll just have to let the little brutes suckle."

"Of course you should let them suckle," George said. "Why else do you think you *have* bosoms?"

"It wouldn't do in France—no lady would think of such a thing," Father Geoffrin mentioned. "The better bosoms *there* are strictly reserved for amatory play."

"As you may have observed, we ain't in France, Father," Tasmin replied. "Vicky and I will simply have to risk scandal and give suck ourselves."

"It might even make a nice picture, George," she suggested. "The two of us nursing our young."

"Why, it might," George said, brightening a little. The fact was, he was growing weary of painting Indians. Necessary as it was to secure a vivid record of these vanishing Americans, the daily anxiety, as he waited to see if his wild subjects would approve of their likenesses, had begun to wear on his nerves.

Of course, he had long wanted to paint Lady Tasmin, and would have no objection to having Vicky sit too—either or both would be a nice change from chiefs and warriors, many of whom were at least as vain as any English lady. Now that both ladies had become better disposed toward him, perhaps something could be achieved.

"I suppose we might call it *Madonnas of the Missouri*," he suggested. "What would you think of having the parrot in it? People do like to look at birds."

"Tush, why not?" Tasmin said. She had come, over the last weeks, rather to like George Catlin. At first his stiffness and pomposity had irritated her so frequently that she delivered some sharp rebuffs—rebuffs that annoyed George so much that he sometimes jumped up and left her company. But she hadn't cowed him; the man defended his opinions, and his resistance earned her respect. With her husband gone and the company thin, having someone to argue with was not a thing to be despised.

"George, if you intend to do us as proper madonnas, you'll have to wait till our brats appear," Tasmin said. "Why not do us now—you could call it *Pregnant Cows of the Missouri*."

At this Vicky burst out laughing, Tasmin giggled, and even George could not resist a laugh.

"I demur, I demur," Father Geoffrin said, with a look of delicate disdain. "No sane person could enjoy looking at those vast bellies. I believe I speak for the civilized public when I say that."

Piet Van Wely, who had all but given up speech, suddenly perked up.

"It is nonsense this Jesuit speaks," he said, a gleam of life in his eye—the first in weeks. "*I* would like to look at this picture you talk about."

"Oh well, listen to our botanist," Father Geoffrin said. "A Dutch botanist, I might add—hardly an opinion we need consider."

Mary Berrybender, fierce in defense of her Piet, flew at the priest and tried to scratch his cheeks with her sharp nails, but Father Geoff, no stranger to Mary's furies, fended her off with a large ladle.

"Hold your tongue, you sickly pederast, or it will be the worse for you," Mary hissed.

"Well, what about it, George?" Tasmin asked. "I've seen a good many pictures, here and there in our country houses, but I don't believe I've ever seen a picture of pregnant women. Why would that be?"

"Goodness, I think you're right," George said. "I've never seen one either—perhaps I have a chance to break new ground."

"Looking at pregnant hussies like these would be rather like looking at a dugong or a manatee," Father Geoff said, with a superior smile. "Who would want to hang a picture of a dugong on their walls?"

"I would—they are gentle creatures," Piet assured him. He had not spoken in so long that the sound of his own voice came as a pleasant surprise.

Tasmin and Venetia, their lovers absent, had lately been experimenting with hairstyles. It was something to do. Tasmin had been trying to persuade Vicky to cut her long hair. In frontier circumstances, why keep such a mane?

"You'll never have time to brush it properly, once the baby comes," she pointed out. Vicky, who regarded her long auburn hair as one of the her chief glories, had resisted the notion so far, but seemed to Tasmin to be weakening.

"George, you must do us at once, before Vicky cuts her hair," Tasmin insisted. "In my opinion such a study will fill a niche: the harsh effects of procreation revealed for all to see."

"Without pregnant women there would soon be no human race," Vicky intoned—a sentiment that Father Geoff considered heavily obvious.

"No human race, exactly," Piet agreed.

"I'm not sure that Vicky and I should disrobe entirely," Tasmin went on, planning the sitting in her mind. "Perhaps we should just drape a shawl here and there, so as not to be absolutely stark naked."

Kit Carson, listening in quiet astonishment, felt his ears turn red with embarrassment. It seemed that Lady Tasmin and Miss Kennet were proposing to undress and allow the painter to draw them, an intention that would surely shock Jim Snow, or any of the mountain men.

"Why couldn't Buffum and I be naked too?" Mary asked. "We could be handmaidens of desire, could we not?"

"Personally I only desire to be my normal shape again," Tasmin said. "If George at some point wishes to draw your scrawny body, that's fine with me."

George Catlin had been racking his brain to see if he could remember a picture that showed a female in the heavily pregnant state. He could not think of one. A noble subject had suddenly been presented him—a subject not only noble but also universal. All mothers, at some point, looked rather as Tasmin and Vicky looked. His own mother must have looked so, though of course he could not remember it.

"I shall just call it *Motherhood*," he said, overcome for the moment by the solemnity of the undertaking.

"Oh tush, George, that's so boring," Tasmin said. "Can't you think of something a little spicier?"

"Why yes, he could draw a prick and call it *Fatherhood*," Father Geoffrin suggested, with a wicked smile.

Titillated, as always, by his own wit, the priest had failed to notice the stealthy approach of Mary, who had snuck into the kitchen and secured a large tureen of gravy, which she promptly dumped over Father Geoffrin's head, leaving the drenched priest too stunned to speak.

"You vile child!" he gasped, before running off to his room to change his dripping vestments.

George Catlin scarcely noticed the incident, so absorbed was he in planning the composition; though idly suggested by Tasmin, it had now quite taken hold of his imagination. *Motherhood*, if delicately yet boldly executed, might be the canvas that would make his name. Perhaps it should be hung in some great building in Washington—the Capitol, perhaps. The more he thought about it, the more excited he became. The allegorical dimension should not, in his view, be ignored. Were not these two Englishwomen, after all, giving birth to Americans—and, by extension, to the new America itself? Would not they represent the newer, the grander America even then being born in the West?

A grand canvas it must be, George decided—in the background there should be a winding river, the broad Missouri that they had just ascended.

Forget the parrot, a bird of other lands. There should be nothing less than an eagle, hovering near, and with luck—no, rather with skill—he might even get in a buffalo.

21

. . . nude except for two long purplish shawls . . .

Venetia Kennet, clad mainly in her own long auburn hair, lounged on a velvet coverlet in the canoe, which was firmly anchored in the Missouri's shallows. Tasmin Berrybender—the Old World bringing its fecundity to the New, or, alternatively, the New World about to offer up its bounty—nude except for two long purplish shawls which she had looted from her mother's wardrobe, was just stepping ashore, behind her the great dun prairies of the West. Tasmin's problem wasn't George Catlin's ambitious concept, it was the shawls. A stiff prairie wind was blowing, frustrating Tasmin's efforts to drape the shawls around herself in a becoming fashion—now and then the two shawls unwound completely, leaving her naked, an obviously pregnant woman, clutching two purple sails—a spectacle so ridiculous that neither Tasmin nor Vicky could contain their mirth. The fact that a great and grave precedent was being set—pregnancy celebrated on canvas for the first time—did not make the proceedings seem less absurd—not, at least, from the models' point of view.

"We're quitting for the day, George—it's too goddamned windy," Tasmin declared.

George had to agree. Though he felt sure the allegory would be powerful, once captured, it was rather too breezy for accurate work. Vicky's hair was always blowing, or Tasmin's shawls.

"Perhaps tomorrow we should try this inside the post," he suggested. "I can always come out and get background—it's the two of you I haven't yet got quite right."

"What if you never get us quite right, George?" Tasmin asked wickedly, pulling on the skins the Oto woman had made for her back downriver.

Somehow the woman had correctly estimated just what her pregnant dimensions would be.

"Why shouldn't I get you right?" George inquired. "It's only a spatial problem—Venetia is so long-legged that she takes up most of the canoe, putting you too far to the right. It just needs adjusting. Perhaps you should be lounging and Vicky standing up."

"No thank you, I prefer to lounge, otherwise my hair would blow," Vicky said. "It's even worse than Tasmin's shawls."

"I doubt the problem is spatial, George," Tasmin said—she was in a mood to tease.

"Of course it's spatial, what else could it be?" George asked.

"Oh, merely that you don't understand women," Tasmin said. "It's why I was such a long time liking you. You're only comfortable with us if you can allegorize us—have me stand for Vanity and Vicky for Lust, or vice versa. The fact that we are many things, not *one* thing, has confused better men than you."

George Catlin was unruffled.

"Be that as it may, I still need to do a little more work on the two of you in this canoe," he said.

"*Do* you, in your pride, suppose that you do understand women, George?" Tasmin persisted. She had no intention of letting the man wiggle off into the technicalities—she didn't care a fig about spatiality.

"Perhaps I don't quite understand them, but I *like* them," George insisted. "I hope you might at least give me credit for that."

"Do *you* think he likes us, Vicky?" Tasmin asked.

"He certainly likes to *look* at us," Vicky said. She had no desire to persecute nice Mr. Catlin, whose many sketches of her seemed to catch a fair likeness. Why Tasmin was so determined to be mean to the man was a mystery—Tasmin just sometimes displayed an inclination to be mean.

"There you have it—likes to look," Tasmin remarked. "I consider that quite a damning comment—likes to look."

"But it isn't at all damning, my dear," George replied. "I'm a painter. If I *didn't* like to look I'd be in a fine pickle. Painters like what their eyes like—or, to put it more strongly, they love what their eyes love. Why should that be wrong?"

"Myself, I'd want more than looking," Tasmin assured him. "Don't mind looking for a bit, but then I'd want a tumble. Your approach is much too pallid, George."

George was studying his rough attempt—Tasmin's badinage did not offend him. So far what he had was a fair study of the glorious curves of womanhood—belly, breasts, shoulders, thighs, derrieres.

"Regard," he said, handing the sketch to Tasmin.

"Regard what?" she said. "It's just a lot of curves."

"Yes, but that's the beauty of women—curves, and generous curves, in the case of you two," he said. "If I can get the curves right, then I've got the woman right. When the curves make a harmony, the spirit will have been caught—insofar as the spirit of woman can ever be caught, of course."

"Surely you can't suppose there's much harmony in *my* spirit, George," Tasmin said. "Vicky is a fine cellist, perhaps replete with harmony, but I'm all kettledrums and cymbals myself—so is my husband. The cymbals clashed so loudly that he ran off, as you know."

She *did* like the balance of the opposing curves, though—hers and Vicky's.

"What about it, Venetia—is it better to be painted, or to be courted?" Tasmin asked her companion.

"Why, I can hardly say, Tasmin," Vicky replied. "I don't think I've ever been courted—I've merely been assumed. That's the way it is, I fear, for women of my station."

Tasmin was startled. Vicky had not spoken in sorrow, particularly, and yet, if her remark was true, sorrow there must be.

Vicky Kennet stepped out of the canoe and wrapped herself warmly in a velvet coverlet.

"Tasmin, I've just decided—I want to cut my hair. I want to cut it all off! All! Will you help me?"

Tasmin was shocked, not because Vicky had decided to be sensible and rid herself of such a burdensome mane, but by her tone—a tone of bitter resignation, the resignation of one who would always be not courted, just assumed.

"Of course, Vicky—I'll help," Tasmin said, but George Catlin, in a panic, broke in.

"Cut off your hair—but you can't," he protested. "I mean, you can cut it, of course, but couldn't you just wait until I've finished my picture? I'm sure with one more sitting I can get it right. You've such splendid hair, my dear—far better than any drapery we could find. Couldn't you just allow me one more day?"

"Perhaps, but I'm not sure, we shall have to see," Vicky said, in sudden bitterness.

"But please—just one more sitting?" George pleaded, but Tasmin took his arm and led him away.

"Don't pester her, George. Let be for now," she advised. As they watched, Vicky Kennet, wrapped in the coverlet, hurried back to the post, her long hair dangling down.

22

"How grotesque pregnant women seem."

Buffum, Mary, Piet, Kit, Father Geoff, and Pierre Boisdeffre had been allowed to watch the painter painting the two women in the canoe, but they had been warned not to come too close, lest their idle commentary distract the artist—in his case the models themselves were sure to supply sufficient distraction.

Near the group from the fort were several Assiniboines, who had ridden in from the north to do a little trading. Being in no hurry, they stopped to watch the strange proceedings on the Missouri River's shore.

"How grotesque pregnant women seem," Mary declaimed. "I shall remain a virgin all my life in order to avoid that awkward state."

"I doubt your resolve will hold if you keep encouraging Piet," Buffum warned. "Males not infrequently misinterpret our good intentions."

"No, no . . . not the little one—she merely eases my anxieties," Piet protested, though not with much force.

"I don't yield the point, Mary," Buffum said. "There's Tasmin, there's Vicky, proof positive. No doubt a great number of anxieties were eased while they were getting themselves in that state."

Kit Carson felt that his ears might burst into flame, so hot were they with embarrassment. Tasmin was some distance away, but, unable to handle the shawls, she now and then stood quite naked, and so, more or less, was Miss Kennet. If Jim Snow were to return at such a moment, murder would no doubt occur—perhaps more than one murder. He himself, entrusted with Tasmin's care, might come under attack, and he felt that he deserved to be attacked, for allowing Lady Tasmin to display herself so shamelessly—but how to stop her? None of the people watching seemed to be disapproving, a thing that puzzled Kit. Apparently if a painter like Mr. Catlin wanted to make a picture of women with their clothes off, then women simply took their clothes off and let him, with no embarrassment even.

More and more often Kit was troubled by the suspicion that the English were not really sane. Mountain men were thought to be wild, and they did get drunk and spit and fight, but no mountain man would simply take his clothes off and allow a painter to draw him in his nakedness. Kit had seen a good many of George's Indian paintings, and in those the opposite approach prevailed: the Indians piled on all the finery they could get their hands on, bear claw necklaces, eagle feather headdresses, fine buckskin robes, and lots of paint. He would have suspected the English ladies to do more or less the same thing, don their best gowns and finest gems, not scamper around naked on the muddy banks of the Missouri River. The whole business was quite disturbing. Every few minutes Kit scanned the plains to the south, half expecting to see Jim Snow arriving, murder in his eyes.

The Assiniboines, for their part, were divided in their opinions about the strange activities in and about the canoe. A young warrior named Skunk claimed to have once used that very canoe, which he said was an ill-balanced bark of the utmost impracticality.

"That canoe will capsize if they're not careful," Skunk declared.

Bad Head, who had had more experience with whites than the boy Skunk, doubted that the pregnant women meant to go anywhere in the canoe.

"They're not trying to go anywhere," he pointed out. "I think they're just playing some game."

Red Crow, the leader of the little group, had recently had his portrait painted by the likeness maker. It was obvious to him that the painter had persuaded the women to take their clothes off so he could look at their big bellies, a desire that was beyond Red Crow's comprehension. He had never liked to look at his wives when their bellies were big.

"Maybe they want to have their babies in the canoe," Bad Head suggested—it was not reasonable, but then nothing the whites did struck him as particularly reasonable.

"It could be religious," Red Crow said. "They could be offering themselves to the river spirits, to make their babies come easier."

"I don't think so," Bad Head countered. "The river spirits like virgins—at least that's what I was taught."

In his view the river spirits, which were quite powerful, had a right to unsullied females. The two white women were English—perhaps the English didn't understand that the spirits were finicky in such matters.

As they watched, the painter and the women and the other white people began to walk toward the post. The two large women who had been naked had finally covered themselves, a relief to Red Crow, who didn't like seeing large white bellies.

Then the painter said something to Kit Carson and old Boisdeffre and the two of them picked up the canoe and began to carry it toward the trading post, an action that made no sense at all. A canoe belonged in the water.

"Maybe it has a hole in it," Skunk said. "They probably want to patch the hole."

Bad Head rode over to the river, hoping he might hear the river spirits the whites had been attempting to entice, but all he heard was the low murmur of the Missouri River, flowing over some rocks.

23

. . . light and graceful Molière . . .

I only supposed it to be a deer of some kind," Bobbety explained, looking at the dead horse. "I didn't want to come on this hunt, or shoot at beasts. I far prefer to collect fossils, or even rocks. You're the one who insisted I shoot, Papa. I merely shot to please you."

Lord Berrybender was shocked almost beyond speech. His horse, the great Thoroughbred Royal Andrew, descended in a direct line from the Byerly Turk, a horse that had been carrying him swiftly among the buffalo all day—he had knocked over at least forty of the great beasts—now lay dead, shot by his own son.

Lord B. had come in, as was proper, and given Royal Andrew to Tim, who rubbed him down. Then they allowed the horse just a bit of a scamper—it was while he was scampering, not far from camp, that they heard the report of a gun.

"My Lord . . . the savages . . . where are they?" Lord B. cried. He felt certain that they must be under attack, but Señor Yanez shook his head. He knew exactly which of His Lordship's rifles had just been fired.

"It's Master Bobbety," the Spaniard said. "He's only got the one eye now."

Bobbety had spent much of the day hiding in a small hummock of grass, near the camp. He remembered that the vast American plain had swallowed up Gladwyn, Fräulein, Tintamarre, a boatman, and at least two Indian chiefs. His one ambition was to avoid being swallowed up. From his hummock of grass he could clearly see the wagon and the buggy—at least he could see them when his one eye didn't water. Of course, various animals ambled by his post during the day—buffalo, elk, and antelope, plus several scurrying creatures. It was only as the day wore on toward evening that Bobbety decided to shoot a large beast—then he would have been "blooded," as his father put it, and, once blooded, perhaps he would be allowed to return to the trading post, whose comforts he sorely missed.

So, when a large brownish beast rather like an elk scampered within easy range, Bobbety, myopic from birth, shot it—only to realize, from a whinny the dying beast gave, that it hadn't, after all, *been* an elk or a deer, but only a horse. Not until confronted with his father's shocked face did Bobbety realize that he had killed Royal Andrew, the finest horse in his father's famous stud. There before them the great horse lay, dead as any of the forty buffalo that had fallen that day.

Lord Berrybender turned ash white—he attempted speech.

"My horse—my best horse," he said—of all the losses suffered by the Berrybenders since their arrival on the Missouri River, none struck home like this one.

Lord Berrybender stared at Bobbety, but had not the strength even to curse. He wavered, he wobbled, then he dropped the glass of brandy in his hand and slowly sank down across the still-warm rump of Royal Andrew, in a dead faint.

"Smelling salts, smelling salts," Signor Claricia demanded, snapping his fingers at Tim—the stable boy, fervently hoping that Lord B. was as dead as his horse, sauntered over toward the campfire, where Milly, the laundress, was attempting to cook a kind of hash which Lord Berrybender favored and which Cook had taught her to make, only Cook had not had to make it over an open fire with a strong wind blowing.

"The old boy's fainted—got any smelling salts, Milly?" he asked. Now that he was out of the chilly stables his own spirits had improved so much that he was not above attempting familiarities with the buxom Millicent. Seeing her bent over the campfire, he sidled up and rubbed himself briefly against her ample backside, only to receive a stinging slap for his efforts.

"None of that now—I ain't your whore, Tim," Milly said. "Just stir the hash like a good boy while I see to His Lordship."

"Oughtn't to be so high and mighty with me, Mill," Tim said. "Wasn't it I that carried water for you, and helped you all these years?"

Milly ignored that plaintive cry and hurried over to the dejected little group standing around the dead horse and the fallen lord.

"It *did* look rather like an elk," Bobbety insisted, to Signor Claricia. The carriage maker had been kicked or nipped several times by the dead Thoroughbred—his passing caused Signor Claricia no grief at all.

To everyone's surprise the forthright Milly bent over Lord Berrybender and administered a number of vigorous slaps, first to one cheek and then the other.

"Gets the blood moving, a smart slap or two," Milly said, continuing with the smart slapping until His Lordship began to stir. His cheeks were soon red, rather than white. With a little heaving and tugging Milly and Señor Yanez soon had him on his feet.

"There now, sir, you're fine—I'd best get back to the hash," Milly said. Tim, sulking from his rejection, attempted to make a grab for her as she went by, but Milly shrugged him off without breaking stride.

"Come now, no languishing, men—you've got a good deal of work to do," Lord Berrybender said, once he had picked up his brandy cup.

None of the company knew what Lord Berrybender meant. The day was over, the bold big sun just sinking, in flaming glory, into the green plains to the west. Earlier Signor Claricia had gone 'round and taken the tongues from a number of fallen buffalo—Lord B., tired of kidneys, now preferred to breakfast mainly on tongue. The guns were cleaned—Señor Yanez had promptly seen to that. What work could His Lordship possibly mean?

"What do you mean, Papa—it's rather near the dinner hour," Bobbety inquired.

"No dinner for you, you myopic whelp!" Lord B. thundered, suddenly livid with anger at the thought that his own son had put an end to the life of Royal Andrew, the finest prize in his stud.

"No dinner for any of you, not till my fine boy is buried," Lord Berrybender decreed. "Get the spades, Tim—and the picks."

"Bury a horse?" Bobbety asked, very surprised. "Why would one bury a horse?"

"Of course you'll bury him—all of you get to work—you'll not have a bite until you finish. You don't suppose I'd leave Royal Andrew just lying out, do you? He must be buried honorably and promptly—so get to it."

"But, Father, it will soon be dark," Bobbety pointed out. "Couldn't we bury him in the morning? I'm sure we'd all be fresher."

"Didn't ask your opinion and don't give a damn how fresh you are," Lord Berrybender declared. "Bury my horse—bury him now."

"Good-bye, I leave now," Señor Yanez said in decisive tones.

Lord B. had been just about to hurry off and enjoy a good plate of Milly's hash when the small Spaniard made his announcement.

"I leave too," Signor Claricia said, no less firmly.

"My work is with carriages," he added. "I don't want to cut out buffalo tongues no more, or bury horses."

"Oh damn, now you're both acting like Cook," Lord B. said. "You think you can just leave me at your whim, I suppose. You'll mutiny when the task displeases you. Hardly reflects credit on your countries, I might say! Come back here! You're my servants—knuckle under now and do as you're told. Otherwise you won't get a cent."

"What good is cents if you're dead?" Signor Claricia asked, but he made the comment to Señor Yanez, as the two of them were strolling off toward the wagon, to secure their kit. Without addressing a word to Milly they took their blankets, a fowling piece, and old Gorska's fine Belgian gun and strolled away into the deepening dusk.

"Fools!" Tim said. "They won't get far—where is there to go?"

"I'm afraid I can't answer precisely," Bobbety said. "I don't know where there might be to go—but I rather believe Señor and Signor are going anyway. There has indeed been a small mutiny, and Papa has failed to quell it."

When they strolled over to get shovels, Lord B. was tucking heartily into Millicent's hash. He viewed the departure of the gunsmith and the carriage maker as a very temporary thing.

"Too excitable, these Mediterraneans," he declared. "Likely to flare up at the slightest provocation. Of course, they're both gifted craftsmen—I suppose one has to expect a bit of temperament, now and then, else one has to make do with indifferent guns and rickety carriages—never able to tolerate either, myself. Must have my guns cared for properly, and my carriages too. Those two will soon be back, I assure you—got their backs up merely because I asked them to dig a bit of a hole for fine old Andrew . . . a direct descendant of the Byerly Turk, finest bloodline in England, though I suppose the Godolphin Arab may have had his points."

Bobbety and Tim took advantage of Lord Berrybender's indignation at the gunsmith and the carriage maker to gulp down as much hash as possible, lest they had to dig all night, but their worries were unfounded. After another brandy or two Lord B. began to fumble with Milly. Thus the night ended as most nights ended, with Milly and Lord B. tussling in the tent, making, to Bobbety's taste, much too much racket with their rough copulation.

The prudent Tim took a blanket and rolled himself up in it, near the carcass of Royal Andrew. The fact that Lord Berrybender had found temporary distraction with Millicent did not mean that Royal Andrew would be forgotten. Tim's prudence proved wise—several wolves had to be discouraged during the night, and Lord Berrybender was out at dawn, ready to direct burial operations. These, in Bobbety's view, proved laborious in the extreme. Fortunately for all of them the energetic Milly was as handy with a spade as she was with a skillet or a laundry basket.

She and Tim dug all morning, while the old lord sat around, shooting at anything that came in sight. Bobbety attempted to throw out a spade or two of dirt, an effort that caused large blisters to form on both his hands. To Lord Berrybender's intense annoyance there was no sign of either the Spanish gunsmith or the Italian carriage maker. It was becoming apparent that their mutiny had not been a bluff.

"Can't think where those fellows can have got to," Lord B. complained. "Expected them back by now. Don't like work, that's their problem."

"I'm afraid I don't like it either, Papa," Bobbety declared.

A final embarrassment awaited Royal Andrew. The hole, once dug, was ten feet from his noble carcass, around which a good many flies had begun to buzz. When Tim, Milly, and Bobbety attempted to drag the carcass over to the hole, they found that they couldn't budge it.

"Timmy, you dolt, why didn't you put the hole closer to the horse?" Milly inquired: inexpert work always infuriated her.

"Don't know," Tim admitted—he had just started digging at Lord B.'s insistence. It had not occurred to him that a dead horse would be so hard to move.

Bobbety thought the hole looked rather comfortable. The strain of such close relations with the servants had set his nerves on edge. Were it not for the finality of the matter, he would not have minded resting in the hole himself.

"What, not buried yet? My great steed will begin to rot pretty soon," Lord Berrybender announced. He had stumped over in a state of considerable annoyance: one of his rifles was misfiring, and there was no Señor Yanez to fix it.

Millicent was of the opinion that there were few problems that could not be solved if a smart laundress addressed herself to them with a clear head. Royal Andrew was not the only horse in the company. It was only necessary to hitch one of the geldings to the carcass and Royal Andrew could at once be plopped into his grave. This was done with dispatch, after which all the dirt that had been shoveled out had to be shoveled back in, an effort that still left something wanting, in Lord Berrybender's view. The prairie 'round the grave looked very level, very bare, a fact which troubled him considerably.

"He ought to have a stone—never find this place again unless there's a marker of some sort," he complained.

"Why would you want to find it again, Papa? There's nothing here," Bobbety observed.

"I'm rather attached to my horses, always have been," Lord B. admitted, his eyes not entirely dry. "I might want to stop and pay my respects to Royal Andrew someday—take a moment out of the hunt, you know?"

"Loved my horse," he added, as the tears began to course down. "Hate to leave him in this lonely place—so unlike England, you know."

His tears flowed swiftly, and yet more swiftly, until Lord Berrybender was racked with sobs; he began to pull at his hair and rip at his clothes. Bobbety watched it all, appalled: his own father was going berserk, right before his eyes, and all because of a horse that had too much resembled an elk. Lord Berrybender's despair seemed very nearly Shakespearean, though the latter was an author with whom Bobbety was not deeply familiar. He and Father Geoffrin were of the opinion that the light and graceful Molière or even the somewhat heavier Racine was an author with considerably more wit than the bard of Avon.

Bobbety's concern did not lessen. Lord Berrybender had begun to cry to the heavens, cursing his fate—in his frenzy it might not be long before he began to curse his children, starting, very probably, with the child who had shot his favorite horse.

Fortunately Milly, who had been carrying a bucket of water up from the Yellowstone River, heard the commotion and came striding over.

"Here now, silly boy, stop that!" Milly said to Lord B. "Come along now with your Milly—we'll just slip into the tent and see what we can find to do."

"I believe I'll just go in search of a suitable stone now, Father," Bobbety said, strolling quietly off. More rough copulations he did not care to hear.

24

. . . they could not afford to strike out wildly . . .

Señor Yanez and Signor Claricia, having abruptly decided to cast their lot together in the New World, decided it was time to dispense with the strict formality which each had felt compelled to maintain while with the English.

The two men, once out of the Berrybender camp, made haste over to the Yellowstone River and hurried south along its banks for a few miles, enough to discourage the old lord if he should miss his prized Belgian rifle and attempt to chase them down. One thing they knew with certainty was that they could not afford to strike out wildly, into the empty land. As long as they kept close to the riverbank and followed it upstream, they had a chance of running into some of the trappers who had set out in that direction.

"Now that we are not with those English we don't have to be so stiff," Señor Yanez said.

"You may call me Aldo," Signor Claricia replied. "With all that riffraff on the boat it was better to be formal."

"Yes—that Pole, the German woman, the Dane—I didn't like any of them," Señor Yanez replied. "You may call me Pedro."

"Pedro, okay," Aldo said. "That's not so different from Aldo. We might get our selves mixed up." He meant it as a joke, but the solemn Pedro Yanez didn't laugh.

"I have always been Pedro, and Pedro I will always be," he declared firmly, looking sternly at the Italian, in the event that he had objections.

Aldo Claricia had none. Pedro, Aldo, Aldo, Pedro—at least they were both Europeans, and from the south. Though night had come and it was very dark, he felt that the two of them ought not to stop until they were well out of range of His Lordship's wrath.

"Do you want to walk awhile?" he asked Pedro. "It might be better to get farther away before we stop."

Hardly had he said it before a terrible roar was sounded, directly in front of them. A huge dark shape suddenly loomed up so close that they could have touched it—but it was a moonless night and neither of them could see the beast that roared. Terrified, both fired their guns, though Aldo Claricia had only a fowling piece, a weapon hardly likely to save them from this leviathan of the prairies—Pedro Yanez thought he saw a flash of great teeth. Though both wanted to flee, they stood as if paralyzed—what if they fled right into the maw of the beast? Though wide awake, they thought themselves to be in the sort of dream where flight offers the only hope—and yet their limbs refused to move.

"Pedro, why don't you reload your gun?" Aldo requested.

"Be still, don't blab your mouth," Pedro said. "We may have killed it."

Pedro didn't believe that they had killed the great beast, though. In shock, expecting death, he had fired both barrels of his gun straight up into the air. Unless the creature with the great roar was a bird, it had survived unharmed.

The prairie had become totally silent. Aldo could hear Pedro breathing, and Pedro, likewise, Aldo.

"Are we alive?" Aldo asked. He was so frightened that it seemed to him that death might have stolen over them imperceptibly, as he had always hoped it would, when it came.

Pedro Yanez was annoyed by the question. Only Italians could be so slipshod as to doubt their own existence. The important question was not whether they were alive, but where the great beast had gone who made the roar—it was, he felt sure, one of the great grizzly bears: even the mountain men feared them. But the two of them were in unknown land—it wouldn't do to draw hasty conclusions. In Spain there were plenty of bears—the

Gypsies had them—but they were small bears, nothing like the size of the beast that had made the roar. On the other hand it wouldn't do to guess wrong: what was it, if *not* a grizzly?

"What if it was something *worse* than a grizzly bear?" he asked.

"Don't be silly—nothing could be worse than a grizzly bear," Aldo assured him.

"Well, *el tigre* could be worse, or elephants," Pedro replied.

"Not elephants—there are no elephants here," Aldo assured him.

"How do you know?"

"Because Lord Berrybender never spoke of them. He didn't bring a gun for elephants."

Pedro made no comment—his silence suggested that he was unconvinced.

"The mountain men didn't mention elephants," Pedro said, less confidently. It seemed to him that the great shape that had risen in front of him had been as large as an elephant—but did elephants roar? He didn't know.

The two of them had been standing stock-still since the great fearsome beast had roared at them.

"Where do you want to go?" Aldo asked. After all, the great beast hadn't killed them. Maybe they should move on.

"I think we should stay here till daylight," Pedro said. "If we move we might disturb it again."

"I mean tomorrow," Aldo said. "Where do you want to go when the sun comes up?"

"Let's go to Santa Fe," Pedro said. The name just popped out. Many people on the boat had spoken of Santa Fe—there would be plenty of Spanish there.

"I don't know about Santa Fe—think of another place," Aldo asked.

"Well, we could go to California—lots of Spaniards there too."

That was just what Aldo Claricia didn't want to hear. Though he had thrown in his lot with a Spaniard and was prepared to travel with him on equal terms, he was not at all eager to go to a place filled with Spaniards— after all, a race of thieves, in his considered view. He would have been far happier to travel to a place where there was an abundance of Italians— only where would that be, in the New World? What if he were the only Italian in all of the West? It was a sobering thought.

"Let's just sleep here and decide in the morning," he said. "Maybe then we can see the beast that made that roar."

"I don't want to see it," Pedro said. "I just want it to go away."

They sat down back to back, feeling that it was important to keep watch in both directions, though it was now so dark that neither could see a foot in any direction. Both vowed to remain alert through the perilous night.

"Vigilance, amigo—vigilance! It is our only hope," Pedro said. Then he fell sound asleep—Aldo Claricia soon slept too, just as soundly.

Bright sunlight woke them up.

"I only nodded for a moment," Pedro claimed, chagrined. "I'm glad you were able to stay alert."

Aldo saw no reason to mention that he had slept soundly for several hours.

Only a yard or two from where they had spent the night the spring grass bore the imprint of a great body. The beast had been resting. Another step and they would have stumbled over it—but now, fortunately, there was no great beast in sight. The plain around them, from horizon to horizon, was entirely empty. They seemed to be the only two living things in the world. There was not even a bird in the sky.

"A beast that large must have made a track," Aldo said. "You Spaniards are such good trackers. Perhaps you can find its track."

"No, amigo, I am only a gunsmith," Pedro admitted. "I have never tracked a thing in my life. *You* track it, if you know so much."

"I'll certainly know if it was an elephant we woke up," Aldo told him, confidently. He peered at the ground in a careful, studious manner.

"I don't see even one track," he was forced to admit. "Perhaps this beast made a great jump, just to fool us."

"It was too big to jump much," Pedro assured him. "Who knows where it went?"

"If it comes at us, shoot good, amigo," Aldo said. "Don't miss next time."

"For that matter, you missed too," Pedro reminded him.

25

. . . Little Onion came walking demurely . . .

When Little Onion came walking demurely up from the birthing hut to tell old Charbonneau that his wife, Coal, had at last been delivered of a healthy baby boy, Charbonneau wept in relief, somewhat to the astonishment of Jim Snow. The labor had taken two days and a night—perhaps Charbonneau was so glad to have the long wait over that he was crying in relief.

"Hard to get into this world and easy to get out," Joe Walker observed. Only Jim and Joe and Toussaint Charbonneau were left in camp—Pomp and the rest of the boys had gone south with Drummond Stewart, into the high Rockies, in search of bighorn sheep.

"It ain't always easy to get out, Joe," Charbonneau said, once he had calmed down. "If you was tied to a Comanche torture stake I guess you'd think getting out was about as hard as getting in."

"I grant the point, that's why I never go anywhere where there could be a Comanche," Joe replied. "What will you name your boy?"

Charbonneau had given the matter no thought. Coal's labor had been so long that he half expected a death—the baby's or the mother's or both—such was not uncommon. Fortunately there had been two experienced Shoshone women in the camp, and their skills had at last prevailed. Jimmy Snow's demure Ute maiden Little Onion was too young to have much experience as a midwife. Now that the matter had been resolved happily there was plenty of time to think of a name.

"Don't know," he admitted. "What are you planning to name yours, Jimmy, if it comes out a boy?"

Jim pretended not to hear the question—he had given no thought to naming, and in any case, it was none of Charbonneau's business. To hide his annoyance he wandered over to the creek to try his luck with a little fish spear he had made.

"Jimmy's a touchy boy," Joe Walker said. "I ought to charge him a hundred dollars for riding my mare halfway around the world."

The little mare, looking as fit as ever, grazed not far from the birthing hut. All the mountain men had been astonished that Jim had passed so quickly from the Knife River to the Green, skirting winter, skirting the Rockies, skirting the Sioux. Joe Walker found that, thanks to Jim, his mare was famous. Several of the trappers tried to buy her from him, but Joe made it clear that she was not for sale.

Jim Snow thought highly of the mare, but he didn't regard the ride as anything unusual. Mountain men tended to amble when they traveled—good hunting, an untrapped stream, native women, or general laziness might slow them down. They moved in fits and starts, capable of hurry when they needed to hurry, but otherwise taking their time and picking their way. They rarely held a steady pace, which is what Jim had done on his ride. He had known exactly where he was going and had no reason to linger along the way. Also, he had been lucky: the weather had been unusually warm, and he had not seen a single Indian in his crossing from the Mandan villages to the Ute country. The little mare liked to go, and go they did, straight across South Pass and into the Ute country, where, upon arriving, he discovered to his dismay that he only had one Ute wife, not two. Sun Girl had died the previous winter, only a few days after he had visited her for the last time; neither Little Onion nor anyone else in the camp could say exactly what it was that carried Sun Girl off. She was well one day, a little shaky the next day, and gone the second night.

Jim was disappointed by this news—disappointed and a little disturbed. It was Sun Girl, mainly, whom he had ridden across the West to rejoin. She had been his first woman, and had always exerted herself vigorously to make him a good wife. Her sister, Little Onion, he scarcely knew; a plan had been afoot to sell the girl to an old man of another tribe; Jim had agreed to the marriage at Sun Girl's request. Little Onion had been his wife for less than a week when he and Kit and Jim Bridger had trekked out of the mountains. It was Sun Girl he had counted on to give Tasmin instructions; Little Onion was very young, not more than fifteen, and very shy, something Tasmin wasn't. Mortality had destroyed his whole plan. Uncertainly and a little reluctantly he had been traveling north with Little Onion when they ran into Drummond Stewart's party. The tall Scot immediately offered Jim a place in his company, but Jim declined.

Now old Charbonneau, relieved that his own wife had narrowly survived childbirth, had reminded Jim that his other wife, his English wife, would soon face a similar ordeal. He had told Tasmin he would be with her when their child came—then she had been freshly pregnant, and such a promise easy to make. Now he had come a long way south, and the wife he had hoped would help Tasmin learn proper behavior was dead. Her little sister, though polite and obedient, was not as experienced as Sun Girl had been.

It was all vexing—deeply vexing. Jim stabbed with the little spear at several trout, but missed them all. Life had seldom presented him with situations that were so unclear. Usually, if it was a matter of guiding some company, he either took the job or didn't. Weather conditions might affect his choice, or the makeup of the group, or something he had heard about Indian hostilities along the way; the choices were seldom hard to make. But here he was now with two wives, neither of whom he knew well. One morning, by the Missouri, he had seen a girl bathing; she had seen him at the same time. He had not found her particularly likable—she talked too much, and often acted foolishly—but they had come together in pleasure—come together often, for a period—and a child was coming, his child. Now that he had been away from Tasmin for some weeks, what had occurred between them seemed almost like a dream. His place, to the extent that he had one, was with the overland guides, or the mountain trappers, categories that frequently overlapped. He belonged with Kit and Pomp and Jim Bridger and the rest. What business did he have being married to an English girl? It was not that he didn't like Tasmin. For all her boldness, he liked her; when she took him into her arms he felt feelings he had never felt before. But what was he to *do* with her? Should he bring her and the child with him on his treks? Would she live in whatever shelters he could throw up, with Little Onion? And what would Little Onion think of a woman who blabbed so much and yet could do little of a practical nature? There was such confusion in his thoughts that he missed and missed with the fish spear—and yet there had been many times when he fed himself with no more equipment than a fish spear and a flint.

"Jimmy's a strange lad," Joe Walker observed to Charbonneau. The latter was trying to whittle himself a whistle out of a section of reed.

"Maybe it was the lightning done it," Charbonneau suggested. "I guess being struck by lightning would make a fellow a little strange.

"That's what the Hairy Horn thought, anyway," he added.

"Oh, that old fool!" Joe burst out. "His opinion is bound to be wrong.

"Jimmy had a hard raising," he added, after some thought. "That old preacher was a rough one—put Jimmy off people, I guess."

"Mostly," Charbonneau said. "But it didn't put him off that English girl. That's his problem now."

26

Often she walked out beyond the stockade . . .

In the last month of her pregnancy, with the weather warming daily, Tasmin slowly withdrew from the chatty group at the trading post. She ceased teasing George Catlin, ceased insulting Father Geoffrin, ceased responding to anything that Buffum or Mary said. In the main, she waited, a dual waiting: for Jim Snow to come back, for the baby to come out. Often she walked out beyond the stockade and sat with her back to the poles, watching for her husband. She didn't doubt that one day he would appear—rumors had already reached the post that he was on his way north, with old Charbonneau and his Hidatsa wife, Coal, who had borne her child.

"Coal was first—I wonder which of us will be next, Vicky?" Tasmin asked. The two of them often sat together, saying little, glad to have a chair to support their increasingly substantial weight. To Tasmin it seemed extraordinary that women could *be* so stretched and not burst open—it was only with difficulty that she could see her own feet.

"Perhaps they'll come at the same time," Vicky said. "The madonnas of the Missouri bringing forth their young in tandem."

"Yes, accompanied by a good deal of screeching, I fear," Tasmin replied.

Mary Berrybender, hearing that prediction, smiled in her sinister way.

"Papa won't like that, now that he's back," she said. "Papa is not one to tolerate undue noise."

"Then let him leave again, the old brute," Tasmin said. "I intend to holler as loudly as I can—it's said to help."

"Señor Yanez and Signor Claricia seem to have made good their escape," Mary said. "Now Papa has no one to load his guns or harness his buggy horses. You shouldn't have sent Kit Carson away—he might have helped Papa in this hour of distress."

"Kit was left here by my husband to be helpful to *me*," Tasmin reminded her. "I sent him off to locate Jim and make him hurry back. This child is not going to be willing to remain unborn much longer."

"Perhaps Millicent can learn to load His Lordship's guns for him," Vicky remarked. "At least she's become proficient at *unloading* a certain gun, if you take my meaning."

"I take it," Tasmin said. "I suppose you're happy to have been relieved of that chore, Vicky."

Venetia Kennet *was* relieved—it *had* been tedious to have to always be copulating with Lord Berrybender, at best, in recent months, an uncertain stud; nonetheless she could not but feel rather moody when she observed the stout laundress cooing over him, murmuring endearments, and even making so bold as to sit on His Lordship's lap. Drummond Stewart had made, for a time, a fine copulator, but the Scot had then left abruptly, with no promises made; it might be that she would never see him again, in which case, once the baby came, she would have to bestir herself and recapture Lord Berrybender's interest. She had no doubt that she *could* reclaim the old lord—after all, there was her skill with the bow—but a general sense of vexation, of the order of things not being quite right, beset her anyway.

In idle moments—and most of their moments *were* idle—Tasmin and Vicky addressed themselves to the problem of names.

"I doubt I shall bring forth a girl," Tasmin said. "I've always rather fancied myself as the mother of sons. I think 'Edward' might do. He would, of course, be called Eddie until he attains his growth."

"I too rather expect a son," Vicky replied. "I was thinking 'Gustavus' would be nice."

Father Geoffrin happened to overhear her remark.

"No, no—that's an odious name, reminiscent of the northern emperors," he objected.

"No one invited you to vote," Tasmin reminded him. "I guess we can name our babies without any help from you, Geoff."

"Venetia can, she's a commoner," Father Geoff said. "You, however, have dynastic obligations to consider—at least you will once you get back to England."

"Who says I plan to go back to England?" Tasmin asked. "I married an American—for all you know I'm here to stay."

Father Geoffrin merely smiled wickedly and drifted off to find Bobbety, who was trying to explain to some Piegans what fossils were—he was hoping they'd bring him some.

As usual, the catty Jesuit had managed to upset Tasmin in ways that caused discontent long after he himself had left the scene. Normal musings about what to name her baby now gave rise to a growing anxiety about what, in fact, the future *did* hold for herself and the child soon to come. When Jim Snow was actually with her she rarely worried. Even if he insisted on an inconvenient life in a tent she didn't feel seriously troubled. Physically she had complete confidence in Jim—he would handle whatever came along. The slap and the sock he had given her the day he left had almost been forgotten—after all, *everyone* told her she was intolerable—Jim Snow had just made that point physically rather than verbally. Spats between husband and wife would occur—that one hadn't dampened her enthusiasm where Jim was concerned at all.

And yet, once he returned, then what? Lord Berrybender's plan was to hunt in a generally southern direction through the summer and fall, going up the Yellowstone and across the Platte.

Where would she and Jim and the baby be, while that progress was occurring? And after it occurred? Her father seemed to be planning to pass through Santa Fe and then hunt on down the plains and the southern forests until they came to New Orleans, where a ship could be procured to take such survivors as remained back to Portsmouth.

Just thinking about the future—Platte River, Santa Fe, New Orleans, England—left Tasmin feeling low and confused. Jim Snow had once seemed willing to take her to Santa Fe. Would he still want to? Would he agree to stay with the Berrybender party, or did he mean for them to strike out on their own?

The more Tasmin thought about these vague prospects, the gloomier she became. After all, it was only a rumor that Jim was on his way back. Perhaps he wasn't. Perhaps her cursing and chattering had driven him off for good. What if he had decided that he preferred the simpler women of the Utes?—if they *were* simpler?

George Catlin observed Tasmin, sunk in her low mood, sitting alone by the fireplace. There was melancholy in her gaze. It was in such low moments that he found Tasmin most appealing; with her brash self-confidence momentarily subdued she seemed vulnerable to any kindness.

After watching her for a moment, George attempted to sneak out, but Tasmin sensed the movement and beckoned him with a lift of her chin.

"Don't be sneaking out, George—I need you," Tasmin said.

"You need *me?*" he asked, surprised.

"Yes. I feel as though there's a crowd inside me. I am extremely stretched. Could you just rub my back?"

"Rub your back? Of course," George agreed. But when he did put his hands on Tasmin's back his pressure was very tentative.

"No good—can't you do anything right at all, George?" Tasmin chided. "Rub harder—much harder."

George rubbed harder, but still not hard enough.

"Hard, George, really hard!" Tasmin insisted; she gave a sigh of pleasure when George complied, pressing his fingers into her back as hard as he could.

"That's good, keep it up," Tasmin said, her eyes half closed.

George Catlin was in the process of keeping it up, digging his fingers as hard as he could into Tasmin's bent back, when he looked around and saw a young man step into the trading post, a stout young Indian woman just beside him. The young man said something to Pierre Boisdeffre. Tasmin, her eyes in a half doze, didn't notice. George did another push or two and then looked at the young man a second time; then he at once jerked his hands away. The young man was Jim Snow.

"I think you better wake up, Tasmin," George said. "Your husband just came home."

27

But then Tasmin, overjoyed . . .

Jim Snow stepped out of bright sunlight into the dim trading post and almost bumped into Pierre Boisdeffre, who was trying to untangle a heap of beaver traps. Once his eyes adjusted Jim saw George Catlin, over by the fireplace, but he didn't immediately see Tasmin, who was bent over. Jim was, for the moment, most concerned to ease Little Onion's intense anxiety. Shy anyway, Little Onion had never before been inside a trading post. For a minute Jim feared she might bolt back outside, but Little Onion, though extremely frightened, just managed to control herself.

But then Tasmin, overjoyed to see him, came hurrying toward them, as fast as she could move in her heavy state.

"Oh, Jimmy . . . it's been such a wait!" she said, opening her arms to him. She saw a young Indian girl standing just inside the door but didn't connect her with Jim Snow—Indian girls often showed up at the trading post.

Just as Tasmin was about to fall into a long-awaited, long-imagined embrace, Little Onion, seeing a large white woman coming toward her husband, did just what Jim had been afraid she would do—she bolted back out the door, to the safety of the plains and the sky.

Tasmin's surge carried her close to Jim—though he grasped her arms, he did not embrace her.

"Oh now, you've run her off," he said. "Maybe Kit will slow her down."

"Run who off? Can't I even kiss you?" Tasmin said in frustration, managing only the briefest peck.

"Little Onion," Jim told her. "She's skittish. Quick too. If Kit don't stop her there's no telling where she'll get to."

"I don't understand," Tasmin admitted. "Is she a friend of Kit's? I don't understand why he should stop her."

Jim felt awkward—he thought he must at some point have mentioned Little Onion's name; he must have told Tasmin that she was one of his Ute wives—but perhaps he had not actually said her name. Even if he *had* said it, long ago in the Oto village, it would be natural enough for Tasmin to forget it.

"She's my Ute wife," he said. "My only one. Her sister was the other one, but she died."

Tasmin started to press forward, determined to kiss her husband, when what he said struck home.

"Your wife? That young girl is your *wife*?" she asked.

"Yes, Little Onion," Jim said again, calmly. It seemed he considered it no news at all, that he should show up with an Indian wife.

"I thought you'd be down at the tent—the mice have about et it up," Jim said; in his tone was a mild hint of censure, just enough that Tasmin heard it and felt annoyed.

"I left to be closer to Cook," Tasmin said. "Did you really expect me to walk a mile once my labor starts?"

There it was already—Tasmin's contentiousness. And meanwhile, there was no telling where Little Onion was getting to.

"Boisdeffre could have stored the tent," Jim said mildly—now a good enough tent had been virtually ruined by neglect.

"You left rather abruptly, Jim," Tasmin reminded him. "I received no instructions about the tent. Am I supposed to read your mind? If so, I fear this whole adventure is a failure. I *can't* read your mind, especially not when you take it hundreds of miles away.

"And now, without a word of warning, you just show up with another wife!" Tasmin said with some vehemence; but just as she said it, the room began to swirl. The walls seemed to be turning and turning around her, like a carousel. Tasmin swirled with the walls for a moment and then fell forward, in a dead faint. Jim Snow and Pierre Boisdeffre just managed to catch her.

"Oh dear, more smelling salts needed, and we have none," said George Catlin. "I'll go ask Cook for a wet rag."

Jim left Tasmin with Catlin, Cook, and Boisdeffre—he wanted to run Little Onion down before she got too far away. To his annoyance not a soul had seen her leave the fort—both Kit Carson and Toussaint Charbonneau were mystified when told that she had left. Kit ran down toward the Yellowstone, Jim toward the Missouri, but Charbonneau soon waved them both back—Little Onion had been sitting quietly behind the stables.

Jim hurried back inside the trading post to see about Tasmin—he felt that he might have been too stern about the matter of the tent. But when he got inside Tasmin was gone.

"Now, where'd *she* go?" Jim asked, exasperated by his wives' tendency to disappear.

"Just into her quarters, with Cook," George said. "It seems her labor has begun. I guess you'll soon be a father, Mr. Snow."

28

Jim Snow crept in shyly . . .

Tasmin's labor was no easier than Coal's had been. Jim Snow crept in shyly and received one kiss before he was firmly banished by Cook, who needed all her skills and didn't propose to tolerate any husbands underfoot.

More than thirty hours passed—Tasmin had long since screamed her-self hoarse; the screams left Venetia Kennet atremble, well aware that the same agonies soon awaited her.

Little Onion felt sure she knew what to do—the old Shoshone women who had delivered Coal's child had taught her a few things—but at first she could get no one to understand her. She spoke no Hidatsa, Coal no Ute. So when Little Onion first showed up with a rattlesnake rattle, Cook was baf-fled. Tasmin was weak, half uncaring; she had come to doubt that she was going to live. But Little Onion was insistent that the rattlesnake rattle could resolve the situation, and Tousssaint Charbonneau finally understood. He remembered that that very substance, ground-up rattlesnake rattle, had been given to Sacagawea when she was being delivered of Pomp.

"Won't hurt to try it," he told Cook. She put no faith in such remedies, but, aware that Tasmin was slowly losing ground, agreed to grind up a little and give it to Tasmin in water.

"It isn't poison, is it?" Tasmin asked, too weak to care very much. To her astonishment and Cook's, only a few minutes later, Tasmin's pains sharp-ened again and then ended. The child was a boy—in only a few minutes Little Onion herself had cleaned him up, wrapped him in a soft bit of flan-nel, and laid him on Tasmin's breast.

Tasmin, exhausted but triumphant, thought it passing strange that she should be receiving her newborn son from her husband's other wife—the baby itself gave out a cry scarcely louder than the squeakings of a mouse.

"I saved just a wee bit of that rattle," Cook said. "It might be that Miss Vicky will need it, rather soon."

The baby—Tasmin had decided to call him Montague, or Monty for short—was for a time reluctant to take the nipple, and again, it was little Little Onion who proved most helpful, teasing the baby with a tiny bit of milk squeezed on a rag. At last he took hold of the nipple and they were all rewarded with the sight of some greedy suckling. Jim Snow was allowed—and seemed to want—only the briefest of peeks.

Cook, of course, still had the company to feed; it at once developed that Tasmin's main helper, as she slowly got back on her feet, was Little Onion. Shocked as she had been that Jim would show up with another wife just as she was about to deliver their child, Tasmin soon found that she could not regard Little Onion with the hard eye that she would normally have turned on a rival. Partly it was the girl's youth, but even more, it was the gentle and loyal attention that she paid to Monty that deflected any jealousy that Tasmin might feel. Tasmin could not get enough of her baby, nor could she be unkindly disposed to a girl who paid him attentions that were as keen as—and, perhaps, a little more expert than—her own. Though the two women had no language in common, they muddled through together, as Monty surmounted his first small crises. He had not an easy stomach, and would sometimes spit up almost as much milk as he took in; also he had a tendency to colic in the night.

Jim had had to go away on a hunt—Tasmin did not quite understand why—and there were nights when Tasmin still felt so weak from her labor that she could scarcely deal with the crying baby. At these times Little Onion walked the baby for her, and cleaned him when he fouled himself. Jim's Ute wife became Tasmin's nursemaid—and, for Little Onion's part, it was only when she was with Tasmin and the baby that she felt at all relaxed. She slept in a corner of Tasmin's room, ate little, and did her best to avoid everyone else in the fort. She could not for the life of her understand why people chose to live crowded up in such a place, when it would have been so much healthier to be outside, on the airy plains.

Jim had been gone for almost a week when Mary revealed to Tasmin that he had been sent on a moose hunt by Monsieur Boisdeffre. The horns of the moose were thought to contain broad medicinal properties, when ground up; Monsieur Boisdeffre foresaw immense profits if only he could obtain a few good racks.

"You mean Jimmy left me for a moose?" Tasmin exclaimed, her mood alternating between anger and amusement. In fact she and Little Onion had all they could do to keep young Monty on an even keel—at this particular time the absence of a husband was not of much concern. Cook even expressed the opinion that it was best thus.

"The menfolk, they've no interest in bairns," Cook told Tasmin cheerfully. "Once the little one is big enough to work I expect Master Snow will find a use for him."

This attitude was shared by Lord Berrybender, who had bestowed upon his grandson only the most casual glance.

"Bring him to me when he's ready to get on with his Latin," Lord B. said. "Can't be much use until then, that I can see."

If the males in the family were more or less indifferent to Monty's arrival, the females were anything but. Buffum was intensely jealous—now Tasmin had acquired a tiny plaything, while she herself had neither infant nor lover.

"How like you to have produced such a greedy brat, Tasmin," Mary said, watching Monty attack a nipple. "No doubt he will become a great criminal and be hung at Tyburn. People will pelt him with ordure."

"That's rather stretching things, even for you, Mary," Tasmin replied. "I should think you yourself are the main criminal in the Berrybender family. In a wiser age you would have been burnt as a witch for your habit of talking with serpents, if nothing else."

George Catlin, at Tasmin's request, came and did a few hasty sketches of Monty at the breast, but the nursery was so thick with females that he felt rather smothered, what with the two Indian women and Mary and Buffum and Cook and the immensely pregnant Vicky Kennet: the place smelled of milk and baby shit and so much femaleness that he could scarcely draw a clean masculine breath.

When, a little later, he attempted to describe the scene to Bobbety and Father Geoffrin, they both rolled their eyes at the thought.

"Why, it's a regular gynocracy," Bobbety exclaimed.

"Females—so *fecund*," Father Geoffrin complained. "They exude—they *drip!*"

"Yes, excessively fecund it sounds," Bobbety went on. "A moderate fecundity must be maintained to secure the continuance of the race, but trust my good sister Tasmin to take things rather too far."

"Now, now . . . it's only one baby," George reminded them—he felt he must come to Tasmin's defense.

"For now," Bobbety said. "But Vicky will soon bring forth, and there's that tiny brat of Coal's. Civilized discourse will soon have to compete with the squallings of several infants."

Bobbety's prediction about the imminence of Venetia Kennet's delivery was very soon borne out. That very night, after a labor that, to Tasmin's envy, lasted a mere eight hours, Vicky brought forth a fine son, whose little head was already covered with fine auburn hair. He was thought, by the ladies who examined him, to have, distinctly, the Berrybender nose.

"No necessity for resorting to the rattlesnake rattle," Cook said. "Miss Vicky was so quick. I suppose I had best save it for the next one."

"Yes, whose ever that may be," Tasmin said, with little Monty snuggled at her breast.

29

"Don't you see how the light's too thin . . . ?"

Don't you see how the light's too thin, up here in Canada?" Kit Carson asked. "The air's not very thick either. Makes it hard to breathe."

"Why'd you come, then?" Jim asked. "You knew we were headed north, to the moose country. If you don't like north as a direction why didn't you go south, with the boys?"

Jim Snow liked and respected Kit Carson, but he had forgotten how picky and hypochondriacal he could be. Last night black ants had gotten into Kit's clothes—they had had to waste half the morning applying mud poultices to Kit's various bites.

"I came because I don't have any money and I need a new gun," Kit explained. "I can't shoot a bow and arrow, the way you can. My old musket misfires half the time. If I don't get a better gun a grizzly bear will eat me—or else I'll lose my scalp."

"You could learn to shoot a bow and arrow if you'd just practice," Jim told him. "Thousands of Indians learn to shoot bows and arrows. I don't know why you couldn't learn."

It was a conversation the two had had before, so Kit didn't answer. He didn't exactly disagree. Skill with the bow would be useful. Jim had just killed three good-sized moose with arrows. But when Kit picked up a bow he just felt silly. When he shot at targets arrows flew every which way. If he had to be dependent on such a weapon, he felt sure he would starve.

"It's hard to see good, in light this thin," he said, returning to his original complaint.

Jim ignored him—if offered a sympathetic ear he might never stop complaining. They had three moose down, all bulls with good racks; except for one small catch, their commission was as good as fulfilled. The catch was that each of them had thought the other was packing a saw—now they had no saw.

"We'll just have to chop them out," Jim said, picking up an axe.

"I can't chop, you'll have to chop," Kit said. Ever since his bad nosebleed at the fort he had been leery of large quantities of blood, such as would surely result if some moose racks were being chopped out.

Jim was exasperated. First Kit failed to pack the saw, then he complained about the light, and now he refused to chop.

"You're a dead loss then, I guess," he said.

Kit, ever sensitive to criticism, wanted to remind Jim that he had looked after Tasmin pretty well while Jim was off meandering, but before Kit could speak in his own defense Jim began to chop. Within a minute or two blood seemed to cover an acre. Kit retreated, so as to stay clear of the blood and bits of flying bone.

"Are you sure my little boy didn't have any hair?" Jim asked, once he had the racks detached. Kit had reported that fact as the two of them were traveling north—he had caught just a glimpse of the baby as Little Onion was greasing its navel.

"Nope, no hair—I didn't see none," Kit repeated.

"That can't be right," Jim said. He walked over to a trickle of a creek and washed the blood off his axe.

"I've seen plenty of Indian babies and they all had hair," he said. He had had a quick look at the baby but Monty had been swaddled in flannel at the time and his head scarcely showed. Now he was disturbed by the news that he and Tasmin had somehow produced a hairless infant.

"Oh, my Lord!" Kit said, in a tone of deep apprehension.

Jim turned, expecting to see Indians, but instead saw two bears—grizzlies, a mother and a sizable yearling with a yellowish coat. The bears were about forty yards away.

"I knew we'd get killed if we came up here where the light's so thin," Kit lamented.

"We're not killed—those bears want the moose, not us," Jim pointed out. "Let's pack up these horns and let them have the moose meat. These old stringy bulls ain't fit to eat anyway."

The bears advanced another ten yards and stopped. Kit was trying to tie the moose horns to their pack animal, but in his haste was making a sloppy job of it.

"Take your time with those knots," Jim cautioned. "I don't want to lose these horns if we have to run for it."

Once the horns were secure the two mounted their skittish horses and rode away. The bears didn't follow.

"I ain't coming up into this thin air no more," Kit said. "We're lucky to be alive."

"You can say that any day," Jim reminded him. "How big was that boy of mine?"

Though happy to have escaped the grizzly bears, Kit was irked by Jim's attitude. Why would the man question him about a matter he should have investigated for himself?

"He wasn't big at all," he replied. "He just got borned. I suppose he weighed about twelve pounds."

"I hope he's stout," Jim said.

What annoyed Kit most was that Jim showed so little concern for Tasmin, who, after all, might have died in childbirth, as many women did; nor did Jim express much gratitude for his own sacrifices in staying by Tasmin's side. The boys had gone south; they were probably trapping beaver by the hundreds. He, Kit, by choosing to stay with Tasmin, was losing money—lots of money. But Jim Snow lived in his own world. He didn't seem to realize that Kit had done him a whopping big favor.

"I expect that baby of mine will grow quick," Jim said. "Tasmin eats hearty—she's probably got plenty of milk."

Jim Snow had always been the most pessimistic of mountain men. He always expected the water holes to be dry, the Indians hostile, the beavers absent. Yet here he was predicting that his baby would be fine. And when two grizzlies showed up with hungry looks on their faces he hadn't turned a hair.

"Do you think you're such a good shot with the bow and arrow that you could have killed those two grizzlies, if they'd come at us?" Kit asked.

"Why no, Kit—I don't think nothing of the sort," Jim said. Kit seemed in a pouty mood, not uncommon with him. Such moods were best ignored.

"I think you might have got that young bear with an arrow—I don't know about the mother," Kit said.

"The fact is, when it comes to bears, I prefer the rifle," Jim replied.

30

. . . three fresh infants . . . hung from pegs . . .

It took Jim only a moment to discover, with relief, that Kit had been wrong about Monty's hair. The three fresh infants, each in its own pouch and cradle board, hung from pegs on the wall of the nursery—one of Bois-deffre's half-empty storerooms had been hastily converted. His little Monty had only the lightest hair on his head, it was true, but it was hair—brown like his own, rather than black like Tasmin's. It seemed to him that a totally hairless infant could not have been expected to last long.

The three babies were all sound asleep, hanging from their pegs and watched closely by Little Onion, who had brought her blankets into the nursery. She considered the infants her charges, whisking them off to their respective mothers when the time came to nurse. Even Cook, a stern judge of nursemaids, approved of Little Onion, a mere girl but with an expert eye for the problems of her young charges.

"Vicky's has got the most hair," Jim pointed out to Tasmin.

"Yes, that's Talley," Tasmin said. "His mother's got the most hair too."

Venetia Kennet had not cut her hair after all. With the birth of her child her mood of resignation passed. She sometimes brought her cello into the nursery and played Haydn for the babies.

Tasmin, though glad that Jim appeared to take an interest in their child, found herself unaccountably awkward in his company. Partly this was because Jim could not really be at ease indoors—not even for an hour. Only under the open sky did he seem himself, the assured plainsman who had won her heart. The smell of the wild was on him, and the need for the wild in him. Indoors, he seemed diminished—seemed a shaggy awkward boy whose hair and beard had grown long since Tasmin had last had an opportunity to trim them.

"I suppose you just aren't meant to be inside four walls, Jimmy," Tasmin said, noting his restlessness. "Would you prefer that we move back to the tent? Coal and Little Onion have done a good job of patching those holes."

Jim was staring at their son—he was shocked by his tininess. For a moment Tasmin had to struggle to choke back tears. The thing she had hoped for had happened; her husband had come back to his family, and yet somehow she still felt disappointed. Cook had explained that women who had just given birth were prone to sudden weepings; she didn't want to cry just then, in front of Jim. He would take it wrong, and why not? What did she have to cry about now? Little Monty was a healthy baby—indeed, all three infants were fit as fiddles, a thing which Cook assured her was quite exceptional. And Jim himself seemed in a mild mood, diffident in relation to his son—so diffident that, so far, he had not dared touch him. And yet, the disorder within Tasmin's breast persisted. Somehow the birth of Monty had made Jim Snow seem younger—perhaps weaker, also. She was now a mother, heir to responsibilities both great and grave. Her child must be kept well nurtured, protected, taught: all things Tasmin felt confident she could do, given an even chance. But would her Jimmy, whom she kept wanting to kiss, whose hair she still wanted to trim, really be a helpmate in this long endeavor? Would he stay with them, or would there be more casual departures after spats or quarrels, or in response, merely, to trapping opportunities or other vicissitudes of the plainsman's life?

It was only two weeks since Tasmin had given birth—a little kissing she would have welcomed, some touching, some tenderness, but, for the moment, not more. Still torn from her long birthing struggle, she felt none of the swelling passion that had linked her so tightly to Jim Snow. Of course, she would soon heal; their ruts, as he called them, might bind them again; but, as they stood together looking at the three infants hanging from their pegs, Tasmin felt a great tumult of feeling, and yet contented herself with holding her husband's hand, while his other wife, Little Onion, watched cheerfully from her corner of the room. Tasmin wanted to ask Jim how things could have gotten so complicated, yet she didn't speak because she knew it was a question he would have no way to answer, and no interest in anyway.

Tasmin had become a woman—little Montague Snow was evidence of that—but her Jimmy, though formidably skilled, was still mainly a boy. How would it end? What would they ever do?

31

. . . Tasmin had lifted little Monty from her purplish nipple . . .

Jim Snow, though relieved that his son, Monty, had at least the beginnings of a normal head of hair, tried not to show his own perplexity as he stood in the improvised nursery with his two wives. That he even had two wives, both of them in the same room of a trading post on the Yellowstone River, was a fair enough mystery in itself. Tasmin, his English wife, was slow of movement, not yet solidly back on her feet after her long labor—he had heard that it was often so with white women. Indian women were supposed to recover from childbirth more quickly, and yet Coal hadn't. One reason they had been so long getting back to the post was because of Coal's weariness. Joe Walker had been kind enough to lend the Charbonneaus a mule, otherwise Coal and her infant would have had to be left behind.

Now Tasmin had modestly offered to go back to the tent with him, since she knew he would be more at ease there himself, but of course he couldn't take one wife and leave the other. When he first came into the nursery after the moose hunt all three women were giving their babies suck, Coal sitting on the floor and Tasmin and Vicky sitting in chairs. It was Little Onion who handled the babies after their milky meal, expertly causing each to belch before returning them to their cradle boards. He had felt uncomfortable in the nursery and was about to leave but Tasmin had lifted little Monty from her purplish nipple so Jim could see his face, the wrinkled apple face of a small baby.

"So, should we pack up?" Tasmin asked, a few days later. Jim didn't know what to say. He was annoyed with himself for having drifted into such a morass of responsibility—it was all the result of having taken Sun Girl to wife in his first hard winter on the Green River. The snows had been heavy, the trapping hard. Having an energetic young Ute woman to do the camp chores was a big help—but then the situation with Little Onion had cropped up, just before Jim left the valley. Thanks to his effort to be courteous to Sun Girl he now had two wives, neither of whom he knew well, and he didn't have Sun Girl, the most competent of the three. What made matters even more sticky was the Berrybender party itself—or what remained of it. Lord Berrybender was determined to set off on a big summer hunt up the Yellowstone valley, linking up with Drummond Stewart at some point; and Kit Carson, like a fool, had agreed to guide the Berrybenders all the way to Santa Fe, although he knew well that to go overland to Santa Fe meant passing through the lands of several tribes of Indians who were likely to be full of fight. None of it made sense to Jim. The old lord had already killed many buffalo, and every other game animal except the grizzly bear and the mountain sheep. In Jim's view he would do well to avoid grizzlies, build a pirogue or two, and float his party back downriver to one of the normal disembarkment points for Santa Fe. Why strike out into the wildness of the West along one of the most dangerous routes of all? But when he said as much to Tasmin she merely shrugged.

"I doubt Papa will turn back," she said. "I think he's keen to go shoot some woolly sheep, or whatever else he can find."

"Death's what he'll find, most likely," Jim told her, but Tasmin shook her head.

"No, but that's what the rest of us will find," she said. "Our help has dropped like flies already, but what is that to Papa? He'll just hire more help."

As they stood before the drowsing infants Jim could feel Tasmin waiting, though not in the snappish way she had waited before the baby came—now, temporarily weakened, she was waiting for him to decide what to do.

"We don't need to put up the tent," he said. "It's warm enough—just bring a blanket or two and come outside with me."

"But, Jim, what about Monty? When he wakes up he'll be hungry," Tasmin reminded him. "He's very young—he doesn't sleep long."

She watched her husband closely, hoping to see that he was really happy to be a father. For a few minutes it seemed that he was. When told that Monty had weighed just seven pounds at birth, he was startled.

"Seven pounds? Why, Kit thought he weighed at least twelve," Jim said.

"Nope, and if he had weighed twelve I doubt I would have lived," Tasmin told him. Jim, so practical in most matters, clearly had no very clear notion of what babies weighed, or what the weight meant for the mother.

They strolled out of the nursery, leaving the cheerful Little Onion in charge of the babies, and walked out of the post for a few minutes. Tasmin was still nervous, still diffident, only a little troubled by Jim's evident indecisiveness where their future was concerned. They had not even settled where to sleep, much less any of the larger questions. When they were alone Tasmin did press a few mild kisses on him; Jim accepted these with an air of distraction, but he shook his head abruptly when she suggested that his hair and beard could use a trim.

"Hush about my dern beard," he said. "It's just now growing good again."

Although rebuffed on that score, Tasmin was relieved to see that, outside the fort, under the bluish skies so high and wide, Jim did seem to be his full self again—not a talker, not easy, but not just a boy, either.

"We ought to bring Monty out," he said. "It's too stuffy in there—he needs to get a good breath of this breeze."

Tasmin's heart lifted. Jim wanted their baby to breathe the air that he had breathed all his life—the fine, windy air of the plains.

"I'll go get him—or do *you* want to?" she asked. At the question Jim looked dismayed.

"You get him—he'll recognize you," he told her.

32

"Seven pounds ain't enough to weigh."

Moving faster than she had moved since her lying-in, Tasmin hurried to fetch the baby before Jim's fatherly mood passed.

Once back outside, she took Monty out of his pouch and cradled him in her arms. He awoke and uttered a few of his little mouse cries—protests that stopped instantly when Tasmin opened her shirt and gave him the breast.

"He's greedy, this boy of ours," she said.

Jim watched as Monty's little mouth attacked Tasmin's swollen nipple.

"Seven pounds ain't enough to weigh," he said.

"No, but he's growing fast—I expect he's already put on a pound or two," Tasmin said. "When we go back in we can weigh him on Monsieur Boisdeffre's scales."

She was not, though, in a hurry to go back in. It was a fair day, the long afternoon just beginning to wane. High white clouds spread shadows across the wavy plains, which were yellowish in places with the first wildflowers. Jim allowed Tasmin to rest her back against his chest—for a few minutes she dozed in unaccustomed peace. For the first time the two men in her life were in the same place. Monty's mouth slipped off the nipple, he had gas, he wiggled and squirmed; Tasmin woke and patted him until he belched; but he still fretted, he was still hungry. When she lowered him to her bosom he eagerly attacked her other breast. So tiny, her little boy was, she thought, and yet a will was there—a young will, of course, but a will all the same. And Jim had a will too. She herself had been called willful many times in her life; now she wondered if she would ever again have the freedom to be willful in her own interest. In passion she had mated with Jim Snow and given birth to Monty; now, sitting in the waning sunlight of evening, looking south to the place where the Yellowstone River lost itself in the brown Missouri, she felt that her own always sharp identity was no longer either sharp or distinct. Like the waters, she was now a kind of junction, a place of merging, the channel through whom Jim and Monty had become part of each other—or at least she hoped they would. Rather as the two rivers constantly caved in their banks and ate whole acres of prairie, now these two males were doing as much with her. Their needs would soon cave her in, sweep through her, suck her away as Monty was sucking even now. Of course, it was peaceful and right that Monty would put on the weight that his father wanted him to have. It was right, too, that Jim would want to bring her out of the fort, under the vast sky—it was being outdoors, attentive to all that there was to attend to in nature, that made Jim Snow whole. And yet, beneath the peace and the feeling of rightness, Tasmin felt a bubble of apprehension forming in her—a small bubble, like the little milk bubbles Monty sometimes blew for an instant with his young breath. What chance did she have, in the circumstances she faced, to remain herself, Lady Tasmin Berrybender, mother but more than mother, wife but more than wife, a woman whole but also a woman separate from the needs of men?

"Ho, now! Tom's coming," Jim said, suddenly alert.

Tasmin looked where he pointed. Sure enough there was a kind of bobbing dot on the prairie—in her opinion it might just be a buffalo. She was reluctant to have their rare idyll interrupted by a bobbing dot—and yet it already had been, for Jim's attention had shifted away from herself and the baby.

"That's Tom Fitzpatrick—I recognize the limp," Jim said. "A mule kicked him when he was young and the leg never healed properly. It don't slow him much, but it's a limp."

Tasmin did her best to suppress her irritation. She had been enjoying her first moments with her young family, and now the mood was lost.

"He's hurrying along, Tom—that's odd," Jim told her. "Tom don't usually hurry."

"I can't help wishing Mr. Fitzpatrick would just leave us alone," Tasmin said, with a touch of her old asperity. "You were gone such a long time, Jimmy. I was enjoying having you back, and I'm sure Monty feels the same way."

If her husband heard her, he gave no sign. His eyes were focused on the moving dot—lost from time to time in the dips of the prairie, but now clearly a man.

"If Tom's in such a dern hurry, it probably means bad news," Jim said.

Tasmin's irritation soon faded into a kind of listlessness. The sight of Tom Fitzpatrick had caused Jim to forget her and the baby completely.

"If you want, we'll sleep out with you tonight," she said. "Monty's such a regular feeder—I have to keep him close."

Jim Snow leapt up suddenly—aquiver, as a hound might be, with some new scent the wind had borne him.

"Tom's running for his life," he said. "We have to run too. Hold the baby tight."

"But why?" Tasmin asked—she could only just see Tom Fitzpatrick across the plain of waving grass and yellow wildflowers. She didn't argue, though. Monty was hastily stuffed into his pouch—as soon as he was secured to the cradle board, Jim pressed her into a run. They were more than one hundred yards from the post; Tasmin feared her strength would give out before they reached safety. But she held out, half supported by her husband. She was gasping for breath—her legs trembled. Monty peered around him in puzzlement. They just made it inside the open gate of the stockade.

"Go find Kit . . . find Boisdeffre, find Charbonneau," Jim instructed. "Tell anybody who can shoot to get their guns."

Then he left her. As Tasmin stumbled on, meaning to do as he instructed, Jim raced across the wagon yard to the stables, where a laggardly Tim was in the process of shoeing Lord Berrybender's fine mare Augusta. Buffum stood nearby, occasionally delivering a tart criticism.

"I'd like to see you drive a horseshoe nail if you'd lost half your fingers," Tim was saying, when, to his astonishment, Tasmin's shaggy husband came racing over. Tim had just been just about to lift the mare's foreleg, but before he could, Jim Snow grabbed the dangling halter and swung onto the filly's back. Her nostrils flared in surprise, but in a moment Jim was racing through the gates of the stockade, the filly running flat out.

"What can it mean, Tassie?" Buffum asked, running over to her sister. Tasmin, quite out of breath, couldn't answer, and, in any case, didn't know.

Lord Berrybender stumbled out of the trading post on his crutches just in time to see his filly racing as if for the prize at Ascot, his American son-in-law clinging to her bare back.

"What ho! Look at her run!" he said, rather pleased by the sight in spite of his disapproval of the son-in-law.

"There are few things in life better than watching a good horse run," he said. "But where's he going, Tasmin? What's he up to?"

"A rescue," Tasmin said. "Mr. Fitzpatrick is endangered. Jim says you should all get guns."

"Get guns—damn it, where *are* my guns? Call for Milly, she'll know," Lord B. said. "That traitor Señor Yanez *would* leave just when I need a gun in a hurry."

Mary, the quick sprite, raced up to the lookout tower in the corner of the stockade, and was rewarded with a fine view of the impending conflict.

"Hey up there, you brat! What do you see? Tell us!" Tasmin demanded.

"I see a fine sight!" Mary cried, making no effort to suppress her flair for histrionics. "The Sin Killer races to save the Broken Hand, who appears to be near the end of his strength. Many painted savages are in close pursuit."

Kit Carson ran out of the trading post carrying his musket. Pierre Boisdeffre and Toussaint Charbonneau were close behind. The latter two were both clearly in their cups. At the same moment Tasmin heard ululating war cries, high and chilling, suggesting that indeed many Indians were not far away.

"Go hide—go hide! They're Blackfeet," Kit Carson urged, but Tasmin shook him off and ran to the gate, determined to see her husband as he raced into battle. Just as Tasmin reached the gate George Catlin came stumbling up, nearly exhausted. He had been painting a prairie landscape and happened to look up just as Jim Snow came racing out of the post. Though George could not see the Indians, one look at Jim was enough; abandoning easel, canvas, and paints, George ran for the fort as fast as he could go.

"Too late!" Mary cried. "The Broken Hand will soon be speared by the fleet Piegan."

Tasmin, losing sight of her husband in the prairie's dip, pulled herself up the steps to the tower where Mary was. Below her the men were all fumbling with their rifles while Tim, Buffum, Bobbety, and Father Geoffrin watched apprehensively.

Once high in the lookout tower, Tasmin finally saw the scene which had caused her husband to jump up in excitement: thirty or more Indians, still producing the ululating war cries, were closing in on the old Broken Hand. There was a long gap in the pursuit. One warrior, especially fleet, was many yards ahead of his fellows. He held a long lance and was almost close enough to touch Tom Fitzpatrick with it. The Broken Hand still ran grimly, though not very fast.

Then Jim Snow flashed out of a dip and was on them just as the Piegan drew back his arm for the thrust. Startled in the extreme, the Piegan not only stopped, he dropped his lance. Jim Snow set the mare on her heels, jumped off, picked up the lance, and ran the fleet Piegan through with his own weapon, leaving him still standing and very surprised—the shaft of his own lance protruded from his chest.

The other Blackfeet, though, were closing rapidly—this time, Tasmin thought, there were no stick-figure gods scratched in the rock to turn them. Jim remounted, swept up Tom Fitzpatrick with one arm, and held him across the filly's back as they raced for the fort. Arrows began to fly, several of which hit the riders, but Jim didn't slow and neither did the horse.

Tasmin had reckoned for a moment that her husband's startling rescue would take the fight out of the Indians—after all, one of their own was staggering around mortally wounded, his lance stuck through his innards. But the Indians showed no sign of slowing, even though they were charging a well-fortified stockade where several riflemen were arming themselves for battle.

"Shoot, Papa, why don't you shoot?" Tasmin cried, wishing she had had the forethought to take the baby inside to safety.

"Can't yet—your husband and my horse are in the way," Lord B. told her. "Can't risk hitting my filly—already lost Royal Andrew, after all."

"Ravishment awaits, as I have long predicted," Mary said.

Tasmin thought that Mary might be right, for once. The Indians were not slowing.

Jim Snow flashed through the gate, still holding grimly to Tom Fitzpatrick, and, at once, the riflemen fired, but with puny—indeed, counterproductive—results. Lord Berrybender's rifle exploded, causing him to fall backward with a great yell, his face black with gunpowder. Kit, Boisdeffre, and Charbonneau all fired but no Indians fell, though one did brush at his sleeve, as if brushing off a wasp.

Tasmin went running down. She had seen the arrows hit her husband and thought he might need immediate succor—but the arrows, it appeared, had merely stuck in Jim's buckskins—he and the other men bent themselves to closing the large log gate—and none too soon. The Indians were not more than one hundred yards away.

"Shut it, let's make 'em climb!" Jim said. He seemed startled to see Tasmin coming down from the tower, but closing and barring the large gate was a task that couldn't wait.

"I'm blinded, I'm blistered. Where's my Milly?" Lord B. yelled.

"You better go hide our baby—and hide them others too," Jim said in a businesslike tone. Before Tasmin could get inside, Little Onion came, took Monty, and at once scurried back into the post. An old bin that had once held corn had been chosen as a hiding place.

Jim, Tom Fitzpatrick, and the rest all hurried up to the lookout tower, fully expecting the Blackfeet to press the conflict. The Broken Hand, having caught his breath, seemed eager to go on with the fight.

Then, to everyone's surprise, the attacking warriors stopped, all of them waiting in a group just out of rifle range. They were watching the lanced man, who was walking slowly toward them, the two ends of the lance protruding from either side of his body.

"Now, there's a sight," Charbonneau said. "Stuck clear through and still walking. Ever see anything like that, Tom?"

"No, but my brother was shot clean through with a bullet—that occurred in a barroom in Cincinnati, Ohio, and my brother is as active today as any man you'd want to know," Tom said. "The bullet missed his heart, missed his lungs . . . and there you are. I suppose a lance like that could go through and miss the vitals—that's what it looks like happened."

"No it couldn't—no it *couldn't*," Kit Carson said. He did not like the sight of a man who must obviously be dead walking around on the prairie.

"They do say the Blackfeet are tough as bears," Charbonneau announced.

Jim Snow, though not apprehensive, was as startled as Kit Carson at the sight of a lanced man walking. The Blackfeet warriors seemed startled too—who could blame them?

"Perhaps that wicked Piegan is filled with such a power of sin that even the Sin Killer cannot subdue him," Mary Berrybender suggested, with her usual, slightly insane smile.

"Shut up, that's nonsense," Tasmin insisted—but Jim refused to second her objection. He just looked hard at Mary, a girl he had been suspicious of ever since he came upon her talking to a snake. He knew that he had been very lucky in his race to save the Broken Hand. It was not often that a warrior dropped a lance—surprise had caused it. Luck, not skill particularly, had decided *that* struggle. And here the man came, walking slowly—but walking.

"I'm in a hurry for that man to die," Kit Carson said. "It's way past time for him to die."

"I guess Piegans don't feel like they have to die just because you want them to, Kit," the Broken Hand said. "I would have died this afternoon myself, if Jimmy hadn't come on that fast mare."

The Indians were talking to the wounded man, who seemed to be delivering a firm opinion. Then one of the older Indians came walking slowly toward the post. The other Blackfeet watched. The fighting urge seemed to have left them, for a time.

"Well, I'll swear, they want to parley, after chasing me five miles," Tom said. "Do you want to go talk to them, Sharbo?"

"I can't talk much Blackfoot—just a few words," Charbonneau admitted. "What about yourself?"

"I'm no better at it," Tom said. "The Blackfeet don't have many whites as guests. There's not much opportunity to learn their lingo."

"I can talk a little," Pierre Boisdeffre said. He was a trader—his job depended on getting along with Indians; otherwise they might burn his trading post down.

"All three of you go, then," Jim said. "Just don't wander out far enough that they can cut you off."

"I suppose we all know better than that, Jimmy," the Broken Hand said, with a touch of impatience.

Charbonneau, Boisdeffre, and the Broken Hand all walked out of the stockade. After a few minutes of conversation in sign, they all came slowly back.

"They want a horse," Boisdeffre said. "That fellow with the lance stuck through him wants to go home to die—I guess he don't think he can make it if he has to walk."

"They're not having my mare Augusta—or the carriage horses either," Lord Berrybender announced. Though severely blistered, his face peppered with gunpowder, he was not blinded—though he did have gunpowder on his eyelids, a circumstance that did not improve his temper.

"No need—give them Joe Walker's mule," Boisdeffre suggested. "I'll pay Joe for her myself." What was the price of a mule compared to the distress of watching his trading post burn?

Tasmin, Jim, and all the rest went up to the lookout to watch Pierre Boisdeffre deliver the mule. The animal was duly turned over, and the wounded man carefully lifted onto its back.

"I doubt we'll ever see a thing like that again," Charbonneau said, as they watched the party of Blackfeet move slowly off to the west.

"I hope not," Kit Carson said. "Once is enough to have to look at a dead man who won't die."

33

The wounded man was called Antelope . . .

Old Moose, the leader of the little band of Blackfeet who had been trying to chase down the trapper known as the Broken Hand, led the small mule that the wounded warrior rode. The wounded man was called Antelope, because he could outrun anyone in the tribe—or anyone in any tribe, for that matter. Antelope was a very fast runner, though it was not likely that he had much more fast running to do. How fast could a man run with a long stob stuck through him? That he was still alive was wonder enough. Old Moose and everyone else in the band expected Antelope to fall over dead at any moment. Old Moose tried to pick a smooth route, so as not to jostle Antelope too much—a man with a lance through his breast would not enjoy being jostled.

In fact, though, to everyone's surprise, Antelope did not seem to be feeling too bad.

"Let's go a long way before we camp, otherwise the Sin Killer might come and stick spears in all of you," he suggested.

"I'm not sure that was the Sin Killer," Old Moose said. "He was moving so fast I didn't get a good look at him."

"Of course it was him," Two Ribs Broken said. "He killed a bunch of moose up north—the Assiniboines told me. They call him the Raven Brave. They were mad because they wanted all those moose for themselves."

"Don't be in a hurry to camp," Antelope repeated.

There was a bright moon, so the Blackfeet traveled deep into the night. Even if the Sin Killer wasn't following them, someone might sneak up on them and try to steal their mule. Everyone still expected Antelope to give up his ghost any minute, but he didn't—instead, he began to eat jerky—tough jerky from an old mountain goat Two Ribs Broken had killed.

Antelope's main problem was that he now had to sleep on his side—the protruding lance made it impossible for him to turn on his back.

"I don't like sleeping on my side," he complained, and yet he was up at dawn and walked over to a nearby creek, where he drank plenty of water.

The band began to face the fact that they were likely to have Antelope on their hands for at least another day. He was not particularly well liked. Thanks to his speed of foot he got a lot of attention from the women, including the wives of several members of the party. In general the man was aloof, but there he was, with a lance stuck through him, just as difficult as he had always been.

"I think we could pull that lance out of you if several of us pull," Old Moose suggested. Antelope's state of health struck him as ridiculous. Was he really going to have to walk along leading a mule all day because Antelope was too stubborn to die?

"No, if you did that my soul might fly out," Antelope said. "I don't want my soul to get away."

Antelope's comment provoked much debate—when it came to the tricky business of souls, opinions differed. Who knew what might prompt a soul to leave? Two Ribs Broken sided with Antelope this time, though he had never cared for the man much.

"He's right—it would be risky," he said.

The band traveled all that day, shot a doe, and wounded a buffalo; at night, though he complained about having to sleep on his side, Antelope was still very much alive.

Some of the warriors were of the opinion that Antelope wasn't really a human being, since a human being would undoubtedly have died of such a wound. A small warrior named Red Weasel was now firmly convinced that Antelope was some kind of witch. Red Weasel thought the best thing to do was to cut the witch's throat, a plan he had to abandon because no one would agree to help him.

"If we had a saw we could saw off this lance right where it goes into my body—then I wouldn't have to sleep on my side," Antelope remarked.

"There are saws at the camp," Old Moose told him. "I guess we can try something like that when we get home."

When they reached their main camp the next day there was, of course, much comment about the fact that Antelope had come back with a lance sticking out of his body. The strongest man in the tribe, Bull, thought he could give the lance one good jerk and pull it out, but Antelope refused to allow Bull to try it, on the grounds that it would provide too good an opportunity for his soul to escape.

A saw was found, and duly sharpened; the lance ends were sawed off so close to Antelope's body that a few scraps of his skin were sawed off too. But such discomforts were minor. Instead of a floppy lance handle, Antelope now merely had a neat plug, could sleep on his back again, and even decided to change his name. His new name was Man with a Plug in His Belly. The women, to Old Moose's disgust, paid him more attention than ever.

34

"Dern 'em, they should die when they're supposed to!" he insisted.

People won't always die when they're supposed to," Tom Fitzpatrick insisted. All those who had watched the young warrior ride away with his own lance sticking out of his chest were confused in their heads about what they had just witnessed. Kit Carson was terribly agitated—he had stayed in the lookout tower until the little band of warriors was out of sight, hoping to see the wounded man fall dead; but he didn't.

"Dern 'em, they *should* die when they're supposed to!" he insisted. "Right's right!"

"Now, Kit—just look at Hugh Glass," the Broken Hand argued. "I'd never seen a man that torn up, and neither had Jimmy Bridger. Hugh's chest was ripped open, most of his ribs were broken, and his scalp was nearly torn off. I thought he was dead and so did Jimmy, or we would never have left him, Sioux or no Sioux. But then, six months later, here he comes, as alive as I am."

"I 'spect you all know Tom Smith," Charbonneau remarked. "A horse fell on him and he busted his leg so bad that it couldn't be set, so Tom sawed it off himself. Not only that, he got up the next day and whittled himself a fine peg leg."

"One of Ashley's men had to have his guts sewed back in after that big fight with the Rees," Tom remembered. "Hugh Glass helped hold his guts in and Jedediah Smith did the sewing."

"I have seen a few sights in that line myself," Lord Berrybender remarked. Though Milly had done her best, his face still looked as if it had been nastily peppered.

"The Spaniards, you know, are cruel to their own peasants," Lord B. continued. "Stick 'em on sharpened tree stumps and leave them to die. Picked a fellow off that had been stuck on a stake for two days—the surgeon sewed him up and off he went. Never know what humans will stand until you've seen a bit of war."

Though Jim Snow listened to all this talk about combat wounds and mutilation, he did not contribute. Some men were tough, there was no denying that, but his failure to kill the young warrior still puzzled him. A bullet was a small thing—it might pass straight through and do little damage. But a lance? Yet the man had walked almost a mile, got on a mule, and rode away.

Pierre Boisdeffre was fretting that this miracle would embolden the Blackfeet, who were plenty bold anyway. The medicine men would use the incident to belittle the power of the whites. A hundred warriors might move against them tomorrow—he doubted that his little stockade would stop a hundred warriors.

"I expect it's time to start south," Jim said to Kit.

"I don't see why," Kit said, and then he got up and walked off. Everyone agreed that lately young Kit had been impossible to deal with.

"There's not a better guide in the West than our Kit," Tom said. "Only he takes bossing. What he can't do is boss himself."

Jim walked back to the nursery, which had been undisturbed by the brief attack. The mood in the nursery was calm, so calm that Jim felt awkward about going in. Monty had just nursed; he hung from a peg, waving his tiny hands. Tasmin was drowsing; she hardly yet had her strength back, which discouraged Jim's inclination to strike out on their own and let the Berrybender party follow Kit and Tom. With Tasmin still weak, it might be best to stay with the group.

"Can't I just trim your beard?" Tasmin asked, waking. Jim had the confined look he got when he was indoors.

The request annoyed Jim—she could immediately see it. Men were prickly about the least things, it seemed. Why would a snip or two cause him to draw away? Nothing made her feel as wifely as cutting Jim's hair, and yet he did his best to withhold the privilege.

"You and your snippin'," he said. "You need to get packed—you all do. We need to get out of here while the getting's good."

Tasmin refused to give up—she felt that she *must* put up a fight, else Jim would never let her do the things she wanted to do.

"Please, just a trim," she said. "I have very little to pack."

"If he won't let you cut his hair, I'll let you cut mine, Tasmin," Vicky said. She had been happy for a bit with her babe, but Lord Berrybender's brutal indifference, plus the absence of Drummond Stewart, had caused her to sink back into glum resignation. If she was to have only the love of her baby, why bother with three feet of hair?

Jim Snow turned and left, his beard unsnipped, which left Tasmin furiously annoyed. When Vicky made it clear that she meant what she had said, Tasmin grabbed some scissors and applied herself with such vigor that virtually the whole floor of the nursery—not a large room—was soon covered with Vicky's shorn locks. Coal and Little Onion watched in amazement—neither of them had ever seen so much hair come off one head.

As Tasmin clipped and cut, Buffum came in to watch, and then Cook and even Eliza. Only Milly missed the cutting—as usual she was busy with Lord Berrybender, who was just getting fitted with a wooden leg, the work of the skillful Tom Fitzpatrick, who had been shaping it for several days.

"It looks a good fit, you'll soon be hopping about like a cricket," Millicent assured His Lordship, who did not welcome the comparison.

"Perhaps not quite like a cricket," he said. Helpful as she was, Millicent did not exactly have a way with words.

When Vicky Kennet first saw her new self in the mirror she could not hold in a shriek.

"I'm shorn like a nun—though I don't *feel* like a nun," she admitted.

"As usual, Tasmin has overdone it," Mary commented. "She has cut off far too much."

"Tasmin should have left you a bit more on top," Buffum ventured. "To me you look rather rabbity, I fear."

"Oh, I don't know," said Father Geoffrin, who had just wandered in. "In fact you look quite Joan of Arc–ish. I hope you won't be foolish enough to attempt martyrdom."

"Look at all this hair on the floor," Bobbety exclaimed. "It's as if a great yak has been sheared—or a musk ox, even."

"I might remind you skeptics that Venetia's hair will *grow*," Tasmin said. She was annoyed by the superior tone everyone was adopting.

From Coal's point of view, and Little Onion's, the great pile of shorn hair was the most exciting thing about the whole procedure. When Vicky indicated to them that they could *have* what had once been her great mane, the girls were almost overcome with excitement. In no time they had sacked up every hair—when Tasmin tried to find out what they meant to do with it the girls gave merry shrugs—they didn't know, really, but were firmly convinced that they had secured a treasure.

Then, almost at the same moment, to the surprise of all the onlookers, both Tasmin and Vicky began to cry.

"What in the world is it *now*, in this year of our Lord 1833?" Buffum wanted to know.

"It's . . . it's . . . ," Tasmin gasped—but then she stopped.

"It's . . . just . . . that life seems so wanting—I think I'll smash my cello," Venetia Kennet said.

35

". . . and now he's chopping up the buggy."

Before Vicky Kennet could carry out this desperate action—one which would deprive them all of music for a very long time, as Tasmin, Buffum, Bobbety, Father Geoff, and even Mary pleadingly informed her—who should rush in but the large laundress, Millicent, sporting a large bruise on one cheek and blubbering loudly.

"Oh, please help me, Lady Tasmin," Milly pleaded. "First Lord Berrybender claimed that his peg leg was too short, and now he's chopping up the buggy."

"What?" Tasmin asked. "Has the old fool gone mad? We need that buggy."

"It's just that he's drunk and in a violent temper, I'm afraid," Milly cried. "When I tried to grab the axe from him he hit me quite a solid lick—not with the axe, of course, else I'd be dead."

"Being Papa's bawd is a rough job, just ask our Vicky," Mary said, with her mad grin.

They all rushed to the courtyard, where Milly's statements were soon confirmed. Lord Berrybender, swinging the axe wildly, had almost succeeded in reducing the fine London buggy to a pile of kindling.

Kit Carson and Tom Fitzpatrick stood nearby, solemnly watching the destruction. Of Jim Snow there was no sign.

"Very good, Father—I see you've been acting with your usual thoughtfulness," Tasmin said. "We've three infants in our company, thousands of miles of wilderness to negotiate, and you suddenly destroy our buggy—what's the sense in that?"

Lord B. ignored her remarks.

"I never liked that buggy," he informed them. "Felt damn good, chopping it up."

"I suppose this means you intend to cram us all in the wagon, then?" Tasmin inquired.

"Not at all—the wagon is for Millicent and me and my guns and shot," Lord B. replied. "No squalling brats invited—might scare the game. Besides, Milly and I will be wanting a little rest now and then—a little time out for human nature."

"Fornication, you mean—spare us these vague euphemisms," Tasmin said, in high indignation. "I do think you're the most selfish old bastard I've ever encountered. So Vicky and Coal and the rest of us will just have to walk, if we hope to get anywhere."

Lord Berrybender ignored her. He was staring at Venetia Kennet's shorn head.

"My God, Vicky, where's your hair?" he asked. "Did a red Indian scalp you?"

"No one scalped her—I cut it," Tasmin told him. "It's that much less she'll have to carry on our long walk."

"But I *liked* your hair," Lord B. said, with a look of distress. "You used to tickle me with it—it was one of our pleasant games."

Vicky didn't answer. The old brute had ruined her, ravished her, gotten her with child, and then abandoned her for a fat laundress. Now, no doubt, he meant to mock her for having cut her hair.

"Oh, I see—perhaps Tasmin was right to cut it," the old man said, hobbling over for a closer look. "I never noticed those pert ears—they were always covered up. Surprised you could even hear your own chords."

"I heard them quite well, thank you," Vicky said—she recognized all too well the rather husky tone that had come into His Lordship's voice. Husky compliments were sure to be followed by fondlings and gropings.

Milly recognized the lustful tone as well—though she stood only a yard from Lord Berrybender, it seemed he had quite forgotten her. Thanks to a haircut, he was intending to grab the prissy Vicky again. It would be back to the tubs for her.

"I'll be going now, Your Lordship—my little one needs me," Vicky said, turning quickly away.

"But wait, my girl!" he said. "Just wait till I get my crutch—damn peg leg doesn't fit right, Mr. Fitzpatrick will have to whittle on it some more."

Vicky Kennet didn't wait, didn't turn, didn't slow.

"What's wrong with that girl? She might just have waited a moment," Lord Berrybender said, frowning. "Always liked Vicky—talented in more ways than one."

"She no longer wants you, Father—if she ever wanted you," Tasmin said coolly. "I think that's plain."

"Oh, nonsense—of course she wants me!" Lord B. exclaimed. "Many a fine tussle Vicky and I have had. Why wouldn't she want me, I'd like to know?"

"Because you're a disgusting, selfish, one-legged old brute," Tasmin told him. "I see you slapped Millicent—and no doubt you'll slap her again."

"Slap any woman I want to, I guess, starting with you, you whore of Satan!" His Lordship thundered. He advanced on Tasmin, hand up-raised, but before he could strike, Tasmin grabbed the axe and held it high.

"Slap me and I'll cut off your arm, or whatever appendage I can reach!" she warned him. "Like to lose an arm, to balance off the leg?"

"Grab her, men, she's daft!" Lord B. said. "Childbirth has addled her!" He looked at Kit and Tom, but neither man moved or spoke.

Toussaint Charbonneau sauntered slowly over, meaning to inspect the ruins of the buggy.

"It's a good thing old Claricia's gone," he remarked. "He was mighty fond of that buggy."

Just then Jim Snow stepped back into the stockade. He had been check-ing around a little, thinking it might be just like the Blackfeet to return and launch a sneak attack.

The old parrot, who sometimes liked to follow Jim around, flapped back too, and settled on the ruins of the buggy.

"There, sir—a timely arrival, I must say," Lord Berrybender said. "Do oblige me and take your wife in hand—saucy wench that she is, she seems to have found it necessary to threaten her own father with an axe."

"What fool chopped up the buggy?" Jim asked, glaring at Kit Carson.

"Not me," Kit said at once.

"You see how my nose is swollen?" Lord B. asked. "A hornet bit me—put me rather in a temper. I'm afraid I took it out on the buggy—inferior vehicle in any case. Never could get comfortable in it."

"Be careful with that axe," Jim said to Tasmin. It was a tool he knew her to be inexpert with, from having tried to teach her to chop firewood.

"I am being careful with it—do you see any blood, Jim?" she asked. "It is merely that Father intends to pester Vicky, and I won't have it. Vicky must not be agitated—it could well affect her milk."

Tasmin lowered the axe. Lord Berrybender looked sulky, but he made no move to follow Vicky.

Tasmin had hoped for a moment that Jim would take her side and pum-mel her father, but she soon saw that he meant to take no side. He strode over to Kit and Tom and asked them why they had stood by meekly while a perfectly good buggy was being chopped up.

"It's *his* buggy!" Kit pointed out, a little annoyed. In his view Jim Snow was far too hard to please.

"Most of us will be walking, it looks like," Jim said. "Let's try and get an early start."

36

Sticking to them close as a tick . . .

Jim could not sleep in the close, stuffy trading post, so Tasmin gathered up their son and a bit of bedding and walked with him about half a mile on the prairies for a night under the stars, which were as brilliant as they had been on her first evening in the West.

Sticking to them close as a tick was Little Onion. The girl, Tasmin realized, wasn't following them out of any impulse toward rivalry, or in order to usurp their privacy. She came because she thought it was her duty to stay near the baby, and, of course, to be available in case Jim Snow, her husband, had some chore he needed her to do. For a time Monty fretted and squirmed, alternately wanting the breast and then not wanting it. Weary, Tasmin let Little Onion take him—she walked him and soothed him until he was quiet, though from time to time throughout the short night, Monty woke and wailed briefly again.

"What's wrong with him? Indian babies don't cry like that," Jim insisted.

"Oh, Jimmy—of course they do," Tasmin said. "All babies cry sometimes. Monty's not used to sleeping out."

"He best get used to it—we'll be sleeping out till the snows come," Jim said.

"Do you wish you could just be rid of us—we're all such nuisances?" Tasmin asked. She knew it was the kind of question Jim didn't know how to answer, but she asked anyway. It was clear that the presence of two wives and a baby left him anything but happy. She knew she probably should keep quiet at such a time, but keeping quiet was not her way. She had mated with this man—surely it was not wrong to try and understand what he felt.

"I led you to this place—I guess it's my job to lead you out," Jim said. Why *would* Tasmin keep asking questions that had no good answers?

"That's what I feared," Tasmin said. "We're just a burden to you, all of us: Monty and I and Little Onion too. You don't want her any more than you want me."

"Less," Jim admitted. "I just married her because her sister asked me to . . . and now her sister's dead."

"That's hardly fair to Little Onion," Tasmin continued. "She's a very proper girl, and pretty in her way. She must find it very sad to have been given to a husband who doesn't want her."

"That's silly thinking," Jim answered. "They were going to give her to an old man who would have spent half his time beating her. I've never hit her once—she's better off with us."

Tasmin liked it that he said "us."

"Unlucky me," she said. "You've slapped me twice and punched me once. Did you ever hit her sister . . . the one who died?"

Jim could not remember that he had. Sun Girl had been an excellent wife—she rarely spoke and never provoked him.

"No, she knew how to behave," he said, being honest. "So does Little Onion, mostly."

"I see . . . and I quite clearly *don't* know how to behave," Tasmin said. "It's certainly odd that you accepted me as your wife, considering how worthless I must seem."

"I had to, so we could rut," Jim said simply. "Rutting's a big sin unless you're married."

"Well, at least you're frank," Tasmin said. "What about Little Onion—you just have to explain a few things to me. I've never been in a bigamous situation before."

"What?" he asked. "What kind of situation?"

"Bigamous—one of two wives," she replied. "When it's time to rut again will you be rutting with us both—or how will it work?"

"She's not much for rutting—too young," he assured her.

"Even so, she has a woman's heart and she's given it to our son if not to you," Tasmin pointed out. "If you and I do a great deal of rutting, as I suspect we might, and you do none with Little Onion, it's likely that she will soon be feeling left out. I know I would, if it were the other way around."

"We don't need to be talking about things like this," Jim said.

"You obviously don't, but I do," Tasmin said. "You left me alone for a long time when I was feeling very married to you. In your absence my married feeling went away, but now it's coming back. I feel married to you again. But there sits Little Onion, singing to our son, and she feels married to you too."

Jim made no response—he was staring into the dark distance.

"I suppose I just want to know that you have some kind of married feeling too," she went on. "That you still want me, in other words."

"It's a far place to aim for, Santa Fe," he said finally.

Tasmin sighed.

"All right, I give up," she said. "There's just no answers in you. I suppose it's just that I ask the wrong questions."

Then she got up, went over, sat down by Little Onion, and sang to Monty too.

37

The stars sent down a kind of fairy light.

In the night, while Jim, Little Onion, and Monty all slept, Tasmin awoke, stood up, and walked away a few steps, to relieve herself. The stars sent down a kind of fairy light. While she was squatting a skunk waddled by, passing Tasmin without alarm. She saw the white blaze of the skunk's tail move off into the grass.

For a time she had been too angry to sleep—angry at Jim for his refusal to address her concerns—they were concerns that seemed to be important for her future. But anger was followed by resignation: what was the use of even talking to the man? His intentions were not cruel, particularly, but his way of living had been so different from hers that they had little common experience from which to frame a discussion. The old patterns of English life—a life still being led by her own family—left many avenues for adjustment. Much was allowed, including frank discussion of what was or was not allowed. Conflicts there might be, but breakfast, lunch, tea, dinner followed inevitably. Tasmin could not be sure that her parents, Lord and Lady Berrybender, had ever been especially close, yet they had produced fourteen children while leading lives that were, in the main, separate. They met at table, at cards, to procreate; conditions of life were very orderly. Despite Lord Berrybender's bluster, extremes of emotion were rarely attained.

But her mate, Jim Snow, knew nothing at all of social pattern—how could he? Survival seemed to be his principal goal—he was not even interested in making money, as the other mountain men were. On his terms he was successful: he had survived where many another man would have fallen. Only the day before, with her own eyes, she had seen him come within an inch of death from the Blackfoot arrows. More than that, she had seen him, in effect, kill a man—that the man hadn't died immediately was only due to some fluke of anatomy. Jim admitted that he had been lucky—surprise had made the warrior drop his lance, otherwise Jim might have been the one speared. The conflict, though brief, had involved life and death. Death in battle—a thing several of her noble ancestors faced—had been a likelihood for all of them. Only by the accident of the warrior's survival had a pitched battle been avoided; the defenders might have been overwhelmed, and she and her sisters taken into captivity or killed, with dire consequences for Monty, Coal's baby, and Vicky's.

Finished, Tasmin sat for a while in the rippling grass. Her anger at Jim subsided. With life or death in the balance, as it had been on many days of Jim's life, why would she expect him to worry about the kind of concerns she had expressed? Mating with Little Onion would be the last thing on his mind. Tasmin had been drawn to Jim in the first place because of the foppish English suitors she had rejected at home. They were men so positioned as to think only of their pleasure. Jim Snow was not indifferent to pleasure—Tasmin was wife enough to know that—but it was not unnatural that he should think mainly of danger, when there was such a lot of it around. What might happen conjugally if she and Little Onion and Monty were all in a tent together was a problem he had so far not even considered, and if he did focus his mind on it, he might be the one surprised the next time he faced a warrior with a spear.

Subdued by such considerations, Tasmin went back to where Jim rested on his blanket—Monty had begun to emit a few little mouse squeaks, meaning he was hungry, so Tasmin took him from Little Onion and sat down cross-legged and fed him. Her milk flowed easily, but her thoughts were not so easy. What of the little boy at her breast, a child they had made in reckless pleasure? What did she want him to be—an English gentleman, or a hardy frontiersman? This too was something she would be unlikely to get Jim to talk about. How could he? Excepting her own monstrously selfish father, he had never seen an English gentleman. The frontier had been his only school. He was anxious to read better, in order to comprehend more of the Bible, but how would he react if she suggested that Monty needed to make a beginning with Latin and Greek? What did she think about such an issue herself? She had always been an eager learner, and had resented having to more or less steal Greek lessons from her hapless brother's tutor. *She* wanted Latin and Greek, but did she want them for her son, a boy conceived on a blanket spread on the prairie grass, while buffalo roared in the distance and hawks soared high above? What *did* she want for Monty: the English life with its order and pattern, or the frontier life with its vast beauty and frequent danger? Of course, Monty had only just been born, there was time to consider many possibilities, but it would *need* to be thought about soon enough, and she was the one who would have to do the thinking. Jim Snow would be busy enough just keeping them alive.

Tasmin wished for Pomp—she could have talked it all through with him. After all, Pomp knew both worlds. He had admired an Italian princess, dead on the Brenner Pass. He had been to plays and operas, and studied philosophy and science—his tutor, Pomp told her, had been a student of the great Kant himself, of whose profound speculations Tasmin had not the slightest notion. Pomp had been given by the generous Prince Paul of Württemberg, who adopted him, every benefit, everything Europe could offer—except, of course, noble birth; and yet he had come back and submitted himself to the spartan rigors of the American frontier. No one else of Tasmin's acquaintance had mastered both lives, both ways. Surely her sweet Pomp would give her good advice—so anxious was Tasmin to have it that she felt impatient for the morning, when, if there were no unexpected delays, they would start south, where Pomp and his patron might be found.

"Where'd you go?" Jim whispered, when Monty had been returned to Little Onion and Tasmin had returned to the blanket where he lay.

"Just to make water," she said.

"Lay back, while it's still dark," Jim said, still whispering.

Puzzled at first, Tasmin then realized that Jim didn't want Little Onion to hear him, though she would not have understood his words.

Obediently, since she felt she had taxed her husband enough for one night with her questioning, she lay down beside him and was startled, when, at once, his hand began stroking her, in the place that had recently made her a mother. Months had passed since Jim had caressed her so— Tasmin was startled—the last thing she had expected to receive from her husband that night was such a caress. For a moment she was nervous—almost resentful. How dare the man be so familiar! Nearby, Monty squeaked, and then quieted, as Little Onion walked him. Slowly, under the stroking of Jim's hand, Tasmin relaxed, forgot Little Onion, forgot the baby. Never passive, she turned and reached her hand inside Jim's leggings, so as to grasp her husband. And yet she was doubtful: Cook had advised her not to rush conjugal relations.

"You'll need just a bit of healing—a month I'd allow, if I were you," Cook had advised—the words had been meaningless at the time, when Tasmin had not even been sure she would ever see her husband again. They were not so meaningless now. Jim's hand worked, Tasmin sighed. Little Onion heard, but didn't care. She was happy to avoid men, when they were in that mood. The tiny male in her arms now was her dearest love, and he, in his squirmings, gave her plenty to do.

38

"You garlic fool, you should have kept it sharp."

If the English don't leave today I think we should go back anyway," Aldo Claricia suggested. "I'm hungry—I need to eat. Boisdeffre would give us food."

"Surely they'll leave today," Pedro Yanez said. "Lord Berrybender might shoot us, if he sees us."

The two of them were holed up in a kind of excavation they had made for themselves, under the west bank of the Missouri River. Their excavation, a tiny cave, was hidden from prying eyes by a thicket of briars and berry bushes. They had been huddled there for four days, expecting, every minute, that the English party would depart. After all, the plains to the south were covered with game—surely Lord Berrybender would not ignore such good hunting.

Their own plans to follow the swiftly flowing Yellowstone south had stalled after only three days because of the lack of adequate knives. Though, when they left the hunting party, they had made off with the fine Belgian rifle that had belonged to Old Gorska, the Polish hunter, and had plenty of powder and shot, they had been negligent in the matter of knives. When, on the second day out, Pedro had brought down a fat doe, they discovered that they had only one small knife between them—a pocketknife that Aldo used mainly for whittling sticks into toothpicks.

This pocketknife, though a fine instrument for making toothpicks, proved wholly inadequate when it came to slicking up a fat Western deer.

"You garlic fool, you should have kept it sharp," Pedro said testily; the comradeship they had proclaimed the night they left the company had quickly begun to fray. Almost everything Pedro did—or didn't do—irritated the sensitive Italian, and that applied in reverse to the testy Spaniard. The slightest contretemps led to heated quarrels. Here, at the very outset of their bold adventure, they were faced with a very formidable problem: a dead deer they couldn't get the hide off, though they were both starving.

"This knife was not meant to cut a deer," Aldo remonstrated—he was bitterly disappointed in the performance of his own knife.

"I don't care, go sharpen it on a rock," Pedro commanded. "This venison is going to waste."

Aldo tried, but the famous yellow rocks which gave the river its name proved poor grindstones. The little knife, despite much grinding, did not become sharper. Finally, driven mad with frustration, Aldo began to stab the carcass blindly, aiming at the belly, where the skin seemed a little less tough.

"Keep stabbing, you made a puncture," Pedro said. "Tripe is better than nothing."

Working in tandem, the two were soon able to pull out many yards of intestines, while the roasts, the steaks, the saddle—all the parts of the deer they had looked forward to eating—remained as inaccessible as ever.

Desperately they sliced the gut into sections—even that taxed the potential of the little knife. They ate the gut, along with its greenish contents, while they sat on the ridge where the deer had fallen and contemplated their unenviable situation. They were just by the blue-green river—they could see it winding far, far across the plains.

"How far do you think it goes, Pedro?" Aldo asked.

"I don't know—a thousand miles, ten thousand, what does it matter?" Pedro said, overcome, for the moment, with the fatalism of his race. However far the river went, they would never get there.

"We will starve before we get to the end of it," he said, becoming lachrymose. "We will never get to the end of this river."

"There are many knives in Boisdeffre's trading post," Aldo reminded him. "We could go back and get some."

"No, it's in the wrong direction, and besides, the English are there," Pedro said, in his gloom.

"Direction? What difference does direction make, in this country?" Aldo exclaimed. "One direction is as good as another. Boisdeffre doesn't like the English any better than we do—at least he'll feed us."

Pedro soon grasped the wisdom of that suggestion. Here was a fat deer, well killed with one shot from the Belgian gun, and yet all they could eat of it was the guts.

So, talking of all the buffalo roasts they would eat once they got back to the post, the two turned north, followed the river, and then crossed and dug their little cave in the bank of the Missouri—from there they could watch the post without being seen.

Once in sight of the post their rage increased in keeping with their hunger. Why wouldn't the English leave? Lady Tasmin they saw twice, walking out with her husband and her infant, followed by the young Indian girl. Millicent, the fat laundress, made trips in and out, loading the wagon, which suggested that departure would soon occur. But when?

"Curs and bitches," Aldo raged. "This is a free country. The old bastard doesn't own us. Why can't we just go in and eat? Think of those beaver tails Boisdeffre cooks."

The Spaniard, though, was more cautious.

"Who knows what the laws are here?" he said. "We took the gun—the old fool might hang us."

"No," Aldo protested. "The gun was Gorska's. No one said His Lordship could have it. You could tell him Gorska willed it to you."

"Me? Why me? Why don't *you* say it, then they'll hang you," Pedro argued, his suspicion of the treacherous Italian coming to the fore.

On their fourth day in the hole, with the English party no closer to leaving for their hunt, both men tried to screw up their resolve and march into the trading post—yet they were still lingering when help suddenly appeared from an unexpected quarter. Who should come strolling along the riverbank with a butterfly net and a pouch filled with specimen bottles but the dumpy figure of Piet Van Wely, clay pipe in his mouth. And that was not all: accompanying Piet was Mary Berrybender, carrying what appeared to be a substantial picnic hamper.

Neither Aldo nor Pedro liked the finical Dutchman, who, for no better reason than that he knew the Latin names of plants, gave himself airs, refused to drink with them, seldom took snuff, and held aloof from all coarse badinage concerning the women on the boat, even though he was known to enjoy the caresses of the spindly Mary.

Nonetheless there Piet was, a fellow European. Surely he would be sympathetic to their need.

"If not, we'll beat them both and take the food and run," Aldo said with dignity. "Why should he get to feast with that English girl while we starve?"

"I hope they have sardines. . . . I could eat a hundred sardines . . . no, a thousand sardines," Pedro bragged, his mouth watering at the prospect.

Hastily they crawled up the bank, knocked the dirt off their clothes as best they could; a week in the wilderness, with no access to a laundress, had left them not exactly dressed for a parade.

But when they presented themselves in all their soiled dignity to Piet Van Wely and the young Miss Berrybender, their scruffy appearance caused scarcely any comment.

"Ho, fellows . . . so you're back, eh?" Piet said, looking far down the Missouri River.

"Back . . . very hungry too . . . I wonder if the young miss would perhaps spare us a bit of a loaf, or even a sausage?" Aldo asked.

"Of course I won't, you grubby beasts," Mary said. "Not a bite shall you have! Shame on you, you treacherous slaves! Deserting my good papa in his hour of need. You would both be bastinadoed if I had my way."

"She's a witch, let's cut her throat and take the sardines," Pedro whispered. Then, to his surprise, Piet Van Wely suddenly dashed off into the prairie grass, waving his butterfly net wildly at anything that moved: butterfly, grasshopper, moth, wasp, bee.

"Ha, Piet, you sluggard!" Mary yelled, with a sinister smile. "Now that the tiny prince comes, you at last bestir yourself. Hurry now, grab the grasses, the flowers, and any beetles that you see. Perhaps we can beat these rivals yet."

Greatly startled, Aldo Claricia looked around.

"What prince, Miss?" he asked, confused—Mary Berrybender deigned merely to point. Where there had been only the broad brown river, there was now a smudge, beneath which there was a speck that might be a boat.

"It's the steamer *Yellowstone,* more successful than our poor boat," Mary explained. "It carries, unless I'm mistaken, Prince Maximilian zu Wied-Neuwied, so celebrated for his researches in the dense Brazilian forests. Now he's caught us, and Piet is very likely undone, for the prince is a most determined explorer and will surely have brought with him many specialists: botanists, lepidopterists, entomologists, a painter, a mineralogist, and Lord knows how many others. Papa will be most vexed: first the lecherous Drummond Stewart quite turned the head of his mistress, Vicky Kennet, and now the little prince of Wied will no doubt usurp us in many sound fields of knowledge, for Piet is but one man and the Germans will likely be many."

"If they are so many, why can't we just shoot them, these Germans?" Pedro Yanez suggested. "The fat beasts, what right have they to crowd us out here, we who have trekked through the snows?"

"Good for you, señor," Mary said. "A fine idea indeed, though of course there might be a bit of an outcry in the embassies. But we Berrybenders have never let a few outcries stop us. For that you'll get your picnic, señor! My good Piet has got to be about his collecting quickly—I doubt he will want to eat."

"We'll eat, he can chase!" Pedro said.

A moment later, mustache dripping, he was just finishing the first tin of sardines, while the more fastidious Italian, Aldo Claricia, was slicing himself a healthy hunk of sausage with his ridiculous little pocketknife.

39

". . . I swing with the net, and the bruin looks up . . ."

Exactly how his large butterfly net managed to get round the head of a grizzly bear was something Piet Van Wely could never adequately explain, not even to himself.

"I am in the weeds, I reach out to scoop a big gray moth who is on a weed, I swing with the net, and the bruin looks up and gets his head stuck in the net. So I *run!*" he said.

The bear, after pawing at the confusing net for a moment, ran too—after the screaming botanist, who raced with all the speed his short legs could muster right toward the startled picnickers. Mary Berrybender, who could usually find no wrong with the plump Hollander, found much wrong in this instance: he was leading the loping grizzly right toward them!

"Fie! Fie! Piet!" she cried. "Can't you see we're picnicking? I must insist that you take your great bear elsewhere!"

"Kill him, Pedro, we'll be gulped!" Aldo said, but Pedro Yanez, as was his custom when in a state of great fear, grabbed the Belgian rifle and fired both barrels straight into the air.

"You miss again!" Aldo said, dropping his sausage. Pedro likewise dropped his can of sardines. Then both men joined Piet Van Wely in flight. Somehow the fleeing Spaniard ran into the fleeing Italian, who tripped the fleeing Dutchman—all three went down in a heap, expecting at any moment to feel sharp teeth rend their flesh.

But the grizzly stopped, attracted, it seemed, by the smell of sardines. He ate up those Pedro had spilled, and then began to lick the can. Then, as the big beast lapped up the delicious oil, a shot rang out, from the direction of the river. A man in a somber black coat, his pant legs muddy from an abrupt leap into the shallows of the river, was hastily reloading his rifle, keeping one eye on the bear. He fired again, reloaded again, fired a third time. The first two shots the bear ignored, but the third provoked a rumble of annoyance, as he nosed among the ruins of the picnic.

"These big bruins, they are very reluctant to die," the rifleman said, nodding to the three men, who were just picking themselves up. To Mary Berrybender he made a deeper bow. She had been watching the contest silently.

Once more the man reloaded, watched the bear closely, stepped within twenty feet of him, and fired a shot directly into his brain.

The grizzly, a sardine can still in its paw, fell dead.

"These big boys only agree to die if you shoot them in the head—they are tougher than all the bears of Europe," the rifleman told them.

"Correct—that is why they are called *Ursus horribilis*," Mary agreed. "Very terrible beasts they are, and my good papa will be most vexed that you have killed one while he has not."

"Not one, young miss . . . six now," the hunter said, permitting himself a small smile. "Perhaps we ought not to mention it to His Lordship, though, or he might want to shoot *me*! And then where would you all be the next time a grizzly bear spoils your picnic?"

"Oh, I never lie to Papa, he is far too clever, Herr Dreidoppel," Mary said. "It *is* you, isn't it?"

The hunter made another small bow. "David Dreidoppel, at your service," he said, removing a small tape measure from a worn leather case.

"We heard about you in Saint Louis—they say you are the best taxidermist in Europe," Mary said. "Are you going to stuff this fine bear?"

"That is a decision for my prince," the hunter said. "I certainly am going to measure him, though—if one of these gentlemen will just help me stretch him out."

"I don't like him, he ate my sardines," Pedro complained, but before any of the others could offer an excuse Mary herself stepped forward and obligingly held the tip of the tape measure right against the dead grizzly's cold, wet nose.

"He is long, but not our longest," Herr Dreidoppel said, as he quickly rolled up his little tape. "Probably we won't stuff him, but that my prince decides."

"And did you once kill an anaconda thirty-four feet long?" Mary asked, excited.

"What a well-informed young miss you are—thirty-four feet seven and one half inches, that boy was—an anaconda of the Orinoco River," Herr Dreidoppel said. "How did you learn such a thing?"

"From the illustrated papers, of course," Mary told him. "Your beard was not so gray in the pictures they showed."

At this the somber hunter laughed aloud, rather to Piet Van Wely's annoyance—he was beginning to be rather jealous of the way the bearded man was bantering with his Mary, without whose protection his position in the Berrybender ménage would be a very shaky one indeed.

"It's wrestling with these big boys, these bruins and those snakes, that made me gray," the hunter admitted. "Ah—here comes my prince. He too is somewhat gray."

At first all any of them could see was a high, round black hat, of European make, making its way as if by magic along the tops of the high prairie grasses. But then, as they watched, a head emerged, wearing the hat, and a man of very modest height, dressed exactly as the hunter was, in a somber coat and muddy pants, appeared. One hand was stuck inside his coat, the other he held behind him.

He stopped, looked briefly at the dead bear, and bowed to Mary.

"I am the prince Max," he said in clipped tones. "I have something for His Lordship, your father, that I think he will very much like to have."

"Claret, I hope, Prince," Mary replied. "It's claret Papa misses most."

"Claret I have," the prince of Wied said.

40

. . . thick necks, eel eaters, fart bags . . .

Lord Albany Berrybender was seldom of a divided mind when it came to women or Germans. Women he mostly liked, if they were not reluctant in the matter of fornication and did not aspire to win at cards.

Germans he roundly detested: filthy Teutons, he called them, thick necks, eel eaters, fart bags, two-legged pigs. Should a German attempt to interfere with his plans in any way, terms of abuse would be heaped on him, accompanied, if necessary, by violent action. In the courts of the Georges, portly fools themselves, many thick-necked German courtiers had come to England—they were even seen in the best clubs. Lord B. had fought duels with a number of them, wounding three with his dueling pistols. He himself had yet to receive a wound or even a scratch. Once or twice, though, stolid princelings from one or another of the piddling German duchies had gained an advantage over him at the gaming tables, and once a German mare had beaten his fine filly Augusta in a race. The final indignity was that two of his greyhounds had been outrun by the fleet whippets of the Germans.

These last indignities came fresh to mind as His Lordship stood in Monsieur Boisdeffre's trading post, looking at the six large bearskins spread on the floor—a sight that astonished even Kit and Tom and Jim, none of whom had expected to see that many bearskins in one place. All had been killed, it seemed, by the cool and accurate marksmanship of the prince's hunter, Herr Dreidoppel.

Lord Berrybender's instinct had been to fly into a great rage and demand to know by what right a German prince had wandered out of the forests of Europe and invaded the rich hunting range which he supposed would be wholly his to plunder. Finding the annoying Scot Drummond Stewart already ensconced in this paradise of game was shock enough; *must* he now really tolerate German princes too—and one, moreover, whose hunter was clearly a very superior shot?

And yet, the fact was, this rather dumpy, unimposing prince had just made him a present of a dozen cases of rich red claret, the blessed elixir that he had so long been without. A noble who had had the forethought to bring such an admirable gift all the way from London could not simply be brushed off as a bad fellow, Teuton though he unmistakably was.

Still, the fact that Herr Dreidoppel had already shot six grizzlies—bears that, by rights, should have been his—put Lord Berrybender's tact to a severe test. The more he thought about the six lost bears, the more the great vein on his nose throbbed, pulsed, and finally turned red, as it only did when His Lordship suffered profound agitation. Lord B. rarely felt that he ought to be grateful; the need to balance gratitude with dismay was a very unaccustomed thing. Was he to overlook entirely the six bears that should have been his? He himself had yet to dispatch even one. On the other hand there was the claret, a bottle of which he had already quaffed, filling and refilling one of Boisdeffre's pewter goblets.

"Grateful, I must say, Prince," Lord B. finally managed. "Don't mind allowing that I was rather starved for the grape—you know your vintages, I see. Lucky you weren't victim to thieving *engagés*, as I was."

"Oh no, we Germans don't take such chances on our good boat *Yellowstone*," the prince replied, in English that lacked nothing of correctness.

"The liquor was kept in a special room, and only I had the key," he went on. "Human nature is everywhere very bad, you know. It is best to remove temptation."

"Bad, yes, bad—human nature's a rotten thing, and particularly rotten if you have to deal with Mediterraneans," Lord B. said, glaring at Signor Claricia and Señor Yanez, whose excuse for their long absence—that they had gone off to relieve themselves out of sight of Milly and had become hopelessly lost—he knew to be an arrant lie.

Pierre Boisdeffre, Tom Fitzpatrick, Kit, and Jim all walked around the six bearskins, saying little but filled with amazement nonetheless. They looked at the skins, looked at one another, and shrugged. None of them, in all their years on the prairie, had ever heard of one man killing six grizzly bears. And yet the man responsible, an ordinary-looking fellow with an iron gray beard, stood quietly at the counter, leaning on his rifle and drinking a little of Boisdeffre's grog.

"That fellow must be the best shot in the world—what do you think, Jimmy?" Kit asked.

Jim Snow had been rather put out that the arrival of the prince had meant a delay in their departure, but, so far as shooting went, it was hard to disagree with Kit. It was obvious that the quiet fellow at the counter must possess unusual steadiness. Grizzlies had a habit of making even experienced hunters panic. He himself, having been much in bear country, had never killed one, though he had shot at several and had been chased twice for his pains. Once he had had to jump off a high riverbank, in order to escape a charge. A man who could down six grizzlies was no run-of-the-mill hunter.

"Look at his eyes," Kit whispered. "Icy blue. I bet that's his secret, good eyesight."

Looking once more at the bearskins, Lord Berrybender could not entirely suppress his sharp annoyance—why had *his* hunter, Gorska, been so incompetent, while the prince's hunter was a lavish success? His first thought had been to approach Herr Dreidoppel in private, perhaps attempt to hire the fellow—and yet there was a chilliness in the man's eyes that gave him pause. Claret or no claret, Lord Berrybender's vein was soon throbbing so violently that he could not suppress a complaint.

"I say, Prince," he began, "this hunter of yours has been helping himself rather freely when it comes to the bruins. I might have fancied killing one or two of these brawny fellows myself."

Prince Max remembered how coolly the old lord had greeted him, before the gift of the claret had caused him to change his tone. Now, it seemed, English ice was to be followed by English bullying. The one-legged old fool was trying to drive him out of the rich hunting grounds of the Yellowstone. Malice, cunning, brutality, chill: that was what one could always expect from the English.

The prince of Wied contented himself with the smallest of bows.

"We have counted thirty-two of these bears since leaving the Knife River," he said. "Your Lordship will soon find that there are many left— perhaps too many. As you journey up the Yellowstone I'm sure you will find all the bears you want.

"As for us," he went on, "we work only for science. I am, as you know, a zoologist. Herr Dreidoppel is not only a fine hunter, he is also the state taxidermist of Wied. We will not be bringing home a live zoo, as your friend Drummond Stewart hopes to do. But we *will* examine everything we kill. In fact, now we must go and open the stomach of the bear Herr Dreidoppel killed today, so that I can analyze his diet. We expect to find fish, berries, prairie dogs, even mice—imagine such a giant feeding on something so small. Would you like to come and watch the examination?"

"Oh hardly, Prince—don't care what the brutes eat," Lord B. said, signaling for Boisdeffre to uncork another bottle of the excellent claret.

Then a dark thought struck him. What if the small prince with the excellent hunter planned on traveling to the south, the direction he meant to travel and would have been traveling already had it not been for the distraction of his rabbly entourage?

"Not heading south, I hope, Prince," he said—better to speak plainly to the fellow. "No room in the south. My good friend Drummond Stewart is, as you know, already there. Very active man, Drum—distinguished horseman and all that. Expect he's already wiped out the game down that way— it's crowding up a bit to the south, I can assure you."

The prince of Wied, well aware that he was being told where he couldn't go by a man who had no more rights in the country than he did, refrained from smiling.

"Oh, no, Your Lordship, we are proceeding west," he replied. "Fort Mackenzie is our goal. No zoologist would neglect the region of the Marias River, where there are said to be enormous herds. Besides, my painter, Herr Bodmer, wants to paint the white cliffs, which lie in a westerly direction.

"We have a fine keelboat to take us," he added, lest the old fool suppose that a proper German expedition would go off ill-equipped.

The notion that the dumpy little prince with the superlative hunter planned on traveling west, into the very heart of Blackfoot country, startled the three trappers a good deal. Six grizzly bears were one thing, but a challenge to the Blackfeet was bold indeed.

"Mackenzie? Marias River—you really mean to go *there*, sir?" Tom Fitzpatrick asked. "It's woolly doings in that country—Blackfoot country, you know. Woolly doings to the west."

"Yes, we hope to shoot the woollies, the big sheep of the mountains," the prince said modestly, although he knew perfectly well what the old trapper meant.

41

Six bearskins was big medicine.

Weedy Boy and the other Minatarees were becoming impatient. The three of them had come to the trading post to see if Boisdeffre would give them tobacco, and the trader did give them a little—he rarely refused them tobacco. But when they saw the six bearskins on the floor, Weedy Boy and the others wished they had not bothered coming to the post that day. Six bearskins was big medicine. When Boisdeffre told them that one man, a hunter with icy blue eyes, had killed all six of the bears, the three became even more agitated—the young warrior named Climbs Up was particularly upset. It was Climbs Up's opinion that whatever bears were near the fort would be wanting to do a lot of killing to revenge such a slaughter. The great bears would not be likely to discriminate, either. They would just kill whoever they met, which could as well be Minatarees rather than whites. Climbs Up, who was pessimistic at the best of times, thought that they ought at once to move their camp farther down the Missouri River. The presence of bears bent on revenge was never welcome.

Weedy Boy was more or less in agreement with Climbs Up, for once, but he thought they ought to talk the whole matter over with Otter Woman before doing anything rash. The two wanted to hurry right back to their camp, but the woman who was with them, Squirrel, was looking at some beads and refused to be rushed, even though she could see the bearskins with her own eyes.

"Let's leave her—she'll be here all day looking at those beads," Climbs Up said.

But Weedy Boy didn't want to leave Squirrel. He was thinking of marrying Squirrel, even though she was rather moody. He told Climbs Up to wait a minute, which Climbs Up did reluctantly. Then, when Squirrel was finally ready to leave, who should show up but old Sharbo, who asked them if they would mind posing for a few minutes for a new likeness maker who had come on the big boat. This likeness maker was young—he wore a brown mustache, a brown cap, and smoked a pipe with a big bulge in it, like a pelican's belly. Sharbo said they could have the beads Squirrel wanted if they would just indulge the likeness maker for a few minutes. Weedy Boy and Climbs Up were disinclined to comply, but before they could leave, a short man appeared and began to hand out such excellent presents that they soon forgot the bears. Squirrel got her beads and a blue blanket, and Weedy Boy and Climbs Up got excellent hatchets with fine sturdy handles, as well as a couple of pipes like the one the likeness maker smoked. Such largesse was unexpected and did much to take their minds off the danger of bears. They went outside the stockade and arranged themselves as the likeness maker directed, with nothing behind them but blue sky and waving grass. Sharbo and the little present-giving man were in the likeness too, pretending to trade with the Minatarees, who of course had nothing to trade. Very quickly the likeness maker made a likeness of the group, which he freely showed them. Squirrel refused to look at the likeness—she thought such business could lead to bad things. In fact when the likeness maker approached with the likeness Squirrel took her presents and ran off, which was foolish, because the little present-giving man soon passed out some nice blue beads. The blue beads emerged from a magical pack that the little man wore over his shoulder. The new gift was really something special: Boisdeffre only had white beads and red beads; blue beads had not been seen by any of the Minatarees since they had left the camp of the Bad Eye in order to hunt upriver.

Weedy Boy took a string of the blue beads to give to Squirrel—Climbs Up didn't think she deserved them because of her impatient behavior, but then Climbs Up was not the one interested in marrying her.

What interested Climbs Up even more than the blue beads was the dark marking stick the likeness maker used to do his likeness. The marking stick marked very dark.

"It wouldn't take long to put on war paint if we had that marking stick," Climbs Up pointed out. "Maybe we could steal it."

Weedy Boy tried to pretend he didn't even know Climbs Up—they had just been given some very fine presents, and now the greedy Climbs Up wanted to steal a marking stick. It was all too typical: Climbs Up had never been able to resist just grabbing anything that took his fancy. Now he wanted to insult the likeness maker by stealing his marking stick, which was nothing they really needed, since they rarely put on war paint, being too few and too weak to make war on any of the neighboring tribes. Much as Weedy Boy hated the arrogant Assiniboines he was not so foolish as to make war on them while his band only possessed two guns that would fire with any regularity.

"But the likeness maker is rich," Climbs Up pointed out. "He has many marking sticks. I only want to take one, to help with the war paint."

Weedy Boy pointed to the large boat the likeness maker had come in. It was anchored just below the place where the Yellowstone came into the Missouri.

"See that boat?" he asked. "It is the biggest boat in the world."

"So what?" Climbs Up said. "I don't want to steal the boat. A small canoe that doesn't leak is good enough for me when it comes to boats."

Weedy Boy was disgusted. It had always been hard to carry on a conversation with Climbs Up—he could never keep to any subject. Who would think of stealing a boat so large that it would take all the warriors from many bands just to row it across the river?

"I don't want to *steal* the boat," Weedy Boy protested. "I just want you to think of all the presents that could be on a boat that big. If we are patient and let the likeness maker do his work, and if we don't do anything bad like stealing a marking stick, then the little man with the magic pack might give us many *more* presents. Maybe if we are polite to him he will even give us a few guns. If we had several guns we could even go after those sneaking Assiniboines."

Such a fine possibility had not occurred to Climbs Up. He had to admit that what Weedy Boy said made sense. He still longed to snatch one of the nice marking sticks from the likeness maker, but he restrained himself, in hopes of getting, pretty soon, a fine gun that would make a buffalo or an Assiniboine dead with one shot. Such a gun would be worth waiting for.

42

Day after day he had gone out in bitter weather . . .

Karl Bodmer, the likeness maker, hurried to put the finishing touches on his hasty little charcoal sketch of his prince's meeting with the three Minatarees, one of whom, the girl, was now in full flight. Winter in the Mandan encampments, during which, despite the terrible cold, he had done much sketching, convinced him that only the most vain of the Indian warriors and chieftains really wanted to have their likenesses captured—and even the vain ones fidgeted too much, which is why the young Swiss artist devoted himself whenever possible to landscapes—the somber, pallid, and yet powerful landscapes of the wintry plains. Day after day he had gone out in bitter weather, attempting to solve, in the medium of watercolors mostly, why such a featureless land should yet be so powerful.

The two Minataree boys standing with his prince were clearly restless. Karl Bodmer focused on his sketch, looked at the group, drew; and then, to rest his eyes, glanced upward into the infinity of the great Western sky. The tones of the plains might be muted, a challenge to his sensitivity, but the skies were always wonderful—only this time, when he glanced up, instead of having his vision cleansed by the skies, he saw the very thing he most dreaded: a man with an easel strapped to his back, coming toward the group.

Then the man disappeared into a dip in the prairie. For a moment Karl thought he might have imagined him. A great white cloud the size of a galleon sailed over and floated on. Thinking, perhaps, that he had been mistaken, Karl looked again. The grass was waving, the sunlight was shining strong, and there came the man, with an easel strapped to his back.

Annoyed—indeed, furious—why *would* the fellow interfere when it was plain that he was not through sketching?—Karl Bodmer slapped his sketchbook shut. Teeth clenched on the stem of his fat pipe, he nodded once to his patient prince and strode off without a word toward the steamer *Yellowstone*, which was anchored not far away.

"Whoa, now! What's got into that fellow?" Charbonneau wondered.

"Here comes George Catlin, he's *our* painter—he's got a big start on your man, Prince. George figures he's done three hundred Indians, so far."

Prince Max, imperturbable, watched the skinny painter approach. He was annoyed that young Karl had behaved rudely, but then rudeness was apt to go with youth—even Swiss youth.

"Of course, Mr. Catlin," he said. "We heard much from Captain Clark about this eminent man. It will be my pleasure to greet him."

All winter, the prince reflected, young Karl had challenged the ice and cold that held them in the Mandan villages. Almost every day, in defiance of the bitter chill, he had gone into the bleak hills, or among the shivering villagers, seeking scenes to paint. But now, on a fine spring day, on a glorious plain, off he stalked, unwilling to meet a rival painter.

"I suppose our Karl was hoping to be the first one to paint these wild peoples," he said.

"Oh no, George has got a good jump on him here," Charbonneau replied. "On the other hand, you were lucky that the ice stopped you at the Mandans'—otherwise you'd have been chopped up, like George Aitken and the others we lost. And there's plenty of Indians George *ain't* painted. If you push on to the Marias River that young fellow will have the country all to himself—there's plenty of these wild boys over that way. Don't know if they'll sit still for a painter, though."

"I rely on presents," the prince admitted. "Good beads, good hatchets, maybe once in a while a musket to some great chief. If the presents are good they'll let Karl paint."

George Catlin saw a young man with what looked like a sketchbook stalking off toward the steamer—young Bodmer, he supposed. He was too weary at the moment to care whether he met the young fellow or not. He had heard that a large herd of buffalo were crossing the Missouri six miles or so below the trading post and had hurriedly tramped down that way to watch the enormous procession. He was not disappointed. Thousands of buffalo in a continual stream surged across the muddy river while he sketched and sketched. One wobbly calf, evidently just born, was swept downstream by the current and seen no more. George had hurried off without grabbing any vittles—he had tramped at least twelve miles on an empty stomach and was, as a consequence, very hungry. Nonetheless he stopped and greeted the small prince courteously.

"Why, hello—you're the prince, I suspect," he said. "Didn't mean to run that young fellow off."

"How do you do, Mr. Catlin," the prince said. "Our Karl is sometimes hasty."

"I've just been watching thousands of buffalo cross the river," Catlin told him. "What I want now is a bite to eat."

"We'll just stroll together, then," the prince said. He bowed to the two Minataree boys, who, seeing that no more presents were likely to come out of the magical bag, hurried off to find Otter Woman and tell her about the bears.

"Shall you go south with His Lordship, Mr. Catlin?" the prince asked. "Will you be the first to paint the beauties of the Yellowstone?"

"Not me, Prince," George said. "Much as I will miss some of the Berrybenders, I've a living to make, after all. I plan to go back downriver on that steamer, make a run at the Comanches perhaps, and then get along home."

"I see," the small prince said, hoping that the news would be enough to cheer up Karl Bodmer. Another day or two and his rival would be gone.

43

"A low thing, addition," Mary insisted.

Tasmin was first astonished, then amused, when it developed that there was one member of the Berrybender family who had not the slightest difficulty in getting Jim Snow to do what she wanted him to do. The lucky person, with the style of command that was needed to domesticate the sulky frontiersman, turned out to be their sister Ten, aged barely four years, the little girl who had cheerfully lived for some weeks amid the cabbages, training her mouse.

With Tasmin Jim was moody, with Lord Berrybender angry, with Mary suspicious, and with little Monty tentative—only rarely would he consent to hold his child, fearing, it seemed, that he might damage him, although Monty was already proving himself to be a sturdy customer.

Little Ten, a stout girl, possessed, to everyone's surprise, an early flair for mathematics—though Mary pedantically insisted that it was only a flair for addition.

"A low thing, addition," Mary insisted. "It's hardly Newton."

Ten began her rapid conquest of Jim Snow by refusing to call him Jimmy—his name, she insisted, was James.

"Mr. James Snow, are you ready to hear me do my numbers?" Ten asked in a loud tone.

"Ready as I'll ever be, I expect," Jim said, amused by the bold tyke. He was working with Signor Claricia to see whether the buggy Lord Berrybender had smashed could at least be fixed enough to make a workable cart.

"I shall begin with two plus two," Ten announced. She doubled and doubled and doubled, usually getting up at least into the thousands before Buffum or Mary or even Tasmin ran and clapped a hand over her mouth. If it was Mary who chose to interfere with Ten and her numbers, a sharp tussle was likely to ensue, there in the yard of the trading post, ignored by the various Indians and trappers who came and went.

Sometimes when the scuffles became too violent Jim would pick the small girl up and sit her on his shoulder. Ten's little gray mouse would sometimes perch on *her* shoulder, watching the proceedings inquisitively.

Usually Jim delivered his small admirer to Tasmin—on fine days Tasmin and Vicky and Coal all brought their babies out and allowed them to finger tufts of grass or test the textures of dirt.

"Do you know mathematics, Mr. James Snow?" Ten asked.

"No, but I know how to give you a better name, little girl," Jim replied. "If you're going to call me James, I'll just call you Kate."

"Very well then, Kate I'll be," the girl said. Then she grabbed Monty and thrust him high in the air a few times, an exercise his father would never have dared try. Monty burbled with excitement and then spat up on Kate's gray mouse, which chattered indignantly.

"Oh drat, now he's soiled my mouse," the newly christened Kate complained.

"It's unwise to bounce a baby up in the air just after he's nursed," Tasmin commented.

"I shall marry Mr. James Snow as soon as I grow up," Kate informed the little circle of mothers.

"But *I'm* married to him," Tasmin pointed out. "What about me, you brat?"

"I shall insist that you relinquish Mr. James Snow and go marry someone else," Kate told her. Then she went over and squatted near Jim, watching in silence as he worked on the cart.

"I believe you have a rival, Tasmin," Vicky said.

"Yes, and I mustn't underestimate her," Tasmin replied. "Little girls seem to be able to get their way with even the most recalcitrant men—even Papa sometimes feeds Kate the best morsels, if there's a goose to eat."

In fact, she was soon amazed at how rapidly Kate Berrybender managed to domesticate her husband, a task Tasmin herself had quite failed to accomplish. He whittled Kate small toys—a rabbit, a chicken—and made her a whistle from a reed, an instrument she insisted on playing loudly, despite Monty's distress.

"I do believe you like this little witch better than you like me, Jimmy," Tasmin said one evening, as they rested under a full moon. Not one hundred yards away, clearly visible in the moonlight, several deer were gamboling.

"I like Kate plenty, but she ain't my wife—you're my wife," Jim told her. His other wife, Little Onion, sat not far away, crooning a singsong tune to Monty. Kate was wandering around blowing her whistle. Jim didn't say it, but having the two young children with them made Tasmin considerably easier to be with. She was less apt to tax him with her queries. Her desire had come back, though—sometimes the two would walk well out onto the prairie to couple; otherwise Tasmin, still noisy in her pleasure, would wake the children. Little Onion, absorbed by her duties with Monty, seemed not to care a whit what they did.

Little Onion, keen of hearing, sometimes did pick up distant sounds of pleasure, but she felt no jealousy. She had Monty to care for, an easier thing than dealing with the lusts of men. Several times, before Jim married her, she had been ambushed and taken in heat by old warriors who smelled bad. The old ones had been excited by her youth. These encounters had been brief but unpleasant. Caring for a plump, jolly baby was more satisfying than what men did with her in the tent or on the grass. She was an obedient wife to Jim Snow and would have lain down with him had he required it, but she was glad she had Monty to deal with, and that Jim had Tasmin.

"She don't take her eyes off that baby," Jim commented, on the night of the full moon. "He'll be growing up thinking he's Ute. Do you think he knows you're his mother, and not Little Onion?"

"I expect Monty takes the practical view," Tasmin told him. "I'm where he gets his vittles—that's enough for now.

"Besides," she added, after giving the question some thought, "it's good that Monty has two mothers that he's thoroughly comfortable with."

"Why's that?"

"This is a dangerous place, that's why," Tasmin told him. "Life's unpredictable—one of us might get killed."

She took his hand and squeezed it tight.

"After all, *your* mother got killed," she said, taking a risk. She had never discussed his past with him.

Jim didn't answer.

"Two mothers are safer, and even three wouldn't hurt," Tasmin went on. "You wouldn't want our Monty to be hidden in a cactus patch, would you?"

"How'd you know that?" Jim asked, startled that Tasmin knew something he had labored to put out of his mind.

"Captain Aitken told me, poor soul," Tasmin replied. "He didn't tell me much—just that Mr. Drew found you."

Jim remained silent. Far away buffalo bulls were roaring in the night.

"Poor Captain Aitken wasn't lucky enough to have someone hide him in a cactus patch," Tasmin said. "I rather miss him."

Jim was thinking about the baby, and also about little Kate, who had so determinedly taken up with them. Tasmin was right about the dangers—she had, for once, shown good plain sense. What had happened to George Aitken—who wouldn't desert his boat—could happen to them. For Monty, and Miss Kennet's baby, and Coal's, extra mothers wouldn't hurt. He lay back and put his hand on Tasmin, happy, almost for the first time, in the thought that he had taken a sensible wife.

44

"My cart, bought and paid for . . ."

Lord Berrybender, furious rather than thorough, had not destroyed the buggy quite totally, as he had meant to. The cab he had thoroughly smashed, but the wheels had only lost a few spokes and the sturdy axle was undamaged. There was nothing to be done about the bonnet, but Jim and Kit went off and cut some logs, which Signor Claricia shaved and lathed until he had a smooth floor for a fairly commodious cart, a process Lord Berrybender watched in sour temper.

"That's not your cart, gentlemen," he warned. "Not your cart at all."

"Don't be so tiresome, Father," Tasmin threatened. "It's the *only* cart."

She did her best to act the diplomat in all proceedings involving Jim and her father; she knew that Jim was not likely to tolerate much guff from her father—her hope was to get them away on their journey south before serious violence could erupt.

"*My* cart, bought and paid for in Lincolnshire," Lord B. repeated. "Besides, even if it *was* yours, you have nothing to pull it with. There's only my good team, and I shall need them for the wagon."

"We'll use the mare," Jim told him.

"Which mare, sir?" Lord B. asked, surprised. "I know of no mare except my Augusta, and of course you can't mean her."

"That's the one—only her name's too long," Jim told him. "We'll just call her Gussie. She can pull a light cart like this one well enough, I guess."

Lord Berrybender was not disposed to let any man cow him—particularly not an American—but he did recall quite clearly the hard shove Jim had given him; he also remembered that Jim had threatened to cut his heart out. Such a degree of frontier irrationality must be dealt with gingerly, His Lordship felt, well aware that he had had little practice with gingerly dealings. He thought that his best bet might be to appeal to Tasmin, who certainly knew that a fine Thoroughbred mare, eligible to receive any stallion in England, could not be made to pull a cart. Nothing so ill-bred had ever happened to a Berrybender Thoroughbred; he felt sure his daughter would realize that and intercede, so as to spare the elegant Augusta such an indignity.

"Not right, Tassie . . . not right at all," he said, in rather a stammering manner. "Augusta's a mare of high lineage . . . Byerly Turk, you know. Not suitable to have her pull a cart."

"Gussie's pulling the cart, Papa," Tasmin replied firmly. "There's three of us with infants to consider—no reason we should tramp a thousand miles, toting our infants over mountains and swamps, while you idle along in a wagon, shooting at everything that moves and tupping Millicent rather too frequently. Millicent, by the way, was quite a competent laundress before you corrupted her—now Buffum and Vicky and I have constantly to deal with mildewed garments that have not been properly aired, although there is an abundance of excellent air available, as you can well see. If you would just keep your big nasty, as Mama called it, in your breeches for a day or two, we might yet get our clothes done properly before we set off to trace the wild Yellowstone to its source."

Jim and Kit, who had been reinforcing the cart wheels, stopped and listened, as they generally did when Tasmin delivered one of her forceful speeches.

"How'd she ever learn to talk like that?" Kit wondered. Jim, a good deal awed by his wife's fluency, just shrugged.

"Shut your mouth, you impertinent harlot—how dare you be disrespectful of the organ that begat you?" His Lordship protested.

"Maybe it begat me and maybe it didn't," Tasmin warned him, coolly. "I intend to investigate that matter thoroughly, at the appropriate time."

"Beside the point, anyway," Lord Berrybender snipped, in no mood for a discussion of Tasmin's paternity, particularly not in front of a sizable company. He meant to keep to the point, and the point was his highbred mare.

"I won't allow it!" he added. "You and your ill-bred mate are not welcome to disgrace my filly."

Jim simply ignored the old man—let him rant and rave. They had given Joe Walker's mule to the Blackfeet, meaning that the pretty mare would have to be their cart horse.

Kate Berrybender, Jim's new champion, at once came to his defense. She marched over and planted her square little person directly in front of Lord B., whom she fixed with a firm, green-eyed glare.

"Take heed, Papa!" she declaimed. "Speak no ill of Mr. James Snow! Take heed! Do you hear me?"

"Not deaf, Puffin," Lord Berrybender said amiably, amused despite himself at the small creature's temerity.

"Where have you come out from, anyway?" he continued. "I thought we kept you in the pantry, amid the cabbages, potted meats, ham . . . some dim lair in the pantry. Why should your good papa need to take heed?"

"Mr. James Snow is my beloved," Kate informed him. "If you speak ill of him I will put a curse on you and it will be a bad curse, I assure you."

"Too late, Puffin—merely having children is a curse, and a bad curse," Lord B. remarked. "Ungrateful brats, every one of them, but Tasmin is the worst."

That a young child could speak to a parent as Kate had spoken to Lord Berrybender was evidence enough, in Kit Carson's view, that the English belonged to a different race.

"How does a curse work, now, Katie?" he asked.

"It turns you black and you become rot," Kate replied. "And you smell very bad and no one wants to take supper with you."

"There, Papa—be careful how you speak of my husband," Tasmin said. "Indeed if you're wise you'll be careful in general. We're about to start a dangerous trip—it must be evident that you can ill afford to lose much more of yourself."

Jim fetched the pretty mare, Gussie, and put her in harness for the first time in her life. The mare was perfectly docile, even nuzzling Jim Snow from time to time.

"I ought to shoot her—rather see her dead than watch this!" Lord B. said, flushing a deep red.

But the company, who had absorbed so many of Lord Berrybender's threats, paid no heed to this one. Mary Berrybender was chasing Kate, meaning to box her ears for having delivered such a melodramatic performance. Kate, shrieking wildly, proved unexpectedly fleet. Signor Claricia was nailing some rude sideboards onto the cart, so the babies wouldn't fall out. Venetia Kennet was tuning her cello, Cook was salting down some trout Tom Fitzpatrick had trapped in an ingenious seine, Father Geoffrin was reading Bobbety a particularly heretical passage of Voltaire, and Little Onion worked the skin of a lynx, brought in by an Assiniboine hunter—she had bargained for the skin with Boisdeffre, thinking it would make an excellent warm cap for Monty. Buffum, low in spirits, intoned a catechism, while Toussaint Charbonneau was talking with several Mandans who had wandered in after breakfast. Boisdeffre was in the process of receiving a gloomy report from some trappers who had just crossed from the Snake River, where, they said, the beaver were much diminished. Lord Berrybender felt quite left out. Everyone, after all, was doing something; no one was heeding his grumbles about the horse, or about the trials of paternity, or about his unfortunate son-in-law. Not only did he feel left out, he felt, on the whole, sad. Born to command, at the moment he commanded no one except a laundress. On his own children he made an ever-diminishing impression; on the rabble assembled in this remote trading post in the West he made no impression at all. He wasn't gone, he still breathed the air, and yet he was, if not entirely forgotten, disregarded—disregarded entirely. His late wife, Lady Constance, would never have disregarded him so. He found he rather missed Lady Constance—fortunately the feeling, though sharp, passed quickly. If Constance happened to disregard him—she had been, it must be said, very idle—a smack or two had been enough to bring her to attention. He thought he might just go seek out the cooperative Milly, who was herself perhaps not so meekly cooperative as she had been at first blush. Lately Milly had shown signs of acquiring airs—mistresses, however lowborn, frequently forgot themselves and took on airs—in Milly's case it was nothing that a smack or two wouldn't correct.

Feeling rather droopy, rather lorn, a man forgotten in his prime—and he felt sure he *was* in his prime—Lord B. went slowly inside. He turned at the door, but no one seemed to be aware of his departure—not a soul cared that he was leaving. Life seemed to be going on, but mainly in contradiction to his wishes. There stood his fine filly, Augusta, very evidently in harness but not seeming to care much about her degradation. It all seemed rather lowering, distinctly lowering, so much so that he thought he had best hurry on and find Milly—get those skirts up over those ample thighs. Airs or no airs, his Milly would pay him some attention—rarely reluctant to attend him, his Milly—unlike everybody else.

Mary Berrybender, however, took note of her father's slow departure.

"I believe we have made our old papa sad," she observed. "He is getting quite ancient, you know, Tassie. We must try to be a little more thoughtful of him in the future."

"That's bosh and twaddle," Tasmin said emphatically. "Let *him* be thoughtful for a change. He's never been thoughtful once, that I can recall—not while I've been about, anyway. Here's his fine bouncing grandson, Montague, even now at my breast."

"Yes, sucking—always sucking . . . he's little more than a bag of milk, I fear," Mary replied.

"Shut up, we were talking about Papa," Tasmin reminded her. "Do you think he's bothered to look at Monty? He hasn't, not once."

"Mr. James Snow, are you ready to hear my numbers now?" Kate asked, beginning to add immediately, but she had only got to thirty-two plus thirty-two when her sister Mary rushed over and covered her mouth.

45

The prince of Wied and his company had departed in their keelboat . . .

That German's got us beat by a mile, when it comes to getting up and getting off," Kit Carson reckoned, surveying the chaos of the Berrybender expedition as it attempted to assemble itself in the wagon yard of Pierre Boisdeffre's trading post.

"A mile? He's got us beat about twenty miles, I'd say," Jim replied. The prince of Wied and his company had departed in their keelboat well before dawn, Toussaint Charbonneau with them. The latter still had hopes of finding Blue Thunder, the third of his charges, whose people ranged not far from where the prince hoped to go. Coal and her baby he left with the Berrybenders; he meant to rejoin the party as soon as Blue Thunder had been accounted for.

"It's plain why that prince was so much faster than us," Jim stated. "There's no women in his bunch—that's why."

The Berrybender party, whatever it might lack, could not be said to lack women. Tasmin, Buffum, Mary, Vicky Kennet, Cook, Eliza, Millicent, and even the tiny Kate were doing their best to cram their many necessities into one wagon and a cart. None of them were at all satisfied with the packing. Tasmin feared that Cook's jugged hares might somehow leak onto her precious stash of books. Millicent, meanwhile, was carefully packing the claret, under Lord Berrybender's exacting supervision.

"Crack a bottle and I'll crack your head," he informed Millicent sternly. "I like you fine, y'know, my dearie—but claret's claret."

Bobbety paced about in a state of high anxiety, the source of that being the wishy-washy behavior of Father Geoffrin, who had, even at that late date, not fully committed himself to the trek up the Yellowstone—a steamer bound for Saint Louis, after all, lay at hand.

"Oh please, Geoff—I'll be so wretched without you," Bobbety pleaded. "Besides, there's a great many natural wonders we might investigate: geysers and hot springs and who knows what. Tell him, Piet—you've been telling me about them for weeks."

"Oh, quite so, geysers and maybe dinosaur eggs," Piet said. "The eggs are very likely petrified, of course. And there may even be the lost sons of Madoc—who knows where those might be."

"And who cares, frankly?" Father Geoffrin said. "The Welsh, lost or found, do not entice me—and you can't make omelettes from petrified eggs, even if a dinosaur did lay them."

"I can't bear for you to leave me, Geoff," Bobbety begged.

"Well, I hadn't been planning to, but then I see that fine boat anchored there and I think: luxury, luxury. All I would have to do all day is read, and perhaps now and then scribble a quatrain."

"That's if the Indians don't catch you and mince you very fine," Tasmin told him.

"Yes, they might just mince you, Geoff," Bobbety seconded, thinking that for once his big sister might make a useful ally.

"But Mr. Catlin's going back on this boat and nobody's trying to stop *him*!" the small priest cried. "Why must I be the only one expected to tramp thousands of miles and get grass burrs in my vestments?"

"What are you talking about—George can't go back," Tasmin said, in shock. "George travels with me!"

She had long since come to take George Catlin's affection for granted; what nonsense that he would ever consider leaving them. There he stood, not fifty yards away, watching some small Indian children shoot tiny arrows at their skinny dogs.

"What's this, George—you're not leaving us, surely?" Tasmin asked, rushing over; but, in an instant, from the painter's sad expression, she realized that it was true and that he was leaving.

"Have to go, Tasmin, I fear," George said. "I'm a poor man, after all—have to take my daubings to market as soon as I can."

Tasmin, totally unprepared for this news, was at once overcome with feeling. She squeezed George Catlin in a desperate hug and gave him a kiss smeared with her tears, which were flowing freely.

George could but hold the weeping woman close—he himself was too moved to speak.

"Oh, George, how I'll miss you!" Tasmin cried. "I don't believe I meant a single one of all the wicked things I said to you on our trip—a devil gets into me somehow and I can't resist heaping abuse, even on you, who have been such a faithful friend."

Much touched, the painter managed a rather sorrowful smile.

"Oh, now . . . that was all just sport, Tasmin," he managed. "Just sport. Fine ladies can't seem to resist having a bit of a tease, with me. I'm sure it wasn't meant to wound."

"Shut up, of course it was meant to wound," Tasmin commanded. "It was beastly behavior, and you know it."

Kit Carson, observing this scene, was astonished—Tasmin was still crying.

"Why's she crying—I thought she despised that silly fool," Kit asked Jim, who just shrugged. What was there to say about a woman given to such loud moods? He was just backing Gussie into her traces, and was hoping that the babies, two of whom were squalling at the moment, wouldn't spook the filly.

"Besides, George, I can't understand it," Tasmin said. "Surely there will be Indians along the Yellowstone that you ought to paint. I promise I won't ever be mean to you again, if you'll just come with us."

It confused her that she felt such a deep pang of sorrow at the thought of parting from this skinny, awkward man—he was not young, his hair was thinning, his complexion splotchy, his teeth not the best—and yet she had watched him risk his life many times on the Missouri's banks, struggling to capture the likenesses of savages any one of whom were capable of killing him. She knew George had often been pained by her chilly rebuffs; she also knew that he was in love with her and had been in love with her almost from the moment they met. Was her husband, Jim Snow, in love with her? It hardly seemed so, although of late he had been an amiable, courteous, and fervently passionate male. Yet the fact was, love was reckoned differently on this raw frontier; the harsh practicalities that must constantly be dealt with left little time for the higher sentiments, the refinements of anguish or ecstasy that Father Geoff was always finding in the pages of Crébillon or Madame de Lafayette. These could hardly be indulged if one was fighting Indians or trying to scrape together adequate meals.

George Catlin, who was unmarried, and too old and too poor to enjoy especially good prospects in the matrimonial line, loved her—more than that, he was, in his skeptical and thoughtful way, a kindred spirit, the only one she could claim in this large, rabbly company. George had a brain, he had thoughts, he was smart—even if his little jests and mots rarely came off. That she would have to part with him in only a minute or two left her feeling greatly confused.

George Catlin patiently waited out Tasmin's little storm of feeling. He *did* love her, and in moments of foolish optimism had aspired to her—after all, there had been cases, even in staid Pennsylvania, where lovely women had bestowed their affections on rather unlovely men.

"Tell me again why you won't go with us, George," Tasmin asked. "I'm by no means convinced that your reasoning is sound."

"Poverty's a pretty sound reason, my dear," George said. "I'm poor—I need to sell some pictures. I have a sizable portfolio to hustle, and hustle it I must, while there's still much interest in the red men back East, where people have money. Might sell the whole thing to the nation, if I'm lucky."

"If you must leave me adrift in this wilderness, then I don't care for you to be lucky," Tasmin replied, not yet absolutely convinced that the cause was lost.

"We've heard that there's smallpox among the Choctaw," George said, attempting to give her a comforting pat, which only infuriated her more.

"Then, damn it, come with us—don't bother about the stricken Choctaw," she said.

"The point is that if smallpox comes up the river, there won't be any more Indians for me to paint—or for Herr Bodmer, either," he told her. "Sorry I didn't manage to meet the fellow—wouldn't have minded comparing techniques. Never too old to learn, you know, Tasmin—though I suppose it is possible to be too *young* to learn—probably Herr Bodmer didn't think he had anything to learn from an old dauber like me."

"Damn it, you're not saying anything I want to hear, George!" Tasmin retorted—then she caught herself and looked around apprehensively at her husband—if he had heard her curse he would surely come over and smack her. Fortunately the Sin Killer, in his domestic mode, was cleaning out one of the mare's hooves, and didn't hear.

"Will you ever finish that picture of Vicky and me parading our fecundity on the virgin prairies?" she asked. "And if you do finish it, will I get to see it?"

"Oh, it's not abandoned," George assured her. "I'm still having a bit of difficulty with the perspective. I might bring it to England when it's done— I've been thinking of bringing some of my Indian pictures to England, in a while. I might be hawking old Blue Thunder and the others in Piccadilly when you get home."

"*Will* I get home, do you think, George?" she asked. "I don't know that I shall. Jim talks of proceeding to Texas, which I judge is not too distant from Santa Fe."

"Texas? Now, there's a place brimming with Indians," George said. "I might go there myself—want to look at the Comanches and the Kiowa. Perhaps we'll yet bump into each other on the trail."

Tasmin suddenly felt foolish. Why was she arguing so, trying to keep this poor man from earning his living? She was rich—George wasn't. She gave him another hug and a slightly less smeary kiss.

"At least this leaves us two prospects for meeting again—Texas and Piccadilly," she said. "I'll be hopeful, George."

"Texas or Piccadilly," George said, with an awkward smile.

Tasmin hurried to the cart, yanked up a startled Monty, popped him into his pouch, strapped the pouch to her back, and strode off to the south, saying not a word to anyone. Behind her the others dawdled, packing and repacking. Pierre Boisdeffre was still trying to persuade Cook to accept a position with him, but he had made the mistake of attempting unwanted familiarities, a behavior Cook had no intention of accepting. Besides, it was hard to know when the company might again need her skills as a midwife.

Mary came striding out with Piet, both of them equipped with nets and bottles, but the mass of the company still dawdled.

Annoyed with this lagging, Tasmin turned and vented some of her irritation in a good loud yell.

"Say! You at the post! Ain't we leaving?" she yelled.

Then she resumed her march toward the purplish, distant mountains, and did not look back.

46

Tasmin marched off briskly . . .

Tasmin marched off briskly, but after a bit, her anger and confusion began to subside and she slowed down. Monty soon made hungry sounds. The plain was barren of anything to sit on, so Tasmin simply sat down in the long waving grass and gave him the breast. In the distance the Berrybender expedition could be seen leaving the post, widely strung out, as if each member of the company, vexed beyond endurance by the proximity of the others, had decided to seek his or her own path toward the mysterious south. Millicent drove the wagon, Kit Carson the cart. Jim Snow was nowhere to be seen, a fact which troubled Tasmin for a moment. She had not forgotten with what ease and rapidity Jim disappeared when he felt in the mood to go. But then, suddenly, there he was—the almost imperceptible swell of the prairie had concealed him for a bit. Better yet, he was alone, which was less and less the case now that Kate Berrybender had attached herself to him with the tenacity of a leech.

"I thought that sluggish bunch would never start," Tasmin said angrily. "I do hate dawdling."

"They're pokey packers," Jim agreed. "The Sioux could roll up fifty lodges and be up in the middle of Canada in less time than they took to get started."

He squatted beside her and urged a kiss on her, such a long kiss that it flustered her slightly. Lately it seemed that her angers awoke his lust—she had only to flare her nostrils like the mare and he would be at her. It seemed Jim had not known much of kissing before she taught him, but now he liked it and was frequently apt to surprise her. In this case his kiss was particularly reassuring: she had been cursing loudly over having to part with George Catlin. Jim might just as well have walked up and slapped her. He was welcome to her soft mouth, though at the same time she felt slightly embarrassed, with Monty nursing just below. Two males, it seemed, were feeding on her at once; which was all very well, except that a mite of some sort was attacking one of her armpits—she badly needed to scratch. Also, the company was coming closer—she could hear the steady creak of the wagon. Sitting in the tall, wavy grass, her baby nursing and her husband kissing insistently, Tasmin felt sweaty and muddled, half yielding, half resisting. Jim's kiss was no casual peck—he wanted her, if not instantly, then soon. But how were they to manage?

"Jimmy, the baby's not through," she said, withdrawing her mouth long enough to switch Monty to the other breast. "Besides, the expedition's coming."

"Let 'em pass," Jim said. "We're in a hollow. They won't see us."

That was true: the company, each member babbling about his or her own concerns, passed fifty yards to the west. Geoff had decided, after all, to stay with Bobbety—the two were chattering about Congreve.

"Let him guzzle all he wants to," Jim said. "Then I'm taking him to Little Onion."

"We mustn't rush him, now," Tasmin warned. "If he doesn't finish he'll get colic, and we don't want that." Though half pleased by her husband's desire, she was also half annoyed. Why must she have to manage these conflicting streams of need? Though she let herself be kissed, she was fully determined to allow Monty to finish; finally he belched and sighed sleepily before she surrendered him to Jim, who took him and at once ran off to hand him to Little Onion.

By the time Jim returned Tasmin was irritated.

"What *is* your hurry?" she asked. "You can have what you want, but you can't have it while the baby's nursing. I can't do everything at once. And besides that, this is a mighty scratchy place to copulate—couldn't you have at least brought a blanket?"

Jim looked around. The Yellowstone River was not far—there was sure to be a soft, shady spot along its banks. He had started to pull down his pants, but he pulled them back up and helped Tasmin to her feet.

Just such a soft, shady spot was soon found. Tasmin ceased hesitating, and, in time, the peaks of passion were scaled, though not quite mutually. Tasmin's ascent, eventually satisfying, required a bit of straining. It was not until her ardor was subsiding that she at last got to scratch the itchy mite bite in her armpit.

Later, the two of them bathed together in the cold green water, slipping now and then on the slick yellow stones from which the river got its name. They were as naked as they had been when they first glimpsed each other on the shallow Missouri's shore. Tasmin could not help noting that Jim looked just as he had looked then—it was *her* body that had registered change. Then, though not virginal, she had been a girl; now she was a woman and a mother, a change attested to by the fact that her breasts were still dribbling milk. Under the press of Jim's kisses she probably had rushed Monty a bit, after all—if it turned out to mean a colicky night it would be herself and Little Onion, not this man who had been in such a hurry to couple with her, who would deal with the colic. The fact that she liked being a wife and enjoyed her ardors did not entirely banish her annoyance at the general selfishness of men—little Monty not excepted! When he wanted the teat he wanted it immediately and was capable of violent protest if denied.

The slow-moving Berrybender expedition had gained perhaps two miles on them while they were coupling and washing up. The company was still spread out, straggling on across the plain.

"You're getting pretty forward about your lusts, Jimmy—kissing me like that when I've got our baby," she informed him. She had not, on this occasion, quite attained the dreamy state that sometimes followed their lovemaking. She felt, on the whole, rather grumpy. Though she harbored no physical attraction for George Catlin, she had, nevertheless, been gripped by a powerful affection at the moment of their parting. And then Jim Snow, like an insistent bee, had slipped in and buzzed and buzzed until he had succeeded in stealing George Catlin's honey. She had gone along with it, lavished her sweets on the bee—but now she felt annoyed.

Jim made no response to this mild complaint. Why wait to rut, if it was rutting you wanted? When he and Tasmin married she had been in such a hurry to couple that she had been annoyed with old Dan Drew for mumbling so over the service. Of course, she was right that the child needed to finish nursing, but, other than that, he couldn't quite make out why Tasmin now sounded annoyed.

"Just look at us, Jimmy," she said. "Please consider us in all our oddity. You're lost in my world and I'm lost in yours. I can barely make a fire, you can barely read a book. I know reams of history better than you ever will, and you know the world of nature better than all our scientists. We're very able copulators—but that seems to be the one skill we share. Without our ruts what would we be?"

Jim got the old, tired feeling he usually got when Tasmin began to complain. Though he had certainly enjoyed their coupling on the riverbank, he felt he might have done better, on this occasion, to just go drive the cart and let Kit Carson attempt to answer all his wife's questions—though of course Kit wouldn't know the answer to any of them, any more than himself.

"Nobody but you talks about things like this," he told Tasmin, though mildly, with no rancor.

Tasmin had been holding his hand, but now she snatched it away.

"Well, but I *do* talk this way and that's just your bad luck, Jimmy," she informed him. "I strongly suspect I shall always talk this way—I fear you're just going to have to put up with it."

They were just coming up on the stragglers of the spread-out expedition—in this case Vicky Kennet and Buffum Berrybender. Kit had stopped the cart for a moment so the two could pick wildflowers, of which a great profusion adorned the plain.

"Why, Tasmin—we thought you were lost," Vicky said. "I have a little gift for you, from George Catlin—he's such a nice fellow—he gave me one too."

She handed Tasmin a rolled-up sheet, which proved to be a lovely watercolor of herself and Vicky, both clearly with child, disporting themselves by a green river.

Tasmin saw that at the bottom of her painting George had written: "Texas or Piccadilly—let's be hopeful! George."

"Oh, he was the dearest man—and we were both so mean to him, Vicky!" Tasmin said, tearing up again.

"I know," Vicky said. "Somehow it's hard to resist making decent men suffer—perhaps it's because there are so few to practice on. I fear we don't deserve such thoughtfulness."

"Well, we won't get it, either, now that Mr. George is gone," Buffum said. "He was even decent to me, whom no one else even notices, and yet I too teased him cruelly."

"Perfidious females, all of us!" Tasmin cried—and then the three of them hugged one another and wept.

47

"How far is Scotland, now, Drum?"

Pomp was high on the shoulder of one of the high peaks of the Wind River range when he came upon the two little grizzly cubs. He was tracking mountain sheep at the time—his patron, Drummond Stewart, was particularly anxious to take a pair of bighorn sheep back to Scotland; and not just sheep alone. Drummond Stewart hoped to bring back breeding pairs of all the mammals of the mountains and the plains, from the tiniest chipmunk to the mighty grizzly bear, for the great game park he contemplated on his northern estate. His plan puzzled the trappers who had come south with him—Eulalie Bonneville, the Sublette brothers, Joe Walker—who could not figure out why an apparently sensible man would want to haul a bunch of wild animals such a distance. Hugh Glass, who was the oldest of the trappers, and a man who had seen much in his life, thought Drum Stewart's plan to be the wildest piece of folly he had ever heard of.

"How far is Scotland, now, Drum?" Hugh asked.

"Five thousand miles, I suppose," the Scotsman replied casually.

"Too far," Hugh concluded. "A buffalo could be born and grow up and get old and die and not travel *that* far. It's too far to think about."

"What are you, Drum? Some kind of dern Noah, gathering up critters two by two?" sophisticated Joe Walker asked.

"Why yes—I suppose I could be considered a kind of Noah," Drum said. "Only I won't need the flood. Anyway, I don't have to walk my pairs all the way to Scotland—but only to a place where we can catch a steamer, and didn't that Indian say there was a steamer nearby Pierre's trading post, even now?"

"That's what Skinny Foot says and he's a Ute," Bill Sublette told them. "Utes don't usually lie."

"Good news for us, if it's true," his brother said. "A boat big enough to take Drum's critters could also take our pelts—be easier than hauling them overland."

The flanks of the high peak where Pomp was tracking the sheep were never easy to ascend; thick bracken, fallen trees, tangled underbrush had to be fought through before he could reach the high sheep paths. Even then, once clear of the tangles of foliage, he might have to climb all the way to the snow line before spotting the tracks of the bighorns.

It was while struggling through a wicked tangle of brush that Pomp heard a rustling just in front of him. He could see nothing, but he kept his gun ready. It was in such a thicket that Hugh Glass had surprised the grizzly that had mauled him to within an inch of his life. On alert, Pomp stopped and waited. He could see nothing, but he had the strong feeling that he was being watched, whether by human or animal he couldn't be sure. Very cautiously he peered into the tangled bracken and was startled to see two brown furry faces staring back at him—the bear cubs were only three feet away. The little bears regarded Pomp solemnly; at first his chief concern was to spot the mother—in the whole West there was no animal so feared as the mother grizzly with cubs to protect.

For several minutes he waited, peering now and then at the cubs, whose solemn looks had not changed. There was no roar, no charge from the mother, but still Pomp waited. He remembered that his own mother, Sacagawea, had cautioned him about how sly the grizzlies were. He watched and listened; it was finally the buzzing of many flies that led him to the dead mother bear—she had been dead at least a day. Pomp looked, but could not determine what had killed her. Bears, like other creatures, sometimes just died, as his own mother had.

Catching the cubs—which would make a wonderful addition to Drummond Stewart's menagerie, proved no easy matter. Even though Pomp spoke soothingly to the little bears, they retreated deeper into the underbrush, where he could not follow. When he went around to the other side of the thicket, the cubs moved back to the side where they had been.

Pomp soon concluded that the best thing to do was wait. He had some venison with him—with their mother dead at least a day, no doubt the cubs were hungry. When he held it out to the cubs they merely stared at him with solemn caution.

Finally Pomp left the venison in the middle of a small clearing, and then hid himself close by. Though the little bears had no doubt been suckling still, he thought they might at least sniff at the meat. He waited more than an hour, hardly moving, and at last his patience was rewarded. Very cautiously the cubs edged out of their thicket and sniffed the meat. Then Pomp pounced—the little bears turned to flee but then floundered into each other and fell in a heap. Weak from hunger, they suddenly gave up the struggle, whining sadly when Pomp picked them up by their scruffs.

"Now don't be crying, bears—we'll soon have you fattened up," Pomp assured them. Having, by one stroke, captured the one species Drum Stewart had only faint hopes of securing, Pomp decided to give up on mountain sheep for the day and hurry to camp. He didn't want the bear cubs to die, as young animals sometimes would if weakened or discouraged.

Fortunately Billy Sublette had just returned from California, where he had purchased a dozen Spanish horses to help pack out whatever furs they took. Three of the horses were mares in foal.

When Pomp got to camp Jim Bridger was so delighted with the little bear cubs that he milked two mares himself. The two cubs, starving, at once lapped up the steaming milk and followed it with a big bowl of porridge that Joe Walker had whipped up, sweetened with a daub of wild honey. Both cubs whined piteously the first night, even though Pomp held them and stroked them; but on the second day, after more mare's milk and more porridge, plus much friendly attention from the trappers, the cubs accepted their role as camp mascots. After some sharp debate they were named Andy and Abby. By the third day they were thoroughly at home, getting into everything, laying waste the cooking supplies, and even eating a plug of tobacco that Joe Walker had left lying around, a feast that put them both in low spirits for a time. But they soon recovered and were as pesky as ever. The only trapper who didn't immediately lose his heart to the friendly cubs was old Hugh Glass, who at first refused to let them lick his face.

"Being kilt by a bear has rather put me off the species," Hugh declared. "These cubs will grow up pretty soon and eat one or two of us, if we're not lucky."

"Why, Hugh—how can you hold a grudge against our little Abby?" Jim Bridger asked.

"It wasn't you that was kilt, Jimmy," Hugh Glass replied; and yet, not more than three days later, he was spotted slipping choice bits of buffalo liver to Abby, who was soon trailing him like a puppy wherever he went. If Hugh slipped away for a day to hunt, Abby whined unhappily until he returned. They even had to chain her by one foot to keep her from plunging off after her friend Hugh.

"I wonder why she likes that old raunch so much," Jim Bridger asked— he was a little jealous.

"Hugh's half grizzly himself—that's why," Milt Sublette suggested.

"More than half, I'd say," Eulalie Bonneville declared. He had had some lively disputes with Hugh Glass over the years.

Andy, though friendly with everyone, attached himself mainly to Pomp, his rescuer, and Pomp was especially careful that no harm came to the cub, whose mother, like his own, had died.

48

He had been born in the wild, and then taken from it.

Excited by Pomp's capture of the two grizzly cubs—sure to be the noblest specimens in his great game park if only he could get them back to

Scotland alive—Drummond Stewart tried again to get Pomp to agree to come back home with him and manage the park. None of the trappers was as good with animals as young Pomp. Already they had elk, deer, moose, antelope, and buffalo—all fawns and calves Pomp had taken—penned up in an ample box canyon, well watered and barricaded with logs. The other trappers seldom bothered with these young creatures, but Pomp went into the enclosure every day, his pockets stuffed with little cubes of sugar, which he dispensed to the spindly calves, none of whom showed any fear of the man. When the little bear cub Andy, Pomp's special pet, followed him into the enclosure, the young quadrupeds were skittish at first, but soon settled down and accepted the cub, who even romped a bit with the spindly buffalo calf.

"I'll never manage them without you, Pomp," Drum insisted. "I'll lose them all if you desert me."

"But I won't desert you, sir," Pomp assured him. "I'll stay with you until you are all safely on the boat in New Orleans—that was my promise."

"Well and good, but what will happen when I get them back to Scotland?" Drum Stewart asked. He was a man used to getting his way, by charm if possible, by bullying or by the expenditure of a great deal of hard cash if charm didn't work; but, in Pomp's case, none of the three worked. At a certain point in the discussion Pomp's mobile, handsome face and liquid eyes ceased to be mobile or liquid. He was never rude, he never shouted or cursed; but when implored to do something he had no intention of doing, his face became a mask, mild in aspect but glazed like porcelain. When that happened discussion proceeded no further.

Pomp respected Drummond Stewart, whose desire to bring the animals of the New World back to a park in the Old World—rather than merely slaughtering them, as Lord Berrybender did—seemed to him an ambitious thing. And yet, even as he devised traps and set lures, Pomp began to develop mixed feelings about the project. The innocence of the young animals touched him. Far from being too cautious, they were, in the main, too trusting, yielding their freedom too easily. Of course, he knew that both losses and gains were involved: the two appealing bear cubs would have soon died had he not found them. Cougars, wolves, or bears would have succeeded in dragging down many of the young quadrupeds. In capturing them he had saved them—and yet a feeling of disquiet wouldn't leave him. He saw the trusting creatures who learned to eat sugar out of his hand as being rather like himself. He had been born in the wild, and then taken from it. His parents had delivered him to Captain Clark in order that he might have schooling; a little later, kind Prince Paul of Württemberg had taken him to Europe in order that he have better schooling: he himself had been like a small animal in a game park, though a park with a gentle and amiable keeper.

Like the little bears or the spindly young elk, his life had been without the risks that would have been his every day if he had grown up with the Shoshone—his mother's people—or even the more settled Mandans or Rees. With those peoples he might have died any day, from attack, bad luck, arrows, weather, bears. He would have been free, but that might only have meant free to be dead if he had been careless, or merely unlucky.

Which was better: freedom with its risks, or the settled life with its comforts? It was not a question he could fully answer, but he did know that now he himself belonged to the wild. He did not intend to go back to Europe. When he returned from Stuttgart, when he stepped off the boat at Westport Landing and looked again at the great Western prairies, it seemed to him that those prairies had been there all along in his head, even when he hunted in the forests of Germany. At once Pomp rid himself of European clothes and went back to the Osage band he had been hunting with when Prince Paul found him. The Osage welcomed him—though many of the young braves who had been his friends were dead, victims of the wild way of life.

Very soon after coming back Pomp realized he was a man whose worlds were mixed. He spoke good Spanish, which meant that he had a value to anyone needing a guide for Santa Fe; he spoke fair French, which put him in demand with trappers who meant to trap the waterways of the north—and he quickly picked up a smattering of the tribal dialects of various Indian bands. Many customers of means—rich travelers like the Berry-benders—would have been happy to hire such a well-spoken and competent guide. Of many possibilities Pomp had chosen Drummond Stewart because the project seemed interesting. Merely helping rich people indulge themselves didn't interest him. But exploring little-known pockets of the West *did* interest him, as did the chance to catch, rather than kill, animals. One of the few things Pomp could remember his mother telling him was that the animals were his brothers and he should treat them with the respect he would owe a brother. It was that duty that made him uneasy, as he walked through the box canyon, letting the young animals eat sugar out of his hand. Was it respecting his brothers to cage them, even if eventually they would roam free in a spacious Scottish park? Was it respecting them to move them from their homes, even if it allowed them longer lives? His kindly tutor, Herr Hanfstaengl, had tried to interest Pomp in philosophy, particularly the philosophy of Kant, of which Pomp grasped almost nothing. And yet, there on the slopes of the Wind River range, walking with his innocent brothers—elk, antelope, buffalo—Pomp wondered, even as Andy, the jealous little bear, tried to snatch cubes of sugar out of his hand before he could give them to the other animals—whether only some philosopher, some very wise man, could resolve the question he himself could merely formulate.

He knew that his parents had been trying to do their best by him, when they took him to Captain Clark to be schooled—his father had had little education and his mother none. Sacagawea had been of the wild—as purely of the wild as the bear cubs or the little elk. The Hidatsa, to be sure, had stolen her from the Shoshone, but the Hidatsa had not taken the wild out of her, because they were wild themselves. Sometimes, walking amid the young animals, pestered by Andy, Pomp felt an ache inside—an ache so deep that he feared he would never be free of it. He had been removed from the wild, and had come back to it, and yet he had not come back to it wild—even some of the mountain men he camped with every night were closer to the wild state than he could ever be. The animal in Hugh Glass was barely subdued—nor was it subdued in Jim Snow. Those two at least, Hugh and Jim, were more like Indians than Europeans. It was a thing he envied them, since he himself was neither the one nor the other. He could fight, of course, if his life was threatened, and yet he didn't like to. Unlike Jim and Hugh, he had been tamed— yet in the West, where he was making his life, the tamed were of little consequence. The wilderness, the wild, only truly welcomed the wild. It seemed to Pomp that the best loyalty he could make his mother was to live where she had lived, on her plains, in her mountains. He didn't want to feed tame animals in some misty Scottish valley. There were times when he felt like kicking down the barricades and turning all the animals free—they were his brothers and they might prefer to stay wild. Though he felt the impulse, he didn't kick down the barricades because he knew it was already too late. The captured creatures were not wild enough to survive; they would all be immediately eaten by keener creatures who had never been anything but wild.

Drummond Stewart, watching Pomp with the deer and elk and ante-lope, knew that in this case he had not won his man. Pomp Charbonneau would see him to New Orleans, as promised, but not a mile farther.

When he said as much to Eulalie Bonneville, the trapper at once agreed.

"Pomp will never go back, but you might tempt Jimmy Snow," Bonney said. "He's got that English wife."

"No thank you," Drum said. "Mr. Snow seems to me to be wilder than these animals. I doubt he'd take kindly to the kilt and the kirk."

Drum had often found himself thinking of Tasmin, though—the woman had from the first looked at him with scorn in her eyes. He didn't like Tasmin's attitude, but he was not disposed to challenge it—not yet, any-way. His thoughts more often turned to the long-legged beauty Venetia Kennet—their frolics had livened up the dullness of a northern winter. Her ardor had surprised him, indeed almost worn him out, but now that he had been absent from her for a few months, she had begun to swim through his thoughts again. He remembered her long legs, high breasts, avid mouth, untiring loins.

Lady Tasmin might look at him with scorn, if she wished. He thought he might just revisit the tall cellist, play a few new tunes between those long legs—for one thing, he liked her stamina. She had survived not only Albany Berrybender's rough treatment, but a northern winter too. Per-haps, if the two of them found that they still got on, he might even take Venetia Kennet to wife. It would outrage rigid home society, but then he had never been obedient to that home society's narrow rules. A man who aspired to be a proper Scot laird would not like be camped by the Wind River, trapping animals that he would then have to transport for thou-sands of miles.

"It'll soon be high summer—I expect old Berrybender and his company will be showing up any day," Eulalie Bonneville said. "That tall girl with him had a considerable fondness for you, as I recall."

Dummond Stewart didn't answer. Bonney was as big a gossip as any woman—might as well cry a secret to the mountains as tell it to Bonney. Let the Berrybenders come—time enough then to see if the tall lass, Vicky Kennet, still favored his rod.

49

. . . Black Toe, a cautious yet proficient man . . .

Blue Thunder had always flourished in winter—the cold sharpened his senses, made him feel keen. To a man brought up amid all the bounty of the northland, winter—so long as one was healthy—was a season to be welcomed.

Blue Thunder even enjoyed blizzards—when a good northern blizzard was blowing, at least there was some privacy to be had—and he liked privacy. In any band of warriors—even Piegan warriors—there were sure to be several chattering fools: just the kind of people Blue Thunder didn't welcome. Even if a man didn't happen to be at home in a well-banked lodge when a blizzard struck, anyone who knew the country could always find shelter under a creek bank, or in a thicket where firewood was plentiful. It was true that blizzards sometimes blew in rather quickly, but then Blue Thunder too was quick—the minute he sensed a lift in the wind, of the sort that made the snow fly, he chose his shelter and made his fire. Then, if there was time, he might catch a porcupine, a hare, or a couple of fat squirrels at least.

Blue Thunder had learned the ways of weather, and how to survive blizzards, from his wise old grandfather Black Toe, a cautious yet proficient man. Black Toe was by far the best snare maker in the whole of the Blackfoot nation. In all his life Black Toe had only been careless once—he had failed to look where he was going one morning and had been bitten on the toe by a small but venomous prairie rattler. Before that accident, which caused his toe to rot, he had been called Leaping Elk, a far more flattering name than the one he ended up with.

The injury to his toe in no way impaired Black Toe's skill as a snare maker. He carefully explained to his grandson that though it might be all very well for hunters to kill big animals—buffalo, moose, elk, even bear if they dared—the fact was that, to a man of sensitivity, the flesh of large animals was often stringy and tough. If there was nothing else to eat, of course, people had to make do; but for those with more delicate palates, who cared to pick and choose, the flesh of birds and small animals was almost always better. Old Black Toe liked geese, green-headed ducks, plump prairie chickens, quail, porcupine, hare, squirrels, curly green snakes, chipmunks, and tiny songbirds so small they could be eaten in one bite. Mice, too, could be eaten in one bite, but Black Toe had little fondness for mice, unless a bunch of them could be roasted together in their nests under a brush pile or somewhere. Of course, the fetus of any animal was apt to be tender—now and then he would roast part of an unborn fawn and leave the mother doe to be eaten by the tribe.

What Black Toe liked best was making snares, and not crude, all-purpose snares, of the sort a clumsy hunter might resort to, but intricate, delicate snares fashioned after long study of the habits and personalities of the various creatures that might be snared. Snares for hares could be made in a few minutes. Porcupines were so stupid and slow that it was not really necessary to snare them. Porcupines were best taken on the end of a lance and their needles carefully saved. Snares for waterbirds had to be carefully secured under the water, a tedious business, especially if it was winter and the water cold. Sometimes Black Toe preferred to net waterbirds, in order to avoid cold work in the water. Once, while setting a snare for geese, he had accidentally snared a small owl, a mistake that disturbed him so badly that he gave up snaring birds for some years. It was after he snared the owl that the snake bit him—the former Leaping Elk felt very lucky that his brush with the owl resulted in nothing worse than one lost toe.

Owls were the worst medicine of all, of course—confusion in one's behavior toward owls almost always meant that death would be coming soon—and yet Black Toe lived thirty years after his brush with the owl, plenty of time to instruct his grandson in the proper use of snares.

When Blue Thunder decided to leave the steamer and enjoy a nice walk home in the crisp winter weather, he took a sack of the white man's excellent axes, and a pouch full of good snares. To the expert snare maker the big boat had been a treasure house, with strings and ribbons and small ropes and other cordage available for the taking. Blue Thunder took plenty, and in fact spent the last week of his stay with the whites making a good assortment of snares. He meant to take his old grandfather's advice and live off small game and tender birds. He didn't really expect to have to defend himself on his walk—the great bears would be sleeping in their dens, and if he should run into some warrior who was in a mood to fight, he had his sack full of axes.

Walking away from the noisy boat into the quiet of the snowy country brought Blue Thunder immediate relief. Putting up with the loud Hairy Horn, and the even louder company of whites, had severely taxed his patience. Very likely Sharbo, the old interpreter whose care he was supposed to be in, would try to catch up with him and attempt to persuade him to come back, but Blue Thunder left at night, so as to get a good jump on the old man. Since Sharbo would probably look for him to go west, he angled north into Canada. Almost at once a blizzard blew in, a good thing from Blue Thunder's point of view. In such weather Sharbo wouldn't pursue him far. In a day the blizzard blew out and the sun shone once more on the plains.

Blue Thunder meant to take his time and have a nice, leisurely trip back to the land of the Piegans. One thing he had agreed with Big White, the Mandan, about, was that going back to one's people after a long absence was a very uncertain thing. Younger leaders would have had time to emerge, chiefs and proud warriors who would not be especially happy to see him return. He had left three wives at home, but any number of things could have happened to reduce that number in the years that he had been gone. He might have a child or two whom he had never seen—but, on the other hand, he might return to discover that he had neither new sons nor old wives. None of his wives had possessed much patience—they might have divorced him by now and taken other husbands. Or they might have died, been killed in raids, been captured. He would have to wait to find out all that until he got back to his old band.

In any case it was good to be once more in the spacious, beautiful northland, where the air was cold, and free of all the taints that air took on in the white man's cities, or on their boats. At his first camp he immediately snared two hares—enough for a meal. He saw a porcupine ambling by in the snow but he was not in the mood for oily porcupine meat, so he let the creature go.

In four weeks, moving slowly, enjoying his privacy, Blue Thunder arrived at the edge of his home country. Far away—perhaps fifty miles farther—he could see the faint outlines of some humpy mountains; much of his life had been lived in sight of those humpy little hills. Now he saw them most plainly at dusk, when the light was not so bright on the thin snow—the hills became reddish, then purple, as the light faded.

That night, although there was plenty of game around—the snow was crisscrossed with tracks—Blue Thunder made a fire but didn't kill or cook anything. He thought he might do better to begin a fast. When he left the boat Blue Thunder assumed that he would go find his old band and re-sume the life he had once led—a life of raiding and hunting, of trying to advise his people about where to camp, or see that they gave themselves good opportunities for hunting.

Now, though, that the hills of his boyhood and maturity were in sight, he felt uncertain. Usually a fast helped at such times of inner confusion. It cleared the head and the body and put a man in the mood to do some sharp thinking. But, on this occasion, fasting only made Blue Thunder feel more confused and uncertain. He had a feeling that going home might turn out badly. It made no sense that he should feel so pessimistic, and yet he did. Once he had been an effective and respected chief, which was why the president in Washington had asked him to come for a visit. But when he had agreed to accept the president's invitation he had no idea that he was setting out on a journey that would cover so much of the world. Sharbo had explained to him that Washington was far, far away, but everyone knew that Sharbo exaggerated. Discovering that, this time, Sharbo *hadn't* exaggerated came as a bad shock. Even after descending the one great river and ascending another for many days Washington had still been far away.

Now Blue Thunder was discovering what he should have been smart enough to figure out to begin with: that leaving one's destined country was not a wise thing to do. But he had gone—and now coming back was hard. Even if his people welcomed him and encouraged him to sit once more with the councils of the tribe, there was something even deeper that would need to be put right, if it could be.

People, of course, were restless—they were always coming and going—his whole band moved according to the needs of the hunt. But the land it-self—the country itself—the land, the hills, the streams, the grasses—didn't go anywhere. It was always there, faithful to its children as long as they respected the earth, the animals, the seasons.

Intolerant of criticism, disdainful of most human opinion, Blue Thun-der nonetheless felt that in this instance he had committed a disloyalty, not to his people, but to his place itself. He had been given certain responsibili-ties in relation to his place; he had been meant to live and die in uninter-rupted contact with his own part of the earth, the prairies that surrounded those stumpy hills.

Many chiefs, of course, had been to see the president—Blue Thunder had foolishly let Sharbo persuade him that it was his duty to go also. He hadn't liked the whites, or their boats, or their cities, but what he had learned about them was sobering. For one thing, they were a huge tribe, as numerous as ants or lice, and, besides that, they possessed magic so strong that it was uncomfortable to be around.

One afternoon he and the Hairy Horn and Big White had been taken to a huge tent, where they had seen magic so powerful that it stunned all three of them. There was a man who swallowed fire. The same man could stick a great sword down his throat and yet not be cut. There were bears in the tent who danced to drums and whistles, and people who swung high in the air like birds, always catching themselves on short swinging branches. Most frightening of all, however, was a great beast out of time—it was called an elephant—a small brown man rode on its head and controlled it. The great beast had a nose many feet long that it could curl up if it wanted to lift its small rider down. Also, the beast had white tusks of great length. When the Hairy Horn saw it he wanted to leave at once. He thought it likely that the elephant would soon go berserk and trample all the people in the tent. Sharbo chuckled at their fears—he assured them that the great beast was really tame, and also very old—older than any living man.

Later, when the three chiefs were on their way back down the Ohio River, they had spent much time discussing the elephant. The Hairy Horn maintained that far to the west, in the hills sacred to the Sioux people, there were drawings on rocks which showed just such a beast. He had not seen them himself, but the medicine men knew they were there. His own brother, the Partezon, had seen the drawings, but of course the Partezon had not gone to Washington and so had not seen the living elephant. When the likeness maker Catlin heard about the drawings he became very excited and wanted to go there at once. Sharbo had had to point out to him that the Partezon was very hard on white people caught in the Sioux country, and even harder on anyone, white or Indian, caught in the Holy Hills. The likeness maker, being foolish in such matters, might have gone anyway had it not been for the approaching cold.

Now that he was almost home, Blue Thunder felt that all the knowledge he had gained on his journey—knowledge that some whites could swallow fire, others fly like birds—sat heavily on him. If he had stayed in his native country he would not have known of such things, or of the elephant, the beast from out of time itself. In his own country, in his lifetime, he would not even have had to deal with many whites—only a few trappers, probably, or, now and then, a daring traveler. His sons would have to deal with whites, but he himself would have been dead before whites came too close to the Piegans' range.

Until he went to Washington and saw the whites in their great ant heaps, he had supposed that they were merely a scattered tribe—any notion that they could ever mount a serious threat to the power of the Blackfeet would have seemed silly.

But now, nearing the end of his journey, Blue Thunder was forced to admit that all his calculations about the whites had been wrong. The whites were much stronger than he or anyone in his tribe had supposed; they were coming west much more quickly and in much greater numbers than anyone would have imagined possible, even three summers ago. What Blue Thunder now knew was that the power of the Blackfeet was as nothing to the power of these whites, men who could make boats that moved without being rowed. They could make guns that could kill buffalo at distances no arrow could travel; they could even tame the elephant, greatest of beasts.

The nearer Blue Thunder came to the valleys of home, the more heavily these thoughts oppressed him. What he knew was that the time of his people, the proud Blackfeet, was nearing its end. He didn't intend, though, to tell this to the people of his band—not even to the elders. This weight, this boulder of knowledge, was something best carried alone. There was no point in disturbing the old ones, whose lives would end before they had to witness too much change.

In three days more, traveling slowly, Blue Thunder saw the smoke of campfires ahead, with the stumpy mountains now not far away. Very likely the camp smoke was from the campfires of his own band. A little river, a clear, skinny stream, ran through this particular valley; his band often camped beside it.

Blue Thunder had no intention of making a big show when he arrived home. Human beings always came and went—it was rude to mark their reappearances with undue celebration. Blue Thunder intended just to walk in, greet an old friend or two, pay his respects to the elders, and go visit his wives, if he still had wives. When a man came back from a long journey it was better just to slip in quietly and not interrupt the important routines of tribal life.

Having decided on this simple plan, Blue Thunder felt a little better— he could see several lodges ahead, and some frames where women were working skins. Life was going on for these Piegans as it always had, with no thought being given to steamboats or elephants or men who swallowed fire.

It had been a long and complicated journey that he had made, but Blue Thunder gradually began to feel a little better. He had returned to where he belonged and could soon, he hoped, realign himself with the country he had deserted. He was west of the Yellowstone, a long way west, and with a little luck could enjoy some good years before the whites became a problem for his people.

As he walked toward the village he made no attempt to conceal himself—he expected that, at any moment, some of the young warriors would spot him and come racing out with lances ready, to determine if he was friend or foe. Indeed, he was a little surprised that the young braves had not yet spotted him—such carelessness on their part was a little imprudent.

But then he did see a horseman coming—but it was not a young warrior. The man coming toward him was old, wore a dirty cap of some kind, and rode an old, spavined, piebald horse, so ancient that it could barely stumble through the grass. To his horror Blue Thunder realized that the man coming toward him was his cousin Greasy Lake—the one person in the whole of the Western plains that he would have walked many miles out of his way to avoid. But there he was, Greasy Lake, appearing, as usual, just at the moment when he was least wanted. He was singing cheerfully, too, quite indifferent to the fact that the horse he rode was too old even to trot, or that the man he was coming to see had no desire to see him: for Greasy Lake had always been a man indestructible in his happiness, a man who wandered through massacres eating plums, serene and untouched, as better men were being hacked to death all around him. Some considered him a shaman or a prophet, others knew him merely to be a fool.

Why me? Why is he here? Almost home and he has to show up, Blue Thunder thought, well aware that the moment Greasy Lake was in earshot he would begin to mooch.

"You don't have a spare coat in your camp, do you?" Greasy asked. He had not seen Blue Thunder in seven or eight years. It had been chilly the night before, but here came his cousin, who had been to see the president, who might have given him a coat or two. Blue Thunder carried a good-sized sack over his shoulder; perhaps the sack had a coat or two in it, one that his cousin could easily spare.

"I don't have a coat, and if I did I'd give it to your horse, not you," Blue

Thunder told him. "A horse that skinny needs a coat worse than you do—you should be ashamed of yourself for riding a horse that skinny."

"Oh, he'll fatten up in the spring," Greasy Lake replied. "In fact there's plenty of good grass under the snow but my horse is too lazy to dig for it."

Greasy Lake remembered that Blue Thunder was always quick to change the subject when it came time to be generous with his family. He was carrying a sizable sack—if the sack contained no coat perhaps it at least contained some good knives or a few green beads.

"What's in that sack?" he asked. Sometimes just asking point-blank was the best way to make a stingy person part with a gift or two.

"Axes," Blue Thunder said, continuing his slow advance on the village.

This was disappointing news from Greasy Lake's point of view. On the other hand an axe was better than nothing. He might find a woman willing to slip into the bushes with him if he gave her a good axe.

"I hope you'll give me one, then," he said. "All I have now is a wobbly hatchet with a loose handle. The head of my hatchet might fly off at any time."

"I'll give you an axe, all right," Blue Thunder told him, testily. "I'll split you wide open with one if you don't leave me alone."

In the end, though, he let Greasy Lake choose an axe—giving the old fool what he wanted was sometimes the best way to get rid of him. Naturally Greasy Lake took a long time making his choice—taking too long to choose was another of his irritating habits.

"These are white men's axes, they're all exactly the same," Blue Thunder told him, as Greasy Lake gave each axe a close going-over.

"No two things are ever quite the same," Greasy assured him. Like his horse he was piebald in color. Part of him was almost white, part brown, and part bronze.

Blue Thunder was hoping someone from the village would spot them and hurry out to rescue him, but no one did. The day of his homecoming seemed to be passing pointlessly, as his cousin examined six identical axes. In the village some women were stretching a buffalo hide over a frame. He thought he saw one of his wives in the distance, but she went strolling off to the river without once looking his way.

"This one is much the best, I'll take it, thank you," Greasy Lake said. The old horse's legs sagged when Greasy mounted, carrying his new axe.

"Do you live with these Piegans now?" Blue Thunder asked, wondering how long he would be expected to put up with the man.

"Oh no, I don't live anywhere, my horse and I prefer just to travel around," Greasy Lake told him. "When it warms up a little I am going down to the Green River—some trappers are having a powwow there, later in the summer. There'll be some rich traders there, I expect. If I'm lucky one of them might give me a good coat."

"That horse doesn't want to travel," Blue Thunder pointed out. "That horse would prefer to die."

Greasy Lake merely chuckled. The suggestion that his horse was played out just amused him. In any case Blue Thunder had never been a very good judge of horseflesh. The fact that his horse had a few ribs showing didn't mean anything.

"Didn't that horse have a funny name?" Blue Thunder asked. It seemed to him Greasy Lake had ridden the same poor old horse all his life.

"His name is Galahad," Greasy Lake said. "It's hard to say until you get the hang of it."

"That's a terrible name," Blue Thunder complained. "Why give a horse a name that's so hard to say?"

"Oh, I didn't name him, that Englishman named Thompson named him—he had that little trading post up on the Kootenai, remember? I think you and some boys burned that trading post down."

"We did burn it down—but just because a white man gave a horse a bad name doesn't mean the animal has to have a bad name forever. You could have changed it."

Greasy Lake decided it was time to be going. He had a new axe, which might enable him to seduce a girl, an activity that would certainly be more enjoyable than talking to Blue Thunder—the man had never been easy to talk to. What was the point of arguing with somebody just because they didn't like your horse's name? In fact, Greasy Lake had little occasion ever to use the horse's name—the horse could be given all the directions he needed without the name ever being uttered.

"Do you know if any of my wives are alive?" Blue Thunder asked.

"I don't know a thing about your wives," Greasy Lake confessed. "I haven't been here long enough to get the gossip."

Then he whacked the old horse with the axe handle and went trotting off toward the camp.

Blue Thunder watched the odd pair go. Being whacked with an axe handle seemed to have put a little life in the skinny old horse. He trotted for perhaps fifty yards and then slowed to a walk, his legs sagging with every step. For a time Greasy Lake and his horse traveled at such a slow pace that it didn't seem as if they were moving at all—but eventually they reached the camp and disappeared.

Blue Thunder himself felt very tired—throughout his life, just talking to his cousin Greasy Lake had the effect of making him tired. His band's camp was right in front of him—a ten-minute walk would put him there— and yet a thing occurred which had often occurred when Blue Thunder talked to Greasy Lake: he lost track of the point of whatever he had been doing. His home village was right there, and yet, for a time, Blue Thunder could not remember why he had thought there was any point in going to it.

50

His welcome was modest and dignified . . .

Though it took a little while for Blue Thunder to recover from his talk with his cousin Greasy Lake, he eventually proceeded on home. His welcome was modest and dignified, as was appropriate. No one asked him a thing about his visit with the president, the cause of his long absence. To inquire about such a thing would have been presumptuous; and Blue Thunder himself made no mention of this great white man because to have done so would have seemed like bragging. An absence of comment about the honor he had been given seemed to be the best approach—it allowed Blue Thunder to settle gently back into the life of the tribe—to settle down slowly, as a great heron settled when it glided toward the surface of a pond where it might soon begin to catch many frogs.

In time Blue Thunder meant to catch a few frogs himself; that is, he meant to catch up on the gossip. A leader, after all, needed to know what was going on—and soon, much to his surprise, he discovered that he was expected to be the tribal leader once more. This was unusual—normally a challenger would have come along and attempted to lead the tribe, and, in fact, one had: a warrior named Cloud. But Cloud, being very hotheaded, had foolishly decided to fight some Shoshone on a day when it was rainy and muddy. Several warriors advised Cloud that this was not a good day to start a fight, since the Shoshone were better mounted than they were, but Cloud could not be made to see right reason. He rushed straight into battle, his horse slipped in the mud and fell, and Cloud was immediately hacked to death by the surprised Shoshone, who were astonished that any leader as badly mounted as Cloud would be so foolish as to fight them on a muddy, slippery day.

Cloud had been placed on his burial scaffold only a few hours before, leaving the tribe with several wise elders but no war chief to inspire the young braves. Blue Thunder was soon given to know that if he thought he still had the mettle of a war chief, then he was welcome to assume the task—he *did* assume it, once he had determined that there were no young rivals skulking around to become a source of trouble.

Fortunately all three of his wives were still alive—though a little subdued at first, his wives seemed glad enough to have him back, though his oldest wife, Quiet Calf, who had always been snippy with him, at once informed him that during his absence she had passed the age of mating—she no longer intended to be with him in the way of a wife with a man.

Blue Thunder knew better than to believe his sneaky old wife for a minute. No doubt she had no intention of being any use to *him* in the way of a wife with a man, but Quiet Calf had always been by far the most lustful of his three wives, and it seemed unlikely that her strong lusts had worn themselves out. Blue Thunder made no response to her big lie, but he resolved to watch her—very likely she had a boyfriend, and he meant to discover who it was. He had never allowed his wives to have boyfriends; it might be the way of the world but it was not his way, and it annoyed him that Quiet Calf would speak so deceptively to him on his first day back. If he happened to catch her with a lover he meant to beat her soundly with a good heavy piece of wood.

Except for this annoyance, which he had more or less expected, his homecoming went pleasantly enough. His wives killed two of the fattest dogs in the camp, in order to make a tasty stew. Blue Thunder sat in front of his lodge most of the day, watching the young warriors at sport: they were racing horses, wrestling, doing a little archery. Mainly they were showing off for the old chief who had returned and become the new chief. To Blue Thunder's critical eye these youngsters did not seem to be especially well trained, but what bothered him most was that there were so few of them—only about ten, not much of a fighting force. He mentioned this to old Limping Wolf, a friend who happened to stop by, and Limping Wolf agreed.

"The Piegans aren't making enough babies," Limping Wolf said, before limping off.

That would have to change, Blue Thunder thought. A band with only ten warriors could not make much of a show. Even the ridiculous Shoshone had many more young warriors than that, and the Sioux were said to have hundreds, probably an exaggeration but worrisome nonetheless.

Just as Blue Thunder was about to allow his wives to feed him the tasty stew, who should return but Greasy Lake. There had been no sign of him all day, which had lulled many people into supposing that the old pest was gone.

"I thought you left!" Blue Thunder said, a little rudely.

"Oh no, I was just down by the creek," Greasy Lake replied. As a guest it was necessary to give him the first bowl of stew. Codes of generosity *must* be observed, even if the guest was unwanted, a category Greasy Lake certainly fit into.

"I found a girl who needed a new axe," Greasy Lake went on. "I offered her that axe that you gave me and she agreed to copulate with me, so that's where I've been all day. She got a bargain—she's already chopping wood with that axe."

Greasy Lake ate so much of the stew that Blue Thunder's wives thought they might have to kill a third dog, but finally he got his belly full and wandered off somewhere to sleep. Quiet Calf was indignant at the way the old man had hogged the stew.

"Is he going to live with us?" she asked. "If he is, I'm moving out."

The remark merely confirmed Blue Thunder's suspicion that the old hussy had a boyfriend, but it had been a long day and he was not up to a big domestic blowup, after walking so far.

"He is my cousin, what can I do?" he replied.

Quiet Calf finally shut up—but as Blue Thunder was preparing for bed, Limping Wolf and Red Rabbit came by and voiced some doubts about having Greasy Lake in the camp at all.

"I just got home," Blue Thunder said. "Do I have to hear about this before I even sleep?" It had just come back to him that being a war chief was a never-ending job. People thought they were welcome to show up at all hours and have their complaints heard.

"I know he is your cousin but I think he brings bad luck," Red Rabbit explained. "Who knows what will happen to us if we let him stay?"

"He's just an old man whose skin happens to be different colors," Blue Thunder replied. What else could he say?

"He stayed with a bunch of Shoshone for one night and in the morning, when he left, some Assiniboines fell on the camp and killed every single Shoshone—except the women, of course. If he stays here those Assiniboines might fall on us."

"That doesn't prove anything except that Assiniboines are mean, and we already knew that," Limping Wolf objected.

"Does that mean you want him to stay?" Red Rabbit asked, annoyed by his friend's sudden softening where Greasy Lake was concerned.

"Well, he is a prophet and a shaman," Limping Wolf answered. "It's not a bad idea to have a prophet around."

"If he is such a good prophet, why didn't he tell those Shoshone that the Assiniboines were about to kill them?" Red Rabbit wanted to know.

"I don't think he liked the Shoshone," Limping Wolf conjectured. "They probably didn't feed him enough."

"What has he ever predicted, can you tell me?" Blue Thunder asked. He was more than a little annoyed at being kept up on his first night home.

"Well, forest fires," Limping Wolf offered. "He's predicted several forest fires."

"So what, forests are always catching on fire," Red Rabbit protested. "I can predict forest fires myself."

The two oldsters droned on, but Blue Thunder ceased to listen. He had his own solution to the problem of Greasy Lake. In the morning he would sneak off and see the girl who had the new axe; his plan was to advise her not to copulate with Greasy Lake anymore. If he had no one to copulate with Greasy Lake would soon go—he would look in other camps for women he might seduce.

Limping Wolf and Red Rabbit finally left and Blue Thunder prepared to turn in. His youngest wife, Wing, had been watching him with a certain look in her eye. Blue Thunder was considering indulging her in a bit of pleasure when a horrible thought occurred to him. What if Greasy Lake were Quiet Calf's new boyfriend? Such a thing would be irregular, but Greasy Lake had a big reputation with the women and irregular things did happen. Greasy Lake only followed rules or codes of conduct if they happened to work in his favor—such as arriving just in time to be served the first bowl of stew. In matters of carnal behavior he had always been quite shameless.

This thought disturbed Blue Thunder so much that he stretched out on his robes and did nothing about the look in Wing's black eyes, inaction which left Wing keenly disappointed. Had she waited chastely all these years—though opportunities abounded—just to hear this old man snore?

"Go to sleep," Blue Thunder told her. "This is what happens when Greasy Lake comes around. He tires everybody out."

"What makes you think I'm tired?" Wing said, but by then it was too late. Blue Thunder was sound asleep.

51

"Oh, woe betide! Oh doom!"

Oh, woe betide! Oh doom!" Mary Berrybender gasped, racing back to the cart.

"What is it, imp?" Tasmin asked, but Mary was, for a time, too out of breath to answer.

"It's Cook—Papa shot her!" Mary gasped.

"Oh horror, not Cook!" Bobbety exclaimed. "What shall we do for vittles now?"

"In my opinion it was foolish of the prince of Wied to replenish His Lordship's claret,"Father Geoffrin commented. "A bibulous nimrod is hardly likely to contribute to the health of the party."

"Piet is attending Cook," Mary said. "Perhaps the wound won't be fatal."

Cook had been inspecting some promising berry bushes, not fifty yards away. Tasmin and Buffum raced over and were relieved to see that she was sitting up—Piet Van Wely fanned her with his big floppy hat. Cook's face wore a look of mild surprise, and there was a spot of blood on her skirt.

"Merely a flesh wound—hit her in the fatty part of the thigh . . . it's not bleeding much," Piet said, to reassure them. He bent to show Tasmin the wound, but there was the crack of a rifle and a second bullet whacked into Piet, knocking him directly into the lap of the wounded Cook.

"Oh no! Now the old assassin's shot Piet!" Buffum cried. "Mary will be hugely distressed."

"Didn't hit me, hit my knapsack," Piet assured them. "However, he *might* hit me, if he is allowed to keep shooting."

"He won't be allowed—Jim's got him, and just in time," Tasmin said, as Jim Snow ran up to the wagon. He pulled her father off the wagon seat and shook him like a terrier might shake a rat. Tom Fitzpatrick and Kit Carson were close behind Jim, though their assistance was by then little needed. Lord Berrybender, after a severe shaking, was flung to the ground and left to consider his misdeeds. Tom and Kit, with the help of Señor Yanez, took all the guns out of the wagon, a precautionary action that caused Lord B., very red in the face, to struggle upright and begin a protest.

Monty giggled in his pouch as Tasmin hurried toward the wagon. Buffum and Piet were left to attend Cook, who was insisting that she ought to be allowed to pick berries.

"I'm sure they would be nice in a pie," she said, in a voice that had lost some of its accustomed force. It was no particular surprise to Cook that Lord Berrybender had shot her—relations between them had been chilly ever since she informed him that she might leave his service. Long experience with the senior Berrybenders had taught her that such inconstancy would not likely be forgotten, much less forgiven.

Mary fell in with Tasmin and the baby. When informed that her beloved Piet had been hit by a bullet, Mary looked grim.

"Let us puncture the old brute's eardrums and leave him wandering deaf on the heath," she suggested.

"Calm down, he only shot Piet in the knapsack," Tasmin told her.

"I shan't calm down, not at all!" Mary said. "We keep our bottles and entomological specimens in Piet's knapsack—it will be a costly loss to science if they are damaged. Valuable bugs might be lost."

"Hang science!" Tasmin replied. "I'm more concerned about Cook. There are plenty of bugs for you to capture, but there's only one Cook and she's now slightly wounded in the thigh."

Jim, Kit, Tom, and the two Mediterraneans stood near the wagon, beside a formidable stack of guns.

"That's the stuff, Jimmy—confiscate his guns before he kills us all," Tasmin remarked. "What excuse did he have this time?"

Jim was calming, but the red of anger was not quite gone from his face, nor the flint from his eyes.

"He's dead drunk—it doesn't matter what he says," Jim told her.

"He claims he shot at a stag," Tom informed her. "But there's no stag—if there *had* been, Jimmy or I would have shot it ourselves."

Kit Carson made a fish face at Monty, winning a smile from him. Monty liked Kit but was less certain about his father, who never made fish faces.

"He shot Piet too, the old bastard," Mary declared. "Piet was struck in the knapsack, the repository of valuable scientific specimens."

"Did he, the damned scamp!" the old Broken Hand said to Mary—he had conceived a considerable fondness for the girl.

"Oh look, now he's beating Milly—come help me restrain him, Kit," Tasmin said, pointing.

Jim Snow looked as if he might go do the restraining himself, but before he could, Tasmin thrust Monty into his hands, an action that startled both child and father. Jim was getting a little better with Monty, and Monty a little more used to Jim, but fully harmonious relations had not yet developed. Tasmin thought it was high time—and past time—that they did. She thrust the two of them together whenever she could, hoping something would click.

"Let them puzzle it out—after all, they're related," she told Kit, as they strode off to the wagon. "Don't you think it's about time that they made friends?"

Kit hardly knew how to answer. He himself liked Monty, and Vicky Kennet's baby, little Talley, and Coal's wild mite, whom they called Little Charlie; but the notion of Jim Snow being friends with a baby wasn't easy to imagine.

"Jim, he keeps busy," he said, thinking his comment might strike a reasonable compromise.

It was, as usual, not the answer Tasmin wanted to hear.

"Why, yes—he hunts," Tasmin replied—for every day, as the company plodded southward over the long plain, Jim and the Broken Hand hunted far ahead; they hunted for the table, usually with success. It was necessary that they be far ahead, Jim told her, to be out of hearing of the fusillade Lord Berrybender fired off every day, to slight effect when it came to securing wild provender. Lord B. had not the patience for exact marksmanship—shooting a lot, in his view, was more likely to be effective than aiming well. Also, it was more fun. By hewing to this principle, he scared away more game than he killed. Even the stolid buffalo, which he had once knocked over like wooden ducks, were keeping well clear of the wagon, from which Lord Berrybender issued wild bursts of gunfire aimed at very distant animals.

Tasmin knew Jim had to range ahead, but saw no reason why this fact should inhibit relations with his son. Evenings on the summer plains were long and soft; there was plenty of time, after Cook had worked her magic with spits and skillets and Dutch ovens, for Jim and Monty Snow to get acquainted.

"It doesn't take long for us Berrybenders to develop our likings," Tasmin said. "After all, Kit, I liked you the minute I met you. I do wish Jim and Monty would show more signs of liking each other."

"Well, Monty don't speak yet, and Jim ain't much of a talker himself," Kit replied.

"You can say that again," Tasmin replied moodily, but before Kit could say anything more they reached the wagon and had to grapple with the problem of what to do with her father, who was still petulantly attempting to box Millicent's ears.

"Father, if you don't stop that nonsense this minute I'm going to have my husband come and give you an even worse shaking than the one you just received," she began, grabbing his arm.

Lord B., wild with anger now, shook free of his daughter.

"No impertinence now!" he said, virtually frothing with rage. "Have that young lout fetch my guns at once—there's a fine red stag about. I suppose I'm still free to shoot at stags."

"There's no stag, Father," Tasmin told him. "Our Bobbety mistook a horse for an elk, which is bad enough, but you've mistaken Cook for a stag, which is a great deal worse."

Before Lord Berrybender could reply, Milly jumped off the wagon seat and ran off, skirts flying and tears drying, to the cart, toward which Cook, assisted by Piet and Mary, was making slow progress.

"What's all this—why did Constance run off—don't like her running off . . . it was just a small little spat we were having," Lord B. said.

"Millicent, you mean, Father . . . It was Milly who ran off, not Constance," Tasmin replied.

The old lord, her father, looked at Tasmin with mild puzzlement. He was very drunk, his nose was peeling from repeated sunburns, his shirt-front was stained red from many drippings of claret, and his white hair was wild and tangled; but what startled Tasmin was his eyes: his look was not the look of a sane person.

"Who's Millicent?" he asked. "I'm afraid I don't know any Millicents."

"Millicent's our laundress—the large girl you were just slapping," Tasmin reminded him, looking quickly at Kit. She felt a sudden apprehension: something was afoot with her father, something beyond the brusque rudeness and habitual selfishness to which they were all long accustomed.

"I really can't fathom what you could be talking about, Tasmin," he said. "Your mother and I were just having a small quarrel—not an easy state, matrimony. Stubborn, both of us, your mother and I. Constance won't give way, and neither will I. Had many a fine row, over the years. Best just to leave Constance be. She'll calm down in a bit."

Tasmin looked at Kit again. Kit, who had always considered Lord Berrybender more or less crazy, just shrugged. What was there to say about such an old scamp?

"Father, that wasn't Lady Constance you were slapping," Tasmin told him, speaking calmly, even soothingly. Her fear was that some link was broken, the link that attached her erratic parent to his sanity. Usually Lord Berrybender's look was that of a selfish old brute, but better that, she thought, than the look of a madman. Perhaps if she spoke softly and addressed him gently she might be able to help him reclaim his wandering spirit.

That hope was very soon dashed.

"Look there, Tassie! It's the stag of Glamorgan—he's eluded me many a year," His Lordship said, pointing. "Can't think where I've left my rifle. Don't see the stag of Glamorgan every day."

Tasmin looked and saw only the Thoroughbred, Gussie, which Tim was leading to water.

"No, that's merely your mare, Augusta, Father," Tasmin informed him, still speaking quietly. "We are presently in America, fast by the Yellowstone River, you know. This is the American plain, not some Scottish glade. And our dear Lady Constance, your wife, my mother, lies buried far away, on a hill by the Missouri."

At this Lord Berrybender looked weary, and suddenly sat down, his back against the wagon wheel.

"It's very strange that you should say such things, Tassie," he told her. "Hard to think why you'd go on with such nonsense unless you've been into the brandy. Wouldn't surprise me if you *have* been into the brandy. I was often into it, when I was your age. Guzzled down quite a quantity, I assure you."

He sighed.

"You know, I feel like taking a good nap," he said—a moment later, head tilted back, mouth open, he was snoring.

"God damn the luck, he's gone off! Crazy as a loon . . . and don't you be telling Jimmy I cursed," Tasmin declared to Kit.

"I won't, I won't," Kit promised.

52

Both stared into the distance, solemnly.

When Tasmin got back to the cart she found that Jim and Monty had established a stable if rather stiff peace. Both stared into the distance, solemnly.

"My goodness, couldn't you at least whistle him a tune or something?" Tasmin asked. "He's really not *that* hard to amuse."

"Never could whistle good," Jim admitted.

Vicky Kennet, on the other side of the wagon, was nursing her Talley, whose meal taking was interrupted briefly by screams from Cook, as His Lordship's bullet was extracted from her thigh. The successful surgeon, to everyone's surprise, was Father Geoffrin, who, after a minimum of probing, captured the bloody slug with his tweezers.

"Why, good for you, Geoff," Tasmin applauded. "It's the first useful thing you've done in six months."

"Oh, I was rather a keen student of anatomy once—attended several operations," Father Geoff said lightly. "I might have made a fair surgeon, I suppose, only I lacked application. Still do."

Cook, who had not thought it quite proper that a French Papist should become familiar with her naked limb, nonetheless thanked him sincerely and promised to remember him when next she made a pudding.

Millicent, for her part, could not seem to stop crying, though her copious tears earned her scant sympathy from the Berrybender party, since she had been quick enough to put on airs and boss them about since Lord

B. had made her his mistress. Finally Tom Fitzpatrick, whose sympathies were broad, took the troubled laundress for a walk by the Yellowstone.

Tasmin did not at first reveal her suspicions about her father's sanity. Soon she got her baby to laugh and her husband to smile. When Tasmin was near, Jim became somewhat more playful with Monty, tickling his bare feet with a blade of grass or letting him grab at a brass button on his hunting shirt. Vicky Kennet went off to help Cook with the meal; no one wanted to trust the preparation of vittles to the clumsy Eliza. In the distance all could see Lord Berrybender, slumped against the wagon wheel, sound asleep.

Long after the evening meal was eaten and the sun lost beyond the distant hills, light seemed to cling to the long grassy prairies. Faint stars appeared, and the call of night birds was heard, though it was not yet fully dark. The sky deepened to rose and purple; the white orb of the moon shone, as if to assist the lingering light.

Though nothing had been said directly about Lord Berrybender's sanity or insanity, a deep collective melancholy seemed to seize the Europeans, starting with Tasmin, who wondered if she would ever have the pleasure of showing off her fine son to old Nanny Craigie, who had raised all the Berrybenders and had been left behind to deal with the several children who had not been invited to travel.

Pedro Yanez, sitting not far away, feared that he would not live to taste again the oily sardines of Barcelona.

Aldo Claricia, his companion, felt that he would give much to eat just one luscious tomato from the fertile fields of Italy.

Venetia Kennet, rocking little Talley in her arms, thought that if she could have just one wish it would be to enjoy once more an opera at Covent Garden.

Father Geoffrin pined for a glimpse of the excellent milliners of Paris, while Bobbety missed most opportunities to attend lectures at the Royal Society—he feared he had not yet quite mastered the complex systems of Linnaeus.

Mary Berrybender, deprived of her helpful tutorials with the late Master Thaw, felt a wish to get back to her Greek, while her friend Piet Van Wely, sweaty from the day's heat, imagined an icy skate on the frozen canals of Holland.

Cook longed to be back in the great kitchen in Northamptonshire, where there was an abundance of ladles and pots, and of reliable kitchen maids as well. At home such a bumbler as Eliza would have been immediately sacked.

Buffum felt that the time had come for her to secure adequate drawing lessons, while her old lover Tim dreamt in the night of musky milkmaids, eager for his embraces.

The weepy Millicent's more modest hope was merely that Lord Berrybender would refrain from pinching her so cruelly.

In short they all of them, wanderers from the old country—Tasmin, Buffum, Bobbety, Mary, Vicky, Geoff, Piet, Pedro, Aldo, Cook, Eliza, Millicent, and Tim—were, for the first time on their long journey, in one mood: the homesick mood. Would those cherished pleasures and traditions, so longingly imagined, ever be theirs again? All were inclined to doubt it—had not the violent prairies already claimed Fräulein Pfretzskaner, stout Charlie Hodges, Old Gorska and his son, Gladwyn, Master Thaw, the somber Holger Sten, Lady Constance Berrybender, many *engagés,* and even the able Captain Aitken? Big White had fallen, it was said. Bobbety had only one eye, and Lord B. himself was much whittled down—Lord Berrybender, whose enthusiasm for the hunt had carried them across the Atlantic, down the serene Ohio, up the muddy Missouri, and now along the swift Yellowstone. Had he now drifted free of his senses, as Tasmin feared? And what would become of them all if, indeed, the master was mad? Only little Kate Berrybender, secure in her attachment to Mr. James Snow, had betrayed no interest in the question.

Even now the old lord was up, bellowing for Lady Constance, whose neck had been broken so long ago.

Jim and Kit and Tom Fitzpatrick had all seen bear tracks that day—in the long twilight Jim and Kit went off for a walk—it wouldn't do to have a grizzly shuffle in and snatch a baby. The old parrot, Prince Talleyrand, who had attached himself to the Broken Hand, wandered around the campfire, occasionally snapping up a scrap.

Tasmin could just dimly see, as twilight finally turned to full dusk, the tall figure of her father, stomping around the wagon on his peg leg, yelling dimly heard curses. He would not lower himself to visit the common campfire but insisted on Cook bringing his vittles, which Cook reluctantly did.

When Jim returned, having seen no bears, Lord Berrybender, though now well fed, was still roaring for his wife to present herself.

"He's gone off, you know, Jimmy—he's insane," Tasmin told him.

"I expect he's just drunk," Jim replied.

All the claret was in the wagon, of course. Lord Berrybender guarded each bottle as jealously as an eagle might guard its eggs.

"There's more to it," Tasmin insisted. "Listen to me! He thinks Milly is my mother. He thinks Gussie is a Scottish stag. He's gone off, I tell you. I'm afraid Berrybenders have rather a tendency to do that. All of us might be considered rather eccentric, but some of us actually go mad."

"Happens here too," Jim assured her. "It's womenfolks mostly, it seems like. Old Maudey Cockerell, who helped raise me, was mostly cracked."

"What happened to her?" Tasmin asked.

"She wandered off in a blizzard and froze," Jim said.

"At home we've a castle where we're sent, when we go off," Tasmin informed him. "Fortunately we're rich. Castle Dismal, it's called—a great pile on the Scottish coast. Poor folks, of course, are just packed in Bedlam. My own beloved cousin Cimmie went off on her wedding day and had to be sent to Castle Dismal—it's stuffed with maiden aunts, second cousins once removed, batty uncles, dim younger sons, demented bastards, and the mildly deformed. I went there once to visit Cimmie. They're all waited on by servants not much less crazy than themselves. Cimmie insisted on being served fried mice on toast, and so she was. Nothing to do but listen to the wind wail over the North Sea. Papa's own brother, Elphinstone, went out and flung himself off the cliff. They hear his lonely spirit wailing in the storms, and there are a great many storms."

"That won't help us with your pa," Jim observed. "Too far away."

"Correct," Tasmin said. "Castle Dismal, I fear, is rather out of reach."

Venetia Kennet overheard the conversation—indeed, soon the whole camp was alerted to the fact of Lord B.'s derangement. When Cook took him his vittles he mistook her for Gladwyn and demanded that she serve the port.

"I wonder if he'd respond to a little Haydn," Vicky conjectured. "I might just try my cello. It used to calm him when I practiced my scales."

"Have a go, Vicky, if you dare," Tasmin said. "You alone have some chance of calming him, though I doubt it will be with your scales."

53

The heat had been blistering all morning . . .

The heat had been blistering all morning; the women, even Cook, had reduced their garb to the minimum that modesty required. Even the thinnest shifts were quickly sweated through. The babies were itchy and fretful—of shade there was none.

Little Onion was the first to hear the tremors. She was walking with Coal, who soon heard them too. They both began to run toward the wagon, Coal holding Little Charlie tight. Tasmin was driving the wagon that morning, thinking she might just be able to manage her father, who was now clearly crazed. But she began to feel uneasy, and so did the horses. The ground seemed to be vibrating, a thing she had never experienced before. At first she thought she might have a broken wheel. She had just got down to look when Jim and Kit came racing up.

"Run to the cart, go!" Jim commanded. "Tom will whip up that mare."

Then he and Kit began to fling things out of the wagon—everything portable went, including Lord Berrybender's claret.

Lord Berrybender, waking from a short nap, saw his precious claret being flung out and opened his mouth to protest, but then thought better of it. He felt they might be experiencing an earthquake—though how could an earthquake happen on such open prairie?

Tasmin stood for a moment, paralyzed—she felt in terrible danger, but could not identify the peril—although the ground was shaking.

"Run, I said—don't stand there!" Jim said, giving her a shove.

For the first time since her marriage Tasmin realized that her husband, too, looked scared. The Indians hadn't scared him, the blizzards hadn't scared him, bears didn't scare him, but now he was scared—a realization that put Tasmin to flight. If Jim was scared they must all flee. The cart was near—Tom Fitzpatrick was urging the women into it, telling them to hold tight to their babies. Pedro, Aldo, Tim, Bobbety, Geoff all made for the wagon.

"We might just make the hills—might just, if we fly," the Broken Hand said. Little Kate jumped out of the cart and dashed for the wagon—Jim hastily yanked her aboard.

Tom lashed Gussie, who at once broke into a run—Jim was driving the wagon, urging the horses on. Tasmin just glimpsed the terrified white faces of Bobbety and Father Geoffrin as they raced.

The swift Gussie soon outran the struggling wagon horses. The irregularities of the prairie caused the cart to bounce, as Tom had warned, but he didn't slacken his speed.

Then Tasmin smelled the dust and heard the rumble. To the west the whole horizon was dust—clouds of it rose high in the sky. It was a moment more before she saw the buffalo, throwing up the dust as they raced in a great stampede, right toward the two puny, speeding vehicles—thousands and thousands of buffalo, running as one beast and shaking the ground as they came. Tasmin clutched Monty tight, convinced that they were all surely doomed. The sight that had caused even her husband to blanch froze her with terror, though not for long. It took all her strength to cling to the bouncing cart while holding her child. Tasmin wished she had stayed with Jim—if they were all going to die, let it be together. The little hills they were racing toward seemed infinitely distant, the buffalo not nearly so far—she already felt choked by the smell of the dust.

Yet the old Broken Hand had not given up, and neither had Jim and Kit—Tasmin saw them flogging the wagon horses, now stretched into a full run.

Now and then the Broken Hand would glance at the buffalo and then at the hills that were to be their salvation, if they could only reach them. Tasmin remembered how grim Tom Fitzpatrick had looked when the Blackfeet were chasing him—yet he had won out then, with the help of her husband—perhaps if Gussie didn't fall or the cart break apart he would win out again.

Tasmin found that she could not take her eyes off the charging buffalo—their beastly concentration as they raced many thousands strong held her spellbound. She had no idea how far away the herd was—perhaps half a mile, at most—but she felt no hope. Against such a maelstrom of brute nature, who could possibly stand?

Then she saw several antelope, racing, as they were, for the hills—several antelope and six wolves. The beasts had made the same judgment as Jim and Tom and Kit.

"If we just don't hit a gully we might beat them!" Tom yelled, lashing Gussie afresh.

Once or twice they bounced high but they didn't hit a gully; the women clung grimly to the sideboards Jim had had Signor Claricia build.

Little Onion, with no baby to worry about, was by far the calmest person in the cart. She kept her eyes fixed on the charging buffalo—then she grabbed Tasmin's arm and pointed. Tasmin was at first puzzled—the buffalo were now very close—but what Little Onion drew her attention to was that the herd did have an edge, and along it the beasts were not so thickly packed. There were gaps in the wall of brown.

Then the Thoroughbred, Augusta, racing strongly, suddenly seemed to see the buffalo herself—for a moment her nostrils flared and she flung up her head in surprise, but, in a moment, as if having assessed the danger, her strides quickened, her legs became a blur of motion—everyone hung on, teeth gritted, and then Augusta zigzagged between a few straggling buffalo on the herd's edge and raced up the slope they had been making for.

"My God, what a horse—saved us all!" Tom said, as the mare, sides heaving, slowed and finally came to a stop.

"She saved *us*, but what about Jimmy and the rest?" Tasmin asked, looking back with apprehension—the wagon, considerably slower, was not yet to the slope or free of the pounding herd.

"Whip 'em up, Jimmy! You'll make it! Whip 'em up!" the Broken Hand yelled.

Jim and Kit *were* whipping them up and were just at the edge of the herd as the full tide of beasts swept by.

It was just as safety seemed at hand that catastrophe struck: a lone buffalo suddenly veered from the herd and ran straight into the struggling, straining cart horses. Tasmin watched with horror as the wagon bounced high and came down on top of the bewildered buffalo, whereupon the wooden vehicle simply burst apart. Everyone—Jim and Kit, her father, Millicent, Bobbety and Geoff, the Mediterraneans, Tim, even little Kate—flew out of the wagon in all directions.

"Now there's an odd bust-up for you," the Broken Hand commented. "They get past ten thousand buffalo and then one old cow's brought them to grief."

"I must help Jimmy!" Tasmin said, jumping out of the cart. "Do you think any of them could be alive, Tom, after such a crash?"

"Oh, certainly they'll be alive," Tom told her. "Might have to set a limb or two, a task Cook and I can handle, I suppose."

Dust had drifted so heavily on the prairie between the cart and the wagon that, for a moment, Tasmin had to stop. She coughed and choked—she could see nothing. But when a breeze thinned the dust a bit and she felt confident enough to stumble on toward the wreck, her heart leapt: there were Jim and Kit, working to try and cut the two horses loose from the busted wagon. The buffalo had evidently wandered on. Here and there the company could be seen, picking themselves up—all seemed pleased to be alive, and Jim was not slow in expressing his admiration for Gussie.

"I never saw a horse run that fast," he said. "She saved those babies, for sure."

"Why, she did *go*, didn't she, splendid old girl," Lord Berrybender remarked amiably. "A tribute to her breeding, Byerly Turk, you know. Where's my Milly? Don't see *her* anywhere. I was rather in a fog, yesterday—hardly myself. Kept wondering where your mother was, Tasmin. Clean forgot she was dead."

"Well, Mother is dead, I fear, Papa," Tasmin told him.

Tasmin, Jim, and Kit exchanged looks, but said nothing. His Lordship seemed to be sane again—the great fright and the great race had brought him out of the fog.

"Great pity about the claret, though," Lord B. lamented. "Hope we run into that prince again—no doubt he'll have some to spare."

To the east the buffalo still ran, a brown river a mile wide, thousands and thousands.

"Why do they run like that, Jimmy?" Tasmin asked.

Jim just shrugged. "Something spooked them, I guess—might have been Indians," he told her.

"Or lightning," Kit suggested.

"Can we fix it?" Jim asked Aldo Claricia, who was poking around in a discouraged fashion in the ruins of the wagon.

"Gone . . . *finito!*" the Italian said. "We can only use it to make a fire."

"We don't have the guns, either—threw them out," Pedro Yanez reminded them.

"Well, we can go back and find the guns—maybe one or two of them ain't broke," the Broken Hand said.

"Best count up the people, first," Jim advised. "We need to be sure nobody's missing."

"I don't see young Miss Mary, or the Dutchman," Tom Fitzpatrick mentioned. "We didn't *leave* them, did we?"

Everyone looked around. There was no sign of Mary Berrybender, or of Piet Van Wely.

"They weren't in the cart," Vicky remembered.

"Oh dear, I think I saw them walking off a bit earlier, with their nets," Buffum said. "I'm not at all sure that they came back."

"You can't mean it! My dear brat lost—and she was doing so well with her Greek lessons, too," Lord Berrybender said. Then he sank down, sobbing, eyes wild again.

"Slap him, Milly, will you? You're a good touch," Tasmin said. "We don't want him slipping into the fog again, just now."

Milly carried out her commission with a will, peppering Lord Berrybender's cheeks with a succession of stinging slaps, until he waved her away.

"Not now, Milly—not now," he protested, thinking the pesky laundress was attempting to arouse him.

"I'm going back to see if I can find any guns that ain't broken," Jim said. "I lost my bow, too—if we don't find something that will shoot, then we're looking at starvation time."

Just then Prince Talleyrand, very dusty, landed on Tom Fitzpatrick's shoulder. When the buffalo came he had risen high in the air, but then so had the dust.

Tasmin insisted on hurrying off with Jim and Kit in the cart, determined to do her best to find Mary and Piet.

"You won't mind if I look for my sister, will you, Jimmy?" she asked.

"You can look," Jim said, "but if they got caught in that stampede there won't be much to bury."

The Belgian rifle and two other guns were recovered undamaged, as were a number of skillets and cook pots. All the clothes had been trampled to rags, and of Lord Berrybender's claret, only a few shards of glass remained. All the books had been thoroughly trampled—only a page or two, blown by the breeze, fluttered here and there in the grass. Tasmin gathered up every page she saw—there a page of Byron, here one of Mrs. Edgeworth's, there several pages of Father Geoffrin's beloved Marmontel.

"I'd rather read a page than read nothing," she said, tucking the pages into her bosom.

Jim and Kit, with Tasmin following hopefully in the cart, searched from one border to the other of the area of stampede—a thing easily done, since the buffalo had beaten away most of the grass—but not a trace of either Mary or Piet could be found.

"If they're alive at least they won't starve—Mary can sniff out tubers, you know," Tasmin reminded them.

"She can even talk to snakes—and some snakes are good eating," Jim pointed out.

Kit Carson had always been famed for his keen eyesight and his acute sense of smell, and yet he had never sniffed out a tuber, and was not entirely sure what one looked like. In love with Tasmin though he was, somehow just being with her made him feel that his own gifts were slightly inferior. Usually this made him mopey, but on this occasion he was too glad to be alive to mope.

Far to the east, the buffalo that had almost trampled them had run themselves out and were grazing quietly on the sunny plain.

"Kit saved us, as much as the mare," Jim pointed out. "The minute he seen the dust we knew we had to run."

They were in the cart—Kit was roaming around by the river, hoping to pick up clues as to what might have happened to Mary and Piet.

"Good for Kit—I'll try to control my urge to pick on him for a day or two," Tasmin said. "Right now I confess I'm rather atingle with the pleasure of being alive. Can't we celebrate?"

Jim looked at her curiously, not at once catching her meaning.

"It's how I felt after the hailstorm, shortly before we were married," Tasmin recalled. "I might have been dead, but instead I was alive and atingle! It calls for celebration."

When he started to answer, Tasmin stopped his mouth with a passionate kiss. Lately, due to the dust and the dirt, to Monty and the various frustrations of travel, their amours, from her point of view at least, had become rather sluggish, pleasures that occurred when she was half asleep, or else sweaty and rather more in need of a bath.

Now, though death had been close at hand, it had been defeated.

"We could have been mashed quite flat, but we're alive, Jimmy!" she continued.

Jim realized what she meant—what she wanted. Kit Carson was only one hundred yards away, scanning the riverbank.

"But Kit's right there," Jim said.

"Hang Kit! I'm so atingle I can't wait!" Tasmin said, giving him another long kiss. "Quick, quick—I'll help you get it out."

Jim barely had time to stop Gussie before Tasmin had it out.

54

Mary Berrybender whacked and whacked . . .

Mary Berrybender whacked and whacked with the thorny briars—her dear Piet's naked back and rump were quite streaked with blood: provident man that he was, Piet had noted the location of an excellent thicket of thorny briars the day before. The two of them had wandered off early, in order to hurry to the briar patch and select just the sharpest thorns so that Piet might enjoy a thorough scourging, a pleasure not always available on the trackless and, in some regions, thornless plains.

At first Mary had been reluctant to thoroughly cut Piet up with these thorny briars, but he had convinced her that such whippings were commonly practiced in his native Holland, both in public gymnasia and in the basements of many stately homes. Some of the wealthier Hollanders, Piet claimed, even employed a special servant to see that there was always a good supply of nettles, briars, or stout flexible switches cut from young trees. Sometimes the servant was even required to do the scourging, although that would normally be handled by the lady of the house—or, in some cases, by a cousin.

"Oh, yes, it's quite necessary for healthy circulation," Piet assured Mary, the first time he stripped down and persuaded her to lash him savagely.

"Keeps the blood flowing . . . keeps us warm during our cold winters," Piet said. "Harder, little one. No need to hold back."

Not wishing to disappoint, Mary soon learned to lay on vigorously and expertly with either briars or switches.

Evidently there was a sound biological basis for Piet's claim of improved circulation; by the time Mary had the blood flowing good, from a few sharp strikes to his rump, Piet would exhibit as perky an erection as could be expected from a man of admittedly modest dimensions. Often it was necessary for Mary to bloody Piet's whole back, from neck to thighs, before an effusion resulted—after which the two of them would bathe in the cold, swift Yellowstone; then Mary would carefully apply a little of Cook's useful salve to Piet's many scratches.

"A healthy life is the best life, little one," Piet would invariably remind her, after which he might nap for a bit, naked on a rock, while Mary, never idle when there were scientific investigations to pursue, would set off with her net in search of dragonflies, mantises, or even the lowly grasshopper.

There were, however, times when Piet's circulation was very slow to improve; by the time Mary noticed the great dust cloud thrown up by the stampeding buffalo, her arm was already quite tired from whipping, and many of the thorns had broken off during her scourge. They had nothing to fear from the buffalo themselves—the herd passed at least a mile to the south—but for some reason Piet's dimensions were very slow to expand, though his back and hinder parts were thoroughly bloody.

And then, most inconveniently, who should appear on the plain to the west of them but Monsieur Charbonneau, accompanied by a piebald man on an equally piebald but very slow horse.

"Here comes our long-lost interpreter—what shall we do, Piet? He might consider these healthy exercises somewhat unorthodox," Mary said.

"Damn Charbonneau, why *will* he appear at such inconvenient times?" Piet complained. "My circulation is very reluctant today—an excess of bile, I fear. Too much bile is sure to drag down one's constitution."

"On this occasion nothing seems to have come up," Mary admitted. "Wasn't it more effective when I merely fondled you under your smock?"

"Effective, yes . . . but is life to be merely efficiency?" Piet asked, before dashing into the river to wash the blood off his back. Mary felt rather downcast—she hated for her Piet to suffer disappointment.

"I suppose I'm about of an age to copulate," she told him. "I'm as old as Coal, and she has had a brat."

Piet at once shook his head.

"Not the same," he replied. "I must have my rigors. Rigor! It's what has made the Dutch a mighty race."

"Even so, I think I'll ask Tasmin what's the best way to copulate—Tassie copulates all the time and perhaps could provide useful instruction," Mary told him as she proceeded to rub a good bit of Cook's salve on his scratched-up nether parts.

Much as he liked his little English dewdrop, Piet was horrified by this suggestion. Tampering with a Berrybender's virginity would very likely get him fired.

Besides, he liked to be whipped, and one of the few things the New World didn't lack was excellent brambles. A good scourging was far better for a fellow than any form of contact with the female pudendum—so dark, so dank, so hairy.

"Your friend rides a very slow horse . . ."

Now there's a sight, Greasy," Charbonneau exclaimed, as the two of them came slowly down the slope toward the Yellowstone. "Why do you suppose our little English miss is whipping that Dutchman so?"

Greasy Lake, plodding along on his good horse Galahad, of course observed the whipping—the naked man's back was streaked with blood—but he could make no sense of such a proceeding. He had seen many men beat girls—old men almost always beat girls, if they happened to have one handy, as a wife or a slave. But, among his people, men who submitted to beatings by women—much less girls—quickly became laughingstocks. Occasionally one would be laughed right out of camp.

In his many years of travel up and down the plains, Greasy Lake had seen so many strange happenings that he did not get upset if something a little out of the ordinary happened. Once he had found a live eagle, trapped in the horns of two dead elk. The elk had huge racks and must have locked them in the course of a fight; then both starved to death. But an eagle certainly had no business getting himself caught between the horns of two elk. Greasy Lake had worked for more than a hour to free the bird, which was young; and then, instead of being grateful, the eagle had gashed his hand with its beak before it flew away. The rescue had occurred at a little creek that ran into the Beaverhead River. Greasy Lake immediately washed his wound in ice-cold water, but the gash became infected and his whole arm began to swell. The situation was serious enough that Greasy Lake sought out an old Shoshone woman who was good with herbal poultices. When she found out how he had got the wound she gave him a lecture about presuming to interfere in the problems of eagles.

"That eagle would have died if I hadn't saved it," Greasy Lake protested, but the old Shoshone woman continued to address him spitefully.

"What do you know—you aren't an eagle," she pointed out. "If you are going to go around letting eagles bite you, then quit wasting my time."

None of that explained why the English girl was whipping the Dutchman—it just meant that Greasy Lake had learned to take a calm attitude toward things that seemed a little bit unusual.

"Perhaps they made a sweat lodge," he suggested. "Sometimes the Sioux and even the Assiniboines hit themselves with branches when they come out of a sweat lodge."

Toussaint Charbonneau had been in sweat lodges, and knew that warriors sometimes whacked themselves afterward, but the Dutchman Mary Berrybender had just scratched up was no warrior. He was a man who studied centipedes and grasshoppers, weeds and seeds. Why would he need a whipping?

"That was a fine flogging you just gave our friend Piet," he remarked when he and Greasy Lake finally arrived at the river.

"*Bonjour*—yes indeed, monsieur," Mary said. "Piet finds it extremely hygienic—many Europeans enjoy a good spanking, I believe. I don't care for the practice myself, though it is said to relieve the menses."

"This is Greasy Lake," Charbonneau told her. "As you can see he slicks himself up with every kind of grease he can find—keeps off the skeeters, he claims."

Piet found it odd that the old Indian who accompanied Charbonneau was so splotchy in color. One of his cheeks was nearly white, the other bronze, his arms rather mottled. As a keen student of genetics, Piet would have liked to question the old man about his ancestry, but decided that it might be prudent to wait for a few days until friendly relations could be established.

"You're lucky you didn't get caught in that buffalo run," Charbonneau told them. "Where's the rest of the party?"

"South, I suppose," Mary said. "We lingered here because of these excellent briars."

Greasy Lake was not much interested in the Dutchman but the young woman was a more singular case. He had heard rumors among the Mandans that a sorceress was traveling with the English party, a young woman who befriended turtles and could converse with snakes. He had a notion this young woman was the sorceress. As a gesture of politeness, he tipped his cap to her.

"Your friend rides a very slow horse, monsieur," Mary observed, staring fixedly at Greasy Lake, who immediately began to feel regret that he had decided to accompany Sharbo to the Yellowstone. By so doing he had come to the place of a witch, and now he was stuck. In order to leave he would have to turn his back on the small English witch, and he did not think that would be wise. She might locate one of the Snake people and instruct him to bite Greasy Lake's organ while he slept; such a thing had happened to Big Muskrat, of the Crows. Big Muskrat had made an enemy of a powerful old witch, as a result of which a snake had wiggled into his blankets and bit his organ, which had turned black and stayed black for several years. Big Muskrat had never again been able to be of use to women.

"It might be wise to rejoin our party," Mary said. "Will you be coming with us, monsieur?"

"Oh yes," Charbonneau said. "I wonder if that little boy of mine can crawl around yet."

"Indeed he can," Mary said. "I'm afraid he crawled into a rather sharp cactus only yesterday."

As Sharbo, the witch, and the Dutchman proceeded south along the riverbank, Greasy Lake thought he might use the fact that his horse was so slow to good advantage—he might just gradually fade from sight behind them, without exciting the attention of the witch.

That plan failed because—to Greasy Lake's dismay—his horse, Galahad, suddenly acquired new energies. The old nag began to prance and even trot—instead of dropping back behind the three foot travelers, he was soon bouncing ahead of them. Galahad, who, to most observers, seemed little better than dead, began to behave like a colt again. This behavior on the part of a horse that was at least thirty years old strengthened Greasy Lake's conviction that he was dealing with a powerful witch.

But there was worse to come. Just beyond the dusty patch of prairie where the buffalo had had their run, Greasy Lake looked around and was startled to see, not far to the south, the Wandering Hill. This was a very bad shock indeed—it was the third time in his life that Greasy Lake had seen the Wandering Hill—and to see it even once usually meant death, for the small devils who lived in the hill were known to loose their deadly arrows at the slightest provocation.

Long ago, near the Little Sioux River, Greasy Lake had seen the Wandering Hill, just a small, conical mound with a single tree on top, and he had escaped the devils' deadly grass-blade arrows by crawling for more than an hour on his belly in the same tall weeds; years later, near the holy mountains of the Sioux, as he was building a burial scaffold for his second wife, he had seen the hill once more, this time many miles farther to the west. And now here the deadly hill was again, on the Yellowstone, and, what's more, his prancing horse was carrying him right toward it, a thing that would be sure to affront the short, large-headed devils who lived in it; they would hardly look tolerantly on a man who had been so forceful as to come near their hill three times in his life.

He stopped his horse at once, but Sharbo and the two others passed him and walked right toward it.

"Stop! It's the Wandering Hill—don't go near it," he cried, but only Sharbo understood him, and even he didn't stop.

"Why, I thought the Wandering Hill was supposed to be way down on the Cimarron, where Jedediah Smith got killed," Sharbo said. "Or was it by the Platte—I can't be sure."

"It wanders, that's why it's called the Wandering Hill!" Greasy Lake chided. How stupid could Sharbo be? The fact that the devils kept the hill moving was well understood by all the tribes of the plains and mountains. The presence of the Wandering Hill explained why ten thousand buffalo had suddenly taken it into their heads to stampede; for it was known to the tribes that the devils inside the hill could bring disorder in the natural world whenever they chose to. At their whim water holes suddenly dried up in a day, or dry rivers suddenly surged with floodwaters. The devils could shake the highest mountains, causing walls of snow to come sliding down. Sometimes small bands of native people who had carelessly camped too close to the mountains were buried alive when the devils sent snow walls plummeting down.

Once past the Wandering Hill the old nag Galahad suddenly lost his newfound energy and became, again, an old horse who could barely lift his feet. Greasy Lake well understood that the devils were toying with him now. The stampede of the buffalo had been merely a small demonstration of their power. These large-headed devils, he knew, were very old. They had been in the hill even before the People had slid off the back of the great turtle who had borne them to their places on the prairie.

But it occurred to him that the small English witch might, for the moment, have a power of her own sufficient to hold the devils in check. It was not only large things that had power. The small rattlesnakes that abounded in the spring had venom much more powerful than that of the old fat snakes who lounged around their dens eating rats and ground squirrels. It was a tiny rattlesnake who had bitten Big Muskrat on his rod and turned it flaccid and black.

"You shouldn't have walked so close to the Wandering Hill," Greasy

Lake scolded, when he and Sharbo finally left the small yellowish mound behind them. "Powerful devils live there! It's a wonder they didn't shoot you with their grass-blade arrows."

Toussaint Charbonneau was usually respectful when Indians talked to him about mystical matters and things that went beyond what could be learned through the senses; but in his view the notion of a wandering hill was nonsense. There were several small conical hills, here and there on the prairies, that just happened to have a single tree on top of them—none of them moved, of course, but it was possible to believe that they moved because they looked so much alike.

Nothing annoyed Greasy Lake more than to have some ill-informed white man try to explain away knowledge that the People had held for hundreds of summers. Hadn't his own grandfather seen the Wandering Hill, far to the south by a stream called the Brazos? If Sharbo wanted to remain ignorant of the deeper truths of existence, that was, of course, his right; but he would regret his ignorance someday, when next he came upon the Wandering Hill; perhaps next time he would have no small English witch to protect him. Then he would see how quickly the merciless devils filled him full of arrows made from poisonous grass.

"Explain it to me, Greasy," Charbonneau asked—he knew the old man was annoyed by his dismissive attitude. "How could a hill that was over by the Little Sioux get clean across the country to the Yellowstone?"

"It is easy for a hill to move," Greasy Lake explained. "All it takes is for the devils inside it to summon up a big wind. A hill is only so much dust—even in a bad storm, dust is always moving. In the land of winds it is easy to blow a small hill from one place to another. The spirits just take the dust from the hill on the Little Sioux and whirl it over this way. The hill dissolves and then forms again—who knows how far the dust will have gone?"

Greasy Lake stopped his lecture—Sharbo was not really listening to him. Travel was an odd thing, he reflected. The plains were a very large place. It was possible to climb a high hill and see many miles, from one mountain range to another, and the plains would seem to be perfectly empty, so empty that it should have been easy to travel great distances across them and see no one. But the truth was different—indeed it was seldom possible to travel even for a few days without running into other human beings, people like old Sharbo, whom he had not particularly wanted to meet. The plains that seemed so empty were actually crawling with people. Being alone on the prairies had never been easy, but now it had become impossible. Even the Wandering Hill was harder and harder to avoid—and that, in Greasy Lake's opinion, was a development that didn't bode well.

56

. . . talk of supernatural evil put Kit Carson off his feed . . .

Here we are in the middle of a virgin wilderness, and yet some things never seem to change," Tasmin remarked, watching Little Onion rock Monty to sleep in her arms.

That day Jim had shown them several spurting geysers, after which all the women had a good bath in the deliciously warm, bubbly pools nearby.

"What things?" Jim asked. Watched by the ever-present Kate, he was just finishing the wrappings on a new bow—his old one had been broken by the stampeding buffalo.

"Your friend Kate won't go away—that's one thing that doesn't change," Tasmin replied. "It might just be, Kate, that now and again my husband and I might welcome a moment or two of privacy."

"I'm just working on this bow—I don't guess it hurts if she watches," Jim replied. "She might have to wrap one herself, sometime."

"That's highly unlikely, I'd say," Tasmin objected.

She considered Little Onion, who sat not far away with Monty. Had it not been for Little Onion's cleverness in devising an excellent travois from the wreckage of the wagon, all three babies would have had to be carried all the way across the valley of the Yellowstone. Thanks to the travois, the infants traveled in some comfort. Little Onion looked lovingly at the baby—her devotion to Monty was profound. And yet Tasmin thought she saw a sadness in the young woman's face.

"Get, brat!" Tasmin said to Kate, with such force that for once Kate obeyed—she was soon to be seen sitting on the knee of the Broken Hand, another of her favorites among the mountain men.

"Your other wife looks sad, Jimmy," Tasmin said. "I like our Little Onion very much and I don't wish her to be sad—I suppose it's because I get so much of you and she gets so little. Close to nothing, in fact. Glad as I am that it's me who gets the most, I do feel rather troubled for our Little Onion."

Jim continued his wrapping for a moment, and then looked up at Tasmin.

"She thinks I'm giving her back," he said to Tasmin, in low tones.

"But back where?"

"To her band," Jim said. "We'll probably meet them soon. Her people will think I'm returning her because she's barren."

"But you're *not* taking her back!" Tasmin declared. "She's a very fine girl, and our son's most loyal friend. She shan't be delivered up for some old man to abuse."

Jim said no more—he concentrated on his work. But Tasmin's agitation would not subside.

"She's no older than Mary, I wouldn't suppose," she said. "She has plenty of time to have babies—in fact no one's tried to give her one. How can she have them if no one mates with her?"

Jim said nothing. He regretted giving in to the pleadings of his deceased wife, Sun Girl, who was insistent that he marry her sister; and if he hadn't, Little Onion *would* undoubtedly have been sold to the violent old man who wanted her. Now he had come to like Little Onion himself. She was unfailingly helpful, quick to take the initiative when it came to any of the camp chores. And yet Tasmin was the wife of his heart—he was not sure how best to proceed with Little Onion. It was just one of the puzzling dilemmas that were apt to arise when a man ceased to travel alone, as Jim had for long preferred to do. He had had no way of predicting that he would ever meet a woman like Tasmin—yet it had happened: they mated, they had a child, and now he could not foresee a time when he could again travel alone. His great trip on Joe Walker's little mare, from the Knife River to the Green, might have been a last clean fling. Then, there had only been himself, the horse, the prairies, the snowfields, the winter sky. Life seemed simple again for a few weeks, although the forces that would destroy simplicity forever had already been set in motion.

Now, as they neared the place of the rendezvous with Drum Stewart and the other trappers, Jim was far from sure what to do next. He and Kit and Tom had had to hunt hard, just keeping the Berrybender expedition supplied with meat. They had done no trapping, had no furs to trade; they would have to rely on credit if they were to supply themselves for the winter ahead. They had three guns but not much powder; they had his bow, one cart, three horses, and a passel of people who had a tendency to quarrel with one another. At least Charbonneau was back—if they did run into Indians he could talk to them, in speech or in sign.

For some reason Charbonneau had brought with him old Greasy Lake, a wanderer of the plains whose origins now no one knew: most tribespeople shied away from the old man, either because they thought he brought bad luck or possibly just because his rambling prophecies were extremely boring to listen to. His horse was so old it could barely walk. No sooner had he and Charbonneau arrived than the old man began to talk about the Wandering Hill, a cone of earth that seemed now to be in one place, now another—Pomp Charbonneau knew the legend and had even spotted what he thought was the hill when they were hard by the Missouri; and Tom Fitzpatrick, usually skeptical, had been startled in the extreme to hear that the hill had moved once again.

"They say Jedediah Smith saw the Wandering Hill the day before the Kiowas killed him," Tom remarked.

Any talk of supernatural evil put Kit Carson off his feed at once. News that the deadly hill might be nearby stirred Kit to such an extent that he borrowed one of the wagon horses and hurried on down to the rendezvous, meaning to return with a few borrowed horses so that the party could make better time.

Tasmin soon saw that Jim did not want to talk about Little Onion. He never liked to talk about matters emotional—they were things not easily fixed. Jim's habit was to ignore such difficulties, to do nothing and hope that a solution would somehow turn up. It was this passivity in regard to awkward human situations that annoyed her most about him. One thing she could never be was passive. Jim Snow liked to slip by human problems, whereas she preferred to fling herself at them.

Unable to bear the melancholy look on Little Onion's face, Tasmin went over and hugged the girl and joined in humming, for a time, the little song that Onion was crooning to Monty. When Monty slept, and had been laid on the soft grass, Tasmin took Little Onion in her arms. She had never done such a thing before—Jim was startled to see it, and so was Little Onion, who kept quite still, like a captured fawn.

"We are not taking you back," Tasmin said.

She had learned a little sign; now she made the sign for sister. It seemed to Tasmin that she could feel this young woman's loneliness; it was there in the resistance of her body, and, of course, she had good reason to be fearful. Already she knew the hard ways of men—and they were in dangerous country. The future could always darken, and not only for their Little Onion. Tasmin wished she could explain to the girl that she was a loyal friend who would not desert her; yet she felt that she lacked the language to get the message across. Little Onion smiled, but in her eyes there was still a sadness.

That night, after an embrace, Tasmin couldn't sleep—she felt agitated rather than soothed. The mountain nights were already chill, so she took a blanket and walked down to a little grassy meadow where deer had been grazing at sunset. She felt she had failed to assuage Little Onion; now what she needed to do was take a sounding of her own emotions. How *would* she feel, for example, if Jim gave Little Onion a child and secured her place, as it were? Hadn't her own father produced thirty bastards? What if Little Onion produced a half brother or sister for Monty? Tasmin found that she could not predict what her feelings might be, should such occur. She knew that she herself would like more children—though perhaps no more children just now, when comforts were so scarce. In the security and order of their great manse in Northamptonshire, with Cook and Nanny Craigie in attendance, of course she would desire more children. But they were not at the moment in Northamptonshire. They were in wild, mountainous country, where great snow-tipped peaks seemed to stretch south forever. Her first delivery had been hard enough, but then she had at least been well sheltered during her lying-in. Now she was in a place where there were not even trading posts. What if she got pregnant again, which was not unlikely, due to Jim Snow's recent enthusiasm for their rutting? Where would they be when the child came—Santa Fe? Or in any town at all?

Moonlight shone on the great snowy peaks beyond the meadows. This wilderness of high mountains and green valleys was extraordinary—and yet, to Tasmin's eye, there was just too much of it. How much longer must they go tramping through it? Were there never to be clean sheets, frequent baths, and well-laid tables again? She remembered clearly the moment of exaltation she had felt that first morning on the Missouri; the feeling had carried her far without regret, and yet how much farther must it carry her? It was not so much England she missed as simply the minimal comforts of civilization: something as simple as a bed, a wash pitcher, or a new novel by Mr. Scott.

The little rill beyond the meadow where she went to bathe was so small that Tasmin could almost straddle it. The water was like moving ice—she dropped her shift and squatted in it, dipping her hands and splashing the chill water over her dusty, sweaty face and body. The air, with its mountain chill, soon had her covered with goose bumps—and yet the cold and the sense of being clean were delicious. Even in her most tomboyish years she had always liked to come home and get clean, an ideal that now, as wife, mother, and wilderness traveler, was often impossible to attain. Dust, sweat, blood, babies' drool, breast milk, the rich oozy seed of the male, and trail dust would likely be hers for some time to come. Only now and again, when she happened on a mineral pool or an icy stream, could she enjoy the fine feeling that came with having clean skin, fresh cheeks, puckered nipples, dripping legs.

When Tasmin stood up and reached for her shift she suddenly saw the great bear, standing only a few feet away, in the meadow through which she meant to pass as she walked back to camp. Too late she remembered that Jim had told her bears were likely to be on the prowl at night, particularly in places where there were many deer.

Now there a bear was—a large, dark shape, its coat shining silver in the moonlight. For a moment Tasmin froze, afraid to move; she held her dusty shift in front of her, longing to have her able husband by her side; but her husband, sated by their embrace, was sleeping soundly some distance away. She was alone with a grizzly bear, the most feared animal in the West.

Yet the bear was not attacking—it had not advanced even a foot. It merely watched her. Kit had told her that the great bears were very curious. Probably this one had never seen a young English lady at her ablutions before. The bear looked at Tasmin, Tasmin looked at the bear. She thought of yelling—and yet, once the first shock passed, she didn't feel like yelling—it might only provoke this great bruin, who could be on her long before anyone from the camp could arrive.

"Shoo, bear," she said in a tiny voice. "Shoo, now . . . shoo. Do go about your business elsewhere. I have a young child. I have to be going soon."

The bear merely watched.

"I suppose that wasn't a very respectful speech," Tasmin added.

Then she waited—and the bear waited too.

Tasmin had hoped to slip back into camp naked—she hated to have to slip the dirty shift over her clean body—in the morning she meant to huddle in their blankets while Little Onion washed a few clothes. But what should she do now that there was a bear? Would the bear care whether she was clothed or naked? Jim had told her that Indian women had to take serious precautions when their menses were flowing, lest bears be drawn to the blood. Tasmin had no immediate worry on that score—at the moment her menses weren't flowing.

Several minutes passed, with neither Tasmin nor the bruin advancing at all, though once the bear did turn its head. Little by little, Tasmin became less frightened. Somehow, perhaps wrongly, she had come to believe that her bruin meant her no harm. She might, to the bear, be no more than a novelty, her bathing a spectacle of a new sort, interesting enough to briefly interrupt whatever hunt had been in progress.

"All right, Sir Bruin, if you are a sir," Tasmin said. "My baby will be crying for me soon. I fear I must end our charming interview."

Yet she hesitated to move, hoping the bear would move first.

It didn't, so gathering all her courage, Tasmin walked straight across the meadow, passing, as she did, within ten feet of the bear, a proximity the bear found too startling to be borne. With a snuff it turned tail, splashed across the creek where she had just bathed, and was gone.

In the morning, once news of the encounter spread, almost the whole camp company tramped down to the meadow to examine the bear's footprints, two of which were clearly visible in the mud by the little creek.

Jim Snow was so flabbergasted that he could scarcely speak—his wife, while he slept, had walked right by a grizzly bear, and yet been spared.

"Your bruin will do strange things," Tom Fitzpatrick said. "I guess its belly was full—that's why it let you go, Lady Tasmin."

"Why, its foot's bigger than mine—what a huge brute it must have been," Lord Berrybender declared. "I have few rivals in the world when it comes to foot size, you know."

"I think it liked me—that bear," Tasmin said. "It was perfectly well behaved—in fact I liked it too. Nothing wrong with a bruin if the niceties are observed."

Just then came a whoop from the south. Kit and Billy Sublette, Pomp Charbonneau, and Drummond Stewart came loping up the slope, leading several horses.

"Good for them, I'm plumb tired of walking," Tom Fitzpatrick announced.

At the sight of Drummond Stewart, Vicky Kennet produced a deep blush, evident to Tasmin, though none of the men noticed.

"Why, your fine gallant returns," Tasmin remarked, smiling. "I suppose the last weeks have been rather a bore for you, Vicky—an absence of frolics takes its toll on us avid girls."

"Do hush, Tasmin—I'm just glad to see him," Vicky said.

57

Then, at the big rendezvous in the Valley of the Chickens . . .

I'm telling you what I saw with my own eyes," Greasy Lake said loudly—he was filled with passion for his mission, an important mission upon which the safety of the People depended.

"Go on with you—you never bring anything but bad news," Walkura said. He was the greatest chief of the Utes—he and some of his warriors had once run off with more than a thousand horses in a raid into California; and now here was old Greasy Lake, upsetting his village with some wild talk about an English girl who could talk to a bear.

"I try to warn people when there is danger, that's all," Greasy Lake insisted. His feelings were hurt that Walkura was behaving so coolly to him, and acting so skeptically about the news he had ridden hard to bring. Of course, Walkura had always been a difficult person—though a great raider, of course. Greasy Lake would rather have taken the news to Blue Thunder, his cousin, but the camp of the Piegans was many days north and Walkura's camp only half a day's ride west.

"Not only that, there's more," Greasy Lake declared. "They don't just talk to one bear, they talk to three."

He had ridden on to the rendezvous with the other whites and seen the two bear cubs, which were as friendly with the trappers as two dogs would be. They didn't even try to eat the three babies, but merely licked them in their faces as a dog might.

Greasy Lake had had no intention of getting into a dispute about the Bear people when he followed the English girl to the creek that night—he followed her because he had always liked to watch naked women bathing themselves. The Englishwoman happened to be too tall and stringy for his taste—he liked short, compact women, young ones about fourteen or fifteen summers when possible. This particular English-woman was shapely enough, as such women went; it was interesting to watch her as she squatted naked in the stream. But of course Greasy Lake ceased to care how she looked the minute he saw the bear, a male grizzly, one of the largest he had ever seen. Yet the bear made no attempt to attack the woman, and when she told it to leave, in her firm voice, it trotted right off, a shocking thing to see.

Then, at the big rendezvous in the Valley of the Chickens—so called because of the abundance of prairie hens—there were the two bear cubs, being petted and made over by all the trappers. This obvious alliance be-tween the white people and the Bear people was such a shock that he didn't even wait to secure the presents that he was sure William Ashley, the chief of the traders, would be happy to give him. Instead, he had rushed right over to the Ute encampment to warn the People, a warning Walkura received with unseemly rudeness, although several of his elders, old wise men who knew how extremely uncommon it was for any humans to suc-cessfully ally themselves with the Bear people, paid respectful attention and listened closely while Greasy Lake told his story.

"And listen, that is not all!" Greasy Lake insisted to his audience of elders. "There is a small witch there who can talk to snakes—according to the Sin Killer himself she is even friendly with the Turtle people."

"It sounds like a story somebody made up while they were drunk," Walkura replied. "White people playing with bears and little witches talk-ing to snakes. What next?"

"It is a family of witches, I tell you," Greasy Lake went on. "The Piegan Blue Thunder traveled with them for many weeks. He says there are even whites who can swallow fire and not be burned."

"Now that's silly talk," Walkura said.

But then old No Teeth, himself a powerful medicine man—he had once made a mistake with a poisoned root, a mistake which caused his gums to turn black and all his teeth to fall out—remembered something impor-tant.

"If the Sin Killer is with them, that's really not good," No Teeth claimed.

"The Sin Killer has eaten the lightning, remember. And now he's married to a witch who can talk to the Bear people—that's not good."

"Oh, that Piegan was probably lying," Na-Ta-Ha remarked. "The Piegans are all liars and Blue Thunder is the worst of them."

"How would you know—have you met him?" Greasy Lake asked. He was becoming more and more irritated at the stupidity and rudeness of these Utes. Of course, it was nothing new—no Ute had ever been particularly nice to him. Now he had ridden his horse hard to get to this village and warn the Utes of a big danger, and yet only one or two old men were bothering to take him seriously. No Teeth seemed to believe him, but No Teeth's reputation as a medicine man had fallen off in recent years. A medicine man foolish enough to consume a poisoned root could not expect to command much respect. Medicine men were supposed to know about such things.

Though Walkura and a few other strong warriors were more or less indifferent to the news Greasy Lake brought, the young braves of the band were another matter. They were young and ready for any fight. There was nothing they would like better than to race over and kill all the trappers; perhaps they could even capture a few women, young women they could copulate with.

High Shoulders, the boldest of the young braves, the one Walkura expected to have the most trouble with, made so bold as to offer a comment, although young warriors were supposed to be quiet and respectful when their elders were holding a serious discussion.

"It sure sounds like a family of witches to me," High Shoulders said—"and besides, those trappers have no business being in our country anyway. I say we round up some warriors and go kill them all."

"Who asked you to say? You don't make decisions about war in this tribe," Walkura told him sharply.

The young brave's comment was particularly irritating because the part about the trappers being in Ute country without permission was true. These big rendezvous had been going on for several years—various chiefs had proposed attacking them but too many of the Ute women had got used to getting nice presents from William Ashley or Eulalie Bonneville or whoever had the best presents at any particular time. The presents, it was true, had begun to have a corrupting effect. Some Utes now claimed that they couldn't possibly catch a fish without the white man's fishhooks, an absurdity, since even the warriors making the claim had caught hundreds of fish on nice homemade bone fishhooks. Or, if not on bone fishhooks, in big reed fish traps.

The problem of the trappers and their big annual party was one Walkura had worried about in his mind for several years. It was true that the Utes ought to get together and kill all these trappers—they had trapped many of the streams and ponds so hard that it was not possible to find even a single beaver in some of them. All the furs they took ought to have been Ute furs, by right, and yet, in Walkura's experience the trappers were vigorous fighters—any force that moved against them had to be ready for serious fighting, with, very likely, considerable loss of life.

It was a lingering, troubling problem, and one Walkura had never quite got around to dealing with, and now here was that old pest, Greasy Lake, stirring up the young men and giving them dreams of battle.

"There is one more thing—I nearly forgot," Greasy Lake told them. "It's the worst thing of all."

"What does that mean—did one of those witches get ahold of your penis and pull it off?" Walkura asked, hoping to get a laugh. The young men were all getting in a war mode; a little comedy might cool them down.

"I don't go near witches—no one pulled my penis off," Greasy Lake countered indignantly. "What I was going to say before you interrupted me was that I saw the Wandering Hill."

His remark at once silenced the crowd. Old No Teeth was so startled that he let some tobacco fall out of his mouth. Na-Ta-Ha looked worried. Of course, medicine men knew better than anyone that a sighting of the Wandering Hill was no joke.

"Are you sure?" Walkura asked.

"Of course I'm sure," Greasy Lake told them. At last he had the tribe's attention.

"Where was it?" High Shoulders asked—he looked nervously around him, as if he expected to see the Wandering Hill sneaking up on the camp.

"Back on the big plain, two days north of the Shooting Water," Greasy Lake informed them. "And that's still not the worst."

"Go ahead—I know you're dying to tell us the worst!" Walkura remarked sarcastically—too sarcastically, in Greasy Lake's opinion. Sarcasm was well enough when some warriors were just joking around, but it was definitely something a leader ought to resist when real danger was being described.

Still, Greasy Lake did his best to hold his temper.

"The English witch walked right by it and the devils didn't kill her," Greasy Lake reported. "The little witch even climbed it partway, and yet the devils did nothing."

There was silence.

"To my mind that proves that all the English are witches—we ought to catch them and put them to death right away," Greasy Lake insisted.

"It would be easier if the Sin Killer and all the trappers weren't there to protect them," a third elder, old Skinny Foot, observed.

"The trappers stay drunk all day," Na-Ta-Ha observed.

"Drunk or not, those trappers are hard fighters," Walkura remarked. "Are you sure it was the Wandering Hill?"

"Of course—it even had that little tree on top," Greasy Lake told them.

Walkura hadn't paid much attention to Greasy Lake's talk of the Bear people and the English witches—that kind of information was often only a matter of opinion. Things could easily be exaggerated—in fact most of the bad news Greasy Lake spread around was exaggerated. All serious leaders knew how unreliable his information was likely to be.

But no one, not even Greasy Lake, would be so foolish as to lie about the Wandering Hill. Only last year three Crow warriors were said to have fallen victim to the devils' deadly arrows. Greasy Lake, though irritating, was not an utter fool. It might be that there *was* a connection between the English witches and the Wandering Hill.

As a leader such a problem was one he couldn't entirely ignore, though that was a pity, because Walkura was feeling lazy. He had caught a new wife while on a recent raid to California, a fine girl of the Modoc tribe. She was a plump, jolly creature, and, once she got over the fact of capture, had become increasingly amorous. Walkura had planned to spend the rest of the summer doing a little fishing, a little hunting, and a lot of copulating. The last thing he had contemplated was the need to make a hasty war on the trappers, most of whom were formidable fighters. The presence of witches made matters even more complicated. The first thing he needed to do, Walkura decided, was to send a reliable man up to the big rendezvous, to see how many trappers were there and what kind of weaponry they had.

The young braves, of course, had no interest in a sober assessment of the situation with the trappers.

At once they set about sharpening all their weapons, honing axes and knives, fitting new strings to their bows, and firing off what few guns they had to be sure that they would still shoot. A few even began to paint themselves, though nobody had told them a battle was imminent.

After watching all this militant behavior for a few hours, Walkura—who was not young—began to be affected by what he was seeing. Watching the young men prance around with tomahawks and race here and there on their horses, he began to feel the tingle of war feelings himself. Was he not the greatest war chief of the Utes? Had he not taken thousands of horses from the Californians? Wasn't the big powwow of the trappers a brazen affront to Ute sovereignty? Little by little his mood shifted. Soon he began to gather up his own weapons, making sure they were as they should be. Was he not still the leader? How dare the young braves act as if they could just go make war anytime, whether he approved or not! Soon he had dispensed runners to other Ute bands nearby, telling them to gather up their battle gear and get ready for a good fight. He didn't bother to send a man to the rendezvous to check out Greasy Lake's reports, or ascertain the strength of the mountain men. As he got more and more steamed up, it seemed to him that the more mountain men there were, the better: however many there were, the mighty Ute warriors would soon make an end to them all. Then, once more, the ponds and streams would fill with beaver, whose furs would belong only to the Utes.

Walkura did not have to wait long for a response from the other bands, either. By the next afternoon warriors began to stream in, ready for a fine war against the trappers.

Seeing that his words had not gone unheeded, Greasy Lake caught his horse, who had been grazing on good summer grass, and slipped away. It was good that the Utes were finally going to act like men and kill the trappers. He hoped they killed the various English witches too, or at least took them captive, so they could be tortured properly, as witches should be. But he himself was a shaman, not a fighting man; his task was merely to understand the nature of the world, and the many things in it, from clouds to spiders. His policy had always been to stay as far as possible from the scenes of battles. Once men got to fighting they were apt to be careless—bullets or arrows might easily fly off in the wrong direction and kill whoever happened to be in their way. Greasy Lake wanted to avoid such dangers; he thought he might go south and meditate awhile beside the Platte River, on what his cousins the Sioux called the Holy Road. Along the Holy Road he might enjoy a quiet time, and do some thinking, without having to worry about arrows or bullets flying out of some big battle to wound him. News of whatever happened near the Green River, between the trappers and the Utes, would reach him soon enough. In the more and more crowded plains there would always be somebody to bring the news.

By the time he left the Utes, just at dusk, the encampment was already filling with warriors from other bands. The whites were going to be in for a hard tussle with these angry Utes, that was for sure.

That night, to be safe, Greasy Lake climbed up in a tree to sleep. He had come back east, meaning to slip quietly past the camp of the trappers, but then he bethought himself of the big grizzly bear that had been in that vicinity only the night before. That bear might still be near. The best thing to do was find a good stout tree and doze for a few hours high in its branches. A bear that large would probably not be able to climb high enough to get him.

In fact no bear came to trouble his slumbers, which were light in any case. He never slept deeply, or long—his life required alertness from him; deep sleep could make a man slow to respond.

Just as he was dozing off Greasy Lake thought he heard a flutter above him, which annoyed him somewhat. The bird mostly likely to be hunting at that time of night would be an owl—and if it was an owl he would have to change trees at once—owls were extremely bad medicine, and particularly bad if one happened to be a shaman. Owls were very jealous of shamans, because the shamans rivaled them in knowledge; as a consequence owls always did what they could to arrange shamans' deaths. There was some moonlight, just enough so that, when he wiggled around, he could clearly see the bird, only a foot above him; it was not an owl but only the white witches' talking bird. He himself had heard the bird speak two or three times—it mostly seemed to talk to the Broken Hand, and usually just cackled out a strange word or two, in a tongue the shaman could not understand. Greasy Lake was relieved that he wasn't dealing with a great horned owl, the most deadly owl of all— on the other hand he wasn't happy that the talking bird had followed him. It might be a sign that the witches didn't intend to let him get away. Greasy Lake thought he had a good solution to that problem: while the old parrot dozed, Greasy Lake reached up, grabbed him, and with one motion wrung his neck, making a speedy end to the witches' talking bird. If those English witches wanted to keep track of an experienced shaman such as himself, they would have to come up with something better than an old green bird who was slow to fly.

58

. . . she indifferently bared a breast . . .

The three little boys—Monty, Talley, and Charlie—two of them new to the complex art of crawling, and the third, Charlie, just beginning to walk, were all of them struggling, each at his own pace, to reach the bear cub Andy, who lolled on his belly, regarding their approach without alarm, when, to the blank astonishment of the grown-ups who were idly watching—in this case Jim Snow, Jim Bridger, Billy Sublette, and Eulalie Bonneville—the blow was struck that was to echo in mountain legend for many seasons. Tasmin Berrybender, a little unsteady on her feet from having quaffed two glasses of William Ashley's cool champagne but firm of purpose nonetheless, walked up, made a fist, and, without a word being said, drew back her arm and struck her husband such a solid and forceful punch in the eye that he fell backward off the log where he had been sitting.

The mountain men could only gape in dismay, but the bear cub, Andy, not liking what he saw, at once wandered off to seek protection with Pomp Charbonneau, to the shocked disappointment of his three small pursuers.

Lord Albany Berrybender, several sheets to the wind himself, thanks to the generosity with which William Ashley dispensed his excellent champagne, merely chuckled at the sight, though William Ashley himself was as startled as the mountain men.

"Good Lord—she's knocked Jimmy over—I confess I never expected to see *that*!" Ashley remarked.

"Not wise to cross Tassie when she's in her cups," Lord B. remarked. "Apt to be bellicose when she drinks. Gets it from me, I fear. I've challenged many a man as a result of good champagne. Frankly didn't expect to meet with such excellent champagne this far out in the wild."

William Ashley, who had long since sold his interest in the Rocky Mountain Fur Company, but continued to come to the rendezvous just for love of the wild, had not expected the Berrybenders, either. He knew they were in the West but had supposed that Lord Berrybender would long since have had his fill of hunting and would sensibly have gone back down the river to Saint Louis. And yet, there they were, Lord Berrybender shorn of part of a leg, much of a foot, and three fingers of a hand—and there stood Lady Tas-min, a ruddy, well-browned Western girl now, her fists doubled up, clearly prepared to do battle if her husband—by common consent one of the most volatile of the mountain men—chose to stand up and fight.

Jim Bridger, Billy Sublette, and rotund Eulalie Bonneville, though deeply puzzled, were nonetheless well aware that they were in the com-pany of a very angry woman, a creature as much to be feared as any bear. Quietly they got up off the log and moved away. It would be impolite to run, as Andy, the bear cub, had done, and yet all of them were rapidly mak-ing tracks.

Jim Snow was so startled that he merely sat where he had fallen. That Tasmin was very angry he had no doubt—but why? They had finally strag-gled peacefully enough into the big camp in the Valley of the Chickens. Of course, Will Ashley had lots of liquor handy: many of the boys only bothered to show up at the rendezvous because of Ashley's whiskey. The champagne Ashley kept cool in a nearby stream was weak stuff compared to the raw spirits most of the trappers drank. Hugh Glass in particular scorned champagne, which he contended was no more than sour water. Thirsty from her long trip, Tasmin had quaffed a glass or two, as did the others, but Jim did not immediately connect the fact that Tasmin punched him to Will Ashley's champagne. The morning had been peaceful. Their son had been trying to pet the little bear cub, and then Tasmin had walked over, her face suddenly dark with fury, and knocked him off the log where he had been sitting with the boys. It was a wrong thing to do, of course—a wife shouldn't strike a husband; but there she was, her fists doubled up, quite prepared to punch him again. For the moment Jim was too shocked even to attempt to correct her—it occurred to him that she might some-how have lost her mind.

"That's for striking me last winter and knocking me out of our tent and causing me to scrape my leg quite painfully on the ice," Tasmin said, her blood up. She was fully prepared for a fierce fight. The minute Jim stood up she meant to slug him again. But Jim didn't stand up. Most of the camp was by now watching the conflict. All heads turned, all conversation ceased. Kit Carson looked especially worried.

"All right, then, coward," Tasmin told him. "But if you ever strike me again, I'll certainly do worse."

Then she whirled on the trappers, who were staring from what they had supposed was a safe distance.

"You are all invited to stop looking at me as if I've lost my sanity—I'm speaking to you, Mr. Bridger, and you, Mr. Bonneville. I have not lost my sanity, I was merely revenging an old injustice. Perhaps you too would like a punch."

Tasmin felt very much in the mood to throw something—she was filled with the same ugly and frustrated feelings that had once caused her to heave her father's hunting seat as far as she could throw it. In this instance the only thing she could see to throw was the jug of coarse whiskey which the trappers had been passing around. She at once picked it up and heaved it; by luck it smashed on a rock, which gave her a feeling of great satisfaction, though this feeling diminished once she saw that neither Jim Snow nor any of the trappers seemed inclined to fight. The sharp smell of whiskey stung her nostrils. Irritated beyond endurance by the mildness of these men who were supposed to be so fierce and wild, she walked up and gave Eulalie Bonneville a good hard punch in the mouth, then walked away, right past her son. Frustrated by the departure of the bear cub, and seeing his mother near, Monty reached out, hoping to be picked up, but his Tasmin strode right past him. She crossed the meadow and continued into a little glade, deep enough that she felt sure no one could see her; she then burst into a torrent of tears, but a brief torrent. The fit passed, her head began to clear, she felt happy to have finally got her own back with Jim, and she looked out with amusement at the scene she had created. Several of the mountain men were peering uneasily at the glade into which she had disappeared. But no one followed her, least of all her husband, which showed a serious lack of instinct vis-à-vis the female, she felt. She had stopped being mad but was yet filled with a feeling that an experienced seducer could have turned this to his amorous advantage. Her husband was not such a seducer—why could men not learn?

Tasmin resolved to stay right where she was. She did not mean to apologize, be meek, explain. She waited, deep in her glade, to see what the trappers, those terrors of the mountain, might do about her. Would her husband venture over? Since the moment when anger might have become lust had passed, Tasmin ceased to care. She suspected that the eventual mediator would be the mild, passionless Pomp Charbonneau, or, if not Pomp, perhaps it would be the rather prissy fur trader William Ashley.

Jim Snow finally stood up—he went over and began to talk to Pomp, whom Tasmin had come to regard more or less as her own possession. Then Pomp went over and chatted a bit with Ashley. Monty, meanwhile,

began to fret. With no bear handy to play with, he remembered that he
was hungry. Jim picked him up, failed to soothe him, and passed him
off to Little Onion, who quieted him but, of course, could not give him
suck. Looking rather annoyed herself, Little Onion handed the baby to
Pomp. Then he and Will Ashley together wandered over toward the glade
where Tasmin watched. That the men felt the need to come in twos annoyed her again so that when they walked up with her hungry baby she
indifferently bared a breast and delayed a moment or two before putting
her child to the teat. This was mainly meant as a challenge to the affable
Pomp, who had once told her that he was rarely troubled by lust, a stupid thing to say to a woman, even if true. Let him look at her breast and
reflect on what lay below—that a man should decline to lust she considered an insult. Tasmin was of half a notion to see if she could change
Pomp's mind on that score but for the moment, with Ashley there, she
merely regarded the nervous ambassadors with all the hauteur she could
muster.

"I guess you had your reasons for punching Jim," Pomp said—"but
why'd you hit Bonney?"

"Because he's fat, I suppose," Tasmin said. "Besides, I needed a second
victim to complete my attack on male complacency. It's your fault, really,
Mr. Ashley, for providing the champagne."

Monty, by now, was guzzling heartily.

"When I drink champagne," Tasmin continued, "memories of old injus-
tices—and there have been many—just seem to bubble up. Claret makes
me amorous, but champagne makes me mean."

William Ashley managed a negligent shrug.

"Our esteemed captain, William Clark, has ever maintained that there is
no wildness equal to the wildness in women," he said.

"How exquisitely philosophical," Tasmin replied coolly.

"Perhaps he said it about my mother—the two of them were close
friends," Pomp remarked, hoping to change the subject, or mollify Tasmin
somehow.

"I met Captain Clark," Tasmin reminded them. "He did not strike me as
being a man who was free of lust."

"Oh hardly," William Ashley agreed. "No stranger to the battery of
Venus, our Captain Clark, I can tell you that."

"How quaintly that sounds, how romantic," Tasmin replied. "The battery of Venus. My own first lover, Master Tobias Stiles, had little of the poet

in him, I'm afraid. 'Cunt' was the term he preferred: blunt but adequate, like himself."

Both men retreated a step.

"Goodness, Tasmin," Pomp said, too deeply startled to hide a blush. "Goodness."

"Don't you chide me, Pomp," Tasmin remarked menacingly. The fires of her anger had been banked but were not extinguished.

"We Berrybenders *will* speak as we please," she continued. "I fear I've come rather to distrust the poetical when it comes to amorous matters. Plain speech and stout action are what's wanted—none of this battery of Venus folderol. You yourself, Pomp, would be a happier man if there were a bit more coarseness in you."

Pomp *was* shocked—he looked, to Tasmin's eye, virginal. Could it be that he had never even had a look at the article being discussed? It was the seat of life, of course, but rather likely to disappoint those who thought in terms of lovely locks, perfect breasts, and other goddesslike attributes, as imagined by the painters and the poets.

Then, in a moment, her mood turned, where Pomp Charbonneau was concerned. The thought that he might indeed be a virgin, might never have ventured into the wilderness between a woman's legs, made her feel protective of him suddenly. Shy Pomp, sweet Pomp—she wondered if she mightn't yet have to help him, guide him in.

"Do excuse me, Pomp, and you too, Mr. Ashley," she said. "I have a rough tongue—hope I haven't bruised your finer sensibilities. I keep forgetting that it is men who are tender souls. We women have our babies to make, and the brute necessities of the business may make us rather coarse."

She shifted Monty to the other breast, half of a mind to pour out more abuse—but the two men were careful to offer her no challenge, so, as an alternative, she went and sat in the sun with Coal and Vicky Kennet. The two bear cubs, seeing the prospect of attention, came over and licked the babies' faces, causing all three to sneeze.

Tasmin looked around for Jim, wondering when he might get around to taking up the difficult challenge of their marriage again. But Jim was shoeing horses, with the help of Joe Walker and Milt Sublette. He glanced her way once or twice but clearly didn't seem to feel that they had to have a reckoning, just then. In Tasmin's view, once she calmed down, that was just as well. Probably her punch took him so completely by surprise that his temper had failed to flare. Shock smothered it. When they could talk she meant to warn him that she could not be trusted when she drank champagne.

When Pomp next strolled by, Tasmin went over and took his arm, to show that no hard feelings remained.

"Don't you be telling on me, Pomp," she said quietly. "Don't be mentioning my coarse speech to Jimmy—he's rather a Puritan when it comes to such things."

"I won't," Pomp promised—in fact the unexpected scene with Tasmin had left him feeling somewhat sad.

"Anyway, you were right," he continued. "I'm the one who doesn't know anything about love."

There was a droop in his voice when he said this, an admittance of loneliness and inexperience that touched Tasmin's heart. She put a friendly arm around him.

"Now, Pomp—cheer up," she said. "You're young—no need to pine. I expect we just need to find you a girl."

Pomp smiled, but did not reply.

Jim Snow, punched in the eye by his wife, supposed that he would forever be a figure of fun among the mountain men. His wife had hit him and he had done nothing about it—of course, she had struck Eulalie Bonneville too, but Bonney was not married to her and bore no responsibility for her behavior.

Jim had hustled over quietly and begun to help out with the horseshoeing, expecting ridicule from the likes of Hugh Glass or old Zeke Williams, who had just arrived at the rendezvous, but, to his surprise, the fact that he was married to a woman of such pure fire produced the very opposite of the effect he had feared. Instead of falling, his stock rose.

"That's some fine gal, that wife of yours," Hugh Glass said. "Must be like living with a she-bear—wild and wilder."

"I suppose it makes Indian fighting seem like a picnic," Jim Bridger ventured. He felt lucky to have avoided being struck himself. Tasmin had favored him with an angry look just before she punched Eulalie.

Jim didn't reply—he worked. But it was clear that the fact that he had gone so far as to father a child on such a woman made a big impression on the mountain men, a few of whom had been a bit skeptical of his abilities, previously. Several of them didn't think he was actually much of a Sin Killer, but Tasmin's utter fearlessness when she walked over and hit him at once banished all skepticism. A man who could hold his own with such a woman was indeed a man to be reckoned with. Jim shrugged off these awed remarks. He himself wasn't so sure that he *could* hold his own with Tasmin—but it was a welcome thing that so many of the boys thought he could.

In the afternoon an Indian wandered into camp and reported that there was a good flock of mountain sheep on the lower slope of a large hill just to the east: at once Jim and Pomp and Drum Stewart grabbed horses and guns—the bighorn sheep were the one species that had successfully eluded the restless Scot.

Tasmin was determined not to let Jim go without his at least acknowledging the fact that she had punched him in the eye.

"I suppose you're mad at me for having punched you," she said, as Jim was tightening his girth.

Jim had the look in his eye that men get when they have more important matters to attend to than anything that might possibly involve women—a maddening look.

"I guess I'll stay out of your way next time you're drunk," he told her. "I bet Bonney stays out of your way, too. He claims he's got a sore tooth."

Jim then raced off—once the hunters were gone, Tasmin went over and made a fine apology to Eulalie Bonneville.

"I'm so sorry I struck you, Mr. Bonneville," she said. "I fear I was very drunk."

"It is of no importance at all," Eulalie said. "I too often strike people when I'm drunk—particularly fat people."

Tasmin laughed. "How's that tooth?" she asked.

"Thank you for inquiring—the agony has somewhat abated," Eulalie said, with great formality. In fact he was terrified of well-spoken ladies such as Tasmin—his preference was for silent Indian girls who scarcely said a word a week.

The hunters did not reappear that evening—it had been late in the day when they left to go chase the sheep.

In the white foggy dawn Tasmin and Vicky Kennet sat by a low campfire, sipping coffee, their babies in their laps, when William Ashley wandered up, an unlit cigar in his mouth. He picked up a burning stick from the fire, lit the cigar, and took several deep puffs as he surveyed the layer of fog that enveloped the Valley of the Chickens.

"Ladies, what say we breakfast on a little champagne?" he suggested, just as Lord Berrybender appeared.

"I mustn't—it makes me mean," Tasmin told him.

"I'll drink hers, then, Ashley—and mine too," Lord B. said. "I'm rather past the dueling age, so I guess I can drink all the bubbly I want."

The trappers who had not gone on the hunt had drunk and caroused all night. Vicky Kennet and her old lover, Lord Berrybender, wandered down to a big campfire the mountain men had built, but Tasmin stayed with William Ashley—she was curious why a man who was said to be so wealthy would put himself at risk every year to journey to such a wild place.

"You're not a hunter, like my papa," Tasmin said to him. "Why do you come?"

William Ashley considered the question.

"Addiction, Lady Tasmin," he replied. "Some men can't stop drinking whiskey, some can't stop taking opium, and I can't stop seeking the wild. I like to be where I can smell it . . . imbibe it . . . the pure wild, if you will."

"But, sir, you've come so far," she reminded him. "Is there really such an insufficiency of wildness between Saint Louis and this remote place? And besides, if we're here—all the way from Northamptonshire—how pure can the wildness be?"

William Ashley smiled—he *did* like the way this English girl put things. One moment she might be calling a cunt a cunt, and the next referring coolly to such a concept as an insufficiency of wildness.

"That's an excellent point—you're here and your civilization will soon follow along," he said. "That's the sadness, Lady Tasmin—there's not much time between first man and last man, between wild and settled. Jed Smith and Zeke Williams and I were the first white men to see this pretty valley here. We saw beaver who had never had to fear the trap, and buffalo that had never heard the sound of a gun. That was scarcely twenty years ago, and yet the beaver are almost gone and the buffalo will go next. Then, if there turns out to be gold or silver or anything a merchant can sell in these hills, they'll tear the very mountains down and rip out whatever it is."

He looked, for a moment, sad.

"I come so I won't forget, ma'am," he said. "I want to remember the wonderful country as it was before it changed."

"Personally, I find it quite wild enough," Tasmin told him. "I can easily imagine a tribe of painted savages pouring out of those trees to kill us all, which would be *more* than wild enough for me."

"Oh no, Lady Tasmin—that sort of thing won't happen," Ashley assured her. "We've been having our rendezvous here in this valley for eight years—

the Utes and the other tribes have come to tolerate us pretty well. I have never been one to underestimate the need for presents, when you're treating with the native peoples. Everybody likes presents, you know. A wagonful of good presents, properly distributed, will take the fight out of most savages, given time."

Scarcely had he finished speaking than he heard the sound of thundering hooves and the scream and yip of war cries—along a ridge at the far eastern end of the valley, bent low over their horses, Jim and Pomp were racing for their lives, pursued by a wild horde of painted savages, such as Tasmin had just mentioned.

William Ashley, looking extremely startled, dropped his cigar—few of his statements had ever been contradicted so immediately.

"I can only think that you must have chosen the wrong presents, this year, Mr. Ashley," Tasmin said, with some indignation. "And now, worse luck, we're all going to be murdered, as a result."

59

. . . the deep grass of summer would cover him with its peace . . .

From Walkura's point of view the attack on the trappers could not have got off to a better start. The minute the big raiding party saw the three hunters and sent up their first war whoops, the tall hunter's horse bolted, carrying him right into the midst of the Utes. There was nothing the man could do to turn his panicked mount. The Utes were startled by this piece of luck, but not so startled as to miss such an easy chance to count coup. They immediately hacked the unhappy rider to pieces—it was what he got for choosing an unreliable horse. High Shoulders tried to scalp him and made a botch of it—he had never taken a scalp before—but already, with the battle just joined, several Ute hatchets were dripping blood, the best possible encouragement when one was going into battle.

"I wish it had been the Sin Killer," Na-Ta-Ha said, but of course that was only wishful thinking. The Sin Killer, and the hunter they called Six Tongues, because he could speak easily with many tribes, had a good jump on them. Both rode fleet mares, and were not going to be easily overtaken.

Still, with one easy kill under their belts, Walkura led the Utes in a wild charge into the Valley of the Chickens, confident that the day would be theirs and there would be many scalps to take home.

Unhappily this confidence only lasted until the charging warriors dropped off the ridge at the eastern end of the hunters' encampment and saw that the valley was covered with a thick white fog from one end to the other. Walkura had only seconds in which to make a decision. What to do? His warriors were in full charge—to halt now, after they had already made a kill, would very likely dampen enthusiasm for the battle ahead. If the Utes had to pull up and wait for the fog to clear, many of the warriors would probably lose interest in the fighting and go home. Some of them were so greedy that they might wipe off their war paint and claim innocence, in the hope that the generous Ashley would give them presents. After all, it was only because of an erratic horse that they had killed the white man—what were they supposed to do when a white man with a rifle rode into their midst?

"The witches made it foggy!" old No Teeth yelled—he had no business even being in the battle but had not been able to resist a chance to deal with the white witches.

Walkura ignored him and charged into the fog. He didn't need witches to explain a fog—the days were warm and the nights chill, and that explained the fog—which didn't make the problem any less disastrous to the Utes' battle plan, which involved taking the trappers by surprise and hoping they were too drunk to react quickly. In the night, getting himself ready for the fight, something had been nagging at Walkura's mind, something pertaining to the battle, but everyone in the camp was talking at once and the young warriors were placing bets on which mountain man they would kill—Walkura could never quite remember the factor he felt he might be failing to consider; but now, as his horse raced off the ridge right into a wall of thick white fog, he remembered what he had forgotten: the likelihood of early morning fog!

Only, now he was *in* the fog, and his warriors were in it too, still in full cry—and there was not a thing to be seen. It was as bad as going into battle in a white blizzard. Walkura didn't know what to do—the warriors were pressing on, right behind him; he now rather regretted that his vanity had prompted him to lead the charge. Now, if he wasn't lucky, he might be struck down by his own men; their blood was up, they would strike at anything they could see, and perhaps, once they got nervous, at things they *couldn't* see. Walkura was actually less worried about the danger of the mountain men, who were not likely to shoot their guns unless they could see a target. The Utes, with their dripping hatchets, were, for the moment, a worse threat.

Walkura cautiously pulled up his horse. He didn't want to race along and smack into a rock, and, as he remembered, there were several rocky outcroppings at the eastern end of the valley—it occurred to him that he might do well to veer to the north, where there was higher ground. He might get higher, above the fog, and gain at least some sense of where the combatants were as the battle proceeded.

Cautiously, Walkura turned north—the fine fury that had led him to charge into battle was quickly giving way to a feeling of glumness, even failure. What had he done now? He might have been home enjoying a bit of amorous activity with his Modoc girl, but, instead, he had let old Greasy Lake's wild talk of bears and witches and the Wandering Hill lead him into launching a foolish raid into the Valley of the Chickens. Those who questioned his leadership anyway—and there were always people who questioned a leader's decisions—would point out the obvious fact that he should have expected to find fog in such a valley in the early morning at that time of year. The fact that they had only launched the charge because they had jumped the three hunters would not matter to such people, who made a pastime of finding fault with his leadership. Even though they had killed a hunter, the naysayers would claim that this was no excuse for forgetting about the likelihood of fog—never mind the fact that once a bunch of Utes had killed a white man and were yelling their war cries and racing their horses, the last thing they would want to hear was that it was foggy up ahead.

Overhead, the sun was only a pale yellow ring—how Walkura wished it would gather strength and burn away this fog while there was still a chance of fighting. But the sun was weak yet, and everyone, whites and Utes alike, was groping around in a clinging mist, their weapons useless, their spirits sinking, as his were.

On one or two occasions Walkura thought he saw a shadow that might be a person—he had an arrow ready, but then realized, each time, that the shadow was only a tree. What amazed him was how totally this fog had managed to swallow his war party of nearly thirty warriors. They had all plunged into the fog and now there was not a trace of them—not a sound could be heard. For a moment Walkura thought he might locate a warrior or two by whistling like the prairie hens for which the valley was named; but he soon discarded that option. He had never been able to do birdcalls very well—if he flubbed his imitation he would only give his position away. What he had begun to wish for, as he inched his way north, was a means for just calling it all off and starting the day over. Only one life had been lost, and that had been an accident. There was no real need for this battle. The whites were irritating, of course, but at least they brought good presents. Why couldn't they just explain the accident, smoke a peace pipe, do a little trading, and perhaps have a few horse races once the fog lifted?

It was fun to plan a battle, rattle weapons, and dance and puff oneself up, but when something like this fog comes along and spoils everything, why try to pretend that there is still a chance for a glorious fight? If a warrior bumped into a trapper and they wanted to go at it, Walkura had no objection. But the big Ute assault had failed; the fog had just swallowed it up.

As Walkura picked his way carefully north, thinking these gloomy thoughts, the fog began to lighten a little. He thought he heard something like a bear, though not a full-grown bear. Then, for a moment, the fog broke in front of him and he saw not one but two young bears, cubs still, growling and rolling around with each other, having a playful tussle. When he realized that the bears were just cubs, his annoyance with Greasy Lake increased. Were *these* the Bear people the witches were supposed to be talking to?

Then Walkura saw one of the little witches, a girl just old enough to begin to be a woman, standing not far from the cubs, watching them roll around in play—he wondered if he ought to capture this girl—it wouldn't hurt to have two young wives, after all. But then the swift Six Tongues appeared out of the fog. He had a gun but didn't raise it—he seemed to want the girl to help him catch the cubs and carry them down into the safety of the fog.

Walkura at once loosed an arrow at Six Tongues—a good shot, too—but before his arrow even struck Six Tongues, Walkura suddenly tumbled off his horse. To his surprise, when he tried to rise, he saw that a limb had grown out of his chest. It took him several moments to focus his eyes and determine that the object protruding from his chest wasn't a limb, it was an arrow; and there stood the Sin Killer, ready to loose a second arrow from his bow. Walkura could not see Six Tongues, who must have wandered down into the fog. Walkura thought he had probably killed the man, but there was no way to be sure. What he *was* sure of was that the Sin Killer, a man some Utes scoffed at as being no very good fighter, had just drawn his own heart's blood. Walkura felt mildly surprised: few white men could use the bow so well. He got to his knees and tried to grip the arrow hard and rip it from his breast; but quickly and quietly his grip loosened, his strength left him, his hands fell away; he slumped to his side and then lay back. He wondered if the Sin Killer would want to scalp him—but no one came, no scalp knife bit; the sky that should be growing lighter grew darker instead, grew as dark as deepest night. For a time, with the steady pulsing out of his blood, Walkura felt a sense of rise and fall, of soaring and dipping; beneath his palms he felt the grass, the good grass of summer, wet a little from the fog, the grass that fed buffalo and elk, antelope and doe—soon, Walkura knew, he would be one with all that had been, and the deep grass of summer would cover him with its peace; he did not feel sad, though he did regret, a little, that he had not had more time with that lively Modoc girl.

60

"I'll see that he wants to!" she said.

Na-Ta-Ha was not one to suppress his criticisms when he thought a raid had been handled badly; and few raids of recent years had resulted in such a complete botch as the raid Walkura had led on the trappers who were gathered with Ashley in the Valley of the Chickens. It was true that they had made an immediate kill, but that was the result of panic on the part of the hunter's horse—panic that brought the victim right into their midst.

Then, after that promising beginning, Walkura had insisted on plunging the warriors into a fog so blinding that they had to slow their horses to a walk, after which the whole war party picked its way timorously through the Valley of the Chickens, never making contact with a single trapper.

"I might have hit one trapper," High Shoulders said. "I think I ran over somebody just as we ran into that fog."

"You think, but you don't know," Na-Ta-Ha countered. "You probably just ran over a dog."

The Utes, who had ridden east to west through the valley, were on their way home. Nobody could expect warriors to fight in fog that thick—there was no reason to apologize for their retreat. Walkura had been in the lead when they all plunged into the fog, so everyone assumed he was somewhere up ahead.

"You watch—he'll be sitting there ready with a lot of excuses when we get home. He's an old man. He's been to the Valley of the Chickens before. He should have known there would be fog."

Most of the warriors, disappointed because there had been no chance to kill trappers or witches, agreed wholeheartedly with Na-Ta-Ha's criticisms.

But then Walkura's horse came galloping up from the rear, and Walkura wasn't on him, a fact that immediately contradicted Na-Ta-Ha's theory.

It was then that High Shoulders remembered that old No Teeth had been with them—they had all tried to make him stay at home but he defied them and had been racing along happily when they all dashed into the fog.

"I don't see No Teeth, either," High Shoulders said.

There was an uneasy pause—their war chief and their medicine man both seemed to be missing.

High Shoulders, with the boldness of youth, spat out a harsh opinion.

"We were chasing the Sin Killer, remember?" he reminded everyone. "The Sin Killer probably killed them both."

Na-Ta-Ha felt uncomfortable with that theory. What if the boy was right? What if he himself had just been criticizing a war chief who had died heroically, a victim of the deadly Sin Killer, the man who had driven a lance through a Piegan? If that turned out to be the case, Walkura's relatives, some of whom were in the war party, would never let him forget his wild criticisms. Na-Ta-Ha immediately changed his tack.

"We have to go back," he declared. "If those two are dead we have to recover their bodies—or else we'll be disgraced."

"And if we do go back we'll probably be killed ourselves, by the Sin Killer or Bridger or the Broken Hand," High Shoulders announced.

Bitter as the prospect was, the war party immediately turned back toward the Valley of the Chickens. They would be disgraced forever if they failed to see that the body of their great war chief, Walkura, was brought home and given proper burial.

When they reached the Valley of the Chickens the fog had long since burned off and the whites were themselves conducting a burial down by the river. A tall woman was playing an instrument that gave off very mournful music. The music was so sad-making that several of the warriors were close to tears, although they had no idea who was being buried.

When the whites noticed that the Utes had come back, Na-Ta-Ha hastily made the peace sign and old Sharbo, looking very sad, walked over to parley with them. He told them it was the old lord's son they were burying—he had been returning from the creek and had been fatally trampled in their wild charge.

"There—I knew I ran over somebody," High Shoulders observed.

Sharbo confirmed that both Walkura and No Teeth were dead. It seemed that Walkura had shot an arrow into Six Tongues, who was Sharbo's son. Six Tongues was not dead, but the arrow was near his heart and had not been removed, which was why Sharbo looked so worried.

"But if Walkura shot Six Tongues, who shot him?" one warrior wanted to know. Walkura had always been quick to discharge arrows—it was hard to imagine anyone beating him at that game.

"The Sin Killer," Sharbo said—his face was drawn and gray.

By the river the Englishwomen and a few of the mountain men were singing over the dead boy—their voices carried far. The Utes did not consider it polite to linger any longer, or parley anymore—not while death songs were being sung. One Ute asked Sharbo if he thought that, after a day or two had passed, it might still be possible for them to do a little trading with Ashley. Sharbo said he didn't think Ashley would object—trading was the point of the rendezvous, after all. The Utes solemnly gathered up the two bodies and rode away with them. It was not clear what had happened to No Teeth, but he was known to be a reckless rider, more reckless than expert. Probably his horse had run into a tree, or pitched him off into some rocks. There was not a mark on him—he even seemed to be smiling. The cynical view was that he had overmatched himself when it came to the white witches. No Teeth was always bragging about how slowly and professionally he would put the white witches to death—and yet now it was No Teeth who was dead. No doubt the white witches had known the old shaman was coming and had used the fog to lay a clever—indeed, fatal—trap for him.

Tasmin sang dutifully over the grave of her unfortunate brother Bobbety Berrybender, whom she had so often ridiculed. He had been calmly
pursuing his interest in freshwater *Mollusca* and had started to the camp
for breakfast when he happened to walk right in front of thirty charging
horses. Buffum was nearly hysterical with grief, and Father Geoffrin not
much better. How sad it was, Tasmin thought, to be dead on a day of such
beauty, for, once the fog lifted, the valley was so lovely that merely looking
at it produced a kind of ache. The fog that had doomed young Bobbety had
saved the rest of them from attack—beauty and death thus closely bound
together, as Tasmin supposed it often must be.

"He was ever my ally in family quarrels, Tassie . . . I shall be very lonely
without him," Buffum sobbed.

The little priest, sad, small, and trembly, seemed shrunken with regret.

"I knew we ought to have taken that nice boat back down the river,"
Father Geoffrin said. "We could have gone straight to Paris and bought lots
of clothes—and now we never shall."

Jim Snow had carried Pomp down the hill and laid him on blankets
in William Ashley's wagon. Several of the mountain men looked at the
arrow and shook their heads, so close to the heart was it. Hugh Glass
was the only other trapper to have sustained an injury—he had stepped
on a shard from the whiskey jug Tasmin had broken and cut his big toe
to the bone.

As soon as the last hymns of requiem were sung over Bobbety, Tasmin
rushed back to Pomp. She was torn by the knowledge of how cruel she had
been to him, only the day before—he who had been so loyal through so
much. As she rushed up the slope she was hoping that somehow Jim had
pulled the arrow out, and that she might see Pomp smiling his diffident
smile again. Instead she found Ashley, Jim, and the two bear cubs, both
whining miserably, sure that something was wrong.

Pomp was still alive, but his breathing was shallow and irregular, his
pulse anything but strong.

"What can we do, Jim?" she asked; but her resourceful husband for
once had no answer.

"You might ask the priest," Jim told her. "He got that bullet out of
Cook—maybe he could ease this arrow out."

Tasmin went to look for Father Geoffrin, who was still down at Bobbety's grave. The mountain men all sat around disconsolately, talking in
low tones, drinking little. Joe Walker incautiously voiced the opinion that

they might as well start digging a second grave—Tasmin at once whirled on him.

"No such thing, Mr. Walker," she said. "Pomp Charbonneau is going to live—I'm just hurrying off to talk to his surgeon now."

Father Geoffrin still sat by Bobbety's grave, sipping from a cup of brandy, which he at once offered to share with Tasmin. She took a searing swallow.

When Tasmin asked him if he would at least try to cut the arrow out of Pomp, Father Geoff flexed his fingers thoughtfully.

"It's the arteries that worry me," he said. "If I nick one, our good Pomp will quietly bleed to death."

"Yes, but if you don't make the attempt, he will certainly die," Tasmin said. Just then old Charbonneau joined them, trailed by Pedro Yanez and Aldo Claricia, neither of them sober. Charbonneau seconded Tasmin's point.

"A Ute put that arrow in my boy, not you," he told the priest. "If my good son dies, it'll be the Ute's doing, not yours. I fear you're the only one among us who has the skill to save him."

Father Geoffrin looked thoughtful for a moment; then he handed the brandy to Tasmin.

"Very well, monsieur," he said. "I had better get to it while the light's good."

Charbonneau, dirty and disordered as ever, tears coursing down his cheeks, sat down wearily by Bobbety Berrybender's grave.

"Here I've been traveling thirty years in these wild places, and not a scratch on me," he said. "And now it's my young Pomp who gets an arrow in him."

"We were nearly killed by a great bear ourselves," Aldo remarked sadly.

Up the slope Tasmin could see a flurry of activity. Cook was heating water. Jim Snow and Kit Carson took the sides off the wagon, so it could be used as an operating table. Jim Bridger fetched more firewood. Father Geoffrin was painstakingly sharpening his knives and laying out his tweezers.

"If only Janey was here," Charbonneau remarked. "Janey could pull him through."

"Who?" Tasmin asked. She had never heard Pomp speak of a Janey. Could it be that he was not so virginal, after all?

"His mother, I mean," Charbonneau continued. "Captain Clark called her Janey—could never quite manage her Indian name."

"I'm going to be with him now," Tasmin said. "Will you be coming, monsieur?"

Charbonneau shook his head—he was staring, blank-faced, at the hills across the river. The two short Europeans lingered with him.

When Tasmin reached the arena of the operation, William Ashley was prancing around, looking officious and bossy.

"The danger will be when the arrow comes out," he was saying. "Very likely our Pomp's life will come with it."

"Get out of here and don't talk like that, you goddamn fop!" Tasmin yelled, suddenly furious. There was something she didn't like about Ashley—he seemed the kind of man who might wear scent.

Shocked, William Ashley backed away. Hugh Glass's mouth dropped open—he had been with Ashley on the day of his great defeat by the Arikaras, ten years earlier, but had never seen the man so dismayed—although, on the former occasion, men had been dropping dead all around him.

Tasmin looked around for her husband—as she always did, when she let slip an oath—but Jim was not there.

"Him and Kit went to stand guard," Eulalie Bonneville explained. "Drum Stewart's dead, you know—killed in the first minute, horse bolted, right into the Utes, Jim says."

"Jimmy will never trust the Utes again," Milt Sublette remarked.

The news of the Scot's death barely registered with Tasmin. She moved around by Pomp's head and kept her eyes fixed on him as Father Geoffrin began his work. Tasmin put her mouth close to Pomp's ear and whispered to him.

"I'm here, Pomp," she whispered. "I'm here to help you—don't die, don't you dare."

Very quickly, Father Geoffrin made two cuts and, to everyone's surprise, lifted out the arrow; but before anyone could speak he shook his head.

"Save the bravos," he said. "There's a tip I failed to get—the arrow must have hit a rib. If Cook will just let me have those long tweezers . . ."

Silently, Cook handed him the tweezers—the probe was longer this time. Tasmin kept her eyes on Pomp—she whispered again in his ear. She did not want him to get the notion that he was allowed to go.

Pomp, drifting in deep and starless darkness, heard Tasmin speak softly in his ear, saying she was here, she was here; but he couldn't answer. The easeful darkness held him in its lazy power; he floated downward, deeper and deeper into it, as the soaked leaf sinks slowly to the bottom of a pool, to a place deeper than light. Helpless as the leaf he sank and sank, until, instead of Tasmin's voice, he heard, "Jean Baptiste . . . Jean Baptiste!" Then the darkness gave way to the soft light of dream, and there was Sacagawea, his mother, sitting quietly in a field of waving grass, as she had so many times in his dreams. Though her dark eyes welcomed him, the look on her face was grave.

As always in his dreams of Sacagawea, Pomp wanted to rush to her, to be taken in her arms, as he had been as a child; but he could not move. The rules of the dream were severe—old sadness, old frustration pricked him, even though dreams of his mother were the best dreams of all.

As usual, when she visited him in dreams, Sacagawea began to talk in low tones of things that had happened long ago.

"When we were on our way back from the great ocean I took you up to the top of those white cliffs that rise by the Missouri," she said. "I wanted you to see the great herds, grazing far from the world of men; but you were a young boy then, not even weaned, and I held your hand so you wouldn't step off the edge of life and go too soon to the Sky House, where we all have to go someday. Now that old Ute's arrow has brought you to the edge of life again, but the woman who whispers to you wants to pull you back, as I pulled you back when you were young."

Sacagawea was looking directly at him—Pomp wanted to ask her questions, and yet, as always in his dreams of his mother, he was gripped by a terrible muteness; he could ask no question, make no plea, though he knew that at any time the dream might fade and his mother be lost to him until he visited her in dreams again. With the fear that his dream was ending came a sadness so deep that Pomp did not want to wake up to life, and yet that was just what his mother was urging him to do—she wanted him to listen to Tasmin.

"I did not wean you until you had seen four summers," Sacagawea told him. "My milk was always strong—I filled you with it so that you could live long and enjoy the world of men, the world I showed you when we stood together on the white cliffs. Obey the woman who whispers—it is not time for you to come to the Sky House yet . . ."

Then, with sad swiftness, his mother faded; where her face had been was Tasmin's face, leaning close to his. Pomp tried to smile, but couldn't, not yet. Even so, Tasmin's eyes shone with tears of relief.

At last Father Geoffrin, who had been probing very carefully, withdrew the long tweezers, which contained the tiny, bloody tip of a flint arrow.

"There . . . it's out—and he's not bleeding much," Father Geoffrin said. "I think our good Pomp can live now—if he wants to."

Tasmin had been watching Pomp's face closely. Her heart leapt when he opened his eyes.

"I'll see that he wants to!" she said, overjoyed that her friend had lived.

Father Geoffrin—priest, surgeon, and cynic—raised an eyebrow.

"I expect you will, madame," he said. "I expect you will."

VOLUME THREE

BY
SORROW'S
RIVER

Contents

Characters

Berrybenders

Tasmin
Bess (Buffum)
Mary
Kate
Lord Berrybender
Monty, *baby*
Talley, *baby*
Piet Van Wely
Father Geoffrin
Cook
Milly
Eliza
Tim
Signor Claricia
Señor Yanez
Venetia Kennet

Mountain Men

Jim Snow (The Sin Killer)
Kit Carson
Jim Bridger
Tom Fitzpatrick (The Broken Hand)
Eulalie Bonneville
William Ashley
Maelgwyn Evans
Hugh Glass
Bill and Milt Sublette

Ezekiel Williams
Joe Walker
Pomp Charbonneau
Toussaint Charbonneau
Rabbit, *baby*

Indians

High Shoulders, *Ute*
Coal
Little Onion
Greasy Lake
The Partezon, *Sioux*
Red Knee, *Pawnee*
Rattle, *Pawnee*
Slow Possum, *Pawnee*
Duck Catcher, *Pawnee*
The Bad Eye, *Gros Ventre*
Fool's Bull, *Sioux*
Hollow Foot, *Brulé Sioux*
Draga, *Aleut*
Takes Bones (The Ear Taker), *Acoma*
Thistle-Pricks-Us, *Pawnee*
Prickly Pear Woman, *Laguna*
Corn Tassel, *Chippewa*
Owl Woman, *Cheyenne*

Miscellaneous

Charles Bent, *trader*
Willy Bent, *trader*
Amboise d'Avigdor
Benjamin Hope-Tipping, *journalist*
Clam de Paty, *journalist*
Obregon, *slaver*
Malgres, *slaver*

Ramon, *slaver*
Maria Jaramillo
Josefina Jaramillo
Lieutenant Molino, *Mexican soldier*
Captain Antonio Reyes, *Mexican soldier*
Doña Esmeralda, *duenna*

1

It was a day of fine sunlight.

La vie, voyez-vous, ça n'est jamais si bonne ni si mauvaise qu'on croit," said Father Geoffrin, relaxing, for a moment, into his native tongue. His patient, Pomp Charbonneau—educated in Germany, competent in several languages—spoke good French. Tasmin Berrybender's *français*, while decidedly casual, was probably adequate, the priest felt, to such a common platitude: life was never so good or so bad as one thought—a proposition which no one who had much acquaintance with the French classics would be likely to dispute.

Tasmin, with a flare of her eloquent nostrils and a cool glance at Father Geoffrin, at once disputed it.

"What foppish nonsense, Geoff!" she said. "Are you going to argue that I wasn't in hell when I thought Pomp was dying, or that I shan't be in ecstasy when I know he's out of danger?"

Though Father Geoffrin, no mean surgeon, had very skillfully removed a flint tip from very near Pomp's heart, the crisis caused by the Ute Walkura's well-placed arrow had not ended there. For three days Pomp's fever soared; except to relieve herself, Tasmin never left his side. Monty, her baby, was brought in to suckle. When Pomp's fever rose she bathed his face and neck from a basin of cold river water; she covered him with blankets when he shivered with chill. Only that morning the fever had at last broken, leaving Pomp calm but very weak. In his dream deliriums he had several times had visits from his mother, Sacagawea, dead many long years, who insisted that he heed Tasmin's anxious whispers and stay with her in the world of the living. His mother and Tasmin together held him in life—without them he would have slipped into the easeful shadows. At the height of his fever he felt some resentment at the two women's tenacity—couldn't they just let him go? But the women, one dead, one strongly alive, were more powerful than the fever. So there Pomp was, weak but still alive, in the big camp in the Valley of the Chickens, though his employer, the sportsman William Drummond Stewart, had been hacked to death by the invading Utes. Bobbety Berrybender, Tasmin's brother, was also killed, trampled as he wandered in the fog by thirty charging horses. Now, in the crisp air of a sunny morning, Tasmin and Father Geoffrin were quarreling volubly, as they often did.

"I accept that some women are not quite suited to the life of moderation," Father Geoff told her. "It's why your Shakespeare is so popular—all that raging. And of course there's opera—same raging. I fear you're the operatic sort, Tasmin—if you can't have passion you'll have torment. Personally, I'd be happy just to buy some nice clothes."

"Not much opportunity for clothes shopping here," Tasmin told him. The trader William Ashley, frightened of Tasmin because she had cursed him violently when he suggested that Pomp was unlikely to survive his wound, had lent them his tent for Pomp's convalescence. With Tasmin supporting him, Pomp had just taken a few steps out into the bright sunlight and the clean mountain air. Once he was settled comfortably on a buffalo-robe pallet, the two bear cubs Pomp had caught, Abby and Andy, shuffled up, eager to be petted. Below them, the same party of Utes who had attacked them a week earlier were placidly trading pelts with Eulalie Bonneville, William Ashley, Jim Bridger, and the other mountain men. From the river came the low, melancholy notes of Venetia Kennet's cello, playing a dirge for William Drummond Stewart, who had been her lover.

When the Utes, whose village was nearby, had come diffidently back to trade, Tasmin had been too focused on Pomp and his fever to pay attention to what went on in camp, but now that she saw their attackers milling around among the mountain men, exchanging peltries for hatchets, tobacco, blue and green beads, she felt incensed.

"Aren't those the same savages who trampled my brother and hacked up poor Drum Stewart?" she asked. "Why are those fools giving them hatchets, the better to brain us with?"

"Ah, there's your extreme nature getting in the way of good business sense," Father Geoffrin chided. "Last week the Utes were enemies, but now they're customers. Bill Ashley has his profits to think of, after all."

It was a day of fine sunlight. Tasmin looked around the camp but failed to spot her husband, Jim Snow, who had wisely left her to her nursing when Pomp was in danger. She didn't see Kit Carson either, but her father, Lord Berrybender, was down by the river, listening to Vicky Kennet's mournful music—soon, no doubt, he would be trying to coax the tall cellist back to his bed, his dalliance with Milly, their buxom laundress, having quickly run its course.

Little Onion, Jim Snow's young Ute wife—though a wife in name only—sat not far away, keeping an eye on Monty, Talley, and Rabbit. Monty was Tasmin's, Talley was Vicky's, and Rabbit belonged to Coal, Toussaint Charbonneau's Hidatsa wife, who was, at the moment, drying the meat of an elk Tom Fitzpatrick had shot the day before. Rabbit could toddle about uncertainly, while Monty and Talley were still at the crawling stage. All three little boys were extremely fond of the bear cubs, but the bear cubs, far speedier than the three human cubs, either adroitly avoided the boys or licked their faces until they sneezed and crawled away.

Bess, called Buffum, was helping Cook pick berries from some distant bushes, while Mary Berrybender, their sinister and uncompromising sister, was helping her Dutch friend, Piet Van Wely, chip with a small hammer at some rocks that, Tasmin supposed, might contain interesting fossils.

"I don't see Jimmy. Where could he be?" Tasmin asked. "I don't see Kit, either. I hope they haven't left, just as Pomp's feeling better."

Toussaint Charbonneau, Pomp's tall, shambling, much-stained father, had been drinking whiskey and dipping snuff with old Hugh Glass, oldest and rawest of the mountain men. Old Charbonneau, officially the party's interpreter, was a tenderhearted parent; for days he had been shaking with worry, fearful that Tasmin would come out of the tent and tell him that his son was dead.

"Why, look, there's Pomp!" old Charbonneau said, tears springing to his eyes as he saw Tasmin ease Pomp down on the comfortable pallet.

"That English girl's got more brass than all of us put together," Hugh Glass observed. "I wish she liked me better. Maybe she'd take the trouble to pull me through, next time I find that I'm dying."

But Toussaint Charbonneau didn't hear him—he was stumbling up the hill, excited to see his son alive—the son he soon enfolded in a tight embrace.

"Careful, monsieur—he's weak," Tasmin said. "We don't want that wound to start bleeding."

"We don't—I'll be careful," Charbonneau assured her, wiping the tears off his face with snuff-stained fingers.

Father Geoffrin took Tasmin by the arm and strolled away a few steps, so father and son could have a bit of privacy. Tasmin had taken to guarding Pomp as an eagle might guard its egg.

"William Ashley has some nice silk shirts," Father Geoff remarked. "And also a rather well-stitched pair of whipcord trousers."

"So what? They're *his* clothes, not *your* clothes," Tasmin said. "You'll have to wait for Santa Fe before you can buy clothes . . . and who knows when we'll get to Santa Fe?"

Monty, spotting his mother, whom he had not seen much of for days, began to crawl toward her as fast as his hands and knees could carry him. Tasmin met him halfway, swooped him up, wiped dirt off his nose, gave him several enthusiastic kisses, but then, to his dismay, handed him back to the patient Little Onion—his other mother, so far as Monty knew. Tasmin then walked away, skirting the traders and the Indians, heading for the river, noting as she passed near Vicky and her father that Vicky Kennet's hair was getting long again. Once it had hung in a rich mass all the way to her derriere; then, in a frenzy of dissatisfaction at being always a rich man's mistress, she had insisted that Tasmin cut it off. Tasmin had done as requested—for a few weeks Vicky Kennet had looked almost as scalped as her unfortunate lover, Drum Stewart, victim of the rampaging Utes.

As she walked down to the rapid, shallow, greenish river, which foamed here and there as it tumbled over rocks, Tasmin kept an eye out for her husband, Jim Snow—called Sin Killer by the Indians and some of the mountain men too. It was Jim, as good a bowman as most Indians, who had killed the Ute chief Walkura only a second after Walkura shot his near-fatal arrow into Pomp Charbonneau. Tasmin walked a step or two into the icy water, stooping to bathe her dusty face and throat; washing was a luxury she had not bothered with or even thought of during her days at Pomp's bedside. The icy water felt good—having her cheeks and throat clean felt good also, so good that she felt like stripping off and bathing the rest of her body as well. Of course, she couldn't do that with the trappers and Indians watching; besides, she had brought nothing clean to put on.

Standing in the shallows, the cold waters numbing her feet and ankles, Tasmin realized that she was, on the whole, relieved not to see her husband. Normally, in the course of a day in camp, her eyes sought him out frequently—even glimpsing Jim at a distance would provide clues to his mood. Jim never hid his feeling; vibration of what he was feeling could be picked out of the air, like the notes of Vicky's cello; then, when it came time for Tasmin to be a wife, she knew whether to approach her husband modestly and shyly or boldly, teasingly. Some moods she could slip around, kissing him if she felt like it, avoiding his hands if she didn't—though it was rare enough that she avoided his hands.

She might, she thought, have avoided them today, if he had approached her suddenly and tried to draw her into the bushes for a rut, as he liked to call it. It struck her, standing in the cold water watching the Indians and the trappers casually trading hatchets and beads, that the one thing she really knew about Jimmy Snow was that he craved her. That was good; she craved him too; but she had been with Pomp Charbonneau for five days, intensely with Pomp Charbonneau; she had felt nothing and thought of nothing except the necessity of keeping him alive. Her child she suckled automatically; the rest of her life she stepped away from, compelled by her determination that Pomp not die. Pomp had been her friend, her protector in times when Jim Snow was away. She had not expected the great bird of death to come swooping at Pomp; but when the bird swooped and nearly carried Pomp off, Tasmin had at once thrown her whole self into the struggle for Pomp's life. Death came so close, at times, that Tasmin was even nervous about stepping out of the tent to make water. Except for the thirty-hour struggle to bring Monty out of her womb, no fight had ever been so intense, so crucial, so starkly a contest between life and death; it required her to call up a level of will that had never been required of her before; it had needed her deepest strength, and she had prevailed, but it was well, she felt, that her husband was not there to want her, just at that moment.

Fortunately, the struggle had ended in victory. Pomp was sitting up, talking with his father and scratching the belly of the bear cub Abby. Once his wound was healed he might be exactly the same Pomp: friendly, kind, urbane, amused, amusing, supple of mind. The sight of him with his father and his pet slowly eased Tasmin's mind, where Pomp was concerned. The bird of death had been driven back to its eyrie. But if he was the same, what of herself? What of Tasmin? It seemed to her she had traveled a great distance during the struggle—thus her relief at not immediately having to deal with Jim, to be a wife again suddenly, as she had eagerly been for a year and a half. Father Geoffrin, at the end of his successful surgery, had seen something of this traveling in Tasmin's face, and had made a cynical French joke about it; the little priest, as sensitive to emotions as Vicky was to tones, had seen in Tasmin's look something unexpected, something that went beyond a nurse's determination to save a patient. Father Geoffrin lifted an eyebrow, he made his joke, but as soon as Pomp's fever broke he moved the conversation into safer waters—that is, he talked of clothes. It had annoyed Tasmin slightly. Once more a man seemed to be avoiding an important question, leaving her to struggle with it alone. *Had* she fallen in love with Pomp Charbonneau as he lay near death? Had she perhaps already been in love with him, but only dared to recognize the feeling when it seemed that she might lose him? Now, her cheeks cold from the icy water of the mountain stream, she wondered what became of deathbed emotions once death itself had been avoided. Would she again walk with Pomp along the mild path of friendship? Or had an emotion much less mild been seeded between them—feelings that would lead to who knew what tumult? Her husband, after all, was Pomp's best friend. It was obvious from Jim's brief visits to the hospital tent that he hoped Tasmin and the priest could save his friend's life. But Jim Snow assumed that feelings were settled things; Tasmin knew they weren't. What if she no longer wanted her vigorous young husband? They had enjoyed a fierce and finally blissful rut only the day before the battle with the Utes—the pleasure had lingered in Tasmin's body for hours afterward—and yet, what of it? Even the most passionate conjugal connection imposed no permanency. Desire was not a guarantor of much—desire might fade, perhaps always did fade; besides, she was her father's daughter, the child of Lord Albany Berrybender, a man who had scattered his seed liberally enough to produce fourteen legitimate children and perhaps as many as thirty bastards—and he was by no means through. On this very expedition into the American wilderness he had already given Vicky Kennet one child and might well give her more, if she wasn't careful. Tasmin, though now a mother, had never been prudish. What if she proved as prodigal in her appetites as her father?

Only the winter before, when Pomp had insisted on walking from Pierre Boisdeffre's trading post to the tent a mile away where Jim Snow insisted they live, Tasmin had sometimes wondered if Pomp was walking her all that way because he wanted to kiss her. Reckless in mood, she had sometimes dawdled on their walks, holding Pomp's arm and half hoping he *would* kiss her. But he didn't, and Tasmin had not quite worked up to kissing him, although she considered it more than once, in part, perhaps, out of annoyance with her husband, Jim Snow, who calmly allowed her the company of this shy, handsome Pomp, Jim oblivious to the fact that kisses, and more, might pass between them. Pomp had once shyly admitted to Tasmin that he was a virgin, a condition that, considering his sweet attractiveness, any helpful woman might wish to alter. When Pomp admitted that he seldom felt lustful, Tasmin took it almost as an insult to her sex. She complained, but she didn't actively set out to *make* him lustful, though she felt quite sure that she could make him lustful, given a little privacy.

So here they were, as summer neared its end, in the Valley of the Chickens, west of South Pass, with the big fur-trading rendezvous winding down and with the rather vague intention of heading off to Santa Fe pretty soon, so that her father might shoot yet more buffalo, elk, moose, deer, antelope, and whatever else might cross his path. Her husband was nowhere to be seen, nor was the helpful Kit Carson, and there she stood in a cold stream, wishing very much that Pomp Charbonneau *had* tried to kiss her at some point, even though, in his eyes, she was the apparently contented wife of his best friend.

Then the pesky Father Geoffrin, who surprised everyone by his competence as a surgeon, had tried to tell her that life was never as good or as bad as one thought it to be. Tasmin was in no mood to tolerate French equivocation; she felt muddled, so muddled in fact that she failed to note the quiet approach of Mary Berrybender, a girl with unusual powers, capable of sniffing out edible tubers and perhaps also capable of sniffing out nascent loves, such as might be said to exist between Tasmin and Pomp.

"Now that you've saved Pomp, do you mean to have him, Tassie—I mean carnally?" Mary inquired; she had her full share of the Berrybender directness where the appetites were concerned and had sensed the rising feeling between her sister and Pomp long before either of them would have admitted that they *felt* such feelings.

So there Mary stood, a half-wild look in her eye, asking Tasmin straight out if she meant to seduce Pomp Charbonneau.

"Shut up and get back to your Dutchman," Tasmin warned. "And don't be playing nasty games with him, either."

She referred to the fact that Mary had been lashing the pudgy Dutch botanist on his bare bottom with some brambles, an activity the two claimed to thoroughly enjoy.

"Shame, Tasmin," Mary said hotly. "You were no older when you were tupping Master Tobias Stiles in the stall of father's great horse Charlemagne. You *did* do it, you know!"

"Of course I did it, and lucky to get the opportunity," Tasmin replied. "When it comes to forthright tupping, I suspect Master Stiles set a standard your Dutchman would be hard put to match."

"Being whipped with nettles is a common practice among educated

Hollanders," Mary reminded her. "I can't think why you'd mind about it, Tassie."

"I've just come through an ordeal—Pomp nearly died," Tasmin said. "I'm not in the mood to discuss our amatory futures, yours or mine. I don't see my husband and I don't see Kit Carson, either. Do you know where they might be?"

"Oh yes, they're gone on a scout," Mary informed her. "It's the Sioux, I believe, that they're investigating. Santa Fe seems to be a great distance away—Jim doesn't wish us to blunder into too many Sioux—they're very irritable at the moment, it seems."

Just then another sister came trailing up, the sturdy Kate Berrybender, aged four. Tasmin was thinking that while her face and throat felt very clean, the rest of her felt soiled and smelly. The desire to be clean all over rose in her; there were bushes thick enough to hide her up the river a ways. She could bathe in discreet seclusion, but would need clean clothes once she stepped out.

"Mary, go find Buffum—I believe she's picking berries. Ask her to have Milly, our amorous laundress, get me a clean shift," Tasmin asked.

Mary, obliging for once, had hardly left to execute this errand when stout little Kate arrived, wearing her usual look of fierce belligerence.

"Mr. James Snow left a message for you," Kate informed her, without preamble. "He says he is going on a scout and will not be back for three weeks, if then."

"Three weeks? And he didn't think it worth his while to say good-bye to his own wife?" Tasmin complained.

"Mr. James Snow does not say good-bye," Kate informed her, with quite exceptional firmness. "When Mr. James Snow wants to go, he just goes."

"So I've noticed, you insolent midge," Tasmin replied. "This is not his first abrupt departure, since taking me as his wife. Inasmuch as you seem to be his emissary, perhaps you wouldn't mind giving him a message from his wife, next time you see him."

"Perhaps—unless it's an order," Kate said. "You are not allowed to give orders to Mr. James Snow."

"The next time he goes heigh-hoing off, he better leave me Kit—that's the message," Tasmin told her. "Little Onion and I could use Kit's help."

Instead of replying, Kate picked up a rock, intending to heave it at her sister—but something in Tasmin's look caused her to check the impulse. She stood, glared, and finally turned away.

Tasmin hurried upriver, got squarely behind the bushes, stripped, and took a chill but refreshing bath. She had goose bumps all over by the time Buffum finally trailed down the slope with her clothes.

2

Tear his throat out? His Vicky?

Lord Berrybender was nonplussed: Venetia Kennet, long his darling, his pet, his bedmate, mistress, whore, inamorata—a woman whose languid beauty had always quickened his juices, who even employed delicate skills to arouse him when arousal seemed beyond reach—had just flatly refused him. She had made no effort to be polite about it, either. In fact, she had threatened to tear his throat out if he so much as touched her.

Tear his throat out? His Vicky? Of course, when he approached her she happened to be sitting by the grave of her lover, Drum Stewart, whose unfortunate death at the hands of the Utes had caused her much grief. But then, Lord B.'s own son Bobbety had perished too. Bobbety had not, perhaps, been very imposing, yet he might have led a mild life of some sort, collecting fossils and looking up Latin names for butterflies or shrubs. But Bobbety was dead, and Drum Stewart was dead, but he himself was not dead, nor was Vicky, whose long white body he had enjoyed so often. Wasn't life for the living? Mustn't it be lived to the hilt? He was not getting younger—it was no time to allow the juices of love to dry up. It occurred to Lord B. that his hearing was no longer as keen as it had been—perhaps he had misheard his lively friend, whose face seemed suddenly red with anger—but why?

"What was that you were saying, my lovely dear?" he asked, hoping a compliment would help.

"I said I'd tear your throat out if you touch me," Vicky said, in icy tones.

"But Vicky, think for a minute—let's not be rash," Lord Berrybender replied—sweet reason had never been exactly his métier, but he thought he might try it, for once. His experience, after all, was considerable—there had been hundreds of copulations, in several countries; women had been angry with him before, perhaps even violently angry. The Gypsy woman in Portugal, perhaps? The fiery Neapolitan countess who kept a dagger in her undergarments? Would either of them have offered to tear his throat out? Lord B. could not be sure, though he felt quite certain that his good wife, Lady Constance, would never have threatened such a thing. For one thing, though not entirely devoid of temperament, Lady Constance had been singularly inept—she would not have known how to begin to tear a man's throat out. The most Constance had ever done was whack at him feebly with the fly swat when he awakened her too quickly with copulation in mind. No, the worst that could be said of Lady Constance was that after the fourteenth child she had become sadly less ardent; in many cases, if she had too much laudanum and her usual bottle or two of claret, she even dozed off while they were copulating, leaving him to labor to a lonely conclusion. Sometimes, in fact, Constance had even been known to snore while he was laboring, a rather deflating thing for a husband to have to put up with. Their tupping took at most ten minutes—was it asking too much of a wife that she stay awake for such a modest interval? Lord Berrybender didn't think so, but Lady Constance was beyond persuasion or complaint. Her snores became habitual, which is one reason he had transferred the bulk of his attentions to the tall cellist with the long white legs and the raspberry teats in the first place. And yet this same Vicky, a mother now, her breasts heavy with milk but her legs still just as long, had threatened to tear his throat out, though as far as he could see, she had nothing to tear it out with, only her cello and its bow. It occurred to him that the bow did bear watching—he himself had accidentally poked one of Bobbety's eyes out with a turning fork. He was in the American West mainly for the hunting—he could not easily spare an eye.

Prudently, Lord Berrybender retreated a step, meaning to fend her off with his crutch if she came at him suddenly.

"Now, now, Vicky—I've a tough old throat after all," he told her. "You've not got a pair of scissors in your pocket, now have you? You've not got a knife, I hope?"

By way of answer Vicky bared her strong white teeth and clicked them at him menacingly, ending the performance with a hiss loud enough to give Lord B. a start.

"I've got these teeth," she said. "It's only one vein I'd need to nip, and out would pour your lifeblood. Surely Your Lordship has seen a seamstress nipping a thread. A good sharp nip at the jugular and it's done."

Lord Berrybender was shocked, so shocked that for a moment he felt quite faint. His dead son, Bobbety, lay buried not twenty feet away, and yet his sweet Vicky, so delicate in her strokings, had threatened to go for his throat.

It was all so topsy-turvy, this new world he had blundered into; perhaps it was the fault of democracy or some other American sloppiness. Vicky, for all her musical gifts, was merely a servant girl. He now began to see that democracy might indeed be the problem—didn't the system actually encourage servants to forget their place? Hadn't his own cook threatened to leave him and take a position with Pierre Boisdeffre? Hadn't the gunsmith and the carriage maker simply walked away one night, while on a hunt, as if they had every right to please themselves? Of course, the Mediterraneans had come back and Cook in the end had stayed in his service; and yet Cook *had* threatened, and now here was Vicky exhibiting violent defiance.

"I know just where that vein throbs, Your Lordship," Vicky declared, in chillingly level tones. "There you'd be, rutting for all your worth, and not three inches from my teeth that big vein would be throbbing. One nip, I've often told myself—one nip and the old brute is dead and I shall never have to be so bored again."

"Here now, that's damnable, calling me boring!" Lord Berrybender complained. "I fancy I give thorough service, most of the time, though lately I know I've developed rather a tendency to haste. But damn it Vicky! You're acting like a regular Charlotte Corday—kill me in my bath, I suppose—that'll be the next thing!"

"You're safe enough in your bath—but you ain't safe in my bed," Vicky told him bluntly.

"I ought to whack you, you insolent bitch," Lord Berrybender protested. But he didn't whack her—the look in her eye discouraged him. Women, after all, were quick as cats. What if she sprang at him, got her teeth in his neck? A ripped jugular was bad business, not easily repaired. So, instead of delivering several solid slaps, Lord Berrybender turned and made his way up the hill, traveling as fast as he could on an ill-fitting peg leg, a crutch, and half a foot. The more he thought about the matter, the more convinced he became that his analysis of the problem was correct. These damnable American freedoms—this democracy!—were clearly inimicable to sound English order. Democracy could ruin a good servant faster than gin, in his view. Forgotten her place, Vicky had: made threats, gave him mutinous looks; intolerable behavior, on the whole. He meant to speak to Tasmin about it, perhaps get Tasmin to deliver a stern reprimand. Tasmin would defend her old pater, of that Lord Berrybender felt sure. Only, for now, he thought he might just trouble William Ashley for a bit of his excellent champagne; a little bubbly might settle his nerves, which, at the moment, were far from being in a settled state. Tear out his throat, indeed! A shocking thing to hear. In his father's day proud wenches such as Vicky had been flogged at the cart's tail for less—or put in the stocks, where the mob could pelt them with filth. It had been an admirable form of punishment, the stocks. As a boy he had seen plenty of people pelted: low types, criminals, drunken old women. What a pity there were no stocks anymore—Lord B. couldn't think why they had fallen out of favor. They'd be just the thing to correct a proud wench like Vicky. *Then* she'd bend her head; *then* there'd be no talk of tearing out the throats of her superiors. A day or two in the stocks, with the villagers pelting her with rotten eggs and sheep shit, would soon take the sass out of her. Then the silly wench would be happy enough to accommodate him, he supposed—even if, of late, he had developed a tendency to be rather too quick.

3

Among the wild, undomesticated company . . .

Among the wild, undomesticated company of the mountain trappers, it was generally considered that rotund Eulalie Bonneville knew the most about women. Bonney, as he was called, was no mean gambler, besides. None of the mountain men could recall seeing Bonney actually trapping any beaver, much less skinning them out. The icy ponds and streams where the other trappers waded to set their traps did not tempt him— keeping his feet warm was a first principle with Eulalie Bonneville; yet at the end of the season, through a succession of clever trades and successful card games or dice rolls or random bets, he generally trekked out of the mountains with more furs than anyone—and better furs too; and yet his prowess as a fur trader drew considerably less attention from his comrades than his expertise with women—for it was exactly *that* expertise that few of the others could claim, their amours for the most part being brief and drunken wallows with river-town whores or compliant Indian women, engagements seldom free of anxiety, since several of their colleagues had had their scalps lifted as a result of lingering too long in the toils of Venus with dusky maidens. And yet Eulalie Bonneville, as broad as he was tall, was said to have at least one wife in every tribe from the Kaw River to the Marias: Minatarees, Otos, Hidatsas, Teton Sioux, Assiniboines, Shoshones, Pawnees, Cheyennes, and Utes. So far only the women of the Piegan Blackfeet were absent from his scattered harem, a fact old Hugh Glass found curious.

"I'd have thought you'd have taken a Blackfoot wife by now, Bonney," Hugh remarked. Hugh and Joe Walker, the Sublette brothers, and young Jim Bridger were all lounging around camp on this bright morning, the bulk of their trading completed for the summer. The bear cub Abby lay at old Hugh's feet. From time to time all the men directed their glances at the clump of bushes near the river, behind which Tasmin Berrybender was assumed to be bathing her lovely body. The bushes were one hundred yards away—even if Tasmin had chosen to exhibit herself naked, the trappers would not have seen much, and yet they couldn't stop looking.

"I wish I did have a Blackfoot wife," Bonney replied. "Marrying into a tribe is the best way to get a little trade started, but the Blackfoot won't have me."

"I figured that was why you collected all them wives," Joe Walker commented. "It was the trade you were after, I expect."

"I don't despise the trade, but I also happen to like a rut, when I can get it," Bonney admitted.

"So how many wives are you up to, Bonney?" Jim Bridger asked. He himself lacked even one wife, and could not but be envious of the chubby trader's progress.

"An even dozen, unless some of my Missouri River wives have died," Eulalie admitted. "I fancy I could handle about twenty wives, if I could keep them spread out well enough."

Just then Tasmin and her sister Bess, both fully clothed, stepped out from behind the distant bushes. Tasmin bent for a moment to shake the water out of her wet hair.

"Now there's a wife and a half, I'd say," Hugh Glass remarked. "Too dern much of a wife for that young whelp Jimmy Snow."

None of the mountain men spoke. Several of them, in their mind's eye, had been imagining Tasmin naked; she *wasn't* naked, but the trappers were reluctant to let go of the exciting images they had been constructing. All of them considered that it had been Tasmin alone who saved Pomp Charbonneau. She had beaten back death, a rare thing. She had also scared the pants off William Ashley by cursing him, and Ashley, though a rich man now, had weathered several desperate Indian fights. One and all, the trappers admired Tasmin; many wondered how it had been possible for a shy fellow like Jimmy Snow to get her to marry him. Kit Carson, of course, was head over heels in love with her, and many of the other trappers a little in love too, and yet her close approach made them nervous. Now here she was, walking up the slope, right toward them, stopping from time to time to squeeze more water out of her wet hair, the droplets making tiny rainbows in the sunlight.

"What do you think, Mr. Twelve Wives Bonneville?" old Hugh asked. "Think you could handle that much of a wife?"

Bonney, as it happened, was deeply smitten with Tasmin, yet he felt a shy uncertainty overwhelm him when she came near or spoke to him. That the mountain men considered him an expert on women did not displease him; but of course, there were women and women. A Minataree girl or a Ute girl might be one thing, Lady Tasmin quite another.

"She's married to Jimmy—I don't think about her," he replied, a comment that drew skeptical looks from several of the trappers. Abby left Hugh Glass's side and went scampering down the slope to meet Tasmin.

"Them grizzlies are growing fast," Joe Walker observed. "I expect they'll eat a few of us, one of these days."

"Suppose Jimmy Snow got his scalp lifted," Hugh Glass remarked. "That girl'd be a widow. Would you court her then, Bonney?"

"I've always been cautious of Englishwomen," Bonney remarked, vaguely. "Besides, I hear the old lord means to make for Santa Fe—myself, I favor the North."

Tasmin, meanwhile, passed within a few feet of the group—she was complaining to Buffum that, once again, her husband had left without troubling to tell her good-bye.

"You *were* rather intent on Pomp, Tassie," Bess reminded her. "I expect Mr. Snow was loath to interrupt."

"He's your brother-in-law, you don't need to call him Mr. Snow," Tasmin said. "Jim's his name, and his habit is to leave when he wants to leave—the rest of us must muddle along as best we can."

She glanced at the mountain men, all of them still as statues and as silent as judges.

"You gentlemen seem rather subdued," she remarked. "I thought you all came here to get drunk and make merry."

The mountain men looked at one another sheepishly. One or two shrugged. Finally Jim Bridger decided to venture a word or two.

"We're all married out," he admitted. "I've 'bout danced my legs off, as it is."

Tasmin did remember hearing a good deal of fiddle playing and general carousing while she was waiting in the tent with Pomp.

"This year's party's about over," Hugh Glass allowed. "Time to get back to the trapping, pretty soon"—a remark which drew from young Bill Sublette a gloomy look. A sociable man, he did not look forward to lonely times along distant rivers.

"There won't be no more parties in the Valley of the Chickens," Joe Walker said. "Ashley says he's done—not enough peltries to make it worth coming this far."

"So this is the end of the big rendezvous, I suppose," Hugh Glass remarked.

There the talk stopped. The men seemed suddenly overcome by gloom at the thought that the free life in the high Rockies—a life made possible by an abundance of fur-bearing animals—might be finished, its end come before their end.

Tasmin and Buffum walked on.

"Taciturn brutes, these mountain men," she said. "It's all I can do to get one to speak."

"It's because you're so blunt, Tassie," Buffum said. "No one is so blunt as you. I fear it scares the menfolk."

"Piffle—I suppose it's just because I don't bill and coo," Tasmin replied. "The male is generally insufficient, wouldn't you say? They all seem to be weak with women."

"Here's Papa, scuttling up the slope," Buffum announced. "I wonder why he's in such a hurry."

"Probably Vicky refused him," Tassie guessed. "Her lover's barely cold in the ground. I don't imagine she wants Papa pawing her just now."

"He'll wear her down, though," Buffum said. "He knows her ways."

"I say, wait a bit, Tasmin!" Lord Berrybender demanded, with a wave. Struggling up the slope on crutch and peg leg had left him very red in the face.

"Yes, what is it now?" Tasmin asked, impatiently. She had just noticed, to her chagrin, that her patient, Pomp Charbonneau, was no longer on his pallet. Pomp was very weak—she had given him strict orders just to rest, yet there he was, walking slowly toward the enclosure where the captive animals were kept, the creatures that were to have gone to Drummond Stewart's great game park in the north of Scotland.

"I say, girls . . . do wait!" Lord Berrybender stammered, very short of wind. "A very bad thing."

"We know, Father—our brother was killed," Tasmin began, but Lord Berrybender cut her off.

"No, damn it, not *that*—we've got past *that*," he protested. "It's Vicky I must speak to you about."

"Well, and what about her?" Tasmin asked. "She's just grieving—we all are."

"No, no! Will you listen, goddamn you!" Lord B. burst out. "She's crazy. She's lost her mind."

"I doubt it, not unless it's happened since breakfast," Tasmin told him. "I had a good talk with her while we were nursing our babies. She's just in no mood to be bothered by the likes of you—for that matter, neither am I. Pomp's wandered off—I have to go get him, if you'll excuse me."

"Don't give a damn for Pomp!" Lord Berrybender said, grabbing his daughter's arm. "You'll stand and you'll listen. Vicky threatened to tear my throat out. Said she'd do it with her teeth, if I came close. You'll have to chide her, Tassie—deliver a sharp reprimand. Can't have servants threatening to tear their master's throat out. Kind of thing that leads to revolution—all that French misbehavior. She deserves a good flogging, that girl, but if you'll just speak to her sharply, perhaps she'll come to her senses."

Lord B. was squeezing Tasmin's arm quite tightly—he was very red in the face.

"Now Papa, Vicky was probably just upset," Buffum began, but before she could complete her plea, Tasmin dipped her head and gave her father's clutching hand a quick, hard bite; His Lordship gave a cry and immediately released his daughter's arm. Blood at once welled up where Tasmin had bitten him.

Lord Berrybender was too shocked to speak, rather as he had been when Venetia Kennet first delivered her threat—his own daughter had drawn his blood.

"Being the weaker sex, we women have to use such weapons as we possess, when selfish men attempt to interfere with us," Tasmin informed him coldly. "A woman's teeth are not to be taken lightly, as you've now discovered."

"But . . . but . . . ," Lord Berrybender stammered.

"No buts, Father—just leave Vicky alone," Tasmin told him. "And don't be grabbing me when I have urgent business to conduct."

Then she left, leaving a startled Buffum to bandage her father's bleeding bite.

Wounds were given every day . . .

When Tasmin caught up with Pomp she saw to her dismay that there were tears in his eyes. He was fumbling with the rails that enclosed the small pasture where the captive animals grazed: three young elk, several deer, two antelope, four buffalo, and a clumsy young moose calf.

"Will you wait, please! You're not supposed to do that," Tasmin said, with some impatience; she was afraid the wound in his chest might open if he put himself to any strain. But when she saw the tears she regretted her tone.

"Mr. Stewart's dead," Pomp reminded her. "There's no use keeping these animals penned up any longer—they won't be going off to Scotland."

Of course, Pomp was right. Drummond Stewart's frightened horse had carried him right into the invading Utes, where he was immediately killed. The animals he had collected might as well be let go, but dismantling fences was not something Pomp needed to be doing when he was so weak he could barely walk.

Pomp meekly stepped back and let Tasmin take over—it took only a few minutes for her to scatter the light railing that had been keeping the animals in. Two fawns came over and nuzzled Pomp expectantly—sometimes he fed them tidbits, but he had nothing with him today. His own weakness surprised him—he had scarcely walked fifty yards, and yet, on the return, had Tasmin not half carried him, he would have had to sit down and rest.

Wounds were given every day in the West, and yet Pomp himself had never before suffered so much as a scratch; the fevers, pneumonias, and other ailments that carried off so many, including his mother, had so far spared him. He knew, of course, that the Ute's arrow had just missed his heart, and that he was lucky to be alive, and yet he was shocked at how completely he seemed to have lost his strength. His legs wobbled—they never had before. His breathing was shallow—he felt unable to get enough air. He doubted whether he could draw a bow or lift a gun—and yet, only two weeks earlier, he had won two wrestling matches, beating Kit Carson easily and even outlasting the wiry Jim Bridger.

Pomp could tell, from Tasmin's silence, that she was rather vexed with him; but she stuck with her task and got him back to the pallet. He tried to smile at her, but even his facial muscles seemed tired.

"I'm going to insist that you mind me, and mind me strictly, for the next few days," Tasmin said briskly. She had been not only vexed but scared: Pomp's face was ashen—he looked again as though he might die. Fortunately, once he was on the pallet, his color soon improved. Tasmin ceased to be quite so afraid.

"I'm sorry," Pomp said. "I've never been sick before. I guess I don't know how it's done."

"Obey your nurse, that's how it's done," Tasmin said, though his apology caused her to feel less angry. She herself had always enjoyed splendid health; she had never been sick either; but she *had* borne a child, at the end of a long labor, and she too had been surprised at how exceedingly weak the effort left her—she could at first barely hold her own babe, and it was several days before she could walk confidently across a room.

"In a week I'm sure you'll be fine," she told him. "Just don't rush things."

Pomp's tears had spilled over—there were tear tracks on his face which Tasmin longed to wipe away; and yet, for a moment, she didn't. Pomp might take it wrong—indeed, it might *be* wrong, inasmuch as she was a married woman. One touch, in her experience, was apt to lead to another. She felt somewhat perturbed—why had this question even entered her thoughts?

Pomp seemed sobered from his close brush with death.

"If it hadn't been for you and my mother—and of course, Father Geoff— I'd be as dead as Mr. Stewart," he said.

"Your mother?" Tasmin asked in surprise.

Pomp looked abashed—he rarely spoke of his mother, and in fact had few memories to expose. And yet he felt Tasmin might understand.

"My mother comes to me sometimes in dreams," he confessed. "She gives me advice."

Tasmin waited—it seemed he might consider that what he was revealing was too private.

"In the fever I felt like I was flying," Pomp said. "But then my mother would come and I'd come down."

"What did your mother advise, in this instance, if I may ask?" Tasmin asked.

"She called you 'the woman who whispers,'" Pomp said. Weary, he had slumped against Tasmin's shoulder.

"I was whispering to you, trying to keep you alive," Tasmin told him. "I whispered and your mother advised, and it worked, you see: you're alive, though you certainly caused us both a good deal of worry."

"I was only seven when my mother died," Pomp said. "I didn't know her very long."

Then he gave Tasmin a sweet, dependent look.

"Where's Jimmy?" he asked, as if just remembering that Tasmin had a husband.

Tasmin shrugged.

"Gone on a scout, and he took Kit with him, which is annoying," she told him. "Kit Carson is a very obliging fellow—I can always put him to good use."

"It's because he's in love with you that he's obliging," Pomp remarked. "Nobody else can get him to do a thing."

Then he looked at her again.

"I hope I can know you for a long time," he told her quietly.

"I hope so too," Tasmin said. She looked for their water basin but it was not to be seen, so Tasmin quickly licked a finger and wiped the dusty tear tracks off Pomp's cheeks.

"Hold still, mind your nurse, it's just a little spit," Tasmin told him. It was a small thing, quickly done, but very pleasing to her, the briefest intimacy, which Pomp accepted, though his mind was elsewhere.

"I'm more apt to cry for animals than for people," he said.

Yes, they're trusting, like you, Tasmin thought. The spittle had done no real good; Pomp's cheeks were still a dusty smear, so she jumped up, hurried to the tent, and returned with the washbasin, so she could wash her young man properly—for already, in her mind, she thought of Pomp Charbonneau as hers—though exactly in what *sense* he was hers, she could not yet say.

5

Besides the mule, there was Jim.

You've got longer legs than me—you'd be fine on this tall mule," Kit suggested.

"I'm fine enough on Joe Walker's mare," Jim informed him. It struck him as curious that he and Kit got along perfectly well when they were part of a big encampment but could not manage to advance even five miles without quarreling when they were alone. They had hardly left the Valley of the Chickens before Kit had started insisting that they trade mounts, a suggestion that Jim ignored. Joe Walker himself had warned Kit about the tall, ornery mule, but Kit had chosen him anyway. Jim himself was quite comfortably mounted on the same little mare that had carried him so smoothly, in the winter past, from the Knife River to the Green, a feat so singular that now all the mountain men coveted the little bay mare.

Jim did not expect to do anything particularly challenging on this scout with Kit; he mainly wanted to have a look at some of the Platte River country before attempting to lead the Berrybender party to Santa Fe. What he didn't need was for Kit Carson—the scout with the keenest eyesight of any mountain man and thus a valuable asset if one were traveling in the lands of the Sioux—to start complaining about his mount before they had even been a week on the trail.

"I'll give you a dollar if you'll trade," Kit said. He had chosen the mule mainly because it was tall—it pleased him to tower over Jim Snow when they rode; Jim, of course, towered over him when they were afoot. The big mule's trot was so rough that it had already caused Kit to bite his tongue. They had a vast amount of country to explore; Kit didn't relish the thought of exploring it on a mule whose trot was a threat to his tongue.

Besides the mule, there was Jim. In camp with the other boys, Jim—though prone to moods—was fairly easygoing. He didn't feel that he had to work every minute—he might laze around with his beautiful wife and his chubby little boy; or he might listen to Hugh Glass tell lies. Jim didn't yarn much himself, but he liked to listen to yarns. But the minute the two of them started to go somewhere, even if it was just a moose hunt in the

Assiniboine country, Jim Snow became a demon, relentless and unyielding in his aims. He seemed determined to travel far faster than the accepted norm—fifty miles a day was nothing to Jim, though it represented intolerably rapid travel for a man handicapped by a stiff-gaited mule.

"A dollar's as high as I'll go for a switch," Kit said, annoyed that Jim had ignored what he felt was a reasonable, even a generous offer.

"No thanks, I'm comfortable," Jim replied. "You'll just have to put up with that mule until something better comes along."

"How could anything better come along, when we're out here in the middle of nowhere?" Kit asked, vexed but trying not to let it show.

Jim shrugged. "The Sioux and the Pawnee have plenty of horses," he remarked. "If we run into some friendly Indians, maybe you could trade."

"No, if we run into any Indians they won't be friendly—they'll kill us and take *our* horses," Kit replied. On a scout his outlook was invariably pessimistic, besides which he was still bitterly jealous of the fact that Tasmin had married Jim—in Kit's view the only possible explanation for that union was that Jim was tall. He was unlikely to shrink, either.

"I wouldn't have picked this mule if we hadn't left in such a hurry," Kit pointed out. "You didn't even tell your own wife good-bye, which is rude behavior, in my book."

"She was trying to save Pomp—I hope she saved him," Jim replied. "If I'd told her I was leaving she'd just argue—she always argues when I decide to go someplace. If Tasmin had to take time off to fuss, she might have lost Pomp, and that wouldn't be good.

"When it's time to go, it's better just to go," he added.

Kit's patience, already sorely tried, was further exacerbated by this reply. If he were married to Tasmin he would certainly take the trouble to say good-bye when he left.

"What would it take to get you to switch mounts, you fool!" Kit asked, in hot exasperation.

"Stop pestering me—I ain't switching," Jim said. He glanced at Kit and saw that he was swollen up like a Tom turkey. If they had been on the ground a fistfight would have been hard to avoid, but fortunately, they were mounted. Jim put his heels into the little mare, who had an easy lope, and went on ahead.

Kit's mule, unlike the mare, lacked an easy lope—in fact, had no true lope at all; he seemed to possess only three gaits, rather than the usual four, though it was true that he could sometimes be coaxed into a gait that was just short of a dead run—a "high lope" was what Joe Walker called it. It was difficult to get the mule, whose name was Brantly, into this high lope, and even more difficult, once he was in it, to keep him from accelerating into a dead run—so the high lope had almost no practical value. The hard trot was Brantly's preferred gait, the very mode of travel that had already caused Kit to bite his tongue.

Now there went Jim, loping off on his little mare, as comfortable as if he were rocking in a hammock. Kit reminded himself again that he was a fool ever to travel with Jim Snow, since when he did, he invariably got the worst of it. Annoyed, he deliberately held Brantly to a slow, stately walk, which meant that Jim Snow was soon little more than a dot on the prairie, so far ahead that he could be of no use at all if an emergency arose.

Then Jim ceased to be visible, even as a distant dot—Kit was alone on the great gray plain, just the kind of circumstance in which his pessimism was apt to get the better of him. First he might just feel generally low; then he would begin to imagine various ways in which death might come, in which regard Indians usually came to mind first and grizzly bears second. Indians were so good at hiding that they could be hard to spot even on a bare plain: up they'd jump, with their lances and hatchets, and be on him before he could even spur his mule. Grizzly bears too were wily stalkers, able to creep within a few feet of their unsuspecting prey. Kit didn't suppose that his renowned ability to see farther than anyone else would be much help to him in a crisis, since crises usually happened close to hand. Though it pained Kit to admit it, Jim Snow had superior instincts when it came to sensing trouble, and he was very quick to act. After all, it had been Jim who killed the Indian who had wounded Pomp—killed him so cleanly that the man had not had time to yell for reinforcements.

So now what had Jim done? He had ridden off and left Kit aboard a mule nobody liked, with a gun that was unreliable. Kit was about to put Brantly in a high lope, in an effort to catch up, when—as if to prove his point—the old Indian appeared. One moment the plain was empty, and the next minute there the man was, standing over what appeared to be a dead horse. A swell of the prairie had concealed him. Kit grabbed his rifle but then realized the Indian was only old Greasy Lake, a harmless prophet who was apt to show up anywhere there was a gathering of any size, in hopes of delivering a prophecy or two in exchange for presents. Faintly, over the prairie breeze, Kit could hear the old man chanting. He spread his arms to the heavens and shuffled around the horse, which turned out to be not quite dead after all. Now and then Kit saw the horse raise his head, though it made no move to get up. The horse, if it was Greasy Lake's same old nag, was as famous in prairie circles as its master. Mountain men who had first seen the animal twenty-five years earlier and had not supposed it could last a week were astonished to discover that the spavined old nag still hadn't died. Efforts to figure out how old the horse might be revealed only that it had very good teeth for an animal that had been alive so long.

Kit thought he might as well investigate—it was better than riding on alone, thinking gloomy thoughts. At first Greasy Lake, who, as usual, was in a kind of trance, paid no attention to Kit at all. He was rattling some kind of rattle as he chanted and shuffled. Kit politely drew rein; he didn't want to interrupt a religious ceremony. Perhaps Greasy Lake was singing his trusty mount a death song—giving him a proper send-off. To Kit's astonishment the old horse twitched an ear, lifted its head, and slowly got to its feet. Greasy Lake at once stopped chanting. He tucked his rattle into a little pouch he carried and got ready to mount his horse.

"I wouldn't do that, Greasy," Kit advised. "That horse will die for sure if you put any weight on him."

"He's a strong horse," Greasy Lake assured him. "I just have to sing to him in the mornings, to get him up. He's a horse who likes to sleep late."

"That horse is older than me," Kit replied.

The horse did shiver a bit when Greasy Lake climbed on top of him, but no longer seemed to be about to die.

"That horse beats all," Kit remarked. "If I thought he had a year left in him I'd trade for him and let you have this expensive mule."

Greasy Lake ignored that remark—he was not such a fool as to trade for a stiff-gaited mule. It annoyed Kit that he had chosen a mule that not even this old prophet would take. No one had ever been able to pin down quite what tribe Greasy Lake belonged to—his age, like his horse's, was also hard to calculate. He claimed to be the cousin of various powerful chiefs, but no one could be sure of the truth of anything he said. Because it was his habit to wander constantly over the West, he was known to everyone, from the Columbia River to the Rio Grande. No tribe claimed him, yet no tribe turned him away.

"Where are you bound for now?" Kit asked—at least the old fellow was usually good for a little conversation.

"I am on my way to see the Partezon—he is my cousin," Greasy Lake replied. "He doesn't like me but I don't think he'll kill me."

The Partezon, war chief of the Brulé Sioux, was the most feared Indian in the West. It was the Partezon who had destroyed the steamboat the Berrybenders had been traveling on, once it got stuck in the ice above the Knife River. Fortunately Jim Snow had led most of the party overland to Pierre Boisdeffre's trading post on the Yellowstone, but Captain George Aitken, several passengers, and a number of *engagés* had been cruelly butchered up.

"I've heard that old Partezon's mean," Kit said.

"He is not friendly," Greasy Lake admitted. "But now I am on my way to look for some white people who can fly. All the tribes are looking for them. I am going to see the Partezon to see if he knows about these flying men. They fly in a little basket attached to some kind of cloud."

Kit wanted to laugh—white people couldn't fly. Probably the old prophet had gone a little daft.

"I've never seen a white person who could fly," he remarked. "Where are these fellows supposed to be?"

"They are flying over the Platte," Greasy Lake said. "If we watch we might see them."

"How close are we to the Partezon's camp?" Kit asked—even mention of the old warrior's name caused the prairies to take on an aspect of menace—and now Jim Snow was nowhere to be seen.

"The Partezon is always moving," Greasy Lake said vaguely. "He may have gone to see the Bad Eye, to ask him to make a spell that will cause these flying white people to fall out of the sky."

Kit had never seen the Bad Eye, an old, huge, gross shaman of the Gros Ventres—he lived near the Missouri River, in a dwelling called the Skull Lodge, the whole top of which was covered with buffalo skulls. Blind from birth, the Bad Eye was said to have hearing so acute that he could identify different kinds of flies just by their buzzing. He was now so fat that he could no longer stand up; when he needed information about some distant happening, he relied on a dark woman named Draga, thought to be a powerful witch and known to be a cruel torturer who had sent many captives to painful deaths, pouring boiling water over them in a mockery of baptism if they were priests, or draping them in ringlets of white-hot hatchets if they were traders who had not been judicious in the distribution of gifts. Bess Berrybender had briefly been Draga's captive and had suffered many cruelties before she could be ransomed.

Kit hardly knew what to believe about this story of the flying white men—it sounded like a wild lie, but he was experienced enough in the ways of the wilderness to know that it was unwise to entirely disregard the ravings of old prophets, a few of whom actually had powers whites didn't possess. When they were camped in the Valley of the Chickens, the Berrybenders still had their old parrot, Prince Talleyrand, who muttered a few words in the German language one day while Greasy Lake was within hearing. Greasy Lake had announced to all the mountain men that the old bird would be dead within the week. Sure enough, less than a week later, a Ute warrior, come to trade, showed up with the head of Prince Talleyrand, which he said he found under a tree—a badger had evidently carried off the rest of the tough old bird.

The fact that Greasy Lake had predicted the demise of the parrot so accurately convinced Kit that he ought to think twice before rejecting the old man's prophecies. It occurred to him, as he walked Brantly slowly along beside the old man's decrepit horse, that there could even be something to this rumor of white men who could fly. He had forgotten about balloons. He himself, in his last visit to Saint Louis, had attended a kind of fair in which a magician of some sort went quite a ways up in the air beneath a hot-air balloon. The balloon went higher than any church steeple in town, but the trick had ended badly when a wind came up and blew the balloonist over toward the Mississippi; when the man finally descended, he plopped straight down into the mudflats and emerged covered with mud. Nonetheless he *had* flown, riding beneath the balloon in a basket of some sort. Greasy Lake, not being a city dweller, had never witnessed a balloon ascent—what he took to be a cloud was probably the balloon itself, but of course that didn't explain why people with the ability to make a balloon go up would want to fly it over the Partezon's country, where there could be few paying customers and a fair chance of being subjected to serious tortures. Could the balloon have been blown off course, as in the case of the Saint Louis magician? After all, a flying basket with some silk puffed up above it could not be particularly easy to control. Maybe the balloonist had had the bad luck to be blown into the Partezon's hunting territory.

One result of having to think all this through for himself was that Kit became even more annoyed with Jim Snow for leaving just at a time when two heads might have been better than one.

"Aren't you with the Sin Killer? I thought I saw the tracks of that little mare of his yesterday," Greasy Lake inquired.

"I was with him, but he's gone off—we'll be lucky if we catch up with him in a week," Kit said.

He had no sooner said it than he was made to feel foolish—Greasy Lake was pointing at something.

"I don't think it will take that long," he said. "Isn't that him skinning an antelope, over by those rocks? He must have killed the antelope with an arrow. I didn't hear a shot."

Sure enough, there was Jim, plain as day—Kit had been looking in every direction but the right one.

"It looks like a young antelope—young and tender. We'll have a good supper," Greasy Lake said.

Of course, it was just like this old rascal to invite himself to the feast—Kit supposed Jim would be annoyed when presented with a guest.

"There's some men out here flying—I suspect they've got a hot-air balloon," Kit blurted, when they arrived. He hoped this startling news would distract Jim from the fact that he had arrived with an uninvited guest.

But Jim Snow, to Kit's surprise, smiled at the old shaman.

"Get down, Uncle, and rest your horse," he said. "We got fresh meat."

The remark stumped Kit completely. He had seen Jim chatting with the old fellow once or twice when they were camped at the rendezvous, but had never supposed Jim was *that* friendly with him.

"How'd he get to be your uncle?" Kit asked, when he dismounted.

"He kept me from starving when I was with the Osage," Jim told him. "So I adopted him, once I got grown."

"I never knew that," Kit said, in a reproachful tone.

"No, but I could fill a barrel with things you don't know," Jim remarked.

"Your friend almost rode past me," Greasy Lake said. "My horse was laying down at the time."

"He's got good eyesight but sometimes he don't pay attention," Jim allowed, with some amusement in his look. "He could be building a fire right now, so we could cook this meat, but I guess he's feeling sleepy because I don't see no fire."

"I just got here," Kit pointed out, annoyed. Jim Snow was every bit as bad as his sometime tent mate Jim Bridger; both of them seemed to feel that he had been put on earth expressly to do their chores.

Greasy Lake was not listening to this irritating palaver. He was giving the antelope skin a close examination.

"I can use this skin, if you don't need it," he said. "My old pouch is wearing out. I could make a nice new one with this good piece of skin."

Kit looked around at the bare prairie—he was beginning to wish he had had the good sense to stay with the big group in the Valley of the Chickens, where he would at least have had the beautiful Tasmin to look at. His gloomy feeling was getting worse—there was Jim Snow, an unbending kind of fellow, expecting him to build a fire in a place where there were very few sticks lying around. Of course, there were quite a few buffalo chips, but they yielded a poor grade of fuel, in his view.

"Greasy's off to see the Partezon," Kit informed Jim.

But Jim, still busy with his butchering, didn't seem to hear, so Kit, in a lonely mood, took a sack and wandered off to see if he could collect the makings of a fire.

6

The day had begun hopefully, too.

Benjamin Hope-Tipping, tall and thin, did not much like the looks of the old Indian on the white horse, the one their interpreter, the youth Amboise d'Avigdor, insisted was the dreaded Partezon. Ben looked at his colleague, Clam de Paty, a man who usually bubbled over with French witticisms; he saw that Clam was not bubbling at the moment. And the boy Amboise was plainly terrified.

The day had begun hopefully, too. Clam, something of a dandy, put on his red pants; they had each had a snort of cognac to wake themselves up. Amboise d'Avigdor, a skilled chef, had poached them several plovers' eggs, which they had with bacon and some of the flat bread Amboise baked in profusion whenever they were stopped long enough to allow him to construct a Dutch oven. A fine breeze was blowing, which helped with the gnats and mosquitoes. For a time he and Clam, each on their old palfreys, had ridden along happily, composing articles in their heads for their respective newspapers. Ben Hope-Tipping had just been composing a few paragraphs about hominy, a dish not then known in Europe; whereas Clam, who had been kept awake part of the night by the roaring of buffalo bulls from a herd of many thousands nearby their camp, was attempting to describe, for his Parisian readership, what the roaring of these bulls, angry in their rut, sounded like on a prairie summer night. The two of them discussed whether it might be worthwhile to include a few notes about burial scaffolds—European readers were always apt to be interested in the burial customs of savage peoples.

Their balloon and all their gear was stored efficiently in a small wagon, driven by Amboise d'Avigdor, who, in the weeks they had been traveling, had become an expert packer. If one of the surly wagon horses didn't kick him, Amboise could have the wagon packed and ready in a commendably short time. Of course, one reason Amboise could have the wagon packed in such a short time was that he had become increasingly reluctant to unpack anything at night. They had scarcely left Plattesmouth when Amboise began to argue against the necessity of linen tablecloths and other common amenities, matters which Ben and Clam had long been in the habit of taking for granted.

"No, messieurs, tablecloths are quite unnecessary out here," Amboise informed them, on only the second day out. "Quite unnecessary. Nothing is more likely to cause savages to attack than the sight of a white tablecloth."

"Surely you jest, monsieur," Clam had remonstrated—he hardly proposed to abandon the habits of a lifetime, one of which was to dine off white tablecloths—because of the whims of savages. Liberties might be permitted at breakfast, but dinner, to a Frenchman, was a sacrament.

"I fear I am unwilling to go native quite to that extent," Clam went on, giving young Amboise a look of such severity that Ben Hope-Tipping supposed the matter to be at an end. He himself felt the same extreme unwillingness to lower his standards, which were no more than the standards of any proper civilization. He was not about to betray his convictions by rashly dispensing with tablecloths.

Nonetheless, Amboise d'Avigdor soon had his way, dropping, as they plodded along, whatever linen he felt disposed to dispense with off the back of the wagon; by the time Ben and Clam discovered this treachery, the tablecloths were gone and many of the heavy napkins as well.

"No napkins—we should kill this boy!" the indignant Clam exclaimed. "How does he suppose we are to wipe our faces?"

"Patience, Clam—I don't think we should kill him just *now*, just *here!*"

Ben argued. They were in the middle of a vast prairie, hundreds of miles from any settlement. Matters were inconvenient enough, what with the flies and mosquitoes, and no tablecloths and few napkins; but it was certain that matters would be even more inconvenient if they lost Amboise. They were, at present, in no position to dismiss, much less execute, an insubordinate servant, vexing as the silly creature undoubtedly was.

The necessity of somehow tolerating Amboise d'Avigdor was almost immediately driven home to the two Europeans—Amboise himself being Canadian—by the abrupt and quite menacing arrival of the Partezon and his highly painted band. A Brulé Sioux named Hollow Foot, returning from a vision quest, had happened to notice a trail of white cloths on the prairie. Hollow Foot had hastened over to the Partezon's village to inform him of this phenomenon. The Partezon, who considered it his duty to protect the Holy Road—to the whites merely the route along the Platte—was not indifferent to this information. In fact he gave Hollow Foot a nice young wife, for being so good as to make a prompt report. The Partezon paused only long enough to allow his young warriors to paint themselves appropriately. He himself rarely bothered with paint now, but he was happy enough that the boys of the tribe kept to the old traditions.

Even without the trail of white cloths it was a simple matter to track and overtake the travelers, who were possessed of a slow, heavy cart whose tracks were easily followed. When the Sioux spotted the three travelers, the young warriors wanted to race down and hack them to pieces—it seemed to the Partezon that half his energies as a leader were needed just to restrain the young. Being young, they had little patience with well-planned ambushes or mature battle plans. The young just wanted to strike, and would have under a lesser war chief; but when the Partezon rode with them, they behaved themselves; he had demonstrated many times that he meant to have obedience. Riding with the Partezon was the greatest honor a Sioux warrior could have, but it was also an honor that could be quickly withdrawn.

The fact that thirty savages seemingly popped out of nowhere and surrounded them came as a considerable shock both to Ben Hope-Tipping and to Clam de Paty. The shock did not serve to increase their already shaky confidence in their interpreter, young Amboise d'Avigdor.

"I thought you were supposed to know how to deal with Indians," Hope-Tipping complained, once it became evident that the red men in the war paint were not going to allow them to advance another inch.

"Well, I do possess some expertise," Amboise said. "I know, for example, that these men are Brulé Sioux and that their leader—that's the man on the white horse—is the dreaded Partezon."

"Still, it's quite rude of him to arrive unannounced," Ben pressed. "He seems unwilling to let us pass—why is that? Free country, America, I was led to believe."

"I suppose they've merely come for their presents," Clam de Paty remarked. "Give them a few fishhooks and a few handfuls of beads."

"Yes, quite—that should make them happy," Ben said.

"It *won't* make them happy, monsieur," Amboise remarked, emphatically.

"But why not? They're excellent beads and very effective fishhooks," Ben insisted. "I caught a fish with one of them myself."

"Don't you remember, messieurs, what I told you about the Partezon—he's not your ordinary savage," Amboise insisted.

"Oh, do remind me," Ben allowed.

"Remind *us*," Clam put in. "What's so special about this old fellow?"

"He's the one who sewed Lord Berrybender's butler into a buffalo, chopping off his feet when they extruded," Amboise reminded them.

"Oh, so he's *that* rascal—very regrettable incident," Ben remarked. He and Clam had heard the story of Lord Berrybender's unfortunate butler many times—it was a staple of saloon conversation as far east as Cincinnati. Evidently the valet, Gladwyn, thought to be of Welsh descent, had been left behind on a hunt. He survived the chill of a prairie blizzard by huddling near a dying buffalo cow—when some natives, Sans Arcs in this case, discovered the man, he was so covered with buffalo blood that the foolish natives, in their innocence, supposed that the cow had actually given birth to him. For a time this notion was accepted and the Welsh valet had become a kind of village god; but there were doubters, one of whom was the Partezon, who ordered a buffalo cow to be killed, into whose belly the unfortunate valet was promptly sewn. The Partezon reasoned that if the man were a god he could easily slip out again, but of course he was merely Lord Albany Berrybender's butler, and he couldn't slip out, and in any case was soon dying from loss of blood.

Ben and Clam had discussed this terrible incident many times, agreeing that the fault lay mainly with Lord Berrybender, for being casual with his servants. No responsible Englishman would have left a well-trained valet out all night in such uncertain weather.

"So that's the brute, is it?" Ben said, squinting at the Partezon. He was beginning to feel distinctly nervous.

"If he doesn't want presents, what *does* the gentleman want?" Clam de Paty inquired. "We can't stop here forever."

Clam de Paty had his full share of Gallic impatience—lengthy negotiations with savages put him in a sulky temper.

"But we *might* stay here forever, because he might kill us," Amboise informed them, in a shaky voice. "You see, he *wants* to kill us, probably after a session of fiendish torture."

"Now, now, young man, really," Ben told him. "Neither Clam nor I are in any mood to be tortured this morning. Please tell Mr. Partezon that."

"I dare not! It will make it worse!" Amboise insisted.

What a vexation this will be to our employers, if we succumb, Ben thought. Many of the warriors simply bristled with edged weapons—lances, hatchets, arrows. Their own weapons, two rifles and a fowling piece, were safely tucked away in the wagon, their precise location known only to Amboise d'Avigdor.

"We must use the balloon," Clam said.

He turned to Amboise.

"Tell them we can fly," he said. "They won't expect to hear it—and besides, it's true."

Amboise d'Avigdor did as instructed. The Partezon remained unmoved, but a great hubbub arose among the warriors.

"That's a handy thought, Clam," Ben remarked. "I suppose we had best unpack our balloon."

"When white people are cornered they'll say anything," the Partezon said, addressing himself to old Fool's Bull, a warrior with much experience.

"Sans Arcs made fools of themselves by claiming that little white man came out of a buffalo," Fool's Bull reminded him. "You and I knew better, of course."

"Do you think these white men can fly?" the Partezon asked.

"Of course not," Fool's Bull said. "Don't be toying with me. I am not a Sans Arc."

The Partezon instructed the young interpreter to tell the two men to go ahead and fly, if they wanted to. Amboise explained that it would be necessary to build a fire first, and unpack a certain amount of equipment.

"They want to warm up their wings," the Partezon remarked to Fool's Bull, who shrugged.

"We need to build a fire anyway, in order to torture them," Fool's Bull said. "Let them build it, if they want to."

"I am not going to torture them here—we'll do that in the camp," the Partezon said. "The people will be annoyed if we don't provide a captive or two. It's selfish to torture them all by ourselves, though I suppose we might singe them a little."

"Okay, I wash my hands of it," Fool's Bull said. "Do as you please—you always do anyway."

"Don't be so cranky," the Partezon said.

While the young interpreter built a good fire the other white men unpacked a kind of vast blanket from the wagon and spread it on the ground, tying it to a kind of basket with several ropes. It amused the Partezon to see what desperate stratagems white people came up with when they were in trouble, though claiming the ability to fly was a new one to him.

Ben and Clam did not allow young Amboise to help with their balloon. Amboise was always ripping things. Ben and Clam—internationally recognized balloon journalists—could not afford mistakes; a leaky balloon meant no end of trouble. They got out their bellows and prepared to inflate their balloon, watched by the curious Indians.

Though the Partezon didn't like whites and didn't want his people to be corrupted by a dependence on the various goods they produced, he recognized that the whites were very ingenious when it came to tools and gadgets. Their weapons were excellent. He himself had a fine rifle that he had taken off a dead captain, but he rarely shot it, or even showed it, lest his people become dependent on the gun and lose their high skill with the bow—a skill that was essential if they were to continue in the old ways, the ways of their fathers, who had flourished with no reliance on white men's goods.

To the Partezon's surprise, the whites didn't make their fire on the ground—they made it in a kind of metal pot—then, using some kind of bellows, they began to pump hot air into the great silk blanket they had spread on the ground. To the consternation of the young warriors, the cloth began to swell, moving as if a great beast of some kind were inside it. This unexpected development frightened some of the young men considerably, but the Partezon gave them a stern look.

The white men pumped and pumped until gradually the great silk cloth assumed a kind of round shape and began to rise off the prairie—it reminded the Partezon a little of the floats boys sometimes made from buffalo bladders, floats they clung to as they frolicked in the river.

But the great sphere that was rising above the white man's basket was no small float. Suddenly a great air beast of some kind had risen above them, tethered, for the moment, to some stakes the whites had driven into the ground.

The young warriors were becoming very nervous. What if a great bird emerged and tried to carry them away? The Partezon looked at them with contempt, but he didn't speak. If the boys were such cowards, then let them go—he would deal with them later.

Soon the great air beast was straining at the ropes that held it.

"I believe we're ready," Clam said, checking the lines that tied the balloon to the basket.

"We're ready," Ben agreed. "Do try to keep us in sight, Amboise—we'll hope to alight somewhere beside this river."

But Amboise d'Avigdor was shaking and shivering.

"You wouldn't leave me, would you, sir?" he asked Ben. "I won't last long, if you do. I feel quite sure the Partezon will kill me most painfully, if I'm left."

"Nonsense," Ben said firmly—at such times firmness was always the best policy. The young fellow merely needed to buck up.

"Now, now, none of that," Clam said. "Someone has to bring the wagon and lead our palfreys. And that, after all, is your job, my boy."

"Besides, the basket only holds two, plus a few provisions, of course," Ben reminded the terrified interpreter.

Amboise d'Avigdor, seeing that the case was hopeless, said no more. His masters, the Englishman and the Frenchman, clambered into their basket and gestured to him to unloose the ropes that kept the balloon pegged to its stakes. Amboise, moving like the dead man he now considered himself to be, did as directed—performing a last duty, as he saw it.

As soon as it was released the balloon rose gracefully, fifty feet, a hundred feet, higher and higher.

This was too much for the young warriors of the Brulé Sioux, convinced that a great bird would soon swoop down on them, ignoring the wagon filled with treasures, ignoring Amboise d'Avigdor, even ignoring the Partezon.

Only the Partezon and old Fool's Bull held their ground. Soon they could barely see the faces of the two men in the basket. More from curiosity than anger the Partezon notched an arrow and shot it at the two men in the basket. His strength with the bow had always been legendary among the People—he could drive an arrow completely through a running buffalo if he chose; this time he used his full strength, yet his arrow barely reached the basket, high above them. It hung for a moment and then fell back to earth.

"The time of the People is over," the Partezon said, to Fool's Bull. In his heart he felt bitter chagrin. His lifelong discipline and rigor, all his efforts to protect the People from a weakening dependence on the white man's goods, would now be for naught. The white men, in this instance, had not made a false claim: they said they could fly and they were flying. He had been looking forward to a jolly time, torturing the two flyers and the young man too, but in the face of what he had just seen, it all seemed pointless. The white men, after all, were superior, not in heart but in invention. Many of the People were brave, but none of them could fly.

The balloon, now very high, rode the strong wind that was blowing from the east—already the two flyers were well on their way toward the setting sun. The great air beast was moving through the sky, it seemed to Fool's Bull, almost as fast as the great geese moved. Soon the balloon would be out of sight.

"I don't know why you think the time of the People is over," Fool's Bull said, though without much conviction. "It's just two men."

"Oh, there will be some battles yet," the Partezon told him. "We will win some and the whites will win some. But we can't fly, and they can. Who do you think will win in the end? They can rain down fire on our villages— maybe they could even run off the buffalo."

Amboise d'Avigdor scarcely dared move. All the young Sioux had run away—only the two old men remained, but one of the old men was the Partezon. It seemed to Amboise that if he could just stay still enough, he might be allowed to live, after all. He stood as if planted; he tried not to shake; he even took care to breathe quietly.

The Partezon dismounted and picked up his arrow. It seemed to Fool's Bull that he looked older; he looked as some warriors looked when suddenly faced with defeat.

"Do you want me to kill this boy?" Fool's Bull asked. "We could take him—it could be someone to torture."

The Partezon shook his head. He had no interest in the trembling boy, who probably would not last an hour under torture anyway. He had not yet recovered from the shock of seeing the white men fly—what it meant was that the time for idle amusements was over. If the People were to enjoy much more time as free men, certain steps needed to be taken at once, steps that were much more important than torturing a sniveling white boy.

Though reluctant to ignore such an easy victim, Fool's Bull felt it was not the right time to argue with the Partezon, who, no doubt, was disgusted by the cowardice of the young warriors. In such a mood he would not brook argument—he would probably just kill anyone who annoyed him at such a difficult moment.

And yet, Fool's Bull had a fearful feeling—when he was fearful it was hard for him to hold his tongue.

"What will we do?" he asked, in his uncertainty.

The Partezon knew exactly what he wanted to do next—it was something he had had in mind to do ten years earlier but, for various reasons, had delayed.

"We are going to attack the Mandans and the Rees," the Partezon told him firmly. These were the tribes that controlled the Missouri River—they were the tribes that had encouraged the whites to come, bring trade goods, take away furs.

"They are rich and corrupt, those tribes," he went on. "They want all the things the white men bring—guns, cloth, beads, tobacco, whiskey. It's because of them that so many white men came up the river. I should have destroyed both tribes long ago."

It was clear to the Partezon now how he had erred. Foolishly he had let the white men have the river, supposing they would be satisfied with the peltries they got from these weak tribes, these corn Indians, farmers and traders. He had believed the whites would be satisfied with this safe trade and not bother challenging the stronger tribes of the interior—the tribes whose lands two white men were at this very moment flying over. His calculation had been wrong to begin with: even now the whites were trapping in the lands of the Utes and the Shoshones; eventually they would even be strong enough to challenge the Blackfeet. The truth the Partezon now had to face was that the whites were not going to be satisfied until they had all the People's land. They would not be satisfied with the beaver; when those were gone they would want the buffalo. They would want everything—the rivers, the holy mountains, everything. Even now two whites were directing their air beast directly into the heart of his own country. There were only two, at the moment, but there would be more.

Fool's Bull was startled by the Partezon's statement, though he wasn't disturbed at the prospect of war with the Mandans or the Rees, who had long been trading Indians. They didn't produce many good warriors—and yet the thought of attacking the Mandans particularly made him nervous, not from fear of their warriors but from fear of the Bad Eye, the most powerful prophet in the West, a terrible man whose prophecies, some said, could cause earthquakes and floods. There were even some who believed the Bad Eye had the power to raise the dead. What if the Bad Eye summoned an army of skeleton warriors to stand against the Sioux? Even the Partezon, who feared nothing, might quail if he saw an army of skeletons rising out of the earth to fight against him.

"I'm worried about the Bad Eye," Fool's Bull admitted.

"He's blind and he's fat—they say he can no longer stand up," the Partezon said. "Why worry about *him*?"

"Some say he can raise the dead," Fool's Bull reminded him.

The Partezon merely gave Fool's Bull a scornful look.

"Even if he can't raise the dead, he might make a bad prophecy," Fool's Bull insisted.

"If he does, it will be his last prophecy," the Partezon replied. "He can't raise the dead but he might join them."

Amboise d'Avigdor didn't dare move until the two old Indians were almost out of sight. His fear had been so great, his heart pounded so violently, that it was several minutes before he allowed himself to believe that he was safe. He saw his bosses' two gray palfreys, grazing some distance away, and realized that—since he *was* alive—he had better get busy. Though the encounter with the Partezon had scared him out of his wits, there were his duties to attend to, if he didn't want to be cursed or even cuffed when his employers landed. Ben Hope-Tipping and Clam de Paty did not like to be kept waiting. There was cognac and cheese in the balloon's basket, but little else; his bosses would expect dinner when they landed—it occurred to Amboise that the two might drift so far away that he would be unable to find them before dark, a circumstance to be avoided if at all possible. A night without their amenities would make the two of them very angry indeed. And yet, what was the anger of two Europeans compared to the terror he had just faced? Whatever abuse his bosses might heap on him, it would be nothing compared to what the old Partezon might have done.

7

Below them lay the plains . . .

I say, Clam—handy thing, a balloon," Ben remarked, offering his companion a slice of cheese. Below them lay the plains, an endless expanse of gray grass.

"It startled those red fellows no end—got us out of a scrape," he added. "The dreaded Partezon was forced to turn tail. I believe I'll just write up our little encounter."

"I am already writing it up," Clam assured him, closing his notebook for a moment in order to better enjoy the cheese, which had come all the way from Paris. The tiff with the Partezon had been, in his view, merely a nuisance, the sort of thing that was only to be expected in an uncivilized country.

"Hardly know where we'll post our next reports," Ben worried. "Postal facilities rather scarce out here, I imagine."

So far, thanks to traffic along the rivers, the two journalists had been able to forward a steady stream of reports to their respective papers. In Cincinnati they had been feted; in Saint Louis they were able to interview the famous Captain William Clark himself, who gave them much useful instruction, showing them on his big map how to locate the famous Swamp of the Swans and other well-known points of interest. Their last report had been filed from Plattesmouth, which merely meant that they had handed their pages to a trapper who claimed to be headed downriver.

"I wonder if that trapper actually took our little write-ups all the way to Saint Louis," Ben said. "We didn't pay the fellow much. Wouldn't surprise me if he tossed them overboard. He couldn't read, you know—as illiterate as a pig."

"We have copies," Clam reminded him. "Our readers will get them someday. You should be keeping the lookout, Ben."

"Lookout for what?" Ben inquired. "I can see the Platte River, and lots of grass, but I don't for the moment see anything that could count as copy."

"You must keep the close lookout so we don't float over the people we need to interview," Clam reminded him firmly. He felt obliged to speak rather sharply: Hope-Tipping, though a good journalist in his way, could be at times a bit thick, making it necessary not merely to point out the obvious, but to repeat it frequently as well.

"The prince of Weid is here somewhere—I would like to speak to this prince and also to his hunter, Herr Dreidoppel, who is, I believe, from Alsace. Perhaps they will have seen the grizzly bears. Many people in Paris want to know about the grizzly bears."

"Of course—same's true of London," Ben remarked. "All the same, I hope it's this hunter who meets them, and not ourselves."

He peered down, happy to see that the plain below them seemed to be absent of bears.

"I've heard that the prince of Weid is not a particularly interesting fellow," Ben went on. "Thorough in his way, I suppose, but hardly notorious. We'd do better to find the Scotsman Drummond Stewart, or some rich fur trader like William Ashley, or, of course, the Berrybenders, my own countrymen. Rather hard to say where *they* might be.

"Lady Tasmin Berrybender is said to be a very great beauty," he went on. "And they have a rather prominent cellist with them, a Miss Venetia Kennet."

"May be, may be," Clam agreed. "But we must *find* these people before we can write them up. So far we are not finding anybody except these noisy red fellows—that is why you must keep the lookout."

"Of course I *will* look, as best I can," Ben assured his friend. "Shouldn't have indulged in that cognac, though."

"What's wrong with the cognac? I chose it myself," Clam said—he found that he had constantly to defend French taste against the rather slighting ways of the English.

"No insult intended, my man," Ben said at once. "It's just that when I drink and look down I become rather queasy. The stomach threatens to flop, at such moments."

Clam de Paty made no reply; he wore, as was often the case, a slightly aggrieved look.

"Things really are *so* distant in America," Ben continued. "I fear we still have hundreds of miles to go before we can expect to find these intrepid explorers you propose to write up."

"We should have questioned that old savage at more length," Clam suggested. "Asked him about the more popular tortures. People always like to read about tortures, wouldn't you agree?"

"I agree that people love reading about tortures," Ben allowed, "but I'm not sure it would have been wise to raise the subject of tortures with him— he might have been all too willing to give a practical demonstration. They did some rather shocking things to your Jesuits, I believe."

"Look, *les oiseaux!*" Clam said, suddenly pointing to a flock of very large birds, flapping toward them from the north.

"Why, so they are," Ben said. "What a pity our ornithological books are all in the wagon. What would you say they are, Clam? Herons, perhaps."

"Well, they have long, sharp beaks," Clam began, and then stopped. The birds were closer now, they were very large birds, and they were coming straight toward the balloon.

"Could they be cranes? They're said to be quite large, I believe," Ben said.

"Shoot them, they are going to hit the balloon," Clam said, in sudden panic. "Go down, go down!"

"The gun, I fear, is in the wagon," Ben reminded him, a second before these very large birds, unwilling to vary their course, plunged into the balloon and even into the basket. Great wings beat all around them. Two of the birds, striking the basket, evidently broke their necks and fell to earth. Some hit the balloon and managed a recovery, while two were actually stuck to the balloon, their beaks having penetrated the silk fabric.

"Let us descend at once, monsieur," Clam insisted.

"Oh, we're descending all right," Ben assured him—the two birds stuck to the balloon managed to free themselves and flew on, followed by an audible hiss of escaping air.

"Damnable creatures, why wouldn't they turn!" Clam yelled, his face red with fury.

"Doubt they expected to run into a balloon on their trip," Ben suggested.

"No, don't talk, steer!" Clam demanded. The balloon was deflating rapidly—already its shape had ceased to be spherical. Fortunately they were over the Platte River, broad and shallow at this point.

"We're going to land either with a thump or a splash," Ben declared. "I think on the whole I prefer the splash."

Fortunately, as the balloon descended, the unfortunate collision with the cranes, if that was what they had been, was balanced by a very helpful gust or two of wind, which allowed them to descend directly into the brown river. The splash, when it came, was a rather considerable one.

"There's something worth writing up, wouldn't you agree, Clam?" Ben

Hope-Tipping asked, as the two of them waded out of the cold, shallow water. "Pioneering balloonists felled by whooping cranes—if that indeed is what they were. We'll be the envy of every ornithologist in the world, and not a few reporters."

"Also, my friend, I saved the cheese," Clam de Paty informed him. He held it high, in triumph, as they struggled toward the shore.

8

"If I had a wife as pretty as Tasmin . . ."

If I had a wife as pretty as Tasmin, I wouldn't be traveling as much as you do," Kit remarked to Jim.

They were stopped near the North Platte, considering whether they should go south for several days, to determine an easy route across to the south branch of the river. Greasy Lake ambled along, a mile or two back.

"You've never had a wife," Jim pointed out. "If you ever get one, then you can decide how much traveling you want to do."

"I almost married my little Josie last time I was in Santa Fe," Kit said, in his own defense. The girl he referred to, Josefina Jaramillo, was short but cheerful—she had let it be known, on more than one occasion, that she wouldn't object to a bit of courting from Kit.

"Isn't she the one you said was bossy?" Jim asked.

"She was a little bossy sometimes," Kit admitted.

"Do you think Tasmin's bossy?" Jim asked.

Kit felt trapped. He didn't want to speak ill of Tasmin, which would mean conceding a point to Jim Snow. The one thing all the trappers agreed on was that Tasmin Berrybender was the bossiest female any of them had ever encountered. When they had nothing better to discuss, the trappers often amused themselves by talking about how much Tasmin needed to be taken down a peg—all agreed that Jim Snow was not the man to accomplish this. Tasmin's bossiness had worked out well for Pomp Charbonneau, since she had flatly refused to allow him to die.

Still, Kit didn't want to come right out and admit to Jim what everybody knew: that his wife was bossy.

"She's sharp-spoken, Tasmin," Kit finally allowed.

"No, she's bossy," Jim said. "I've got used to it, but you needn't be complaining about my traveling.

"If you was married to Tasmin she'd have scared you all the way back to Missouri by now," Jim added.

"Are we going down to the South Platte, or not?" Kit inquired.

"I 'spect we better," Jim said. "We've got a passel of people to guide. It wouldn't hurt to know if there's a big bunch of Indians between here and there."

"It's pretty dern hard to get to Santa Fe, whichever direction you start from," Kit admitted.

"We've got three babies and a passel of females," Jim reminded him. "I hope we can get 'em across before it gets too cold."

He didn't want to discuss it with Kit, but in fact marriage and fatherhood had made travel not quite the free frolic it had once been.

Kit could dance around the question of Tasmin's bossiness all he wanted to, but the fact was that Jim missed his son, Monty, more than he missed his wife. A little time off from Tasmin was only a sensible relief. He and Monty were not yet quite confident of one another, but they were slowly forming a sly attachment. With Tasmin he could only be pleasant and hope for the best.

Jim did feel that a certain amount of scouting was advisable—getting the Berrybenders, or most of them, across to Santa Fe would not be a cakewalk. None of the plains Indians were likely to be friendly—and water was no sure thing along part of the route. If all the mountain men chose to accompany them, they could probably bluff most of the Indians, but it was not likely that the mountain men *would* stay together on such a long trek. The West held too many temptations, in the way of valleys never before explored. The mountain men were notably independent. They might start off in a group and then peel off, one by one.

Jim plunged into the Platte and let the little mare pick her way carefully through the shoals. Kit's mule managed to step in a hole—he stumbled, panicked, threw his rider, and splashed on across the river. Once on the south bank he shook himself thoroughly, showering Jim with cold spray— even so, he was a good deal luckier than Kit, who floundered out, soaked, in a worse temper than he had been in to begin with.

"I'm wet as a rat," he complained; it was very annoying to be stuck with such a worthless mule.

They heard a shout and saw Greasy Lake trotting along the bank at what, for him, was a great rate—he was pointing at the sky. When Jim and Kit first looked up all they saw was a flock of cranes far to the north—for a moment, due to the intensity of the white sunlight, the balloon had been invisible. They could just see the faces of the two white men in the basket, high above.

"Greasy Lake was right—there's our flying men," Kit said.

Jim was startled by the sight of the balloon, a phenomenon he had only vaguely heard about—he had supposed it to be mainly a product of Greasy Lake's imagination, but there it was, as real as anything.

"Now that's a fine way to travel," he said. "If we had a few of those we could float right over to Santa Fe."

"I wouldn't know how to steer it," Kit admitted. "If you couldn't steer it proper, there's no telling where you'd end up."

In their astonishment at seeing the balloon and its passengers, the two of them had forgotten the flock of cranes. Along the Platte large flocks of birds were a common sight—campers sometimes camped a few miles off the river, in order not to be kept awake by the quackings of geese and ducks. But as the cranes came closer, the men in the basket became more agitated, and not without reason: the balloon was directly in the path of the cranes—in a few moments, despite all the balloonists could do, the cranes, in close formation, began to strike the balloon. One or two fell in with the men and then flapped out, but at least six struck the balloon itself.

"Uh-oh," Kit said. "You'd think a dern crane could see a balloon that big."

"Two or three's stuck to it still," Jim remarked—very soon it became evident that the balloon was losing air.

High above, the balloonists were trying frantically to keep their balloon—no longer as round as it had been—up in the air.

Greasy Lake came trotting up, very excited.

"You were right, Greasy," Kit admitted. "There's flying men all right."

"They're trying to hit the river—can't blame them," Jim pointed out.

Fortunately the wind came to the balloonists' aid, pushing the balloon directly over the water.

"I hope they can swim," Kit said, forgetting that he himself had just waded out of the shallow Platte. A moment later he realized that he had spoken foolishly.

"If they'd come down in the Mississippi they'd need to be good swimmers," he added, but thanks to the drama overhead, no one was listening.

Greasy Lake began to wail and chant—he thought it might possibly be gods who were descending into the river. An old Miniconjou, a wandering shaman like himself, had first told him about the balloon and the men who flew beneath it; at first Greasy Lake hadn't known what to believe. But as the balloon came splashing down into the brown water, he saw that the sky travelers, after all, were men and not gods. They waded out of the river, holding what goods they could carry above their heads, looking every bit as wet as Kit Carson. One of the men, a rotund man in wet red pants, seemed to be cursing in French, a language Greasy Lake often heard when he was in the North. The other man was taller, and dressed all in black, as men were said to dress whose business it was to carry off the dead. It seemed to him that the fact that cranes had hit the balloon was not without significance. Some of the People believed that cranes were the carriers of souls; they were said to carry off old souls and bring new souls to babies, when they arrived. Greasy Lake himself had seen nothing of particular merit in the cranes he had observed, nothing that would suggest that they could be entrusted with such an important task, but what he had just seen—cranes bringing down a flying boat—suggested to him that he might need to rethink his position in regard to cranes. Perhaps the reason the flying boat had collapsed was that the cranes had dumped too many souls in it. In the confusion there was the likelihood that some of these souls would escape into uncertain territory, the vague, troubling spaces between life and death, where these flitting souls would likely do much mischief. It might be that what had occurred high over his head was some big error of the gods—an error that had allowed many souls to escape. No one had ever claimed that the gods didn't make mistakes. The gods of war, for example, were always getting things mixed up. What occurred in most battles was often the very opposite of what the war chiefs and war parties had expected to happen. Some men died and others lived, all because of errors of the gods.

9

. . . though happy to have saved his fine Parisian cheese . . .

Clam de Paty, though happy to have saved his fine Parisian cheese and also a warming bottle of cognac, nonetheless, once he was safely on dry land, blew up into a frothing rage and filled the air with curses, none of them exactly directed at Ben Hope-Tipping but few of them missing him by a very wide mark, either.

"You should have descended—it was our only hope!" he insisted.

"Frankly, old boy, an ascent would have been the better strategy," Ben replied, unmoved by the Frenchman's frothing. "The ballast was on your side—if you'd only tossed out a bag or two we might have missed them."

"*Voilà!* Who's these peoples?" Clam asked, having just observed that they had human company: a small, wet man, leading a tall mule; a tall, dry man on a wet bay horse; and an old Indian of some sort, rather blotched in complexion, aboard a horse that seemed about to fall down.

"Extraordinary, isn't it?" Ben said. "People do just seem to pop up out of nowhere, here in America."

"Of course they come from nowhere—all this is *nowhere!*" Clam began—and then he suddenly remembered that all their guns were in the wagon, and where was that foolish boy Amboise, whose instructions had been to follow them closely? Of course, they would need dry clothes, and need them promptly—and yet there was no sign of Amboise, who deserved a good cuffing, at least.

"These fellows seem to be friendly," Ben said. "The Indian looks to be rather past warrior's age. Can't think what's keeping Amboise—wouldn't mind a change—fear he's lagging, as usual—such a pity to have to introduce ourselves in wet clothes—you must speak severely to Amboise, Clam, when the lazy boy shows up."

"I'll 'severe' him—I'll bash him," Clam assured him. He twisted his mustache a bit, in order to appear civilized, and advanced on the strangers, who stood watching them—they did not seem particularly welcoming, but at least did not seem hostile.

"Hello, gentlemen!" Hope-Tipping said loudly, as they approached. "Very glad of your company, I'm sure. I'm Benjamin Hope-Tipping and this is my French colleague, Monsieur Clam de Paty. We write for the papers, and as you see, we come before you freshly baptized."

Jim Snow felt slightly depressed at the thought of having to deal with two more fools or idiots from Europe. The fact that they could fly did not mean that they would be competent to take care of themselves now that they were on the ground.

Kit, however, was delighted to see the newcomers—weeks of traveling with his unsociable old friend Jim Snow and the erratic old prophet had put him in the mood for more talkative company.

"Why, howdy, glad to meet you," Kit said, striding right over to shake hands. "I'm baptized too, but we'll dry. The fellow on the bay mare is Jim Snow and the Indian is called Greasy Lake—he's a big prophet. We've been guiding the Berrybender party—they ought to be around South Pass somewhere by now."

"Why, yes—the Berrybenders—we're very anxious to meet them," Ben told him. He shook Kit's hand but was looking past him, at Jim Snow. Clam de Paty did the same.

"Monsieur, who did you say that was?" Clam asked, nodding at Jim.

"On the bay mare—that's Jim Snow," Kit replied.

"*The* Jim Snow—the man they call the Sin Killer?" Ben inquired eagerly.

"Why, yes—he's the only Jim Snow there is," Kit declared, a little annoyed. "Sin Killer's a nickname some of the boys gave him."

The two men were paying Kit no mind at all—both of them were staring at Jim.

"Clam, we're made—we've found the Sin Killer," Ben exclaimed.

Clam de Paty was scarcely less excited.

"All we need now are dry notebooks," he said. "Where is that Amboise? I'll have his ears."

Watching the two foreigners approach, squishing loudly in their wet boots, Jim had the feeling it was time to leave. Kit could take these two intruders back to the main party, which should be on the move by now. He himself far preferred to scout alone—Kit had insisted on coming along on this trip because he was badly on the outs with Jim Bridger and Milt Sublette over his neglect of camp chores. Jim Bridger had pummeled Kit soundly in their last fistfight, cracking one of Kit's teeth, an injury much resented.

To Jim it seemed only fair that Kit earn his keep by escorting these two men back to the Berrybenders.

"Oh, I say, Mr. Snow," Ben began. "*So* pleased to meet you. I am Benjamin Hope-Tipping and this is my colleague, Monsieur Clam de Paty—we've traveled quite a long way in hopes of meeting you."

"*Oui,*" Clam said. "Splashing down just when we did was a miracle. But for the birds we would have flown right over you."

Jim said not a word. He merely looked at the two men, wondering what they wanted. Why would anyone travel a long distance to meet him? And what did they expect from him now that they had found him?

"We're journalists," Ben announced, with a touch of pride.

Jim sat on his mare—he did not change expression. He seemed, to Clam, neither surprised nor concerned by Ben's announcement. He didn't react at all.

Ben Hope-Tipping was more than a little disconcerted by Jim Snow's calm lack of response to his statement of purpose. It occurred to him that the term he had used—"journalist"—might not be current in this wild empty West. After all, he and Clam *were* pioneers; certainly pioneers insofar as their use of balloons went. The two of them might well be the first journalists the Sin Killer had ever met. There were, after all, few newspapers in the West—only an ugly sheet or two in Cincinnati and hardly even that in Saint Louis. This young man, the famous Sin Killer, feared by the red savages for his violent furies—yet a man who had won the hand of Lady Tasmin Berrybender—a fine subject for journalistic treatment if there ever was one, probably had no clear idea what a journalist was. It might even be that he had never seen a newspaper. His concern, after all, would be survival, not amusement of the sort newspapers were designed to provide.

"We're journalists," he repeated hopefully. "We write for the papers, you see."

"You're the Sin Killer, yes, yes," Clam said. "We have many questions for you, if you'll oblige."

Jim remained silent—it annoyed him a little that his Sin Killer nickname had become such a staple of Missouri River gossip that even these two foreigners had heard the term.

But the fact that they *had* heard it was just a mild irritant—it really meant little to him, nor did it encourage him to linger in their company. It had been a year since he left the lower Missouri—whatever the two fellows had heard was most probably wild lies. The two certainly seemed harmless—they did not appear to be armed—but why they would suppose he'd sit still and let them ask him questions, he could not imagine.

He looked at them, nodded as a small gesture of courtesy, and simply rode around them, leaving them looking at him with open mouths.

"Why didn't he speak—is he mute, the young fool?" Clam asked. Had he traveled all the way from France to have some young American ride around him as if he were a stump?

Ben Hope-Tipping had been as startled as his colleague by Jim Snow's blatantly disinterested response. In his shock at being ignored by this legendary fellow—one of the frontiersmen they had most wanted to meet—Ben wondered if they had omitted some ritual or other—the peace sign, perhaps? Trappers and travelers in the West seemed often to speak to one another through hand signs—perhaps that was what the Sin Killer had been expecting. And yet they had been told that he spoke English—what could be the matter with the fellow?

Jim rode over to Kit and shrugged.

"These two fellows are even nosier than Tasmin," he remarked. "She started asking me questions the minute we met, and these skunks are just as bad."

"They sure didn't ask *me* many questions," Kit replied, in a pouty tone. "All they wanted to know about was the great Sin Killer."

"I ain't the great nothing," Jim told him. "And I can't make much of a scout if I have to drag these two fools behind me. You and Greasy slow me down enough."

"Of course you can go faster than anybody else—you got the best horse," Kit said, still aggrieved.

"I think I'll go south for a few days and have a look around," Jim said. "You can handle these fellows, I expect."

"I don't want to handle them," Kit said at once. "I'm glad we got to see the balloon, but it's busted. Why can't these fellows just handle themselves?"

"Suit yourself—I'm leaving," Jim told him.

"You would leave, you selfish fool!" Kit burst out—Jim's habit of doing exactly what he pleased, with no regard for anyone else, infuriated him.

Jim agreed that seeing the balloon *had* been interesting, but some birds had knocked it down, and helping the men fix it was not his business. He turned to leave. Probably the balloonists had a wagon and a servant nearby who would soon arrive and help them out. He wanted to be on his way, an intention which continued to infuriate Kit.

"What am I supposed to do with them?" he asked, a little desperately.

"Take 'em to Ashley—maybe he'll adopt them," Jim suggested. "He likes to blab and puff himself up—I expect he'll give them some yarns they can write in their papers."

"It's a damn big chore to leave your best friend with," Kit announced— he hoped the appeal to friendship would make Jim change his mind.

"They didn't fly all this way without no kit," Jim pointed out. "I imagine their slave will show up pretty soon and help you with them."

Kit suddenly had a thought. Perhaps the two men were eccentric millionaires, out for a long lark in the West. Perhaps they were as rich as or even richer than Lord Berrybender or the prince of Weid. Maybe if some mild danger arose he could hurry them out of harm's way and then convince them that he had been the one thing that stood between them and death. It might be that they'd want to make him rich for performing such noble service. It would serve Jim Snow right if he managed to get rich off these strangers. For that matter, it would serve everybody right.

Kit was so pleased with his new notion that he could not resist trotting after Jim.

"That's right, you go away . . . leave these folks to me," he said. "I bet they make me rich, once I save them."

"I hope they will—if you *do* save them," Jim said. Then he put the little mare in a lope and hurried off, happy not to have to hear any more rattle from Kit.

10

Jim Snow had no sooner ridden off . . .

Jim Snow had no sooner ridden off than the two journalists, wearing looks of extreme dismay, came running over to Kit.

"Where does he go?" the Frenchman in the red pants asked—there was indignation in his tone. "When will he come back, this Sin Killer?"

"We *had* rather hoped to speak to him, you see!" the Englishman remarked, as shocked as he was annoyed.

"It won't be today," Kit assured them. "Not unless you can run as fast as that mare can lope."

"This is an outrage!" the Frenchman spluttered—he was very red in the face, though not quite as red as his bright pants. "If we were in France I would call him out!"

Kit found the remark puzzling.

"Why call him out when he's already out?" he inquired.

"My colleague means he would challenge Mr. Snow to a duel," Ben explained—he had calmed a little.

Kit Carson usually managed to maintain a solemn, even dignified demeanor, easy to do when traveling with an unsociable person like Jim Snow, who was out of sorts most of the time anyway. On the other hand, when some absolutely ridiculous notion was expressed in his hearing he was sometimes given to bursts of hilarity—these giggle fits, as he called them, often lasted so long that they became something of a trial to those who knew him.

The notion that a short Frenchman in red pants could be so foolish as to challenge Jim Snow to a duel was just the kind of nonsense that caused Kit's sense of humor to get the better of him. He burst out laughing, but of course there was no one to tell the joke to except old Greasy Lake, who was over by the river, chanting over the fallen balloon.

"Why are you laughing, monsieur? In France a duel is a serious matter," Clam de Paty insisted—he was finding America less and less to his taste, an awkward thing since, at the moment, he was far out in the middle of it.

Ben Hope-Tipping, annoyed himself by the young fellow's unseemly response, nonetheless realized that his colleague's abrupt mention of a challenge to the Sin Killer *did*, under the circumstances, smack of the ridiculous.

"Not sure a duel is quite the wisest course in this case, Clam," he remarked. "It would seem that the Sin Killer is famous precisely because of his facility in battle. After all, you can hardly write the fellow up if you're dead."

The same thought had occurred, though belatedly, to Clam de Paty himself. Fortunately the man who he had threatened to call out was now almost out of sight—there seemed to be little practical danger of a response from that quarter.

"Pardon," he said, in chilly tones, to his more circumspect colleague. "A duel is no mere brawl, no massacre, no mere thing of fisticuffs—it is, like everything in France, a civilized engagement, a contest with rules. With a pistol in my hand, monsieur, I assure you I am not to be taken lightly."

Ben decided to ignore his friend's absurdly puffed-up conduct—they were not, after all, out with their seconds in the Bois de Boulogne. Still, he could not but be irritated by the young frontiersman's giggling, which seemed to cast their whole enterprise in an undignified light. Clam de Paty, despite his rather erratic temperament, was a leading, perhaps *the* leading, force in French journalism—had he not interviewed Prince Metternich himself, and Czar Alexander, and the empress of France, not to mention numerous Bourbons, generals, and acrobats?

His own credentials, for that matter, were not evidently the poorer. He too had interviewed lords, ministers, Mrs. Jordan, two Rothschilds, a Baring, even the great Wellington himself. It was bad enough to have their fine, expensively made balloon punctured by some wayward American birds—were they now to be reduced to standing around in wet clothes, on the barren American prairies, being laughed at by a young frontiersman and ignored completely by a rather blotchy old Indian? Ben prided himself on his ability to maintain a level temperament—a good, sound Dorset temperament, on the whole, in clear contrast to the frequent oaths and curses his more volatile Gallic companion was apt to burst out with. Just at the moment, though, Ben found that he was becoming rather vexed. After all, the sun was setting, and there was no sign of Amboise d'Avigdor or the wagon, in which were plenty of dry clothes. They seemed to be faced with a long, damp night. Why was this young fool still giggling?

"Do endeavor to control your hilarity, Mr. Carson," he said sharply. "I confess I can't quite figure out what's so funny."

"I just got tickled at the thought of that French fellow in the red pants fighting a duel with Jimmy," he admitted.

"And why is that amusing, monsieur?" Clam asked.

"Because Jimmy would kill you before you could twitch," Kit informed him calmly. "Jimmy don't hold back when life or death's involved."

Jim Snow, already miles to the south, was only visible for a second or two, above the waving grass.

"Will he come back, do you think, Mr. Carson?" Ben asked—obviously there was no immediate hope of an interview, though it was *the* interview of all interviews that would have done most to enhance the authenticity of their great Western expedition.

"Oh sure, Jimmy will show up someday," Kit told them. "He's got a wife and baby back with Ashley and the trappers."

Just then a cloud passed between them and the sinking sun. Though it had been a warm day, Ben felt suddenly chilly. Their not quite fully deflated balloon floated on the river, snagged on a number of stiff branches. The old piebald Indian was still chanting, though not so loudly.

"I suppose we should rescue our balloon, Clam—possibly it can be patched," Ben remarked.

"It's awkward being wet," Clam admitted. "Where could that foolish boy be?"

"He was rather fearful when we left," Ben recalled. "Seemed rather convinced that those red fellows might do him harm."

"What red fellows?" Kit asked, alarmed. He had no idea how far the balloon might have floated before the cranes downed it—with Jim now gone and two obviously helpless strangers on his hands, the thought that there might be bad Indians somewhere near was entirely unwelcome.

"Oh, quite a bunch of painted fellows stopped us," Ben informed him. "Upset our young interpreter rather a lot. An old fellow on a white horse seemed to be the leader. What was it Amboise called him, Clam? The Partezon, was it?"

"That's right—the Partezon," Clam agreed. "No paint on him, though the other fellows were painted up rather grotesquely. That's when we decided to go up in our balloon."

"I believe we rather frightened the savages when we went up," Ben remarked. "They ran off, but the two old fellows didn't."

Kit began to regret that he had burst out so at Jim—if ever the two of them needed to stick together, it was now. But of course, as usual, Jim had left.

"Best think of our balloon," Ben insisted. "Amboise is sure to turn up soon. If a muskrat were to nibble our balloon, it would only be harder to patch. Once we've saved it we can build a roaring fire and get out of these wet clothes."

"No fire tonight," Kit informed them immediately. It was sadly obvious that the two men lacked even the most elementary practical sense.

"I'll help you get your balloon off the snags," he said, "but we can't be building a fire, not with the Partezon around."

"But sir, no Indians *are* around—we flew over several miles of prairie and it all looked quite empty," Ben insisted; both he and Clam were horrified at the thought of a night spent in their sopping clothes.

"How many miles did you come?" Kit asked.

"Ten, maybe," Ben said. "What do you think, Clam?"

Clam de Paty shrugged. Once in the balloon, he had applied himself to the cheese and the cognac—calculations of distance were none of his affair.

"We flew until the birds came," he told Kit. As the guardian of French precision he tried to avoid vague statements.

"No fire tonight," Kit repeated firmly. "Ten miles ain't far enough. An Indian can smell smoke ten miles—*this* Indian particularly."

"But we're very wet, Mr. Carson," Ben reminded him. "And once we wade around saving our balloon, we'll undoubtedly be even wetter. Surely you can't expect us to spend the night in damp garments."

"I should certainly hope not," Clam added. "What business is it of the savages if we enjoy our fire, monsieur? Civilized men cannot be expected to sleep in wet clothes."

"Take your clothes off and sleep naked, then," Kit advised. "If you start a fire I'll be leaving, and the Partezon will probably be coming."

"Sleep naked—in this chill?" Ben asked, horrified at the thought. "Couldn't we make just a small fire, one not apt to roar? What harm could there be in that?"

"The Partezon will come and burn you in it, that's what harm," Kit told them. "He probably didn't think you could really fly off or he would have burned you already."

Without wasting any more time on chatter, he waded into the river and began to disengage the soppy silk of the balloon from the sticks where it had snagged. Darkness was falling and the work was chilling but Kit's imagination had just served up a warming thought. If he helped save the balloon, maybe the balloonists would let him go up in it with them. If he came floating down into Ashley's big camp in a red balloon it would show all the boys—and Tasmin particularly—what a clever fellow he was. None of the mountain men had ever ridden in a balloon. If he returned to the Berrybenders in a balloon his stock was bound to rise—maybe Tasmin would look at him with new eyes.

It was not easy, extracting such a large, floppy object from the snag-filled river. Greasy Lake had no interest in the rescue, but Ben Hope-Tipping stripped off and came in the water to help. He seemed to appreciate Kit's efforts, unlike the Frenchman, who maintained an airy indifference.

By the time they got the balloon safely free of snags and spread it on the grass, a pale moon had risen. Greasy Lake, without a word of good-bye, rode off just as darkness fell.

"Strange old fellow—where do you suppose he's going?" Ben asked.

"He don't know himself—Greasy just wanders," Kit said.

11

Mainly the Ear Taker hunted people . . .

When the Ear Taker was a boy, hunting in the dry canyons, the People called him Takes Bones, because he was always picking up small bones or animal teeth from carcasses in the desert—bones or teeth that he then worked into fishhooks, awls, spear points; but once he reached adulthood some of the People began to call him Who-You-Don't-See, because of the exceptional stealth of his attacks, most of them aimed at lone travelers, white traders, careless soldiers. Mainly the Ear Taker hunted people—white or Mexican usually—but when he hunted animals his stealth worked just as well. He could even surprise antelope, most cautious of animals. If he saw several antelope grazing together he would anticipate the direction of their grazing and go flatten himself in the grass, well ahead of the grazing animals. Hunting naked at times, he flattened himself until he became as much part of the ground as a lizard or a snake. The antelope would sometimes walk right over him, coming so close that he could strike one with a light spear tipped with poison—the poison old Prickly Pear Woman had taught him to make from the secretions of a toad. Prickly Pear Woman was actually white, but she had been taken prisoner as a small girl and had lived with the People most of her life—some of the People even regarded her as the grandmother of the tribe. She had dug herself a little room beneath the roots of a great prickly pear—she had learned to move among the prickly pear so smoothly that the thorns didn't stick her, a feat not even the Ear Taker could manage.

The Ear Taker was short, but it was agreed that he could outwalk anyone in the band. He could walk from moonrise to moonrise, licking dew drops off sage leaves or grass blades if there was no water. Old Prickly Pear Woman had told him of the terrible cruelties the whites had visited on the People long ago—many grandmothers ago. When the whites came into the lands of the People they at once began to order people around—the People, having always been free, didn't like this and made a revolt, killing many whites. But then many more whites came and made all the People prisoners; to ensure that the People could never rise up again, an old governor commanded that all warriors over a certain age must have one foot chopped off—and the chopping was soon accomplished, leaving the People a tribe of cripples. For a generation all the warriors had to hobble on one foot, a terrible humiliation.

To a great walker like the Ear Taker no greater humiliation could be imagined—even though the chopping had occurred many grandmothers ago, and the warriors of the People now walked on two legs again, the Ear Taker decided to devote himself to avenging this old cruelty.

At first he tried to avenge the atrocity precisely in kind, by sneaking up on sleeping traders or soldiers and chopping off one of their feet. It was easy enough, in Santa Fe, to find victims, most of whom had passed out from drunkenness; but the Ear Taker soon discovered that chopping off feet with an axe or a hatchet was not easy to do correctly. Twice he struck too high on the leg and his victims bled to death. Two others he managed to strike cleanly, so that at least two white men had to hobble through their lives as the old warriors had hobbled.

In time, though, the Ear Taker thought of a better, more easily effected revenge: ears. All white men were vain; they fancied themselves lords of the earth—with an ear missing, a white man's vanity could never be repaired. In the Ear Taker's view, the loss of such a prominent feature as an ear would be a humiliation worse than death to many of the proud white traders.

Once the choice was made, the Ear Taker began to build his reputation. He haunted the caravan routes into and out of Santa Fe to the east or the south, using his great stealth to slip up on unwary traders as they slept and quickly remove an ear—before the victims could even become fully awake, the Ear Taker was gone.

He soon discovered that the first essential for such work was a knife that could be made as sharp as a razor; and by great good luck, he soon found such a knife. The Ear Taker joined with some Apaches to ambush a little bunch of soldiers bound for the City of Mexico. More than twenty Mexican soldiers were killed, including a captain who possessed a very fine knife. The Ear Taker kept the knife and spent many days sharpening it until the blade was so keen that he could cut flies in two in the air, or bees or other flying insects.

The Apaches with the Ear Taker had, of course, mutilated the soldiers in the traditional ways, castrating them, poking out their eyes, disemboweling a few of them—but they had no interest in ears, which meant that the Ear Taker had twenty sets of ears to practice removing. And he did practice. Since ears were mostly gristle, it was possible to remove them—if one's knife was sharp enough—while causing the victims little immediate pain. The pain, for the whites, would come when they awoke and discovered that they had received an injury that was conspicuous and permanent. A man with a leg cut off might get a wooden leg, but no one could get a wooden ear. A man's humiliation would be there for all to see.

By the time the Ear Taker had finished with the twenty corpses, his technique was perfect: with his left hand he grasped the ear, stretched it, and with his right hand, cut just at the juncture of ear and scalp. Soon he could perform the motions perfectly, in only a second—then he would be off, into the desert or the prairie, gone before his victims could even figure out why one side of their head was suddenly bloody.

In two months, by stalking the caravans from the east, the Ear Taker had removed a dozen ears. Soon, horrified trekkers, white, black, or Mexican, began to arrive in Santa Fe lacking an ear. The governor and the military could not fail to take note. This singular but terrifying threat to a man's appearance would soon begin to act as a brake on the Santa Fe trade. Traders from east or south had always had to contend with droughts, blizzards, or hostile Indians—but now they faced a new threat: an assailant whose pleasure was to cut off ears. This fiend, this Ear Taker, seemed to be able to succeed no matter how many guards were posted. In a few cases he had even taken ears from some undisciplined guards who had nodded off for a moment.

To the military's dismay, the Ear Taker had one huge advantage: no one had ever seen him, or had the slightest idea what he looked like. Barefoot, dressed like any other Indian, the Ear Taker could walk around the plaza in Santa Fe in perfect safety—a small man, dark, modest, friendly, never questioned or suspected by any of the soldiers whose ears he might eventually take. Except for old Prickly Pear Woman, none of his own people would ever have supposed that Takes Bones, a modest toolmaker exceptionally skilled at working bones, had become the dread Ear Taker.

By the time the Ear Taker had wreaked his vengeance for a year, several once-proud traders had given up the trade and sought safety in the East. In Santa Fe the governor became even more alarmed—he even delegated a company of soldiers whose one duty was to hunt down the Ear Taker. The soldiers marched off, first east, then south—they caught no one, but while they were marching, the Ear Taker took three more ears. The soldiers got lost near the Cimarron River and almost starved—six were killed in a brief engagement with the Kiowa. The survivors came back to Santa Fe, having failed completely. How were they to find a man no one had ever seen? The governor then thought of trying to tempt the Ear Taker into committing a rash act. He had three condemned men taken a few miles out of town and left to wander—they were, of course, being watched closely from a distance. The condemned men were not bothered, but one of the soldiers who was supposed to be watching had his ear taken off while drunk. No one saw anything and there were no tracks to follow, but a few days later, a trader named Bates claimed to have seen the Ear Taker fleeing in the dawn, having just taken an ear from a sheepherder. Bates described the Ear Taker as unusually tall, though in fact he was a very short man, not even five feet in height.

Though confident now of his skill, the Ear Taker knew that all the skill in the world could not prevent accident. Sooner or later, if he continued to take ears near Santa Fe, someone *would* see him. There were Apache trackers so skilled that they could track anything—one of them might be employed to track him. Old Prickly Pear Woman, whom he visited frequently, often cautioned him about the risks he was taking.

"The spirits don't like it when we learn to do things too good," she reminded him. "They set traps—good traps—it's to remind us that we are only people. You have taken enough of these ears around here—I think the spirits are getting ready to trick you. You better go somewhere else, if you want to keep taking people's ears."

The Ear Taker knew she was right. Lately he had had the feeling that someone clever was watching him. Often he caught rabbits looking at him steadily, which was disconcerting. Sometimes he came quite close to the steady-looking rabbits, but they didn't flee. They merely hopped a few steps and resumed their steady looking.

The next day he spent several hours in the plaza, just walking around, chatting with a few people. No one bothered him, or even seemed to notice him, but when he left Santa Fe and walked out into the country, the first thing he saw was a big jackrabbit, watching him. The traders had no interest in him, nor the soldiers, but every rabbit he saw seemed to be looking at him. This was a worrisome thing.

The next day the Ear Taker climbed to the top of a butte several miles from town. The butte was a holy place; men came there seeking visions. The Ear Taker waited all day, but only near dusk did he see anything that might give him a clue about what the spirits might be planning. As the sun was sinking a great dust devil blew up, far to the north, the dust swirling high in the air. Then the sun struck the dust in such a way as to make a kind of dust rainbow, a thing the Ear Taker had never seen. The dust devil headed in a northerly direction and finally dissolved. The Ear Taker believed he had been given a sign, and what the sign suggested was that he go north. Perhaps if he went north, where there were also said to be careless whites—trappers, hunters, families traveling west—the spirits who were annoyed with him for being so good at cutting off ears would leave him in peace for a while.

The minute the Ear Taker made his decision and started north, the rabbits began to run away from him again.

The Ear Taker walked from moonrise to moonrise. At dawn he walked through a large prairie dog town and was pleased to note that there were no small owls to be seen, although owls often occupied the dens of prairie dogs. The presence of owls always indicated that death was near—the fact that he didn't see a single owl gave him confidence that he had made the right decision.

Two weeks of strong walking brought the Ear Taker into the Sioux country, near the Platte River. On his walk he had not seen a single soul, neither white man nor red man, but he knew that when he crossed the brown river and traveled along the Holy Road, he would soon find humans again. On his walk he had mostly eaten wild onions, plus one porcupine. When he came to the Platte River he was hoping to find some berry bushes, but just as he saw the curve of the river he also spotted two antelope. At once he lay down and made himself part of the ground, for the antelope were grazing right toward him. He had his light spear with him, whose

poison should be fresh enough to kill. The antelope had no inkling of the
Ear Taker's presence, of that he was sure, and yet only a moment later
they both raised their heads and at once took flight to the west. He had
been flattened against the ground when the antelope ran—soon he began
to pick up the vibrations made by a number of horses. As the Ear Taker
watched, about twenty Indians came loping out of the south, their object
being to capture three white men, two of them mounted on small horses,
the third driving a wagon. The Ear Taker assumed that the three whites
would either be killed on the spot or else carried off someplace where they
would have to suffer the appropriate tortures. Instead, to his surprise, a
parley took place—the young white man driving the wagon was obviously
making a plea for mercy. The young warriors looked restless; they were
clearly eager to hack up the whites, but an old chief, who rode a white
horse, restrained them.

Then two of the white men dismounted and pulled a huge red blanket
of some kind out of the wagon; then they built a fire in a bucket and began
to pump fire into the blanket, causing it to expand and take on a kind of
round shape—it rose from the ground and hung like a red moon over the
prairie. This sight startled the young Indians very much—it startled the
Ear Taker too. A blanket had turned into a kind of moon, with a basket
underneath it, which two of the white men climbed into. To the Ear Taker
it all seemed like strange magic; but then, he reminded himself, he was in
a new country and should have expected unusual things to happen.

Then, immediately, something even more unusual took place. The young
white man who had been conducting the parley with the Indians loosened
some ropes and the big moon rose into the air, with the two white men sitting comfortably beneath it. Soon the two men were high above the river.
The old Indian shot an arrow at them, but his arrow merely hit the basket
and fell back. A breeze pushed the red moon west—soon the two men were
well out of range of any arrow.

It was all too much for the young warriors, who galloped away, leaving
only the two old men and the young white man who had been driving the
wagon.

Seeing the two white men fly was by far the most astonishing piece of
magic the Ear Taker had ever witnessed. The north country was clearly
where the spirits disposed themselves differently than the spirits of the desert. After a bit the two older Indians rode away, not even bothering to kill
the young white man, who caught the two horses and soon proceeded on

west along the river in his wagon. The Ear Taker would have liked to discuss what he had just seen with old Prickly Pear Woman, but of course that was impossible—he would have to observe the peoples of this strange country a little longer and then draw his own conclusions.

The sun was sinking—it would be night soon, and night was the Ear Taker's element. It occurred to him that he could test the situation a bit by following the white boy, letting him make camp and go to sleep, and then taking one of his ears. He got up from the ground and carefully followed the wagon, though keeping to his side of the river and watching the skies for any sign that the two flying men were returning. He also watched closely for any sign that the young white man had unusual powers—he did not want to allow himself to be tricked, on his first day in the north country. He remembered that he *had* been tricked, not long before in Santa Fe. He decided to take an ear from the famous white trader John Skraeling, known to Indians as the Twisted Hair. Skraeling was a very light sleeper, thus difficult to rob, as many thieves had discovered to their sorrow. Skraeling slept under his own wagon; the Ear Taker thought it would be a good test of his stealth, to sneak up and take one of Skraeling's ears. The trader was a sick man, who coughed a lot; some of his helpers were just waiting for him to die, so they could divide up his goods, but none were quite bold enough to attempt to kill him.

The Ear Taker chose a moonless night on which to make his attempt. He crept up on Skraeling's wagon and listened carefully for the man's breathing, which would tell him where the head was. It was then that the gods played their trick: Skraeling *wasn't* breathing, though surely he had been when he crawled under the wagon. The Ear Taker crept closer, listening. Thirty yards away some trappers were drinking and carousing, making enough noise that the Ear Taker couldn't hear the sleeping man's light breath. Carefully he put his head under the wagon, but still he heard nothing. No living man could breathe *that* quietly, he thought—and then he realized the truth. Skraeling had crawled under the wagon and died of his own sickness; the Ear Taker had waited one day too long to make his attempt. Since he was there, he took an ear off the dead man anyway, but the mischievous spirits had managed to upset his plans.

At dark the young white man stopped and made a hasty camp. It was clear to the Ear Taker that he was a clumsy boy—he had no skill in hobbling horses or making camp. No doubt his job was just to follow the fliers around and do chores for them when they came down.

When dusk deepened, making it easy to move without being observed, the Ear Taker crossed the river, so he could observe the boy more closely. The young man seemed to be a very ordinary fellow. During the hour or more that the Ear Taker watched he became a little annoyed at the thought of old Prickly Pear Woman, who had managed to convince him that the spirits were likely to set traps for him. She liked to stir people up, getting them all worried about disasters that never happened. She told one old man, who had been her lover once, that he had offended the Toad people and would turn black as a result. The old man didn't turn black, but he worried so much about the Toad people that he stumbled into a gully and broke his neck. That very incident had convinced the Ear Taker that it was not wise to believe everything old Prickly Pear Woman said. Probably she was just bored, and had merely been amusing herself when she told him the spirits might be laying a trap.

Once he determined to go on and take one of the young white man's ears, the Ear Taker carefully observed the usual cautions. He waited until the moon was behind a cloud before creeping into the camp. The boy was a loud snorer, making the position of his head easy to determine. Taking the ear took only a second. The young man jerked, but did not wake up. The Ear Taker left immediately, recrossing the river. He walked most of the night and then hid himself in some bushes and slept. The ear taking had gone well, and he felt relieved, but he still had no intention of being careless. After all, he was in new country, where there might be new rules.

12

Amboise felt safe where there were trees . . .

Amboise d'Avigdor was a deep sleeper, particularly so after a day on which he might have died a terrible death. Since the Partezon, cruelest of all Indians, had spared him, Amboise didn't feel he had much to worry about. Of course, his bosses would be in a terrible fury when he caught up with them the next day; they would have expected him to follow their flight, make their fire, cook their dinner, and lay their beds. The dreadful threat posed by the Partezon had not impressed them; they were safe in their basket, applying themselves to the cognac and cheese. It was irritating, but that was just how his bosses were.

Amboise himself was from the Chippewa country, his father a *voyageur* in the land of the *mille lacs*. Amboise felt safe where there were trees; he did not enjoy being alone on this vast prairie. He could handle a canoe better than a wagon, and he much preferred the company of trappers and river Indians to these two rude Europeans.

Yawning, Amboise soon stretched out on a blanket between the wagon and the campfire—he at once began to send his rasping snores out into the night. He slept deeply, cooled by the night breezes—for a moment he felt a sting like an insect bite but did not come fully awake. The sun was high before he opened his eyes and looked about him absently. Then he saw, to his surprise, that the grass near where he had just slept seemed to be red. Surely the grass hadn't been red when he lay down, else he would have chosen a different spot. Then he noticed—what was more puzzling and also more annoying—that his shirt was red too. When he put up a finger to scratch his cheek, his finger came away red. These reddenings of grass, shirt, and finger were quite puzzling to Amboise. He walked off a little distance and relieved himself; time enough to figure out the source of this puzzling redness later. Only when he happened to notice a lot of green flies buzzing over the reddened grass did it occur to him that the redness might be blood. The two palfreys were quarrelsome beasts, always at odds with the sorrel gelding that pulled the wagon. Perhaps while he slept the horses had fought, bitten one another until the blood flowed. But the palfreys were grazing placidly, some distance away, and the gelding didn't have a mark on him. Besides, his own cheek was bloody, which would be an unlikely result, if the horses had fought.

As he stood by the river, perplexed by this odd circumstance, it struck Amboise with sudden force that the blood must be his own. At once he raised his hand to his cheek, and it came away bloody.

Amboise's first fearful thought was that he had somehow been scalped. Perhaps the old Indian who had seemed so uninterested in him the day before had slipped back in the night and scalped him. Astonished that, as a scalped man, he could still walk around and make water, Amboise rushed to the wagon and quickly pulled out Clam de Paty's little shaving mirror, a useful object that he was obliged to locate for Monsieur de Paty every morning when he was ready to shave.

Amboise opened the mirror, which was in a handsome leather case, and quickly had a look at himself, a procedure that only deepened his puzzlement. One of his cheeks *was* very bloody, and yet it was plain that he still had his hair, and looked, on the whole, very like his healthy young self. But what could have occurred to make him so bloody? His bosses were always berating him for his clumsiness, but could he have been somehow clumsy enough to cut himself while he slept? Such a loss of blood seemed to indicate that he had been bleeding most of the night, and yet, where was the cut? Could he have walked in his sleep, fallen on some rocks, or perhaps accidentally cut himself on the axe that he used to chop firewood? None of these explanations really satisfied, since he had awakened exactly where he lay down. Clam de Paty's little mirror was small—until Amboise tilted it at an angle, it hardly showed his whole face. When he did tilt it, what it showed plainly was that one side of his face was bloody and one side normal, if rather stubbly—unlike his bosses, Amboise could rarely find the leisure to shave. The more he tipped and slanted the mirror, the more it struck Amboise that, after all, something *was* rather odd about his face—something just a bit off—but because of the abundance of dried blood he could not at once say what it was. Then he put up a finger, meaning to scratch his left ear, and found that, instead, he only scratched his temple. Very carefully Amboise tilted the mirror and made the astonishing discovery that he no longer *had* a left ear. At first he could not credit his own vision, which was apt to be bleary and not too precise in the first moments of the new day. He had gone to sleep with two ears on his head—he felt quite sure of that fact—and yet now he seemed to have only one, which defied all the laws of nature, as Amboise understood them. For a minute he blamed the mirror, a small mirror, inadequate for close inspection; and yet, play with it though he might, he could not make the mirror contradict his first impression, which was that he no longer had two ears. The right one was there, stiff as an ear should be and even fairly clean. But the left ear was simply not there, a fact so startling that Amboise sat down and fell into a faint, in which he dreamed that he was bathing in a cool river. In this dream, a brief one, he definitely had two ears. He did his best to delay a return to consciousness, but despite him, consciousness soon returned—a glance at the mirror was enough to confirm the dreadful fact: he was a man with only one ear, an inadequacy that was likely to strike his employers as very discreditable indeed. His employers were exacting men, so exacting, in fact, that Amboise found he was worrying more about how to explain the situation than he was about the loss of the ear itself. Bitter as they would be about the fact that he had not presented himself to make the fire and arrange the bedding, they would take one look at him in his altered state and at once draw the worst conclusions. Very likely they would conclude that he had taken advantage of their absence to borrow one of their shaving kits, perhaps had tried to shave using one of their mirrors, and in an excess of clumsiness, cut off his own ear. The fact that he had smeared blood not only on Clam de Paty's mirror but on much of their kit as well would lend strength to such an assumption. Amboise wondered again if he might, somehow or other, have cut his own ear off, concluding that it was impossible. His first suspicion—that an Indian had crept in and cut it off while he slept—was undoubtedly the right explanation. The old Partezon, who seemed so uninterested in him, had had his sport after all. There was no sign of the ear anywhere—whoever cut it off took it away. Who was more likely than the Partezon to commit such a cunning act?

Very hastily Amboise took Clam de Paty's mirror to the river and washed it clean of blood. Then he stripped and ducked himself several times, so that he would be clean too. A quick check in the mirror revealed a hole in the left side of his head, but with no ear to shield it. The gristly appendage that had been with him for all of his twenty-one years was now gone.

He carried a bucket of water up from the river and did his best to clean the blood off the various articles in the wagon, making rather a damp job of it. Then he hitched the gelding to the wagon, put the palfreys on a loose rein, and hurried off as fast as he could go to the west. He was anxious to be back with his bosses before the old Indian came back and stripped him of his other ear—and perhaps a few other parts of himself as well.

13

Restraint was not her way . . .

They trusted me to keep them safe, and I failed," Pomp said, in a voice so low that Tasmin could scarcely hear him, though she stood close to his side in the woods a few hundred yards below the camp. They stood over the remains of the friendly bear cub Andy, who, with his sister, Abby, had been caught by Pomp just before the battle in which Pomp was so badly wounded. Andy had been clubbed to death, skinned, and cut up, no doubt by the same Indians who had killed the other freed animals, once they wandered away from the enclosure where they had been penned. Pomp himself, once he recovered, had freed the animals—buffalo, deer, antelope, elk, and moose, all half tame and no doubt easy prey for the Indians, who were coming to the camp to get in a last bit of trading with William Ashley.

"Damn the Indians . . . they should have seen they were pets!" Tasmin said—Pomp's sadness affected her so deeply that she had to say something, even though she knew there was no logic in her complaint—why expect Indians, who lived by hunting and whose erratic food supply had usually to be earned by exertion and danger, to pass up easy meat? Pomp himself, as the young animals were captured, expressed certain doubts about the semidomestication of these wild beasts, which Drummond Stewart had wanted to put in his Scottish zoo. He knew that the caution wild animals needed would not be easily regained—Andy's death made the point emphatically.

"I know there are zoos and game parks and such in Europe, but out here I think it's best just to let the animals be," Pomp remarked. "Once you interfere with them they forget how to be wild."

As you yourself have, Pomp Charbonneau, Tasmin thought—then she took Pomp's face in her hands and kissed him, a thing she had been wanting to do for weeks and weeks. They were alone in a deep glade, what better chance could she have? Restraint was not her way—she wanted to make Pomp not look so sad. It flitted through her mind, as she drew Pomp's face toward her, that she had done much the same when she could no longer resist the urge to kiss her husband, Jim Snow, now several weeks gone on his scout to the south. He should know better than to leave me, Tasmin thought—Jim knew she was a passionate animal, strong in her appetites; he also knew she cared for Pomp, though perhaps without suspecting in quite what way she cared—she had hardly been certain of the nature of her feeling herself. Jim and Pomp were friends; they had hunted and camped together often. Yet their natures were very different, Jim hard, Pomp soft, and the one not necessarily better than the other. Tasmin had learned to align herself more or less comfortably with her husband's hardness, even if it involved sudden slappings and moments of frightening violence, but Jim's rough masculinity was not the only kind she could respond to. Pomp's shy softness had a deep appeal too. She had thought much about Jim and Pomp and come to the conclusion that she was not likely to find complete sufficiency in any one man. She had seen herself that life was very uncertain—William Drummond Stewart had been a virile man a month ago and now he was as dead as Charlemagne, as was her brother Bobbety. The insistence with which her father, Lord Berrybender, pursued even his most vagrant appetites—which had once seemed the most abysmal selfishness—now, in the light of life's risk, made more or less good sense. Perhaps it was better to honor one's appetites while one could. Had Pomp been clearly happy, at ease in his soul, Tasmin felt she might have chosen to let him be; but he wasn't serene, there was sadness in his eyes— so she stopped thinking about it all and kissed him. If Jim Snow beat her for it or killed her for it, so be it! Her kiss, when she first delivered it, was tentative, soft, shy—for all she knew it was Pomp's first kiss. She kissed his mouth, and then, still soft and shy, kissed his cheeks, his eyelids, his throat just once; and then she kissed his mouth again, a longer kiss this time, if still a soft one. Pomp did not withdraw; she even felt his breath quicken a little, and that slight hastening of breath gave her confidence that she had not misread him or forced on him something he didn't want. Pomp did want her kiss, and even returned it a little, if awkwardly—it was no polished seducer she was dealing with. She drew back and looked in his eyes, in which she saw a startled, boyish uncertainty—perhaps a little fear even. He looked at her alertly, as if trying to pick up an odor or identify the call of a distant bird.

"I've come to love you—I won't lie—I can't help it!" Tasmin said. "I hope you're glad."

She seized his hand and twined her fingers in his, waiting—it seemed that her whole future depended on this soft-souled man who had not yet learned to lust.

"I'm glad—it's all new to me," Pomp said. "I'm not as good a kisser as you."

"Don't be a fool, you're lovely, you're fine!" Tasmin burst out—in her relief she spoke so loudly that she quickly looked around to see if anyone from the camp might be close enough to hear.

Then she kissed Pomp again, longer and with a little more diligence this time, lingering over his mouth. She moved a little closer, locking her arms around him, aligning her body with his; at this Pomp stiffened a little, not the erect stiffening of the aroused male—it seemed merely that he was surprised that anyone would want to be so close to him. She lay her cheek against his breast, listening to him breathe. Just knowing that he wanted her kiss was heaven—she asked nothing more at the moment. She wished she could stand close to Pomp, reaching up now and then for a kiss, all day—and yet even as she enjoyed their light embrace she knew that the larger world and its demands were not far to seek. Her child, Monty, would soon be wanting to nurse—motherhood could not be scanted for long, no matter how keenly she wanted to stay in the quiet glade with Pomp, nuzzling and kissing. She had feared that he might mention Jim—but he hadn't.

"Have you never had a woman? I must ask," Tasmin said, blushing. Pomp merely shook his head—if anything his silent confession made her feel all the more shy. Jim Snow had been no virgin when he came to her, and she herself had been well prepared for the conjugal business of marriage by her vigorous couplings with Master Tobias Stiles, her father's head groom. She and Jim, of course, had had their share of awkwardness and confusion when they first met, but these had to do with clashing personalities; physically they had been primed for one another, evidence of which was that Monty had been conceived in their first blissful weeks.

Yet now it was Pomp's deep physical shyness that she found so delicious—out of respect for it her kisses were delivered softly—she did not want to frighten him.

"I've seen chambermaids do this, in Germany," Pomp admitted. "The prince had thirty servants and the young maids were always getting in love."

"Why, you little spy," Tasmin said. "And what did the sight of all this kissing make you feel?"

"Sad," Pomp admitted at once.

"Sad . . . but it's merely life going on," Tasmin told him.

"Because I thought no one would ever want *me*," Pomp admitted.

"But you were wrong. Many women will want you, although I don't intend to let them get past me," Tasmin informed him.

Pomp gave a tired shrug. "My mother loved me so much that when she died I tried to die too—I was always springing fevers," he remembered.

Tasmin remembered the night when they were walking to her tent by the icy Yellowstone, when Pomp had admitted that he rarely felt lust. His polite neutrality had irritated her then—now, in the warm summer, with her arms locked around him, she thought she understood a little better.

She had wanted, even then, with her husband not two hundred yards away, to kiss him, to push him toward life, to plant him solidly into it and not allow him to be tempted by the other place, death, the mystery that enclosed the mother he still yearned for.

Frightened for a moment, she kissed him again, more deeply this time.

"Those German girls, those maids and cooks, just weren't bold enough," she said. "You're a shy one, Pomp. You need a shameless English girl like me, who ain't afraid to grab you."

Pomp gave her a shy smile, tempting Tasmin to the longest kiss yet, a kiss that seemed to remove them from the normal sphere of daily activity and lifted them to a place where there was only one another. But it wasn't merely daily activity that Tasmin wanted to banish—what she wanted was for him to be tempted by *her*, not by the other place, the place where his mother was. Yet even after this melting kiss, the shadow remained. Happiness, even the extreme happiness she felt when he accepted her kiss, was no barrier to danger. She felt that she would have to be very alert, very forward, so that this young man, her darling, her breath, would not misjudge some dangerous moment because of his old temptation to the shade. Even as she held him and kissed him she wasn't sure that he was quite won.

"You must watch yourself from now on," she told him solemnly. "You mustn't be careless—you mustn't get killed. It would break my heart. I fear we've many dangers to surmount before we reach Santa Fe."

"Yes, and from what I hear, Santa Fe's as dangerous as any other place," he said. "Most of the Mexicans would as soon kill us as look at us."

"Just don't get killed—will you promise?" Tasmin asked, holding his cheeks in her hands so he would face her.

"We mustn't talk about it—it's bad luck," Pomp said. For a moment he looked scared. Just then, in the distance, Tasmin heard Monty wailing. Monty was fascinated by horses—perhaps he had toddled too close to one and been kicked, or else cut himself with a knife someone had carelessly left in his path. Little Onion was the soul of vigilance where the toddlers were concerned, but the little boys had already proven ingenious at injuring themselves, no matter how closely their keepers watched them.

"Damn it, what's wrong with that child now?" Tasmin wondered, annoyed at having her idyll interrupted. "I suppose we can't just stand here kissing forever, although I'd like to. Come with me—I'll feed the hungry brat."

"You go—I want to bury what's left of Andy," Pomp replied. "Besides, I'd be shy around the boys yet."

"You mean you think it shows—that we're in love?" Tasmin asked.

"The boys don't have much to do but gossip and pry," he reminded her. "I guess most people like to gossip and pry. Back at Prince Paul's castle the servants did so much gossiping they barely had time to get the meals cooked, or the horses groomed."

Tasmin was reluctant to stop holding him—she kissed him one more time.

"What a nuisance society is—even *this* society, which is hardly elevated," she said. "I think we deserve a little more time to ourselves, with no comment encouraged."

Pomp smiled.

"You're the most beautiful woman in the world," he told her. "People are going to have something to say about everything you do."

"Oh hush—how many women have you seen, that you should pay me such a compliment?" Tasmin retorted, though she blushed. What with the Indian attack, and her nursing, and her mothering—all the general press of life—it had been weeks since she had had a moment in which to consider her looks. On the boat up the Missouri she had amused herself in all the usual ways: redoing her hair, trying on dresses and jewels, looking in the mirror, worrying that the American climate might affect her complexion. She had also had a bit of time to study herself at Pierre Boisdeffre's trading post. But once on the trek, she had no time for looks—it seemed to her that looks might as well be left out of the equation until they returned to civilization. What she saw the few times she did look was a sunburned, windburned, freckled girl, scratched by weeds and bushes and so pressed by the need to keep her baby well and her husband satisfied that looks hardly seemed worth worrying about. For the moment, energy seemed to matter more, and so far, her energies were still equal to the hundred tasks of the day, whether the tasks were motherly, wifely, or miscellaneous. Still, that Pomp considered her the greatest of beauties was very satisfying.

"I expect there are fine beauties in London or Paris or even New York City that might dispute that comment," she told him. "Of course, there are few of them out here—I suppose I profit from an absence of rivals."

Pomp smiled again—in the distance Monty's wails had intensified.

"I've not paid many women compliments," Pomp said. "I'm just now starting—with you."

"Oh, damn! What could be ailing that child?" Tasmin complained. "I hope you won't be long at your tasks—I want you to come back soon."

"I expect your sisters will be curious, too," he reminded her. "They're always watching, those girls."

"Yes, and they'll be slapped, unless they're careful!" she declared hotly, before she turned away to see what could be the matter with her sturdy child.

14

Tasmin had guessed it: horses!

Tasmin had guessed it: horses! A large one belonging to William Ashley had stepped on Monty's toe. Little Onion had already made a poultice for the damaged digit, but Monty still sobbed and choked, great tears rolling down his plump cheeks, while the two other toddlers, Talley and Rabbit, looked on in shocked wonder. Seeing his mother, Monty immediately flung out his arms to be taken, and Tasmin did take him, though of course there was not much to be done for a mashed toe that Little Onion had not already seen to.

"Little boys should avoid big horses, if they value their toes," Tasmin told him; she then sat down behind a wagon and gave him the breast, which he attacked greedily, as if, by sucking noisily, he could avoid his hurt. The wagon was theirs, purchased from Ashley by Lord Berrybender—it was already half packed with a mélange of their possessions. The Berrybenders, like the trappers, had been inching toward a departure for several days. But with the Ute danger passed, life in the Valley of the Chickens was on the whole pleasant and no one could quite work up to resuming the hardships of the trek, though William Ashley had hurried off finally that very morning, going north to catch a steamer at the mouth of the Yellowstone. He had sold Lord Berrybender four horses and what little champagne remained.

Tasmin had marched through the trappers without giving them a look—a mother hurrying to her injured child was not likely to attract much comment. In her opinion the mountain men would have needed to be a good deal more expert in the ways of women to suspect that she had been enjoying the first blushing kisses of her new, unsanctioned love.

In fact the mountain men were mainly debating which way to go once they left the rendezvous: south with the Berrybenders to Santa Fe, north with Ashley to the Yellowstone, east into the Black Hills of the Sioux, where there were said to be many beaver still, or west over the mountains to California. Tasmin and Pomp were often together anyway—all the mountain men reckoned that Pomp would be dead but for Tasmin's nursing. If he was sweet on his beautiful nurse, that would be only natural. None of them had ever known Pomp to take a woman—the common opinion was that if he ever *did* take one, he would be unlikely to start with Jim Snow's formidable wife. In the end the mountain men who decided on Santa Fe did so at least in part because it meant they'd have the Berrybender women to look at—in their minds no small benefit.

Tasmin had hoped for a few minutes alone, in which to soothe her child and collect her thoughts, but even the modest privacies attendant on the performance of bodily functions were not always easily secured in such a large camp. The bear cub, Abby, who liked to inject herself into every crisis, followed Tasmin around the wagon and thrust her cold nose into Tasmin's hand. It was a lovely, clear day—near the river Tasmin saw her father, in argument with Vicky Kennet. Vicky's violent threat to tear his throat out if he touched her had caused only the break of a day or two in the old lord's pursuit of the long-legged cellist.

Tasmin was just shifting Monty, a little boy who would soon be passing from hunger into sleep, onto the other breast, when his two little friends, Talley and Rabbit, followed the bear cub and stood watching the proceedings solemnly, as if waiting for a chance at the teat themselves.

"Go away, boys . . . you've got the wrong ma," Tasmin commanded. "This fountain will soon be empty."

A moment later Little Onion, who had been drying jerky, swooped over and picked up a little boy under each arm; she carried them, unmoving as logs, back around the wagon so that Tasmin could finish her nursing in peace.

She had scarcely gone when Tasmin's sisters came trailing over, Buffum looking subdued and Mary, as always, looking combative.

"Pa's determined to have Vicky—I doubt it will be long before he wears her down," Buffum remarked.

"Mr. Bonneville fancies her too," Mary remarked.

"Mr. Bonneville is said to have twelve wives, which would mean little time for Vicky," Tasmin said. "Perhaps he merely likes her fiddling."

"The pater is tired of Milly," Mary informed them. "And he does know Vicky's ways."

"Vicky's merely a servant, you know," Buffum reminded them. "Servants finally have to do what masters say—even if reluctantly."

"Where have you hidden Pomp?" Mary asked, giving Tasmin one of her not-quite-sane but nonetheless penetrating looks.

"He's burying the other bear cub," Tasmin said. "The Utes made short work of that friendly little beast. Pomp feels badly about it."

"Our Pomp's too softhearted by half," Mary replied. "I suppose you've been soothing him, Tassie, in your insistent way."

"Suppose all you want," Tasmin replied. "Why don't you go flog your fat botanist and leave the rest of us in peace?"

"Such a careless brat, Monty," Mary said. "Letting a vast horse step on his toe."

Tasmin made no answer. She did not propose to talk to Mary, a skilled interrogator who proceeded by indirection but, in the end, usually managed to extract whatever kernel of information she was seeking. It was better to ignore her than to outwit her, although Tasmin did mean to outwit her when it came to her own relations with Pomp. Since Pomp had not reappeared she thought she might use the time, once Monty finished nursing, to do a bit of packing herself. Jimmy, her husband, always kept his possessions neatly, in one place, a habit that irritated her, since her own managed to get themselves scattered over an acre or two.

By the river her father and Vicky still seemed to be faced off. Tasmin was rather fearful that violence might erupt—and it did erupt, but not from the riverside. It came in the form of a loud fit of sobbing, the source being Buffum, who flung herself into Tasmin's arms.

"Oh hell . . . now what's wrong with you?" Tasmin asked. Buffum, usually wan and quiet, if capable of distinctly sharp sarcasm, had been looking unusually cheerful, even beautiful, for the past few weeks, and had even offered, on more than one occasion, to tend to the little boys for an hour or two, while Coal and Little Onion performed prodigies of labor about the camp.

For a time Buffum sobbed so hard she could not get breath to speak, while Tasmin made soothing sounds and occasionally stroked her woeful sister's hair.

Mary, who hated to see her sister Buffum get even the most cursory attention, soon showed her impatience with Buffum's lachrymose fit.

"Do make her hush, Tassie," Mary insisted. "Nothing is as boring as listening to a rich girl cry."

"Rich girl?" Tasmin said. "What possible good's it being a rich girl here? Show a little sympathy for your sister—for all we know she's grievously ill."

"Not a bit of it!" Mary insisted. "The mater spoiled her outrageously and now we must have our conversations interrupted by all this wailing."

"I don't recall that it was much of a conversation anyway," Tasmin remarked, still stroking Buffum's hair, which was rather lank. "Why can't you just go and beat your boyfriend? Bessie here may not wish to reveal this sorrow, which is likely a profound one."

"It *is* a profound one!" Buffum declared, glaring at Mary. "The fact is I'm in love with a Ute and I don't wish to leave, tomorrow or ever."

"Miscegenation—I suspected it," Mary said. "Father will be most distraught."

"Well, first things first—which Ute are you in love with?" Tasmin asked.

Four Utes still wandered around the camp, hoping to pick up a few last presents. Buffum pointed to a tall, handsome youth who was in conversation with Jim Bridger. Tasmin had noticed the boy herself, several times—his looks were indeed striking, and he wore nothing but a loincloth.

"His white name is High Shoulders," Buffum informed them. "I find him singularly beautiful and I shall love him till I die."

"You evil slut, now you've lain with our brother's murderer!" Mary hissed.

"Oh, do leave off," Tasmin said. "Our brother was run over by a horse. I will admit that if I were inclined to copulate with a Ute, young Mr. High Shoulders would be the most likely candidate. It would no doubt be a good deal more normal than flagellating a Dutchman with brambles."

"Oh, Tassie, he is *so* beautiful!" Buffum declared. "I was by the river when he came to me the first time. As you can see, he doesn't wear much—just that little flap, which he quickly removed. I confess I could not look away—Tim, as you might suspect, is a rather stubby lad. High Shoulders at once presented himself to me and we began to fornicate to the most blissful lengths—I even suspect that I may already be with child."

"They must have been blissful lengths, if you're already pregnant," Tasmin said, not unkindly. She remembered her own blissful lengths with Jim and her surprise at how quickly Monty was planted in her—apparently the famous Berrybender fecundity had not been at all affected by vigorous travel in the West. Lay down with a Berrybender and a child will soon enough arrive, Tasmin thought.

"You are evil hussies, both of you," Mary declared. "I far prefer Piet's mild hygienic practices, myself."

The half-insane light was once again in her eyes.

"Now Buffum will give birth to a wicked little half-breed, further debasing the Berrybender escutcheon," she continued.

"Pomp's a half-breed—surely you don't consider *him* wicked?" Tasmin replied.

"No, but it's plain that you hope to be wicked with him," Mary said. "Perhaps you have been already, even though joined in holy matrimony with Mr. Jim Snow."

"Let's take one imbroglio at a time, if you don't mind," Tasmin said lightly, well aware that a direct or too emphatic denial would only fan Mary's flame. Besides, the fact was that Buffum's dilemma *was* immediate. The company's departure was imminent. What *was* to become of Buffum and her handsome Mr. High Shoulders? Was he to travel with them, far from the land of his people, or was Buffum to be left behind, to live, improbably, as a Ute wife? It was certainly a dilemma Tasmin had not expected to be presented with, but of course such things *would* always happen and a decision would have to be made. She stole another look at the slim youth, High Shoulders—a striking young man in every way. Tasmin could not but wonder whether she would have approved of the union had the Ute been short, squat, and toothless, rather than sharp featured, graceful, and lean. Ugly men might, of course, have fine souls; some she had seen in the London salons, though ugly as frogs, seemed to enjoy clear success with ladies both elegant and highborn. Her sister would not be likely to disregard a fine body, should one present itself.

"This iniquity shall not go unpunished," Mary said, but neither Tasmin nor Buffum paid any attention to her—Mary soon hurried away to make the news known to Piet.

"What am I to do, Tassie? I can't leave him—I can't—and we are to depart tomorrow, Jim Bridger declares."

"Somehow I don't think you'd last long with the Utes," Tasmin told her. "I think we'd better take your handsome savage with us, if he'll go. Jimmy won't much like it—he doesn't trust Utes—but then, who knows when we'll see Jimmy again?"

It was then, as Bess rushed off to her young man, that Tasmin noticed that Monty, unaware of the passion storms swirling around him, had dropped off the breast and was sound asleep.

15

"Stop calling me a wench . . ."

Tasmin found herself secretly pleased that her sister Bess had been so enterprising as to take a handsome lover. This development would give the trappers something to talk about for a while, so that they were unlikely to take any particular notice if she were to wander off in the woods with Pomp Charbonneau, known, in any case, to be her very close friend.

Where was he, though, her Pomp? She found that she could not keep from throwing glances at the glade where they had recently been embracing. Tasmin was not exactly worried, and yet she did wish Pomp would appear—even a distant glimpse of him would be reassuring. When he didn't appear, little by little, anxieties crept in. Was he perhaps having second thoughts—reminding himself, for example, that it was Jim Snow's wife whom he had just been kissing? He had seemed to welcome her kisses— but then, where was he? Being so very inexperienced, perhaps he merely did not suspect how anxious ladies were likely to become, or how insecure they could be, even about long-established affections, and of course, only more so about affections that had only been acknowledged for a few hours.

In Pomp's arms, with his mouth on hers, Tasmin had felt certain enough about his love—though she was not yet entirely sure about his desire. Hadn't he confessed to her himself that he really didn't know *how* to desire? Tasmin considered desire an easy thing, usually; a thing quickly awakened, though perhaps not likely to appear with uniform intensity either among men or women. There were days, after all, when she felt not the slightest desire to copulate with Jim. That need came often enough, and intensely enough, but there were times when it was absent. Pomp had so far been exempt from these rhythms—entirely normal rhythms, in

Tasmin's view. After all, if lovers were constantly at one another, how could work get done and children reared?

Pomp, she felt sure, was merely untouched in that way—she considered that it might be delicious work to get him going and bring him up to speed. But at the moment, she would be content with something simpler: she merely wanted him to reappear, to give her at least a look that might suggest that he wanted to continue what they had begun. The fact that he did *not* reappear was beginning to annoy her. Men, she knew, were rather of the out-of-sight, out-of-mind disposition. She doubted that Jimmy Snow, wherever he might be, had given her two thoughts since he departed; perhaps Pomp, a male after all, was merely trying to catch a fish, or something, quite unaware of the anxious flutters in Tasmin's breast. He was not yet quite back to full strength—he might merely be taking a nap in the cool glade. Tasmin deposited her sleeping child with Little Onion and strolled down toward the trees, meaning to look for Pomp, but before she could put that plan into action, matters came to a head between her father and Vicky. Lord Berrybender gave a loud cry—evidently Vicky had rushed in and bitten the old fool. Lord B., wild with fury, managed to deal her a roundhouse blow, knocking her off her feet and into the shallows of the river. The mountain men, always happy to divert themselves by watching fights, gave a wild cheer, though it was not clear to Tasmin which combatant they were cheering for. Vicky Kennet came at Lord Berrybender again, kicking his peg leg out from under him; she then grabbed his crutch and began to beat him with it—her fighting spirit provoked even wilder cheers from the mountain men. Then Lord B. managed to catch her ankle; he succeeded in upending her. The two of them rolled around near the river's edge, neither able to gain a clear advantage. Lord B. cursed, Vicky screamed insults—a few of the trappers began to stroll down toward the scene of the combat in order to watch the fight at closer range. Tasmin thought she had better go too, perhaps attempt to break up this violent tussle before anyone was very much hurt; but before she could reach the struggling couple, Pomp Charbonneau, the very man she had been hoping to see, emerged from the forest, the carcass of a small deer across his shoulders. He quickly waded the river, dropped his dead buck, and began to urge armistice on the wrestling couple. Much relieved to see that Pomp had merely been hunting, Tasmin hurried along; but by the time she reached the river her father and Vicky had given up punching one another; both sat, wet and exhausted, staring into space. Pomp helped Lord B. get his peg leg adjusted.

"What a tussle, Papa," Tasmin said. "I assure you we've all been most entertained by your efforts to subdue a helpless woman."

"Subdue her? I want to muzzle her—you see where she bit me," Lord Berrybender complained, pointing at a tiny spot of blood on his throat. "I won't be able to sleep a wink, for fear she'll slip in and finish the job."

"Now why would our Vicky do such a thing?" Tasmin asked. "I hope you haven't been suggesting improprieties again—I warned you about that myself."

"That's right—you bit my hand," Lord B. recalled. "I ought to muzzle you and this wench too."

"Stop calling me a wench, you old pile of guts!" Vicky demanded, her nostrils flaring.

And yet, a moment later, when Lord Berrybender struggled to stand up, it was Vicky who helped him, returning the very crutch she had been beating him with.

"I never saw such obstinacy," Lord Berrybender remarked, though in a considerably softer tone.

"So it's the altar or nothing—is that the case, my dear?" he added, thoughtfully.

"That's right—the altar or nothing," Vicky said. "I'll be your wife, I reckon, but I won't be your whore."

Lord Berrybender heaved a sigh. Then he put an arm around Vicky's shoulder and the two of them started up the hill.

"It might as well be the altar, then," Lord B. remarked, to Tasmin's complete astonishment.

The mountain men, far from sure what they were witnessing, nonetheless produced a hearty cheer, as the old lord and the young cellist walked away from their combat hand in hand.

Behind the trappers Tasmin spotted Buffum, standing shyly by the side of High Shoulders, her towering Ute, who seemed to be trying to figure out what the men were celebrating.

"There, do you see that?" Tasmin asked Pomp, with a nod at her father and his bride-to-be.

"I guess they made it up—and there's venison for supper too," he said, smiling.

Tasmin, despite her relief that Pomp was all right, felt a flush of irritation. Made it up? Was that all he saw in the situation?

"It's more than that—he's going to marry her—it's what Vicky's planned for since the moment my mother broke her neck," Tasmin informed him. "I thought my father would elude her, but he didn't. She's won . . . and good for her. Don't you see?"

Pomp got out his knife and prepared to butcher the little deer. He heard a note of irritation in Tasmin's voice and looked up, wondering what was wrong. Tasmin realized that Pomp was merely being practical—getting a meal ready—and yet it irked her that he should have been so untouched by the storm of emotion he had just witnessed; if he was untouched by her father's acknowledgment that he was attached to Vicky, perhaps he was untouched, also, by the fact that they themselves had kissed. If he had strong feelings for her, he was evidently willing to let them wait until the task at hand—cutting up a deer—had been performed properly. It irked her so much that she gave the helpless carcass a vigorous kick.

"Wake up, Pomp!" she demanded. "My father's getting married, my sister's taken a savage lover, and then there's *us*. Rather a lot for an afternoon, wouldn't you say?

"There is *us*, isn't there?" she asked, her confidence slipping.

"There's us," Pomp agreed, calmly. "Do you want to sneak off for a minute, once I get this deer butchered?"

"That's exactly what I do want—to sneak off for a minute, once you get this wretched deer cut up," Tasmin told him. "And you might consider hurrying, if you don't mind. I'm afraid that you'll soon realize that I'm a very impatient person."

"I'll hurry," Pomp said, kneeling by the carcass.

With an effort Tasmin restrained herself—it was on the tip of her tongue to explain to the young Nimrod that in her opinion kissing should come first and mundane chores a distant second. Any of the trappers could easily have butchered the deer. She started to make that point, but held back— she had glanced up the hill and noticed that Father Geoffrin was watching the two of them closely, a fact which irritated her mightily. Father Geoffrin, a great reader of risqué novels, was always the first to spot new currents of emotion, should any happen to swirl through the camp. Tasmin didn't want the nosy priest knowing about herself and Pomp—not just yet. So, instead of immediately drawing Pomp into the bushes, Tasmin waded into the river and washed her face and neck. Even a Jesuit couldn't object to that, or conclude that something might be afoot.

All the same, refreshing as the splash was, Tasmin felt a sag of weariness at the thought of the intractability of men. When she met Jim Snow he had known nothing of women except the bare physical facts. Of course, Jim had grown up in a wilderness—how could he have learned? But Pomp had been educated in a castle in Germany, where by his own admission he had observed cooks and chambermaids making merry with their lovers. And yet it was beginning to dawn on Tasmin that Pomp might know even less about women than Jim had. Was she always, then, doomed to have to be the teacher? Would she never find a man who could teach *her,* someone who would dance her off to bed without her having to forever be leading and expostulating? In the whole camp, the discouraging fact was that the only man who did understand her feelings was a little French priest, whose real interest was in romantical novels and well-stitched French clothes. Must she simply flounder from innocent to innocent until, old and jaded, she accepted one of the cynical old frog princes of the London salons, perhaps for no better reason than that she would at least not have to explain to him the realities of love?

Tasmin didn't know—she still meant to take Pomp into the woods and kiss him to her heart's content—but since that was her plan, she thought it might be wisest to give Father Geoffrin a wide berth until the thing had been accomplished.

How irritating that the priest seemed able to read her emotions as easily as he read his Marmontel!

16

"Not for nothing have I read my Laclos . . ."

But that's *why* I understand your emotions better than you understand them yourself," Father Geoffrin informed Tasmin—who had at once forgotten her resolve to avoid him until her romance had been consummated—if it should be.

The two of them, having attacked the tender venison with their hands, were licking grease off their fingers.

"Not for nothing have I read my Laclos, my Crébillon, the divine Madame de Lafayette, my Restif, and all the others," he went on. "I am so well schooled in the subtleties of love that a peek into your own feelings requires not the smallest effort."

"I suppose what you're saying is that I ain't subtle, like your powdered French ladies," Tasmin grumped. "Is that what you're saying, Geoff?"

She was watching Pomp assist Jim Bridger in doctoring a mare who had something amiss with her foot.

"Would you say that a sledgehammer hitting an anvil is subtle?" Geoff asked, with a wicked smile. "That's about how subtle you are, my beauty."

"It's hardly a flattering metaphor, and I'm not your beauty," Tasmin told him. "I feel like crying and you're not helping, even though that is generally thought to be a priest's duty."

"Tasmin, you can't make Pomp Charbonneau into what he's not," Father Geoff told her affably. "He's not a lecherous man. Perhaps you can maul him into what you want him to be—but perhaps not. After all, not all love succeeds—if it did, think of how monotonous life would be."

"Shut up! I'll make this succeed," Tasmin said. "I'll make Pomp want what I want. Why shouldn't he?"

Father Geoffrin shrugged.

"He's a very calm fellow, Pomp," he observed. "Perhaps he prefers his calm—he won't have much of it if you succeed in entangling him in your lusts."

Though Tasmin had sought the priest out—where else was she going to get an informed opinion about matters of the heart but from this smart celibate? But now she found that she hated everything he was telling her. Why would Pomp Charbonneau, the man she meant to have, possibly prefer calm to passion? He hadn't really even known passion yet.

"If he's as innocent as he looks, you might consider giving him a little time to reflect," Geoff advised.

Tasmin put her face in her hands—in a moment warm tears were dripping through her fingers, tears mainly of self-reproach. She was beginning to fear that she must, after all, be a bad woman to want this young man when she already had an excellent husband. It must be sinful to want two at once—and yet that was the fact: she did want two at once. Whatever he might have observed the German chambermaids doing, Pomp Charbonneau *was* as innocent as he looked; yet now she was determined to besmirch that innocence, and as soon as possible. She *did* want to entangle him in her lusts. She was bad—she knew it—and yet she couldn't change. She meant to have her way—the greedy, sensual way of the Berrybenders. Were her appetites, after all, as selfish and unrestrained as her father's? What had he done, for the last forty years, except seduce every comely woman who caught his eye, in the process betraying his marriage vows as casually as if he were eating a peach? She was younger, but was she any better? She knew she wasn't. Even in England she had scorned ladylike behavior—now, far out on the American prairies, it could only be a nuisance. There were social customs—and then there was one's real nature. What *was* her real nature?

"Cry, you'll feel better," said Father Geoffrin, putting an arm around her shoulders rather tentatively. "Although personally it's the one criticism I have of women—they *will* cry—and then men feel so bad."

"Well, you needn't feel bad," Tasmin told him, flinging off the arm. "I wasn't crying about you."

"But you might, mightn't you? After all, I'm a needful person too," the priest told her. "I cry about myself every time I remember how far I am from Paris."

"That's not important," Tasmin said bluntly—she needed to take out her irritation on somebody. Why not Geoff, her understanding friend?

"There you sit, day after day," she went on, "reading about love in your ill-bred books, and yet you never do love with anyone at all. At least I try to grapple with the thing itself, although I always seem to fail."

"You don't always fail—no self-pity now," Geoff reprimanded. "Sometimes you appear to be *very* happy, as you were this morning when you emerged from your first little rendezvous with Pomp."

"How did *you* know that I was happy?" she asked, for it was true: she had been very happy that morning.

"By your blushing—you reddened like a rose," Geoff told her. "It's mainly happy women who blush to the roots of their hair."

"You spy!—sometimes I hate you—no one else saw me blushing," Tasmin retorted.

"Not so—your sister Mary noticed even before I did."

"The sinister brat, what did she say?"

"She said, 'The fat's in the fire, Tasmin has had her way with Pomp,'" the priest quoted.

"But I *haven't* had my way with him—why are you all so convinced that I'm bad?" she asked, feeling very discouraged.

"*I* don't think you're bad," Geoff assured her. "You're merely very impetuous, and rather forward at times."

"I confess I did kiss Pomp—just kissing, no more," Tasmin admitted. "And you were right—I *was* happy, and I did blush. But it was only kissing."

"Fine—though kissing has been known to lead to even more intimate behavior," Father Geoff reminded her. "And then you went back in the woods with him after he butchered our deer. That was for more kissing, I assume."

Tasmin put her face in her hands again, too upset to voice her disappointment.

"It was like kissing a brother," she confided, when she felt able to speak.

"Now I understand your tears," Father Geoffrin said, putting his arm around her again; this time she let it be, and even rested her throbbing head against his shoulder.

"The kisses of a brother are not always what one wants," he said.

"It was so sweet this morning," Tasmin told him. "But this afternoon it just didn't work . . . he wouldn't even allow me to hug him as I wished to."

"My, my . . . it's so complicated," Father Geoffrin said. "Do you suppose you'd ever want to kiss me? You needn't worry that I'd feel brotherly about you."

Tasmin fairly jumped away—she could not have moved more quickly if she had discovered that she was standing on a snake.

"But Geoff, you're a priest—you can't kiss anybody, much less me," she told him.

"I'm not much of a priest—you yourself frequently remind me of that sad fact," Geoff said. "Besides, there's a whole school of literature based on the unchaste and disorderly behavior of priests and nuns."

"I'm not literature, I'm a woman," Tasmin said, indignantly. "You of all people—trying to catch me when I'm discouraged."

"A catch is a catch," Father Geoffrin said.

Tasmin looked him in the face. His was a thin face, intelligence popping off it like sparks. In his eyes she saw unmistakable desire, the one thing she had not been able to arouse in her sweet, handsome Pomp. A shiver ran through her—she was about to tell Geoff quite firmly that he had better mind his manners when Monty came waddling in their direction. The confusion inside Tasmin was so great that she merely jumped up and hurried toward the river, passing her son without even giving him a pat, a lapse that startled Monty so that he opened his mouth to protest but then forgot to wail.

Father Geoffrin sighed; he thought there might yet be at least a glimmer of opportunity, though opportunity was not likely to present itself anytime soon. As a second best he helped himself to another bloody slice of the excellent, tender venison.

17

In her confusion she first blamed Jim . . .

When dusk fell, Tasmin hurried down to the river and walked along it until she found some concealing bushes; then she sat down and sobbed until she was empty of tears. In her confusion she first blamed Jim—why would he just go riding off and leave his wife the opportunity to develop so many unfaithful feelings? There were several competent scouts in the company—why couldn't two of them have conducted this scout, if it was so important? Wasn't the real reason Jim left that he simply got tired of dealing with her? Of course, their matings were still lively and satisfying—it was her talk, the incessant flow of opinions that poured out of her, which seemed to tire Jim. Indeed, her talk seemed to tire everyone, except perhaps the smart little French priest, whose sudden declaration of interest had just shocked her so. If only Jimmy wouldn't indulge in such lengthy absences she would have much less opportunity to daydream of love with Pomp.

But once she was cried out, which left her calm if tired, content merely to listen to the river rush over its rocks, Tasmin knew that blaming Jim Snow wasn't really fair. She had had just as many daydreams of romance with Pomp Charbonneau while Jimmy was still in camp. Nor could Pomp be blamed, particularly—he had told her months before that he wasn't lustful, a confession she had felt free to ignore, confident that she could make any man lust a little if she applied herself to the task. Young virgins often became old lechers, in her opinion. Pomp Charbonneau simply didn't know what he was missing—once she was able to show him, surely he wouldn't want to miss it anymore.

Sitting concealed behind her bush, Tasmin felt exhausted—a whole day of the surge and ebb of feeling had worn her out—and for what? Here they were, hundreds of miles from Santa Fe, with summer ending, the temperament of the Indians uncertain, the way hazardous, Jimmy gone, herself with a young child to care for, a task that would have usurped all her energies had she not been able to count on the loyalty of Little Onion, a young woman who had nothing in particular to be happy about, that Tasmin could see, but who was unfailing in her devotion to the various little boys while still managing to accomplish a myriad of chores.

Tasmin knew she should have been grateful enough just to be alive and healthy, with a healthy baby. She should be capable of concentrating on just the task of survival, and not go around kissing one minute and sobbing the next, allowing herself to be prey to the sort of hothouse emotions that might better have flourished among the bored nobility of London or Paris, Venice or Vienna, rather than in a remote and rugged valley by a mountain river. Why bother loving, kissing, seducing, desiring, failing, or succeeding in the rare sublimities and frequent disappointments attendant on the attempt to love any man, much less the two intractable specimens she had fixed her feelings on? Why didn't she just stop it, pack up her kit, yell at the trappers until they sprang into action, get the whole company on the road—any road?

She knew she didn't lack character—it must be that her character was just bad, selfish, even brutal. She couldn't stop wanting the pleasure of being loved by a man—even the sneaky little priest had looked at her in such a way as to make her shiver. The first soft kisses she had exchanged with Pomp that morning *had* made her blush to the roots of her hair. She *was* reckless and she couldn't help it—she was going to make trouble for men. Those who didn't welcome trouble would do better to stay out of her way.

Just as Tasmin was reaching this uncomfortable conclusion, she happened to notice a small, squat figure watching her through the bushes. Kate Berrybender, unobserved, had found her out.

"Are you crying because you miss Mr. James Snow?" Kate asked, with her customary bluntness.

"I would be glad to see Jimmy—I mostly am always glad to see Jimmy," Tasmin admitted, wondering why, of all times, she now had to be interrogated by a four-year-old.

"So is that why you're crying, then?" Kate asked, in a tone that was surprisingly sympathetic.

"It's not always easy to say why one cries, my dear," Tasmin said. "I cry because I'd burst if I don't."

"I think it's because you miss Mr. James Snow," Kate concluded. "I often feel like crying myself when Mr. James Snow is absent. When he's here I don't feel that the Indians are as likely to scalp me."

"An accurate surmise, I'd say."

"Pomp Charbonneau is rather worried—I believe he's looking for you," Kate informed her.

"You found me easily enough," Tasmin pointed out. "Surely a skilled scout such as Pomp could locate me if he really wanted to."

"I don't know whether to call him 'mister' or 'monsieur,'" Kate confessed. "At times he seems rather French."

Tasmin chuckled.

"Personally, I don't find him French enough," she confessed. "Nor do I find him American enough. It may be that he's stuck in between, which is why he vexes me so."

"That priest is a wily fellow," Kate remarked.

"Wily indeed—but at least he's French enough," Tasmin told her.

"All the same, I do feel better when Mr. James Snow is with us," Kate said.

"I suppose I do too," Tasmin allowed. "If you see Monsieur Pomp, tell him that I can be found sitting squarely behind this bush."

"I don't like it that you cry, Tassie," Kate admitted, in a quavering voice. "Perhaps you could hug me. I'm sure I'd feel somewhat better after my hug."

Tasmin hugged her warmly—despite the child's bossy airs, she *was* a baby sister.

"I think I'll just call Pomp 'mister,'" Kate said, as she was leaving. "Perhaps it will help him be more American."

It was full dark when Pomp came—Tasmin had been sitting, rather numbly, wondering if he *would* come. He moved so quietly that when he put his hand on her shoulder Tasmin jumped, thinking it might be Geoff.

"Kate said you were crying—I expect it's my fault," he said.

"Not at all," Tasmin assured him. "If there's one thing I can't stand it's men who assume blame when no blame has been assigned them.

"I have my moods, Pomp," she added. "Many of them are just my moods—most of them have nothing to do with you."

"But you *were* vexed with me this afternoon," he reminded her, easing down to sit beside her.

"It would be more accurate to say I was frustrated," she said. "I didn't see why I shouldn't kiss you, and yet when I tried I felt embarrassed. Nothing is more sobering than trying to kiss a man who doesn't really want you to."

"It's just that this is new," Pomp said. "I was afraid someone might spot us."

Tasmin didn't believe him, but she found his hand and twined her fingers in it.

"Pleasure has its risks," she told him. "I don't shy from them, but you big strong men certainly seem to."

"I was only trying to explain."

"No use, no use," she said sharply. "Explaining won't get us where I want us to be."

She forced him back until he lay full length on the grass—then she bent over and pressed a kiss on him that lasted and lasted, as their kisses had that morning. She was gentle at first but not girlish. Soon she kissed his eyelids, his throat and chest, nipped more than once at his lower lip and his neck. Pomp quivered but he didn't draw away. Tasmin, who had daydreamed about many delicious preliminaries that might be drawn out for days or weeks, as Pomp decreed, suddenly felt such a rush of desire that she felt herself go damp and dewy; she at once abandoned the notion of exquisite preliminaries. Keeping him pinned beneath her, her avid mouth on his, she undid his trousers and grasped his shaft. Pomp seemed to shiver, but didn't protest.

"Just let me do what I want," she whispered. "Just let me."

She put her mouth back on his, so as not to let him spoil things by some clumsy word. Dewy as she was, she had only to flex a few times to settle Pomp just where she had been wanting to settle him. Pomp lay very still; he didn't move but Tasmin moved. Her breath grew hoarse and hot against his cheeks—in only a minute, it seemed, his seed surged, and then seeped and seeped and seeped as, for as long as possible, Tasmin held him inside her, calming, her warm cheek against his. They lay thus for several minutes, neither of them speaking, Tasmin stroking his brow, touching his hair, now and then dipping her mouth for a quick kiss. Little by little the worm of his manhood grew smaller, until it finally slipped out.

"Now then, that wasn't so hard, was it?" she asked. Pleasure was still in her voice, just a little hoarseness.

"It's only happened to me in dreams," Pomp admitted, speaking softly. He seemed to be sinking into an even deeper quiet.

"Well, I hope you liked it as much as you liked the dreams," she said. "I assume you *did* like them."

"I liked this more, because I like you," Pomp said. "Only I feel I lost something, somehow."

He didn't say it critically—from the gentle way he held her it was clear enough that he was pleased—and he had spoken honestly, rather than romantically. He felt he had lost something; he admitted it.

"You did lose something, but it can easily be replenished," Tasmin assured him. "In fact it's replenishing, even now. But you're mine now—I suppose you could justly say you'd lost your freedom."

She leaned close but could not really see his eyes.

"If you're just going to accuse me of stripping away your innocence, then I'm likely to box your ears," she threatened.

"I wasn't innocent," Pomp insisted. "I saw too much to be innocent, even before my mother died."

"I don't know what you're talking about," Tasmin said, wondering why they were talking at all. Very likely, with the right kiss or caress, they could be making love again.

"Ma said I was born by sorrow's river," he said. "I seem to carry a weight. It keeps me from being quite like other men."

"Stop it! Don't talk so!" she demanded. "What we just did made me quite as happy as I've ever been. I don't want my happiness to slip away, and it will if you continue to talk so sadly."

Pomp said no more. He accepted Tasmin's kisses and kissed back, gently. Tasmin expected that he would begin to touch her—her breasts, perhaps, or the seeping place below, but he didn't. She told herself she had better not rush him. Once he learned more about passion he would surely be more active. She must be patient with him, a hard resolve, because she was by nature impatient. Now that she had had a little of what she wanted, she saw no reason not to have more—yet she knew it might be best to accept his shyness, for a time. She tried to brush away the shadow that dappled her happiness. What if Geoff was right? What if Pomp valued calm more than passion? What if in his depths he just wasn't sensual? His body had responded to her, but even then, his soul he seemed to keep for himself. He was a man without strategies. Even Jim Snow, no very refined seducer, had more guile and much more temperament. She continued to hold Pomp and kiss him but she couldn't quite get his sad words out of her mind. He had been born by sorrow's river—he seemed to carry a weight other men needn't carry. What could these words mean? She hated all such reflections.

They lay together in the darkness for almost an hour, until finally the evening chill drove them back to the campfire. The mountain men, playing cards and drinking, took no notice. In order to stoke her resolution, Tasmin flew at once into a frenzy of packing—she charged into the mountain men and demanded that they put down their cards and see to the wagons and animals. She wanted a dawn departure.

Tasmin had finally had enough of the Valley of the Chickens. She was up most of the night, packing and hectoring, and might have actually had the party on the move not long after dawn had not Vicky Kennet insisted that her nuptials with Lord Berrybender be performed before they left.

"I rather fear she means it—damned stubborn on that point," Lord B. was forced to admit.

"Oh damn! Now?" Tasmin protested, but Venetia Kennet held her ground—she refused even to come out of her tent, insisting that they become man and wife before risking the prairies.

"All right, be quick, then—Geoff, get to it! Marry them!" Tasmin demanded.

"But I've hardly had my coffee," Father Geoffrin protested; but Tasmin was ablaze with impatience. Father Geoff managed to find a prayer book, lined up bride, groom, and attendants, and proceeded to intone what seemed to Tasmin like rather dubious Latin, while the mountain men listened in wonder. The minute he was done the bride and groom exchanged a lusty kiss, the mountain men cheered again, and the company slowly climbed into wagons or mounted horses and proceeded out of the Valley of the Chickens. Old Hugh Glass traveled on foot, the bear cub, Abby, trailing behind him.

As the bright sun shone on the long plain ahead and struck gold glints off the snow on the high peaks to the north, Tasmin felt her spirit suddenly soar. They were moving again, they were on their trip in this wide, sunny land. They had been too long stopped, all crowded up together. No wonder she had become moody; no wonder she had worried too much about what Jim or Pomp might feel. Now at least they were on the go: travelers, adventurers! What a fine life it was!

Vicky Kennet, the new bride, sat beside Tasmin on the wagon seat. Lord Berrybender, much excited to be loose amid the game again, had converted their old cart into a kind of fiacre; he raced ahead with Señor Yanez and

Signor Claricia, provided with some new guns he had purchased from William Ashley, eager to shoot whatever beasts presented themselves.

"Well, Vic, I guess you're my stepmother now," Tasmin remarked. "I hope you'll attempt to give me motherly advice when I need it, which is apt to be often."

"I will, but it's not likely you'll take it," Vicky said, with a smile.

"At any rate, congratulations—I thought you had about given up on the old boy," Tasmin offered.

"I did give up on him, several times," Vicky admitted. "But Drum was killed and I came to find that I rather missed your father, odd as that must sound."

"Pretty odd, yes," Tasmin said.

Vicky Kennet didn't feel especially victorious. Mainly she felt tired. The struggle with Lord Berrybender had filled some years of her life, and would no doubt go on being a struggle, and yet the sun was bright and the sky above them vast and blue.

"I expect we're suited enough, your father and I," she remarked to Tasmin. "He knows my ways and I know his."

Tasmin wondered if she would ever be lucky enough to say such a thing. Would she ever know Jim's ways—or he hers? Would she ever know Pomp's ways? Did he even want to know hers?

Before she could slip into a funk again from pondering the imponderables of human love, Monty, too unsteady in the bouncing rig to stand up, crawled to his mother, pulled himself up by grasping her long black hair, and began to make hungry sounds. As if on cue, Vicky's little boy did the same.

Tasmin handed Vicky the reins and pulled Monty into her lap.

"If you drive while I feed mine, I'll drive while you feed yours," she offered.

"Oh Talley won't wait," Vicky told her. "He's as greedy as his father. Perhaps Little Onion can drive—then we can nurse our brats together."

Little Onion, stunned at first to be offered such a huge responsibility, nonetheless accepted the reins and was driving the team as if she had been doing it all her life. She drove, the two mothers nursed, and the Valley of the Chickens was soon just a blue shadow, far behind them.

18

. . . two wolves, huge and insolent . . .

Jim Snow had just killed an elk—more meat than he needed, but the only game he had seen larger than a prairie dog for three days. A week earlier he had been among innumerable buffalo, but the great herds were being pressed by so many Indian bands—Sioux mainly—that he had thought it wiser to leave the buffalo prairies and drift back to areas where there was too little game to attract many hunters.

It was an old elk—it had been trailed by two wolves, who were waiting for it to weaken sufficiently that they could attack. The elk's flesh would be barely edible, but prairie dog made poor eating too, and Jim had to eat. The two wolves, huge and insolent, only retreated a few hundred yards at the sound of his shot. They expected to get their share of the elk, and no doubt would.

Jim was just sharpening his knife, preparatory to cutting up this old, tough animal, when he thought he heard a shout—it seemed he could just see a moving speck, far to the east. The speck might be a human or a solitary buffalo—he couldn't yet tell.

By the time Jim was half done with his butchering, the speck had grown and divided: two humans were approaching on foot from the east. It seemed likely that they were friendly, since they were approaching him directly, making no attempt to conceal themselves. Jim continued his work; he felt little enthusiasm for jerking meat that was almost too tough to chew, but nothing better offered, and a man who was too picky about food could easily starve.

Jim had not seen a soul in six days, as he scouted to the south, enjoying the calm of the great empty country. Very likely the Berrybender party would have left the Valley of the Chickens by then—they would be expecting him to rejoin them soon and lead them to Santa Fe. With Pomp and Kit and Jim Bridger and the others with the party, Jim saw little reason to worry; they were all competent guides.

Then he stood up in surprise: one of the two advancing specks was clearly Maelgwyn Evans, a trapper and friend he had last seen in his camp on the Knife River. The larger speck was probably one of Maelgwyn's sizable wives. But why would Maelgwyn Evans and a large wife be hoofing it across these dun prairies, where there were no beaver to trap?

"Ho, Jimmy," Maelgwyn said, in his lilting Welsh voice, when the couple came in hailing range.

"Hello yourself—this is a fine surprise," Jim said. "I didn't know you was much of a hand for taking long walks like this."

"Well, no, I ain't that much of a walker, and neither is my little bride here, Corn Tassel, who was a maiden of the Chippewas. She's the one gave you that good rubbing with bear grease, when you visited me on the Knife."

"I remember Corn Tassel, but you used to brag that you had six hundred pounds of wives," Jim reminded him. "Corn Tassel's no fawn, but she don't weigh six hundred pounds, either."

"She don't for a fact," Maelgwyn agreed. "I guess you ain't been to the Missouri lately, Jim. So you don't know."

"Don't know what?"

"About the smallpox," Maelgwyn told him. "Water don't burn, but the pox swept up that river like a blaze. I doubt there's thirty Rees left, maybe forty Mandans, and not more than a dozen Otos."

Maelgwyn sighed.

"That's it, Jimmy," he went on. "There's been a raging plague—I expect it's in Canada by now. Bodies everywhere in the villages—wolves feasting. The living too weak to bury the dead. I lost four hundred pounds of wives in less than a week—that's how fast people went."

Jim Snow could hardly credit what he was being told. The Rees and the Mandans had been populous tribes, strong enough to hold their positions as river keepers since long before Lewis and Clark made their trip. Barely a decade earlier, the Rees had turned back William Ashley and a boatload of well-armed mountain men, and the Mandans had been courted by traders from as far away as the Columbia River or the Hudson.

"Only thirty Rees?" he said, shocked—it was almost too much to believe.

"If there's that many," Maelgwyn said. "They may have all died by now. People couldn't die much quicker if you shot them. I seen six dead in a bull boat—I guess they meant to paddle off, but they waited too long to escape."

Jim could hardly get his mind to accept it: as long as he could remember, the Rees and the Mandans had been the powers of the North. If they were gone, what would it mean?

one strong enough to help him out of the lodge and into the water. All the warriors were dead—the few children and few old people who were alive had not the strength to support his weight. The Bad Eye felt bitterly angry. He was the great prophet of the Mandans, but the tribe had collapsed and there was no one to assist him in the time of his greatest need.

Then it occurred to the Bad Eye that perhaps there was a chance, after all. He couldn't walk but it might be that he could crawl. Carefully he rolled off the low ledge where he had held court to tribes and traders for so long and managed to heave himself onto his hands and knees. The effort was enormous; sweat poured off him, stinging sweat that mingled with his sores; but he did manage to crawl a few yards before he had to stop and rest.

Three times he had to stop, exhausted, before he was out of the Skull Lodge. All around him he smelled death—it seemed there must be hundreds of cawing ravens in the camp. But he could also smell the water, which gave him hope. It seemed not far. If he stopped and rested from time to time, surely he could reach it and be saved by the nibbling fish. It was not an easy crawl. Several times he blundered into corpses, or parts of corpses. Once he became entangled in a tree that had washed ashore. But he kept on, convinced that he would be healed if he could only reach the water and give himself to the little fish, the nibblers. For a time it was day—he felt the sun—but the river was much farther than he had supposed it would be, and there were many obstacles in his way. A large creature that he supposed to be a dead buffalo, putrid now, had to be skirted. Finally, after much pushing, he got around it.

Near the river he got into some terrible sticky mud. His hands sunk deep into it when he tried to crawl over it. The water was not far—he could hear the song of its flowing, but his strength was almost gone. Night had come; the mud was cold. Soon he began to shake from fever, shivering one minute and burning the next. Every time he rested it became harder and harder to raise himself onto his hands and knees. The mud was a dreadful obstacle; he could only crawl a few yards before collapsing. At one point, on the slick slope, he slid a few feet and almost rolled onto his back. That wouldn't do: on his back he would be as helpless as a turtle who had been flipped over by a raccoon. Feeling that he was going to be too weak to reach the water, the Bad Eye put all his strength into one last effort, and he did reach water, but it was not the river, it was only a shallow pond near the river's edge. The coolness of the water made him shiver so violently that he felt death might be shaking him. With his hands he raked the water of the little pond, hoping to touch a fish, a little fish, who might nibble the poison out of him. But the only fish in the pond was a dead one, who lent the water a stagnant smell. The Bad Eye felt keenly disappointed. He was in water, but not the right water. He knew he must try again, and he did try, but this time his weight was greater than his strength. He could barely even hold his face out of the water of the pond, even though the pond was only a few inches deep. He tried to crawl out of the pond but water lapped into his mouth and nose when he failed to lift his head. Frightened and bewildered, he began to sputter. His face had never been in water before— except perhaps long before, in boyhood, when his mother had taken him into the river in hopes that it would cure his blindness. All his life he had heard the sound of the river, and yet now he couldn't reach it. When he lifted his head above the water he could breathe the humid, smelly, fishy air, but when he tired, when his neck could no longer support the lifting of his head, his face fell into the water, causing him to choke and splutter. He thrashed, but he could not advance: then he began to drink, swallowing the filthy water, gulping as fast as he could so that it wouldn't cover his face when he rested. Perhaps if he swallowed enough he would finally float, as he had floated in his dream.

It was there, in the misty dawn, still fifty yards from the channel of the great river he had been trying to reach, that the Partezon, riding with Fool's Bull through the camp of the dead, found the great prophet of the Mandans drowned in a puddle so shallow that the water hardly came above the hocks of the Partezon's white horse. A frog sat on the drowned man's head; it leapt into the water with a plop when the two horses came to the edge of the pond.

"Look, there he is," the Partezon said, to Fool's Bull.

"So what? He's just a dead man, let's go," Fool's Bull urged.

But the Partezon was not to be hurried; he sat on his white horse, looking at the swollen corpse of the Bad Eye for what seemed to Fool's Bull like a long time.

"He was supposed to be the greatest man in the world," the Partezon remarked. "And now look: frogs jump off his head. He's just dead, like anybody else."

"Yes, dead—like we'll be in two or three days if we don't get out of here," Fool's Bull remarked bitterly.

"You're always in too big a hurry," the Partezon remarked, but he finally turned his horse and rode downstream.

20

Far out on the prairies . . .

Far out on the prairies, a day or even two days out from the river, the Partezon and Fool's Bull had begun to come upon dead people: Mandans, Rees, a few Otos who had fled in hopes of saving themselves from the great sickness that seemed to hang over the river. They were now half eaten; they had failed to save themselves. As the two riders came closer to the river they saw more and more dead—so many that Fool's Bull would have much preferred to turn back, hunt a little more, enjoy the summer prairies. But the Partezon refused to listen—he always refused to listen. The last thing Fool's Bull would have chosen to do was ride through a country where everyone was dead or dying. It made no sense. This plague had already destroyed the people of the river. Why go where people were dying? The sickness might leave the river and follow them onto the plains, in which case even they would die too.

Fool's Bull had said as much to his stubborn companion, but such sensible considerations didn't interest the Partezon at all. He just kept riding east, ignoring, with his usual rudeness, every sensible thing that Fool's Bull brought up. Over and over Fool's Bull vowed to himself that he himself would turn back and leave the Partezon to his folly; but he didn't turn back. Mainly he kept riding east because he didn't want to give the Partezon a chance to call him a coward, which the Partezon would certainly do if Fool's Bull pulled out of this strange quest.

"We'll die ourselves if we're not careful," he said several times. They were on the edge of what had been the largest Mandan village, and yet they saw nothing but abandoned lodges, some of them with dying people laying half inside and half out, too weak to go farther. Old people, young people, warriors, babies: all were dead or almost dead; the few who clung to life looked at them indifferently as they rode past. They were too far gone to struggle.

"I expect to die someday," the Partezon remarked. "I don't know why you think you ought to live forever."

"I don't want to live forever, but I don't want to die right now, either,"

Fool's Bull argued. "I have two young wives, remember. If you had a few young wives, instead of your cranky old wives, you wouldn't be so reckless with your life."

"I am too old for young wives," the Partezon argued—it amused him to see what lengths Fool's Bull would go to avoid certain tasks.

"Your young wives look bossy to me," he added. "I wouldn't be surprised if they wear you out pretty soon."

Conversation with the Partezon was rarely satisfactory, mainly because the Partezon scorned what seemed to Fool's Bull a sensible, simple, reasonable approach to life. Common sense should have told the man that it was foolish to come into a place where all the people were dying of a horrible sickness; and yet, there they were. Only after they had ridden all the way to the river itself, and seen the drowned body of the Mandan prophet, did the Partezon seem satisfied.

"It's a poor prophet who can't even save himself," the Partezon commented, once they had watered their horses and turned back to the prairie.

The Partezon had heard about the Bad Eye for many years; he had hoped to see him and perhaps converse with him a little. The Mandans had always seemed to him a gullible people, easily tricked by the white traders. It would have been interesting to see what kind of prophecies the fat prophet would have come out with.

Fool's Bull, for his part, was horrified by the state of the dead people he had seen. He was long accustomed to seeing men die in battle and had witnessed many captives being tortured; those deaths had seemed clean, in a way: they were honorable deaths, involving defeat but not shame. The dead in the Mandan camp were different: they were foul deaths, putrefying deaths; and there were so many dead that proper burial was out of the question. He didn't want to see any more such scenes.

"I hope the sickness doesn't follow us," he said, several times.

"You should listen when I tell you something," the Partezon scolded. "The minute I saw those two whites fly up in the air, where only birds are supposed to go, I told you that the time of the People was ending. Now that you've seen it with your own eyes, perhaps you'll pay attention when I tell you something important."

"I saw it, but I don't understand it—how can a whole tribe suddenly die?" Fool's Bull asked.

"The whites made the plague, that's why," the Partezon answered. "Maybe they dropped it out of the sky. If they can fly, then it must be easy for them to sow plagues. Maybe they fly over at night and drop the poisons into cooking pots or onto blankets. I don't know how they spread this pox, but I'm sure they do it."

"What if they drop some on us?" Fool's Bull asked, suddenly fearful—the Partezon had voiced an awful thought.

"Then we'll die, as the Mandans died," the Partezon told him. "Only I don't plan to be as foolish as that fat prophet—I won't crawl into a puddle and drown."

"It's all very well for you to be calm about dying—you're old," Fool's Bull reminded him. "I'm a young man with two wives to sleep with. I don't want this pox dropped on me."

"What you are is a liar," the Partezon told him. "We were born in the same summer—they put us in our cradle boards together—it's nonsense to say I'm old and you're young."

Fool's Bull realized he had spoken carelessly. He and the Partezon *were* the same age. And yet he wanted to live a long time and the Partezon seemed indifferent to the prospect of immediate death.

"Even if the whites *can* fly, it doesn't mean the time of the People is over," he argued.

"You're wrong—that's exactly what it does mean," the Partezon told him.

Of course, he himself did not mean to die shamefully, half in and half out of a lodge, as so many of the Mandans had. He had had a full life, killing many enemies, stealing many horses. When it came time for him to pass into the spirit world, he meant to do it in a dignified way. He meant to go alone in Paha Sapa, the sacred Black Hills, and find a cliff high up, where the eagles nested; there he would fast and pray and chant a little until the spirit left him and passed on to the Sky House, the place of spirits, higher than any white man could hope to fly. He had supposed that the life he had always known would last forever, season following season with the old ways unchanged; but that was shallow thinking. Things changed for everything: for the eagles, for the Sioux, for the buffalo.

Even as he was thinking these thoughts he happened to see some dim brown shapes on the far horizon and at once put his horse into a gallop. The brown shapes were buffalo—the Partezon wanted to kill a few more, while his arm was strong and his heart high. The sight of the buffalo excited Fool's Bull too—he forgot to complain. Soon the two men who had hung in cradle boards together, many summers before, were racing full out, bows ready, eager to kill a few more buffalo, in the old way, their way, the fearless and noble way of the fighting Sioux.

21

It was well past noon . . .

It was well past noon when Amboise d'Avigdor finally caught up with his impatient masters, Benjamin Hope-Tipping and Clam de Paty. At once, of course, they noticed that he now had only one ear, and jumped—as he had feared they would—to the wrong conclusions.

"What? You clumsy young fool! You cut off your ear?" Clam exclaimed. "And I suppose you used my razor to do it—an instrument far too fine for your clumsy hands."

"No, monsieur . . . no, I didn't," Amboise protested, "though I did just borrow your mirror for a few minutes, to inspect my head."

"Rot, I'm afraid, Amboise—it's rot!" Ben Hope-Tipping complained. "The fact is you now have only one ear, and how else could you have lost the one you're missing?"

"I don't know, sir . . . I swear I don't . . . it's a great embarrassment to me, I assure you," Amboise pleaded. "The palfreys were recalcitrant, you see, so that I was unable to catch up with you. So I just lay down to rest for a few minutes and when I awoke I was all bloody—quite offensively so—and I am exactly as you see me now, a man with only one ear."

"Now, now . . . stop lying, monsieur," Clam began. "Ears do not simply remove themselves as one sleeps. Ears are well attached, I might add. Quite firmly attached, I insist. One can box them sharply, as I am inclined to box yours, and yet they do not fall off."

"Well, Clam, accidents happen," Ben said. He saw no point in berating this shivering boy, who had at least arrived with their kit intact. "Never mind about the ear—the thing to do now is shave and get into some decent clothes."

"This wasn't an accident," Kit told them, looking carefully at Amboise's head.

"Not an accident—explain yourself, monsieur?" Clam insisted. "You mean this foolish boy cut off his ear on purpose?"

"He didn't cut it off, the Ear Taker cut it off," Kit said.

There was silence on the prairies.

"Excuse me? The Ear Taker? Who is this Ear Taker?" Ben inquired.

Talking to these men often made Kit feel as if he were traveling in circles. Wouldn't it seem likely that the Ear Taker was just what his name implied: a man who takes ears?

"Nobody knows who he is, but what he likes to do is cut off people's ears," he explained. "White men's ears, mostly. He slips up on people while they're sleeping and when they wake up they're one-eared, like this fellow."

"I believe there's a story here, Clam," Ben remarked at once. "I believe I'd like to get my notebook and jot down a few particulars, if Mr. Carson will oblige us."

"Certainly there's a story—what does this fellow look like?" Clam asked.

"I don't know and neither does anybody else," Kit said. "Nobody's even seen him. He works at night and he's so quick with his slicing that he's gone before the victim even wakes up."

"But why haven't the authorities done something?" Clam asked. "Catch him, garrote him! Rid us of this menace!"

"Who's supposed to catch him? There are no authorities out here," Kit reminded them. "He used to work around Santa Fe mostly, but I guess he's moved."

"But that's most disturbing," Ben told him. "You don't suppose he has designs on our ears, do you?"

"Probably," Kit allowed.

"Then we will have to post a guard in future," Ben told him.

"Where would we get a guard?" Kit asked.

Ben and Clam exchanged glances.

"Well, there's Amboise," Ben suggested.

"I can't guard very well, sirs," Amboise admitted. "Can't seem to stay awake."

"If you nod off I expect the Ear Taker will just slip in and take your other ear," Kit announced.

The two Europeans weighed their prospects in silence, looking apprehensively at the long plain and the waving grass. Clam's blood had begun to boil at the thought of this criminal threat. Nothing of the sort would be allowed if they were in France.

"I'll shoot him on sight," he declared.

"There won't be a sight—he works in the dark," Kit reminded them. "You won't see him."

"What must we do, then, Mr. Carson?" Hope-Tipping asked. "I'm afraid neither Clam nor I can afford to lose an ear—we're much in society, you know. It would not be acceptable in the chanceries, I'm afraid."

"Well, we can hurry up and join the Berrybenders," Kit suggested. "Some of the mountain men are probably still with them—they're pretty fair guards, if they ain't drunk."

"We shall have to insist on sobriety, then—won't we, Clam?" Hope-Tipping said. "If you'll just excuse us while we make a bit of a toilette, we can be on our way."

"You better patch that balloon up, if you've got anything to patch it with," Kit suggested. "It might come in pretty handy."

He had not given up on the notion of a dramatic entrance via balloon, once they located the company—Tasmin would be mighty impressed, if she looked up and saw him flying. The two journalists were thoroughly aggravating—it would serve them right if the Ear Taker got one of their ears—but that didn't mean he was ready to give up on a flight in their fine balloon.

22

Tasmin, primed and ready . . .

Tasmin, primed and ready, deeply in the mood to enjoy her new love, would cheerfully have spent all her time alone with Pomp Charbonneau; but thanks to the myriad vexations of travel, the Berrybender party had been proceeding east for more than a week and she had so far spent no time alone with Pomp at all, a situation that vexed her very much. With Jim Snow gone; Kit Carson gone; Lord Berrybender newly besotted with his bride, Venetia Kennet; Buffum Berrybender in constant shy attendance on her tall Ute; and William Ashley and Eulalie Bonneville, nominal leaders of the mountain men, departed for the north, it fell to Tasmin and Cook—herself the object of a circumspect courtship with Tom Fitzpatrick—to manage the day-to-day affairs of the expedition. Tasmin found herself saddled with so many duties that she would have had little time for love even if her lover had been assiduous in pursuit, which he wasn't. This too vexed Tasmin extremely. She had given herself to the man and knew that he had been pleased; and yet, instead of coming back for more, Pomp rode off every morning with Jim Bridger to scout the day's route, and sometimes did not return until after dark, by which time Tasmin had her child to feed and the camp to more or less administer. Of course, it would merely have been prudent to wait and come to Pomp well after dark, when they could have enjoyed one another in secret—but Pomp didn't allow her even this. Often it was late when he returned—he usually just rolled up in a blanket and slept by the campfire with the other men.

Tasmin, never one to be passively thwarted, would soon have developed her own strategies for seduction; she would have intercepted Pomp and cajoled him into making love had she herself not been ground down by the exigencies of camp life, which were constant and mostly negative.

First Monty wandered into a bush and was stung nearly a dozen times by wasps. Despite Little Onion's dexterity with poultices, the little boy ran a high fever; he sobbed fretfully whenever Tasmin left him. Then Coal's little boy, Rabbit, managed to bounce out of the wagon, which ran over his foot, causing him to add his wails to Monty's. Were that not enough, Piet Van Wely, while attempting to chip a fossil out of a rock, was bitten in the calf by a rattlesnake; while the babies whined, Piet groaned and sweated. Hugh Glass made a cut in the calf and sucked out most of the poison, but Piet languished for three days, a stricken Mary Berrybender in panicky attendance. Finally Little Onion made Piet a bitter concoction which purged him thoroughly, after which he soon recovered. Mary held the Dutchman's sweaty head as she cooed to him. Intolerant of children at the best of times, she felt no compunction about kicking Monty or Talley or Rabbit if they crowded into Piet's space.

"These brats have all fouled themselves—I smell it!" she insisted. "And soon Buffum will be giving birth to a red brat who will do the same."

"Not too soon—she just got pregnant," Tasmin replied. "You're Monty's aunt—you could take a hand in his upbringing, you know. It wouldn't kill you to wipe a baby's bottom."

Vicky Kennet, the new bride, seldom rode with them during the day—

Lord B.'s besottedness had reached such a level that he required Vicky to accompany him on his daily hunts. Revived by the fine high air, His Lordship sometimes felt in the mood for a spot of copulation around lunchtime. He could not bear to be without the services of his bride.

"Why is the pater so gross?" Mary asked, a question Tasmin made no attempt to answer. She was uncomfortably aware that, if she were allowed to indulge her natural inclinations, they might not be much less gross than her father's. More than once Tasmin found herself wishing that Pomp would leave Jim Bridger with the company and take *her* on a scout. She could well have tolerated a spot of copulation around lunchtime herself.

But no such notion occurred to Pomp, whose main concern, when he was in camp, seemed to be with his ailing father, who had been taken with the jaundice and was in consequence so wobbly on his feet that he too had to be allowed space in the wagon. Coal and Little Onion combined their skills and gathered herbs for yet more concoctions, which, though beneficial, did not cure the elder Charbonneau very quickly. After a long consultation with Pomp it was concluded that old Charbonneau would profit from sitting for a time in a sweat lodge, where the poisons could be sweated out of him. This required a half day's break in the trekking—Tasmin hoped it might present her with an opportunity to get Pomp to herself for a bit. Old Hugh Glass not only helped build the sweat lodge but, once it was built, casually stripped off and insisted on participating.

"I've a heap too much bile," he announced. "When I lived with the Rees I was often refreshed by the sweats." He at once crawled in with old Charbonneau.

Unhappily for Tasmin they were stopped on an absolutely open plain, with no deep glades that might be suited for romantic interludes, which Pomp, to her fury, showed no sign of wanting anyway. He spent his time happily giving archery lessons to Jim Bridger, who desired to master the bow but, so far, was a long way from doing so.

The night Tasmin seduced Pomp, Jim had not been mentioned—in fact Jim had never entered her thoughts. The moment was hers and Pomp's; at the time she had hardly supposed it would be their only such moment, but now she was beginning to wonder. Was Pomp *thinking* of Jim—his friend, her husband? Was that what kept him away?

When old Charbonneau and Hugh Glass emerged from the sweat lodge Mary Berrybender watched from the back of the wagon, where she was attending to her Piet.

out of arrow range, but the young Ute, hot for the challenge, raced right past him. Pomp jumped down, reloaded, and killed the Pawnee archer, but not before he put an arrow in High Shoulders's hip. Infuriated, High Shoulders ran on and poked the dead Pawnee with his lance several times.

When the five remaining warriors broke for the open prairie, Kit and Jim swung east to attempt to intercept them. Kit's mule was exceptionally hard mouthed—once he got his speed up, there was no stopping him. When he was nearly into the fleeing Pawnees, Kit suddenly realized he no longer had control of his mount—the very thing that had caused the death of Drum Stewart was now happening to him. He pulled back on the reins with all his might but it had no effect on the mule at all. In fact, he increased his speed to a wild runaway's, which very quickly carried Kit straight into the midst of the fleeing Pawnees.

Jim Snow was doing his best to catch up, but knew it was hopeless. The mare wasn't as fast as the big mule. Jim also saw that Kit had lost control of his mount and was fast approaching a collision point. It occurred to Jim that he could shoot the mule, but Kit might be injured in the fall, in which case he would be an easy kill.

Kit himself, as he got closer and closer to impact with the Pawnees, thought of shooting the mule himself, but that would leave him with an empty gun, so he held off.

Rattle was the only one of the fleeing raiders to notice that a collision was coming—Red Knee, flushed with his triumph, was merely running for the fun of it, and the other boys, happy to be alive, were whooping and hollering, giving no thought to the white man on the mule. Rattle thought he might get an arrow into the foolish white man whose mule was running away with him, but to his great annoyance, his horse jumped a bush and he dropped his arrow just as he was ready to string it. Before he could ready a second, the huge mule plunged right into the midst of the surprised Pawnees. Rattle's horse and two others were knocked down. The mule fell to its knees, tried to recover, then fell and rolled over one of the Pawnee boys just as Kit Carson jumped free. Rattle was knocked into the melee but clung to his bow and, as soon as he could scramble to his feet, readied an arrow to fire at the foolish white man whose erratic mount had knocked down and possibly damaged three Pawnee horses.

Kit saw Rattle notch the arrow and fired at him from the hip—the arrow, when released, flew over his head. Two of the Pawnee boys whose mounts had been knocked down were staggering around with the wind knocked out of them. Red Knee and a boy named Duck Catcher because of his skill with snares were the only raiders whose horses were not affected.

Highly annoyed that this white man had spoiled their triumphant departure, Red Knee turned back, meaning to kill the man—whose gun was empty—with his hatchet. He leapt off the horse he had taken from the dead Thistle-Pricks-Us and ran at the white man on foot, hatchet raised.

Jim Snow, in easy range now, saw that Kit—faced off with Rattle—had no notion that he was being menaced from the rear. Jim fired—the bullet took Red Knee in the side, startling him so that he promptly sat down—but that reaction only lasted a second. In a moment Red Knee got to his feet, remounted, and joined Duck Catcher in flight.

Pomp, Kit, and Jim all knew that the battle was won, but High Shoulders, one leg covered with blood from the wound in his hip, raced in and lanced one of the winded Pawnee boys before anyone could wave him off. Rattle, winded too, and wounded in the thigh by Kit's bullet, was unable to find the arrow he had been about to shoot; he began to sing his death song—so did the other young Pawnee, who faced the white men armed with nothing but a knife. Jim came riding up, rifle at the ready, but he held his fire. Red Knee and Duck Catcher, having ridden off a certain distance, pulled up, uncomfortably aware that the battle was not over and that two of their comrades were facing death. They sat on their horses indecisively, trying to decide what to do. Matters that had at first looked simple were now very confused.

For a moment, both sets of warriors were poised in tense indecision; they were ready for blood and death and yet did not feel quite compelled to push matters to a conclusion. The excitable High Shoulders was ready to kill both Pawnees, but Pomp waved him back and Kit merely stood where he was, his gun empty. The conflict could have been rejoined and finished in a few seconds; and yet, no one moved or spoke until Pomp realized that there was something familiar about Rattle.

"But you're the son of Skinny Woman," he said. "My father was married to her sister once. Aren't you called Rattle?"

Rattle, surprised that Pomp, or Six Tongues, had remembered him—they had met for only a few minutes after a buffalo hunt—merely nodded.

"Dern, your pa's been married to more women than Bonney," Kit said. "It's hard to go anyplace without running into some of his kin."

Rattle left off his death song—it didn't seem that the whites were in the mood to kill them, though it annoyed him that Red Knee, who had started the whole thing, was just sitting there watching from a safe distance.

"We tried to steal some horses from the Cheyenne, but they were too much for us," Rattle said—suddenly he felt very tired.

"Yes, it's hard to steal from those Cheyenne," Pomp agreed. He tried to speak very carefully—such situations were tricky to get through. If any one of the combatants, on either side, felt that their courage or honor was being slighted, knives and hatchets would flash and it might be necessary to kill all the young Pawnees, something Pomp wanted to avoid if at all possible. They were just boys, raiding a little; if it became necessary to kill them all, the tribe would certainly attempt to avenge them. The company might be facing a hundred warriors this time, instead of these few youths.

Rattle knew that the whites could easily finish them off, but it seemed their blood had cooled—it might be possible for them to leave.

"We would like to take our dead," he said, addressing himself to Pomp. The Ute, he knew, would have liked to fight on, but the whites did not seem in a mood to support him. Even the Sin Killer was no longer leveling his gun.

Once Jim heard Pomp talking calmly to the young Pawnee he knew that there needed to be no more killing. It was screams and war cries that kept battles going. Once there was even a little friendly conversation, the war mood usually died; unless someone jumped in the wrong direction or accidentally fired a gun, there would be, for a time, an end to slaughter. After the terrible effort of violence a calm seemed to enfold them all. Even Lord Berrybender, who was approaching cautiously in his buggy, a gun across his lap, seemed to feel it.

"There's no calm like the calm of a battlefield, once the killing's over," he remarked, looking around him with composure. There was the great sky, and the light, waving grass—there lay the dead. The living, no longer locked in struggle, had a moment of quiet, of gratitude. After all, they were alive. Even High Shoulders had calmed down.

One horse had a broken leg. It was a Pawnee horse, and it was agreed that the Pawnees should have the meat. When the horse was killed, High Shoulders even helped with the butchering, which was accomplished in a very short time.

In the distance, the apprehensive women watched. Father Geoffrin and Clam de Paty were talking calmly to Ben Hope-Tipping, who still sat upright. Pomp hurried over—just as he arrived, Ben lay back in the grass and died. The Pawnees were now trotting slowly away, with their three dead and their fresh horse meat. Soon the prairie swallowed them up, as a boat is lost in the curving distance of the sea. Pomp's father came ambling over. Clam de Paty was sobbing, bitterly remorseful because he had not managed to warn his friend in time to save him.

"Skinny Woman's son was not hurt badly," Pomp informed his father. "Kit just wounded him in the fatty part of his leg."

Toussaint Charbonneau shook his head, in general regret.

"Those boys are too young to be out raiding on their own," he remarked. "Too young to have any judgment. They thought we'd be easy pickings, but we weren't."

"Dern if I'll ever ride that goddamned hard-mouth mule again," Kit declared. "That big ugly fool nearly got me killed."

"You don't need to be cussing, let's just dig these graves," Jim told him.

"Jim Bridger and the Sublettes would go off just when we needed them," Kit said. He was so happy to be alive that he felt he could indulge in a few complaints.

"I guess you'd complain if you were in heaven," Jim told him. "Only if you don't stop that cussing, you won't be in heaven."

"You could be wrong about that," Kit told him, angrily. "You ain't God— you could be wrong."

30

She had armed herself with an axe . . .

What do they think just happened, a fox hunt?" Tasmin asked, with considerable pique. She had armed herself with an axe, which she still gripped tightly. Coal and Little Onion had skinning knives, Cook a great cleaver, Vicky, Buffum, and Mary sharp hatchets, Eliza a rolling pin. Unlikely Amazons though they were, they crouched behind the wagon, ready to mount a spirited defense of their lives and their virtue; yet abruptly the crisis seemed to pass. The combatants had become more or less at ease with one another. Jim and Kit were helping the Pawnees tie their dead on horses; High Shoulders helped cut up the horse.

"It was the same with the Utes," Tasmin reminded them. "Enemies one day and customers the next."

"I suppose it's merely the frontier way, Tasmin," Vicky remarked.

"More likely the military way, I guess," Tasmin replied. "If battles were fought to the last man, then there would soon be no more battles and the only masculine thing our silly males would have to do is fornicate, and I'm sure they'd soon tire of *that* simple pleasure."

"Not High Shoulders," Bess observed, with a blush. "High Shoulders never tires of fornication."

"Well, then ain't you lucky," Tasmin told her. "Many of us are forced to endure lengthy stretches of abstinence. I suppose we had better go attend to Milly and Tim—or what's left of them."

"And Mr. Hope-Tipping and Señor Yanez," Mary reminded her. "Fortunately my good Piet is safe."

During the anxious moments of battle the babies had been piled in the wagon and enjoined to keep still. Tasmin had looked at Monty so sternly that he opened his mouth in dismay. His mother's stern looks, which came without warning or explanation, usually had the effect of freezing Monty in his place, which was just what Tasmin intended.

Eliza, Cook's clumsy helper, who had only been allowed a rolling pin by way of a weapon, for fear that if given anything sharp she would probably only injure herself, was sobbing hopelessly, in grief at Milly's death. Though lately they had fallen out—Milly then a nobleman's mistress, Eliza just an unwanted servant girl—Eliza wept because she had now lost her one friend, a girl, like herself, born into the service of the Berrybenders. Milly was dead, and where would she ever find a friend in this violent place, America?

Tasmin, Buffum, and Mary, carrying some worn blankets that might be suitable for shrouds, trudged off into the prairie toward where Milly and Tim had last been seen.

Jim and Pomp came hurrying over, anxious to divert this burial party if they could.

"I wouldn't go look," Pomp told Tasmin. "Me and Jim can tidy them up."

"I'm going to go look," Tasmin informed him bluntly. "Who were those Indians, Jimmy? Why did they attack us?"

"Pawnees—just boys," Jim told her. "They couldn't manage to steal any horses from the Cheyenne, so they decided to try and kill a few of us."

"They didn't merely try—they succeeded," Tasmin pointed out. "Are Señor Yanez and Mr. Hope-Tipping both dead?"

Pomp nodded.

"They killed four of us—how many of them did we kill?"

"Three," Jim said.

"Then it's a narrow victory for the savage Pawnees," Tasmin declared. "We women weren't frightened out of our wits for nothing."

Gripping her axe, she had been so scared that she was trembling, but as soon as she saw Jim racing back to join the battle, her wild terror diminished. Her husband might not understand her, but Tasmin had absolute confidence in his ability to protect her.

"Why do you want to be looking at those dead folks?" Jim asked. "They're apt to be chopped up bad."

"That's precisely why I want to see them," Mary told him. "Piet thinks I'm progressing rather rapidly with my anatomical studies—I'm sure a close look at poor Tim and Milly's remains will be most helpful."

"You hush," Tasmin said. She had no real answer for her husband's question. Why *did* she want to see two badly mangled corpses? Pomp and Jim gave up the effort to stop them; soon they were looking at the remains of two servants who, for all their lives, had been entirely familiar: Tim and Milly.

"It's exactly as it was with Fräulein Pfretzskaner," Buffum informed them. "They cracked her skull and then seemed unable to stop chopping."

"The human cranium must be little harder to crack than a coconut," Mary said, staring sadly at the remains of the girl who, for most of her life, had washed and ironed her clothes.

Buffum suddenly burst into deep, gulping sobs—the sight of the mutilated girl brought back hard memories of her own brief but painful captivity by the Mandans. She remembered the terrible cold at night, with herself and Mademoiselle Pellenc huddling under a bit of deerskin they had snatched from the dogs. Then the men had been at her; the terrible witch woman, Draga, had beaten them with hot sticks. Now there lay Milly and Tim: the former she had often abused, the latter was a lover who, though not especially gifted, had done his best. Both were now so gashed about that they might indeed, as Mary suggested, have been cadavers there to be examined by an anatomy class.

Tasmin put her arms around her sobbing sister. The two corpses already had a waxy look, as if figures in a wax museum had been crudely disassembled. Their remains had already become unhuman. Once there was no life in the flesh, only an absence of life, a sort of unhumanity, what was there to say?

"I don't know why they refer to dead bodies as mortal remains—of Lord this or that, of Jack and Jill for that matter," Tasmin told them. "We're only mortals while we're alive. Once we aren't alive, what does remain—these scraps of flesh, these bloody bones—hardly seems worth fussing over."

"Oh, don't be icy, Tasmin," Buffum sobbed. "Don't."

"Sorry," Tasmin said. "I very much regret that those Pawnee boys chose to attack us, the result being that neither Tim nor Milly, nor Mr. Hope-Tipping nor good Señor Yanez, will ever be among us again. But they're *gone*—and their husks don't interest me.

"We'll all leave husks someday, somewhere," she added. "Let's just bury them and go along."

"I suppose they always remove the genitals of the male," Mary remarked.

"Not always—in some cases there is no time for such embellishments," Tasmin told her.

Buffum, still sobbing, still distraught, stumbled off to find High Shoulders, but Cook—an expert with shrouds—soon arrived, accompanied by Tom Fitzpatrick, who had just missed the battle, though he claimed to have had intimations of it.

"I seen some birds fly up, and some antelope start running," he said. "If you've been in as many Indian fights as I have, things like that get you wondering."

Tasmin left the corpses to Cook and wandered back to the wagon where the children were. Her mind was on the anxious minutes when she had stood behind the wagon, gripping her axe. What *would* she have done if the battle had gone the other way—or if the Pawnees had passed up Tim and Milly and come straight for the wagon? Suppose Pomp had been killed? Suppose Jim and Kit had been out of earshot, and her father too slow to mount a defense? Could she and the women have somehow fought off these racing warriors with their flashing lances and deadly hatchets? Would old Charbonneau have been able to sway the attackers? Should she and the women have done better to fight, or to submit? After all, Buffum had survived *her* capture. What if the Pawnees had simply filled them all full of arrows, as they had Mr. Hope-Tipping?

Tasmin stopped for a moment—her legs suddenly became jelly at the thought of what might have happened. She sank to her knees, feeling a throb of relief deeper than any she had ever felt before: the relief of one who had been within a minute of death and yet had been left alive. The plain around her had never seemed more vast and merciless, the sky above never so filled with light and brilliance. And yet, in this place of light, the darkness of death was not more than a minute away. Her survival had not been due either to the craft of men or to the bounty of the gods: it had been absolute luck. Tim and Milly, dragging their fuel sacks around, had blundered right into the path of the warriors—without the brake their deaths provided, the Pawnees would have been at the wagon in only a minute more. Even Pomp and High Shoulders, though they had been quick, might not have been quick enough. The memory of an old book of Greek fables she had had as a child came to her. In it was a picture of Zeus and Poseidon looking down on earthlings through a hole in the clouds, pointing their fingers in an arbitrary way at this mortal or that, far below.

So it might have been that day, Tasmin felt. Señor Yanez and Signor Claricia had been sitting next to one another. Ben Hope-Tipping had been no more than an arm's length from Clam de Paty, yet now the Frenchman and the Italian were alive, the Englishman and the Spaniard quite dead.

She had survived, and so had her child, her sisters, father, husband, lover, and most of the company—and yet the deadly combat had been the work of only seven restless boys. Were not there thousands of Indians somewhere on the plain? What if twenty came, next time, rather than seven? Suppose a hundred came?

In time strength returned to Tasmin's legs; she walked on to the wagon, where her hungry child was waiting. The burials were accomplished without ceremony, Father Geoff merely mumbling a few *Requiescat in pace*s. No one wanted to linger in this spot where death had caught them. Jim Bridger and the Sublette brothers, returning from a fruitless search for beaver, got back just as the company pulled away from the four mounds of earth on the long prairie.

"Was it the Partezon?" Jim Bridger asked.

"Of course not, you fool!" Kit responded angrily. He and Jim Bridger were currently not on good terms.

"I ain't a fool, I just asked a question," Jim replied, doing his best not to inflame the volatile Kit.

"It was just some Pawnee boys, out practicing raiding," Pomp told him.

"That dern big mule nearly got me killed," Kit said, attempting to produce a friendlier tone. He didn't really like being cross with Jim Bridger, his old pard, but for some reason he often did feel distinctly cross with him.

Jim Bridger spat a goodly chew of tobacco juice onto the prairie.

"If them Pawnee sprouts killed four of us just practicing, I don't think I want to make their acquaintance once they get practiced up."

"Amen to that," Billy Sublette remarked.

31

In a while she might be more welcoming.

When Jim put his hand on her, Tasmin angrily knocked it away. It startled him—she sometimes refused him when she was very sleepy, but now she lay beside him wide awake. Jim could see her staring upward. Of course, if she had been violently angry with him, as she sometimes was, he would have known it and kept his hands to himself. But she did not seem angry, merely stiff and distant—indeed, more stiff and more distant than he had ever known her to be.

Of course, Tasmin was changeable. In a while she might be more welcoming. He let her be for a bit, but when he advanced his hand, Tasmin, who had been waiting for just such a move, knocked it away with even more emphasis.

"Stop it," she said. "Can't you tell when I don't wish to be pawed?"

"Not till I try," Jim replied.

"It would be a good thing for you to learn—when to leave well enough alone," Tasmin told him.

Jim was silent. He had hoped to make love, not argue. Tasmin had shown plenty of courage during the fight that day, from what he had seen. She had grabbed an axe, and been ready to use it. But the big fight was over. Why did she think she wanted to fight him?

"I guess it's good night, then," he said.

But Tasmin clutched his arm. To his surprise her hands were shaking, and there were tears on her cheeks. She clutched him hard, crying silently, her body shaking, but not with passion.

"I'm scared . . . I'm scared . . . that's why I don't want you, can't you tell?" she said.

Jim relaxed a bit and held her until her shaking stopped. He felt that for once he did understand her mood. In sudden battle there was no time for fear—it was act or die. But afterward, once the issue was settled, strong men sometimes took the shakes, just as Tasmin had. No doubt it was the recollection of how close death had been. He himself had once had an Osage arrow part his hair: a fraction of an inch had been the difference between living and dying. He had paid no attention to the arrow at the time, though he chased and finally killed the Osage who shot it. But the next day, watering a horse, he recollected that something had zipped right across his scalp, even drawing a few drops of blood. He sat at the water hole a long time, not shaking, but thinking. Once he left the water he forgot about the arrow. Prairie life involved so many close calls that experienced men learned not to dwell on them—surviving them was enough.

"You might get your pa to loan you a gun or two," he suggested. "Indians won't pay much attention to a bunch of women with axes and knives."

"I suppose not," Tasmin admitted.

"What if you and Kit had been farther away?" she asked, sitting up. "What if Pomp had gone off with the trappers, as he meant to do? What if High Shoulders had been hunting?"

"Try not to be thinking about it," Jim said—only to receive a sharp dig from Tasmin's elbow.

"Jimmy, I *am* thinking about it!" she said, pounding him twice on his chest with her fist. "I *have* to think about it. If you can't be persuaded to stay close, then I need to know what to do if some restless Indians show up again."

"I'll be staying close," Jim assured her. It wasn't a chore he looked forward to—he was fond of roaming far ahead, out of range of the squabbles and arguments of the company. But the Pawnee boys, once they got home, would be sure to mention the big party of whites traveling through their country. In the party were several women who might be captured and sold, and also some fine horses. The Pawnee elders might decide they were a tempting target.

"Just tell me what to do if they come and you're not close," Tasmin plead. "Do I fight, or do I submit?"

draw a little water from the barrel, just enough to make a soup, Pomp stopped her.

"No soup for a while," he told her.

Clam de Paty started to launch into another protest, but something about the look of the mountain men stopped him. They all wore looks of taut concern.

Jim and Kit, wielding two spades, began to dig holes in the center of the creek bed. Lord Berrybender watched this activity with furrowed brow. Like Clam he was subdued, in part by the realization that they had drunk the last of the Ashley champagne only the day before. The company was now without spirits of any kind.

Vicky shared the general concern. She and Tasmin stood by Cook, who was extremely distressed. No baths to bathe in, no laundry done, and now not even soup. To Cook, these were shocking things.

At mealtime that evening the whole company was despondent. Cook, for the first time in her long service, had nothing to cook. The little boys made do with mother's milk—for the rest there was only elk jerky and a little corn they had purchased from the Utes. To the mountain men this was nothing out of the ordinary, but the Europeans were faced for the first time with a total absence of anything that could be called dinner.

"Sure you don't have another bottle or two of that good cognac tucked away in your basket, monsieur?" Lord Berrybender asked Clam.

The Frenchman merely shook his head.

Tasmin realized that she was seeing her father sober for the first time in her life.

"Not sure I've ever seen you sober, Father," she said.

"Bad planning, or I wouldn't be sober now," Lord Berrybender replied. "Life seems rather a harsh business, when one is sober, just as I feared it would. I seem to be married to Vicky now—none too clear as to how that came about."

Then a thought seemed to stir him.

"I say, Clam—you've still got your balloon," he pointed out. "What if we puff it up and you and I go sailing off? If we caught a nice breeze it might waft us to Santa Fe—plenty to drink there, I bet."

Clam brightened at this suggestion—but only briefly. The wind that might blow them to Santa Fe could just as easily blow them into some Indians, as it had once already.

"A thought, monsieur—a thought," he replied.

"Never been in a balloon myself—I'm anxious to try it," Lord B. went on—he brightened visibly at this prospect. "I might even bring my Belgian gun. Could increase my bag considerably, if I'm lucky. Sail right over a buffalo herd and pop away at them."

Clam found that he was not much attracted to the notion of ballooning with Lord Berrybender. On the whole he thought he preferred to stick to the mountain men, who seemed to know what they were doing, even though presently there were hardships. But then, life in the Grande Armée had not all been pretty girls and puddings, either.

"A damn pity losing Yanez," Lord Berrybender continued. "He did keep the guns in good working order, I'll say that for him."

Tasmin felt an anger growing—and just when she had been rather sympathetic to her father. Sober, he looked wan and old, almost pitiful—and yet he had immediately demonstrated that he was prepared to be as selfish as ever.

"You mean you'd just leave us, Father?" she asked, in a quiet tone. "You bring us to a desert where we'll likely either starve or be killed by savages, while you propose to fly away—is that really your intention?"

"Can't see much wrong with the notion," Lord B. replied. In his mind he saw himself killing buffalo after buffalo—or perhaps even one of the great bears—while flying along in the cool air.

"Then you *would* leave us, wouldn't you?" Tasmin inquired, in ominous tones. "You brought us here, far from our customary shores, and you propose to desert us just when our prospects are bleakest—it's rotten behavior, if you ask me."

"But I *didn't* ask you, and why should I, you contentious hussy?" Lord B. said, annoyed. Tasmin's accusations were making it difficult for him to concentrate on his own nice fancies of the hunt.

"Rotten behavior, Papa—I feel the same!" Buffum announced, with sudden spirit.

"And I curse you for a black tyrant," little Kate yelled suddenly. Then, to the surprise and shock of the company, Kate rushed at her father, penknife drawn, and began to stab him vigorously in the leg, striking home at least three times before Amboise stepped in and lifted her off, kicking and stabbing, into the air.

Amboise handed her to Jim, who managed to persuade her to surrender the bloody penknife.

Lord Berrybender was stunned. His wounds were hardly serious, but his lap was now soaked with his own blood.

"I've always known it was a mistake to breed," he remarked, to no one in particular. "But Constance *would* breed, and now Vicky will soon be the size of a cow again. It's a bad business, monsieur."

Pomp, Vicky, and Cook managed to cut Lord Berrybender's trouser leg off; to Cook's shame, there were no clean trousers to produce; they were allowed just enough water to wash the wound. Vicky helped her husband off to their tent, while Tasmin gave the violent Kate a lecture on the evils of patricide.

"I say he's a black tyrant!" the unrepentant Kate insisted.

Tasmin noticed that the mountain men seemed unusually subdued, sitting in silence as a sunset faded to a line of pink along the western horizon. Jim Bridger was whittling a stick, the rest of them merely sitting.

"You seem a dispirited bunch," Tasmin told them. "Surely one of you—well traveled as you are—must know someplace where we could find water."

"We know the country pretty well, I guess," Tom Fitzpatrick told her. "We just forgot something, in this case."

"What?"

"That every year ain't the same," he told her. "Some's wet and some's dry."

"And then some's *real* dry," Jim Bridger added.

"I see. And this is one of the ones that are *real* dry, correct?" Tasmin said.

"The driest I've ever seen," Hugh Glass admitted.

"There's springs, though," Kit Carson insisted. "The Indians hunt out here. They must know places where there's water."

"What they probably know is when to stay away," Tom said. "That's why we ain't seen Indians for a spell."

"It might rain," Jim Bridger pointed out.

"Or it might not," Hugh Glass said grimly.

When told that they must ration water, Tasmin had supposed that the worst that might happen was they would all have to be dirty and thirsty for a few days. Now, looking at the grave faces of the men—resilient fellows all, not easily daunted—she realized that their situation went beyond inconvenience. They were clearly in danger.

"We oughtn't to have let Greasy Lake wander off," Kit said. "If there's a spring anywhere near, he'd know it."

"We've got our animals, at least," Jim Bridger reminded them. "I've drunk horse piss before."

Then he suddenly realized that Tasmin had heard him use a coarse term—he turned beet red from embarrassment.

Jim Snow was so annoyed by this lapse that he stood up and led Tasmin away. The word hadn't shocked her, but the vision it called up was very shocking indeed.

"Drink piss?" she asked, when they were alone. "Could it get that bad?"

"That bad and worse," Jim said.

33

As dawn light spread over the plain . . .

As dawn light spread over the plain, only Cook and one or two others were stirring. Even Jim Snow was still dozing. Tasmin gave Monty the breast and then deposited him with Little Onion. She picked up the axe that she had used to defend herself in the Pawnee attack and carried it to the small wagon belonging to Clam de Paty, who was sleeping under it. It was Amboise d'Avigdor, a friendly boy now known as Ambo to most of the company, whom Tasmin shook awake.

"Get up, Ambo, I need you," she whispered. "I want you to help me get the balloon out of the wagon—and the basket too."

Amboise quickly accomplished what he was asked to do, awakening Clam de Paty in the process—but Clam didn't emerge from beneath the wagon, or offer any objection to what Tasmin was planning.

"If you want a ride we need to make a fire," Amboise whispered. "It only goes up if you fill it with hot air."

"Not what I had in mind at all, thanks," Tasmin said. Then she attacked the padded basket with her axe and soon reduced it to kindling. Clam still lay on his pillow, a pleasant smile on his face.

"Got any shears?" Tasmin asked Amboise. Shears were at once produced, after which Tasmin cut several great holes in the fabric of the balloon; she then folded the cut pieces neatly.

"I expect Cook can find a use for these snippets," Tasmin said, before bending down to address Monsieur de Paty.

"I just destroyed your balloon, monsieur," she informed him cheerfully.

"It ain't Methuselah, it's Zeke Williams—why, I thought the Arapaho took Zeke's hair a year ago. It shows you you can't believe everything you hear."

"I don't believe *anything* I hear, particularly not if it comes out of Jim Bridger's mouth," Kit said—he was feeling smug about the fact that his vision had been accurate after all.

There was a mist on the prairie that morning—when Tasmin looked the first thing she saw was the top half of Pomp Charbonneau, seemingly floating on a cloud. At once her spirits rose. There he was, not dead at all. But where had he secured such a noble ox?

To Jim Snow the reassuring thing was not that old Zeke Williams was still alive, but that the ox he rode seemed to be in good flesh, not gaunt like their own horses. That meant there was abundant water somewhere near—oxen sometimes faltered on the Big Dry. For the first time in two weeks Jim felt optimistic about their chances. The sight of a healthy ox suggested that they might survive.

"Hello, Zeke—where have you been this last year, and how did you get so gone that we gave you up for dead?" Tom Fitzpatrick asked.

All of them saw that the old man's feet were swollen and cut—no wonder he had to ride the ox.

"Why the goddamn thieving Rappies caught me," Zeke said—his eyes were bright blue and twinkling.

"Kept me all this time, hoping to sell me," he added.

"Hoping to sell you? Why, who'd pay money for a man your age?" Kit asked. He almost got a fit of giggles at the thought.

"If I was in the market they could sell Zeke to me," Tom Fitzpatrick remarked. He gave Kit a severe frown.

"Zeke came to the Big Horn River with Manuel Lisa a derned long time ago," he said. "He knows every water hole in the West. I'd buy him just for what he knows."

"Got any bacon, boys?" Zeke asked, impatient with the palaver. "I've been on the run from the Rappies ten days—I've mostly et grasshoppers."

Pomp gently eased the old man off the placid ox. Zeke's beard was long and white; he was so bent that, when he attempted to stand, he almost stepped on it. He was almost naked and badly scratched up, but his eyes were lively, and his look, once he spotted the women, was impish.

"Why, look at those pretty gals, what a sight!" he said. "The Rappies don't have that many pretty gals in their whole tribe—and I ought to know. I had to marry up with four of them."

"Four wives?" Jim Bridger questioned. "I thought you were a dern prisoner—why'd they give you four wives?"

"Not enough bucks in the band, that's why," Zeke explained. "The Pawnees killed a bunch off—so they had women going to waste. Women get mean as cats when they're going to waste, and the Rappies know it."

"So they put you to stud, did they?" Lord Berrybender exclaimed. "Clam, you should be taking this down. Put to stud by the Arapaho. It would make rather a good report, I'd say."

Clam de Paty only smiled. In the hard days of hunger and thirst he had lost so much weight that his red pants no longer fit. He had ceased to believe in his own survival, or the company's. He supposed they would either starve to death or be killed in some brutal way, as Benjamin Hope-Tipping had been. Why write anything up? The rain had raised his hopes, but already the day was hot; the horizons shimmered in the distance. Ordinarily he *would* have written up the old fellow's story, made a racy item of it; a lust slave amid the native Eves. It was just the kind of thing Parisians liked to read about over their coffee—but Clam was too discouraged to care. He had fought with the Grande Armée, he had been awarded medals, and where had it all brought him? To a scorching plain, rude company, daily aggravation, even danger. Had he been put on earth so rich Parisians could read racy stories with their coffee? His notebook was in his pocket but he didn't reach for it. Who was Lord Berrybender to tell him what to write?

Clam turned and walked away.

"Moody fellow . . . that's the French, you know . . . can't be bothered," Lord Berrybender observed.

Tasmin had grabbed Pomp and was chattering with him. Jim wanted to know about the ox, an animal in excellent flesh. And he wanted to get the company moving. They could all listen to Zeke Williams rattle when night came.

Tasmin had just started filling Pomp in on the events of the last few days when Jim Snow walked up, looking impatient, practical, and stern. It irked her; why had she married such an impatient person? But there he was.

"That ox don't look thirsty," Jim said.

"He's not—there's a fine spring about twenty miles east," Pomp told him. "A family of travelers found it but the Arapaho wiped them out. Nine dead. Zeke hid in a snake den, or else they would have got him."

"I guess that means the Rappies are still around. But I doubt they'd attack *us*, if we stay bunched up. Seen Hugh and the Sublettes?"

"I saw them—they went exploring," Pomp told him. "Maybe we'll see them in Santa Fe."

Tasmin was annoyed; she wanted to talk. If there was one truth that irked her more than any other it was that men had so little use for women's talk. Even Pomp often looked a little absent, a little bored, when she attempted to expound her views on this and that. Was there any man, anywhere, who really cared to talk to her?

"*I* care to talk to you—surely you'll grant me that modest distinction," Father Geoffrin said, as the two of them plodded beside the slow-walking ox. As a novelty they had sat the three little boys on the beast's broad back, an experience that awed the children into complete silence, afraid to utter a sound in the presence of this great beast god, the ox.

"My husband merely closes his ears—it's as if they have tiny doors—when I start to talk," she went on. "Kit listens, but then Kit is so deeply smitten with me that he hardly counts."

"What about your new love, Monsieur Charbonneau?" the priest asked. "Has he no taste for your enchanting babble?"

Tasmin shrugged. Did Pomp really listen to her? Could he really be expected to, when the trek was so hard, their lives so threatened?

"Sometimes he tolerates it—whether he actually likes it, I can't say. It's goddamn hard to determine what men actually *like*, don't you think?"

"And yet men are open books compared to women," Father Geoff told her. "You know what I miss in America? Frivolity! Out here it's all life-or-death. No time for frivolous kisses, clothes buying, books and plays, *maquillage*, dancing, a little light seduction—all the things that make life so pleasant. No one here will be frivolous with you—I suspect that's your difficulty, my dear."

Tasmin shrugged again. The world Father Geoffrin's words conjured up—a world where women wore rouge and powder, danced quadrilles, went to operas and plays—was so different from the world where she now found herself that in memory it hardly seemed to belong to the same life. Even on the steamer *Rocky Mount*, not a year ago, she and Vicky Kennet had made themselves up and paid a great deal of attention to their hair. But that had been another time. Only yesterday she had been weak from thirst—they had all faced the prospect of dying, not a situation in which one gave much thought to hair curlers and the like.

"It's the reason we get along so well, I expect, Tasmin," the priest went on. "We both like our fun, and it needn't be particularly serious fun. But your husband is not what I'd call a frivolous man, and neither is your new love, Pomp."

"Stop calling him my new love," Tasmin insisted, glancing around to be sure no one had heard him.

"I find all this rather odd," she continued. "Here we are, inching across a prairie where we might be killed on any given day, and you think I ought to be more frivolous. I don't know that this is very useful advice, if it is advice."

"Perhaps not—but we might return to civilization someday," the priest reminded her. "If we do, I hope you'll remember that I, at least, liked to listen to you talk. It's worth something, isn't it?"

"Of course it is—I'm not ungrateful," Tasmin said.

They had by then jettisoned all but one small wagon, in which her father, old Zeke Williams, and the babies rode. Sometimes Toussaint Charbonneau, still yellowish, was allowed to ride for a bit. But mostly Charbonneau walked, with Pomp at his side, carrying his gun and helping him a little if he faltered.

"I suppose there's no one more dutiful than Pomp," Tasmin said, looking back at the pair. "He's far more careful of his father than we Berrybenders are of our own."

"Of course, and it's entirely admirable," Father Geoff agreed. "And yet I do feel that dutiful men are sometimes rather lacking in spirit."

"What nonsense! Nothing of the sort is true of Pomp," Tasmin said, flaring up. "He has plenty of spirit."

Father Geoffrin smiled and shrugged.

"I'm sure you'd know best about that, my dear," he said, with a smile that indicated that he didn't believe her for a minute.

They strode in silence for a while.

"In my experience women tend to favor rascals," Geoff said. "I've often wondered why."

"You're more than enough of a rascal yourself, if you ask me," Tasmin said tartly. "I believe I've had enough of your saucy talk for now."

"I'm sure you'd know best about that," the priest said, but by then Tasmin had already turned away.

36

. . . tears of pain and frustration . . .

But none of us are used to walking, Pomp," Tasmin said, tears of pain
and frustration staining her cheeks—minutes earlier she had done the very
thing Kit Carson had warned her about: she stepped on a small poisonous
cactus, whose thorns pierced her moccasin and stuck deep in her heel.
Now Pomp held her foot in his hand as, probing gently with a needle, he
attempted to perform for her the service she had performed for Kit. One by
one he was working the greenish thorns out of her foot.

"We're pampered gentlewomen, not mountain men," Tasmin reminded
him. "Even the grass here is like spikes, and the sun's so bright I can't possibly spot every vicious cactus that lies in my path."

"You best learn to look out for them," her husband advised, politely.

"Oh, shut up, Jimmy—even the experienced Kit Carson stepped on one
not long ago—why am I expected to be more expert than Kit?" Tasmin
asked.

Jim Snow walked away—any attempt at counsel would only make Tasmin angrier. Let Pomp do the doctoring—she didn't seem to get quite so
angry with Pomp.

"Anyway, I'm not the only sufferer," Tasmin pointed out. "Vicky's feet
are severely blistered and so are Buffum's."

Pomp had almost finished extracting the thorns—her foot was not really
much damaged, but her point was unarguable. Of all the Englishwomen
only Mary Berrybender was used to walking—until their feet toughened,
there were bound to be problems. But with the company now down to two
horses, one wagon, and the ox, there was no alternative to walking.

"It's only about five miles to the springs," Pomp said, hoping to cheer
Tasmin up at least a bit. "We can rest for a few days, once we get there."

"Two or three of you could ride on the ox," Kit Carson suggested. "It's
big enough to carry two or three of you."

"But we'll soon have to eat the ox," Vicky pointed out. "Jim Snow said
so this morning—eat it just as we ate the palfreys and most of the rest of
our steeds. Why get used to riding a beast we will then immediately eat?"

Tasmin let out a yelp—Pomp, probing with the needle, went a little too deeply in pursuit of the last tiny thorn.

"This will pass," Pomp assured her. "Your feet will soon toughen up. Look at Zeke. His feet look pretty bad, but he ran nearly a hundred miles on them."

"And I'd run another hundred, if the Rappies got after me," Zeke Williams piped. Since his rescue he spent most of his time staring at the womenfolk with his intense blue eyes. Cook felt strongly that the old fellow required careful handling if lustful assaults were not to occur.

"I can't be much cheered by the thought that my feet might soon look like Mr. Williams's," Tasmin allowed. Then she yelped again, but for the last time: Pomp had captured the final thorn. He rubbed her foot gently, to be sure he hadn't missed any. The last thorn out, Tasmin at once felt the pain diminish. The group began to drift on. Buffum thought she might try the ox and had Jim Bridger lift her up, but just as she mounted, the ox slung its head to rid itself of flies; a string of slobber struck Buffum in the face.

"I do despise ox spit," Buffum said, immediately jumping back down.

Pomp started to set Tasmin's foot back on the ground, but Tasmin kicked at him with it—just a little teasing kick to make him look at her! Notice her! She wanted just to sit with him for a bit, now that the others had gone.

Pomp didn't immediately realize what Tasmin was about. He set the foot down anyway, but before he could stand up, Tasmin kicked at him with the other foot.

"Remember that I'm a biped," she told him. "Don't neglect the other foot."

Pomp looked up then, right into Tasmin's eyes, something he rarely did. In a place where every day's march carried the threat of death, he didn't feel that he should complicate matters by letting this powerful young woman, Jim Snow's wife, fix her feelings on him. But he only had to look into her eyes for a moment to realize that her feelings were already firmly fixed.

"You're such an elusive gentleman, Monsieur Charbonneau," Tasmin said. "I've not been ignored so adroitly in quite a long time."

Pomp didn't turn his eyes away, and he still held her other foot.

"There's no thorn in this foot," he said, giving the foot a light squeeze.

"No, but there's a thorn in my heart," Tasmin told him quietly. "It aches rather as my heel ached before you operated. You could soothe it as easily as you soothed my foot, if you only would."

In the distance she saw Father Geoffrin walking with Clam de Paty—the priest was looking directly at her, an interference that infuriated her.

"There's that detestable Jesuit," she said angrily. "At last I manage to obtain a brief interview with you, and wouldn't you know he'd be looking. I'd like to slap him, and maybe I will."

The fact that Father Geoffrin was watching put Pomp more at ease, a shift that Tasmin immediately noticed.

"You don't care at all, drat you!" she said. "You are such a frustrating man, Pomp. I fell in love with you and I allowed you to know it—a very forward thing. I'm still in love with you. I thought I detected some interest—you returned my kisses, at least."

"I liked those kisses," Pomp admitted. He still held her foot, but felt rather silly. Kit was watching them too, no doubt jealously. The company was inching on, but Pomp and Tasmin had not moved.

"You're such a rational fellow, Pomp," Tasmin said, with a cutting smile. "I suppose my little importunings must seem silly to you. The geography hardly encourages a grand passion. In the days when we had to drink that horse slop I ceased to care whether you loved me at all, but I've had a cool drink or two and now the feeling's back. I thought love was supposed to fatten on obstacles such as these—isn't that what Mr. Shakespeare says?"

At that Pomp smiled, amused despite himself by Tasmin's steely persistence, her wit, her evident determination to do whatever it took to gain his affection—which, of course, she already had. But not many women would call up Shakespeare when they were on a burning plain, with the Arapahos likely to fall on them at any moment.

"I've been gone from Shakespeare for a while," Pomp admitted. "There's probably something like that in the sonnets, though."

When Tasmin saw his shy, astonished smile she knew her gamble had not been wholly in vain. Perhaps he *did* want her still. He was just such a modest young man.

She took back the foot she had thrust into his hand.

"I'm hardly asking you for a wedding cake, Pomp," she remarked. "After all, I'm married, and we have these numerous perils to surmount. But surely a kiss now and then wouldn't be beyond you—or a confiding word, once in a while. I hate being always rebuffed, and why shouldn't I hate it? It's damned vexing to be able to command the attention of everyone except the one person whose attention I crave."

Together they walked back toward the company, Tasmin limping a little, her foot still sore. Pomp took her arm, a gesture of concern that pleased her mightily.

"I'm worried about Pa," he said, in an effort to explain what Tasmin took to be his inattention. "He's sick. He's traveled many a mile. I fear Pa's playing out."

Ahead—far ahead—Tasmin could just see a green smudge on the horizon—it must be the spring Pomp had mentioned. Trees meant water, and water might mean a bath—clean clothes, even. Her thoughts began to fly ahead, and yet she had to admit that Pomp's explanation was just. Toussaint Charbonneau did look as if he might be playing out. Pomp, the good son, would naturally be worried.

"Perhaps we can rest for a few days, once we get to the spring," Tasmin suggested. "Your father might improve."

Pomp didn't answer. He didn't look convinced. But he still held Tasmin's arm—held it firmly, as she limped on, with a defiant look, toward the journalist and the priest.

37

He felt too tired, too sad . . .

This wilderness has destroy me," Clam de Paty mumbled. He felt too tired, too sad even to make his English precise. What he had mumbled was the truth: the American wilderness had destroyed him. He did not want to walk across it—not even one more mile. He did not want to write about its mountain men, its savages, its grizzly bears, its mountains. He had come to America a famous man, a veteran of the Grande Armée, a man who had won medals; was he not the most famous journalist in the most civilized country in the world? Yet now, thanks to his bosses—always greedy for new information—he was destroyed, broken, finished, ended, afflicted with a numb despair. True, they had found a good spring, had drunk their fill, had bathed many times, had rested. And yet, all around them, the wilderness still yawned. Santa Fe was still hundreds of miles away. The nice young Monsieur Charbonneau could talk to him all he wanted about how easy the rest of the trip would be compared to what had already been endured, but young Monsieur Charbonneau was missing one big point: Clam de Paty no longer cared. The wilderness had finished him. All day and all night, as he shook and trembled, he thought of nothing but Paris, its cobblestones, its wines, its actresses.

"Of course, it's a dratted nuisance to have no claret," Lord Berrybender allowed. "But aren't you rather overdoing this, monsieur? This wilderness is amenable enough, as wildernesses go. I shot three buffalo yesterday—plenty of meat now for our march. Doubt we'll have to eat horse meat again."

Clam de Paty didn't respond. Why should he? The old Englishman was a fool. A Frenchman would have understood at once that when a man is finished, he is finished. There was no more to be said.

"How vexing," Mary Berrybender remarked. "That Frenchman declares that he will go no further. And now Monsieur Toussaint Charbonneau proposes to leave us and take Coal and Rabbit, a decision Pomp opposes."

There had been a sharp frost during the night—the prairie sparkled as if sown with diamonds, and edges of the green pool had a little rind of ice. Monty had cut his foot on a shard of glass, residue from the family that had been massacred near the spring. Monty, howling, raced off, leaving bloody footprints on the frosty grass. Tasmin was forced to run and catch him, and now had the task of binding up his cut.

"Damn it, why did this child have to cut his toe half off?" Tasmin remarked. She was not very cheered by the thought that she soon would have two children to keep up with. Clam de Paty's despair didn't interest her—if he continued to balk, then he should be abandoned—but Toussaint Charbonneau's departure was a matter for considerable concern. Old Sharbo and his cheerful wife, Coal, had been with them all the way from Saint Louis. The three little boys, Monty, Talley, and Rabbit, had never been separated. And then there was Pomp, whose deep attachment to his father they all respected. Now the old man proposed to quit the company and take his wife and child back to the Missouri River, along whose banks he had lived much of his life.

Little Onion helped Tasmin bandage Monty. Jim Snow and Jim Bridger were devising a harness for the ox, so it could pull the wagon—this meant that their two remaining horses could be used by the hunters.

Tasmin expected long faces—she assumed everyone would be doing their best to dissuade the old interpreter from taking such a dangerous course of action; but instead she found the whole group chatting merrily. Tom Fitzpatrick and old Zeke Williams were advising Charbonneau about the likeliest routes. Old Charbonneau himself, who had been stumbling along, yellowish and tired, seemed suddenly to have a spring in his step—he looked on the whole rather jaunty.

"Why, Monsieur Charbonneau, I'm so surprised that you're leaving us," Tasmin said. "Why this sudden urge to travel alone?"

Toussaint Charbonneau tipped his filthy cap to her.

"It's just that I'm a river man, Lady Tasmin," he said. "I reckon I've been up and down our good old Missouri more than thirty times and I'm longing to make another trip or two before I'm done. Our Pomp was born right on that river, you know—I've just got a yen to see it again. It's a fine, fair river, if sometimes a little muddy."

Tasmin gave Coal a long hug—she was very fond of Coal, who had made Monty the rabbit-fur cap that had seen him snugly through a bitter winter. What Coal thought about the sudden departure, there was no guessing. Her look was stoical. Where her husband went, she too must go. Monty and Talley stood watching, solemn as judges, as Rabbit was put in his pouch. Pomp and his father held a long embrace, and then the Charbonneau family walked off east across the frosty plain, equipped with not much more than a rifle and a blanket. The mountain men gave a cheer and got back to their harnessing and packing. The great sunny distances soon swallowed up the little family.

Tasmin expected Pomp to be sad—it seemed such a risky undertaking his father was attempting. And yet Pomp was in a perfectly good mood; like his father he seemed, if anything, rather jaunty.

"But isn't it risky?" Tasmin asked. "I thought there was smallpox along the river."

"Oh, Pa's bound for Saint Louis, not the Mandans," Pomp assured her. "He likes a visit with Captain Clark every year or two. He'll soon be in Osage country, and Pa gets along with the Osage pretty well."

"I still think it's odd," Tasmin told him. "It seems that among you mountain men the best cure for jaundice or most other ills is just to set out—go to a new place. My Jimmy does it frequently. I don't think I shall ever get used to it, and yet it seemed to have a tonic effect on your father."

"Yes—Pa's not really a trapper or a fighter," Pomp told her. "But as long as he can travel the Missouri he seems to get by pretty well.

"Pa's probably just lucky," he added, reflecting. "Of all the men who went on the big trek with Captain Lewis and Captain Clark, only Pa and two or three others are alive. Most of them were better hunters than Pa—he's never been much of a shot. Most of them were better at handling boats than Pa. All of them were better at tracking. And yet he's alive and they're dead."

"I hope some of his luck rubbed off on us," Tasmin said. "I have a feeling we're going to need it before we get home."

38

Just so, as a boy . . .

Clam de Paty, citizen of France, sat calmly by the fine, cool spring, throwing pebbles into the water as the Berrybender party prepared to leave. His weeping servant, Amboise d'Avigdor, had already stumbled away.

Just so, as a boy, Clam had thrown pebbles into the Seine. Last-minute entreaties were pressed on him, but he maintained a dignified silence. Pomp Charbonneau sat with him a minute; he pointed out that many Indian tribes used these springs, not all of them friendly. Clam might have to fight—he could hardly hope to prevail. Also, bear tracks had been found—an old grizzly evidently came to the springs to water.

All this information Clam ignored. He had explained that he was finished, destroyed; and that, it seemed to him, made matters clear enough. He had no more to say. If a bear came, so be it. If Indians came, so be it. He was under no obligation to travel endlessly on. The Americans and the English were welcome to mind their own business.

It happened to be an exceptionally fine day. The mountain men and the Berrybenders were slow to get off, but finally they departed—the noise of the expedition grew faint in the distance. The only sound was the plop of pebbles, as Clam pitched them one by one into the water. A few crickets sounded. Small birds with skinny legs came and dipped their beaks into the greenish pond. After weeks of loud company, the solitude itself was refreshing.

Clam possessed a fine whetstone—he thought it might be a good time to sharpen his saber, the saber he had used when he fought in the Grande Armée. It was a sword of Toledo steel; he enjoyed keeping its edge keen, attending to it whenever he had the leisure. Now, of course, he had perfect leisure. He had last used his saber in the clash with the Pawnees—the edge of the saber had been dulled when he struck the Pawnee boy's horse. But the whetstone would soon restore an excellent cutting edge. When he finished his work he whacked at a grasshopper, cutting the creature in two.

Clam then napped for a bit in the shade of one of the small cottonwood trees. He awoke feeling rather in a poetical mood, so he took out his notebook and a tiny anthology of poetry containing some verses of Voltaire. They seemed to Clam very bad verses—he himself, he felt quite sure, could do just as well. He thought he might compose an ode to the glory of France. When his body was found, as he hoped it would be, the ode would be there in his notebook, so that his public would know that Clam de Paty had died a patriot.

But poetical composition, once Clam got down to it, proved to be a knotty business. His rhymes wouldn't come, and he had little confidence in his meters. A few phrases seemed to hold promise, in an airy way. He thought he might change the ode to a roundel, a form at which he had once been pleased to consider himself fluent. He had composed some racy verses once to a lady's garter—though the lady herself had been no lady; she was a petite actress named Thérèse whose teeth were crooked, causing her to lisp in a manner that, for a time, won the affections of theatergoers; but jaded creatures that they were, the theatergoers soon tired of Thérèse and her lisp. Clam tired of her too, though his little poem to her garter had been much admired by the beau monde at the time. In despair Thérèse took poison, but didn't die. Her crooked teeth turned black—she was seen on the stage no more. Such was the way of Paris: actors, actresses, journalists like himself, even poets and the writers of satires had but a season; many of them took poison eventually, or flung themselves into the Seine and drowned. And yet that old crab Voltaire had lived to a ripe age, spouting his tedious verses all the while. Clam became a journalist; he placed his faith in facts; he succeeded; he made his name; he interviewed the great; he went to banquets—and it all led inevitably, it seemed, to his present situation. Here he sat, in happy solitude, his Toledo blade well sharpened, sitting by a pool of green water in the American West. He thought he might pass an hour or two versifying about the buffalo, a beast little acclaimed in

The journey they were making seemed almost insanely illogical, based on nothing at all except her father's inclination to pursue blood sports. When pressed to put a time for their arrival in Santa Fe, the men were so vague in their reckonings that Tasmin wanted to slap them.

"Six weeks, I'd say, if the Arkansas ain't in flood," Tom Fitzpatrick guessed—Jim and Pomp thought they might be there a week or two sooner, if Indians didn't impede them.

"Ox travel is slow travel," Jim reminded her—the statement was so obvious that Tasmin wanted to kick him.

"I *know* ox travel is slow travel, Jim—I indulge in it every day," Tasmin reminded him. "I just wanted to know how much farther it is to Santa Fe."

"Getting to Santa Fe always takes longer than folks think it will," he told her.

"I just want to get there before I have this baby," she said. "Four walls and a roof are a great comfort when one is giving birth."

"We'll be there way before then," Jim assured her. "You've got nearly half a year before that baby comes."

"I know—it seems that we've a great deal of time," Tasmin agreed. "And yet one day, to everyone's annoyance, Vicky and Buffum and I will be screeching and screaming as we deliver up our bloody brats. I'd just rather not be outside when I'm doing the screeching."

She realized that such a comment could mean little to Jim Snow, who had spent his entire life outdoors. He could not be in a room—even a large room—without becoming restless. Due to lack of opportunity, indoor life was beyond Jim Snow.

"If we don't make Santa Fe we'll at least make the Bents," Jim assured her—the Bents being a company of several brothers who were said to be building an immense trading post near the Arkansas River. Nightly the mountain men allowed themselves to speculate about all the money they could make if the Bent's big trading venture succeeded. Some were of the opinion that the Bents had paid the Mexican authorities a lavish bribe in order to secure their concession.

"What I like about Santa Fe are the señoritas," Jim Bridger announced one night. "It's been a dern long while since I've danced with a señorita—or done anything else with one."

"Bravo, Jim!" Tasmin said. "And while you're dancing with your dusky señoritas, perhaps we ladies can find some handsome caballeros to dance with. There *are* handsome caballeros in this great capital, aren't there, Kit?"

Kit felt embarrassed—Tasmin's unexpected questions always left him feeling tongue-tied.

"Oh, the Mexicans are always dancing," Kit said vaguely.

"Well, and what about these Bents?" Tasmin asked. "Any dancing to be had at their establishment?"

"St. Vrain, maybe," Tom Fitzpatrick remarked. "He's their partner—flatters all the Mexican ladies. I expect St. Vrain can dance."

"If you're such a dancer, how come you've never asked me for a turn?"

"Well, we ain't had a fiddle, I suppose that's why," he said.

"I suppose a cello is not quite the same," Tasmin admitted. Through thick and thin, despite many abandoned goods, Vicky Kennet had insisted that they must make space for her cello, and they had.

At night Tasmin had taken to sitting up late with the mountain men. Reticent at first in her presence, they soon relaxed and went on gossiping and cussing into the small hours. Jim was at first uneasy about Tasmin's penchant for late hours but he didn't attempt to restrict her. Usually, at night, he was the one to keep Monty, spreading their blankets as far as possible from the sounds of carousing.

Persuading Jim to keep Monty afforded Tasmin her only chance for a little time alone with Pomp—the latter would usually be standing guard just out of camp. Tasmin could sometimes manage a word with him while on her way to join her husband and her child. Pomp was usually cool on these occasions, so cool that Tasmin felt like pounding him with her fists in frustration. His responses were more brotherly than not, a thing that infuriated Tasmin—yet she refused to give up. She loved the man and wanted him. What was wrong? Sometimes, leaving Pomp, she didn't make it back to Jim and Monty. She would sit alone on the prairie all night, crying, confused, tormented. Why couldn't she give up? Pomp didn't want what she wanted—probably he never would. All the wanting was hers. It left her feeling hopeless.

One morning Mary Berrybender, who was often out early seeking specimens for Piet's various collections, found Tasmin sitting listlessly in the grass, not crying, merely looking into space.

"Why, Tassie, Monty is squalling for the teat," Mary said. "Why are you sitting way out here?"

Tasmin lacked the energy for any sort of quarrel with her sister, a girl in many ways so perceptive.

"You're wanting Pomp, I suppose," Mary told her. "Buffum and I and Vicky all think so."

Tasmin shrugged.

"You're a highly professional trio, when it comes to matters of the heart, I'm sure," she said. "If you have all concluded that I'm wanting Pomp, then I suppose I am—it hardly means I'll get him."

Monty's hungry cry, faintly heard, increased her dull irritability. She had once had a fine, springing bosom, and yet now Monty had hung on it for months, with another child soon to take his place at the same milky fountain. Was that the problem? Would Pomp have wanted her if she was a girl yet, with a fine, springing bosom, instead of the mother she had become, whose nipples sometimes dripped with milk?

Somehow she didn't suppose it would matter much to Pomp. Such thoughts were idle. Her husband didn't find her lacking in appeal. Why was she not content with Jim Snow's lively virility? Why had she been obliged to seek another? And why had it to be Pomp, a man too sensitive for his own good?

"Poor Tassie," Mary said. "I suppose it's always hard for great beauties to be happy."

"Great beauty indeed! Don't flatter me," Tasmin said. "I was rather beautiful once, but America has quite scraped that away. Now I'm just a peeling, scratched-up wife and mother. We're all scratched up things. Does no good to dwell on what a beauty I was."

"You're young, though," Mary reminded her. "What's lacking is our gentle English climate. You'd soon be beautiful again if we were in a place that wasn't so dry."

"We've another day's trudging to do—why yap about beauty?" Tasmin asked.

"Because you seem sad," Mary said. "I do believe that Buffum and I are luckier. She's very happy with High Shoulders, and I'm most companionable with my Piet."

"Then my discontent must be my fault," Tasmin said. "My Jimmy's an excellent man—he ought to be enough. What's wrong with me?"

"It's that you don't have an accepting nature, Tassie," Mary replied. "I don't believe you accept anybody. Even I put up with my Piet's trifling limitations."

At this Tasmin put her face in her hands.

"What I mean to say—it's that you want more than there is," Mary went on. "You want more than there is."

"That's right," Tasmin admitted. "I don't have an accepting nature, and I do want more than there is. How am I to go about correcting these awkward faults?"

"How could I recommend?" Mary said, looking puzzled. "You're my big sister. Buffum and I look to you as to a paragon."

"Rather a muddled paragon, this morning," Tasmin told her. "I used to believe that I was really a de Bury, you know. Mama and Lord de Bury were said to have enjoyed a *petite liaison* before Papa came along. It's hard to imagine Mama doing much copulating without a brat resulting. I used to suppose I was that brat."

"Why shouldn't you suppose it? Perhaps you're right."

"I no longer think so—I'm too much like Papa," Tasmin said. "He also lacks an accepting nature, and I'm sure you would agree that he wants too much. If he didn't want too much we wouldn't be here."

"He's rather had his comeuppance, though," Mary said. "Vicky's got the upper hand now, physically. Papa spends his day cowering, hoping she won't bloody his nose."

"He's greatly altered by a lack of claret," Tasmin pointed out. "Wait till we get someplace where there's liquor—he'll soon be the one doing the bloodying again. Vicky had better enjoy her dominance while she can."

"What will the Sin Killer do if he catches you with Pomp? The thought worries us extremely," Mary said.

"Oh, stop worrying," Tasmin told her. "Pomp's not interested—he's too pure for me. I am going to try to learn not to assault him, if I can."

"But if you're in love with him, how can you stop?" Mary wanted to know. "It's as if I told Piet I wouldn't whip him with brambles anymore. He would be heartbroken and so would I."

Tasmin saw Little Onion approaching with Monty, who had stopped squalling in expectation of his breakfast.

"Piet's requirements may actually be rather simple when compared to the needs—whatever they are—of the elusive Monsieur Pomp. What does one do with a celibate? I confess I just don't know."

"Piet believes celibacy to be contrary to nature," Mary said. "He plans to make me not a virgin very soon.

"Only he hopes to wait until we're in a more comfortable setting before getting on with penetration," she added.

"Well, that's considerate of him," Tasmin said. "In the end you may be luckier than any of us, Mary."

Little Onion sat Monty down—he began to toddle at his most rapid pace toward his mother, who soon enveloped him in her arms. Here's a person who wants me, Tasmin thought. No doubt about that.

"I wonder if Piet and I will have many brats," Mary mused. "They seem to require such a lot of raising—I really wish Nanny Craigie would have come."

Tasmin's bad mood began to lift—sometimes Monty did amuse her. It was funny to watch such a tiny person making a mad dash over the dewy grass.

Just then she saw Jim Snow, riding off with Tom Fitzpatrick on an early morning hunt. At the sight her spirits lifted even higher. Jim looked so dashing, there on horseback—maybe he'd get them all to Santa Fe, after all.

40

Even the slightest delay had always irked him.

I am the one who has been chosen to keep the stories," Greasy Lake reminded the Partezon, who of course knew it as well as he did. But the Partezon was on his way to seek his death place and would not sit still for any long-winded talk. Already the Partezon looked annoyed. Even the slightest delay had always irked him. The Partezon had lived many seasons, and made many people die, but now he was riding into the sacred Black Hills to die—it was important, Greasy Lake felt, that a few things be made clear to the man before he took his journey to the Sky House.

"I am the one who has been trusted with the stories," he said, once again. "That was decided by grandfathers long ago. You know it yourself. Your own mother brought you to me when you were born. Now my horse has died and I can't get around. You are just going to climb up into those hills and die. You have a fine horse. If you take it way up there, it will just get eaten by a cougar or a bear, which is a waste."

"Why didn't you ask Fool's Bull for his horse?" the Partezon countered.

"That roan of his is a decent horse. But you let Fool's Bull ride off, and now you want my horse. I could find my death place a lot quicker if I didn't have to deal with people like you and Fool's Bull."

"But I am not a warrior, like Fool's Bull—I'm a prophet," Greasy Lake reminded the Partezon. "You have a fine white horse, and I need the best horse I can get. You are part of the great story I have to protect—give me your horse and I promise to make him last thirty years."

"My horse may last thirty years but you won't," the Partezon said. "Don't bother me with talk about grandfathers. Pretty soon the whites are going to kill all the People, including you. What about your stories then?"

"Now you're being selfish," Greasy Lake said—he was becoming exasperated. "The whites aren't going to kill all the People—and the stories are safe. If the whites knew I was a prophet they would have killed me already, but the whites can't tell a prophet from a fool. I will see that the stories are correctly passed on, but I could do a better job if I had a good horse to carry me around."

"You don't weigh much—you should get a young horse," the Partezon told him.

"I'm not heavy—it's the stories that are heavy," Greasy Lake said. "The stories finally broke my old horse down. I carry all the stories—as many as ducks on the Platte. Soon I will be carrying your story too."

For two turnings of the seasons the Partezon had been passing blood, but lately he had begun to pass more blood, and blood of a vivid red. He told no one—he didn't want the People to know that he was dying—but he himself was convinced of it, which is why he had no fear of the pox that had destroyed the Mandans and the Rees. He had no fear that Fool's Bull would get sick, either, because Fool's Bull was the luckiest man among the Sioux. Fool's Bull had ridden through battle after battle without a scratch. Bullets could not seem to hit him, nor arrows, either. The worst injury of Fool's Bull's life was a centipede bite which caused one of his fingers to turn black.

The Partezon didn't like prophets, particularly, but he knew that old Greasy Lake must be a good prophet because he had been able to intercept him as he journeyed to his death place. After their trip to the Mandans, the Partezon had sent Fool's Bull back to the tribe, with instructions to keep them well away from the river. Fool's Bull had been reluctant to go, but the Partezon had insisted, so he went. He was scarcely even out of sight when Greasy Lake turned up, standing by his dead horse. Of course, he at once started talking about the big responsibility he had, as the keeper of stories.

The Partezon had serious business to arrange—his death—and he did not want to waste much time at the foot of the sacred mountains, talking to a puffed-up old prophet.

Abruptly, he dismounted.

"All right—take the horse—load it down with your stories, if you want to," he said. "But let me alone."

But the Partezon had walked only a few yards before Greasy Lake interrupted him again. He pointed at a mountain that stood alone, well to the north of the mass of hills—that, he indicated, was where the Partezon should look for his death place.

"It's the hill where the rocks face north," Greasy Lake said. "That's the one where the eagles nest."

Somewhat to the Partezon's surprise, it turned out to be good advice. It took the Partezon, who was becoming very weak, almost a full day to make his way to the rocky summit where the eagles circled. There were nine of them at least, he saw. The presence of the eagles convinced him that he had done the right thing when he gave Greasy Lake the horse. There they were, the great soaring eagles, flying far more gracefully than the white men had flown in their clumsy machine.

Climbing carefully, applying his disciplined attention for the last time, the Partezon managed to reach the top of a bare rock spur. He thought he would be safe there—it was unlikely that a bear would try to climb the rock spur just to eat an old man like himself. Instead, the great eagles would eat him—in time he would be part of their fine, sweeping flight. At sunset the Partezon lay flat on the rock. He was very weak, but at least he didn't have to think anymore—a great relief. He looked a last time far away, to the plain where the People lived. In the night, without him noticing, his breath became one with the wind.

41

Both brothers were short . . .

Charlie and Willy, they're going to fight!" Josefina announced. "Every single day since we've been here they fight."

Maria Jaramillo, engaged to be married to Charles Bent, peeked off the parapet where she and her sister had climbed. The man she was to marry, Charlie Bent, stood nose to nose with his brother Willy. Both brothers were short, only a little taller than Josefina, who was not quite five feet tall. No doubt Charlie had given Willy an order Willy didn't like. Willy's habit of objecting to Charlie's orders was cause of many fistfights between the brothers—most of the fights, fortunately, were brief.

Maria and Josefina had climbed up to the parapet of the huge adobe edifice the brothers were building with their partner St. Vrain—a building part fort, part trading post, and part caravanserai—in order to smoke their little *cigallos,* cigars wrapped in corn husks, a popular vice with girls of the better class. On the parapet they would be less likely to be caught in this mildly illicit activity by their aunt and chaperone, Doña Esmeralda, an aging beauty who had spent virtually her whole life in the governor's palace, drifting serenely from one intrigue to another. Doña Esmeralda smoked *cigallos* herself but forbade them to her nieces.

"There they go! With their fists!" Josefina said. Maria looked down and saw that, sure enough, Charlie and Willy were raining punches upon one another, to very little effect. The brothers' fistfights, occurring, as they did, on an almost daily basis, aroused no interest at all in the various people at work in the huge courtyard. Ceran St. Vrain, just back from a trip to their warehouses in Saint Louis, was serenely inventorying goods as they were unloaded from the big wagons. Across the way, at the unbuilt gap in the south wall, the small men who worked with adobe went on shaping their mud bricks and setting them in place. A herd of sheep had just passed out of the wide gates, accompanied by two sheepherders and a woolly black dog.

"The fight's over—nobody won," Josefina remarked. Charlie and Willy now seemed to be in amiable discussion.

"That's right, we're in rags and I'm hungry," Tasmin remarked. "Will our captors feed us, at least?"

"*Frijoles,* maybe. Beans," Pomp told her.

Tom Fitzpatrick, watching the riders approach, had stopped looking indignant. His look had become somber. Pomp too stiffened.

"They ain't soldiers—Jim and Kit made a mistake," Tom said. "They ain't soldiers—or am I wrong, Pomp?"

Pomp studied the approaching riders with more care. A few of them seemed to be in military coats, and carried military muskets, with bayonets. The sun glinted off the bayonets, and off the brass buttons on the coats. But they were not riding in a military formation. He had supposed they were going to be faced with the inconvenience of a polite arrest. But now he wasn't so sure.

"But gentlemen, if they aren't soldiers, who are they?" Lord Berrybender asked.

"Renegades!" Zeke Williams suddenly announced, peering at the company with his hard, blue stare. "They're slavers, I expect. I know that big fellow on the black mule. That's Obregon."

"You know him?" Pomp asked, surprised.

"It's Obregon," Zeke repeated. "He came trading for slaves when the Pawnees had me. Didn't want me, though. Wanted women, when he could get them. Or boys, if he couldn't get women."

Tasmin's mild apprehension turned to a chill of fear. Here was the threat that all the women had talked about when they were still safe on the steamer *Rocky Mount*: abduction, rape, slavery. Even Jim Snow, in the first days of their acquaintance, had warned her about slavers. Now the frightening prospect, which they had once talked about in the safety of their staterooms, had become real.

"I count fourteen of them," Tom told Pomp.

"That's what I make it," Pomp said. "We need the two Jimmys back—with them I think we could put up a good fight."

"I'm sure if they hear shooting they'll come running—Jim Snow's just back in the gully," Tom said.

"Maybe I should try to parley with them," Pomp told the group.

"No parleys!" old Zeke piped up. "Parleys don't interest Obregon—not when he figures he has the advantage. He's gonna see all these pretty women, and he'll be thinking of all the money he could get for them down in Chihuahua."

Pomp considered the advice but felt inclined to disregard it.

"I'll be watchful," he said. "It'd be best if all the women hunker down behind the wagon. We don't want to whet Señor Obregon's appetite."

When Tasmin saw that Pomp meant to ride out and talk to the slavers, she walked over and grabbed his rein, a thing she would not have done had she not felt such deep apprehension.

"Mr. Williams knows these men—why won't you listen to him?" she asked. "They might just shoot you down and overrun us."

"Here, signor, hand me my fine Belgian gun," Lord Berrybender said. "At least we have time to prepare for this fight—not like those impetuous Pawnees."

High Shoulders, alerted to the danger, came running to the wagon with his lance, ready for battle. Just as he arrived, Pomp saw Jim Bridger returning to camp at a casual pace. He carried a prairie chicken and a jackrabbit. Though Jim had clearly seen the advancing party he showed no particular concern—in fact, he was whistling, a practice he was much prone to.

Jim Snow, too, was walking back toward the group. It had not taken him long to revise his first estimate of the situation.

When he arrived Pomp dismounted.

"That changes the odds, pretty considerably," he said. "We'll let *them* send someone to parley if they want to talk. Maybe Kit will come back, too."

"Nope, Kit's bound for the Bents'—I sent him," Jim Snow told Pomp. "If those fellows aren't soldiers, who are they?"

"Slavers, Zeke says," Tom Fitzpatrick told him. "Ever hear of a fellow named Obregon?"

Jim shook his head.

Tasmin walked off—she wanted to be alone. Now that her husband was back she had lost her fear. Jim would see that they weren't harmed—and yet she was shaking because it had been such a close thing with Pomp. If she hadn't grabbed his rein she felt sure he would have loped off and been killed. In her mind she saw the bullet strike him, saw him fall off his horse and lie dead. And yet Pomp must have engaged in many such parleys—why was she so fearful on his behalf? He was a grown man, a famous guide, skilled, alert—she could not say why she harbored such a deep fear of his death. She still believed she would lose him if she didn't watch him close. It wasn't that he was weak—Pomp wasn't weak—and yet neither was he hard, as Jim Snow was hard. Even her selfish old father was harder in

45

When the fat man, still smiling . . .

When Malgres turned away from Obregon and loped over to join the other renegades, Jim Snow was more than a little suspicious. The renegades disappeared into the gully where he and Kit had hidden—Jim thought they might be planning to race through the gully and make a flanking attack.

"That was Malgres—he killed Big White," Jim told them. "Be watchful."

Even as he said it, the ragtag group of slavers trotted up the east side of the gully and stopped. They did not look in the mood to charge. They merely sat on their horses, waiting for their jefe to return.

"Hello, my friends, don't shoot!" Obregon yelled, as he plodded toward the waiting company.

"Why, the fellow looks like a dunce," Lord Berrybender said.

"Agreed," Tom Fitzpatrick remarked. "Are you sure this is the slaver, Zeke? He looks like a fool to me."

Zeke Williams did not appreciate having his information challenged by men of small experience, and he considered that most men younger than himself were men of small experience.

"Did I say he was a professor?" Zeke inquired. "He's a slaver. He trades in boys and girls, when he can get them."

"Oh, what we'd call a pimp," Lord B. remarked. "I suppose it's the same everywhere . . . old rich men like virgins."

When the fat man, still smiling, rode up to them on his scabby mule, Tasmin moved closer to her husband, for there was something peculiarly repulsive about the man, something that suggested rot, decay, an unwholesome softness—all the women felt like shuddering, and yet none of them could say quite why they were so repulsed.

"Don't shoot, let's all be friends," Obregon said, in his shrill voice. "You don't need to point your guns at me, señores. Let's all be peaceful together."

"We took you for soldiers, at first," Tom Fitzpatrick said.

Obregon wore a filthy straw hat—he removed it and made a small bow to the women, his eyes lazily assessing them even as he practiced this courtesy.

"Oh no, there are no patrols out here today," Obregon assured them. "They are all out hunting the Ear Taker—he has come back to Santa Fe. You know of him, I suppose.

"I see you do know of him," he went on, looking directly at Amboise d'Avigdor. "Last week he took an ear from the governor's nephew—I wouldn't want to be the Ear Taker, if they catch him."

Tasmin had picked up Monty—she held him close, her arms wrapped around him. She had never seen a man as disgusting as Obregon. She felt almost queasy, and not from morning sickness, either.

"Do you suppose that's how eunuchs look, in harems?" Mary asked.

"Hush, he might hear you," Tasmin warned—though she thought Mary might be right.

"I'm sorry if my caballeros frightened the ladies," Obregon went on. "We are kindly fellows—we didn't come to harm anyone."

"I suppose you're looking for those thieving Pawnees," Zeke Williams told him. "You were mighty friendly with 'em when they had me captive."

Obregon smiled again—he allowed his gaze to drift over the women, especially Tasmin and Vicky. He remembered that the old fellow who spoke had been a prisoner of the Pawnees on one occasion when he had visited.

"No, we are merely going to visit some Cheyenne who are hunting nearby," Obregon said. "Would you gentlemen have any coffee or tobacco to spare—we are running low ourselves or I wouldn't ask."

"Do we look rich to you?" Zeke piped up at him. "We've got nothing to spare."

"Why, I see the English gentleman has an excellent gun," Obregon said. "Such a gun must be very expensive—all we seek is a little coffee."

Tom Fitzpatrick found the man irritating.

"Zeke's right, we've nothing to spare," he said firmly.

"Where's Skraeling—the man Malgres rides with?" Jim asked.

Obregon smiled again, looking not at Jim but at Tasmin.

"Señor Skraeling, he died," Obregon informed them. "He was not a healthy man. Malgres rides with me now."

There was a nervous silence. The men had become as uncomfortable with Obregon as the women. Yet Obregon continued to sit, smiling blandly, as he let his eyes dwell on this woman and that.

"Could I buy this girl?" he asked, pointing at Mary. A small quirt dangled from his wrist—he used it to point.

"Buy her? Certainly not, sir," Lord Berrybender told him. "She happens

"*I'll* be the leader," Ramon said. "I'm smarter than Obregon anyway."

"It doesn't matter how smart you are," Malgres argued. "The Indians don't *like* you, but they do like Obregon."

Ramon thought such talk was all nonsense. He thought he knew the business well enough to win the Indians over.

"Obregon never gave them much—just cheap goods," Ramon argued. "If we give them more than he did, then they'll like us."

Malgres ceased to argue. Ramon was too stupid to grasp the point, which was that *liking* didn't have that much to do with the quality of the trade goods.

Obregon would not stop moaning. Around midnight, kept awake by this irritating noise, Ramon walked over and caught Obregon by his twisted jaw, causing him to emit a piercing scream, which was reduced to bloody gurgles when Ramon cut his throat.

In the morning none of the renegades felt energetic enough to dig Obregon a grave, so they stripped him of all his possessions, left him to the coyotes and the carrion birds, and turned back toward Santa Fe.

49

Josefina had always been the bold one . . .

Josefina had always been the bold one in her family. Maria might be haughty but she was not one to take chances when it came to money. She wanted a rich man and she got one in Charles Bent, the most ambitious young trader to have traveled the Santa Fe Trail. Their mother had not wanted Maria to marry an *americano* but their father, a practical man, saw the benefits of such a union right away. The *americanos* were coming—why not recognize reality and form a union with the most successful of them?

Josefina didn't think of it in those terms—the minute Kit Carson returned and looked at her with his shy eyes, Josefina determined to grab him and get him to marry her. Doña Esmeralda wouldn't like it and her parents would huff and puff, since Kit was only a penniless guide, but Josefina intended to point out to them that if she and Kit got married at the same time as Maria and Charlie, it would save the expense of a second wedding. However, if her parents didn't knuckle under, Josefina was fully prepared to run away with Kit—her father would lose his little Josie, the child dearest to his heart, the girl who was always willing to fetch his pipe and fill it for him.

Kit had followed Jim's instructions—he walked his horse for two miles down the gully; he heard no gunfire and supposed the encounter with the Mexican soldiers must have passed off peaceably. He traveled on through the day and through the night and was rewarded not long after sunrise with his first glimpse of the big trading post the Bents were building. Kit would never have supposed those two scrappers, Charlie and Willy Bent, with their fancy partner St. Vrain, would have built anything as large as this huge adobe stockade he was approaching.

No sooner had Kit wandered in awe through the massive gates than Charlie Bent, without so much as a handshake, came over and began to pump him for information.

"I thought you were traveling with a rich Englishman. Where's he at?" Charlie wanted to know. He had heard about Lord Berrybender from Captain Clark—the thought of doing business with a man that rich appealed to his acquisitive instincts, but now Kit Carson, a fellow not worth a nickel, had arrived without him.

"They're coming—they've got an ox, and that ox ain't speedy," Kit told him. "I expect they'll show up in a day or two."

Willy Bent walked up with a grin on his face and punched Kit in the shoulder. Willy and Kit liked to tussle and wrestle, but with Charlie Bent around there were few opportunities for sport.

"Here, Willy—you and Kit get a buggy and a wagon and go bring in that English party. They'll probably be wanting to replenish their supplies, and we can sure help them out."

"But Kit just got here—let him eat at least," Willy said. "Besides, Kit don't work for you."

"Well," Kit said, noncommittally. He didn't want to ignite a conflict between the brothers, and it was easy to do.

While the brothers were facing off, Kit happened to cast his eye toward the parapet and saw two girls—at once he recognized the Jaramillo sisters, the stuck-up Maria and the merry little Josefina, whom he had once been so bold as to kiss.

"What are those girls doing here?" he asked. "I thought they lived in Santa Fe."

storeroom doing his inventories, hurried out, puzzled. Where had the Indians come from? Which Indians were they? He himself had been out that morning on a long scout and had seen no Indian sign at all. It was true that Kit Carson and Willy Bent were expected to arrive with the English party at any time, but if it was them, why did Maria think it necessary to scream at the top of her lungs? Now the sheepherders had left their sheep and the builders their building. Her husband-to-be, Charlie Bent, a man who hated to see work interrupted, would no doubt have sharp words for his bride when he took stock of the situation—but where was Charlie Bent?

"Where's Charlie?" St. Vrain yelled at the distraught young woman, who was scurrying in and out of the spacious second-floor apartment where she would soon be living with her husband.

"He's dead—I killed him!" Maria cried.

"She didn't—she broke his head a little!" Josefina, her short but usually reliable sister, shouted down at him.

"His head is cut. Maria hit him with a pot," Josefina continued.

"Hit Charlie with a pot? But why?" St. Vrain inquired.

Josefina just shrugged.

"She was angry," she said. "All these pots up here are broken now—every one."

St. Vrain hastened up the main stairway, itself not quite finished, and peeked cautiously into the rooms where the couple planned to live. Charles Bent lay stretched on the floor, bleeding from a gash on his temple. The floor was littered with shards of pottery—the heavy pottery that the local Indians made.

Charles Bent made an effort to sit up, only to fall back.

"Steady now—just rest a minute," St. Vrain advised, kneeling beside his partner. He turned to ask the young ladies for some water so he could bathe Charlie's head, but the two Jaramillo girls were gone. He had to go all the way down to the kitchen to find someone to help him. The cook who brought the water clucked anxiously when she saw all the broken pottery.

Charlie, by this time, was able to sit up, but his eyes were unfocused. St. Vrain washed the cut, which was not serious, and waited patiently for his partner to come back to himself. St. Vrain's first suspicion had been that Charlie had surprised a thief in his apartment and been hit in a struggle—but no. He seemed merely to have angered his beautiful and volatile young bride-to-be. St. Vrain had suspected that Maria had a fiery temper, and here, all around, was the proof.

"I don't go in for this heavy pottery, myself," he said, in order to make a little conversation while his partner was recovering.

"If a woman decides to throw a pot and it's a heavy pot, then heads could get broken," he said.

Charles Bent heard his partner's voice, but the voice, though distinct, seemed to come out of a fog. The fog filled the room. It had been a fine, sunny day when Maria began to throw pots at him, actions which embarrassed Charlie considerably. He didn't want to see his beautiful bride-to-be's face contorted with anger; he had been trying to keep his own temper under control, and so had averted his eyes just as Maria threw the pot that hit him. Now the world seemed foggy, but at least Maria was not screaming at him anymore.

"I expect I can guess why the fair Maria was so angry," St. Vrain told his friend. "It was because of where we decided to put the English, when they arrive."

"How'd you guess?" Charles asked. Kit Carson had informed them that two of the Englishwomen were with child—it seemed in the best interest not only of the travelers but of Bent, St. Vrain and Company to rent the English party quarters for the winter months, rather than allowing them to wander on to Taos or Santa Fe. Kit mentioned that the English party's kit was in bad order: they had few spare clothes, their guns needed attention, they would probably need a new buggy, perhaps a new wagon, blankets, winter coats, cookware, servants, and the like, all things that Bent, St. Vrain and Company could supply for a price. The only rooms yet finished where the English could be properly housed were the handsome second-floor rooms where Charles and Maria had intended to begin their married life. Charles Bent, as Maria should well know, was not a man to put personal convenience over profits. No doubt the English, tired and bedraggled from more than a year of trekking, would be happy to pay well for the lease of such handsome quarters—perhaps they would stay for four months, or even six, in which time, by supplying all their needs, Bent and St. Vrain could recoup a very large part of their expenditure on the post—a large sum made larger by Willy Bent's habit of paying far too much to the laborers—a liberality that horrified Charles when he returned from a trip to Saint Louis and sat down to inspect the books.

Fortunately, there were three small rooms off the stables which, Charles thought, would do quite well for himself and Maria. Willy could assist the firm's economy by sleeping in a tent—and if he didn't like it he could lump it.

Maria Jaramillo knew quite well that she was marrying a merchant—surely, Charles thought, she would see the sense in vacating their domestic suites for a few months in order to take advantage of this God-sent opportunity to make money—lots of money—off the English party. Surely she appreciated that their position as traders was far from secure. The goods caravans they hoped to operate year-round from Saint Louis traveled at great risk. Any one of them might fall prey to Indians, drought, bandits. Their suppliers in Saint Louis had to be paid, and paid promptly. The concession they had obtained from the Mexican authorities had been expensive, and competition was steadily increasing. Boldness, industry, and economy were required, if Bent, St. Vrain and Company were to hold their position. St. Vrain, convinced that they must expand into untried territories, was already looking at the Platte River country. Their coffers, thanks to the building, were at the moment far from full. Playing hosts, for a price, to this English nobleman and his family was an opportunity that must not be missed. Surely a devoted wife would not object to starting married life in temporary quarters so that this chance for enrichment could be seized.

"Maria was mad anyway," St. Vrain reminded Charles. "She didn't like it that Kit and Josefina included themselves in the wedding."

"I'm mad about that myself—it's a nuisance," Charles told him. But of course, as both Kit and Josefina emphasized, it *would* save on expense, and Kit promised to make himself useful in various ways until the wedding. Maria, when she heard the news, yelled and screamed at her little sister, but Josefina, long used to such displays from Maria, ignored her.

When Maria rushed to Charles to complain, he had little to say. After all, Maria's parents were amenable to the plan—getting two weddings for the price of one seemed sensible to them. Charles refused to contest the decision, which is when Maria's rage flowed through her and pots began to fly.

"I never thought Maria would get so mad she'd hit me," Charles confessed.

St. Vrain, a bachelor, merely smiled. "Women like to throw things. One threw a hammer at me, but it missed."

"A hammer?" Charles asked.

St. Vrain nodded—he did not elaborate.

"Where'd Maria go?" Charles asked.

"I don't know, but I'll find out," St. Vrain promised. "You rest, my friend."

He strolled out onto the balcony just in time to see Maria Jaramillo, mounted on the fine gray mare Charles had given her as a wedding present, go racing off through the great gates of the fort.

Charlie Bent had followed St. Vrain. He stumbled out just in time to see his bride-to-be running away.

"Uh-oh, where's she going?" he asked. "She said she was going home to Taos—but it's in the other direction."

"She won't go very far—let's just go about our business and let her have a nice ride," St. Vrain suggested. "I imagine she'll be more friendly when she comes back."

"If she's any less friendly we'll all be in trouble," Charlie observed.

St. Vrain put his arm around his partner, but did not try to offer advice as to his domestic situation.

"These English won't stay forever," Charlie remarked. "It'll just be a few months we have to live by the stables. What's a few months?"

St. Vrain took a cigar out of his pocket and offered it to his friend, but Charlie shook his head. He didn't smoke and rarely drank to excess. Indeed, he had so few of the common vices that St. Vrain found it worrisome rather than reassuring, since it left Charlie vulnerable to the most dangerous vice of all, an attraction to difficult women—such as the one just racing away on her gray mare.

"Now I've got a dern headache—did you finish those inventories?" Charlie asked.

St. Vrain shook his head. "I would have, but your little bride started screaming so loud she scared the sheepherders," St. Vrain told him. "Then she said she had killed you. I figured the inventories could wait."

"Not for long, they can't," Charlie insisted. "We need to know where we stand—those English will show up soon."

He started for the stairs, meaning to go finish off the inventories himself—but after a step or two he stopped and turned back. His fiancée was now almost out of sight—she was only a dot, far off on the plain.

"Don't you think I should go after her? What if she gets lost?" he asked.

"Don't go after her—she won't get lost," St. Vrain assured him.

Charlie nodded and turned away again, only to stop a second time.

"What if she ran into some Pawnees?"

"There are no Pawnees around. Your bride will return, I assure you. She's just riding off her fit."

Reassured, Charlie Bent went back to work. St. Vrain stayed on the balcony, smoking. What he had not thought wise to suggest to his partner was wearying himself trying to please his brother. She had seen for herself how happy Willy was when he could be with the tribe for a few weeks, hunting, racing horses, letting her tend to his needs. Willy never got a bad look on his face at those times; some nights he slept so deeply that even the bright morning sun didn't wake him. Owl felt that if she could just keep him with the tribe long enough, as they moved around following the buffalo herds and enjoying life, Willy would soon lose the habit of thinking so much about money. Of course, it was all right that Willy and his brother had brought white man's goods to the People. She herself loved colorful beads and cloths, blue particularly, and was quick to put to use the various awls and needles Willy brought her. But all it took to procure those goods was a few skins, and with buffalo so plentiful, skins were easily obtained. Just because the whites had attractive goods was no reason to exchange the cool, airy Cheyenne life for some smelly trading post. In her opinion, being crowded together, as white people were, led to disputes and quarrels that were unlikely to arise where people were free to spread out and go where they pleased.

Still, when Willy got a big frown on his face, Owl desisted. She gave him a tickle or two in an intimate place and then popped out of their robes and helped him get his gear together. There was no point in trying to stop a husband from going away—of course, even Cheyenne husbands often went away when they felt like raiding a little, or just riding around without the impediment of womenfolk.

Indian or no Indian, Willy could never leave his Owl without an awareness of how much he was going to miss her in the chill, hectic months of trekking that lay ahead. Never once had he made the long trip across to Westport Landing without various kinds of trouble presenting themselves. Sooner or later Indians of one band or another would show up, demanding presents and hoping to steal a horse or two, or a gun. The weather would either be too hot or too cold, too wet or too dry. Sometimes animals would sicken inexplicably; other times men would turn up gimpy. But despite the troubles and perils of the road, the company was prospering. They knew the route well now, and were more efficient trekkers than their rivals. Willy wasn't quite as single-minded about commerce as his brother was, but Willy wasn't lazy, either, and he meant to be rich someday.

Owl stood demurely by Willy as he saddled up and prepared to leave.

"I'll be quick to track you down when I get back," Willy assured her. Owl did not like for him to touch her in public, so he gave her the briefest of hugs, mounted, and loped away.

For an hour or more Willy traveled with a lump in his throat. He had a lonely feeling and also a worried feeling. Owl could say all she wanted to about the good Cheyenne way of life, but there were no guarantees in the Cheyenne way of life, or the white way either. It was common knowledge that smallpox had wiped out the Mandans and the Arikaras, strong tribes both. The same disease might come to the Cheyenne—besides which, the Cheyenne were a fighting people. Owl might get snatched in a raid, or killed in a battle, in which case he might never again lie with her in their comfortable robes, enjoying being man and wife. Willy always worried when he left Owl—his mind seemed to conjure up nothing but bad images, some of them rather unlikely. Buffalo were unusually plentiful that fall, and the old bulls were unreliable. What if Owl were off doing some chore and got gored by a buffalo? Also, there were panthers that lurked around Indian camps, hoping to snatch a colt or a young mare—what if one got Owl? Such thoughts were so worrisome that it was all Willy could do to keep from turning back—and he might, in defiance of all commercial good sense, have turned back had he not spotted a horseman far ahead on the prairie. The horse was white, an unusual thing in itself. As Willy approached—not before checking his pistol and his rifle—he saw an old Indian man, sitting on a scrap of blanket, chanting. A white man sat astride the horse. As he came closer Willy saw that the white man wore a look of dejection. Perhaps he had been traveling with the old Indian long enough to grow tired of listening to him pray.

When the old Indian finished praying and stood up, Willy recognized him—it was old Greasy Lake, a prophet he and Charlie had encountered several times in their first years as trappers on the upper Missouri. The old man had even helped them out once by informing them of the approach of a large band of Piegans. Willy would not have expected to meet old Greasy—a man of splotchy complexion—so far to the south.

"Hello, Greasy, who's your friend?" Willy asked, nodding toward the white man, who was gaunt, with dark circles under his eyes.

"I am Clam de Paty, monsieur," the white man said. "I am from France and I want now to go back."

"I don't know about France, but I expect we can get you to Saint Louis," Willy told him. "I have eight wagons up ahead—we're Saint Louis bound."

"He was one of the men who could fly," Greasy informed him, nodding at Clam. "He was with the Sin Killer and the Broken Hand and all the English. I don't know where they are."

Horse races were to follow the dancing; the handsome Monsieur St. Vrain was expected to win them all, but Tasmin didn't stay for the races. Once she had drunk the proper number of toasts she went at once to Pomp and persuaded him to follow her upstairs, into her bedroom, where a good fire had been laid. With her door firmly locked behind them, well above the clamor of the festivities, Tasmin was determined to have a long, slow, amorous joust of the sort she had been wanting ever since she had fallen in love with Pomp. At last, she thought, I'll have you—and Pomp followed without reluctance—at first he looked rather amused, which was not exactly what she wanted. Tasmin was determined, now that she really had Pomp alone, to break through the amusement and the politeness and arouse a passionate Pomp. She was ready to do anything—hit him, bite him, fondle him, probe, kiss—anything to break down his pleasant, accommodating reserve. She had had enough of merely being tolerated, obliged. She meant to be *wanted*, as much as this man could *want*.

And yet their fiesta was ill timed; just when Tasmin wanted them to be slow, they were quick. But Tasmin refused to quit. She wouldn't let Pomp up. She meant to keep him in the stained and tangled bedsheets all day and all night, if she could. She bit and she caressed—she insisted on long kisses, for it was when they kissed that she was able to feel that she had at last found him. With her mouth on his she whispered that she loved him and he began to kiss back. He was a young man, easily rearoused after a short interval. Tasmin urged and they enjoyed a longer rut; she was beginning to feel that she knew how to please him—and yet finally she jumped out of bed so abruptly that a long spill of seed came trickling down her thigh; she stomped around the room naked, furious, hurt, sobbing in confusion. She stood in front of the fireplace for a moment and then slumped back on the bed and dried her tears with one of the too coarse sheets. Instead of being filled with feeling, as she had hoped to be, she felt drained of it—she felt blank, felt it was all impossible, couldn't understand why she always had to be the one to start the fiesta with this man—why must she do everything? If she wanted to be touched in a certain way she had to take his hand and move it, much as she had taken Monty's hand when she wanted him to wave at his father. Pomp was a grown man—why must she direct things as if they were actors on a stage?

"I guess I'm not learning very fast," Pomp said, wrapping her in his arms. Tasmin, angry, tried to shrug him off but he tightened his arms around her and held her. Too tired to go on the attack, she rested in his arms.

"I *want* you—it's not something I *learned*," Tasmin said, though listlessly. "It's something that is. I have no one to blame but myself. You told me that night on the Yellowstone that you were not really troubled by desire. I've merely been forcing myself upon you. Why should you want me? I'm married to Jim—and I'm pregnant, probably by you. I've made a thoroughgoing mess, married to a man who constantly leaves me and in love with you, another man, who refuses to arrive. Thank God for Little Onion—she has been more help to me than you and Jimmy put together."

Pomp didn't say anything, but he continued to hold her.

"I wasn't seeking expertise from you, though I wouldn't scorn it," Tasmin said. She had begun to feel comfortable in his arms, though, and when he kissed her lightly she didn't object. It showed that he *was* fond of her, at least—she had always known he was fond of her. Why had she been unable to leave it at that? But she hadn't, and now they were lovers, although only one of them was in love. If pressed, Pomp might claim otherwise, but that was loyalty, not love. Fond he was, loyal he was, attracted he could be, in love he was not. Now that she had touched and considered every part of his body, she could not allow herself to believe that Pomp was going to fall in love with her.

"It's very discouraging to a woman to have to force these things," Tasmin told him, trying not to sound reproachful—it was just something she wanted him to know.

Pomp continued to hold her—she was feeling more and more tired.

"What am I to do, Pomp?" she asked in a low voice. "Sooner or later, unless we're all killed, my father will hunt his way to an ocean where there are boats that go to Europe. By then I'll have my child by Jimmy and my child that I suspect is by you. *What* am I to do then? Stay with Jimmy Snow, who can't bear much domesticity? Pester you, a man who doesn't really need a woman? Leave you both and go home and marry some fop? Stay in America, where, sooner or later, I'll probably get scalped? At least you would fit in my world, if I do go back to England, as I must if my children are to be properly educated. I care for my Jimmy but there's no pretending he'd like England—he wouldn't put up with it for a week. And you don't really want this—*that's* not likely to change."

"That's a big bunch of questions," Pomp said. He looked at her fondly, and twined his fingers in hers.

"Yes . . . a bunch of questions, and you're not helping me answer any of them," Tasmin said.

She sighed, started to sit up, found that she lacked the energy, lay back.

"The worst of it is that I *do* love you, even if I have to teach you every-thing," she said. She reached for his crotch and held him, and was still holding him, her questions unresolved, when the two of them went to sleep.

58

Tasmin was sitting quietly . . .

Tasmin was sitting quietly in her room with Vicky Kennet, the two of them passing a mirror back and forth, when the Mexican cavalry, forty-five strong, swept into the courtyard of the trading post. At first the two women tried to ignore the clatter. Both were contemplating cutting their hair, and for the same reason: resignation, utter resignation. Life—or at least romantic life—had arrived at a stalemate; neither woman could fore-see a time when they could be happy with their lovers, Lord Berrybender in Vicky's case, Pomp Charbonneau in Tasmin's. The two women, amiable as sisters now, were agreed that they paid much too dearly for whatever driblets of pleasure they derived from these two men.

"Let's cut it off—let's be drab—they can hardly like us less," Tasmin complained. Then, intolerably vexed by the clatter from the courtyard, she strode across the room and flung open the door, meaning to shout down whoever was making all the noise below. How were ladies contemplating the decisive step of cutting their hair to be expected to complete their de-liberations when there was such a racket outside?

When Tasmin yanked open the door she almost charged straight into two bayonets, which were attached to muskets aimed at her. As a result of her momentum she only just avoided having her bosom pricked. Both soldiers, though uniformed, were mere boys; both looked shocked when Tasmin came charging at them. Both immediately lowered their muskets. Tasmin, for her part, was so startled at being unexpectedly confronted with naked bayonets that she dropped her mirror, which, fortunately, didn't break.

The boy soldiers who faced her seemed frightened, as if they, not she, were under attack. She saw their legs trembling when she stooped to pick up her mirror. Beyond them, down in the courtyard, she could see a great many mounted soldiers milling around. Her father had evidently been prevented from leaving on his hunt. Red in the face with outrage, he was surrounded by cavalrymen. Signor Claricia and Amboise d'Avigdor were with him, the former looking resigned, the latter looking pale.

"Heigh-ho, Vicky—no barbering today," Tasmin told her. "There's a bunch of soldiers here and they've made bold to interfere with Papa."

Before the two of them could leave the room to investigate, a trim young officer stood in the doorway—after glancing around the room to make sure no men were in hiding, he bowed courteously to the ladies.

"I'm Lieutenant Molino, please forgive my discourtesy," he said. "I'm afraid you are now to consider yourselves prisoners of war."

"War? Us? What war?" Tasmin asked.

Lieutenant Molino, who was quite handsome, smiled at them pleasantly—as if he himself was aware of the absurdity of what he had just said.

"There are angry wars and polite wars," he said. "I hope this will be a polite war. For the moment it would be best if you come with me."

"Now? But we've not made our toilette," Tasmin protested.

"If I may say so, you both look very presentable," Lieutenant Molino replied. "Right now Captain Reyes is about to make a speech—his humor will not be improved if we keep him waiting."

He bowed again and swept his arm, indicating that the two of them were to go ahead of him.

"Let's go, Vicky—how exciting. I guess I ain't been a prisoner of war before," Tasmin said.

Once on her balcony, Tasmin saw that the whole courtyard was filled with Mexican soldiers, the sun glinting off their bayonets. All along the balcony the Berrybenders and their servants were being herded along by boy soldiers such as the two Tasmin had almost charged into. In the center of the courtyard, a small, wiry captain with a ridiculous plume on his hat sat on a large sorrel horse, impatiently popping a small quirt against his leg. Charles Bent, red in the face with vexation, was remonstrating with the captain, who appeared to be unmoved by whatever appeal Charles was making. Lord B., still in his buggy, was red in the face too, but he had stopped shouting and was attempting to follow the argument.

VOLUME FOUR

FOLLY
AND GLORY

Contents

Characters

Berrybender Party

Tasmin
Jim Snow (The Sin Killer)
Bess (Buffum)
High Shoulders
Mary
Piet Van Wely
Kate
Monty, *child*
Talley, *child*
Lord Berrybender
Vicky Berrybender
Little Onion
Petal, *child*
Petey, *child*
Randy, *child*
Elf, *child*
Juppy, *half brother*
Father Geoffrin
George Catlin
Cook
Eliza
Amboise d'Avigdor
Signor Claricia
Mopsy, *puppy*

Mexicans

Governor
Doña Margareta, *the Governor's wife*
Julietta Olivaries
Doña Eleanora, *Julietta's aunt*
Tomas, *footman*
Joaquin, *blacksmith*
Major Leon
Corporal Juan Dominguin
Rosa
Emilio

Mountain Men and Traders

Kit Carson
Josefina Carson, *Kit's wife*
Tom Fitzpatrick (The Broken Hand)
Old Bill Williams
Charles Bent
Willy Bent
Lonesome Dick

Indians

The Ear Taker
Cibecue, *Apache*
Ojo, *Apache*
Erzmin, *Apache*
Flat Nose, *Comanche*
Na-a-me, *Kiowa*
Greasy Lake, *prophet*
Oriabe

Slavers

Malgres
Ramon
Draga
Blue Foot
Tay-ha
Bent Finger
Snaggle
Chino

Texans

Stephen F. Austin
Jim Bowie
Davy Crockett
William Travis
Sam Houston

Miscellaneous

William Clark
Harriet Clark
Toussaint Charbonneau
Joe Compton
Elliott Edgechurch
Inspector Bailey

would happen to his family? And yet Tasmin, indifferent to his presence at first, began to be hostile. She clearly didn't want him around.

Cook, seeing that Mr. Snow was confused, took it upon herself to explain matters to him. Cook liked Mr. Snow. In her opinion it was only his abilities that had brought them safely thus far. She had studied maps. It was clear that Northamptonshire was still very far away. There might be more savages to contend with, more parching distances to cross—in her opinion doom would overtake them if they lost Mr. Snow.

"It's only that Lady Tasmin was such a good friend of Mr. Pomp's," Cook explained, as Jim listened, grateful for any clue that might help explain Tasmin's hostility.

Much as Cook liked Jim Snow, she had no intention of telling him all she knew about Lady Tasmin and Pomp Charbonneau. She was far from the opinion that delivering the whole truth was a good thing. Much harm could come with truth, in her opinion.

"When my husband died, God bless his soul, I hated any woman who still had a husband. If I couldn't have my old John, who gave me eleven bairns, then I didn't see why other women should get to have their men. That's not Christian, I know, but that's how womenfolk are. And maybe not just womenfolk."

Jim looked surprised. Was Cook telling him that Tasmin disliked him at present just because he was alive and Pomp dead? Weren't people always dying? He missed Pomp himself—they had enjoyed many fine scouts together—but it didn't make him hate Kit Carson or the Broken Hand.

Jim felt reluctant to leave the kitchen, with its good smells. Cook said no more—in her view explanation was mostly wasted on men. Though her opinion of the scrawny Mexican chickens was low, she had managed to catch a fairly plump hen, just browning over the roasting pan. She had meant it as a small treat for her suitor, Mr. Fitzpatrick, who had left off suggesting indecencies and was on the whole behaving well. But seeing Jim Snow's despondency, she changed her mind, slid the hen on a plate, and sat it in front of him. "You'll be needing your strength, if you have to climb back over that pass," Cook told him.

They had crossed the pass with five dead men in the wagon. Tasmin, inconsolable, had sat by Pomp's body all the way. Cook remembered the sound of ice crackling under the wagon wheels as they rose higher into mist and cloud. The pass was so high it seemed they were rising to heaven, although, under the circumstances, with five men dead and all of them half frozen, it was more like entering a cold hell.

"I want some!" Monty cried, seeing the chicken. Talley crowded around too. Jim gave each boy a drumstick. Traveling as he did, eating whatever he shot, singeing it, sprinkling on a little salt if he had any, with only now and then the treat of a buffalo liver, he could not but wonder at Cook's skill. She made the best meals he had ever eaten. The plump hen was delicious. He thought he might just have a slice or two, but before he knew it, the hen was eaten and he and the two little boys were licking the greasy bones.

3

Snowflakes swirled around him . . .

All the way to Taos, Jim kept remembering how desperately Monty cried when he realized his father was leaving. Little Onion couldn't shush him—he kept stretching out his plump arms to Jim, who had not expected such a display. He did his best to assure the little boy that he would be back, but Monty's sobs increased until finally Tasmin stepped out of her room.

"Go," she said. "You're just making it worse. Ever since I've known you, you've been an expert at leaving. One looks around to find you gone. Perhaps it's the right way. Babies don't cry for the vanished, just for those about to vanish."

"I had no idea he'd carry on this way," Jim said.

"Nor did he, but I assure you he'll live," she said. "Just *go! Vamos!* Scat!"

Jim went, but he couldn't free his mind of the image of Monty's distress. He had never supposed himself missed. Men had tasks that took them away, sometimes far away. From the heights of Taos the plains beyond looked as if they stretched on forever, yet Jim had just crossed them twice and was about to cross them again. Jim didn't like the bustle and noise of Saint Louis—he was always glad to get back to the quiet spaces; and yet, when he considered the future, he wondered if Saint Louis might be the right place to lodge his family. Tasmin would have some society. Captain Clark admired her and would see to that. There'd be someone to see to the children's lessons. The tiny twins were just mites yet, but Monty had been just a mite not long ago, and now he was a boy possessed of a good appetite.

Coming down toward the Kaw on his recent trip, he had seen a curve and a thicket of reeds that looked familiar, but he couldn't think why until they were well past it and dusk had fallen. It was on that curve that he had first seen Tasmin, stripped off, preparing to bathe in the cool dawn. He had been stepping into the river for the same purpose; he too was naked. He could remember his startlement vividly. He had taken in nothing of Tasmin's beauty, so profound was his own embarrassment. All he had wanted to do was hide. A little later he had killed a deer and fed her its liver.

That had not been very long ago, and yet, in that modest interval, the two of them had married, gone up the Missouri, crossed to the Yellowstone, and then gone all the way back south to Santa Fe. They had three children—it was Little Onion's opinion that it had been the big meteor shower on the plains that had caused the twins. Whatever caused them, they were born, healthy, and in Cook's opinion, likely to live. For the moment they were well provided for, but that might change. Jim had nothing to sell except his skill as a plainsman—he supposed there would always be a need for reliable guides, more and more need as the Americans filtered into the West; but guiding kept him far from his family, and his son's outburst had shown him that absences didn't suit everybody. They had once irked Tasmin as much as they now irked Monty. What the twins might want, as they got older, he couldn't guess. As he approached the little house Kit Carson and Josie had taken he didn't feel at ease in his spirit, as he usually did when he traveled alone.

The small house Kit and Josie lived in was little more than a hut—fortunately, both were short people. Jim thought he might stop in for a night as he headed east. Snowflakes swirled around him as he rode up. It was chilly weather. Kit was behind the house, chopping firewood, a fact that rather surprised Jim. Two walls of the house were already banked high with chopped firewood, and yet Kit was going at it as if he and Josie were down to their last stick. How much wood could they burn anyway, in one small fireplace?

Cold as it was, Kit was soaked with sweat from his vigorous work with the axe.

"If you don't slow up on the firewood there won't be a tree left standing," Jim said. "You got enough chopped to heat a fort, and you don't live in a fort."

Kit stuck his axe in a log and left it. He stared at the towering stacks of firewood as if noticing them for the first time.

"I hate running out of firewood," he said.

Then he sighed.

"There's nothing wrong with having plenty of firewood, is there?" he asked. To Jim he seemed distracted, even rather gloomy.

"I don't know what else to do when Josie's mad at me," Kit admitted. "It's too cold to just sit around. So I chop firewood."

This was the first hint Jim had had that the newly married Carsons were experiencing marital unease—though, once he thought about it, it was not surprising that Josie got mad at Kit. Jim himself was frequently mad at Kit—at least he was if he had to be in his company for a day or so. Josefina had been mightily taken with Kit before the marriage, but now that she actually had to live with him it was no wonder that she found him irritating.

Jim was about to ask what Josie was mad about when the girl herself popped out the door. She looked as friendly and cheerful as could be.

"Come in, Jimmy—we got posole," she said.

Then she looked at her husband.

"What about you, woodchopper?" she asked. "Don't you ever get tired of chopping wood?"

Kit was perplexed. Twenty minutes earlier Josie had been seething like a kettle, so angry with him that she spluttered when she tried to talk. But now she was his old, cheerful Josie again, a twinkle in her eye as she stood beneath the high piles of stacked firewood towering above her head.

"If this wood falls on the house it will be the end of us," she said.

In fact she *had* been furious with Kit, earlier—she had given him a long list of supplies to bring back from the trading post, but he had let the list blow away and had forgotten half the things on it, including the most important item of all, a swatch of soft flannel which she had ordered specially from Saint Louis and had been waiting for for a year. She wanted to make the flannel into a warm nightgown to wear on cold nights, when the north wind howled through Taos. Kit had promised her faithfully that he would bring the flannel, but then he had carelessly lost her list and had returned

"Monty says you don't breathe when you die—but I like to breathe," Petal confided.

"It's the accepted thing to do," Tasmin allowed.

Kate Berrybender came in at that time. Petal, never happy to be interrupted, did her best to ignore Kate—but Kate had little respect for the wishes of children, Petal particularly.

"Cook is wondering about dinner—must it be goat again?" Kate asked.

"Why not a pig? There are plenty of swine running around this town. Have Papa buy one," Tasmin suggested.

"I was talking about how you die," Petal reminded her mother.

"It's too late to cook a pig today—I fear it will have to be goat," Kate remarked. Petal was glaring at her.

"My, such a dark look," Tasmin said.

Petal, her interview ruined, turned and marched out of the room. How one became deaded—the term she preferred—was still annoyingly obscure.

"There's going to be trouble with that child," Kate observed.

"There's trouble with all children, as you'll discover someday," Tasmin told her. "But I agree. There's likely to be rather more trouble than usual with that one."

8

. . . a quick soldier caught his foot . . .

The Ear Taker, the small dark man who had first been known to his people as Takes Bones, knew it was folly to return to Santa Fe. On his way back from the north the jack rabbits began to stare at him again, as they had before he left to explore the northern lands. That was certainly a bad sign. Then, in the space of three days he saw three owls, which was a worse sign. It was foolish to ignore such obvious signs, but the Ear Taker came back to the southwest anyway. He had not enjoyed the north. There were no Mexicans, only a scattering of whites, and Indian tribes which were so wary he could not approach them. Their camps were full of dogs, quick to pick up unfamiliar sounds or scents.

Old Prickly Pear Woman had told the Ear Taker that if he walked north far enough he would come to the edge of the world and perhaps be able to catch a glimpse of the great snowy void where spirits were said to go; but that had turned out to be just an old woman's lie. The Ear Taker walked north for many weeks, but instead of coming to the edge of the world he just came to a place that was extremely cold. If he had not been able to find a snug den that had once been used by a bear, he might have frozen. The bear's smell was still strong in the den. He thought the bear might return and want his home, but no bear came. In his whole time in the north he had only taken two ears, one from a young white boy who had been traveling with some men who could fly in a basket and the other from an old trapper who was extremely drunk. He hated to give up on a place he had walked so far to see, so he stayed through another winter and learned to snare animals that made their lives in the snow. Food was never a problem—the northern ponds were covered with ducks and geese. Now and then he came across an old man or an old woman who had become too old to move with the tribe and so had been left to die. He liked to sit with such old ones, even though he didn't know their tongue. Once he even ran into an old shaman who made his home in the bole of a big tree. Old Prickly Pear Woman had told the Ear Taker that there were shamans who could teach people to move in and out of time, so they could visit their ancestors, but the old man in the tree, though he mumbled constantly, didn't know how to move in and out of time.

The first thing the Ear Taker did, when he came back to the country of his people, was to pay a visit to old Prickly Pear Woman. He intended to point out to her that she had misled him badly in the matter of the edge of the world, which was not in the north, as she had insisted it was. But when he came to the vast field of prickly pears with the narrow tunnel underneath, the hole where she had lived showed no signs of recent habitation. Several rattlesnakes were using the hole as a den; they were irritable when the Ear Taker showed up. He killed one fat snake and ate it, but left the others alone. He remembered that the old woman had a hiding place nearby, under a flat rock; she kept the equipment she used in her spells there: dried-up toads, scorpions, dead mice. The Ear Taker found the large rock easily enough but the only thing there in the hole was some of the bitter cactus buds that the old woman sometimes chewed when she was seeking a vision. The buds he took for himself—now and then he would chew one and feel as if he were flying.

Soon the Ear Taker began to take ears again, slicing ears off drunken drovers, just as he had before. His skills had eroded somewhat; several times he made bad cuts, once by accident even cutting a drover's throat. Once again he became fired with his mission, which was to humiliate whites as the whites had humiliated the People they took captive after the big pueblo revolt many grandfathers back.

The irritating thing, though, was that the jackrabbits continued to stare at him in an unnatural way; also, he kept seeing owls. Once one flew directly over his head, a sure sign that his death was near. He was glad to be back in the country of red canyons and piñon trees, but the owls worried him. Before he could make up his mind to go farther off the now busy trails to Santa Fe, the thing that had been coming happened: a quick soldier caught his foot. He had the soldier's ear in his hand, having just sliced it off, but for some reason he hesitated a moment before springing away. He did not think any soldier could be as quick as this soldier was. The quick soldier hung on to his foot; the soldier yelled out and very soon the famous Ear Taker was caught and firmly tied with rawhide cords. Before they tied him he quickly crammed all the remaining cactus buds into his mouth and chewed them, hoping they would poison him and allow his spirit to float away before the torturers got busy; but he vomited up the buds while the excited soldiers were beating him and kicking him. From time to time, in the days of pain that followed, it seemed that his spirit might fly away, but the feeling didn't free him from the pain entirely. The Mexicans were convinced that he had special powers—to make sure that he didn't escape them, his feet were chopped off and the stumps seared with hot irons. Then they hung him on a gibbet in the center of the Plaza, where all who wished could observe his pain. At first he was hoisted off the ground with hooks through his ears, a fitting punishment for an Ear Taker, it was felt. But the weight of his body soon pulled the hooks through and he fell. Many soldiers, convinced that he was a devil, wanted him garroted right away, but the Governor refused to hurry. Any man who was missing an ear was allowed to come and give the Ear Taker twenty lashes: fourteen men took advantage of the offer. The Ear Taker was by then close to death, but he was not dead. Screws were driven into his skull through what remained of his ears; the screws would hold his weight whereas his ears wouldn't. Thin rawhide cords were attached to the screws, and the Ear Taker, naked and bleeding, hung several feet off

the ground, his facial muscles horribly distorted by the weight of his hanging body. Through it all the Ear Taker scarcely cried out. He sighed great
sighs—but his sighs grew fainter as he weakened. The native people shuffled
about the Plaza, doing their little bits of business. They kept well away from
the gibbet. They did not need to see what was happening to this small man.
Their memories were full of terrible stories about things the Spanish had
done to the People.

But the Mexicans watched: laborers, soldiers, women. The Governor's
wife, Doña Margareta, spent hours at her window, staring at the dying man
whose practice had been to take ears. Watching the blood drip from his numerous wounds gave her an unexpected satisfaction. When two more one-
eared men turned up and claimed their right to lash the Ear Taker, Doña
Margareta watched every stroke. She even sent a manservant to search
about the city and see if one or two more earless men could be found.
When none turned up she persuaded her husband to allow some of his
victims who had already lashed him to lash him again. What were lashes
compared to the loss of an ear?

While the Ear Taker was dying, a process that took four days, the Berrybenders all stayed away from the windows that looked out on the Plaza.
Amboise d'Avigdor, who had lost an ear, declined to claim a turn with the
lash. Lord Berrybender, leaving the Plaza on his hunts, turned his face
from the spectacle.

"Excessively cruel, I sometimes think, the Spanish race," he said. The
sight of the hanging man rather upset his digestion—once he even called
off a hunt without firing a shot.

It was Amboise who happened to notice the stranger, a thin bald man
sitting well back in the shade, with a drawing board on his lap. The man
was watching the Ear Taker's suffering with an almost scientific interest—
he looked down from time to time, sketching what he saw.

"Why, where'd that fellow come from—I'd swear he's English," Lord Berrybender announced, when Amboise called his attention to the stranger.

Then he looked more closely and drew back with a start.

"My God, it's Edgechurch," he said. "Elliott Edgechurch. Met him in
England more than once."

"Is he an artist, then?" Amboise asked. "He's drawing this poor hanging
man."

"I suppose he can draw but he's not precisely an artist," Lord Berrybender replied. "In London he's called the Torture Man."

9

. . . soup would be spilled and wineglasses knocked over.

That man's too scabby!" Petal announced, in what was, unfortunately,
her most carrying voice—the remark embarrassed everyone at the table except the mild gentleman it described, Dr. Elliott Edgechurch, who peered
at the little girl in a kindly way.

"Oh damn, she's escaped again," Tasmin declared, setting down her
fork. Before she could jump up and seize her impolitic child, Petal had
darted under the table, amid a thicket of adult legs. She knew from experience that if she could just get right under the center of the wide table
nobody would be able to reach her, though as various diners made the attempt, soup would be spilled and wineglasses knocked over. Sometimes,
if pressed, Petal might seek sanctuary in her grandfather's lap. Lord Berrybender—though, to Vicky's annoyance, quite indifferent to his own two
young sons—could seldom resist Petal, even when she had just delivered
an embarrassingly accurate description of their distinguished guest, a
man who had been physician royal to several majesties and was generally
thought to be England's most eminent surgeon.

"She won't stay in the nursery—finds the dining room more exciting,"
Tasmin explained. "If I had a dungeon I'd fling the brat into it, but I have
no dungeon."

"Oh, it's no matter, I *am* scabby at present," Dr. Edgechurch admitted.
"It's the harsh American waters. I am from Wiltshire, where the waters are
far softer. Even in London I am sometimes troubled with eczema. I generally carry various emollients and a very delicate soap that can only be
obtained from France—not cheap, my soap, I assure you. But a vital piece
of my kit bounced out of the wagon and the muleteers absolutely refused
to go back and look for it, so here I am, entirely at the mercy of American
waters. The young lady was being no more than truthful, as the young so
often are. I *am* too scabby."

Petal remained under the table, just out of reach of various grabbing
hands. She didn't really object to the scabby man—what she objected to
was being left in the nursery with the five boys while, downstairs, the adults

were eating exciting meals. Sometimes Kate would mind the nursery, but usually that chore was left to Little Onion, the more easily eluded of the two. All that was necessary was to pinch a little boy hard enough for the boy to raise a howl. While Little Onion soothed the injured male Petal could often sneak out and slip down the big staircase; by the time Little Onion realized that a miscreant was missing, Petal could be under the table or in her grandfather's lap. It was an exciting game, one Petal didn't always win. Sometimes Little Onion ran her down before she could reach the stairway.

"Leave her be, the brat," Tasmin said. The tall doctor with the scabby skin seemed kindly, on the whole. He also seemed to know everyone in Europe, including the French doctor who had taught Father Geoffrin anatomy. When he discovered that Amboise d'Avigdor had lost an ear to the Ear Taker he examined Amboise's head carefully and took some arcane measurements.

"The fellow was a specialist, and a sound one," he announced. "He knew how to remove an ear, but I doubt he knows much else. The appendix would stump him, I imagine, or even a joint."

Lord Berrybender was uneasy. Somehow he couldn't quite like this kindly surgeon, though he was certainly vigorous in pursuit of his goals. He had arrived in Santa Fe from California, where he landed after making a long and thorough examination of the elaborate tortures practiced in China and Japan. All the way to China just for torture? It seemed to Lord Berrybender that there was something slightly unwholesome about it, but the Governor's wife, Doña Margareta, found Dr. Edgechurch fascinating—she couldn't get enough of hearing about the many severe cruelties the famous doctor had witnessed. It annoyed her that the little Berrybender girl had distracted Dr. Edgechurch from an elaborate description of how the Ottoman sultans punished women who failed to please them: by tying them up in sacks with wildcats and flinging them off a cliff, or else crushing their breasts with viselike instruments designed solely for that purpose. Doña Margareta meant to encourage her husband to try to keep Dr. Edgechurch in Santa Fe—then she could draw the man out at length. Santa Fe was filled with criminals—it was her opinion that better tortures needed to be devised, in order to subdue this element.

"How much longer do you think that little Ear Taker will hold out?" Lord Berrybender inquired. "Rather puts us off our feed, having him hanging there. My cook is even reluctant to go to market. The sight of him preys on the mind, you know."

"Two more days will finish him," Dr. Edgechurch assured them. "He has no very serious injuries, but it's a strain on the heart, having the muscles pulled out of shape as they are. It's the mistake most torturers make: they don't understand that the nerves grow fatigued. Pain exhausts before it destroys. The Japanese understand this well. They allow their victims regular respites."

Tasmin found that she disliked Doña Margareta intensely. About the English doctor she wasn't sure. He was a surgeon; he cut people for their own good. Torture, of an approved sort, must be all in a day's work for him. While recognizing that humans must sometimes be cut open to remove diseased organs, Tasmin still felt that it must take a curious sort of human being to choose cutting as a profession.

"What drew your attention to torture, Doctor?" Piet Van Wely asked. He saw in Doctor Edgechurch a fellow scientist. But to his dismay, the question drew a frown from the great man.

"I am *not* drawn to torture—as a humanist I strictly oppose it," he replied. "If a criminal must be put to death I advocate doing it humanely, with a bullet or a noose."

He took a long swallow of wine.

"What draws me to the torture chambers—and I've inspected more than one hundred, most of them quite bloodily active—is not torture but nerves," Dr. Edgechurch said. "The human nervous system is as yet poorly understood. I am even now attempting a comprehensive atlas of nerves, but my atlas is far from complete. Nerves are not easily traced. They mainly reveal themselves under extreme conditions—such as torture. There's more to be learned about nerves in torture chambers than in anatomy classes."

"Excuse me, I believe it's time for my devotions," Father Geoffrin said. He had grown pale, he felt queasy; he did not want to hear of any more horrors.

"So tell me, Dr. Edgechurch," Tasmin said, determined to tough this curious diner out, "which nations produce the best torturers? Or do I mean the worst?"

"Oh, that's easy, the Japanese," the doctor said at once. "There's something aesthetical about it. They're very good with cords, for example. Very good with cords."

Doctor Edgechurch paused to reflect on his long experience.

"Of course great specialists do pop up here and there—you might almost call them artists," he said. "There's a Viennese called Schoensiegel.

Extraordinary fellow. Confined himself entirely to feet, and yet he broke the strongest men. Plenty of nerves in the foot, I can tell you that."

Tasmin found the situation curious in the extreme. All the Berrybenders, even the usually unshockable Mary, were looking discomfited. Petal had crawled up in Lord Berrybender's lap and was rapidly polishing off his *cabrito*. Buffum and Vicky looked distinctly peaked. And yet Dr. Edgechurch had said nothing improper or suggestive. He was a famous physician, determined to understand the workings of the human nervous system. Accordingly, as he had politely explained, he went to places where nerves were stretched to the limit: that is, torture chambers. It made sense, and the doctor had been modest and matter-of-fact in explaining it. And yet Geoff, turning green, had to flee. Buffum excused herself, Vicky remained expressionless, and Lord Berrybender was too distracted even to play with his granddaughter. Mary Berrybender, who could talk about the most recondite sexual practices without turning a hair, was now twisting her hair into curls, a nervous habit she was thought to have outgrown. With the exception of Doña Margareta, whose eyes shone more brightly every time a torture was mentioned, the whole table had been quelled.

The odd effect he was having on his hosts did not escape Elliott Edgechurch. He drained his wineglass, stood up, thanked Lord Berrybender, and bowed to them all, in his face a touch of sadness.

"There! I've done it again—spoiled a perfectly good dinner party," he said.

"Now, now," Lord Berrybender said, but the doctor ignored him.

"Healthy people don't want to hear about tortures—and why should they?" he asked. "It's the same with operations. Healthy people don't like to watch them. In both instances there is always the possibility that such agonies will in time be theirs.

"Thus," he added, "my investigations will of necessity have to be of a lonely nature."

"But one day you'll have your atlas," Tasmin told him. "No doubt it will win you great fame."

"I hope not—that too would be a form of torture," Dr. Edgechurch said; then he left the room.

"Too scabby!" Petal said again. In this instance no one disagreed.

19

. . . there he was again, kissing her mother . . .

Petal had almost forgotten the bearded stranger when she came round the corner and there he was again, kissing her mother, who clung to him happily. It shocked Petal so that she walked into the nursery and pressed her face into a corner—her new way of showing extreme displeasure. When people refused to do what she wanted them to she hid her face in a corner until Monty or some big person pulled her out and offered compromise. The only person who didn't seem to care when Petal removed herself to her corner was her mother, who proposed no compromises.

"You can stand there a week, if you want to be stubborn," Tasmin said. "Why should one care?"

Jim thought Petal the very image of Tasmin, with high similarity of disposition too. She looked daggers at him when he tried to play with her a little: it was the same look Tasmin gave him, when she was angry. He not only had a forceful wife, he now had a forceful daughter too.

After enduring another day in which her mother's door was firmly locked, much of which she spent with her face pressed bitterly in a corner, Petal decided to take her concerns directly to the intruder—the man had gained a power over her mother that was not acceptable.

The next day, catching her father alone, she made a blunt demand.

"You go away from here," she said. "And you go quick."

Jim was amused. The child's tone of voice was exactly like Tasmin's, if she happened to be giving Kit Carson an order.

"I been gone so long you nearly got grown on me," Jim told her. "Why do I have to go away?"

"You bother my mother too much," Petal said. "That's why."

"What if your mother likes for me to bother her?" Jim suggested. "Suppose she'd *rather* I bother her."

Petal didn't like this equivocation. Why wouldn't the tall man just go?

"When you go away I can take my nap with Mommy," Petal explained.

"Well, you're welcome to take your nap with both of us, I guess," Jim said. "You and Petey too, and Monty."

The last thing Petal was prepared to tolerate was having her brothers around at nap time. Nap time meant her and her mother—no strangers.

"You bother my mother too much, that's why you have to go away," Petal insisted, returning to her original charge.

A few hours later, clutching the blue rooster, Petal wandered into her mother's bedroom, only to find the tall stranger there beside her mother.

"I told him to go away, he bothers you too much," Petal insisted.

"In fact he doesn't bother me at all, little girl," Tasmin said. "He bothers *you!*"

Exasperated that her mother would take such a tack, Petal went immediately to a corner and pressed her face into it. Her mother and the tall man took no notice. If she threw a tantrum Little Onion would come and carry her away. After a bit she left the corner and approached the bed. She gave the tall man a bit of a smile.

"Lift me up," she said—and he did.

"Now she's going to pile on the charm," Tasmin warned.

Petal tried to put her hand over her mother's bad mouth.

"I have a blue rooster," she remarked, holding it up so Jim could inspect it.

"Here comes the charm," Tasmin said.

Petal ignored her mother. "His name is Cockadoodle," she said.

"I eat roosters," Jim said, deadpan.

Petal was taken aback. She studied her opponent.

"Blue roosters make mighty good eating," Jim said.

Petal put the rooster behind her.

"It was Petey's rooster but he gave it to me," she said.

"What an outrageous lie!" Tasmin said. "You stole that rooster."

"It followed me home," Petal said, keeping a close eye on the stranger.

"She'll argue for hours, you won't wear her down," Tasmin warned.

"I may be hungry when I wake up from my nap," Jim said. "I may want to eat a rooster. I hope I can find a blue one."

He then shut his eyes—in a minute he emitted a faint snore.

"I hope he goes away," Petal remarked.

"It won't help you—next time he goes away we're going with him," Tasmin informed her.

Petal studied the sleeping man. Then she slipped off the bed and hid the blue rooster amid Little Onion's kit. It was going to be necessary to watch this sleeping man.

20

. . . when it came to deciding on a route the two could not agree.

Though they had been absent from Santa Fe for almost a year, Jim and Kit had not attempted California; when it came to deciding on a route, the two could not agree. Kit insisted that the better route lay south, along the Gila River. Jim, who wanted to strike due west, was taken aback.

"The Gila River?" he said. "We'll starve before we get anywhere near the Gila River."

"That's the way I'm going, you can do as you please," said Kit.

A moment later, though, he revealed more conflicted feelings.

"Josie don't want me to go at all," he admitted. "If the dern Bents like California so much, let them go. Josie don't think it's right for a husband to take off and be gone that long."

"I expect most wives would take that line," Jim told him.

While they were grappling with these issues the matter was settled for them by the surprising arrival of a counterorder from the Bents, delivered by the taciturn old hunter Lonesome Dick, who seemed put out that he had had to ride so hard on their behalf.

"I've sweated my horse," the old man said, leaving no doubt that he considered it their fault.

"It don't hurt a horse to sweat," Kit pointed out. "What do they want now?"

"They want you to go to New Orleans," Lonesome Dick informed them. "I'm going to Califorphy. If they'd sent me in the first place I'd already be halfway there."

"Dick's never been friendly," Kit said, as they watched the old man ride off.

Two months later the two of them were on the under deck of a Mississippi River steamer, watching the low buildings of Saint Louis fade out of sight to the stern. It seemed that a large shipment of goods off an English ship that had encountered foul weather had been put off at New Orleans, rather than Baltimore, as had been planned. It was said to contain Lord Berrybender's new guns, as well as a large quantity of cloth and other tradable items.

Kit, who couldn't imagine an easier way to travel than by steamboat, was in high spirits.

"I bet there's a passel of fish in this river," he claimed. "They say catfish get as big as horses."

"If there's fish that big I'd hope to stay out of their way," Jim observed. "A whale swallowed down Jonah, I recall."

He was glad to be out of Saint Louis—its jostle and stench were not to his liking—but he at once took to steamboat travel. He found that he could sit and watch the widening waters for hours, letting his thoughts drift to no purpose. Clouds formed; rainstorms blew in and blew out. Jim preferred the spacious, grassy plains to the thick forests that now covered the shores, but the river itself he liked. Kit felt the same.

"It'd be easy, being a waterman," he said. "You just float along—no tramping."

"We'll get plenty of tramping on the way back," Jim reminded him. Charles Bent, ever hopeful of new territory, wanted them to pack the goods overland much of the way back, crossing a long stretch of dangerous country. It was Charles Bent's opinion that there would soon be a steady stream of immigrants along the southern route, and he meant to have a trading post somewhere along it, preferably near the Canadian River. Scouting possible locations was Jim and Kit's real mission.

"Time waits for no man," Charles Bent declared. "If we don't get us a post down that way you can bet somebody else will."

Neither Jim nor Kit felt any eagerness to see what the southern tribes felt about this—they agreed in advance to avoid these tribes, particularly the Comanches, and concentrate on getting the goods safely back to the big post on the Arkansas. If Charles Bent wanted to persuade the Comanches to lay down their lances and scalping knives, let him do it himself.

As the steamer proceeded south, the gradual widening of the river filled Jim with amazement. He had never expected to be riding safely down such a vastness of water. The constant traffic in all manner of boats, as they approached the port, was in itself a delight to watch.

The gradual spread of the great plain of water had a sobering effect on Kit.

"A river this big could swallow this boat like a pill," he observed. "I could never swim a river this wide. I'd be drownt."

"Or swallowed by one of them big catfish," Jim reminded him. On several occasions the boatmen, using ropes for lines, had hooked catfish that were not much smaller than horses; the fish were so large that they had to be cut up before their flesh could be brought on deck.

"The more I think about all this water the less I like it," Kit remarked.

"We'll be there tomorrow—go away if you're going to complain," Jim protested. "I'd like to enjoy the sights, if you don't mind."

Jim sat on deck all night, watching the starlight on the water, listening to unfamiliar bird cries, wondering why the movement of water was so soothing.

The turmoil on the docks was more intense even than what they had encountered in Saint Louis.

"I am certainly surprised to know there are so many black people in the world," Kit said.

Jim was surprised on that score too—although the shades of color on the New Orleans waterfront were more various than he had seen anywhere. There were very black people, and lightly black people; there were yellow people and people the color of coffee; Spanish people, Choctaw Indians, French sailors, English sailors, large whores and small whores; drunks lying in the mud; wagons being loaded and boats being unloaded; fishermen hawking their catch: such a bustle of people that Jim wished immediately to be back on the broad, calm river. Besides the jostle, he felt closed in by the heavy vegetation. The humid air left them both sweating profusely. Flies and mosquitoes were persistent. They passed a pen full of dusty cattle, and another pen full of silent, apathetic slaves.

All the waterfront was a boil of activity, heaps of goods piled here and there; and yet no one seemed to be in charge. Neither Jim nor Kit had any clear idea of how to locate the goods they were supposed to secure. While they were considering the problem two small men fell to cursing one another in a tongue neither Jim nor Kit could recognize. The men had blue bandannas on their heads. They quickly fell to fighting with knives—a crowd gathered, drawn by the possibility of violence: the crowd was not disappointed. Neither sailor was killed, but both were cut—the dusty ground beneath them was soon bloody. Finally the two combatants stopped and walked away together.

Jim eventually managed to locate a wizened little man with long chin whiskers who seemed to be an inspector of some kind. When Jim mentioned the English boat that had supposedly unloaded, the little man nodded.

"It's about time somebody got here," he said. "It's six months now we've been putting up with that cannibal."

"Where's a cannibal?" Kit asked, not pleased.

The small inspector, whose name was Bailey, led them quickly through an alley where two pigs were quarreling over a fat brownish snake. When they came out of the alley Inspector Bailey pointed to a grassy spot under some huge trees draped with trailing whiskers of Spanish moss. The boxes and bales piled up were being guarded by an enormous black man, who sat comfortably on one of the bales, fanning himself with a hat.

"That's the cannibal—calls himself Juppy," Inspector Bailey told them. "Take him with you, if you don't mind."

Jim and Kit were startled by the size of the man, who was light brown rather than black. They had both seen tall men before, but none as tall as this man—and in most cases the tall men were skinny. But this man was thick in the trunk; his arms and legs were massive, as were his thighs.

"Why do you think he's a cannibal?" Jim asked.

"People don't get that big by eating regular food," Inspector Bailey declared. "There's a witch up the street that's been trying to poison him, but the poison don't take. That's a sure sign of a cannibal.

"Come by my shack and sign the bill of lading when you're loaded," the inspector told them.

"Loaded? Loaded how?" Jim inquired. "We don't have a wagon yet."

"Juppy's got a wagon, and the mules to pull it," the inspector informed them, before departing.

The big black man was walking toward them now, seeming to cover the yards in only a step or two.

"Would you be the gentlemen from Messieurs Bent, St. Vrain and Company, by any chance?" the large man asked, smiling agreeably. "I hope so because I'm ready to travel—too many little old black witches in this town. I'm Juppy."

He extended a very large hand—somewhat at a loss, Jim and Kit shook it.

"I hope you're not a cannibal," Kit told him. He had begun to feel some anxiety on that score and felt it best to be frank.

Juppy laughed an easy laugh.

"See any tasty-looking people around here?" he asked. "All I see are some ugly sailors and a few old skinny witches. Nobody plump enough to eat."

Then Juppy laughed.

"Just joking," he said. "If you're from the Bents I guess we better get loaded so we can be on our way."

Jim and Kit felt uneasy. Charles Bent had said nothing about a black giant named Juppy.

"Nobody told us about you," Jim admitted. The giant seemed perfectly friendly, but he certainly was a giant. On a practical level, bringing him with them posed problems. Could they expect to find a horse big enough to carry such a heavy man?

"Don't be worryin'," Juppy said. "I've made all the arrangements, and I've got my mule, Jupiter—he's been my mount since I was thirteen. My instructions from Father were to give you every assistance, but not to let his expensive new guns out of my sight, and they haven't been out of my sight since I picked them up in London. As you'll see I've not wasted my wait—I've got a good bunch of pack animals and a wagon we can use as long as the terrain permits wagon travel. The upriver steamer leaves at six. We better start loading, don't you think?"

Jim and Kit were deeply puzzled. Juppy was efficient, as well as friendly. He had got things ready. The pack mules looked healthy. And yet he referred to his father's instructions. Who could his father be?

"Why, Lord Berrybender, who else?" Juppy informed then. "I assumed you knew."

Jim and Kit could only shake their heads. Of course both of them had heard that Lord Berrybender had fathered a great many bastards, but no one had informed them that one of his bastards was a brown giant.

"He probably didn't mention me because he wants to surprise the girls— my half sisters," Juppy speculated. "Papa met my mother in a circus—she was the giantess."

Jim and Kit were still startled, but Juppy produced the wagon and the pack animals and loaded most of the bundles and bales. By six they were on an upriver steamer. There had been some awkwardness at the customs shed. Jim and Kit were forced to admit that neither of them could write their name. The bills of lading were incomprehensible to them. Inspector Bailey handed the papers to Juppy, who inspected them closely and signed them "Jupiter."

"Jupiter, same name as my mule," Juppy said, with a smile.

Soon they were aboard the boat, watching the great river pour on toward the sea.

21

. . . knocking over a bowl of pudding . . .

When Petal looked up and saw the brown giant in the doorway of the nursery she screamed as loud as she could and raced for Little Onion, who was rather surprised herself. Jim Snow, just returned, had already been in for a visit with Tasmin, but he had said nothing about the brown giant. Juppy wanted to be a surprise.

Only that morning Petal had caused trouble in the kitchen, knocking over a bowl of pudding in her eagerness to lick the spoon; she compounded her disgrace by allowing Mopsy to eat most of her porridge. Efforts to make her behave were met with the usual defiance, exasperating Cook so that she told Petal that a big black giant would soon arrive to carry her off.

Petal was used to such threats from Cook—indeed, used to threats from everybody. Very few of them were ever carried out; Petal merrily went on doing as she pleased, which was why the sight of the big brown giant was such a tremendous shock. She had never thought a *real* giant would appear—and yet there one stood. Worse yet, he was blocking the doorway. There was no way she could flee the room.

Tasmin was bending over Petey, tending a rash he had broken out with, when Petal screamed. Petal was hoping her mother might know a way to kill the giant, but instead her mother forgot Petey and, with a big smile of happiness, jumped into the giant's arms, kissing him warmly.

"Oh, Juppy!" she cried. "Mary, Buffum—Juppy's come!"

Soon, to Petal's astonishment, her two aunts had run into the room and were hugging the brown giant. Then her grandfather came—he began to weep at the sight of the giant.

"Why, Juppy boy—here you are at last," Lord Berrybender exclaimed. "Did you bring my leg and my guns?"

"Got the leg, got the guns—looks like I should have brought you a few fingers, while I was at it," Juppy said.

Then Cook, who rarely left her pots and kettles, came and gave Juppy a hug. The five little boys watched, astonished. Petey even forgot to scratch his rash. Mopsy raced around, frenzied with excitement, until Kate Berrybender caught him and insisted that he calm down.

"I hid him at Kit's," Jim admitted, when Tasmin wanted to know why he had shown up before her half brother. "He wanted to be a big surprise, and I guess he was."

Despite the fact that her mother and her aunts and even Cook were clearly fond of Juppy, Petal did not entirely lose her initial apprehension. What if the giant was only pretending to be good? What if his real purpose was to carry her off?

"So what's the news from Northamptonshire, Juppy?" Tasmin asked. Petey was sitting in Juppy's lap, a sight that greatly pleased her.

"The worst news is that Nanny Craigie died," Juppy reported—the news sobered them all.

"Not Nanny Craigie!" Tasmin exclaimed. "I don't know why, but I thought she'd live forever."

"She didn't," Juppy said simply.

"Then who's looking after the younger brats?" Mary wanted to know.

"Nobody, they're running wild," Juppy admitted.

Tasmin felt a sudden stab of homesickness, a deep longing to be back in the home of her youth: back in their green and gray England. It was a brief stab, but intense. She leaned her head against Juppy's big arm.

"I'm so glad you came," she said. "We're all glad—very glad."

Petal soon came to be of the opinion that the big giant was harmless, after all. Ordinarily she would have gone over and shoved Petey out of his lap—on principle—but with her mother sitting so close she didn't quite dare. Her mother was too likely to take Petey's side. Petal had three times been spanked, for treating Petey roughly—an outrageous abuse. Still, it was not her way to allow anyone to deny her pride of place for long. After studying the situation for a moment, Petal moved. She marched over to the big man and squeezed into his lap, next to her twin.

"You have a big lap," she announced. "It can hold two."

"It sure can, little miss," Juppy said.

22

Even peasants gave way to hot impulse.

Julietta Olivaries had become Lord Berrybender's mistress without hesitation—the very first time she was seated next to him at a formal dinner, she had signified her readiness by fondling him under the table. She even managed to get his cock out of his pants, and this before the dinner guests had quite finished their soup. Across the table Lord Berrybender's wife was watching them closely—very likely she had fondled him at table at some point herself. Lady Berrybender was a full-bosomed, beautiful woman, if a commoner. Julietta felt no overwhelming physical attraction to the tipsy old lord, but she did like his aristocratic manner, a manner that tolerated no scruples when it came to amorous activity. In Santa Fe only Lord Berrybender and herself could naturally assume the prerogatives of high aristocracy. Her own aunt, Doña Eleanora, was a settled housewife now. Lady Tasmin was certainly aristocratic, and looked to be a creature of hot impulse, but then, in Julietta's view, hot impulse was common. Even peasants gave way to hot impulse. What attracted her to Lord Berrybender was that his impulses were cool, not hot. He simply disregarded rules; he did as he pleased, not fastidiously but boldly.

Julietta felt just as privileged when it came to disregarding restrictions on her behavior. It infuriated her that she had been sent to Santa Fe—she meant to get back to Europe as soon as possible, but in the meantime, she meant to take her pleasures where she found them—and in the case most troubling to her aunt Eleanora, she found them with a blacksmith.

"A blacksmith—a peon! Surely not!" Doña Eleanora exclaimed, when Julietta casually confirmed a rumor that had been going around.

"We'll be disgraced," she added.

Julietta shrugged. "An Olivaries can be disliked but not disgraced," she pointed out. "We can do as we please. You've been stuck in this little place too long. You're becoming dull."

"I'd rather be dull than give myself to a blacksmith," Eleanora replied.

"But that's dull—be dull," Julietta retorted.

The blacksmith looked half Indian. He was very dark; he had sturdy legs. He worked with his shirt off—Julietta had often watched him; sweat made his arms and belly shiny. She watched him for two weeks before she took him, looking down from her window. Watching him work, all sweaty and greasy, Julietta began to excite herself with the thought of how it might be with a peon. She watched him from shadows, gently exciting herself. Then one day at dusk, when the Plaza was all but empty, she walked across to the blacksmith's and simply lifted her skirts. The blacksmith was so startled that he burned his hand on a horseshoe he had been straightening. Julietta pushed past him, into the little dark room where he slept. She waited for him to come. For a bed there were only a few rags. At first the man was so frightened that he couldn't stiffen. His name was Joaquin; his experience with women had been brief and crude. Julietta refused to let his nervousness defeat her. She took his balls in her hand; she bit his lip. Then she took off all her clothing—something none of the whores or native girls ever did. Instead of being as brief as possible in copulation, which was what Joaquin was used to, Julietta, once she had him in her, took her time. She did not seem to mind his sweat, his grease, the scratchy rags. She made him work, offered him her backside, made him lie down beneath her. She returned to her room filthy, soiled, her face and breasts red from the scrapings of the young man's stubble.

Every night for a week Julietta went to the blacksmith's—she offered caresses that Joaquin had never known before. Doña Eleanora thought her niece had lost her mind. She didn't bathe, her clothes were sweated through, she reeked. But when she attempted to remonstrate, Julietta merely looked scornful.

"You should try Joaquin sometime," she advised her aunt. "He's learning a few tricks. If you tried him you wouldn't be so dull."

"You're mad," Eleanora told her. "You should be locked up."

But she did sometimes think of what Julietta suggested.

Joaquin proved to be good for a week, but only a week. By the time he had become bolder, Julietta was bored. One night she abruptly left him; he was erect and pleading—but she left, went home, ordered the sleepy servant girls to draw a good bath. She threw away her sweaty clothes, bathed, slept soundly. Joaquin often looked at her window but Julietta didn't allow him even a glimpse.

A week later she told Lord Berrybender exactly what she had done with the blacksmith. She went into detail, described intimacies that she had not yet permitted His Lordship. Lord Berrybender was eating a bowl of green chili stew at the time. He looked idly up at his outrageous young mistress, but didn't lay down his spoon.

"So that's where you've been," he said mildly. "A blacksmith—sturdy specimens, I suppose.

"And younger than me," he added. "That's the crucial point. Age is rarely kind to lechers. I suppose he was a bit grubby, this fellow—part of the appeal. I enjoy a grubby girl myself, from time to time. Get my fill of ladies with their pouts. Juppy's mother was rather a grubby girl. Giantess from Santo Domingo. Juppy's nearly the size of his mother."

"Now there's a stallion," Julietta remarked. "I wonder what *he's* like."

"Juppy doesn't carry on with women," Lord Berrybender told her. "Never known him to."

"What a pity," Julietta said.

23

. . . *for some hours she could not be consoled.*

I wish you'd just stop meddling," Jim told his wife. "It's better to just let people be."

Tasmin was in a mood to agree. She had made an attempt to settle the matter of Little Onion's divorce from Jim—in view of her obviously deepening bond with Signor Claricia—only to have everything go wrong. When Buffum, with High Shoulders' help, explained the matter to Little Onion, the girl burst into tears—for some hours she could not be consoled. Tasmin was horrified. She had meant to help the girl yet had only hurt her. That bringing up divorce might make Little Onion feel a failure had not occurred to her—and yet that was exactly what Little Onion felt. If her husband no longer wanted her for a wife, then she had not been good enough, and the only thing to do was go back to her people, a discarded woman. That Jim had never tried to be a husband did not seem very important to Little Onion—she had done her very best to be a good wife anyway—she had done the chores and kept the children. And yet it was over; she was not wanted, she had failed.

When it was explained to her that no criticism was intended, that they had merely supposed she might want to marry her Mr. Aldo, Little Onion looked even more horrified and burst into tears again. She shook her head vigorously; she wanted nothing of the sort. Mr. Aldo was her friend, and she wanted it to stay that way. Jim, finding himself in the middle of an unnecessary crisis, went to Little Onion himself and did his best to smooth things over. He assured her that she had been a fine wife—he had never wished to divorce her. Little Onion had already packed her few things, intent on leaving; but Jim persuaded her to stay, and Tasmin and the family, deeply embarrassed, lavished affection on her. Little Onion agreed to stay, but she was skeptical and, for a time, sad.

A little later she realized that her friendship with Mr. Aldo might have just confused the white people. She liked the old man and wanted to see that he took care of himself. She fed him, kept his clothes mended, doctored him when he was ill; but she did not want to lie with him—nothing of the sort. Lately, it was true, he had become feisty; she sometimes had to fight him off. But that was merely the way of men. Finally Little Onion realized that it was Mr. Aldo's behavior, not hers, that had confused the white people. Slowly, she recovered from her sense of hurt. Someone should just have asked her point-blank about her feelings for Mr. Aldo—then they could have all laughed about it together.

All the Berrybender women were sorry to have hurt Little Onion, but Tasmin was the one who felt the deepest self-reproach. Jim was right; she ought not to meddle. She loved Little Onion—she didn't suppose her children would have survived the dark months of her grief without her Little Onion's loving attention. She did her best to win back the girl's trust—and, in time, she did.

"I suppose it's hopeless, trying to know what others are feeling," she confessed to Jim. "I don't even know what *you're* feeling unless you hit me—then I know you're angry. I could have sworn a romance was brewing between those two—and I was completely wrong."

"You got enough to do—don't be worrying about Onion," Jim said. "She can take care of herself."

"I fear meddling is just what families do—particularly families crammed together in a foreign place," Tasmin countered. "In England we'd have drifted apart by now, most of us."

Then Buffum came in, looking tearful. High Shoulders had been gone on one of his hunts. He had not been seen in ten days—Buffum was overcome with worry, as she always was if her husband was absent more than a week.

"I need to know he's safe," she told them.

"Be glad you aren't married to this one," Tasmin said. "He thinks nothing of absences of six months or more."

Jim quietly left. He didn't want to quarrel about his absences. Only yesterday he had quarreled so violently with Tasmin that he struck her. She had suddenly informed him that she and the children were going to accompany him on all future trips, no matter how arduous they promised to be—yet she knew perfectly well he couldn't do the jobs he was assigned with a wife and three babies in tow. It was absurd—and yet Tasmin flared and he flared—Jim felt cornered, as he always did if he was inside a house.

As he walked past the nursery his daughter spotted him. Petal was still feeling her way with her father. He was a difficult conquest; he could not simply be bossed, like other people. Flirting and cajoling didn't work either, though they worked on Juppy, the brown giant her father had brought back with him.

Nonetheless she pointed a finger at Jim, in a commanding way.

"Come see me, I'm a spider," Petal commanded.

Jim did as ordered.

"Spiders sting," he said. "What if I don't want to be stung?"

"Then behave good," Petal advised. "Behave good, Mr. Sin Killer."

Jim was startled.

"Auntie Mary says that's your other name," Petal explained. "Only I don't know what sin is."

"It's stealing your brothers' toys," Jim informed her. She was holding a small leather burro that he had brought specially for Monty. Petal sat the burro on the floor.

"It followed me," she explained.

"Telling lies is also a sin," her father informed her.

"Fibbing—only fibbing," Petal insisted. "But I was good in the kitchen. I didn't turn over the pudding."

"If I was you I'd give Monty back his donkey," Jim advised.

Petal made no move to comply.

"You isn't me," she pointed out.

24

Even as he and Kit stood whispering . . .

Unable to sleep inside the house, Jim usually spread his blankets behind it, near two Dutch ovens Cook sometimes used for baking. Tasmin sometimes joined him there, but not often, since the whole nursery was likely to follow her, trailing along like so many little ducks. All six of the children would soon be shivering in the cold, spoiling Tasmin's hope of spending a quiet hour with Jim. Usually she gave up and led the brigade back inside, leaving Jim in peace. The Plaza seldom quieted down early; horsemen, cavalrymen mostly, would clatter across it at all hours.

Kit Carson could move with stealth if he wanted to, and on this occasion he particularly wanted to avoid sentries and soldiers. He materialized at Jim's side, pressing a finger to his lips, indicating that Jim should follow him. Jim took his gun and did as Kit suggested, wondering what brought Kit to Santa Fe at that hour of the night.

They were on the far side of the sheep pens before Kit felt it was safe to talk. He came right to the point.

"They're arresting the bunch of you tomorrow in the morning," Kit told Jim bluntly. "Josie heard it from someone in the Palace."

Jim didn't question the information. Josie was usually reliable where matters in Santa Fe were concerned. She had lived in the Palace herself at some point. If she said the Berrybenders were being arrested, it was probably true. What it meant could be debated, but that the Mexicans meant to rid themselves of Americans and English alike he didn't doubt and had never doubted. From the Mexican viewpoint, it was get rid of the Americans before the Americans got rid of them.

Even as he and Kit stood whispering, the first hint of dawn showed in the east. Jim would have liked to slip in and warn Tasmin, but knew it might be a fatal mistake. Pomp had let himself be taken; Jim didn't intend to make the same mistake.

"They were already under house arrest," Jim pointed out. "I suppose arrest means they aim to ship 'em out."

"That's it—that's Josie's view," Kit agreed. "Charlie Bent thinks there's going to be a war for Texas anytime. I suppose the Berrybenders would make good hostages—the Mexicans might trade 'em for a general or two."

Day was breaking—Kit grew nervous.

"We better go if we're going," he said.

"I've no time to warn the family but I have to get my mare," Jim said. He crept through the sheep and soon was back with the mare. The tip of the sun just broke the horizon.

"High Shoulders is out hunting," Jim said. "I better go find him or he'll come back and get arrested himself."

In the distance Kit could already see a few soldiers, just waking up.

"I'm going," he said. "If you come to my house, come in the night."

"Thanks for the warning," Jim said. "Thank Josie too—don't let her whup you too bad."

Kit, suddenly nervous, was on his way to Taos—he felt he could not spare the time for gratitude.

25

Lord Berrybender, apoplectic . . .

I'm so glad High Shoulders is hunting," Buffum said, as the whole Berrybender household, considerably disheveled, were being urged into wagons. Lord Berrybender, apoplectic at being disturbed so early, was allowed to use his buggy, with Signor Claricia to drive; but that was the only favor the English were allowed.

"I would have liked a word with the Governor—he's a friend, after all," Lord Berrybender said to the head of their escort, a graying major named Leon, a careful man, not brutal, not young, and not especially familiar with the English gentry and their ways. He had been allowed a skimpy escort of only eighteen young soldiers and was well aware that it might not be enough. Their destination, the port of Vera Cruz, was very distant; the country they had to cross was hard country. The essential thing was to get started.

"I will do my best to make you comfortable," Major Leon assured them—the English had been two hours assembling themselves, and one or another of the women was still darting into the house to search for some important article that had been forgotten in the haste and gloom of the dusty morning. The dog Mopsy was only remembered at the last minute.

"In fact, Major, you've only made us uncomfortable," Lord Berrybender grumbled. "Wouldn't have minded a bit more sleep."

"It's better to travel while the day is cool," Major Leon replied. He felt uneasy. With such talkative, grumbly people it was not easy to choose correct remarks, as Lady Tasmin at once reminded him.

"It's the fall, Major—that's not a summer breeze that's blowing," Tasmin pointed out. They were all swaddled in blankets, the children big-eyed and solemn at the prospect of departure.

Lord Berrybender, very annoyed, had not given up on protocol.

"I still think I ought to be allowed to say good-bye to the Governor—he's been most generous with us," he asserted. "Besides, he's a friend."

"There is a problem," the Major admitted. "He may still be your friend, but he is no longer the governor."

He did not elaborate, but signaled to the drivers to get the wagons going. Soon a buggy, three wagons, and eighteen supply mules, and the escort, eighteen strong, filed out of the Plaza. Joaquin, the blacksmith, just stirring his forge, yawned as they went by.

"But where's Julietta? Stop!" Lord Berrybender exclaimed. It had just dawned on him that his mistress was not in the wagons.

The Major didn't stop.

"We seem to have forgotten Señorita Julietta Olivaries," Lord Berrybender insisted. "We must fetch her. I'm sure she'd want to come."

"Unfortunately that is not the case," Major Leon replied. "The señorita is in Santa Fe for her health. She is staying with her aunt."

The Major's eyes hardened. Who was this old English fool, to think that he could summon a lady of the Spanish nobility at will? It was intolerable. Hauling this old lecher away from Señorita Julietta was a pleasant part of his task.

Signor Claricia had not been feeling well—Juppy was driving the buggy. The reins looked like threads in his big hands.

"I think you better let that one go, Papa," he advised. "The Major wants to be making time."

"Thank you, señor," the Major said. "We cannot go back for anyone. The time for good-byes is past."

Then he trotted to the head of the column and led the party south, into the desert, along the Camino Real—the road that, if they could survive it, would take them to the City of Mexico and beyond.

26

Except for the biting, blowing dust . . .

T ravel is never as neat as one imagines it will be," Major Leon admitted. "Even military travel is rarely neat. One must heed these calls of nature."

"Indeed, and right now she's calling rather too often," Father Geoff allowed. "I've been twenty times. The water, I suppose."

Except for the biting, blowing dust which swirled around them constantly, chapping lips and irritating eyelids, reducing the children particularly to life beneath a kind of tent of blankets, the journey south had not yet been too harsh. Major Leon kept his word about trying to make them comfortable. He exhibited no compulsion to hurry, a relief to the mothers and to Cook, all still trying to organize their resources and equipment for what would surely be a long trip.

"One cannot hurry an ox," the Major pointed out. "We must remember the fine fable of the tortoise and the hare."

Stimulated by this reference, Piet Van Wely roused himself and gave an impromptu lecture on the differences between the tortoise, the turtle, and the terrapin. He too was suffering from bowel complaints—they all were. The precise, well-regulated columns that Major Leon liked to maintain ceased to exist, as the complaint attacked cavalrymen and hostages alike. The English were jumping out of wagons and hurrying desperately through the sparse vegetation, in hopes of finding a bush behind which to answer the frequent calls in private.

"It's quite clear that this is amoebic," Piet informed them, so weak by this time that he could scarcely sit up. "These waters contain bad amoebas."

he should be able to manage. The thoroughbred was more skittish. There were no sidesaddles in the smithy—because of the threat from Indians, the ladies of Santa Fe were not encouraged to ride. Ladies out for a canter might never be seen again.

"If they catch us they will hang me," Joaquin repeated several times.

"If you keep quiet they won't catch us," Julietta insisted. Avoiding the Plaza, she led the horses through the narrowest, darkest alleys she could find.

When it was Joaquin's turn to mount he swung himself onto the horse so awkwardly that the sorrel crow-hopped and threw him hard. Exasperated, Julietta dismounted and steadied the sorrel until Joaquin finally managed to crawl aboard and find his stirrups. The stars were still bright. Her aunt Eleanora was a notoriously late sleeper. It would be noon before anyone realized they had left. She thought the soldiers might conclude that Joaquin had accidentally left the stalls open, allowing two horses to escape; then he fled, for fear of punishment.

The only person who saw the two riders make their way south under the starlight was an old woman whose habit, on starlit nights, was to sit out beside her little hut with her tame goose. She liked to study the heavens; she was called Oriabe, though some of those whose fortunes she told just called her Grandmother. Her goose squawked twice, when the lady and the blacksmith rode by. "Be polite, you're just a goose," Oriabe scolded. She liked to sit out all night, until the stars began to fade. She wished she had not seen the two riders. A large owl was hooting from a nearby tree when the riders passed. Owls, of course, were harbingers of bad fortune—fatal fortune, in fact. She knew this owl, which often hooted from that tree. Oriabe meant to have a word with the bird, some-day soon. She meant to ask it to find another tree to sit in. Owls were sure to scare away people who might need their fortunes told, and besides that, it was hard to make a proper reading of the stars with a big owl hooting all the time.

28

If it seemed a good time to go north, he went north . . .

Jim Snow was usually quick to decide on a course of action; once decided, he worked efficiently to carry out whatever plan he had made. The ability to weigh options and act on his decisions had served him well all during the years when he had acted singly. If it seemed a good time to go north, he went north; and on the whole he preferred north to south. The water supply was too chancy in the south.

Now, though, having slipped out of Santa Fe ahead of arrest, Jim could not immediately decide on a plan. His family were already miles to the south—of course, one of the helpful things about travel in dry country were the dust clouds that any company threw up. Kit Carson was hardly out of sight before Jim spotted the dust of the first patrol—in the clear high air such dust clouds were visible many miles away.

Jim had no difficulty in eluding these young soldiers—he merely went higher into the rocks. The soldiers were not skilled at mountain pursuit. They explored a ridge or two and gave up. Soon the dust cloud was moving in the opposite direction, back toward Santa Fe.

Jim had gone north mainly because he wanted to intercept High Shoulders, who was hunting somewhere to the north. He wanted to prevent High Shoulders' arrest. Jim looked around for a campfire, or some evidence that High Shoulders was in the vicinity, but he found nothing. The hills were empty.

Finally he made a campfire himself and kept it going all night. If High Shoulders was nearby he would notice and investigate. High Shoulders had shown himself to be a skilled reader of country. Together they could easily catch up with the slow-moving oxcarts that were carrying their wives and children away south. Then a plan of rescue could be devised.

Jim felt a mild annoyance with Kit, for being so henpecked that he had gone scuttling back to his Josie when he might have been helpful to Jim and the Berrybenders. Thanks to his association with the Bent brothers, Kit could go in and out of Santa Fe at will. He might easily have found out

30

. . . there was no sign of Mopsy.

Tasmin woke to wailings, grief, six children awash in tears, with several whites also on the brink.

"Oh no!" she cried, when informed that there was no sign of Mopsy.

Even Major Leon had a weakness for the little mongrel. He dispatched his soldiers to search for clues—the soldiers rode in a wide circle but failed to find even a trace of the small dog.

"Let me go, I can find him," Monty pleaded. All six children tumbled out of their wagon, determined to locate their pet.

"But I need him, where is he?" Petal inquired.

Mopsy had been helplessly friendly. If he had an enemy it was only Cook, who found him too much underfoot when she was trying to make a meal under windy or gritty conditions. But even Cook was seen to weep.

"What could have *got* him?" Petal questioned, when the search was abandoned and the trek continued.

"An eagle, perhaps—he was quite small," Mary suggested.

"Or a wolf or a bobcat," Piet added.

"But I'm small and Petey is small and Elf," Petal pointed out. "What if an eagle got *me?*"

"It would soon spit you out—you'd be a difficult mouthful," Tasmin said.

"I think the eagle might get Elf next," Petal concluded. "He's the smallest."

Despite this reassuring thought Petal kept her eyes on the skies—she fled under her blankets with mouselike speed if a big bird showed itself.

The country they had to cross grew increasingly bleak, harsher, in Tasmin's opinion, even than the plains. She had begun to feel fearful for her children—anxiety, like a low fever, was never quite absent. She looked around her often, hoping to see Jim. Major Leon liked Tasmin—seeing that she was worried, he did his best to reassure her.

"For now we have the Rio Grande," he reminded her. "Water won't be a problem until after we come to the Pass of the North."

"And after that?"

"After that we will have to be careful," the Major said.

Tasmin felt a deepening anger at her father, who was grumbling and pettish because he was not allowed to hunt with his new guns. One of the things she liked about Major Leon was that he stood firm against Lord Berrybender's complaints.

"Your guns will be returned to you when you board the boat," Major Leon insisted.

"Board the boat—what nonsense," Lord Berrybender grumped. "What can I hunt from a boat?"

"For that matter, what could you hunt in this desert?" the Major asked.

When Tasmin needed to communicate with her father she did it through Juppy, who continued to drive the buggy.

"I suppose you can tolerate him because you've only had to put up with him for a month," she said. "We've had four years of this, and look where we are. In a desert. The sandstorm gave all the children nosebleeds and sore eyes. And I doubt that's the worst we'll have to put up with."

"You can't hurry life—just got to wait it out," Juppy remarked. "What are you going to do with Jim? Take him home?"

"Oh, don't ask me—I don't know," Tasmin said. "I think about it all the time, but I have no answer. He's used to all this space. I fear he'd feel rather cooped up, on our little island."

Juppy looked over Tasmin's head. He thought he saw a man, a very short man, half hidden behind some dry bushes. But when he looked again he saw only the bushes. Had he seen a man? None of the soldiers betrayed any anxiety. The peculiar thing about the country they were in was that there was so much light that it somehow made it harder to see things. A yucca might look like a man, or a man like a yucca. What at first seemed to be a deer might only be a bush. When he tried to peer into the far distance his eyes soon began to water, causing the horizons to blur. Only things that were close—the horses, the oxen, the soldiers—could be seen clearly. The strange hard light had a blinding effect. The greater the distances ahead, the less precisely it seemed one could see.

Juppy had become a great favorite with the children—sometimes all six swarmed over him at once, like so many little raccoons. During their noon break, while he was playing with them, Major Leon came trotting over.

"We have company," he said.

"Who? Where?" Tasmin asked.

The boy named Ojo was particularly intolerant of Cibecue's words of caution. Ojo was convinced they could easily beat the Mexicans who were guarding the family of whites.

"They have guns—we don't," Cibecue pointed out. It was an argument that convinced the older warriors but it didn't convince Ojo or his three friends.

"Why can't we sneak in and steal some guns?" Ojo asked. "I would like a gun, myself, and I would like to catch one of those white women and do what we did with the Spanish girl."

Catching the Spanish girl had been a huge stroke of luck—the boys were all still excited by the memory of the things they had done to her—they had all been following the wounded mule deer and out of nowhere this girl appeared. They also found a boy with a broken back, farther up in the rocks. It had been a fine afternoon, but it was also a fluke. Cibecue was not young and yet never before in his life had the band caught a Spanish woman.

Catching a lone white woman who happened to be in the wrong place was one thing—attacking a column of Mexican soldiers quite another. Cibecue kept trying to explain to Ojo that luck was never constant. One day it might be good, the next day bad. The fact that they were able to kill the two horses was even luckier than having the girl to rape and torture. The women had done a thorough job with the horses; for once they had an abundance of meat. It was a time of plenty, but it wouldn't last forever. What Cibecue had to make Ojo understand was that he couldn't risk four young hunters in a foolish attack on some Mexican soldiers.

"Suppose they kill three of you?" he speculated. "You are all good hunters and you will get better. You raped that Spanish girl pretty good. You can make the band some babies when we need babies. If I let you go and they kill three of you, then we lose three hunters and three fathers too."

There was a silence. The older men weren't really listening. They were watching an eagle soaring over a good-sized butte to the west. They were thinking the eagle might have a nest there: they might be able to catch some young eagles, which would be a thing of power. They thought Cibecue was wasting his time, lecturing Ojo and the other boys. Young men never believed they could die—even less were they able to grasp that the whole band might die if they lost too many hunters. The band was small and poor, but at least the women were energetic, constantly at work gathering seeds and roots, growing a little corn, and snaring rabbits, which were unusually numerous just then. The boys were not men yet; they didn't want to think ahead. The band had always been there—in their immature heads it would always be there.

"Can't we just follow the Mexicans?" Ojo asked. "We can stay out of sight. The women have to make water sometimes. I bet we could catch one."

Cibecue decided it was hopeless. No matter what he said these boys were not going to be restrained unless he took them far from the source of temptation. They had been too excited by what they had done to the Spanish girl. He did not want to be sharp with them—they were good boys. He didn't want to flatly lay down the law, either. Boys were apt to feel that their pride demanded independence. Tell them not to do something and they would just be that much more apt to do it.

Cibecue was the leader, but he had to lead delicately—he didn't want to make Ojo and the other boys too puffy with rebellion. The simplest thing to do was just go west for two or three days, until the temptation of the white women was not so immediate.

"Are you counting eagles?" he asked old Erzmin, the oldest warrior in the band.

Erzmin had always been unusually attentive to the ways of birds. Once, in a bad time, when deer seemed to have vanished from the country, Erzmin had kept them from starving by collecting the eggs of various birds he had managed to follow to their nests.

"Just two, so far," Erzmin replied. "I think they may be a pair—they might have a nest over there but it's too early for there to be eggs."

"Let's go look anyway," Cibecue suggested. "Keeping up with eagles' nests is a good thing to do."

"The women are still cutting up that jerky—those were fat horses," Erzmin reminded him.

"We don't want the women with us," Cibecue said. "We can go hunt eagles' nests for ourselves."

He started west at a brisk pace—Erzmin and the older warriors right behind him. Erzmin knew what Cibecue was trying to do. He didn't want Ojo or the other boys getting themselves killed trying to steal a white woman.

Ojo and his three companions were bitterly disappointed by this development—but, alone, what could they do?

After a minute or two they fell in behind the older men.

34

. . . Major Leon did not have the aspect of a joker.

Major Leon laughed genially when Jim politely inquired about his status—that is, whether he could expect to be arrested at some point down the trail. Jim thought it best to be clear on that point—he did not mean to be arrested.

"In Santa Fe you might have been an enemy, but here you are an ally, Señor Snow," the Major told him. "We have a long way to go—we might need every fighter we can get—besides which it's my duty to tell you that I've fallen in love with your wife."

With that the Major smiled, made Jim a little half bow, and rode off.

Jim was so startled by the Major's last remark that he would have been hard put to reply. Probably it was meant as a joke, just a rather flowery way of saying that the Major liked Tasmin a lot. And yet Major Leon did not have the aspect of a joker. He had looked, on the whole, rather melancholy when he mentioned to Jim that he was in love with his wife. Jim could not believe that such an absurd statement was to be taken literally, and yet the Major had sounded rather matter-of-fact about it.

With Petal, Monty, and Petey all competing for his attention, Jim had little opportunity to think much more about the Major's startling declaration. It seemed that Major Leon was on good terms with the children too, even taking them one by one on short horseback rides. Petal particularly seemed to enjoy these rides, insisting that she could hold the reins herself and pushing the Major's hands away when he briefly attempted a correction of some sort.

"Take your hands *off!*" Petal insisted, and usually the Major complied.

It was late in the day before Jim finally had a chance to speak privately with Tasmin.

"That's a funny kind of a major," Jim remarked. "The first thing he said to me was that he was in love with you."

Tasmin blushed a little, nervously. She made a little what-can-I-do gesture; she shrugged.

"It doesn't surprise me that he told you," she said, with a heavy sigh.

"He's incapable of concealing anything from anyone—it's part of his problem."

Jim still didn't understand.

"Does he just mean that he likes you a bunch?" he asked.

Tasmin chuckled.

"No, he doesn't mean that he likes me a bunch, as you put it," she told him. "Geoff, after all, likes me a bunch."

She sighed again.

"It's different with Major Leon," she told him. "Major Leon *is* in love with me."

For a moment Tasmin teared up, at the thought of the absurdity of the situation. Here she was in the middle of nowhere; her captor was in love with her; she had three bouncy children, and a husband who was honestly puzzled.

"I hope you'll just excuse it," she said to Jim. "Nothing improper has happened—nothing improper ever will. But the Major *is* in love with me and it's best to just let it wear off. I can't seem to make him give it up.

"At least it's a benefit for the children," she said. "They get little horse rides."

Jim didn't know what to think. He didn't doubt Tasmin's fidelity—it had not occurred to him that anything sinful could have happened—surely not. Major Leon seemed sad and perhaps a little silly, but he hardly seemed like much of a ladies' man.

"I don't understand it," Jim admitted.

"No, you don't," Tasmin said mildly, irritated by the position she found herself in.

"You've never been in love with me, you see, Jimmy," she said, taking his hand. "I believe you do care for me—and then there's *this* that we have."

She moved his hand between her legs and at once felt an old quickening.

"There's this, and I'm glad we have it." She didn't move his hand, but she held it to her. Her boldness stirred Jim a good deal.

"Maybe it's more important than being in love—the poets aren't clear on that point," Tasmin continued. "But it isn't the same. Major Leon is in love with me, as Kit once was—you remember that, don't you?

Jim nodded.

"What's the Major get out of it?" he asked, not angry, just puzzled.

"Oh, I don't know," Tasmin admitted. "A chance to do me small kindnesses, or pay me small attentions," she said. "You remember how Kit was—he was always at his happiest when I gave him a chore to do—the harder the chore, the more it pleased him to do it."

Jim did remember Kit's infatuation. He had not been jealous of Kit's attentions to his wife; but he had thought Kit rather a fool, for doing so much of what was rightly Tasmin's work. Jim had supposed that Pomp was also sweet on Tasmin, though Pomp was far less likely to do her endless favors or hang on her conversation. At first, when he heard Tasmin and Pomp talking about some book or play, he had supposed it was only educated people who fell in love; but then along came Kit, who couldn't read or write a lick, and he was worse sweet on Tasmin than Pomp had been. If further proof was needed that all sorts of people fell in love, there was High Shoulders, a Ute who at first couldn't speak a word of English, and yet had been in a fever to be with Buffum from the minute they laid eyes on one another.

"Major Leon is a curious case," Tasmin went on. "He confessed to me that he has only been able to be in love with married women—and yet he doesn't attempt to make love to them, in the common way. Instead he fetches me extra blankets for the children. Once he brought me a pretty rock. Or he might offer me a tidbit from the stores. He's not read me poetry, though—Geoff is still my only literary man."

Jim looked over at the Major. He always sat alone, apart from his men.

"There's plenty of things I don't understand," Jim admitted.

"And being in love is one of them," Tasmin said. She still held his hand and began to rub it against her.

"It's not dark enough," Jim protested.

"It's dark enough for *something*," Tasmin chided. "Leave me that hand."

Later, in the deep night, Tasmin woke from a doze and saw Jim sitting up—he still wore a look of confusion.

"Jimmy, don't worry about it—being in love isn't everything," she told him. "It can be a terribly painful condition. The poets are clear on that point."

"Kit can do it and Major Leon can do it and High Shoulders can do it—how come I can't?" he asked. "It just don't seem necessary."

"Correct—it isn't," Tasmin agreed. "We've done a bunch without it—though of course I was as much in love with you as you'd tolerate," she told him.

"Though I wouldn't be surprised if you fall in love yet," she added.

"Why would I?"

"You might be given no choice—it might just sweep over you one day. You mustn't underestimate Petal—if any woman can get you, I expect it's her."

"She's a baby," Jim replied—though he did like Petal. She didn't readily allow anyone not to like her, once she took an interest in them, and lately she had taken a strong interest in him.

But being in love with your own child surely wasn't what they had been talking about.

"Best not to think of it too simply, as just being a thing that happens to people who want to rut," Tasmin told him. "It just might be that your own daughter is the only woman capable of sweeping you off your feet.

"Time will tell," she added. "Time will tell."

35

"This makes me feel rather dry and coldhearted . . ."

Don't you be sulking, Geoff," Tasmin warned. "I have enough to do keeping this unruly lot in marching order. If there's one thing I don't need in my life right now it's a rude friend."

"I can't help it," Father Geoffrin replied. "I'm filled with dark forebodings anyway, and now this ridiculous little major has turned your head."

"Not a bit of it . . . my head's *not* turned," Tasmin argued. "My husband is here, remember. Nothing untoward has happened. Major Leon is just a bit smitten, that's all."

"I could be smitten myself with a little encouragement," Father Geoff told her. Then he shrugged and apologized.

"I'm sorry—it just irritates," he admitted. "I'm used to being the one you talk to—I'm jealous that you're talking to someone else."

"Incorrect—I'm mostly *listening* to someone else," Tasmin said. "Yesterday the Major finally told me his sad tale."

"And was it sad?"

"As tales of thwarted love go, yes," Tasmin told him. "He confessed to being very shy, a quality I had already detected in him."

"Prissy, I'd call it," Geoff complained. "He's always stroking his mustache—I notice these things, you see."

Tasmin gave him a stern look.

"You notice—and then you misinterpret," Tasmin scolded. "Major Leon is at ease with me because he doesn't expect to succeed. The impossibility of success is what it takes for some men to relax with a woman. That's common enough."

"Out with the sad tale—I won't interrupt."

"Major Leon was once in love with a girl of good family in Santa Fe," Tasmin began. "But because of his shyness he could not quite work up to proposing. The girl, of good family, who was not unreceptive to his suit, grew tired of waiting and accepted another. But the man she accepted quite abruptly died. There was a period of mourning, and then Major Leon tried again. This time he was just able to mumble out a proposal, which was immediately accepted. A wedding date was set—at last his love had been answered."

Tasmin stopped.

"Why don't you finish the story for me, Geoff?" she teased. "It's suitable for a tragedy. Your beloved Racine would have found it interesting."

"More likely Molière, if that prissy little man is the hero," Geoff said. "There he is stroking his mustache again.

"I suppose the girl died," he added, after thinking for a moment.

Tasmin nodded. "The girl died. Rather sad, don't you agree? He's a decent man, if limited. He finally wins the consent of a woman he could have—and then she dies, after which he has taken no chances in that particular line. He only falls in love with women he can't have, like my humble self."

"And yet you do *like* him, so it's not *so* sad," Geoff remarked. "He gets affection, at least. What does Jim think about the Major and his affections?"

Tasmin laughed.

"The Major told Jimmy right off that he was in love with me—startling news to my Jimmy, who's continually puzzled by the odd twistings and turnings of human emotion. Now and then he attempts to puzzle out what romance might be, but it's so foreign to his nature that he can't quite grasp it."

"I can't see that this bothers you much," the priest said.

"That's because you don't see me when it's bothering me," Tasmin told him. "You may have noticed that I've started caring about my looks again, in the small way that's possible under present circumstances."

"So?"

"It's the result of Major Leon's attentions," Tasmin told him. "It's always nice to have a man who looks at you closely enough to notice small improvements.

"Very small improvements," she added. "But still it's nice."

"This makes me feel rather dry and coldhearted, and I don't like the feeling," Father Geoff said. "I'm sure that's why the Major annoys me. His attentions may be shallow but they please you, and my attentions don't."

"Nonsense, your attentions have always pleased me," Tasmin assured him. "You're the one man I can talk to. At one point I could talk to Pomp, but then I fell in love with him and that spoiled that."

"I wish the man would quit stroking his silly mustache," Geoff said, looking at the Major.

36

Juppy, their giant . . .

Juppy, their giant, who sometimes pretended to be a great fish, rising from the water with all six shrieking children clinging to his back, died first, followed by Eliza—she would break no more plates—and Amboise d'Avigdor, ten of the skinny soldiers, and the shy, sad Major Leon. Signore Aldo Claricia died, even as Little Onion sought frantically for herbs to cure him. Cook was very ill but lived; Piet Van Wely was also at the point of death but survived. High Shoulders died an hour after Juppy; Buffum raged, cried, clung to him, prayed, but nothing helped: the cholera took him, though it spared his son, Elphinstone, spared Vicky's Talley but killed her Randy, spared the twins but took Monty. Jim held his dying son in his arms to the end, but Tasmin could not bear the look on her son's shocked, silent face—she grabbed her twins and ran far out into the desert, convinced that they would all die unless they fled the place of infection, a small, filthy village where Major Leon assured them travelers on the Camino Real often stopped to rest their animals. Jim had not much liked the look of the place—a burial had been in progress as he rode in—but they were short of fodder for the oxen, there were goats that could be bought, and perhaps even a horse or two to replace some of theirs that had gone lame.

"I regret that I left him so often," Jim said to Father Geoffrin, when Monty died.

"None of us are free of regret," Father Geoff told him.

Jim had not tried to stop Tasmin's mad dash into the desert, but now he was worried.

"I wish you'd go find her," Jim asked the priest. "There's Indians around—I wouldn't want them to catch her."

As he sat with his son's body, he remembered what had been done to the Spanish girl.

Lord Berrybender was weeping, stomping, occasionally crying out.

"Oh, my poor Juppy—come all the way from Northamptonshire, only to die like this," he exclaimed.

Vicky stared at him with hatred.

"I regret Juppy, but you might remember that your son Randy died too—a child you scarcely noticed."

Lord Berrybender merely shrugged.

"I loathe you—you will never touch me again," Vicky said. She picked up Talley and ran into the desert, in the direction that Tasmin had gone.

It was near sunset. Father Geoffrin hurried on his errand. He didn't like it. Cold sun shone on the stark mountains to the east. The landscape offered no welcome—it offered its sere implacability. Where was consolation to be found in such terrible country?

Tasmin clutched her two babies tight. She supposed Monty would have died; she wanted to know but dreaded to ask. She looked at Geoff, who nodded, sadly.

"What about Jim?" she asked.

"He's not dead. He wanted to stay with Monty. He thinks the village well is tainted."

He spoke mainly to fill the terrible silence.

"Is Monty gone'd?" Petal asked, nervously. "I don't see Randy—is he gone'd?"

She knew something had gone terribly wrong, but none of the adults would talk to her.

"You remember that tosh about love we were talking only last week?" Tasmin asked. "That talk about love. I will never forgive myself for being so frivolous."

Father Geoff had no wisdom to offer. The tragedy that had befallen them was beyond any words to correct. What were words, set against the deaths of young and old? And yet silence before the facts was terrible too.

"In casual times there's no harm in talk about love," he said.

"It will never amuse me again," Tasmin avowed.

Father Geoff didn't try to speak against her despair, or Vicky's.

"Children so often die," he said. "All three of my brothers died within a year. I suspect that's why I became so odd."

It was true, of course—Tasmin knew. Many children died in the Berrybender nurseries. Cousins died—the children of the servants died. Master Stiles, her first lover, lost a beloved young daughter. Her own aunt Clarissa had lost no less than six children. What Tasmin, in the freshness of her grief, could not fathom was how Aunt Clarissa regained enough interest to keep making more babies. Tasmin certainly did not expect to regain it.

"Please, can we go back to the camp—Jim is afraid there might be Indians," Geoff asked.

"They're no worse than cholera, if they are around," Tasmin said. She felt a deep reluctance to take her two living children back to the place of death. Vicky seemed to feel the same way.

"Look where we are—nowhere!" she said. "That whole wretched village is dying. It seems impossible to go on."

"But we must! For the sake of the living," Geoff pleaded.

The surviving soldiers and one or two men from the village dug the graves. There was no wood for coffins—they sacrificed blankets to make shrouds. Finally everyone but Juppy was shrouded, not up to Cook's standards, of course. Crosses were made and fixed rather unstably in rocks. Tasmin sobbed until she was dry. So did Buffum and Vicky. It seemed terrible to have to leave a dear child, a dear mate, in such a bleak place.

"I hope to come back someday and get him," Tasmin said to Jim. "I want him to be in a proper graveyard."

Petal could not understand it. She thought that Monty and Randy must only be playing hide-and-seek. They were playing too long; she wanted them to come out, be found. She refused to believe that they were, as she put it, gone'd. For the next few days she kept poking her head under blan-

had him tied in his seat. Lord Berrybender was frothing and spitting in his fury.

"I'll have every man jack of you lashed at the cart's tail!" he yelled. "Don't care if you are my own blood. Put you in the stocks! Pelted with offal!"

"Maybe his mind's slipping, Tassie," Mary conjectured. "He's like he was that day Bobbety shot his horse."

"We've just lost seven people," Tasmin reminded her. "One was his son and two were his grandchildren—and yet he still wants to shoot.

"I think most of us are not far from crazy at this juncture," she went on. She meant it; she felt only just sane. It seemed to her she might just hang on to sanity if there was no more trouble, no more loss. But here they were again, facing a wintry plain—a plain that seemed endless. There would be more trouble and, very likely, more loss.

Suddenly they were all startled by a wild ululation from Jim—furious at Lord Berrybender. The Word suddenly poured out, frightening the old lord so that his hair stood on end. Tasmin remembered the sounds of the Word from the day the Osage chased them; to everyone else it was a shock. Lord Berrybender thought his son-in-law must have gone mad. What did it mean?

Petal was extremely startled, but not frightened.

"Petey, listen at Jim," she commanded, and Petey did listen, amazed.

The whole camp fell silent until the Sin Killer finished his cry.

"As I was mentioning, Mary, some of us are not far from crazy," Tasmin said. Jim Snow gave her father a hard shaking before he turned away.

"That's only the third time I've heard you do that," Tasmin said, when Jim, calming, came to her.

"You missed Billy Williams—he's the one who shot High Shoulders," Jim told her. "I yelled him the Word, not long ago."

"Do it again," Petal demanded. "I like it. Do it for me. It's like a gobble bird.

"Some people call them turkeys but I call them gobble birds," Petal added.

Despite her cheerful request, Jim did not do it again.

39

"It just comes out, when I see bad sinning," Jim told his wife . . .

It just comes out, when I see bad sinning," Jim told his wife, trying to explain his crying of the Word.

What he had done so startled the camp that, for a few minutes, they all forgot their grief. Soon enough sorrow edged back into their consciousness, but they looked at Jim differently. Petal was the only one in the company who tried to make him make the strange sounds on command—her command.

"Be the Sin Killer," she asked her father, but he wouldn't obey.

Lord Berrybender was so upset by what his son-in-law had just done that he got an attack of the shakes. He trembled so violently that Cook finally gave him a little whiskey, to calm him down.

"I wish I knew exactly what you think the bad sins are," Tasmin said. "I'm sure we'd all try not to do them if we just knew what they were."

Jim felt shaky himself. In his rage he had pulled his knife, just as he had with Billy Williams. It had been in him to cut Lord Berrybender's throat—he had just managed to stop himself, and yet all Lord Berrybender had done was make himself a violent old nuisance.

"I nearly killed your pa," he said, to Tasmin. "I had the knife out. It's lucky I stopped."

"I believe it made a profound impression on Papa," Tasmin told him. "On all of us, for that matter."

For a second night they scarcely slept. Jim untied Lord Berrybender but didn't speak to him. Lord B. looked pathetically at Vicky, hoping for a word of sympathy, but Vicky turned her back. Cook finally took pity on him. She had been His Lordship's cook for many years; his flaws and faults were abundant, but still he must be fed—though, as she worked, from time to time she found herself sobbing at the thought of dear Eliza and the little lost babies.

"Where will we go now, Jimmy?" Tasmin asked. "Are there no towns anywhere? We're all tired of this wilderness my father's selfishness has brought us to."

Jim had been asking himself the same questions. There were Mexican towns to the west but they would all just be arrested again if he took them to a Mexican town. He knew there were settlements in south Texas—but he didn't know the country and would have to feel his way along, hoping to strike one of the forks of the Brazos River, which he had been told led to the settlements. When he and Kit had come back along the Canadian River country after their trip to New Orleans, they had met numbers of immigrants, but none of them had any very reliable information to pass on. With luck, once they got east, they might chance on a party of immigrants and join up with with them as protection against the tribes.

Tasmin could not remember Jim being as doubtful about how to proceed as he was at the moment. Always before, he had seemed to know exactly where he wanted to go—when decisions had to be made, he made them without hesitation. His sudden lack of certainty filled her with despair. They were caught in a nightmare—a nightmare that had no meaning. If they had come to a place where even Jim Snow felt daunted, then the future looked dark indeed.

"Remember that first morning, when we met?" she asked. "You killed me a deer and we set out in the boat and I became rather impatient. I offered to put you ashore and proceed on my own, but you wouldn't have it—then the Osage got after us and you saved me."

Jim just nodded—of course he remembered.

"If you'd just gone ashore as I wished, none of this would have happened," she went on. "You'd have survived and I'd have been killed. Probably all of us would have been killed, and it would have served us right. We left our place—and a good place it was—for a place where we could not possibly belong. The Indians were right to try and kill us. We were just invaders—spoiled invaders."

She paused—she knew she was just confusing Jim. And yet it was how she felt: better to have died than to have lived to bury her child.

Jim kept his mind on the route. Past times, such as Tasmin was talking about, didn't interest him. He meant to kill several buffalo and have Cook and Little Onion jerk the meat. They might pass out of the buffalo range—they would need meat.

"I wish Kit was here," he admitted. "Kit's been a passel of places. He might even know something about Texas."

Tasmin saw that he did not want to deal with the complexity of her regret, which was hers to suffer alone—yet she knew he grieved for Monty.
As parent and child the two had got off to a slow start, but improvement
had been rapid. Jim often took Monty up beside him on the mare—he had
even tried to teach him one or two birdcalls—calls Jim himself didn't do
well.

Jim after all had the job of saving them. Why should he care about her
moody recollections? And yet the fact that he didn't made her feel lonely;
she abruptly got up and walked away. She felt like giving up—what Vicky
had done under the pretext of recovering her cello. Vicky could not stand
what was—she had sought the cold, hoping it would all be over.

Tasmin stood at the edge of the camp for a long time—not particularly
thinking, just being alone.

"I wish you'd go talk to Tassie," Kate Berrybender said, to Father Geoff.
"She might run away. Couldn't you stop her? She likes you."

Geoff got up and did what Kate asked.

"Go away, Geoff—can't you see I prefer to be alone?" Tasmin said at
once, when he approached.

"Don't leave—we all depend on you," Geoff told her.

Tasmin looked at him so coldly that he turned and went away, fearing
that he had failed in his mission.

Tasmin stood until her feet and fingers were numb with cold—the far-
away stars were brilliant. Finally she went back to the wagon and made
sure her children were covered up.

40

. . . an extremely irritating old fellow.

His nose is too small," Greasy Lake told the Likeness Maker. "He's proud
of his nose—I think you better make it larger."

George Catlin was both exasperated and frightened. He was attempting
the portrait of a Comanche warrior named Flat Nose—the man had been

by the scrutiny, she glared at the white man. Why was he looking at her so?

"But she's blind—she won't be able to see my painting," George said.

Greasy Lake had been watching the old woman closely and was not convinced that she was so blind.

"She just pretends to be blind so people will wait on her," Greasy Lake concluded.

"Wait on her? They left her to die!" George pointed out. "Who do you think is going to wait on her?"

"I think she could see a picture if you painted one," Greasy Lake insisted.

"Even if she doesn't, it will be an interesting challenge," George said. "I should have thought of it myself. Perhaps I can even make it a profitable sideline, when I get back home. The society matron as young belle! Why, my fortune will be made."

At once he set to work, old Na-a-me glaring at him the whole time—she worked her gums and occasionally mouthed imprecations. George found the situation amusing; he wished Tasmin were with him to share the joke. He was trying to use his art to turn an old Kiowa grandmother into a young woman.

Despite the old woman's irritation George took as much time with this portrait as he would have if he had been painting a mighty chief. When he finished he handed the picture to Greasy Lake, who studied it carefully before passing it on to old Na-a-me. At first old Na-a-me was puzzled by what she was given. One of her eyes was gone but one was not quite so bad—peering at the picture, she decided the white man must be a powerful magician. From nothing he had made a picture of a Kiowa girl, such as her sisters and her cousins had been long ago. That the girl was meant to be herself, she did not grasp. Except for a rippling reflection in a stream now and then she had never seen herself as a girl. The Kiowa had no mirrors then—only lately had traders begun to bring them. The girl in the picture was only a girl to Na-a-me at first, and yet the white man had worked hard and brought it into being with his magic.

Then it occurred to her that the white man might be even more of a magician than she had supposed. Perhaps he was offering to make her into a girl again—young like the girl in his picture. Why would this strange magician want to do that?

After thinking about it for a few minutes Na-a-me decided it was all about the white buffalo. The old prophet was trying to bribe her with the gift of youth, if she would only help him find the white buffalo. He wanted the power of the white buffalo so badly that he had gone to the trouble of finding a magician who was offering her what appeared to be a second life. Perhaps this time she would find better husbands than she had found the first time—but if not, she would at least get to live a great many more summers.

There was a problem, though: Na-a-me had no idea where the white buffalo was—nor was she even sure there *was* a white buffalo. But she had always been an accomplished liar, easily deceiving her husbands and her lovers when it pleased her to. It took no time at all for her to invent a big lie about the white buffalo.

"He's in that big canyon over by the Rio Rojo," she said.

"The Palo Duro, she means," George said. "That's not far from here."

Greasy Lake was wary. He wanted Na-a-me to be more specific.

"If the buffalo is there, where do they hide it?" he asked.

"To the west, near the sunset," Na-a-me told him glibly. She didn't like the prophet. He reminded her of her husband Peta, who was always asking questions, hoping to expose her lies. Greasy Lake was the same kind of man. He wanted to pick her story apart, but Na-a-me didn't let him. The buffalo was at the west end of the big canyon. That was all she intended to say. The prophet wanted to know if the white buffalo was well guarded, but Na-a-me refused to elaborate. She considered that she had told them a perfect lie.

That night Na-a-me slept little. She was waiting to feel herself become young again.

Bitter was her disappointment to wake up to find herself still old. The white man and the prophet were leaving. She had seen the picture. Why wasn't she young?

Then it became clear to her. The white man was a clever trickster, but not clever enough to make old people young. He had tricked her into telling them about the white buffalo. Then she remembered that she had lied too. She had no idea where a white buffalo lived. The lies, she saw, had canceled one another out. She would just die, as the People had intended she die. There would be no second life, a realization that made Na-a-me bitter. She cursed and cursed, working her mouth in anger. The white man had left her some food, some matches, some tobacco. What he hadn't left her was a second life.

42

It was easy enough for Charlie to prance around . . .

Charlie will think we're lazy if we give up and go back this soon," Willy Bent argued. "I expect he'll dock your wages."

Kit began to boil at the thought of such an injustice.

"If he tries to dock my wages I'll give him a lickin' he'll never forget," Kit said. "And if he tries to dock yours I suggest you do the same."

"He can't dock *my* wages," Willy pointed out. "I'm his partner. I own as much of the company as he does."

"Then you could dock my wages yourself—just try it if you want a lickin'," Kit told him, still indignant. The high-handedness of the Bents frequently put him in an angry state.

"You deserve to have yours docked," Willy observed. "You're the one who got us lost."

"I ain't lost," Kit protested. "Why are you standing there telling lies?"

"If you don't know which river this is, then we're lost," Willy insisted. "You're the one who wanted to follow it."

The day before they had dropped off a high escarpment into broken country of gullies and washes and salt cedar thickets. They had chosen the rough country because of the abundance of Indian sign on the plains. In the gullies and washes there were places to hide. Charlie Bent had sent them on a scouting trip to the country below the Canadian River, country that was controlled by the Comanches and the Kiowas. Charlie saw it as a major immigration route and was determined to put a trading post somewhere in it. Kit and Willy's job was to look for likely sites, and they had found several; but the likeliest site in the country didn't eliminate the real problem with such a venture: the real problem, still, were the Indians.

Charlie's notion was that they might locate some small poor band and lavish presents on them until they put aside their lances and scalping knives and began to see the virtue of having traders around. Maybe the small bands could then influence the big bands. It was easy enough for Charlie to prance around his secure establishment on the Arkansas and develop theories such as that one; but it was quite another thing, as Willy and Kit could testify, to ride around in constant danger trying to locate this ideal small band.

They had been scared enough just because of the overabundance of sign, but then they ran into Tom Fitzpatrick, on his way back from a trip to Mississippi, and Tom brought news of a bad new war chief, known as Wolf Eater from his habit of chasing down wolves and eating them in order to enhance his power. Wolf Eater had recently wiped out two small immigrant trains, leaving burned and mangled bodies here and there on the prairie.

"He's a bad un," Tom assured them. "Whatever you do, don't try to pow-wow with him."

"I have no intention of speaking to the man," Kit told old Tom.

It was worry about the Wolf Eater that had prompted them to leave the prairie and begin to traverse the badlands, on a day of light snow and cutting wind. In the distance a broadish, reddish river flowed east.

"That'll be the Rio Rojo, I guess," Kit said.

"What if it ain't?" Willy asked. "Charlie's going to want an accurate report."

"If he don't trust me, let him come look for himself," Kit replied hotly. The pickiness of Charles Bent was often hard to tolerate.

"If it ain't the Red, I suppose it could be the Prairie Dog Fork of the Brazos," Kit allowed.

"Whatever it is, it's no place for a trading post," Willy said. "You'd never get wagons through these gullies."

There was no disputing the fact that rocky gullies had a bad effect on wagon wheels.

"There's a big canyon around here somewhere," Kit mentioned. "They say a million buffalo can graze in it without even being crowded."

"I suppose that would be an exaggeration," Willy remarked.

"What's to stop us from having a look?" Kit argued.

Willy thought he might as well humor the man. If he refused to let him visit the canyon he'd sulk all the way back to the Arkansas.

"We can look, but I have no intention of going down in it," Willy told him. "It would be easy to get boxed in by Indians in a hole in the ground like that."

The next day near dusk they found themselves looking down into the Palo Duro canyon—plenty of buffalo roamed the canyon floor, though considerably less than a million, as Willy was quick to point out.

Kit, as usual, was reluctant to give ground.

"I expect it'll fill up in the spring, when the grass is better," he said.

They were near the west end of the canyon when they spotted two

could, he did her favors, performed little chores. He had not seen the Indian girl or the little boy but he liked Tasmin and readily agreed to take one of his men and go have a look. Two of the soldiers were cleaning their rifles—they were hopeful that they might see game to shoot at. Lazily they got up and followed Corporal Dominguin.

Tasmin wished desperately that Jim would show up. For some reason she became frightened—the vast, empty place, filled with perils, was enough to frighten her. She had an urge to race off and find Petey herself, though she realized that she would probably only get lost.

When Corporal Dominguin came back he just shook his head. In his hand he held Petey's little bear.

47

... *trying to call the blue quail* ...

Blue Foot hated whimpering children. He had not wanted to take the child at all but Tay-ha insisted. Women were easier managed if they were allowed their children. Tay-ha was not sure how the brown woman happened to have a white child, but many whites now passed through the country—mixed pairs were not uncommon. They were all disappointed because they had only managed to catch a brown girl when there were at least five salable white women in camp. But there were only four of them, and a number of soldiers with rifles guarded the women.

"You hit her too hard," Blue Foot insisted.

Tay-ha was very good at ambushes. If he didn't want to be seen he wasn't seen. He was already swinging his club when the girl sensed him. She turned and the blow took her in the temple, which was not where he meant to hit her. He swung hard because they were close to the camp and he didn't want her to scream, but he had meant to hit her in the back of the head. Her own movement caused his miscalculation. They had thrown her, inert and unconscious, over the spare horse and put ten miles between them and the camp before they stopped.

Still, Tay-ha was ready to admit that he had hit the girl too hard. She had been lifeless as a sack when they raped her. She had not opened her eyes.

"Draga won't like this—she wanted us to catch some white women," Blue Foot complained.

"I can't do everything right," Tay-ha told him.

The old man, Snaggle, bent over Little Onion, looking at her closely.

"She has blood in her eyes and more coming out her ears—she's dying," Snaggle told them. "It's pointless to take her any farther."

Little Onion faintly heard the talk, which seemed to come from a great distance. She tried to stroke Petey, to make him stop whimpering, but her hands wouldn't fully obey her. She and Petey had been squatting, trying to call the blue quail, and the blue quail were listening. They had stopped, listening to Little Onion's call. Only at the last second did she sense the man with the club who had somehow got behind her. Then she fell into deep darkness, in her head a pain far worse than any she had felt before. In the blackness all she could do was try to soothe Petey so the men would spare him. If they could only survive a day her husband might come.

Blue Foot was thoroughly disgusted. The white women in the camp would have made them all rich, if they could have caught them. But Tay-ha had to go club a brown girl who was making birdcalls with the child. They would have to go back to Draga's great slavers' camp with nothing to show. Any of the white women would have brought big money—but now that prospect was all spoiled. He had wanted to grab one of the white women while she was making water, but the soldiers were too close.

"Are we going to wait all day?" Snaggle asked. "This girl is ruined."

Blue Foot knew it was true. She had blood in her eyes. She could have been a useful slave, but that was not to be.

"Just finish her, since you ruined her," he said to Tay-ha.

He caught the little boy by the ankle, swung him a few times, and threw him as high as he could throw him. While he was swinging the boy, Tay-ha killed the girl. It only required another hard rap.

The little boy hit the frozen ground. Blue Foot intended for the fall to kill him—he didn't seem like a strong boy. Old Snaggle went over and inspected him.

"He's still breathing," Snaggle reported.

Enraged—why couldn't anything go right?—Blue Foot looped his rawhide rope around one of the little boy's feet—then he jumped on his horse and rode off as fast as he could go, through some rocks and some cactus. When he came back Snaggle was quick to report that the boy was dead.

"This has been a wasted day," Blue Foot complained, as the four of them rode south.

"More than that," Snaggle reminded him. "We watched that camp for three days."

"There were just too many soldiers," Tay-ha said.

"We might catch somebody if we went to Mexico," Bent Finger suggested. He was the youngest slaver—no one paid much attention to him.

"We are not going to Mexico," Blue Foot said, in a tone that suggested to Bent Finger that his comments were unwelcome.

They rode south, under a full moon, for most of the night. Here and there they saw campfires—Comanche campfires, probably. They were on the great war trail that the Comanches used when they made their raids into Mexico. A day's ride west of the war trail was the big slavers' camp known as Los Dolores. There, at the moment, the old woman Draga reigned—a woman crueler but more efficient than most of the other slavers.

"I wish you hadn't hit that girl so hard," Blue Foot chided. "I hate going back with no captives to show."

"Shut up about it," Snaggle told him. "Tay-ha didn't mean to kill her, but what's done is done."

48

. . . Tasmin came running out, panic in her face.

I'm eager to see Tasmin and the rest," George Catlin said.

"Me too," Kit Carson put in. "We'll have us a regular reunion."

Old Greasy Lake had refused to leave the yellow buffalo, so Kit and Willy had thrown in with George Catlin and set out in search of the Berrybenders. A few days later they had the happy luck to run into Jim Snow, who was packing home a sizable load of buffalo meat, a welcome sight.

"It's just like Jim to have buffalo when the rest of us are making do with prairie dog," Kit remarked.

Then Tom Fitzpatrick, who had been trapping on the south Canadian with little luck, drifted in, and he also was looking for the Berrybenders.

"I thought I might court that pretty cook a little bit more," he told them. "Absence makes the heart grow fonder, they say."

Kit Carson felt that the sentiment was very dubious.

"It don't make my wife's grow fonder," Kit said. He knew Josefina would soon be throwing things, once he got home—mad because he had been away so long.

Jim was glad to see them all, though he was surprised that George had risked himself in the Comanche country.

"I had a military escort, you see," George said. "And after that I had Greasy Lake."

Jim supposed that the arrival of so many old friends would throw the camp into an uproar of welcome—but he soon saw that there had been trouble. All the soldiers had their rifles at the ready. Before they were even in camp Tasmin came running out, panic in her face.

"Hello, George—I'll hug you in a minute," she said, going straight to Jim.

"Little Onion has been taken, and Petey," she told him. "They've been gone since yesterday. None of us saw or heard a thing. Can you please go find them?"

"I doubt it was Comanches—you'd have heard plenty if it had been," Tom Fitzpatrick remarked.

"Please go find them," Tasmin repeated, her eyes on her husband.

George Catlin was shocked by how the years had roughened Tasmin— roughened all the women. Beauty was still there, but they were no longer peaches-and-cream English girls, fresh off a boat.

While Jim and the others were debating what to do, Tasmin gave George a kiss and a long hug.

"George, I'm frightened—really frightened," she said. "We lost Monty to cholera and now one of my twins is missing—it's very hard."

"I'm sure," he said. "But who's that little girl I see with the wild curls— she must be yours?"

"Yes, that's Petal—make what you can of her," Tasmin said, before rushing back to Jim.

"Tom thinks it's slavers—there's some big camp south of here where

In the afternoon Jim got out his tattered copy of the Book and fumbled through it. There were two verses that he felt sure were in the Book, but he couldn't find them. One was "Vengeance is mine, saith the Lord." The other—he only half remembered it—was "Blessed are the meek, for they shall inherit the earth."

Jim wanted badly to find those verses, but his copy of the Book had so many pages missing that in the end he had to give up. The first seemed to mean that he should let the Lord manage what vengeance need be—but he wasn't going to heed that verse.

It was when he remembered Petey and Little Onion that he thought of the second verse. They had been the meek, as he understood the word, but they hadn't inherited the earth. Instead they had had painful deaths. He had been raised to believe that every word in the Book was true but he couldn't make that belief jibe with what had just happened—much less with what was about to happen.

Jim decided it would be best just not to think about the Book until he got back to the company and could talk about his confusion with someone who was educated. He was about to go into battle, and he didn't plan to hold back. Confusion of the mind was not something he could entertain—not then. The Sin Killer was going to fall upon the heathen, screaming out the Word. His sword and his gun would then accomplish what needed to be done.

54

At once everyone fell silent.

Malgres suddenly had a thought—a notion about the Sin Killer.

Ramon, still frightened, had bought some liquor from Draga, who kept some in her brush house. He was now in a stupor, not quite asleep but too drunk to be talkative.

Malgres gave him a shake.

"What?" Ramon asked, apprehensively.

Malgres pointed to the men who were camped with old Snaggle, the most ancient person in the camp.

"Weren't those men arguing about killing a girl?" he asked. "The one with the club did it—he hit the girl too hard, and she died. I think they killed a little boy too."

"So what? Nobody wants to drag a child around!" Ramon said.

"The girl and the little boy came from that big party of whites—the one the Sin Killer was with when he hit Obregon," Malgres went on.

"I want to go to sleep—I hate talking about the Sin Killer," Ramon told him.

"I think that girl they killed was the Sin Killer's wife," Malgres concluded. "The boy must have been his son. He has come for vengeance."

"I thought he had a white wife," Ramon said.

"Yes, and an Indian wife too. I tell you, he's come for his vengeance. That's why we heard that cry."

"Then let him kill them—I don't like them anyway," Ramon remarked.

Malgres, convinced that the Sin Killer was near, and convinced, also, that he had come to kill the four slavers, at once went over to warn the men. Maybe they would want to try and outrun him.

But the men proved to be rude fellows—they were playing dice and resented Malgres's interruption.

"Can't you see we're gambling?" Blue Foot asked.

"Yes, I can see that," Malgres said. "In my opinion you ought to get on your horses and go. The Sin Killer has come for you."

Tay-ha had begun to develop his own uneasy suspicions on that score. What Malgres said might be true. How could such a sound come from a bare cliff? Probably there was a cave they couldn't see. He tried to talk Blue Foot and Bent Finger into going with him to see if he could spot the cave, but they weren't interested.

"There must be a way up it," Tay-ha said. "We ought to go have a look."

"We'll just kill the man when we see him. What does he want?" Bent Finger said. He was losing at dice—his mood was sour.

"I think he wants the men who killed his wife and baby," Malgres declared.

Blue Foot took offense at once.

"How do you know so much about it?" he asked.

"I don't know much about it—I just had an opinion," Malgres said—he didn't know why he had troubled to warn this quarrelsome bunch.

"He knows because you bragged," old Snaggle said to Blue Foot. "You told everybody you killed a girl and a child."

"I doubt they were the Sin Killer's," Blue Foot answered, but he was beginning to feel shaky. Why had this Malgres been so rude as to interrupt their game?

At once everyone fell silent. Then Blue Foot rattled the dice, but didn't roll them.

"I think the Sin Killer's dead," Tay-ha mentioned. "Some Utes caught him and took his hair. I heard that from somebody."

He didn't know why he had made the remark, because it was the opposite of what he believed, which was that the Sin Killer was in a cave, watching them, probably studying their weaknesses, which were many. Somewhere up there the man was watching, making his plans to kill. It was a bad thought to live with.

"You spoiled a good game and I was winning," Blue Foot pointed out.

"You're too rude—you deserve to be killed," Malgres told him. Then, feeling that his advice had been scorned, he went away.

55

A white man was standing there . . .

Tay-ha had begun to want to own the Mexican woman, whose name was Rosa. At least once and often twice a day he led her a little way from camp and copulated with her. Rosa didn't resist but she refused to look at him while he was about his pleasure; as soon as he finished and withdrew she stood up and walked wearily back to camp.

Rosa belonged to Chino, a small half-breed slaver who was well known to put very high prices on his merchandise. He owned a dozen captives and kept them longer than was normal because he refused to lower his price. Tay-ha offered Chino one hundred dollars for Rosa, an offer that irritated Blue Foot. Not only was the price ridiculously high, but having to take a woman with them would seriously limit their mobility. Chino, however, refused the offer; he sometimes took his own pleasure with Rosa and was not going to let her go unless he got a high price.

Tay-ha believed he could finally talk Chino down, and if he couldn't, he might just kill him. The thought of owning Rosa excited him more and more. He led her out and kept her till late afternoon, playing with her breasts, probing. Rosa still refused to look at him, and she left at once when he finished. Tay-ha had laid his club down while enjoying Rosa's body, and when he turned to pick it up he received a terrible shock. A white man was standing there—the white man had his club and was raising it. The man had covered his body with brown dirt, but it was clear from his hair that he was a white man.

Tay-ha was too stunned even to cry out. Was it the Sin Killer? Already his club was coming toward his face, thick as a log, and fast.

Using the well-sharpened Mexican sword, Jim cut Tay-ha's head off. It was smashed and bloody, as Little Onion's had been. Jim left it for the coyotes and badgers. But he hoisted Tay-ha's small body and carried him to the bluff. As soon as it was dark he carried the corpse along the ledge to his cave.

The next morning, just at dawn, the people in the slavers' camp heard the cry of the Sin Killer for a second time—they heard the Word, emanating from the face of a cliff.

Then, from the same spot, a body flew out and fell with a thud on the hard desert floor.

"I thought so," old Snaggle said, when he went with the others to inspect the headless body. "It was not like Tay-ha to stay out all night. He had already sent that woman back."

Blue Foot suddenly felt seriously worried. Tay-ha's head had been cut off—this suggested that the killer had a plan. He had come for vengeance.

Malgres called for unified action.

"He's just in a cave up there," he said. "If we all go after him we can kill him."

None of the other slavers had the slightest interest in climbing the cliff.

Draga lumbered over and looked at the headless body. She studied the cliff for a long time. An enemy was around. But her eyes had been smoked to dimness. All she could see was rock.

"Maybe we should leave?" Blue Foot suggested.

Ramon approved of that plan.

"If we leave as a group he won't dare attack us," he said.

"He attacked Obregon when we were fourteen against him," Malgres reminded him. "Then he didn't even use a gun, just a club. I think he could have killed us all."

"Let's just leave," Ramon said, almost pleading.

Draga had no intention of leaving.

"There'll be Comanches along in a day or two," she reminded them. "We'll get the Comanches to hunt him down."

"What if no Comanches come?" Blue Foot asked. "What if they're late?"

They all strained their eyes looking up at the cliff, but it just looked like an ordinary red butte, very sheer. That a man could be up there didn't seem possible—and yet Tay-ha's body had been flung down.

"Tay-ha wanted to buy my captive," Chino remembered. "I wonder if there was any money in his pocket."

He began to search Tay-ha's pants, but found nothing. Old Snaggle watched with amusement. He knew where Tay-ha hid his money—he meant to get it for himself when nobody was looking. He had come to admire the Mexican woman—perhaps he would buy her, with Tay-ha's money. It would be a fine joke on Tay-ha, although one he couldn't appreciate, due to being dead.

"What if he kills us all, one by one?" Ramon asked.

Blue Foot was outraged that one white man could disrupt their business so much. It was true that at present he had no slaves to sell himself, but he and Tay-ha had intended to go to Mexico and catch a few pretty soon. Now he would have to go with Bent Finger and old Snaggle, neither of whom was particularly skilled when it came to catching young Mexican slaves. With Tay-ha he could count on half a dozen captives; with the others he would be lucky to get three.

Later, drunk, Blue Foot decided it was all Tay-ha's fault, for carelessly hitting that Ute girl too hard; and as if that were not vexation enough, his own rope was missing. His rope had been right on his saddle but now it wasn't there. Annoyed, he accused old Snaggle of stealing it, but the old man just shrugged. Angrily, Blue Foot made a tour of the whole camp, looking for his rope. It took a long time to braid a rawhide rope—its loss put him in such a foul mood that he cuffed two or three of the captive boys. Then he asked Chino if he could use the Mexican woman and Chino refused, a very annoying thing.

"You let Tay-ha use her often enough—why not me?" Blue Foot asked.

Chino didn't bother to reply. Rosa sat with her eyes downcast; she was tired of being summoned by men but she was a captive. If she refused she would just be beaten and then dishonored anyway. Only her thoughts were private; no man could have those. She was glad someone had cut off the head of Tay-ha, the man who dishonored her most often, but Rosa had forgotten how to hope. She was a poor woman—who would bother to rescue her from such a place? And yet when she saw Tay-ha's headless body she felt a little hope. Someone was up there—the slavers were afraid. She hoped whoever it was would kill all the slavers—then she would never have to accept their stinking bodies again.

56

They gambled and drank; they posted no guards . . .

Jim could scarcely credit the carelessness of the slavers. One of their own had been killed—decapitated, in fact—and yet they made little change in their habits. They gambled and drank; they posted no guards; they staggered around drunk; they didn't even heed the warnings of their own dogs. Jim had crept in in the night and stolen the rope without being challenged, though several dogs barked. When a dog barked in an Indian camp all the warriors were on the alert immediately. But the slavers only kept dogs to eat—they just ignored the barking.

Jim had studied the camp thoroughly and was ready to attack. The rawhide rope had been the last piece of equipment he needed. He meant to drag its owner to death at the end of it, as Petey had been dragged; then he meant to kill the rest of the slavers and attempt to guide the shivering captives to a place where they would be safe.

Jim had prepared one more demonstration—he wanted to spread a little more terror, enough to cause the drunken men to panic—and when they were panicked, the Sin Killer would come among them.

In the night he led the little mare up the narrow ledge to his cave. She snorted once or twice, probably because she smelled the ram, but she didn't falter.

That night he made sure that his sword was still sharp.

At dawn he was ready. He mounted the mare and rode her carefully along the ledge—as he did, he let the Word pour out. Below, slavers and captives struggled to come awake. When they did they saw a man riding across the face of the cliff, seemingly upon air. It was only just dawn: the sun was not up. As Jim yelled out the Word, men scrambled for their guns. Chino even fired a shot, though he knew the distance was too great.

Jim and the mare were off the ledge in two minutes—then he loped a wide circle to the east. He wanted to come at the men when the rising sun was in their faces.

Malgres, Ramon, and Blue Foot decided to flee, but half drunk and gripped by fear, they made a mess of it. Blue Foot's horse was notably skittish—it had to be approached calmly and patiently, but Blue Foot was too frightened to be calm—he rushed at the horse and the horse bolted. The panic communicated itself to Malgres's horse, and then Ramon's. The three men found to their shock that they were afoot at the worst of all times. Ramon fumbled with his gun. Malgres, looking around for a horse he might steal, drew his thin knife and began to stumble toward Draga's hut. But then, to his horror, the Sin Killer came racing directly out of the face of the rising sun.

"A long knife beats a short knife every time," Jim said, as he cut Malgres down.

Ramon dropped his gun. The Sin Killer came racing past him, after Blue Foot. For a second Ramon felt hope—perhaps the man only wanted Blue Foot.

Jim killed Ramon with a backhand slash as he rode by. The mare closed with Blue Foot in only a second. Jim dropped the rope over the man and jerked it tight around his legs. Blue Foot's face hit the stony ground so hard his teeth cracked. Before he could try to free his legs Jim turned and raced directly at the slavers' camp, crying the Word as he came. Blue Foot bounced in the air, hitting rocks, hitting cactus; then he was dragged through a campfire: ashes filled his eyes, coals burned his hands. Jim poured the Word out in full cry, louder than he ever had. He dragged Blue Foot through every campfire as he slashed at the stumbling men. He cut Chino down where he stood. The Word had never poured out of him so strongly—it excited the little mare. Here was her chance to run, and she did run, bursting through Draga's brush house as if the sticks were twigs. The old woman just managed to crawl out of the way.

Too late, the slavers tried to flee—Jim cut them down as they ran. One managed to mount and run but the mare overtook the slaver's horse as a greyhound might overtake a coyote. The fleeing slaver's horse threw him. Jim killed him as he struggled to his feet. What was left of Blue Foot still bounced at the end of his own rope. The Sin Killer was still crying out the Word; he turned back toward the camp, racing down on Draga, who faced him bitterly. No one could stop this man—he had cut through her slavers as if they were merely vegetation, and now he was charging at her. Draga felt a poisonous bitterness: a hard life hers had been, and now this sudden end.

The Sin Killer split her head; he could not stop. He had brought vengeance to the heathen and there were several more, huddled together in terror, screaming. The Sin Killer raised his bloody sword, still crying the Word. He could think of nothing but killing and was about to urge the mare into a last charge into the midst of the heathen, when the Mexican woman sprang in front of him. She grabbed his bridle, fought him for the little mare's head.

"*Señor, no mas!*" she said. "*No mas!*"

The Sin Killer found it hard to stop; he wanted to keep killing until there was no one left to kill. But the Mexican woman was stubborn; she hung on to the bridle.

"*No mas, señor*—they are only captives," she cried, clinging to the frothing, sweaty mare who wanted to run some more. The wild sounds excited her.

The woman would not let go—he would have to kill her to free himself—and he didn't want to kill her, though he had raised a dripping sword. The Word ceased to pour out of him; he began to stop being the Sin Killer. One of the huddled little boys in the group before him looked like Monty. He saw a terrified girl the age of Little Onion. He remembered his children, his dead children, his dead wife. What the woman said was true. The group he had been about to charge were captives, not slavers. Only this stubborn Mexican woman had kept him from cutting them all down. He began to shake, as he realized what he had almost done. The struggle to stop himself from killing was the hardest he had ever fought. The captives still looked terrified. The sword he carried still dripped with Draga's blood. Jim dismounted, shaking, and broke the bloody sword over his knee. Toward the captives he felt a sudden shame.

"It's all right—I won't hurt you," he stammered.

When he snapped the sword he cut his hand on the sharp blade. The brown woman found a little of Draga's whiskey. She washed the wound and bound it. One or two of the captives began to lose their fear. Jim saw that Blue Foot was dead, filled with thorns as Petey had been—it no longer seemed important. For an hour he felt too weak to walk. The captives were cautiously probing among the corpses of the slavers, taking a knife here, a little money there, a belt, a shirt.

Rosa saw that the white man had exhausted himself with his terrible rage. She herself had known rage, but only for a short time. She had raged at her husband for his drunkenness before he died. She raged at her neighbors for letting their goats into her squash. She had raged at God when her two babies died. But she had not raged as this man raged. He had killed every single slaver, and if she had not stopped him he would have killed the captives too—and killed her as well.

Rosa was cautious with the man. It took time to recover from such terrible anger. Meanwhile she did her own canvass of the destroyed camp. There was a boy named Emilio who was good with horses—she made him go catch the ones who had belonged to the slavers. She set one of the girls to assembling pots, and what food had been in camp.

All this time Rosa watched the white man. He seemed spent, able only to sit. His hands still shook. But he did notice that Emilio had managed to bring in the horses.

"Señor, will you help us—we are far from home?" Rosa asked finally.

Jim had never felt such weariness. He felt almost incapable of movement, yet he knew he had to move. He nodded at the woman. Of course he would help them, once the weariness passed.

"Señor, we should go," Rosa told him. "Too many Comanches come here—they are always coming and sometimes they are many."

Jim nodded again. He liked the looks of the boy who had captured the horses.

"That boy's good with horses," he told her. "My packhorse is tied just behind that bluff. If he'll go fetch him we can load up and leave."

Emilio started at once but Jim stopped him.

"You don't have to walk—take the mare," he said.

The mare had calmed too. She snorted when the boy mounted but Emilio spoke to her soothingly. Soon he returned with the packhorse. Jim would have liked to sleep, but he knew it was not the time. The brown woman was directing the packing, helping the captives assemble supplies. They should be able to make good time—or they should if only he could shrug off his strange weariness.

"I don't know your name," he said to the woman. "I'm Jim."

"My name is Rosa," she said. To her surprise the man stood up and offered to shake her hand. The gesture was so awkward that Rosa smiled—she had not expected to smile again. But she took the man's hand and shook it. He did not want to turn her hand loose, but finally he did. He acted like a badly wounded man, and yet he had received no wound. Rosa kept an eye on him, as she worked. She saw that he was dazed. There was a little of Draga's whiskey left. Rosa took the jug to Jim.

"We have a little whiskey—it might help," she said.

"I might turn sinner if I get drunk," Jim told her. But then he felt silly. He had killed a whole company of men. Surely killing was a worse sin than drunkenness. He took the jug and swallowed two mouthfuls of the burning liquid.

"That's like drinking fire," he said. But he felt a little energy return. A few minutes later he led the group out of the camp.

57

He felt a constant need to rest.

The next days were the hardest Jim Snow had ever spent on the trail. The country itself was no harsher than other country he had traveled through—the problem was that he had no energy and no drive. He felt a constant need to rest. He knew he needed to move the freed captives off the great Comanche war trail—and he did lead them east; but compared with other treks he had made, it was a fumbling, uncertain process. He could not seem to keep his head about him: he kept going back in memory to the terrible moment when he had been about to slay the innocent captives with his dripping sword.

After all, he *hadn't* done it—Rosa's stubborn action had brought him out of his killing frenzy just in time. The crisis had passed; yet he couldn't forget it, couldn't quite come back to himself.

"It's a good thing no Comanches found us today," he said to Rosa, as they sat by the campfire the first night out.

"I've got no fight in me now," he added. "We'd be easy pickings."

"The Comanches will see all those dead men—they may not want us," Rosa told him. "You even killed the old witch. She was a cruel woman—you did good to kill her."

Jim knew that was true—Draga's cruelties had been practiced on his own sister-in-law, Buffum, and countless others. Still, he seemed to have no strength and he could not get his mind off the terrible thing that he had almost done.

Three times in the next days they saw Indians—and yet the Indians didn't come close. Probably Rosa was right. The Indians had seen the massacred slavers, Draga with her head split, Blue Foot dragged to death. Rapidly news of the massacre of the slavers spread across the southern plains and deserts—in weeks it spread all the way to Canada. The Assiniboines knew the Sin Killer. They called him the Raven Brave and it did not surprise them that he had killed a bunch of miserable slavers. The Raven Brave was a man to be feared.

Of the captives only the boy Emilio, who was so good with horses, felt at ease with Jim. The two of them talked about the problems of horses. The other captives kept to themselves. They could not forget that this man had been about to kill them. They weren't sure they could trust him. The young women held back.

Rosa managed the trek, managed the camps they made, managed the other captives—most of all, she managed Jim. She was efficient. She knew to make well-banked campfires. With Lord Berrybender's fine new rifle Jim made a lucky shot on an antelope. Rosa took a horse and packed the animal in. She butchered it, fed the others, dried some of the meat.

Jim could not hide how disturbed he felt. He did not like to be without Rosa's company—she steadied him. She rode beside him all day and sat with him at night. There was little talk. Only once or twice did he return to the moment of conflict, when she had jumped forward and stopped the killing.

"'Vengeance is mine, saith the Lord'—it says that in the Bible," Jim told her. "I expect that's the right way."

Rosa didn't answer. She had never liked priests or followed their debates. What she wanted to tell Jim was that she had never been as glad of anything as she had been when she watched him kill the slavers. She didn't intend to speak of it to Jim—it was better not to speak of one's shame—but she had been particularly glad when he had killed Tay-ha, the man who dishonored her most casually, treating her as no better than an animal, even taking her in her bowels. She could never speak of such shame, or hope to be an honorable woman again, but she did not agree that vengeance should only be the Lord's. She was alive because Jim had been vengeful. It was true that he lost himself in a blood frenzy and had almost gone too far—but she had stopped it, and it was over. She was not going to regret the deaths of slavers. In fact she had gone and spat on Tay-ha's corpse, and was happy when she did it.

She saw, though, that Jim was troubled in himself, and she did what she could to help. She brought him his food, sat with him, administered the trek, settling little quarrels and seeing that Emilio took good care of the horses. She saw it as a miracle that they were alive at all, and Jim, sad-eyed now and awkward, had made the miracle. Rosa meant to devote herself to him, to the extent that he would allow it.

One night, to her surprise, Jim asked how old she was.

"Old enough to have buried two babies and a husband," Rosa said.

Jim didn't press her. He had merely wondered. Rosa's silences were comfortable silences. She seemed to have no need to question him, as Tasmin did. When Tasmin went away after some discussion Jim usually felt relieved; but when Rosa went away, to attend to some chore, he felt anxious, and the anxious feeling only left him when Rosa came and settled herself by the fire. In settling herself she seemed to settle him. In a while he would stop feeling anxious. He found it to be a comfort of a sort he had not had in his life before. The thought that, once they were safe, Rosa might wish to go back to her home was unsettling. He began to wonder whether there might be a way to keep her. And yet he was a married man—he had a wife. Why was he thinking such things?

58

Was this ribbon becoming? Would this petticoat show?

Goodness! A ball? What are you thinking about, George?" Tasmin asked. Buffum, Vicky, and Mary were all likewise taken aback. A ball, when they had been in the safety of the settlements only a few days?

"Mr. Austin absolutely insists that you come," George Catlin informed them. "There is much war stir—Mr. Austin feels that a little entertainment would not be amiss. There will be music—even dancing, perhaps."

"All things we once took for granted but have since put behind us," Tasmin said.

"Not so behind us—we danced in Santa Fe, Tassie," Buffum remarked.

"I didn't—I mourned—but never mind," Tasmin said. "I wouldn't mind consenting if I had a dress. What does Mr. Austin propose that we come to the ball *in*? We've all emerged from barbarism very nearly naked, it seems to me."

"Well, you aren't naked but you are perhaps a little begrimed still," George allowed. "Mr. Austin is sensitive to the problem of attire. Some nice Texas ladies are being dispatched to the rescue. They may desire to loan you frocks. Also, there's a kind of haberdashery here in Washington-on-the-Brazos. Not up to London standards, of course, but you might be able to obtain some cloth that would do to be sewn."

"I guess it's not a very long step from barbarism to civilization, down here in Texas," Mary remarked. "I would like to take one hundred baths before considering the matter of adornment."

"I suppose that means you'll be wearing your tiara," Tasmin said in jest—but at the mere mention of a ball their mutual spirits *did* rise.

"I suppose, after all, it's what we were bred to do—go to balls," Tasmin remarked.

"I hear it will be quite thick with heroes," Father Geoff put in.

"Oh, Davy Crockett's here," Lord Berrybender informed them. "I quite hit it off with him in Washington. The man likes to drink—so do I. He's quite the hunter too. A killer of bears, I believe."

"And then there's Mr. Bowie, who's invented quite a formidable knife," George told them. "It's the kind of weapon your husband, Jim, could put to good use."

"I shall want to bring Juan—I hope it will be no problem," Buffum announced. It was now understood that she and Corporal Dominguin were betrothed.

"Mr. Austin is a man of great sophistication—I'm sure your corporal will be welcome," George said.

A hasty trip was made to a tiny general store, where cloth of various kinds was purchased. Cook was soon sewing. When the local matrons showed up with frocks for loan, all were in the end rejected by the very particular Berrybenders.

"When we go to balls around here we must manage to be queens of them," Tasmin instructed; but then, as she was trying to pull a brush through her recalcitrant hair, she suddenly put down her brush and burst into tears.

"But Tassie, what is it?" Kate asked. She found her sister's tendency to tears something of a trial.

"It's too soon—much too soon," Tasmin sobbed. "Two days ago—forty-eight hours—I hoped for nothing more than to keep my daughter alive. I had buried two sons. And now Mr. Austin gives a ball and I'm expected to care how my hair looks, and to observe that my frock is too tight in the bosom? I can't do it! I can't care about these fripperies. I've lived where it's life-or-death too long."

Then she began again to brush her hair.

"You are wrong, Tassie," Mary told her. "Those who survive *should* dance—it's a blow for life! Right, Geoff?"

Mary considered that she herself looked rather elegant, her pregnancy just showing.

Father Geoffrin, having seen the Berrybender women in all their states, had been permitted access to their boudoir so that he might advise about certain perplexities of fashion. Was this ribbon becoming? Would this petticoat show?

"Mary's right," he said. Tasmin's frock *was* too tight in the bosom, but then, she had a splendid bosom.

"It's a strike for life!" the priest agreed. "It may feel like disloyalty to the dead, but it isn't."

Buffum was not quite able to resist her own looks, now that she had freshened up a little.

"I wish Juan had better shoes," she said.

At the last minute, as they were all making final adjustments to their wardrobes, Cook, in a panic, announced that there had been an escapee from the nursery: Petal could not be found.

For a moment Tasmin felt a wild flutter of panic—children were sometimes kidnapped even from the villages by clever Indians. But Petal?

Fortunately the miscreant was at once plucked from her grandfather's buggy. She was determined not to miss this exciting ball and negotiated a compromise: she would attend the ball for one hour and then be returned to the nursery. In fact Petal charmed so many of the officers that Cook waited long in an anteroom before the little minx was finally surrendered. Even the austere Mr. Austin was seen to be reciting Petal a rhyme.

Tasmin danced a dance with Davy Crockett but did not warm to the man—his breath was so heavy with brandy that she felt she might be made drunk.

The Berrybender women, though feeling themselves much reduced in vivacity by their recent ordeal, nonetheless swept the young men of Texas before them. Piet sat rather forlornly on the sidelines, watching Mary dance dance after dance with the lively young blades.

Tasmin allowed a few of the young blades too, but then found herself being gracefully led round the floor by James Bowie—his look was melancholy but his dancing expert.

"My goodness, Mr. Bowie," she said, "I'd forgotten how pleasant it is to dance with a man who can dance. I wouldn't be surprised if you were the best dancer in Texas."

James Bowie smiled—a happier light came into his face for a moment.

"My wife would not tolerate inept dancing," he said.

"Of course not—is she here?"

"She's dead—cholera—and my two daughters as well."

"Then we have tragedy in common," Tasmin replied. "I lost a son to cholera—he's buried in New Mexico. Lady Berrybender also lost a son, and my sister Elizabeth a husband."

"It's a wearying thing to see loved ones go so quickly," he said. "It's because I couldn't fight the cholera that I'm here to fight the Mexicans, I guess."

"And do you think the Texans will win?" she asked.

"Oh yes, they'll win—and it won't take them long, either," Bowie said. "If you stay around a few weeks you'll be guests of the Republic of Texas."

"My husband's behind me somewhere—I intend to wait for him," Tasmin told him. "We lost a second boy—this one to slavers. My husband's gone for his revenge."

Jim Bowie merely nodded. Though his dancing remained graceful, the melancholic look was back on his face.

Buffum came hurrying over, in some distress.

"Tassie, you must talk to father—Mr. Crockett is trying to persuade him to go fight the Mexicans," she said.

"What nonsense! Papa's a cripple—he'll just be in the way," Tasmin declared. "I consider old Crockett a bore, and he's nowhere near as good a dancer as Mr. Bowie here."

"Davy's feet are too big," Bowie said, with a smile. "We used to call him Bucketfoot. No fun dancing with Bucketfoot."

By the time they reached Lord Berrybender, their persuasion was useless. Lord Berrybender's blood was up—he was determined to go.

"Father, that's ridiculous," Tasmin said. "You're too old for the barricades."

"Not a bit of it—stirs my blood just to think of a good fight," Lord B. told her. "Can't wait to see action, in fact. The blare of bugles, the thud of cannon. Bowie and Crockett and I will go tomorrow—Crockett assures me it will just be a skirmish—be back in a day or two. The place is called San Antonio."

Tasmin went at once to Davy Crockett and attempted to persuade him to leave her father, but Davy Crockett showed more interest in her bosom than in her opinions.

"Oh, we won't have much of a scrap in San Antonio," he assured her.

"Why not?"

"The big battle will be farther east," he assured her. "Sam Houston's over on the plain of San Jacinto, getting ready. He'll show General Santa Anna what's what—no question of that."

"Still, it seems foolish to take a crippled man into battle," Tasmin persisted.

"Nonsense—it'll be a tonic for your father," Crockett said. "He was just telling me about some of his adventures in Spain. Nothing like the smell of gunpowder to get an old warhorse stirred up."

"Getting Father stirred up has never been a problem, Mr. Crockett," Tasmin told him. "I think you would have done better to leave well enough alone."

Davy Crockett was taken aback. Young women with fine bosoms seldom talked to him so brashly—and from the look in this one's eye, worse might be to come. Though it was not his way, he strove to be diplomatic.

"I assure you there's no danger, madam—nothing serious is likely to happen at all," he told her. "The fact is I like your father's company. If he doesn't come I'll have to ride seventy miles with Jim Bowie, which is like riding seventy miles with a mute. Jim's run out of conversation. With your father along we can get drunk and tell lies and we'll be there in no time. There's nobody there but Billy Travis and a hundred or so of his men—hardly enough for Santa Anna to bother with."

James Bowie was of the same opinion.

"I've no great opinion of Billy Travis, which is why I felt Crockett and I ought to lend a hand."

"It all seems very casual, I must say," Tasmin told him. "It seems that Mr. Crockett anticipates a picnic—or better yet, a carouse—rather than war. What if he's wrong?"

"You've hit it!" Bowie told her. "Davy's whole life is a picnic or a carouse. He'll fight well enough, though, if he can find a fight."

Later, Tasmin allowed George Catlin a dance, which was not a success.

"Stop stepping on me, George—good Lord, why can't you dance?"

"I don't know—it's a puzzle," he said. "I do keep trying, though. I've noticed that ladies seem to reserve their greatest contempt for men who won't even try to dance. So I try."

"I don't like Mr. Crockett," Tasmin said. "It seemed to annoy him that I questioned his decision regarding my own father. Every time I ask a man a question I'm greeted with annoyance, if not worse. I don't see why that should be."

"I can't deal with these philosophical questions when I'm doing my best not to step on your feet," George said.

Later, dancing with a young soldier who didn't step on her feet but who didn't utter a word during the dance, either, Tasmin found herself thinking of Jim. She tried to imagine him dancing and couldn't. The surroundings were hardly fancy, just a half-formed army base near the Brazos River, and yet Tasmin could not picture her husband joining in even such a primitive soiree—much less some grander ball in Washington or London, or even Saint Louis. It was a perplexing dilemma. Jim had the skills that enabled him to pursue killers in a wilderness, and yet, she considered, how much easier it would be for her to be happy with him if he could just dance with her at a party—only something as normal as that.

"If we ever get anywhere where there's a dance instructor I mean to insist that you take dancing lessons, George," she told her friend.

"I could try, if you insist," George said. "But it won't do any good. The flaw is within."

The next day in midmorning Davy Crockett, Jim Bowie, and Lord Albany Berrybender set off for San Antonio. Lord B. was in the best of spirits. It was decided that, once General Houston routed Santa Anna, the Berrybenders would proceed on toward Galveston and look into the possibility of getting a ship.

"I'll catch up with you, never fear," Lord Berrybender assured them. "I just want a whiff of battle one more time—takes me back to the great days of the duke."

"What do you think about this, Vicky?" Tasmin wanted to know.

Vicky had received so much attention from young soldiers at the dance that she had become a little flustered, fearful that she might have exposed too much bosom.

Nonetheless she was not happy to see Lord Berrybender drive away.

"Impossible as he is to live with, I still wish he hadn't gone," Vicky said.

"I feel the same," Tasmin told her.

59

. . . signs of settlement began to appear . . .

When signs of settlement began to appear—a farm here and there, some already abandoned—Jim reckoned that the worst of the danger was over. They were on the Brazos. One grizzled farmer met them with rifle in hand, offered no food, but did tell them where they needed to go.

"You're on the right river," he said. "Another week and you'll come to Mr. Austin's colony. I expect your people are there—they came by a week ago."

Jim was heartened by that news. Tom Fitzpatrick had brought them through. He himself still felt his strange fatigue. He led the party, but Rosa did most of the work, making the campfires, cooking, keeping the captives in order. One wintry day she went off with Lord Berrybender's rifle and came back with two wild turkeys.

As they drew nearer and nearer to the settlements Jim realized he would soon have different problems to consider. He had rescued eleven people, including Rosa. They were all Mexican, their clothes were rags, they had not a cent, although Rosa had collected what money she could find on the slavers. What was he to do with them? More particularly, what was he to do with Rosa? He had become so needful of her that he couldn't imagine being without her. Somehow her presence was comforting to him, easing, as no other woman's had ever been. The best times of the day were at night when all the chores were done and they just sat by the campfire. They spoke scarcely at all in those times; and yet her presence was a deep comfort. He did not want to lose her; but she had been kidnapped: she might want to go home. The others, perhaps, could find employment of some sort in the Texas settlements. Even if they succeeded in getting back to their homes, the raiders might take them again.

Jim found it hard to reconcile his need for Rosa with the fact that he had a wife and daughter not many days ahead. What could he do? What would Tasmin want? What would Rosa want?

Rosa knew that Jem, as she called him, was troubled. He had told her that he had a wife and daughter. He had made no move to use her, as the slavers had used her. She herself felt sad—what could she do, when Jem returned to his family? Her home was far—even if she could find it, it was no place she wanted to be. Her husband's wicked old mother blamed her for his death. His sisters hated her. Vaqueros she didn't want were pressing her to go with them. She had to fight them, and some of them were strong. If she went home she would finally have to accept one of them, or she would starve.

Rosa had come to be fond of Jem—but since he already had a wife he wouldn't want to stay with her. Besides, she had been dishonored. How could she be a wife to a good man after the stains she bore? She even worried that Jim might have witnessed her shame. He had a spyglass. He might have seen her when Tay-ha led her out. She didn't want to ask him.

Jim, in his years with Tasmin, had rarely been able to figure out what she was feeling, except when she was angry. But now he had a sense that he *did* know what Rosa felt. When she sat by the campfire at night she wore a look of quiet sadness, as if she felt that her prospects were very bad. She did not want to look beyond the chores of the day. She would be happy to serve Jem, be a servant in his household, but probably his wife would not want such a thing.

Jim knew he was not a good talker, when it came to explaining things; and yet he had become so dependent on Rosa's company that he felt that he had better try. He didn't like the sad looks he saw on Rosa's face. Also, he didn't believe he could ever be at ease with Tasmin, in the way that he was with Rosa.

Besides, the Berrybenders were tending homeward. He didn't want to go to England and he doubted Tasmin intended to stay in America. The two boys' deaths had cut her too deeply. He didn't know how it would all work out but he knew he did not want to lose Rosa. He wanted to keep Rosa. One night he looked up and told her so in the simplest words he could find.

"I don't want to send you home," he told her. "I want you to stay with me and go where I go."

Rosa was shocked. What was Jem thinking? He had a wife. Was he asking her to stay with him as his whore? Her face showed her disappointment.

"It's not what you're thinking," Jim told her. "I guess my wife and I will be parting. She's going to England and I can't. She won't be my wife always."

Rosa was too startled to respond at once. She had not let herself hope that Jem might want her as his woman, but that seemed to be what he did want. And yet it didn't seem credible. Why would he want to leave a rich woman for a poor Mexican who had been misused?

"I am . . . surprised," she told him. "You are no longer to be with your wife?"

Jim shook his head.

"You saved me when you grabbed that bridle," he told her. "Otherwise I would have killed all these people."

"Yes, I did that—but it's past," she told him. "You are not killing any-body now. I expect your wife is a good wife. Why would you leave her for a poor woman like me?"

"I'm better with you than I am with Tasmin," he said.

Beyond that he couldn't explain.

Rosa waited, but he said no more. Yet she thought she must make him be clear.

"Jem, are you asking me to be your woman?" she asked, watching him closely as she said it.

Jim nodded.

"And you mean to send away your wife?"

He nodded again.

Rosa said no more. Jim waited, nervously. He wanted an answer, but Rosa didn't immediately give him one.

"Will you, then?" he asked.

"I don't know," Rosa said quietly. "I am glad that you want this, but I don't know."

"When will you know?" he asked.

Rosa took his hand and squeezed it, to show that she was not being hard.

"When I've met this wife you want to send away—then I'll know," she said.

60

Davy Crockett, sober and somber . . .

Y ou know, Crockett, it's rather odd," Lord Berrybender said. "I started my military career attempting to shoot small brown men through the dust and the smoke, and here I am at the end of my military career, still attempting to shoot small brown men through the dust and the smoke. There's a certain symmetry to it, wouldn't you say?"

Davy Crockett, sober and somber, mainly wished the old lord would stop talking. The siege of the Alamo had lasted almost two weeks, and the mood inside the old mission was not optimistic. Inside the walls of the mission's courtyard Mexican bodies were piled in heaps; and yet there seemed to be an endless supply of soldiers, ready to fling themselves at the Texans as Santa Anna commanded. Jim Bowie was sick, they were almost out of ammunition, and yet old Albany Berrybender went on babbling end-lessly about battles he had fought in Portugal and Spain. Probably half of what he said were lies, Crockett thought; but then perhaps the old fellow was wise to relive old battles: it might distract him from the fact that he was likely to die in this one, a fact for which Davy Crockett knew he bore some responsibility.

"I fear I rather misled you, Albany—I supposed this would be mainly a lark," he admitted. "I would never have supposed General Santa Anna would have come at our little company in such force—not when he has Sam Houston waiting for him on the plain of San Jacinto."

James Bowie, very weak from typhus, sat up on his cot and began to sharpen his knife—the big knife with the handle guard that he had de-signed himself.

"Why, Crockett, this is just a warm-up," he said. "Santa Anna thought he'd get an easy victory—probably wanted to get his soldiers' blood up. I doubt the man supposed we'd be this tough."

Around the shadowy interior of the old church, Texans were grimly counting bullets. William Travis, their leader, spent his day at a little lookout post, with his spyglass. What he was looking for was some slight sign that Santa Anna might be tiring of the siege. He knew he could overrun the Tex-ans eventually, but on the other hand, the cost in men was not small—Travis had no time to count bodies but he supposed the Mexican casualties must be approaching a thousand men. The Texans had most of them lived by the rifle—they could shoot, and they had, day after day, for almost two weeks. A wise general would not sacrifice a thousand men to overrun a force of less than two hundred; and yet generals were not always wise, and the men were being sacrificed. The wisdom of generals was a topic Lord Berrybender was happy to expound upon, on chill evenings, in the old church.

"Napoleon—brilliant of course, but hardly wise," he said. "Got cocky after Austerlitz and let the Russians suck him in. I suppose that's what we've done with General Santa Anna. We've sucked him in and your Gen-eral Houston can mop him up."

"Rather rough on us, of course," Lord B. added. "Fortunes of war and all. Luck bound to run out sometime."

The last remark set Davy Crockett grumbling.

"Speak for yourself, Albany," Crockett said. "I'm not ready to have my luck run out. I didn't come to Texas to die—always rather fancied dying in a brothel, if you must know."

"An original choice, certainly," Lord Berrybender replied. "I expect we could find a few whores around here, if only the Mexicans would give us a pass. Easy enough to get passes at such times in Europe—officers' honor and all that, but it doesn't seem to have caught on here."

"Nope, they mean to have our gizzards, and no entertainment allowed," Jim Bowie remarked.

"If we're to be slaughtered I hope it happens before the brandy runs out," Lord Berrybender remarked. "I have rather an enviable reputation as a drinking man. I'd hate to be sober when I draw my last breath."

Davy Crockett didn't like the cheerful tone in which Lord Berrybender spoke of the likelihood that they would all be killed. It might be true enough, but why talk about it? The thing to do was keep one's focus on life.

"Well, America's a grand place—my only regret is that I never got to shoot a grizzly bear," Lord Berrybender said. There was every sign that another charge was coming. The Texans had repulsed many, perhaps they would repulse this one—and yet, perhaps not.

"Deplorable uniforms!" he yelled, when the Texans' guns had all but fallen silent—the brown men, at last, began to pour in.

"I'd speak to somebody about those uniforms—they make you look like clowns!" he yelled to the fellow who was rushing at him with the shining bayonet. Jim Bowie, he saw, was up and whirling like a dervish, jabbing and striking with his big knife.

Lord Berrybender just managed to parry the bayonet with his rifle, but another soldier came rushing just as fast and this time the blade went into his chest with a thunck, as if someone had stabbed a big ripe melon. Very surprising it was, that melon-struck sound. He thought he must remember to mention it to Vicky; but then, as he sank down, he realized that he would not be mentioning much else to his Vicky—how he had always liked that long, slim body of hers. The soldier in the clown uniform was trying to pull the bayonet out of his chest, but the bayonet seemed to be stuck. It was all more surprising than painful. He remembered the look on Señor Yanez's face when the Pawnee boy ran at him and stuck the lance deep into him. Surprised was how the small gunsmith had looked: perhaps that was how *he* looked at the moment—surprised. Then the boy did jerk the bayonet out and Lord Berrybender sank to his knees. All around him men were struggling, but he himself felt rather like stretching out. Time for a nap, gentlemen, he thought—time for a nap.

61

. . . dark rumors began to reach them . . .

The Austin colony was all in a turmoil, would-be soldiers arriving almost hourly to fight for the Texas Republic—volunteers departed at an equal rate, hoping not to miss the glorious fight, though uncertain as yet which battle offered the best chance for glory. Petal and Elf particularly enjoyed the confusion. Both were popular with the soldiers—they were given frequent horse rides by men homesick for their own children. George Catlin was impatient—he wanted to press on to Galveston and see what boats were going where, but Tasmin and Vicky were reluctant to leave without their husbands. Vicky expected to see Lord Berrybender come up the road from San Antonio any day.

Then dark rumors began to reach them—the Texans were said to be besieged in something called the Alamo; the Mexican army was said to have an overwhelming advantage. And yet the news was all vague. It was reported that William Travis had drawn a line in the sand with his sword, with all those prepared to die for Texas independence on one side of it while those on the other side, who didn't care to commit themselves, were free to leave. Some said Jim Bowie was with the stalwarts, some said Crockett was with him, but no mention was made of Lord Albany Berrybender at all.

Vicky Berrybender became deeply apprehensive—her husband, after all, was notably reckless. When Mr. Austin, even more grave than usual, came to deliver the sad news—not only Lord Berrybender but nearly two hundred defenders of the Alamo all dead—Vicky was not really surprised. What surprised Lord Berrybender's daughters was the depth of Vicky's grief. She not only sobbed, she screamed so loudly that her frightened son, Talley, ran to Buffum for reassurance. Tasmin could do nothing with Vicky, nor could Father Geoffrin or anyone else.

"What do you suppose she would do if Father had ever been nice to her?" Tasmin asked.

"Perhaps there was something about him that we missed," Buffum suggested. "After all, Mama had all of us by him."

"The ability to get women with child is a very common one," Tasmin remarked. "It's useful insofar as it keeps the race going, although whether that is a good thing might be debated."

"*Is* debated—that's what philosophy is all about," Geoff told her.

"Drat you, I don't care about philosophy!" Tasmin told him. "That old brute, my father, has now left us stranded in a place we have no reason to be. I'm his daughter. I wish I could feel something positive, but I can't. His life was one long selfish folly, and we're the victims of it."

"That's harsh, Tassie," Mary said. "Speak no ill of the dead."

"An absurd sentiment," Tasmin answered. "I cannot subscribe to it."

In fact she felt bitterness, not grief, when she thought of her father. The roll call of those who had died because of his selfishness—which included three of his grandchildren—would not be short, once it was tallied up.

"Almost two hundred heroes died at the Alamo," Mr. Austin intoned, in his sententious way.

"If you're counting our father, make it one hundred ninety-nine," Tasmin said, not caring if the comment shocked her sisters. "I'm sure he shot plenty of little Mexican soldiers before he died—children most of them, like our Corporal Dominguin."

Mr. Austin was deeply offended.

"Hardly a patriotic view, under the circumstances," he said, frowning.

"Not meant to be patriotic—but not unfair, either," she retorted. "What could you know about the trail of dead we've left behind us?"

"I merely meant that it would be an inconvenient thing to say just now, when everyone is hot to kill Mexicans," he said, shocked by the English-woman's temerity.

"Not everyone *is* hot to kill Mexicans—it's just you intemperate Texans," Tasmin told him, whereupon Stephen F. Austin turned on his heel and went away.

Geoff, George, and Tasmin's sisters all seemed stunned by what they had heard.

"Well, am I expected to be polite to a fool like that?" Tasmin asked. "I suppose I ain't polite enough for this fine new republic."

"I ain't polite either," the cheerful Petal said.

62

She felt a stir of unease.

Vicky didn't try to explain to Tasmin why she grieved so when the news came that her husband, Lord Berrybender, was dead. She found it easier to talk to Buffum, who, after all, had lost a husband also—perhaps a better husband than Albany Berrybender could ever have been. There were men who dissembled and men who changed, and then there were men who could only be what they were. Lord Berrybender was a man of the latter sort. He had been many things that were not nice. He had been violent and he had been cold; he had been drunken, unfaithful, and brutal; he begged shamelessly when she refused him, yet he thought no more of lying to her than he would have of lying to a fly. Cruelest of all, he had shown no interest in their children, had scarcely ever invited either boy into his lap, where Tasmin's brash Petal installed herself without bothering to ask permission.

"There is always more than people on the outside can see," Vicky told Buffum. "He was so sweet sometimes, Buffum—so infinitely sweet. I vowed a thousand times not to forgive him, and yet when he looked at me in a certain way I could not hold to my purpose. I forgave him countless times. Do you think I'm wrong?"

"No," Buffum said. "When men are sweet there's no holding out."

"They say the flesh is weak—it's a true saying," Vicky told her. "And yet if one is not weak—if one is strong, like Tasmin, it seems one must be mainly alone."

She sighed.

"I was not made to be alone," she said.

"Nor I," Buffum told her. "I fear that Tassie is very likely to end up alone. She is so very unbending."

"I'm certainly nothing of the sort," Tasmin said indignantly, when Mary repeated the remark to her. "How dare she say that? I've yielded, I've compromised, I've abandoned position after position in order to avoid being alone. I don't know what Buffum means. Even now all I can think of is when my husband will appear. I've spent more than half my marriage waiting for Jimmy to appear. I won't have Buffum telling me that I don't bend."

Cook was out early the next morning, hoping to find a few eggs—the hens in Washington-on-the-Brazos were skinny things. Cook felt it was better to rely on them for eggs than to attempt to cook such wiry specimens.

It was when she looked up from a nest with a single egg in it that she saw Mr. Jim coming. Behind him, on other horses, were some very ragged people. Riding beside him, at his elbow, was a brown woman. Something in the way the two looked at one another caught Cook's attention. She felt a stir of unease.

Nonetheless she at once woke Tasmin, to give her the news.

"What? Where is he?" Tasmin asked, jumping out of bed.

"He's just stopped to speak to Mr. Fitzpatrick," Cook said. She was in rather a quandary about what it was best to say.

"Why do you look that way?" Tasmin asked. "Is Jimmy hurt? Tell me."

"No, he's not hurt," Cook assured her, wishing she had never spoken. But Tasmin had known Cook so long that dissembling was impossible.

"There's a woman with him," Cook at last said.

"A woman? What do you mean, a captive?" Tasmin asked, more puzzled than concerned.

"Just a woman—I shouldn't have mentioned it," Cook said.

63

She had been fearful of being scorned . . .

Petal, friendly as could be, put her short white arm next to Rosa's brown one, comparing the two tones.

"I wish I was brown—it's prettier," she concluded.

"You better just stay white," Rosa told her. "If you're white maybe you can be the queen someday."

"Yes, and she'd certainly like that," Cook observed. "She acts like a queen already, this little miss does."

"I boss her," Petal said, smiling. "I boss everybody. I even bossed my grandpa, only now he's gone'd."

"Your pa's dead?" Jim asked, very startled, when Tasmin told him the news. "I didn't think anybody could kill that old man."

"There were said to be five thousand soldiers with General Santa Anna—I suppose it was enough to do the job," she told him.

Tasmin refrained from asking Jim about Rosa, who had met all the Berrybenders and now sat with Petal and Cook. Jim was just back. Tasmin intended to resist her impulse to be the prying housewife. Tasmin assumed Jim had rescued Rosa, and then came to like her. It was easy to see that he *did* like her. Meeting the Berrybenders had made Rosa a little nervous, but not very. What they all noted about her was that she seemed very calm.

"I suppose it's because she's had to put up with worse things than meeting a bunch of half-addled Europeans," Geoff remarked, trying to put his finger on the quality of Rosa's calm.

"But does she want my husband?" Tasmin wondered. "It's clear that Jim wants her—but it's not clear that she intends to accept him. What do you think, George?"

"She was taken by slavers—undoubtedly a rough experience," George said. "Remember what happened to Buffum at the Mandans'. These hothouse questions probably mean nothing to the woman. She's far from home—she has nothing but the clothes on her back. What Jim wants or doesn't want may be the least of her problems."

"But it's not the least of mine," Tasmin told him. "I'm not criticizing her, George. I think I like her. Whatever she is, one can see that she's not cheap. Jim didn't bring back a whore."

Though Tasmin didn't say it to the company, the questions she wanted to ask did not all have to do with Jim. The man who had ridden away, flinty faced, to revenge the murder of a wife and son was not the man who had come back, leading ten captives and a dignified Mexican woman. Jim had always been lean—it was one source of his appeal. Tasmin had always disliked fleshy men. Master Stiles had been lean, Pomp had been lean, Jim was lean. But now he seemed a skeleton, hollow-faced, haunted. He wore a look of deep unhappiness, which only changed when he looked at Rosa, or sat by her for a moment. Tasmin felt perplexed. Jim had fought fierce battles before: with the Piegans, with the Pawnee boys, with Obregon and his men. He blazed with rage, became the Sin Killer, then slowly came back to being Jim. Only this time it was clear that he had *not* come back.

He was not the old Jim—even Petal could not quite reach him. Whatever they had gone through together had left Jim in great need of this quiet woman.

Despite her curiosity, Tasmin felt hesitant about trying to get the story from Jim—he never liked it when she questioned him. While he was busy with the horses, listening to Tom Fitzpatrick fill him in on what was known about the terrible massacre at the Alamo, Tasmin saw an opportunity and sat down by Rosa.

"Will you tell me what happened?" she asked. Why not be direct? "My husband doesn't seem quite like himself."

Rosa was relieved that Jim's wife could speak to her in a friendly, frank way. She had been fearful of being scorned, perhaps even beaten, although she had done nothing sinful with Jem. But a wife wouldn't know that—a wife might have suspicions. She had had plenty of suspicions about her husband—and well-founded ones, too.

"I was taken by the slavers, like the others," Rosa said. "They were very bad men, cruel. Jem came in the morning and killed them all, every one. No one escaped him."

"That's no surprise," Tasmin told her.

"He spilled much blood—he couldn't stop," Rosa went on. "He was going to kill everybody—those women—even those children."

She nodded toward the other captives, who were sitting listlessly nearby, waiting for someone to tell them what to do.

"I was able to stop him," Rosa told Tasmin. "I grabbed his bridle—in time he came back to himself. When he realized what he had been about to do, he broke his sword. Now Jem thinks I saved him."

"It sounds to me like you *did* save him," Tasmin said. "You kept him from killing innocent people. So it's no wonder that now he needs you very much."

"Yes, he needs me," Rosa agreed. "I don't know for how long. He saved my life. He killed the men who dishonored me. He kept us all from starving. He told me he had a wife. I'm glad you are friendly toward me. I am not a husband stealer. I told Jem I would be his servant. I can cook and make fires and do the things a servant does."

"But do you have a home to go to?" Tasmin asked.

Rosa shook her head. "My little ones are dead," she replied. "So is my husband—he was no great loss. So if you and Jem need a servant I will stay and work for you, to show that I am grateful."

Tasmin didn't immediately answer, because she didn't know what to say. That Jim wanted to keep Rosa was obvious. What was less certain was whether he wanted to keep his wife. He had not kissed her, not touched her. He *had* kissed Petal, but that was all.

Cook soon took to Rosa, who immediately set about making herself useful. Tasmin could only brood and wonder.

Jim was aware that he needed to explain things to Tasmin. She *was* his—when night came she would expect him in her bed. And yet he meant to do as he had been doing, spending his nights by the campfire with Rosa.

Finally Tasmin bearded him—indecision and uncertainty were states not to be born.

"Jimmy, I'm not angry—I just want to know what you want."

"I have to stay with Rosa," Jim said, relieved that Tasmin didn't seem angry.

"She saved me, now I need her," he added. "I guess we should marry."

"Well, that might work in the Ute country, where men are allowed various wives—but it won't work here," Tasmin said. "It would make you a bigamist, and bigamy is a crime, I'm sure—besides, I imagine Rosa's Catholic, and the Catholic Church certainly frowns on bigamy."

"Rosa saved me from slaughtering the women and children," Jim said. "She's the real Sin Killer—she killed the big sin I was about to do."

Tasmin walked away, perplexed. She needed to talk to her counselors—George and Geoff.

"Jim's been through a crucible—the slaughter in that camp must have been terrible," George said. "He's had a moral crisis and it's left him not himself. He badly needs Rosa to lean on, but of course that may be temporary."

"She seems a nice woman," Geoff added.

"She is, but I don't know that *I* am," Tasmin told them. "It's so complicated. She's very grateful to Jimmy, of course. She offered to be our servant, to show her gratitude. Besides that, she has no place to go. I don't think a servant is what Jimmy wants. I think he wants to take her to wife. He said as much. And yet here I am, the old wife but hardly the easy wife. Rosa seems to want to be as Little Onion was. She's been misused, and Jem, as she calls him, saved her. So she wants to help him. I don't think she means to mate with him."

"That could change," Geoff told her.

"Of course, given enough time—but enough time might mean years," Tasmin said. "What am I to do right now?"

Her counselors looked stumped. They ceased to counsel.

"It's very peculiar, the situations life presents one with," Father Geoff reflected.

Night fell, the company ate. Tasmin slept alone. Rosa built a campfire, and she and Jim sat beside it.

64

. . . Tasmin woke up tearful . . .

In the night Tasmin woke up tearful, from an aching pain—but the pain was not because her husband was sitting by a campfire with a quiet Mexican woman. She cried from the grief that woke her two nights out of three—her grief for her boys. It was a grief she had come to doubt she could bear and remain sane. If Jim had known how to help her, she felt she might get better—but Jim didn't know how to help her—never had. When, yesterday, he had casually said that he wanted to marry Rosa, Tasmin suddenly realized that words such as "marry," "husband," "wife" had, for Jim, neither legal nor sacramental weight. Those words didn't mean to Jim what they meant to people brought up in settled societies. All he meant by "husband," "wife," "marry" was that he and the woman in question might travel together for some while. But his scanty reading of his tattered Bible had given him no sense of holy matrimony as it was understood by settled people. His agreeing to get "hitched up" with her had been, for him, a light thing. He was a mountain man; he saw no reason not to add wives when a pleasing new woman came along—it wasn't a fault exactly, merely the fruit of his unparented upbringing. Tasmin didn't hold this against him—how, under the circumstances, could it have been otherwise?—but it did make her feel lonelier when she woke up in the night grieving for her boys. She now considered that she should have known all this at once, on their first night together, when she had got slapped for attempting to explain what theology was. Jim had no theology, just a notion or two: that sin, whatever it was, should be punished; that wives should be silent and obey their husbands. He had the merest scraps of belief and he couldn't help her when she felt sad in the night.

When dawn came she went straight to the fire Rosa was already building up.

"Excuse me for inviting myself into your company this early," Tasmin said. Jim looked tired and a little wary. Rosa offered Tasmin coffee.

"I've got to say this, Jim," she told him, trying to control her voice, trying not to begin to cry.

"I can accept the death of our boys because I have to—they're dead," she said. "What I can't accept is how they're buried."

Jim looked perplexed. The boys were buried where they died, as most travelers were buried.

"Here it is, Jim," she went on. "I can't bear to think of them buried lonely and far apart, far from either of us. I want them buried together, in a churchyard we could visit. A nice churchyard, with grass, and a headstone for each of them."

"I buried my girls that way," Rosa said. "I put up little crosses.

"If I am ever in my village again I will visit them," she said sadly. "But I don't know if I will be."

"You see, Jimmy?" Tasmin said. "That's how any good mother would feel."

Jim waited, not sure what the women were telling him.

"I think I have the resources to be happy again, sometime in my life," Tasmin told him. "If I can just visit my boys from time to time and know that they're together in a proper graveyard I can reconcile myself to what's happened and go on. But if one poor tyke is over by the Rio Grande and the other I know not where, in time I think I'll go mad. It's a thing I just can't bear."

"You should go get them for her—you can find them," Rosa said. "If you buried them you can find them—it will help her."

"That's just what I intended to ask—that you go gather in our boys," Tasmin told him, grateful to Rosa for smoothing the way. "I haven't asked you for many favors—I'm sure you'll agree. But I'm asking this."

Jim thought the request strange, but had no objection to doing it so long as Rosa would come along.

"I would be grateful if you'd go with him," Tasmin said, to Rosa. "As their mother I know it's my job. But it would mean leaving Petal in the lap of this infant republic and I fear she would soon bring it down. They'd be trying to recall General Santa Anna if they had to cope with Petal for a month."

"You mean you want to wait here?" Jim asked.

"No—not here," she said. "I mean to leave Texas and I hope never to come back. I'll wait for you in Saint Louis. I'll make George or Geoff wait with me, and perhaps Buffum and her young corporal as well."

Jim looked at Tasmin several times—she had a wild, desperate look, like a mare that had been locoed. Her face was thinning, making her eyes even larger, wilder.

"Please, Jim," Tasmin asked. "We've got Petal to think of. I don't want to become a crazed mother. If you can't find the time to bring them all the way to Saint Louis, then take them to Bent's Fort. I'm sure Kit would bring them the rest of the way."

Jim thought he could see the right in it, brothers laid together in a settled place.

"No, I won't send them by Kit—they're our boys," he told her. "I'll go get them and bring them wherever you want them."

"Thank you," Tasmin said.

She turned to Rosa.

"It'll be a hard journey, I know. I'm grateful to you for attempting it."

"I never took no journey till I was stolen," Rosa said. "That trip was hard enough."

"This one will be easier," Jim told her. "The weather will be easing, and I'll get you a better horse. That old sack of bones you're riding barely made it this far."

He talked for a bit, discussing the practicalities of the journey. Tasmin and Rosa listened with only half a mind, half an ear. Jim was thinking of guns and blankets, meat and bullets. The women were thinking of dead children, those they had brought into being, had suckled, had cleaned when they soiled, but had lost.

"I expect it will take four months," Jim concluded.

"I'll be in Saint Louis by then," Tasmin promised.

65

. . . they were still good shoulders, she considered.

I think it pays to be particular about cocks," Buffum told them. "I've been lucky twice." She was pregnant again and glowing. Corporal Dominguin was evidently given little rest. Somehow Buffum had turned into a beauty; no one seeing her now would suppose she had ever been plain. Whether this change was a result of a particularity about cocks no one could say; but Buffum was rapidly becoming the beauty of the family. Tasmin, feeling old and dowdy, was too distracted to do much about herself, although, once they got to Galveston Island, where some adornments were available, Father Geoff urged a few purchases on her: a new hairbrush, scent, a frock. Still, when General Houston gave a ball for the Berrybenders as they passed through, Tasmin had as many young men petitioning her for dances as Buffum. Tasmin bared her shoulders; they were still good shoulders, she considered. She let herself be swept up in the dancing for an hour—it took her mind off other things.

General Houston, rather grumpy, somewhat dyspeptic, did not dance. Tasmin had hoped that someone would recover her father's body from the Alamo, but the hope was forlorn. The heaps of dead had been thrown into common graves. Vicky still teared up when Lord Berrybender's name was mentioned, which was more and more seldom as they straggled on toward the port of Galveston and began the confusing business of attempting to decide which of them were going home to Europe and which merely to Saint Louis with Tasmin and Petal.

"George and Geoff have no choice," Tasmin said. "I need them until Jim brings me my boys."

The two men made no protest.

"After that you two can go anywhere you please, with my gratitude," Tasmin told them.

"I'll have to go somewhere where I can sell my pictures," George told her. "And pronto, else I'll be bankrupt."

"Somehow bankruptcy suits you, George," Buffum joked. "I doubt any of us could stand you if you were rich."

Cook was the first member of the company to declare herself resolute for England. Tom Fitzpatrick's suit, in the end, had been firmly rejected.

"He's not young, he's not handsome, and he has no money at all," the ever-practical Cook informed them. "I can't see the point of it, miladies."

"I should have thought the point of it might be that he cares for you," Tasmin said, a little taken aback by Cook's firm refusal of the man who had loyally helped her across thousands of miles.

Mary and Piet also opted for Europe.

"I want my child to be born in a safer country," Mary told her sisters.

"You once were almost wholly demonic, Mary," Tasmin reminded her. "How odd that you should have become the most practical among us."

"We may come back," Piet suggested. "The arachnids attract me—spiders. I may just want to do a study."

Buffum refused to hear of England.

"Afraid of being disappointed by the cocks?" Tasmin joked.

Buffum merely chuckled, in her new, sultry way.

Vicky chose England.

"I suppose I had better go see if there is anything left in Northampton-shire," she said. "And I do need a new cello."

In the evenings Tasmin and Petal, sometimes accompanied by Elf, took long walks on the gray beach, looking at the gray sea. Petal and Elf busied themselves collecting shells.

"That sea looks *too* big," Petal declared. "Why don't we go back and find my Jim?"

"He's not just *your* Jim—I had a share in this too," her mother told her. "Besides, our Jim is hard to find."

"I still think this sea looks too big," Petal said.

Kate Berrybender was the last family member to choose Europe.

"It's my mathematics, you see," Kate explained. "Piet assures me I shall have much better tutors in Europe—he suggests perhaps Göttingen. I should like to advance my mathematics and I fear a lack of advanced tutors here."

But as the ship was loading Kate burst into tears.

"It's because I don't know if I shall ever see Mr. James Snow again," she sobbed.

"*We* will see him, and anyway he's not *yours*," Petal insisted.

"You ought to smack that impertinent brat," Kate advised.

66

. . . a frustrated trinity . . .

On the voyage to New Orleans both George and Geoff were desperately seasick. They could seldom drag themselves to the card table. Buffum, wilder and wilder, spent the voyage sequestered with Corporal Dominguin, now merely called Juan. Petal and Elf wandered the ship, fighting like cats and dogs. Petal persuaded a sailor to help her up into the rigging, where she clung to a rope. Tasmin shouted herself hoarse but Petal refused to descend. A team of sailors was finally dispatched to fetch her. One of the sailors was so exhausted by the effort that he fell into the sea.

Tasmin had begun to feel rather guilty about her shameless use of George Catlin and Father Geoffrin; and yet for her it was an intensely lonely time, her husband far away and with another woman, her sister occupied with a lover, her daughter opposing her every wish. George and Geoff were old and well-trusted companions. When they were well they were able to provoke at least a semblance of gaiety in her—a bit of the old, teasing Tasmin would return. Yet the cruel fact was that both men were in love with her and were not going to get what they wanted. She resolved to send them away when they reached Saint Louis, and yet they reached Saint Louis and she didn't send them away. They had been welded, through travel and travail, into a frustrated trinity from which none of the three could find the strength to leave. Except on her waspish days, Tasmin was kind to her old friends. They avoided all talk of romance except when the vibrant Buffum—who was actually having a romance—joined the discussion. The better Buffum looked, the more sour the three of them felt.

Once in Saint Louis, they settled into a large house, lent them by Captain Clark, and settled in to wait. Petal and Elf immediately stuck themselves in a chimney, finally emerging very black. Once off the water, George's and Geoff's health improved; there were card games again, and a semblance of levity. George made a great many sketches of scenes along the docks and the riverbank. Geoff and Tasmin shopped, buying things neither much wanted. Buffum paid a visit to the great Bent brothers warehouse, being run by two younger Bents—Buffum considered the warehouse so very dis-

"You little deserter," Tasmin told him, the next time she caught him alone.

Father Geoffrin merely laughed.

"Oh, you've been so bitchy to me," he reminded her. "I'm not like humble George Catlin. I don't turn the other cheek."

"If you did turn it I'd slap it," Tasmin replied.

Later, they made up, but it was clear to Tasmin that the newly beautiful Buffum was in the ascendance where Geoff's attentions were concerned.

A week later, having loaded up a great load of goods from the Bent warehouse—all meticulously accounted for by Buffum—Charlie, Kit, Jim, and Rosa got ready for their journey up the river and across the plains.

Tasmin and Petal came down to the Missouri docks to see them off. While Petal did her best to charm her father out of going, Tasmin gave Kit another tight squeeze.

"I'm sick of good-byes—but I hope your next baby lives," she told him. "I've a notion you'd make a fine pa."

Kit choked up. Tasmin was so changed, sadder, yet kind to him. He could only mumble a good-bye.

Rosa gave Petal a little white cap made from rabbit skins, much like the one the young Hidatsa girl Coal, wife to Toussaint Charbonneau, had made for Monty when he had been an infant. Tasmin thanked Rosa again for the shrouds—then she suddenly ran out of words. She smiled, Rosa smiled, Tasmin turned away.

When the boat was ready to leave, Jim put Petal down. Tasmin felt desperate to say something—anything—since it seemed Jim wasn't going to make even the simplest farewell.

"I'll be sure to let the Bents know when we get back," she told him again.

"That'll be fine," Jim said. He stuck out his hand—startled, Tasmin shook it. Behind him Tasmin saw Rosa put a hand to her mouth, shocked—perhaps even appalled. This was a wife he was leaving! Was that all?

It was all. Tasmin turned away—hurt, confused, crushed. Jim Snow seemed to her quite the oddest man she had ever known—Rosa by now had probably realized as much herself. Tasmin tried to buck up. It was just his shyness, his deep unease with females, she told herself. And yet she felt not merely lonely: she felt negated, as she had that day when Jim left to go kill the slavers.

Soon the boat pulled away. West of them the Missouri's shores were vague with summer heat. Jim Snow stood in the rear, with Kit and Charlie

Bent. Petal stared, silent. Tasmin remembered going ashore at dusk that
first evening, to inspect the great dun prairies. She remembered her ecstasy at the first sunrise—that had been but a scant four years ago. Then,
she had been wholly innocent of the brutalities the distant vistas hid,
though only the next day the Osage tried to kill her. And yet, for long, it
had seemed a grand adventure, rather than the death march that was to
bring her two sons to their new grave in Saint Louis. And not just her sons:
Pomp Charbonneau, Little Onion, Fräulein Pfretzskaner, Old Gorska, Signor Claricia and Señor Yanez, Tim and Milly, their big Juppy, and all the
others who had fallen to the implacable land.

Thinking of Jim and Rosa—she could still just glimpse Jim; Petal was
hopelessly waving—Tasmin wondered if she could have displaced Rosa
and kept Jim, had she cared to throw her whole self into the fight. She
knew him; she had her wiles; she might have summoned all the ruthless
brilliance of the Berrybenders, pitched everything into the effort. And yet,
even assuming that she could still summon that pure force, what would it
have accomplished? It was not the sad, kind Mexican woman who kept her
husband from her: it was the merciless land, where Rosa was at home and
she wasn't. She could never, it seemed to her, win Jim, her American, from
this place that he fit and she didn't. Rosa could go with him, be useful in
the ways that Little Onion had been useful. She could make him fires, cook
his prairie meats, mend his buckskins, accept him if he wanted her, doctor little wounds. Tasmin herself might still love the man—it was the land
she couldn't love. Perhaps it was better, though it was terrible, that she
lose the man with whom she had had much pleasure, pleasure that now
seemed hard won. They had begun their lovemaking far out on the prairie,
where the buffalo bulls in hundreds roared in their rut. Naked, those first
few times, Tasmin had been convinced that she was now a child of nature—and there was the folly hidden under the glory: she was a daughter
of privilege, English privilege, and Jim was a son of necessity—American
necessity. Such a combination might thrill, but could it endure?

Petal had stopped waving.

"My arm got tired," she said.

"I shouldn't wonder."

"You made Jim go!" Petal accused.

"Not so—he made me go," Tasmin said.

"Will I ever see my Jim again, or is he gone'd forever?" Petal asked.

Tasmin picked her daughter up and looked at her sternly.

"You mustn't ask me that, my dear," she said. "It's rather too soon to know."

Petal cried; but later, for the next many months, she made good use of her mother's formulation. When anyone taxed her to explain some ambitious mischief, Petal would look them in the eye and say: "You mustn't ask me that, my dear. It's rather too soon to know."